FOREVER FANTASY ONLINE:
LAST BASTION

BOOK 2 OF 3

RACHEL AARON / TRAVIS BACH

Bastion was supposed to mean safety...

It was supposed to mean a break from fighting for their lives and a chance to talk to someone who might actually know what's going on. Access to their gold and some beer would have been nice, too.

They got none of those things. When Tina and James arrive in the capital, they find a city on fire in more ways than one. Players and non-players hunt each other in the streets, while the king who controls the city's all-powerful artifact cowers from the chaos in his castle. Desperate to warn somebody about the Once King's coming invasion, James wants to try to talk to the king anyway, while Tina just wants to meet the royal portal keepers who might be able to send them home.

It shouldn't be hard to get an army of the world's best-geared players through one city, but when they discover that the captain of the Royal Knights has been massacring low-level players in revenge disguised as justice, James and Tina will have to decide which is more important: the lives of their fellow gamers, or the stability of their new world's last great city. Both choices deserve a champion, but with the Once King's armies closing in, taking the wrong side may doom everyone to an eternity as slaves to the Ghostfire.

Series Information

Forever Fantasy Online

Last Bastion

The Once King

Copyright and Publishing Info

Aaron Bach, LLC
"Writing to Entertain and Inform."
Copyright © 2019 Rachel Aaron & Travis Bach

ISBN Paperback: 978-0-578-56833-1
ASIN eBook: B07Q24W76N

Cover Illustration by Daniel Schmelling,
Cover Design by Rachel Aaron,
Editing provided by Red Adept Editing

Content Warning

A note from Rachel Aaron

This a book about gamers. The characters talk like gamers, think like gamers, and act like gamers, which--as any gamer knows--is sometimes not very well. As such, this book will contain far more cursing, sexual situations, prejudice, and blood than my novels usually do.

That said, it's still us. Travis and I do not tolerate hate in our fiction any more than we do in real life. Just because a character says/does something awful does *not* mean that we agree with it, or that that person will not have to pay for their actions. This book deals with difficult issues many real people face, and we tried our best to give those issues the gravitas and realism they deserve. We might not have done everything perfectly, but Travis and I did our best to get it right.

The FFO series is our love letter to the online games we played obsessively for years. We wanted to show the amazing strength and resourcefulness of the gaming community without painting over its pitfalls. This book reflects that, and we hope that you love it as much as we do.

Thank you for reading and enjoy the story

Prologue

Six years ago.

Why do they all have to be so much taller than me?

Tina Anderson, aged fifteen, glared at the wall of yakking high school boys blocking the sidewalk to the school bus loading zone. Normally, she could have cut through the grass to get around, but the rain was pouring like a wall beyond the roofed walkway. If she didn't want mud up to her knees, the sidewalk was her only option.

"Excuse me," Tina said, tapping on the barrier of backpacks.

No response.

"*Excuse* me," she said a bit louder, glancing nervously at the line of yellow buses, which were starting to edge forward. "I need to get to the--"

Before she could finish, one of the boys turned around suddenly and walked straight into her. Since he had a good eleven inches and eighty pounds on her, the impact sent Tina flying. She managed to catch herself before she went sprawling butt-first into the mud, but one of her sneakers still slipped in, flooding her foot with warm, slimy water.

"Watch where you're going, kid!" the boy yelled as he shoved past her.

"We were in the same class, idiot!" Tina yelled back, but the boy was already jogging away. Glaring at his retreating back, Tina shook off her soggy foot and plunged into the gap he'd left in the wall of backpacks, shoving her way through the mob to the pickup zone.

Just in time to see her school bus drive off without her.

"*Wait!*" she cried, diving into the rain. She ran down the sidewalk, waving her arms, but the driver must not have seen her, because the nacho-cheese-colored vehicle just picked up speed, leaving her soaked and panting at the end of the school's driveway.

i

Cursing the red taillights as they vanished into the rain, Tina turned around and started trudging back up the flooded road to the dubious shelter of the covered sidewalk. This wasn't the first time the bus driver hadn't seen or remembered her, but the fact that it had happened today, on the last day of school, felt like a personal insult from the universe. All she wanted was to get home so she could log into Forever Fantasy Online and play until exhaustion forced her to stop. Was that too much to ask?

Refusing to admit defeat, Tina shook the rain off her backpack and dug out her smartphone to message her mom.

I missed the bus, she typed. *I know you're working, but it's the last day of school, and it's pouring rain. Can you or Dad come get me, please? I'll do the dishes to make up for it.*

Satisfied she'd offered sufficient bribery, Tina pulled up a book on her phone and settled against a post to wait. Thirty minutes later, she'd finished her book and there was still no reply from her mother. Frustrated, she messaged again and sent a text to her dad as well this time.

Another thirty minutes crawled by. The school's pickup line was long since empty, leaving Tina alone with the pounding rain and a low battery symbol. She checked her messages for the millionth time, but they all showed as delivered. There was just no answer.

Heaving an enormous sigh, Tina pushed herself off the pole. In hindsight, she knew a mid-afternoon reply was a lot to ask of her busy parents. They'd been working overtime like crazy this year to pay for her brother's college tuition. They probably weren't even looking at their phones right now, but she didn't want to wait out here alone until they got home and noticed she was missing.

Going to wait in the library, she texted her mom. *Pick me up after work?*

Putting her phone away, Tina waved goodbye to Mrs. Hamilton in the front office window. The principal's secretary gave her the merest flip of a hand in acknowledgment. Adults-who-didn't-care pacified, Tina pulled the tiny emergency umbrella out of her bag and set out into the Seattle rain. Her still-damp sneakers were instantly soaked through again, but she consoled herself with the reminder that school was actually over. Starting tomorrow, she could binge FFO as much as she wanted. Compared to that, losing one afternoon wasn't such a big deal. Her parents had picked her up from the library before. She just had to kill time until they got off work at six, and then the whole evening would be hers.

That thought was *almost* enough to cheer her up as she squished her way onto the main road, tilting her umbrella sideways to block the spray from the cars driving past.

***

Four hours later, Tina was officially panicking. She'd made it to the public library just fine, but it was nearly eight-thirty now and there was *still* no reply from her parents. As the second child, Tina was used to being ignored, but this was ridiculous. Even her busy, distracted parents were never *this* bad.

Something horrible must have happened while she was at school. Her thoughts went immediately to her uncle Vernon, who'd been in the hospital for skin cancer. Maybe his operation had gone wrong. Or maybe there'd been an accident, something that left her parents unable to text her back. She was racing through all the worst-case scenarios when her phone buzzed in her hands.

Tina snatched it to her ear. "*Dad!*" she cried desperately. "Are you okay?"

"What?" her father replied, his voice tired and distracted. "I'm fine, but you picked a hell of day to miss the bus."

"What's wrong?" Tina demanded. "Where have you been?"

"I'm sorry, Tina," he said, ignoring her questions. "But I can't come get you right now. I'm going to call a ride share to take you home, okay?"

"Why?" she asked frantically. "Is Mom okay? Did something happen to Uncle Vernon? What's going on?"

Her dad fell silent for a moment, building her dread even higher.

iii

"It's your brother," he said at last. "He called this morning and told us he was coming home for the summer."

Tina's heart stopped. "Is James hurt?"

"He's fine," her dad assured her. "But something happened at the university. James won't tell us what, and he's really down about it. Your mom and I are driving out to the airport to pick him up right now, and then we're going to take him to dinner at Lucas's Bistro to cheer him up. There are leftovers in the fridge, so you should be all set for dinner, but I need you to get the air mattress out of the attic when you get home so James has somewhere to sleep tonight. Also..."

The list of chores kept going, but Tina wasn't listening anymore. She couldn't decide what made her more upset. There was just so much.

James was *feeling down,*so he'd just decided to fly home to be pampered by Mom and Dad? After three god-awfully expensive years of college, James was terribly behind in his classes, mostly because he played FFO all the time. Tina did, too, but she still managed to do her homework.

James had been slowly sliding into slackerdom ever since he'd gotten into the FFO early beta, but things had gotten *really* bad this year, like fail-all-your-classes bad. He'd promised at Christmas that he'd make up the courses this summer, but apparently Tina was the only member of the family who remembered that detail. Given how hard they were working to pay for his stupid fancy education, you'd think their parents would be taking his possibly flunking out more seriously, but *no.* As always, James was their precious baby. All he had to do was say he was feeling "down," and their parents dropped everything to comfort him. They were even taking him out to one of the best French restaurants in the city, and she was supposed to eat leftovers and make his bed for him?

"Tina, are you listening?"

She was so angry it took three tries to unclench her jaw enough to answer. She wasn't entirely sure what she said, but her dad didn't seem to be listening, anyway, so she just hung up, dumping her battered old phone into her soggy backpack. She shoved herself out of the library chair and stomped over to put up the book she'd been nervously half reading. When she tried to put it back on the shelf where it belonged, though, she couldn't reach. At four feet nine inches, she was just too short, and the stool she'd used earlier was nowhere to be found.

That was the final straw. Tina burst into tears. She just started sobbing right there between the stacks. It was loud enough that the other patrons turned to look, which only made everything so, so much worse. After shoving the book onto the return cart, Tina grabbed her backpack and fled, pulling her the damp strands of her tangled brown hair to shield her face as she raced down the rubberized stairs toward the library doors.

***

Things only went downhill from there.

The first weekend of Tina's summer vacation was spent *un*-renovating her mother's new art studio back into a bedroom for James. Her parents were supposed to be helping, but they'd had an emergency at work, which meant the whole job had fallen on Tina.

Since it was *his* room, fixing it up should have been James's responsibility, but other than a few brief interactions on the way to their house's single bathroom, Tina hadn't seen her brother at all. He'd looked terrible when she had seen him, all sunken eyes and pale skin, but any sympathy Tina might have felt was destroyed by the fact that James spent every waking moment lying on their parents' bed, playing FFO instead of helping her. When she pointed this out to their parents, though, they'd just told her to stop being childish. And then they'd taken James out for dinner. *Again.*

By the third day, Tina didn't even care anymore. She just wanted the work to be over. Thankfully, the morning of the fourth day, her mother had finally declared the bedroom fit for her darling, leaving Tina free to do what *she* wanted, which was to run down the hall to her own room and flop on her bed to *finally* play some FFO.

All of her anger and resentment vanished the moment she put on her VR headset. FFO's brassy, repetitive loading music was the most glorious thing she'd ever heard when the updates finally finished and she was able to log in. All that was left now was to decide who she wanted to be.

There were a lot of options. Despite playing FFO obsessively for a year, Tina had yet to find a character she really liked. She had one of almost every class, but she hadn't leveled any of them up to max. The best she had was a level forty-five elven Cleric named ClaraSpell. Her goal this summer was to get *someone* to level eighty, and as her highest character, ClaraSpell was the logical choice. When Tina moved her virtual finger to the elf's selection button, though, she paused.

Normally, Tina liked playing a Cleric. People always wanted a healer in their group. Considering how ignored she usually was in real life, Tina relished the popularity, but she kind of regretted making ClaraSpell an elf. She'd picked the race because she'd loved how graceful their animations were, but despite setting all the character customization sliders to the minimum, ClaraSpell still looked like a busty Fantasy pinup girl. A misconception that was only made worse by the armor she was currently wearing, a combination that everyone on the forums jokingly referred to as the "Holy Harem Girl" set.

Usually, the power the magical armor gave her was enough to make Tina overlook the constant boob talking and accidental "bumping" into her ass from other players, but she just didn't know if she was up for dealing with the harassment today. If she didn't focus, though, she'd *never* get a character to max level. She was still going back and forth over it when a chat window popped into the corner of her vision.

"Hey, Tina!" her friend David's voice came over her speakers. "You logged in yet?"

A grin spread over Tina's real face beneath the VR helmet. She wasn't even in-game yet, and David was already trying to jump the line to get her in his party. After days of being used as a mover-bot by her parents while her brother slacked, the preferential treatment felt like a drink of water in the desert.

"Getting on right now."

"Great. Make a new Knight and join me in Bastion."

Tina scowled. "A Knight? Why?"

"'Cause I need a tank, and no one else is on. Just make something and get in here."

"Dude, I'm not making another character! I need to level Clara up."

"You can level your Cleric anytime," he said irritably. "I need a Knight to tank the first dungeon, and you owe me for letting you have that Azure Starlight Staff the last time we did Red Canyon."

Tina rolled her eyes. She should have known that would come back to haunt her. David never let you have anything for free.

"Okay, okay," she said, clicking the Create New Character button. "Just give me a few minutes to make something that's not hideous."

"No one cares what you look like," David scolded. "Just hit the randomize button and get in here."

"*I* care," Tina snapped. "And why are you in such a rush? Even if I logged in right now, my Knight's only going be level one. The first dungeon is for level tens."

"Don't worry," David said smugly. "I've got a ton of enhancement scrolls. We'll just pump up your health bar so you don't die every time something hits you and wing the rest."

That sounded like a stupid plan, but Tina hadn't really wanted to level Clara, and Knight was the only class left that she hadn't tried.

"Okay," she said with a sigh. "I'll be right in."

"Great, just be quick about it."

Tina rolled her eyes as the chat window closed and clicked on the Knight Class button to check out her options.

There were a lot. Unlike Clerics, Naturalists, and Sorcerers, which were limited to the mana-using species, every race in the game could be a Knight. Tina's first thought was to just make another elf, but the chainmail bikini the level one female Knights started out wearing wasn't much better than the Holy Harem Girl set. If she didn't make an elf, though, that didn't leave many options.

Schtumples were out. The tiny, pug-like characters were cute in a hideous, stumpy, bug-eyed way, but Tina couldn't stand the idea of her fantasy self being even shorter than her real life self. The ichthyian fish people looked gross, humans were boring, and Tina didn't want to have anything to do with the jubatus. The male models weren't so bad, but the females all looked like porny cat-girls. Total cringe.

That left the towering stonekin race. Tina had seen them around, but the rock people were much more popular with guys than girls. She couldn't remember the last time she'd seen a female stonekin, actually. Looking at the rock lady's hulking, body-builder physique, Tina could understand why. Stonekin girls were intimidating, but that might be fun in its own way. She usually only played elves, which meant David was probably expecting the chainmail bikini. If Tina showed up as a giant stonekin, he'd freak his shit.

That settled it. After clicking the female stonekin, Tina messed with the customization settings until she had a beautiful but stern-looking lady with emeralds for eyes and copper-metal dreadlocks for hair. Maybe it was her shitty week doing the decision-making, but she set all the sliders for muscles and height to maximum.

The result was an eight-foot-tall monster with legs the size of tree trunks, which was actually pretty exciting. ClaraSpell had been only four inches taller than Tina. She had no idea what playing this beast was going to be like, but just thinking about piloting that much power around was thrilling. She also liked the full-coverage chain armor her new Knight was wearing. The stonekin lady was still strangely busty--why did asexual rock-people even have boobs, anyway?--but there were no bare midriffs or exposed cleavage in sight, a vast improvement over her elf's pinup girl costume. All she needed now was a name.

Since this character was only being made to annoy David, Tina went with the first cheesy thing to pop into her head.

"Roxy."

Name already in use, the game system replied. *Chose another.*

Tina sighed in disappointment. Stonekin weren't exactly popular, but FFO had been out of beta for two years now. It made sense that all the good rock pun names would already be taken. "Okay," she said, passing her fingers through the glowing keys of her virtual keyboard. "How about 'Roxxy?'"

Name accepted, the system said cheerfully. *Would you like to log in as Roxxy?*

Tina clicked YES and leaned back in relief. By FFO character creation standards, that hadn't taken long at all, which was good. David was an impatient guy, and he seemed to be in a particular hurry today. Tina was ready to get into the game and see what the rush was about when the virtual world around her suddenly went dark, and then spacey music started to play as lines of white text began to float past her face.

> *Infinity has no ending and, thus, no beginning.*
> *Such as it is for the Sky, knowing no limits of time and place.*
> *The Unbounded Sky is infinite. It reaches all worlds and all worlds lie within it.*
> *Or so once was believed by Sun, Moon, Wind, and Water...*

"Oh *no,*" Tina groaned.

It was the , the stupid, cheap, scrolling text intro all new characters had to sit through before they could play. Desperate, Tina looked around for an escape, but she was already trapped inside FFO's character-loading sphere, a milky-white bubble floating in a vast sea of endless stars. It was very pretty, but there was no way out of it until you actually loaded into the game. Normally, that only took a few seconds, but when you made a new character, the game held you hostage until you'd sat through the entire , which was *still* going.

> *The Celestial Elves were born to wander infinity, their spirits endlessly curious and enduring.*

The Birds were born of the Moon. Theirs is a nature of always returning.

Neither knew why the Sun burned the Moon, but both knew it was the end of forever.
And the Sky beyond the tragedy grew cold...

"Gahhhh," Tina groaned, mashing the escape key on her virtual keyboard as the text crawled by. "Why is this unskippable?"

All were trapped. Bounded by limits and cut off from eternity.
The immortal elves learned that their nature could not withstand the finite.
With no other choice, they descended to the last unknown realm.
But the Birds fought back...

Some developer must have threatened to quit if they didn't include his literary attempts, she decided. When she couldn't take it anymore, she brought up her chat client to message David that she was stuck in Vogon poetry torture, but he didn't reply. She was trying him again when the last stanza of the poem finally scrolled past her nose.

Good luck, hero! May you bring new hope to this tragic world.

"Finally," Tina said, grinning as the stars and the loading sphere vanished. But the grin slid off her face as the world around her lurched. "Whoa!"

The purpose of the loading sphere--when it wasn't trapping you in word torture--was to let FFO's Sensorium Engine take over your senses so that when you entered the game, you felt as if you were actually *in* your character, not lying on your bed with a helmet on. The process was always a bit disorienting, but loading into her elf had never felt like this. The moment the game started, Tina felt like she'd been thrown on top of a pair of stilts. Very, very *tall* stilts at the top of a very large stone statue.

"Whoa," she said again, throwing out her arms for balance as her senses finally settled into her new character's body enough for her to look around.

She was standing in the sun-drenched expanse of Founder's Square, the crowded, colorful central hub of FFO's capital city, Bastion. Beside her, a large fountain burbled at the feet of giant white marble statues portraying the heroes of the Battle of the Heraldsford River in overly dramatic, physically impossible poses. Beyond them, the square itself was lined with elegant white limestone buildings interspersed with tall palm trees swaying in the warm equatorial breeze. It was the same bright, cheerful scene Tina saw every time she made a new character, except now she was seeing it from a totally new angle--one from eight feet up.

"This is freaking *sweet*," she said, turning her character's giant stone head, which stuck more than a foot above rest of the crowd of milling players looking for groups. Grinning at her new-found power, Tina messaged David to let him know she was in and started pushing her way through the crowd, only to discover that no pushing was necessary. She didn't even have to say, "Excuse me." People just took one look at her giant stone body and moved out of her way on their own.

It was pretty fantastic. She'd never even considered playing a stonekin before because they'd seemed inconveniently huge, but for perks like this, Tina could handle bumping her head on a few doorways. She'd never been interested in the melee combat classes before, either, but now she was starting to see the appeal. Even with the weird feeling of being on stilts that came from having to pilot a virtual body so much bigger than her real one, she could feel the strength flowing through her stone arms and legs. She felt as if she could crush anything, and that was unexpectedly intoxicating. She'd made this character because David had pushed, but now that she was in the game, Tina was legit excited to play Roxxy. Now she just needed David to message her back so they could get to that dungeon.

When he failed to respond to multiple texts, Tina rang him on voice chat. "Dude," she said when he finally picked up. "Where the hell are you?"

There was a lot of blasting and other combat noises over her speakers, and then David's frustrated voice sounded in her ear. "Sorry, Tina," he said in a rush. "I tried to wait, but you took a million years, so I had to go without you."

"Are you shitting me?" she cried. "Dude, I made this character just for you, and you couldn't wait for me? And it was *not* a million years!"

"It is when I've bet my brother I can get a Cleric to level thirty before he can," David said distractedly, his voice muffled by the swelling sound effects of a healing spell. "He's already a level ahead of me cause you were dragging your feet. I had to pay another group to take me along."

Tina felt zero sympathy. "What am I supposed to do, then?"

"Just wait there," he said. "My current tank has to go to work after this dungeon. We'll switch you in on the next run."

"But you just started," Tina said in disbelief. "You want me to wait here doing nothing for an *hour* just so you can have a tank the moment you pop out?"

"Pretty much," David said without a hint of shame. "And after you tank two runs for me, I've got a level-thirty guy lined up to carry me through the whole Red Canyon quest line. Anyway, I gotta shut up and heal. Just wait there, and I'll TTYL."

"Jerk!" she yelled at him.

This player has activated Do-Not-Disturb mode

Tina closed the conversation with a punch of her new, giant fist and glanced at the clock floating at the edge of her character's vision. It was already eleven a.m. She'd wasted her entire morning on this bullshit. She should've just told David no and played ClaraSpell. At least then she'd be doing something useful right now. As it was, she might as well log out and go get lunch. Hopefully her parents had remembered to leave something out for her today. With James home, leftovers weren't a thing she could rely on anymore. She was trying to remember if there was any more instant mac and cheese in the pantry when someone cleared his throat behind her.

"Excuse me, good Knight," someone with a formal, stilted voice said. "Are you occupied at this moment?"

Blinking in surprise, Tina looked down from her interface to see a golden-haired elf standing beside her. He was dressed in starter armor just as she was, and the lower half of his face was obscured by the Assassin's starter Bandit Bandanna. Encouraged, Tina glanced at the status bar over his head. Level one, just like her.

"Nah, I'm not busy," she said, turning to face him. "What's up?"

"I was hoping to enlist your aid," the elf replied, his voice lilting in the "ye olde" manner that was a sure sign he was using the in-game translator. Some people would see that as a reason not to play with him, but Tina was fine with the translator. It did a perfectly acceptable job most of the time and a *hilarious* job when it messed up.

"Our group wishes to move through the starter tasks with efficiency," the elf went on. "As such, we are in dire need of a Knight. We would be honored to have one as mighty as you to lead us."

The Assassin finished with a bow from the waist, and Tina smiled awkwardly, holding up a finger in what she hoped was the universal signal for "wait a second" while she did a quick check of her skills.

Thankfully, the Knight's gameplay looked pretty straightforward. She had a starter sword and shield in her backpack, both of which grew enormously to match her stonekin's physique when she equipped them. Chuckling at the ridiculousness of it all, Tina turned and saluted the Assassin back.

"I am the stonekin known as Roxxy, and it would be my pleasure to spearhead a band of heroes against the great evil which dwells in the darkness," she replied, matching his ye olde-ness just for the fun of it. Fortunately, the golden-haired elf didn't seem to mind at all. He just extended his hand.

"Then let us vanquish Bastion's foes together," he said, blue eyes twinkling.

Tina's giant hand engulfed his as they shook on it, and her interface dinged to let her know she'd joined a party.

"I am known as Silent Blade," the elf said, triggering the game's privacy settings to reveal the nameplate floating above his head, which Tina noticed was actually spelled *SilentBlayde*. "I travel in the company of a Ranger, a Naturalist, and another Assassin. We are all new to this world but not lacking in bravery. I have already procured us potions and food. Shall we join the others at the entrance of the first leveling zone?"

"Potions *and* food?" Tina said, breaking into a smile. "You're exceptionally well-prepared for a level one. I'm hella impressed, dude--I mean, SilentBlayde."

That earned her a jaunty thumbs-up. Tina flashed her own thumbs in return, but the Assassin didn't move. He just stood there expectantly, and then Tina realized he was waiting for her. She was the tank, the group's default leader. He expected her to go first.

The rush that followed that was unexpectedly powerful. In her real life, Tina *never* went first. It wasn't that she didn't want to, just that no one ever let her. Now, though, SilentBlayde was looking at her as if he expected nothing less, and Tina nearly bowled him over in her rush to grab her chance.

"Come on," she said, striding out of the Founder's Square toward the Bastion starter zone. "I've done these starter quests a dozen times, so I know exactly where to go. Let's rock'n'roll!"

SilentBlayde chuckled when the translator program finished processing that for him. "Rock is what you do, stonekin, so I will have to provide the roll."

He jumped as he finished, doing the flip animation all elves did when they hopped, and Tina burst out laughing.

It looked like today wasn't going to be a total waste, after all.

Chapter 1

Tina

Present day.

Tina stepped through the massive arched entry of the Portal Keeper's Sanctum in the city of Bastion. Her left boot squelched in a pool of congealed blood as she stopped atop the building's front stairs. Her right boot left a massive scrape in the thick layer of ash. There was more ash on the wall beside her, a sticky coating that turned the once beautiful rose-colored stone as black as the rest of the city before her.

The sight made her shake in her armor. Sitting upon a high hill in East Bastion, the Sanctum normally gave an excellent view of the capital to new arrivals teleporting in from other places in the game. Now, though, black smoke billowed from the countless building fires, obscuring the view and blanketing the once-beautiful white limestone of Bastion's upper city in a grimy layer of soot. In the distance, she could hear the clash of steel and cries of pain echoing from the narrow, smoke-clogged streets. In the square in front of her, though, the only movement came from the buzzards hopping and squawking over bloody piles in the street with none of their usual fear of people.

Putting a hand over her nose to keep out the stench of rotting flesh, Tina forced herself to keep looking, her sharp stone eyes flicking between the gaps in the smoke to the only point in the city higher than the Sanctum: the king's royal castle.

Protected by eighty-foot-tall walls of solid granite, the soaring towers of the castle's inner keep seemed to be the only structures left in Bastion that were still white. Behind them, verdant mountains rose like green knives from the plains beyond Bastion's walls. The mountains were a big part of why the city was here. They surrounded the city on three sides, hemming it in like a bowl. Unfortunately, this also kept in the

1

smoke, blocking the winds and turning the sheltered capital into a cauldron of smoke and ash, most of which seemed to be concentrated in the lower city. But while Tina could see fires rising above the roofline to the south, nothing moved in the streets immediately in front of the Sanctum except scavengers.

As bad as it looked to her, though, the blood- and ash- covered street must have been a lot worse for the fleshy races behind her. Tina heard several people from the raid break ranks to retch behind the soaring pillars. Those who didn't lose their breakfast seemed to be shocked still, pushing through the arched doorway as they fanned out on the sooty and scarred landing of the Sanctum's front steps to get a look.

"Jesus, Mary, and Joseph," Frank said quietly, crossing himself.

"Why'd this happen?" a Ranger demanded. "Bastion is supposed to be safe! PVP isn't even allowed here!"

"Who's fighting?"

"What are we going to *do*? There's nowhere else to go!"

"We're totally fucked!"

Tina couldn't say they were wrong. All through the grim, desperate march through the Deadlands, the mantra had been "Just get to Bastion." Even Tina had clung to it when she'd had trouble putting one foot in front of the other. Bastion represented safety, wealth, order, and possibly even a good time.

She'd worried there would not be a kind welcome for them here, but she'd hoped that the Roughnecks' contract from working with the Order of the Golden Sun could be used to smooth over the initial mistrust. In all her worst case scenarios, though, she'd never imagined *this*. She never would have thought the game's safest city--the entry zone for new players, the one place where you could go AFK without fear--would be torn by anarchy in the streets. It was the damn Order Fortress all over again. Everything they'd done, all that sacrifice and pain to get here, and once again, *here* was not worth having.

It was so damn unfair.

Clenching her armored fists, Tina turned her back on the ravaged city to face her guild. They looked how she felt: horrified, shocked, as if the whole world had been yanked out from under their feet. But she absolutely understood they couldn't afford to fall apart here, so she banged her armored hand on her shield, filling the smoky air with the harsh clang of metal until she'd dragged their gazes back to her.

"Listen up, people," she began in her usual booming voice, but then she stopped. Something was different. Everyone gave her their attention--a nice change from the Deadlands--but people also winced or pulled their hoods up defensively. Tina wasn't sure whether they were traumatized or she'd just stepped in something again and didn't know it yet, but after the mess she'd made at the Order Fort, it was enough to make her change her tone.

"We'll be okay, folks," she said in a much gentler voice. As gentle as a stonekin could sound, anyway. "This isn't the Deadlands. We have food for several days, we have water, we have ammunition, and most importantly, we have each other."

She pulled out the contract she'd had Commander Garrond of the Order sign. Flipping it over, she showed the crowd their golden signatures they'd had to sign to officially be part of the Roughnecks.

"Don't forget," she said, holding the paper high. "We've already fought an end-game raid boss and won. That makes us one of the deadliest things in the world right now, so don't let this banged-up city intimidate you. Whatever did this to Bastion, it should be afraid of *us*, so buck up."

"But what are we going to *do*?" a Cleric in the back wailed.

"That's what we're trying to figure out," Tina said, pulling out her sword to use as a pointer. "For now, I want everyone to--"

She froze. She wasn't even in reach, but the moment she'd drawn her sword, all the players in the front row twitched. Some even jumped back, putting up their hands to ward her off. Tina frowned at this new reaction. She was trying to think of what to say when she noticed Zen

watching her with her arms crossed and her sharp eyes disapprovingly
wary, as if the Ranger was gearing up for another fight.

Damn, what have I done this time? Confused and on guard, Tina shot
a look at SilentBlayde. He was watching the crowd as well, his slim blond
eyebrows scrunched in a frown, which perversely made her feel a little
better. Whatever she was missing, at least it wasn't obvious to him, either.

But as much as she didn't like it, Zen's watchful gaze was an
annoying reminder that Tina had officers to appease now. After years of
running her own show, that was going to take some getting used to. At
least she could make them work for her this time.

"I'm going to talk with the officers, and *we're* going to figure out a
plan together," Tina corrected. "But we're not going to do it out here. It
stinks, and it's too exposed. For now, let's all go back inside the Sanctum--
where it's safe--while we figure out our strategy."

To her relief, no one flinched at that order, and Zen unfolded her
arms at last. Catching her eye, Tina made a tiny "Over here" gesture. Zen
nodded and made her way over, threading silently through the
Roughnecks who were filing past on their way back down into the
Sanctum.

"Zen," Tina whispered when the Ranger reached her. "Did I do
something wrong just now? Everyone's as jumpy as shit. I know the city is
bad, but--"

"It's not the city."

Tina jerked back, but the elf just raised her hand and waited until
the last of the Roughnecks--everyone except SB, who was still waiting
stubbornly for Tina in the doorway--had gone inside.

"There's no nice way to say this, Roxxy," Zen said when they were
finally alone. "So I'll just give it to you straight: people are afraid of you."

"*What?*" Tina said. "Why? I'm the one who got us here safely!"

"Yeah, by terrifying everyone into following you." Zen shook her
head, bright-green curls swishing in the smoky air. "You yelled, bullied,
and beat us down that road for three days straight. Lots of people had

planned on leaving the guild once we made it to Bastion. Now we're trapped again, so it's only natural people are upset. They were looking forward to getting away and not having to deal with you anymore, but everyone knows we can't fight anything serious without you, so they're stuck. It's hard to cope with."

Each word that left Zen's mouth hit Tina like a shard of ice in her chest. She knew the Ranger wasn't just saying this to hurt her. First, the former nurse was above that sort of pettiness, and second, she'd seen the truth herself in the others' eyes. End-game raiders who shouldn't be afraid of anything had flinched at her gestures like abuse victims, and that made Tina sick to her stomach in a way the stench of the decimated city surrounding them hadn't.

"I'm sorry," Zen said quietly. "I know it's tough to hear, but--"

"No," Tina said, running a hand through her copper dreadlocks. "Don't apologize, Zen. I asked, and you were brave enough to tell me the truth to my face. Thanks for being so stand up. Um, can you post guards and gather up the officers for a meeting, please? I... I need a few minutes alone before we get to business."

Zen patted the plate armor on her shoulder. "I'll take care of it. See you inside."

The Ranger had barely started down the hallway after the rest of the guild when SilentBlayde appeared in the space where she'd been.

"Tina," he whispered, his voice deep with concern. "Are you okay?"

She couldn't even meet his eyes. "You're an officer too, SB," she said, looking down. "Please go with Zen."

When he didn't move immediately, Tina was afraid he was going to push. But then the Assassin turned and started down the hallway. He paused only once to look over his shoulder. When she didn't call him back, his whole body slumped, and he walked inside, vanishing down the hall that led to the Sanctum's portal chamber.

Finally alone, Tina sank to the ashy ground, plunking down on the bloody step to put her face in her hands. This was her fault. All through the Deadlands, she'd told herself that playing the monster was the only way to make these idiots save themselves. To their eyes, though, she hadn't been playing. She'd actually *been* their monster, the thing worse than Grel, who kept them moving. As she thought back on the last few days, the memory of all the abuse she'd heaped on her raiders in the name of saving them made her insides twist. No wonder they were more horrified at being stuck with her than facing a city full of dangers. Those threats were as yet still hypothetical. She was the devil they knew, the necessary evil they were forced to put up with to survive.

Tina let out her breath with a curse. She wanted to say she didn't know which hurt more, the shame or the guilt, but she did. A better person would have regretted the pain she'd caused, the hurt. For Tina, though, it was the 'stuck with her' part that stabbed the deepest. The last thing she ever wanted was to be someone's baggage, and it hurt all the worse because she knew she'd earned it.

Raising her head, she looked bleary-eyed out at they bloody, burning city. The blackened, vacant windows of what had been Bastion's most luxurious shops stared back at her, their lovely limestone facades scarred with slashes and blast marks. Shapes scurried about in the darkness of the empty, looted rooms--more scavengers if they were lucky, who-knew-what if they weren't. It wasn't the sort of place any of them could be alone, which meant Zen was right. They were still stuck together, which meant no one could run. Not even her.

That sucked in the context of her current pity party, but it was also a relief, because it meant she still had a job to do--a job people needed her for so badly, they'd put up with her despite the way she'd behaved. She could never say no to that kind of need, even when all she wanted was to run away and hide in shame. There was nothing for it but to step up, and maybe if she did so well enough, this time, she could fix things.

Wiping her stone eyes, Tina braced her stone muscles and rose to her feet. Her magical armor scraped as she moved, the glowing, rune-covered plates of sacred sun-metal grinding together like old bones. When

6

she was standing again, she tucked the charter Commander Garrond had given her carefully back into her bag. She wasn't sure if it was legally binding--who knew what the laws of this world were now--but it was the only thing she had that said they were a guild. So long as everyone kept buying into that idea, she had a chance, which meant there was still a shot at making this right.

It was a thin thread of optimism, but Tina clung to it like a rope as she marched back inside the Portal Keeper's Sanctum. As she clanked back down the main corridor to the Room of Arrivals, Tina realized that the floor here wasn't the same pinkish red as the rest of the building. It was much darker, more red than pink. Her stonekin senses told her that it was the same rock as the rest of the building, though, which meant the discoloration had come from something else, and a *lot* of it.

Back inside the cavernous Room of Arrivals, Tina was relieved to see that Zen had organized things even better than requested. A Knight in armor with glowing green runes, two Rangers, and a Cleric with a Sunlight Staff stood guard by the main entrance. There were guards on both of the narrow side halls as well, while the rest of the guild had circled in the middle of the large, open area that had once held all the portals back when the portals had been open.

They all gave her scared looks when she passed by. Tina tried to answer their unspoken concerns with confidence, though now that Zen had told her what to look for, she could see the damage running deep in the raid, which made confidence a challenge. It didn't seem possible that she'd messed this up so badly, but she remembered every choice that had gotten her to this position. It didn't matter how good her intentions had been at the time, this was still the fallout, and it made her want to run harder than ever. The only reason she didn't was because running would shatter the group. As ironic as it was, right now, "stuck with Roxxy" was the only thing holding everyone together, so she sucked it up and kept going, marching over to the circle of her officers with her chin held high. Or as high as she could manage.

As always, SilentBlayde was the first to look up at her, and the first to smile. "What's the plan, Roxxy?" he asked confidently.

"That's a good question," Tina said, leaning on his support as hard as she could. "I think it's time we had the talk we didn't have time for in the Deadlands."

"Which is?" Anders, the ichthyian Cleric officer whose beating had been the first of Tina's many bad decisions, asked.

"We need to discuss how we're getting home," Tina said. "There weren't--" She stopped when she realized the whole Room of Arrivals had gone silent. Silently cursing all the cat- and elf-eared players with amazing hearing, Tina stepped a bit closer to her officers and continued as quietly as she could.

"There was nowhere to go except forward while we were running from Grel'Darm," she continued, hoping Zen wouldn't bring up the swamp. "But that's not the case anymore. I don't know what's up here in Bastion, but we're strong enough to make it to the South Gates. From there, it's just a starter zone, but really, it's the whole world. We're all max-level players. Other than the Deadlands, we out-level and out-gear everything out there. Wherever we need or want to go to in order to find our way back home, we can. We just have to figure out where that is."

The nervous shifting vanished as she mentioned "home." It was as if they'd all forgotten that getting back was a goal they could have. Now that Tina had put it back on the table, though, everyone snapped to attention. Killbox stopped wringing his hands on his massive ax, and KatanaFatale, the Sorcerer officer, ceased gnawing on his fingernails.

"Home would be really nice," NekoBaby said wistfully, crossing her arms over her prodigious bosom as if she were trying to shove it down. "I want my real body back, dammit."

"But how do we get back?" Zen asked pointedly. "We don't even know what brought us here in the first place."

8

That was a lore question. Tina wasn't the best at those, but she knew people who were. All it took was a glance over her shoulder to find her brother and his pet NPC hovering nearby.

"James," she said, waving at him. "Can you join us?"

James jumped at her question and glanced at his angry cat-warrior guy whose name Tina had already forgotten. That was awkward considering the NPC was supposed to be James's brother now or some bullshit, but honestly, she couldn't bring herself to care. She was just happy James was safe and close enough for her to keep him that way.

That thought was enough to make her grin as James and his cat-bro came over. But then her brother waved his staff at her happily while making a strange series of whooshes and clicks as he walked up. When Tina frowned, James turned to his NPC and made a different set of whistling, clicking noises. She was wondering what new madness she was facing--and what she'd have to do to stop it--when SB came in with the save.

"James," the Assassin said gently, "not all of us can speak of Wind and Grass."

James blinked his slitted cat eyes in surprise, and then his ears went back in embarrassment.

"Oops, sorry. I'm not used to being multilingual yet. Switching back and forth is surprisingly hard. Is Central okay? I'm pretty sure we all use that regardless of race or nationality."

"Central?" Tina asked, confused. "Central what?"

"You mean you didn't know?" James asked, tilting his head sideways in a catlike motion. "You've been speaking English since we got here, but we all have our racial languages and Bastion's Central Tongue as well now."

"What?" Killbox said excitedly. "No way!"

"Try saying 'the merchant's way' or 'king's blessing,'" James said. The words came off his tongue strangely, and Tina jerked in surprise when she realized he'd said them in Central, and not only could she

9

recognize that now, but she understood what he was saying. She mouthed the words to herself next, in English and Central, marveling at the difference in the sounds her tongue made even though her brain translated both the same.

She wasn't the only one. The entire room exploded in noise as the whole guild started trying out all the different words they now knew, especially the dirty ones. NekoBaby in particular was happily cursing up a linguistic storm, much to Angry Cat's stern disapproval. To her amazement, Tina was able to pick out the meanings of most things, even from languages she didn't think her character technically knew. For the most part, though, the chatter was a cacophony of whistling, bubbling, and yowling. She was trying to filter it out when she noticed SB watching the chaos with a smug smile.

"You knew, didn't you?" she asked, leaning closer to him.

"Sort of," he replied in Elven. "I knew that I could read."

Tina's eyes went wide. "Hey, I can speak elf!" She grinned and switched to Elven as well. "This is so cool! But wait, why do I speak Central and *Elven*?"

SB shrugged. "The FFO Wiki suggested that the stonekin's creators--the Bedrock Kings--were once fallen Celestial Elves. I bet that's why you know it. It was their language first."

"Yeah!" James chimed in. "Wasn't there an ichthyian scholar who referred to Old Elven as the Unbounded Language?"

"As in the Unbounded Sky? I'd forgotten that quest!" SB said, getting excited as well. "If all Elves originally spoke a central language, that would make sense why Old Elven is on so many old magical items."

"It's on my bow," Zen said, holding up her beautifully carved weapon. "I'd noticed I could read it back in the Deadlands, but I thought that was because it was bound to me."

"Yeah, yeah, cool, cool," Neko said, pushing her way back over now that she'd finished cursing Angry Cat into an apoplexy. "But let's get back to the important stuff, like how we're getting home." She turned on

10

James and SB. "You guys are no-life nerds who've basically memorized the wiki, right? Is there any mumbo-jumbo in there that explains what the fuck brought us here?"

Frank, already on edge from all the cursing, winced again. "That ain't how you ask for help, young lady." Neko waved his admonition away and honed in on James, who was looking decidedly uncomfortable with all the attention.

"I've actually been pondering that a lot recently," James said, his tail lashing self-consciously. "FFO's lore has a lot to say about other dimensions, mostly as a way of backsplaining all the alternate timeline quests, but there's nothing specifically about our world that I can remember. The only official entry that even acknowledges Earth's existence was that Japanese cereal commercial that claimed the power of the Once King was pouring into your bowl. It's hardly credible."

Tina rolled her eyes, but SilentBlayde started to bounce on his heels. "I have something!" he said eagerly. "The Origin Poem says, 'The Unbounded Sky is infinite. It reaches all worlds, and all worlds lie within it.' If that's true, then maybe FFO touches our world somehow. Or maybe our world is inside the Unbounded Sky, kinda like how the nine worlds of Norse mythology all fit inside of Yggdrasil."

Tina and James both looked at the Assassin in awe. "Dude, how the hell do you know the Origin Poem that well?" Tina asked. "It's only shown once during character creation."

"I don't remember the *whole* thing," SB said. "I just know that particular saying because the portal keepers quote it as part of their default interaction dialog."

Tina gaped at him. "You actually listened to that?"

"I couldn't ignore it," he said with a shrug. "I did every single one of the 'Ages Relived' events for four years running. You can only listen to the same dialog so many millions of time before it gets drilled into your head."

11

"It is a beast of a grind," James agreed. "I only made it half way before I gave up." He scowled at SB. "I'm *still* jealous of your Unfallen Cloud pet, by the way."

SilentBlayde flexed his arms in a show of gamer superiority, and Tina felt something inside her soften. Current disaster notwithstanding, it was nice to talk like this again. Things between her and her brother had always been tense, but FFO was the one place where Tina got to see the James she actually liked--the one who was clever and knowledgeable and wasn't messing up her life.

It was the only way she'd gotten through that horrible summer. James wouldn't even look at her after he came home from college unexpectedly. He'd tromped around the house like a zombie, barely coming out of his room even to eat. Inside FFO, though, he'd been a different person, always volunteering to help her through instances and quests even though he was already at max level. He and SB were the reason she'd been able to level Roxxy up to eighty in less than two months despite never hitting the level cap on any other character. With her tanking, James as healer, and SB as their DPS, there'd been nothing they couldn't do. Things had slowly fallen apart again after she discovered raiding, but for a few golden months, the three of them had been inseparable.

It had been so long, she'd almost forgotten all about it. Now, though, listening to her brother and SB nerd out over lore and their collections was painfully nostalgic. It made her homesick for a time when things hadn't been so serious, when she'd just been able to log out and go to sleep after a bad night and try again the next day. But this wasn't that world anymore, and if Tina ever wanted to get back to it, she needed to keep them on track. Her brother and SilentBlayde were already off on a tangent about where in this world they might be able to get a full copy of the since no one could make new characters anymore when Tina stepped in to steer them back to the matter at hand.

"However the connection happened," she said sternly, "what I still don't understand is why it happened through Forever Fantasy *Online*. You're talking about magically connecting worlds. This was just a game."

"I don't think where we are now was ever a game," James said quietly. "I think this world touched our reality somehow, and the game was just how we interpreted it." As he said this, all the playing-with-languages conversations behind them suddenly died out.

Her brother blinked nervously at the new attention.

"I can't prove it," he said quickly. "It's just a feeling I have. But if this world wasn't real before the Nightmare, how do you explain everything that's going on? The languages are a great example. I know thirty different words for wind, and not lazy, made-up words like whind, wynd, and winda, either. Of Wind and Grass is a fully functional, non-Romance language with its own unique grammar and alphabet, and it's not the only one. Even Central, which would have been the easiest to skimp on since it's basically the human common tongue, has zero conventions stolen from Latin, English, German, or any other language I'm familiar with."

"There's no hints of Japanese, either," SilentBlayde added. "Or Chinese or Korean, though I'm not as good at those."

"Exactly," James said, nodding rapidly. "FFO isn't *Lord of the Rings*. The game developers didn't sit down and invent multiple brand-new, completely functional languages just for the sake of world building. The only logical explanation is that these languages were already there *before* the game. And they're not the only ones. There's also the matter of all the extra land, people, and buildings that popped up. I played in FFO's early beta. I *know* they didn't make millions of square miles of world design and then chuck it all right before launch. This is all stuff that had to have been here before the Nightmare, er, FFO started."

"Damn," Tina said, looking up at the beautifully hewn stone arch soaring over their heads. "I knew this wasn't the game anymore, but I was still hoping that it was generated somehow. You know, a rogue simulation or some crazy psychologist's social experiment gone wrong. Something we could still just wake up from."

"We still haven't ruled that out," James said. "I just feel that the evidence points to this being a real world that was shoehorned into a game. I could be completely wrong, though. I can't prove anything."

"And either way, it doesn't help us with our real question," Tina said with a sigh. "How do we get *home*?"

"The royal castle," James said immediately.

Tina arched a metal eyebrow. "Why there? I came here betting on the Portal Keepers, but as you can see, they're AWOL." She nodded at the empty room.

"They're gone from *this* Sanctum," James said. "But there's one keeper I'd bet money is still in his place."

"The dimensional adviser to the king," SB finished for him.

"Bingo," James said excitedly. "He's the guy in charge of the people who made portals for every alternate timeline, lost dimension, and that really weird celestial dungeon series three expansions ago. The dimensional adviser is always with the king, *and* he has a personal library in the royal castle that might hold our answers. Especially now that all those books aren't static art objects, but things we can actually pick up and read."

Tina's eyes lit up as her brother talked. She wasn't sure which NPC her brother was talking about--they were all just interchangeable quest fountains to her--but a library was something she could get behind. Even if the king's portal dude didn't know how to help them, she had a whole raid full of super-smart, Intelligence-geared casters. With the right books, she was certain one of her people could figure it out. She just had to get them there.

Grinning at the brilliance of her new plan, Tina clapped her hands together. She'd just intended to get people's attention, but the moment her metal gauntlets crashed together, the whole room flinched. Tina flinched

14

as well. Apparently it was still too soon for sudden loud noises. If she wanted to fix things, she'd have to watch that.

"James, SB," she said, taking great care to keep her voice upbeat and nonthreatening. "This is great intel. Thank you very much. Going by what you've said, I think we should make for the royal castle and seek out the king's dimensional adviser. It's probably too much to hope that he'll be able to portal us all home, but he's the best lead we've found yet. Even if he doesn't know, his library is sure to have something. I say we go for it."

Most of the raiders seemed to like that idea, but while almost everyone else was nodding excitedly, KatanaFatale worriedly raised a hand.

"I hate to be a downer," the Sorcerer Officer said, "but how are we going to get *into* the castle?"

"What do you mean?" Zen asked.

KatanaFatale hefted up the side of his dirty purple robes and put a finger through the large arrow-hole above his right leg. "Remember the Order Fortress? All the NPCs blame us for wrecking their world. I don't think they're going to just let us use their library."

Tina and the whole group turned to look at James's NPC companion--the tall jubatus warrior whose only facial expression seemed to be "glare daggers."

"This is Fangs in the Grass. He was labeled as Arbati in the game," James said quickly, stepping between Angry Cat and the group. "I'm his adopted brother now. He's cool."

"But what about the NPCs here in Bastion?" Killbox asked.

Ar'Bati's sharp expression grew even sterner as he squared his shoulders. "You players appeared right after the Nightmare imprisoned our world," he said in weird-sounding Central. *Accented* Central, Tina realized with a shock. "For eighty years, we have had to fight and die endlessly for your entertainment. Even if you were not directly responsible, you were the face of our suffering. I have learned better and forgiven you, but do not expect others to have done so."

15

Tina ran a hand through her copper dreadlocks. "Yeah, that's about what Commander Garrond said too."

Everyone's expressions turned grim after that. Then NekoBaby popped up. "Hey, wait," the cat-girl said to Ar'Bati. "What do you mean, 'eighty years'? FFO has only been out for eight. Ten if you count that ridiculously long beta, but *definitely* not eighty. Full-sensory VR didn't even exist back then."

"I know the length of my imprisonment!" Ar'Bati snarled, baring his teeth at Neko as if the cat-girl's very existence offended him.

Tina stuck her giant armored arm between them. "Chill, dude," she said flatly. "She's not calling you a liar. FFO the game had two-hour-long day-night cycles so players wouldn't have to wait an actual day to do the daily story quests, so it would make sense if there was a time disparity between the real world and this one. It sucks if it was real-time for you, but it doesn't mean Neko's wrong."

That argument earned another growl from Ar'Bati before James put a hand on his shoulder and pulled the warrior back. Not that Tina cared. The cat could hiss all he liked. They were moving on.

"Okay," she said, raising her voice so everyone could hear but not so loud that it counted as shouting. "Unless anyone else has objections, we're going to the castle to talk to the portal guy. If we're lucky, maybe we can find a common enemy again and get some kinda team-up going with the king like we did with the Order."

"Or we could try conning our way in," suggested Anders. "King Gregory *is* called the Buffoon King. I bet he's super gullible."

"That's an idea," Tina said. "Anyone else know how we can--"

"I do!" James cried suddenly, digging into his backpack. "I know a way we can get into the castle. Take a look at these." He pulled out what appeared to be a pile of dirty looking papers.

Tina scowled. "What are those?"

"Letters," James said eagerly, opening the first scroll to show her the text written in elegant slanting script on the inside. "You remember the Once King's invasion plotline the devs were going to unroll at the end of this expansion? Well, it's still going, and it's gonna go down soon. According to these letters, the undead are planning to get around Bastion's defenses by portaling their armies straight into the Room of Arrivals. They've already bribed a portal keeper named Star Fall to open the door for them."

"Yeah, but that was in the game," Tina said skeptically. "That stuff doesn't matter anymore, dude."

"It does to the Once King," James argued, pointing at the letter. "The game might not be controlling things anymore, but he still wants to kill all the living, and this plan is already set up. Why would he abandon it?"

"Um, because we already wrecked it," Tina said. "Weren't you listening? We already beat the Once King's army back in the Deadlands. That's how we got our portal here."

"Yeah, but he has more," James said. "This was the undead expansion. The Once King has a presence in every zone, and they're all planning to--"

"Maybe they were planning to," Tina said, exasperated. "But I keep trying to tell you, this isn't a game anymore. The old plot doesn't matter. Those aren't even real letters you're holding. They're written in English! They're just leftover quest items and flavor text for players. They don't mean anything now."

"But they *do*," James argued furiously. "Some are in English, yes, but the rest are in Old Elven, which means they were written by the lich himself. This is a real plot that's going down *right now*, and if no one warns the king, Bastion will be defenseless when it shows up! The quests are all still..."

There was more, but Tina didn't bother to keep listening. There was no point in arguing when her brother got like this. Once he got something into his head, he never listened to her. She couldn't remember how many times she'd warned him something was a bad idea only to

17

watch him charge ahead and have it blow up in his face anyway. She just wished he could be this stubborn about things that actually mattered, like school.

That said, maybe James's obsession could work to her advantage this time. After all, the king was an NPC too, and those scrolls did look super official. If James could convince the bigwigs of Bastion that the undead were coming to kill them all, then it would be easy to pitch hiring the Roughnecks as the next logical step. And while James and his gullible NPCs were all waiting around for the plot to kick in, Tina could do the actual work of finding them a way home.

Her face split into a grin. Well, well, it looked as if her brother *was* useful after all. Now that she'd figured out how to use them, though, there was no way she could leave those letters with James. Whatever was waiting out there in Bastion, it was bound to be rough. Her flighty brother could barely handle raiding stress back when this was a game. Being subjected to the real thing might shatter him completely, and the last thing she needed was for James to freak out and run off with her ticket to the castle.

No. It'd be far better for everyone if the vital documents were given to someone who could actually handle the stress. James was still yammering on about "multi-pronged global offensives," though, which was why Tina just reached out and took the bag full of letters from her brother and then immediately handed them to SB.

"Wait!" James said frantically as she took them from him. "Those are--"

"Super important," Tina finished. "You made your point. But that's why I'm giving them to someone who can actually protect them."

SilentBlayde's eyes flicked toward James as he accepted the bag, but he didn't say a word. The Assassin just quietly put them into his backpack. Shoulders drooping, James turned back to Tina, but she didn't give him a chance to complain. He was getting what he wanted. He could be happy with that. Meanwhile, she had a raid to take care of.

"Listen up," she said, turning back to the crowded room full of players. "We've got our plan. The king's portal keepers are still our best shot at getting home, so they're our target."

Lots of people smiled when she said the word "home." Tina smiled back, happy to finally be getting something out of them other than fear.

"We've only got a few days of supplies," she continued. "But the royal castle has all of Bastion's four- and five-skull badasses, so if anywhere in this city is safe, it's there. James's letters should be enough to get us in the door. Once we've got the king's attention and a big new undead threat to scare him with, it should be a breeze to convince him to hire us as mercenaries. That way, we can eat *his* food and shoot *his* ammo while questioning *his* portal keepers on how best to get *us* all back to where we belong."

She finished with a smile and was immediately rewarded. Now that there was a concrete plan for going home, the nervous pall that had hung over the raid since they'd seen the burning city vanished like morning mist. All around the room, people were talking excitedly and readying their weapons to move out. Just seeing it made Tina feel ten times better. Then Zen opened her mouth and ruined her good mood.

"We should vote on it."

Tina barely clenched her jaw just in time. She'd been about to scream at the Ranger for throwing a speed bump into what was otherwise the best reaction to a plan she'd ever had. But yelling at people was what had gotten her into so much trouble in the first place, so Tina swallowed her frustration and gave Zen a polite look instead. "Why? Looks like everyone's already in agreement."

The willowy elf lifted her chin stubbornly. "You're deciding on a course of action that determines all our fates. That sounds vote-worthy to me."

In her head, Tina was cursing herself for ever allowing this stupid officer-vote bullshit to happen. But she must have made *some* progress

19

during the Order Fortress mess, because she managed to keep it inside as she turned to the rest of the officers.

"Fine," she said, only growling a little. "Is anyone against going to the royal castle and getting hired by the king so we can talk to his portal master?"

Five hands stayed down, but one went up.

"What is it, Killbox?" Tina asked, glaring at her Berserker officer.

"I think we should hit the bank first," Killbox said, his handsome face splitting into a greedy smile. "You know how much loot there has to be in there? We need to get it before someone else does. Also, there's a brothel over on Shadow Street that--"

"No," Tina said flatly.

"But they have elf chicks there with giant--*oof*!" He stopped with a pained grunt as Zen elbowed him in his chain-covered stomach. "Okay, okay," he said, rubbing his abs. "Let's go to the castle."

"Great. We're all in agreement," Tina said, turning back to the rest of the raid before anyone else could bring up a stupid idea. "All right, folks, we're moving out! I want heavy-armored people on the outside. Rangers, casters, and other squishy types are in the center. We're not going far, so small heals are okay, but *don't attack* anything unless ordered. We don't know what's going on out there yet, and I don't want to earn random enemies if we don't have to."

Everyone nodded and started sorting themselves out. Satisfied with her raid's quick compliance, Tina started forward to take her place at the front and nearly ran James over.

"What?" she asked, looking down at her brother and his pet cat, who wouldn't stop glaring at her.

James glanced nervously at the readying raid, gripping his staff, which was oddly wrapped in white sheets and what appeared to be some kind of a binding charm. "Where do you want us?"

Tina shrugged. "You're a caster, aren't you? So get in the middle with--"

20

She paused. Her first instinct was to stick him with Zen since she was the most responsible, but Tina really didn't want to ask the Ranger for a favor right now. SB was the next logical choice since she trusted him implicitly and he and James were friends, but he was her best Assassin, and she didn't want to waste his talents on brother-sitting. She was struggling to think of someone she could trust who wasn't going to be busy or inconvenient when she got a wicked idea.

"You know NekoBaby, right?"

James winced. "You mean the jubatus healer from the old Roughnecks who does nothing but troll people?"

"That's her," Tina said cheerfully. "Here's the thing: she's a great healer, but she's reckless and prone to antics. I need you to keep an eye on her for me. You've got a warrior NPC, and even if you're stuck as a healer, you're still a black belt in real life. That's a lot of muscle, and it'll make me feel a lot better knowing Neko has an escort that can fight."

That was laying it on super thick, but sure enough, James straightened up proudly at the request. His cat-warrior also seemed less bristly now that they had a seemingly respectful assignment.

"Can do," James said. "We won't let you down, T."

Tina nodded sagely as the two jubatus started walking toward Neko, fighting not to smirk at her own cleverness. NekoBaby didn't need an escort any more than Tina did, but the Naturalist was a drama-bomb of the worst sort. If she got her claws into an earnest mark like James, she'd never let him go, which would keep them both occupied and out of Tina's hair. Two cats with one stone.

Grinning at how nicely everything was going for once, Tina walked to the doorway to take her place at the front of the raid. When she made it to the doors, SB was waiting for her.

"Do you want me to scout?"

Tina glanced at the hallway where the smoke from the burning city was curling into the Sanctum. "No. I don't want anyone out there alone just yet. For all I know, the city is flooded with three-skull monsters."

21

Blayde smiled and stepped into *her* shadow, vanishing completely. "What if I do it this way?" he asked from the dark.

Tina jumped a foot in the air. She couldn't see him at all, but she could have sworn she could still *feel* SilentBlayde standing behind her, like a breath on her neck. It should have been as creepy as hell, and if it had been anyone else, it would have been. But this was SB. He was the only person in the entire world Tina trusted to have her back no matter what, and that made his presence in her literal shadow comforting rather than freaky.

"That's super cool, dude," she said, waving her arm through the empty place where he should be. "When did you learn to go into other players' shadows?"

"Just now," he said proudly, his disembodied voice a whisper against her ear. "I could never get this close in the game because of the limits the devs put in for PVP balance, but that's all gone now. Also, we're in the Holy City of Bastion, which is blessed by the Sun itself. The Lightless Realm is ultra-tame here, and that lets me get right up on top of people without them noticing. You can't see me, right? I can spy on lots of stuff for you this way."

"I can't see a thing," Tina said, grinning. "Right on! Invisible recon teams it is, then! But take ZeroDarkness with you. Invisible or not, I still don't want anyone out there alone. And don't stray too far from the raid, okay?"

Saying that made her feel like a clingy idiot. What was the point of having invisible scouts if you ordered them to stay close? But as much as she trusted Blayde's Assassin skills, she couldn't shake the two times she'd found him dead or nearly dead back in the Deadlands. "Find SB's body" was not something Tina wanted on her to-do list *ever* again, so even though it was dumb, she didn't take the orders back.

"I'll be careful," SB promised, vanishing from her shadow.

Tina missed him as soon as he was gone. There were gasps behind her as their other Assassin, ZeroDarkness, vanished from the raid as well,

22

and then Tina felt a slight breeze as the two of them slipped past her out the door. That was only because she knew what to look for, though. If she hadn't been hunting for invisible Assassins, she wouldn't have noticed a thing, which made her feel better. Good enough to draw her sword and point it at the smoky doorway.

"Roughnecks! Move out!"

No one sounded particularly excited by the order, but the raid did as it was told, following her nervously out of the stone Portal Sanctum building and into the still-burning city beyond.

Chapter 2

James

Surrounded by raiders, James shuffled out with the crowd following his sister for his second look at the ruins that had once been the Holy City of Bastion. Avoiding the slippery blood, he walked down the ash-coated stairs behind the swishing tail of NekoBaby into the small cobbled square outside. Back in the game, this had been where all the fruit vendors stood. Now, the only movement came from the packs of carrion birds. James wasn't willing to look close enough to see what they were eating, but the smell told him plenty. The whole square reeked of rotted meat and cold ash, making him regret his sensitive jubatus nose all over again.

Fangs looked even worse than he did. The jubatus warrior's eyes were huge and round above the hand he'd placed over his mouth in an attempt to block the stench. "This is even worse than Red Canyon."

James nodded silently, keeping a tight grip on his Eclipsed Steel Staff, which was still wrapped and bound to keep the voice inside from whispering. The wards also kept him from using his weapon's stat bonuses, but James didn't remove them. As useful as the raid weapon's boost would be to his casting, he could already guess what the nihilistic weapon would have had to say about this situation, and he did *not* want to hear it.

"What could have done this?" Fangs went on, looking up at the shattered windows and burned-out shops, their famous white walls now black and broken. "Bastion is the greatest city in the world, the seat of the king! It's protected by the Royal Knights. How did they let this happen?"

"I don't know," James said quietly, nodding down the eerily empty street Tina was leading them down. "But I bet we'll find out."

He was not looking forward to that. His twitching ears had picked up the sound of distant fighting somewhere to the south, but here, in what

24

should have been the richest shopping district in Bastion, he heard nothing. Even the vultures were gone, leaving the street bare save for the smashed skeletons of carts and the stumps of the scorched palm trees.

The silence grew deeper the farther they walked. In a few blocks, the buildings stopped being so badly burned, but that was almost worse. Now that the walls weren't solid-black soot, James could see the blood splattered across them. Gashes from swords and axes marred the once elegantly painted wooden shutters over the windows, and the doors of the houses had all been kicked in, the rooms inside raided and smashed when they weren't burned-out entirely.

"It looks like a war zone."

"It looks like a slaughter," Fangs corrected, looking pointedly down at the perfectly laid cobbles, which were covered in rust-brown stains. "This is--*was*--a residential street. Where are the townspeople? The shop-keepers?"

From the anger in his voice, it was clear Ar'Bati already knew the answer to that. James did too. There was too much blood on the ground *not* to know, but he couldn't bring himself to say the truth out loud. After what had happened at Red Canyon, he'd thought he'd toughened up, but there was something about this emptiness that got to him in a way that violence hadn't. He felt like he was walking through the ghost of an atrocity, but he was far, far too late to do anything about it. The whole thing made him feel infuriatingly helpless. The only good thing he could say was that at least they weren't being attacked.

He should have known better than to think that. Only seconds after the relief crossed his mind, a whole piece of building crashed to the street in front of them. Tina was ready at once, her towering stonekin lifting the huge shield until she filled the narrow street like a wall. The rest of the raid was still scrambling to react when SB suddenly appeared, stepping out of Tina's shadow as if it were a doorway.

"*Above you!*"

He pointed at the roof to their left, and James whirled around just in time to see a figure step out from behind a crumbling gable. He was tall and willowy, which meant he was almost certainly an elf, a player one. James recognized his crimson robes: a mid-range Sorcerer's set popular with fashion-forward players despite its sub-par stats. But just as his shoulders slumped in relief that they'd found someone who might be able to tell them what was going on, the player raised his hands and summoned a beach-ball-sized sphere of fire.

"I'm going home!" he cried, his eyes wild in the glare of his fire.

"*Shit!*" Tina cried, moving her shield over her head as the elf's fireball grew into a car-sized tornado of roaring, blistering flame. "*Fire!*"

Before James could ask if that was a description or a command, five bows twanged. The blinding swirl of flame vanished a second later as the Sorcerer toppled off the rooftop and fell to the street below, his body riddled with arrows. He hit the ground with a stomach-curdling *thump*. But while he didn't move again, the raid did, their formation dissolving as everyone freaked out.

"Oh shit!" one of the Rangers shouted. "We killed him!"

"Why did he attack us?"

"I think it was a suicide."

"Must have been lower level. Didn't have the health for five arrows."

"I can't believe we just killed a guy!"

"Calm down. We can rez him."

"Yeah! Can we use Raise Ally?"

"I'll do it!"

"*Stop! Stop!*" Tina shouted, shoving her way through the circle of panicking players. "What are you doing?" She waved her arms in the face of the Cleric who'd already started casting the Raise Ally spell. "No rezes!"

The Cleric bit his lip. "But--"

"But nothing," she said sternly, glaring down at the dead Sorcerer, whose crimson robes were now even redder. "This idiot just appeared on a roof and cast Fire Tornado at us unprovoked. He's clearly deranged. If we bring him back, he might just attack us it again. We don't have the mana to waste on--"

There was more, but James didn't hear it. He was already gathering magic into his hands, wrapping the green ribbons around his fingers until it went off in a flash, lighting up the entire alley with the golden-green explosion of the Naturalist's version of the Raise Ally spell.

"*Who did that?*" Tina roared.

"I did," James said, using his bound staff to push through the crowd until he reached the red-robed Sorcerer, who was now gasping in the middle of a bright-green patch of magically glowing moss.

The look on his sister's face cut him to the bone. It didn't matter that she was a giant stonekin. Her expression of disappointment and disgust was exactly the same as the one she'd given James back home, right before she'd slammed her door in his face.

"Of course," she said through clenched teeth. "Of *fucking* course it was you."

"What else was I supposed to do?" James yelled back, dropping down beside the coughing Sorcerer to help him sit up. "You were going to let him die!"

"That's what happens when you attack my raid!" Tina roared back. "You die! It's his own damn fault! And for the record, I wasn't planning not to rez him. If you'd let me *finish*, you would have heard me say that we shouldn't waste magic bringing back someone who tried to kill us without securing him first! You know, get a rope and tie him up or something. Not just dump our magic into a crazy person who might fireball us the moment he wakes up!"

As she spoke, James's stomach started to sink. Maybe he had jumped to conclusions, but he didn't regret it. "There was no time for that," he argued. "Raise Ally has a six-minute timer, and none of us have clocks anymore. He could have been lost forever while you were searching for rope!"

27

"Better that than risk one of my healers getting cooked!" Tina yelled. "You just endangered everyone by ignoring orders!"

James flinched. His little sister's anger had always been a thing to behold, but it was even more terrifying now that she was eight feet of solid stone. The only reason he didn't scramble away was because he was still clutching the Sorcerer--the person who was alive because of him.

"I'm not in your guild," he told her, voice shaking. "I don't have to take your orders. Especially bad ones."

If her anger had been terrifying before, it was monstrous now. He could actually see the fury spreading through her as she clenched her giant fists. "Goddammit, James," she said in a voice that shook the paving stones. "Why do you always do this? Why do you *never* listen to me?"

It was on the tip of James's tongue to say he *did* listen, except he couldn't say that, because he hadn't. He'd rolled right over her in his rush to save the Sorcerer, and while he refused to regret that, he probably should explain himself better.

"I wasn't trying to undermine you," he said, striving to be reasonable. "But we don't know why this person attacked. You heard what he said before he fired, right? He said he was going home. He had to know he didn't have a chance against us." He looked down at the shaking elf. "This was suicide by raid. You've got to be really desperate to try something like that."

"That's not our fault," his sister said coldly. "He attacked us! He's the messed-up one!"

"We're all messed up!" James cried. "We're all trapped in strange bodies in a strange world that hates us. You had a raid to help you, but plenty of people had to go through all of that alone." He nodded down at the Sorcerer, who'd curled his thin body into a ball. "He's a victim of this just like we all are! He deserves our sympathy."

"Then you can give it to him," Tina snarled, turning her back on him. "I'm not having an unsecured mad bomber in the middle of our group. You rezzed him. He's your responsibility. Leave him or drag him along. I don't care, but the next time he shoots a fireball at one of us, he's dying for good. Understand?"

James thought that question was aimed at him, but it was the Sorcerer who answered. "I won't do it again," the elf promised, his voice shaking so badly, the words were almost unintelligible. "Just please don't leave me alone. I can't be alone anymore."

He started to cry after that. James rubbed his back and looked up at Tina, hoping she'd see what he meant about people breaking, but his sister had already marched away.

"Everyone back in formation!" she yelled at the raid. "We're moving on!"

The other players scrambled to obey, picking up the bags and weapons they'd set down while they warily scanned the rooftops for more surprises. Up front, SB said something to Tina and vanished again, presumably to resume scouting. When he was gone, Tina started down the street again, leaving everyone else to hurry after her.

"Hup to," NekoBaby ordered, glaring at James, who was still kneeling beside the Sorcerer. "Rocky Road is in a fuck-it mood, and she will absolutely leave your ass behind if you don't get a move on."

"Tell your boulder-woman James will move when he is ready," Fangs snarled at her.

"Whoa, kitty, don't get feisty," Neko said. "I'm just telling it like it is." She looked back down at James. "Even Roxxy isn't this touchy. You must have some kinda great talent for pissing her off, dude."

James winced with how on-the-nose the cat-girl's comment was. "She's just trying to keep everyone together," he said quietly. "I'll handle this. You keep going. I'll catch up."

Neko ignored his excuses, sauntering off so she could stare judgingly at him while leaning against a burned palm tree. But at least she was no longer hovering, so James shook his head and turned back to the Sorcerer.

"Can you stand?"

29

The elf nodded and pushed himself to his feet, clinging to James the whole way up. The magic had healed the arrow wounds and the damage from the fall, but Raise Ally only returned people to life with twenty percent health. For this player, that didn't seem to be a lot.

"You should be ashamed," Fangs said when the Sorcerer was on his feet. "Suicide is cowardly and honorless. What would your family think of this?"

The elf winced, and James closed his eyes with a sigh. "Not helping, Fangs."

"It is the truth," his adopted brother said stubbornly, crossing his arms over his chest.

"I'm with Angry Cat," NekoBaby chimed in from her tree. "Trying to blow us up was a dick move."

"*Guys,*" James said sharply, but the elf shook his head.

"It's my fault," he whispered, looking down at his bright-red boots. "I'm so sorry. I didn't mean... I wasn't planning to attack. I was just desperate, and when I saw you all, I just sort of..." He sighed, rubbing a sooty hand over his face. "I'm sorry. This was all my fault."

He sounded broken by the time he finished, and James's heart went out to him all over again. "It's okay now," he said gently, squeezing the Sorcerer's arm. "You're with us now. You're not alone. I'm James, by the way. What's your name?"

"Flameboyant."

"That's your character's name, right?" James said, pulling the elf gently down the road so the raid wouldn't actually leave them behind. "This isn't a game anymore. Do you want to go by your real name now?"

Flameboyant shook his head violently, sending ripples through his long crimson hair. "I don't want anyone here to know who I am IRL."

"Why not?" Fangs demanded, eyes narrowing. "Are you a criminal?"

"It's 'cause you're ashamed of your character, isn't it?" NekoBaby said at the same time, her high-pitched voice surprisingly bitter. "Neon-red hair? Stupid fancy gear? You're a dress-up character, aren't you? I bet you don't want anyone back home finding out that you made the prettiest pretty-boy elf possible. I'm gonna guess you're a girl in the real world. You know girls can play guy characters without getting laughed at, right? It's not the same for dudes."

That was an awfully specific accusation, but before James could tell Neko to lay off, the Sorcerer fought back. "That's not it at all," he said angrily. "I am a guy, but I can't tell you my real name because everyone who knows this character knows I'm gay."

NekoBaby's mouth snapped shut at that, but James was more confused than ever. "How is being gay a problem?"

"It is in my country," Flameboyant said wearily. "Where I live, homosexual acts are still illegal. If anyone finds out what I've been doing in this game, they'll have me arrested. I can't risk my real identity getting out."

"Then your country is stupid and wasteful," Ar'Bati said. "At Windy Lake, we have no problem with men who like men or women who like women so long as they still sire children to grow the clans."

James couldn't cringe hard enough at that. "So close, Fangs," he muttered. "And yet so far." But as he turned to apologize to Flameboyant for his brother's complete lack of tact, the elf laughed.

"A point in your favor, then," he said, smiling for the first time. "Your medieval village is more progressive than my supposedly first-world home."

Ar'Bati looked mortally offended at Windy Lake being called a village, so James cut in before things could escalate. "What level are you, Flameboyant?"

"Forty-five," Flameboyant said proudly, brandishing his ruby-studded staff. "I'm fire spec!"

"No kidding. Never would have guessed that from the fire storm you tried to *kill us* with," Neko said as she fell into step beside them. "And

31

can you hobble any faster? We're getting dangerously close to the back of the group."

"Is this your alt or main character?" James asked, ignoring her.

"Main," the Sorcerer replied, though he did start walking slightly faster. "I'm just a casual player. I mostly log on for my friends and the cyber. Kinda wishing I'd ground to level eighty now, though."

"How are you feeling?"

"Physically or mentally?"

James shrugged, and the Sorcerer sighed, reaching up to rub the back of his neck awkwardly. "I'm not suicidal anymore, if that's what you mean. To be honest, it's a huge relief just to confirm I don't have Leylia's. I haven't been able to talk with another player since this happened, so part of me was still convinced this was all in my head. It's easy to talk myself into crazy things when I'm alone."

"I feel ya," James said, putting a hand on the tall elf's shoulder. "That was my worry when this started too. But we can't *all* have Leylia's, so you're good."

"Oh yeah, super good," Neko grumbled. "Just trapped as your character in a violent world that hates us. Real summer picnic."

"Don't listen to her," James said, shooting a glare at Neko, which the Naturalist ignored. "You're surrounded by level eighties with top gear. That's as safe as any of us can get. Roxxy, the big stonekin up front, is our raid leader. She's also my sister, and despite what she said earlier, I know she'll take care of us. You just scared her, that's all."

"She's right to be wary," Flameboyant said angrily, glaring up at the burned-out buildings. "This city is a nightmare."

"What happened?" Neko asked, suddenly nosing in. "You were here, right? Who did all this hacking and slashing? Was it an undead army or something?"

The Sorcerer bared his perfect white teeth. "Shitheads happened. The non-player characters all hate us now. They started messing people up

32

bad while we were all down and no one could move. They killed a lot of players outright, but they kept a lot more for their revenge."

The way he said that made James's blood run cold. "What happened?"

"A lot of stuff," Flameboyant said, his amber eyes getting that dangerous, far-away look again. "I was in the instanced player housing waiting for friends to 'port over for a good time when it hit. One minute, I was pouring drinks for three, then wham-spin-wham, and I woke up in some random warehouse on the east side of the city. My first thought was that I had Leylia's disease, so I was terrified to move. Eventually I got over it and crept outside to check. That was when I saw how lucky I'd been to be in that warehouse."

James didn't want to ask, but he had to know. "What was outside?"

"This," he said, spreading his hands at the bloody destruction around them. "Everyone was going crazy. Some players came out of the transition early and started fighting back, but others were like me. They thought this was just a dream caused by Leylia's, so they just did whatever they wanted. I've seen murder, theft, kinky slavery stuff, you name it. Not all of the NPCs were killing players for fun. Some were just trying to stop us from rampaging."

Flameboyant started to shake. "There was this one family. I think they were the elves who used to run the manawine shop. Anyway, they ran into my warehouse with their kids to hide, but a Berserker and a Ranger came in after them..." He trailed off, rubbing his hands over his face before turning desperately to James. "You have to understand, I still thought this was all a hallucination. Even if it wasn't, those players were level eighty. I couldn't stop them, so I just stayed hidden." He dropped his eyes. " It...it wasn't pretty. Wasn't quick, either. I prayed for Leylia's after that. Insanity seemed kinder than facing the truth, you know?"

He looked at James as if he wanted him to agree, but James didn't know what to say. Ar'Bati did, though.

"Where were the knights?"

33

Flameboyant blinked. "The who?"

"The Royal Knights!" Fangs snarled. "The protectors of Bastion! Brave men of integrity and uncompromising honor sworn to serve the king! Why didn't they stop this?"

Flameboyant stared at him as though he'd started speaking another language. "Dude," he said at last. "Who do you think was slaughtering us?"

Before James could process that, the whole raid ground to a halt as Tina raised her hand.

Chapter 3

Tina

Tina had spent the last twenty minutes stewing about her brother.

It wasn't just that he'd rezzed the Sorcerer or that he'd disobeyed orders. It wasn't even that he'd argued with her in front of her raid. It was everything. The whole *Jamesy-ness* of the situation. He always, always, *always* found a way to take something simple and screw it up. And then, when she pointed out his failings, he'd somehow turn things back around on her to make it look like it was *her* fault.

Now the whole raid was probably talking about how Mega-Bitch Roxxy wasn't going to rez that poor guy, all because James couldn't wait three *fucking* minutes for her to secure the situation like a goddamn responsible leader. It was the broken record of her entire childhood all over again. Even trapped in another world, everything was still about what *James* wanted. How *James* felt. All Tina needed now was for their parents to show up and make a fuss over how brave he'd been to stand up to her, and the circle would be complete.

Just thinking about it made her want to turn around and scream at him all over again. She tried to distract herself by keeping her eyes on where they were going, but that was almost worse. She'd liked Bastion well enough back in the game, but the city had been a horror show from the moment they'd stepped out of the Portal Sanctum, and it was only getting worse.

The farther they went into the old part of town by the castle, the taller the stone buildings got, looming over the streets and cutting off her view until she felt like she was walking through a canyon. The smoke was thicker in here as well, and the silent, blackened buildings were full of shadows and hiding places. It was the perfect place for an ambush, but aside from the suicide Sorcerer, she hadn't seen a soul.

35

Even SilentBlayde was quiet. She could feel him whenever he passed through her shadow. His slight touches were her only comfort on what was otherwise a horrible, paranoid march. Tina was wondering how much farther they had to walk before they reached the castle when SB's touches suddenly ceased.

She stopped in her tracks. "Blayde?"

A hand reached out of the shadows to grab her arm, making her jump.

"*Don't do that!*" she hissed as SB came out of her shadows. Then she saw his face. "Whoa, what happened?"

SB's blue eyes were haggard when they met hers. "Founder's Square is around the corner."

That was a relief. The Founder's Square had been one of the main player hubs back in the game. It had been right next to the Portal Sanctum, but Bastion had been hit by the same annoying spatial expansion as everywhere else, which meant a lot more walking. Still, Founder's Square was one of the main stops on the road to the castle. It should have been good to confirm that they were headed in the right direction, but Tina didn't think anything good was coming when SB looked like that.

"How bad is it?"

"Bad," he whispered, reaching up to tug his mask higher over his face. "You'll see."

She wanted to ask why he wouldn't just tell her, but she'd learned the hard way never to push with him. So instead, Tina held up her hand to stop the raid.

"Wait here," she said as the group came to a halt. "I'm going to check ahead."

No one argued, though Anders did step up to follow her, staff clutched nervously in his webbed hands. Technically, she should have told him to follow orders and stay back, but Tina didn't mind having a healer along, so she let him follow, holding her breath as she walked around the corner.

And into hell.

"Fuck," she whispered, hand shooting up to cover her mouth.

For the most part, Founder's Square looked how she remembered. It was still huge and had the fountain in the middle with its giant statues of the heroes of the ancient Battle of Heraldsford. Oddly, the fires that had ravaged the rest of the city didn't seem to have been as bad here. The tall, elegant buildings flanking the square were still sooty, but they were mostly intact, as were the ornamental pavilions where the NPCs who sold armor tokens used to stand surrounded by swarms of bored players browsing for new gear or showing off their elite pets and mounts. It had always been a popular place, crowded and busy.

Now it was full of bodies.

The football field-sized square was carpeted in corpses. They were so thick on the ground, Tina could barely see the blood-drenched cobblestones. Someone had stacked them stonekin-high around the fountain, making it look as if the heroes of Heraldsford were standing knee deep in a mountain of the dead.

Behind her, there was a horrible noise as Anders emptied his stomach. If she hadn't been subsisting on a diet of magical rocks for the last few days, Tina would have joined him. Whatever had happened here, it must have been days ago, because all the bodies were rotting. Even by her stonekin's dulled standards, the stench was horrific, overpowering even the smoke, but what really got her was the way they'd died.

"Blayde."

Seconds after she said his name, the Assassin stepped out of her shadow, his face pale above his mask. "Look at this," she said, kneeling down beside the body of a jubatus Knight whose throat had been slit open. "His sword is still in his sheath."

"A lot of them are like that," SilentBlayde said, his voice shaking. "Whatever happened here, they didn't fight back."

"I don't think they could," Tina said, moving to the next body, a Cleric with a very nice staff that was still on his back. "That's the Solace of the Sun," she muttered, eyes roving over the dead. "Glorious Plate of the Defiant, Aracneweaver's Robes, the Amulet of Discord... These are *all* players." Her eyes went back to the ugly knife slits that marked each throat. "No one just stands there passively and lets someone slit their throat. I bet whoever did this came through and killed them while they were collapsed during the transition."

"They do seem to have been here for a few days, so the timing matches up," SB agreed, waving his hand at the flies that were swarming over the square like a sandstorm. "But why would someone do this?"

"Why did the soldiers at the Order keep attack us?" Tina said darkly, looking over her shoulder at Anders, who'd finished emptying his stomach. "Go get the rest of the guild."

"Are you sure?" SB asked quietly as the Cleric ran off. "There're other streets. We could go around."

"No," Tina said, shaking her head. "They need to see this, and we need to search for survivors. Maybe someone managed to escape this." And if they had, maybe they could tell her who'd done it.

There was a wave of gasps when the raid came around the corner. Several players followed Anders's lead and lost their breakfasts. Others just stood and stared glassy-eyed, unable to process the sheer magnitude of death. A few ran out into the carnage, crying out in rage and horror as they discovered the bodies of friends, even family, but the true incarnation of rage was Zen.

Tina had never seen an elf do anything other than flow from place to place, but the dark-skinned Ranger *stomped* across the square to check the bodies, her lovely face as hard as steel as she turned over the bodies one by one with the cold, precise, channeled fury of a medical professional. When she'd made it through a good quarter of the square, she turned on her heel and stomped back to Tina.

"They're all higher-level players," Zen said. "I didn't see a single body wearing gear for less than level forty five, and there's no NPCs at all. Also, look at this."

The Ranger shoved a scrap of fabric into her hands. Tina looked down in confusion, fingering the scrap of bright-red wool. *Actually* red, not just bloodstained, and carefully lined with elegant gold-colored trim.

"What is it?"

"I don't know," Zen replied. "But I had to pry it from an Assassin's cold, dead hands. He was probably just aware enough to grab whoever attacked him, and a bit of their clothing ripped off in his fingers. Not that it saved him."

Tina clenched her jaw and turned to SB, who was still hovering beside her. "Do you recognize this?"

"It's too small to say for sure," the Assassin replied, leaning in for a closer look. "But those are the king's colors."

That didn't bode well. "Keep looking," Tina ordered, putting the cloth in her backpack. "See if you can find anything else. And check everywhere someone could hide. Maybe we can get a witness."

The raid nodded and fanned out. Since she didn't mind blood so much as a stonekin, Tina volunteered to check the pile by the fountain. She was gently looking through the piled corpses for any sign of life when a shout rang out across the square.

"I found someone!"

Her head shot up to see Zen digging at the rubble that had slid down in front of the door of a collapsed inn. "*Help me!*" she cried.

A half dozen Knights and Berserkers ran over to help her clear the fallen stone. Tina charged in as well and shoveled the ash-stained white stone aside to get to the weak voices she could now hear calling from inside. It took her, Frank, and Killbox working together to heave the final bus-sized hunk of solid limestone wall out of the way, revealing the main room of the inn. The falling rocks had smashed a hole in the floorboards, and down below, huddled like dogs in the cellar, was a knot of filthy, gaunt-looking people wearing the comically mismatched armor of low-level players.

"We're saved!" a human Ranger cried, her red-rimmed eyes wet with tears.

"Thank you," a gaunt Assassin sobbed as Killbox reached down to pull him out.

The Roughnecks rushed forward, lighting up the grim Founder's Square with the vibrant golds and greens as heals rained down on the battered survivors. James was there as well, adding his Naturalist spells to the mix. Tina didn't even mind that they were vastly overhealing and wasting mana. She was too busy hauling the group's lone stonekin up into the smoky sunlight.

"Thank you," he whispered, stone voice cracking.

"Our pleasure," Tina said, looking over her shoulder at SB. "Get these folks food and water from our supplies, please."

"On it," the Assassin said and disappeared, then he reappeared just a few moments later with a bag and a waterskin bearing the mark of the Order of the Golden Sun.

The players fell on the food as though they hadn't eaten in days, which was probably accurate.

"Thank you *so* much," the thin Assassin who'd been pulled out first said. "I thought we were done for."

"You're welcome," Tina said, flashing him a marble-toothed smile. "You're lucky Zen heard you down there."

The Assassin nodded, his face haggard, like he knew just how slim that chance had been. "Did you guys find BlastBarry yet?"

"Who?" Tina asked.

"Whoa," Killbox said at the same time, suddenly looking up from the rocks he'd been moving to prop up the structurally unstable inn's upper story. "Did you say BlastBarry?"

"Is he alive too?" Tina said hopefully.

All the survivors looked down at their feet.

"No," the Assassin whispered. "He's dead. But we wanted to find his body."

"He's the only reason we're alive," the girl Ranger added. "He died saving us."

"He's dead?" Killbox asked, eyes going wide. "*Fuck.*"

"Did you know him?" Tina asked.

Killbox nodded, covering his face with a burly arm. "BlastBarry was in the Red Sands PVP guild with me. We did arenas together all the time. Dude was such a great asshole with his long-range fire tornado spec." His deep voice started to crack. "I can't believe he's dead."

He fell quiet after that, and Tina put a comforting hand on his shoulder before turning back to the survivors. "Who did this?"

"The Royal Knights," the Ranger said, baring her teeth. "Those sons of bitches started cutting throats the moment the wham-spin-wham finished. I was still stuck in sensory hell, but I heard them laughing about it. I also heard someone order them to take the low-level ones alive. They were trying to grab me when some of the players started to snap out of it."

"A bunch of us woke up early," the thin Assassin continued, his face haggard. "I was one of them, but this isn't my main. I just started this character, so I couldn't do anything against the high-level Knights. The players who could fight back did, but we were badly outnumbered and popping up one by one. I dragged as many people as I could here to the inn, but there was a whole squad of knights out there slitting throats and grabbing people, and soon it was down to just BlastBarry. He was holding the doorway, dumping fire into the knights and screaming for everyone to get to the cellar before he ran out of mana. He took as many of the bastards out as he could, and then he blew up the inn instead of letting them take us. I heard the Royal Knights digging for a while afterward, but they eventually gave up and left us for dead. We tried to run away after that, but we're all too low-level. None of us had enough strength gear to move the rocks and get out. If you hadn't shown up..."

His voice trailed off, and Tina put a hand on his shoulder. "Thank you for telling us."

41

"I just hope you can do something about it," the Assassin replied, his red-rimmed eyes vengeful. "You guys look like serious raiders. I hope you kick the shit out of all those Royal Fuckers. I'd do it, but I'm stuck on my damn alt. There's not much I can do as a level thirty when all the knights are level eighty."

"Well, you're all with us now," Tina said, patting him gently on the back. "So you'll get to see it if we do."

"I'd like that," the Assassin said.

With that, Tina left the survivors to their meal, walking back to the door where SilentBlayde and Zen were waiting. "You catch all that?"

"We did," SB said darkly, glancing at Zen, who looked equally murderous. "Sounds like the Royal Knights were killing the ones who could fight back and taking the ones who couldn't."

"They were probably mad about the Nightmare," Zen said. "Remember how the Order treated us? We saved their bacon, and they still acted like we were Nazis."

"I think the Knights hate us even more," Anders said as he joined them. "Remember the April Fool's Day quest line? The whole game teamed up to humiliate and harass the Royal Knights every spring to stock up on luck potions."

"Those quests were hilarious," SB said, then his shoulders slumped. "Not so funny now, though."

"Being mad about pranks doesn't excuse this," Tina said hotly. "*Nothing* can excuse this."

"So what are we going to do about it?" Zen said. "And what about the low-level players they took alive?"

Before Tina could answer, someone cleared their throat behind her. When she looked over her shoulder, James was standing in her shadow.

Just seeing him set Tina's teeth on edge. James's antics were the last thing she needed right now, and to make matters worse, he had his pet NPC in tow. The Angry Cat looked shocked by all the death, which Tina

42

supposed was a very small mark in his favor, but he was still glowering with an attitude she absolutely did not want to deal with right now. She was about to tell James to take his circus back to Neko when he announced, "My brother has something to tell you."

Tina was about to tell him that his *brother* could go to hell when SB put a hand on her arm. "Does he know anything about this?"

"No, for I was not here," Ar'Bati replied, pulling himself taller in a futile effort to match Tina's stonekin. "But I heard others outside saying that this was the work of the Royal Knights, and I knew then I had to speak with you."

Tina's eyes narrowed suspiciously. "Why?"

"Because it cannot be true!" the jubatus said fiercely. "The Royal Knights are a noble order, protectors of the king himself! To be elevated to their ranks is the greatest honor in Bastion. They would never commit such atrocities!"

"Well, *they*"--Tina pointed at the huddled survivors--"say otherwise. Are you calling them liars?"

The cat opened his mouth, undoubtedly to say exactly that, but James got there first.

"He's saying there must have been some kind of misunderstanding," her brother said tactfully. "And I agree. You remember how the knights were in the game. They're the quintessential Lawful Good guys of FFO. They were always on our side in every quest zone. Why would they just go crazy and kill everyone?"

"Ask your cat," Tina snarled. "All the NPCs went nuts when the game turned real. Why should the knights be different?"

"The Nightmare changed everything for the worse," Ar'Bati agreed. "But the Royal Knights are *not* murderers! It could be that some were driven mad, as I was, but you cannot condemn an entire order for the acts of a few!"

"This was a lot more than a *few*," Zen said hotly, stabbing her finger out at the square full of corpses. "You think a handful of bad apples

43

could have done all that? This was clearly a coordinated effort to kill off all of a specific group of people. Where I'm from, we call that genocide."

"I know how bad this looks," James pleaded. "But Ar'Bati has a point. I can't vouch for the individual knights who did this, but the Royal Knighthood as a whole has always been unrelentingly good. They ran all the starter quest hubs around Bastion, and they serve the king directly." He turned to SB. "You have the 'Hand of the King' achievement, right? That means you've done *all* of King Gregory's quests, including the stupid lost-cat ones. You *know* he's not a bad guy. Do you think for a moment that he would tolerate this?"

"I can't say," SB replied cautiously, glancing at Tina. "I know the quest text made King Gregory *seem* like a decent man, but does that mean anything anymore?"

"But you have to admit that it doesn't add up," James pressed. "None of this does. It just doesn't make sense for the Royal Knights to slaughter players when we've always worked together. I'm not saying the individuals who did this aren't guilty if it's true. I'm just saying we should make an effort to investigate before we declare the one force who's always been our stalwart ally to all be evil murderers."

Frustrated, Tina blew out a breath. On the one hand, she thought James was grasping at straws. Between the scrap of cloth with the king's colors and the eyewitness testimony, it was pretty obvious who the guilty party was. On the other, though, the King of Bastion was the one who had everything they needed. Their plan to get home depended on gaining access to *his* portal keeper and *his* library. If her gut was right, then they were screwed, but if her brother was actually on to something and this was a horrible but *isolated* incident committed by a handful of knights gone nuts, they might still be able to salvage the situation.

"I hope you're right, James," she said tiredly, glaring down at her brother. "But there's no way to know for sure from here. We'll just have to keep going and see how things shake out. The Royal Knights' barracks are in the royal castle. If they've all turned against us, we'll know soon enough."

James closed his eyes in relief. "Thank you, T."

"I'm not doing this for you," she snapped. "I'm just not willing to give up yet on the only good plan we have. If we can't work with the king, we're back to wandering in the wilderness."

"I'm fine with that," Zen said, folding her arms stubbornly. "I refuse to work with anyone who does this."

"So do I," Tina agreed. "But so long as there's a shadow of a doubt, we should honor it. Innocent until proven guilty, right?"

Zen's scowl said she'd already made up her mind, but she didn't say anything else. When Tina was sure she wasn't going to have rebellion in the tanks, she turned to the rest of the raid, who'd crept close to the broken inn to listen.

"Let the survivors finish eating and then get back into formation," she ordered. "The plan is still on. We keep going to the castle."

No one looked happy about that, but no one seemed willing to fight her over it, either. It wasn't the reaction Tina had wanted, but she'd take it, walking out into the square to search for a clear spot where she could get her traumatized army back together.

***

The raid that marched out of Founder's Square was very different from the one that had walked into it. The players were no longer a huddled mass looking at the ruined city in fear. They were an army, marching in formation with weapons drawn. If the reason behind it hadn't been so gruesome, Tina would have been delighted, but she'd been changed as well, stalking down the increasingly chaotic ruined streets with her fists clenched and her eyes dead ahead.

The death hadn't stopped when they'd left the square. They were in the oldest, nicest part of Bastion now. Back in the game, the tangle of ancient streets and elegant houses surrounding the castle had been charming and expensive, the home of the city's most exclusive and ridiculous vanity item questlines, like the Duke's Turban. Now, they were a warren of smoke and blood.

Bodies had been shoved into every narrow alley. Just like in the square, the corpses were all players, but these people hadn't died of a quick slash across the throat. Their killers had been much more creative. The bodies had been mutilated, some with obvious signs of torture, others simply hacked to pieces in a frenzy.

The scale was totally different, but in its own way, the walk through the narrow streets was even worse than Founder's Square. At least there, people had just been dead. This violence was sadistic on a level Tina could not comprehend. Even the Once King hadn't treated his victims this badly. With every torn-up corpse she passed, her hatred for whomever had done this grew and grew. She was trying to get a hold on her rage before it caused her to do something stupid when she felt SB enter her shadow.

"The Royal Mile's just ahead," he whispered, his voice like a ghost in her ear.

The Royal Mile was the name of the big parade boulevard that ran north and south through the middle of the city straight to the castle gates. Despite the name, it was a lot longer than one mile, but it was the most direct path to the castle. That should have made it a good find in these mazelike streets, but SB's tone told a different story.

"How's it look?"

The Assassin took a shaky breath. "Not good. There's a ton of NPCs. They've got a big camp set up in the middle. There weren't enough good shadows to get in without being seen, so ZeroDarkness and I didn't get as good a look as we wanted, but it's definitely not a place we should just walk into."

"Well, shit," Tina said, looking up at the looming buildings caging them into the narrow street. "Good call on not risking yourselves. Is there any way around?"

"Not if you want to get to the castle," SilentBlayde said, stepping out of her shadow to point down the street. "There is a big building two blocks north that's still structurally sound. We could probably see what we're up against from there. Zero's already got it staked out."

"Good work," Tina said, holding up her hand.

The raid behind her stopped at once, feet and claws scraping nervously on the sooty street. Considering the last time she'd stopped them had been for a field of bodies, Tina didn't blame them one bit for being anxious, but she didn't have anything to say to soothe their fears. So instead, she ordered them to stay on alert and called her officers forward. She was about to lead them to the building SB had pointed at when she saw James walking toward her behind Neko, even though the cat-girl was hissing at him.

"Whoa," Tina said, putting her hand on her brother's chest. "What do you think you're doing?"

"Going with you," James said, looking obnoxiously determined despite his flattened ears. "I want to help."

"Then stay where you're told," she said sharply. "This is for officers only, and as you just told me an hour ago, you're not even part of my guild."

James winced at the reminder, but he didn't back down. "I have business with the king as well," he said stubbornly, pointing at SB's backpack. "Those are my letters in there. Ar'Bati and I risked a great deal to get them so that we could warn Bastion of the Once King's invasion. I can't do that if you take one look at the situation and decide to bail."

The moment he mentioned the Once King, Tina rolled her eyes. "Enough with the stupid plot crap already," she snapped. "For the *last time*, we already took care of the Once King's army in the Deadlands."

"And *I* keep trying to tell you that wasn't his only one!" James said frantically. "The Once King is the primary source of conflict for every zone in the game. All of those questlines are still going, and now that they're not being reset with the server or foiled by players, there's nothing to stop them from moving into their final stage." He looked around at the alleys full of bodies. "I know things here look *really* bad, but even if this was all the Royal Knights' doing, we still have a duty to warn the king about what's coming. I'm not part of your guild, but I am walking through this city with you. If you're going to make a decision that involves my future, I want to be there."

"Well, you don't get to be," Tina said coldly, crossing her huge arms over her chest as she glared down at him. "This isn't home, James. You don't get to dictate what happens here. This is *my* raid, so you're going to listen to what *I* want for once and *stay put*."

James sank lower. "But--"

Tina didn't stay to hear the rest. She just turned on her heel and stomped off down the street. It felt uncomfortably like running away, but if she'd stayed, she would have just ended up yelling at him, and that wouldn't help the new responsible-leader image she was trying to cultivate. Also, Tina *hated* yelling at her brother. It always ended up making her feel even worse, which was saying something, because no one got to her the way James did. Even when he wasn't trying, he always managed to wheedle into the worst parts of her, which was why it was better for everyone if she kept him at arm's length and preferably out of earshot. He'd be safe with the raid around him. Meanwhile, she had work to do.

The building SB had picked out for them was a tall, skinny tower at the corner of what had once been a charming intersection. The wooden door was charred and hanging off its hinges, making it easy to kick out of the way. Tina stepped over a fallen sign skillfully painted with a loaf of bread and crunched across the glass-strewn floor. The others followed right behind her, but while they all went up to the second floor with no problem, Tina paused at the human-scale stairs.

Stonekins had always been too big for the rest of the world. Back in the game, it had only been a minor inconvenience since she couldn't actually feel her shoulders scraping and her weight never broke anything because game physics weren't real physics. Now, though, all of that had changed. In her new perspective, the tiny wooden steps looked perilously fragile, like strips of balsa wood.

There was no other way up, though, so Tina turned her giant metal-booted foot sideways and placed it gingerly on the first step, easing her weight onto the board. The stair groaned and creaked as her weight came down, but the wood held, as did the next one. She had to hunch her shoulders and slide sideways to fit her body up the staircase itself, but eventually she reached the third floor, where everyone else was already waiting.

The six of them were crammed into what had been a small sitting room. ZeroDarkness was there as well, crouching beside the large cracked picture window that looked over the Royal Mile, the reason they'd come up here. Someone had pulled the curtains, which was good, because with all their glowing magical equipment, they would have stood out like disco balls to anyone who looked up. The multicolored light did a nice job of illuminating the room, though, enough to see that there were no bodies or blood. That was a welcome relief after the last hour, and Tina let out a long breath.

"Okay, Zero," she said, easing forward to stand at the window beside their other Assassin. "What've we got?"

The jubatus gave her a haunted look. "It's easier just to show you," he said quietly, pulling the curtain open a crack to reveal the Royal Mile below.

"Fuck," Killbox said.

"Fuck," Tina agreed, dragging a hand down her haggard face.

49

The Royal Mile was a four-lane flagstone road that ran from the southern city gates on her left all the way north to the castle's outer-wall gates on her right, which were shockingly close. It had been impossible to tell from deep in the narrow streets, but they were only a few blocks away from the royal castle, so close that she could no longer see the green mountains behind the towering eighty-foot white outer walls. Directly in front of them was the Grand Square, the largest expanse of open flagstone in the city. It was the place where all the big in-game events kicked off, which meant it was always decorated for a party. Now, though, it looked like a concentration camp.

It was jam-packed full of tall men in shining armor and wearing the king's red and gold: Royal Knights. As SB had mentioned, they'd set up a full military camp in front of the castle, complete with hundreds of tents and two large ballistae pointed south down the Royal Mile. All the roads leading into the square had been blocked off with ten-foot-high barricades made from piled rubble scavenged from nearby buildings. Only one section had been left open, and that was guarded by a full squad of Royal Knights armed with long spears in addition to their normal swords and tower shields.

Moments later, Tina saw why. As she watched, a wooden wagon carrying a large cage full of scared, sweaty players rolled up the Royal Mile to the defended camp. When it stopped at the checkpoint, the Royal Knights driving it, one elven and one human, went around back to open the cage. As the human knight approached, the low-level players pressed themselves against the farthest side of the metal enclosure, but gate guards were already there, using their sharp spears to drive the players forward to where the other guards could reach. The human driver laughed at their shouts of pain then plunged his armored arm into the crowd and yanked an elven Sorcerer still in her starter robes out by her hair. He dragged her kicking and screaming out of the wagon and handed her to his elven friend, who was waiting with a blood-stained rope to tie her hands behind her back.

Zen clenched her fists. "What are they doing to her?"

"I think we'll find out soon enough," Tina said, looking farther into the camp, where a dozen more wagons were parked in a circle, their metal cages full of player prisoners watching the newcomers in horror.

Back at the first wagon, the guard squad was using their spears to force the remaining low-level players out of the cage. There were a lot more of them packed in there than Tina had realized at first. By the time the cage was empty, the knights with the ropes had tied up over two dozen players. The last one out, an ichthyian Sorcerer, fell to his knees, clearly begging for his life, but the knights just kicked him into line, beating his face until it was bloody before binding his webbed hands behind his back and attaching him to the long rope with all the others. When all the players from the wagon were bound together, the guards marched them into the camp past the wagons full of other players and up toward the gate to the royal castle, where a gallows had been hastily assembled.

The long board platform had twenty nooses in total. Without a word from their executioners, the weeping players were hauled up the stairs one by one and fitted with thick ropes around their necks. The gruesome spectacle was being overseen by an astonishingly tall Elven knight. Even from this far away, Tina could see that he was at least a foot bigger than his fellows. When all the players were noosed, he stepped forward, brushing his graying black hair away from his face as he proceeded to read something off a scroll. Tina couldn't hear what, but as he read, all the players who hadn't been weeping already started to bawl.

"That's Captain Malakai!" SB hissed.

Unable to tear her eyes off the spectacle, Tina tilted her head. "Which one?"

"The really tall elf reading the scroll," SilentBlayde said. "You remember the four-skull mini-boss we had to kill on our way to fight King Gregory for the 'Drunken King' event every Oktoberfest? That's him. He's the officer in charge of all the Royal Knights."

51

"Oh yeah," Tina said, eyes narrowing. "Looks like we didn't kill him enough."

Back on the gallows, Captain Malakai had finished reading his decree. He rolled his scroll back up and walked to the edge of the gallows. Then, with a final sneering look at the condemned, he turned and kicked the metal lever, dropping all the players through trap doors. They kicked and swung at the end of their ropes for several moments. The higher-level players lasted longer than the lower ones, but eventually they all went still. When the kicking stopped, the Royal Knights standing guard nearby set down their shields to applaud. They were taking down the dead to make room for the next round when Tina reached out and snatched the curtain closed.

"Well," Zen said darkly. "I think that settled the question of whether or not the knights are guilty."

Tina nodded, clenching her fists.

"What are we going to do, Roxxy?" Anders asked in a stricken voice behind her.

"What do you mean, 'What are we going to do?'" Killbox asked. "We're going to go in there and start breaking things!"

"Yeah, fuck those guys!" Neko cried in agreement. "I say we roll 'em!"

The room was soon full of calls for violence, and Tina put her hand up for quiet. "I want to kill them too," she said. "But let's think this through. That camp is packed. There have to be hundreds of enemies down there, and not stupid zombies this time. Those are level-eighty NPCs in heavy armor with swords and shields, *and* they have prisoners. It's not the sort of situation we can just plow into."

She glanced back through the gap in the curtain to take a better look at the enemy. It pissed her off how much the Royal Knights' armor looked like Roxxy's. Since she was a Knight-classed character, it made sense that they'd look similar, but the more she studied them, the more certain she became that the men down there were *nothing* like her. Unlike

52

player Knights, who came in every race, the Royal Knights were all human or elven, and their weapons and armor didn't glow like hers did, a sure sign that they were made from mundane steel. They had to be stronger than normal people, given how easily they were able to drag the gearless low-level players around, but Tina was sure that she was a hell of a lot stronger. When a jubatus player got free and scrambled under a wagon to hide, no one lifted the wagon off him as she could have. Instead, the knights used their spears to stab the guy to death in his hiding spot. When they were done, they fished out his limp corpse and tossed it onto a wagon full of player bodies that was trundling out of the encampment, destination unknown.

"We have to get down there."

Tina jumped. She hadn't realized SilentBlayde was so close, but when she looked down, he was peering through the curtain right beside her, his handsome face twisted with fury like she'd never seen. And he wasn't the only one. All of her officers looked ready to murder. Killbox was grinding his fists together, and even Anders was flexing his spines menacingly. Tina didn't know KatanaFatale well yet, but apparently the fire Sorcerer could literally steam when angry. It was quite the unified front, and for once, Tina was right there with them.

"The king can go to hell," she announced as she turned to face them. "I don't care if he's our ticket home or not. We're not working for anyone who would order this shit." She pounded her fist into her open palm. "We're going to clean them out."

"I'm all for it," SB said immediately. "But how? You were right when you said that we couldn't rush in. There's an army down there, and our track record versus armies isn't so good."

"I don't know about that," Tina said. "There's a lot of them, sure, but these guys are nothing compared to Garrond's Order of the Sun. They've got mundane gear, no archers, no high ground, no magic users, and I know for a fact that the royal castle's main gate takes *forever* to open, so reinforcements won't be quick. We, on the other hand, are freshly loaded, as pissed as hell, and we've got the element of surprise." Her face split into a wicked grin. "I bet we *could* just roll 'em."

That earned her a *whoop whoop!* from Neko and a high five from Killbox. Everyone else seemed less gung-ho, but the only person who actually spoke up was Anders.

"And then what?"

The whole room turned to glare at him, and Anders cringed, but his bulging fish eyes never left Tina's. "Say we do roll the knights and free the players--what do we do with them?"

"We take them with us, duh," Neko said. "They're baby lowbies. If we set them loose in the city, they'll just get caught again."

"Okay, but *how* do we that?" Anders pressed, keeping his eyes on Tina. "You said yourself that our food won't last forever, and that was before we added the survivors from the Founder's Square to our ranks. There are a dozen more wagons full of low-level players down there. That's a lot of extra mouths to feed who can't contribute to the raid. We'll be greatly increasing our liabilities by saving them."

"Well we can't *not* save them," Tina said fiercely. "What are you saying? That we should just leave them to die?"

"No, no!" The ichthyian Cleric put up his webbed hands. "This is an atrocity, and it absolutely has to stop! But we're not saving anyone if we rush in blindly, use up all our mana and ammo, and then collapse while wandering through the city, trying to get away. Even if we kill every knight in that camp--and that's a stretch--the FFO wiki defines the Royal Knights as the king's private army, which means there have to be a lot more of them around than the hundred or so we can see down there. There are also the normal city guards and Bastion's soldier NPCs, all of whom will be after us once we do this. Again, I'm one hundred percent for wrecking that camp. I just also want us to have a plan for what comes next."

Tina didn't have a good answer for that. She leaned back to the window, glaring through the curtains at the extermination camp to see if

54

there was something she'd overlooked, some big weakness they could exploit to their advantage like the corridor they'd used to trap and kill Grel. She was still searching when Killbox snorted.

"Why are you getting all complicated about it?" he asked. "It's not like we haven't done this before."

Tina glanced back at him in confusion. "What do you mean?"

The Berserker shrugged his huge shoulders. "I'm just saying that this shit fest is no different from every other shitty zone in FFO. Here, see if this sounds familiar." He straightened up and schooled his face into a stern frown. "'Hero, there's an enemy camp in the square below! You need to kill the guards, free the prisoners, arm them with the enemy's weapons, and feed them with the enemy's food. And while you're doing that, burn fifteen tents and kill the named officers X, Y, and Z. Oh, and if they have any cool magical thingies lying around, rig those into a bomb as you leave.'" His stern scowl slid into a smirk. "See? This is just another quest zone. Boo-fucking-yah."

Tina's jaw was hanging open by the time he finished. She didn't know whether to laugh at his stingingly accurate summary of things quest givers wanted them to do in what felt like every zone of the game, or to be astonished that Killbox had actually suggested a viable plan.

"I can't believe I'm saying this," she got out at last, "but I think Killbox has a really good idea."

Killbox stuck his thumbs in his belt, grinning at her praise. Meanwhile, everyone else was staring at her in shock.

"I'm serious," Tina said. "If we smash the place up and give all the freed players the knights' weapons and supplies, that lets them join us as fighters instead of liabilities. Also, breaking their stuff and killing their officers means the knights can't easily follow us or counterattack. And if they *do* have a magical thingy, we can totally rig it to explode. It may not blow up big, but having to worry about defusing a bomb is just one more thing they'll have to do instead of chasing us. It's a legit good plan!"

"But what happens after that?" Anders asked, pressing his webbed hands together nervously. "I don't mean to keep being Captain Bringdown, but you *do* realize that attacking the king's knights means we'll be starting a rebellion, right? We're in the heart of Bastion's territory. All the surrounding zones are sworn to support the king. Even if we make it out the gates, if King Gregory names us enemies, we'll have nowhere safe to run."

"We're not going to run," Tina said firmly. "If we can't go to the castle, we'll go to the bank."

"I don't think withdrawing your savings is gonna help," Frank said nervously.

"We're not going there for money," Tina clarified. "The bank is a magical vault that stores all of the stuff players want to keep but can't fit in our backpacks. It's literally packed with loot! Plus, since it was always meant to look secure, the building itself is a fortress." A smile broke over her face. "Think about it: we're about to free and arm a hundred players who hate the knights as much as we do. Once we've loaded up on the enemy's weapons, we'll take our *army* and march to the bank. Once we take control of the building, we'll have a bitchin' base with all the food, magical supplies, and weapons we could ever need. Do you know how much sweet armor I've stuffed into my vault over the years? I could probably gear an entire raid by myself."

The whole room started buzzing excitedly at the prospect of getting their loot back, but Zen still looked unconvinced. "That might work against normal NPCs," she said. "But what if the king decides to come out and kill us himself? He's a five-skull raid boss, remember?"

"If he comes out, we'll deal with it," Tina said confidently. "We're a raid. Bosses are our *thing.* And I've already tanked him hundreds of times. I've spent the last five Oktoberfests chain killing him, trying to farm his stupid endless beer stein, which he *still* hasn't dropped. Gregory has got a lot of HP, but he's nothing on Grel. We've totally got--"

56

She cut off when SilentBlayde suddenly stepped into the center of the room. "They've hung twenty more people while we've stood here arguing," he said darkly.

"Enough talking, then," Tina agreed, looking around at her officers. "Let's vote on it."

Zen's eyes went wide. "*You're* asking for a vote?"

Tina gave her a firm nod. "This is a course of action we're all bound by. Everyone has to be in, not just following my orders. That's vote-worthy in my book."

For the first time ever, Zen beamed at her. "I vote yes," she said, raising her hand. "I don't care if we have to fight the knights and the king at the same time. I couldn't live with myself if we abandoned all those people."

"Same here," Killbox said, thrusting his armored arm up so fast, he punched a hole in the low ceiling.

"Me too," KatanaFatale said.

"You know my vote already," SB said, putting his hand up.

"Thanks for letting me ask the devil's questions," Anders said. "No matter what, I want to stop the knights. Let's do it." His webbed hand went up.

"I'm still not entirely sure what's going on with the boss monster king and what not, but if we're saving people, I'm all in," Frank said cheerfully.

"It's a hell yeah for me," NekoBaby said, throwing her hand into the air. "I'm *so* down with killing those assholes."

"That's everyone, then," Tina said with a bloodthirsty grin. "The vote passes. Now." She cracked her stone knuckles. "Let's go teach this city not to mess with players."

The others cheered and rushed down the stairs to tell the raid. Not wanting to crash three stories to the ground, Tina followed more slowly, easing her weight down the not-rated-for-stonekin steps. For once, though, even being forced to lag behind couldn't dent her mood.

She'd hated this voting thing when it had first been forced onto her, but now Tina was starting to see its usefulness. Having to make her case for big stuff was annoying, but letting the officers have their say at the beginning seemed to eliminate dissent afterward. *And* since she could always count on SB to take her side, it was impossible for her to actually lose a vote since it took *all* of the officers voting together to override her say as Guildmaster. She still hated that she'd had to give up power, but this wasn't actually a bad system now that was getting used to it.

Figuring that out made Tina feel like she'd already won. By the time she got to the ground floor of the destroyed bakery, she was stepping lighter than she had since this disaster started. True, her plan to get them home had fizzled, but she finally felt like she had her guild back in hand, and they were about to go pound some fuckers who *truly* deserved it.

"You look surprisingly happy," SB, who'd been waiting for her at the door, said.

"Of course I'm happy," Tina replied. "We finally get to be the goddamn heroes for once." She flashed him a grin. "You ready to do this?"

"*Oh* yeah," he said, patting his blades. "Just give the word."

"Let me get my raid ready and it's given," she said, breaking into a jog as she hurried back to her players to whip them up for the kill.

Chapter 4
James and Tina

"**T**hey're doing what?" James hissed. "*We're* doing what?"

NekoBaby gave him a wicked fanged grin. "Stomping the yard, fool! These NPC knights are player-killing creeps, so we're gonna trash their shit and save our peeps. The plan is easy: we're gonna stay in formation and kill everything sleazy. Healers and ranged are gonna take the barricades so we can support the melee throwing down like grenades."

She finished with her hands out, miming a mic-drop motion with her staff. "There," she said, standing up normally again. "That's our strat. I even rapped it for you, so don't fuck up."

James still couldn't believe what he was hearing, and not because of Neko's awful rhymes. "But that's a *rebellion*!" he cried, slamming his own staff down on the cobblestones. "It's the worst course of action possible! Even if we win, we're going to split the city into armed factions right before the Once King's invasion!"

"Meh," the cat-girl said with a shrug. "You're the only one who thinks the invasion is still going to happen. I'm with Roxxy. The O. K.'s corpse brigade already got beat, which means all the scripts are off. We're writing our own plot twists now."

"But why are we going straight to *attacking*?" James demanded. "We should at least talk to the king first!"

"Um, dude, they're the *Royal* Knights," Neko reminded him. "Unless the king is seriously AFK on his duties, it's kind of obvious he's in on this."

James shook his head violently. "I can't believe that. King Gregory is a famously kind man. Hell, half of his quests are for solving problems caused by him being *too* nice. There is no way he'd be party to his knights committing war crimes."

Neko rolled her orange eyes. "Yeah, well, they kind of built an industrial-strength hangman's scaffold on his front door, so 'scuse me if I don't believe you."

"There just has to be some mistake," James pressed. "This isn't normal behavior for them! We should at least try to find out what's going on before we--"

"Why the hell are you defending them?" Neko demanded, jabbing him with her claw. "They're mass-murdering fucks!"

"I'm not defending their actions!" James cried. "I'm just saying we shouldn't engage in vigilante justice when we haven't tried *anything else* first!"

Neko crossed her arms over her chest belligerently. As she did, James realized for the first time that the healer wasn't actually wearing a white dress, but a giant undershirt with a belt over it. Her actual robes, worn over her shoulders like a long open duster, were ripped open down the front. He was wondering what had happened to her when Neko turned up her nose.

"You can bitch back here all you want, but I take my orders from Roxxy, and she says we're gonna murder the shit out of them for what they've done."

Frustrated, James dragged a hand through his fur. "Then I'm going to talk to Tina."

"So much nope on that one," Neko said, snagging his shoulder. "Roxxy told me to keep you out of trouble. I've got the lightning sub-talent, so don't make me Taser you."

She waved her other hand at him, which was now wreathed in lighting, and James froze. Despite her tattered robes, the cat-girl still had ten times better gear than he did. Even specced for healing, one blast of her lightning would be enough to put him on the ground. He was still backing away when Ar'Bati suddenly jumped up from the step where he'd been sitting beside the silent and grim Flameboyant.

"What do you mean 'keep us out of trouble?" he demanded. "*We* were supposed to be escorting *you!*"

"Yeah, that's what we in the business call 'being handled,'" Neko said sweetly, batting her eyelashes at the furious warrior. "I'm actually the cat with the power, and just so you know, I'm a blast first, heal second kind of girl. But we can still be cool. Just don't try anything stupid, and I'll keep you nice and safe."

By the time she finished, Fangs was growling deep in his throat. If James had given him even the slightest hint of a go-ahead, he probably would have thrown down right then and there, which was why James kept his arms firmly at his sides. It wasn't just fighting Neko that would be futile. They were in the middle of a whole raid of Roughnecks, any one of whom could tie both of them into pretzels. Any efforts to force their way anywhere would be doomed from the start, so James lowered his bound staff.

"Okay, okay. You win," he said, fangs clenched in frustration. "We'll stay put."

That earned him a pat on the head and a "good boy" from Neko. It also earned him a punch in the arm from Ar'Bati. The hit was enough to make him stumble, but James didn't even say *ow*. He just waited patiently until Neko was distracted by some other drama--which took precisely ten seconds--before turning his attention back to his adopted brother.

"Listen--"

"No!" Fangs in Grass snarled. "*You* listen! I refuse to fight against the king, and you must too. Anything less is treason!"

"I know," James said. "But--"

"Since you aren't panicking, it's obvious you do *not* know," Ar'Bati said. "King Gregory's rule doesn't stop at Bastion's walls! The Savanna is also part of this kingdom. Our father is addressed as 'Lord Rends of Claw Born' outside of Windy Lake for a reason, and our mother was the Four Clans' ambassador in Bastion for years. You were adopted into a noble and powerful family! We are not commoners who can flirt with questionable acts. *Especially* treasonous ones! You heard the idiot Naturalist's rhyme. We risk dishonoring our entire clan for generations just by standing here!"

"I don't want to do this, either," James assured him. "But Tina is my sister. I can't abandon her."

Ar'Bati made a cutting motion with his claw. "Your *sister* is a power-drunk mercenary with no loyalties who chases whatever benefits her at the time! Stopping her would be far kinder than abetting this crime!"

"Roxxy would kick your ass if she heard that," NekoBaby informed them.

James and Ar'Bati both whirled around, and the jubatus healer, who was still a good ten feet away, batted her large, pointed ears. "I have *cat ears*, remember?" she said, rolling her eyes. "You want to talk shit behind Roxxy's back, do it more quietly."

"I will tell her my opinion to her face when the chance arrives!" Fangs yelled back, puffing out his chest. "I do not fear her like the rest of you, cowering in her shadow!"

Neko sneered at him. "Go ahead and try it, fur ball. She'll turn you into Angry Cat tacos."

Ar'Bati hissed at her for that, and James grabbed his arm. "Leave it," he whispered angrily. "It doesn't matter what we want, anyway. We're prisoners."

"Then we should be making escape plans!" Ar'Bati whispered back.

"I can still heaaar you, Angry Cat!" Neko called in a singsong voice

"*My name is Fangs in the Grass!*" Ar'Bati bellowed back.

Whatever new insult Neko was about to yell back got cut off when Tina climbed up on an overturned wagon and banged on her shield for attention.

"All right, people, listen up!" she yelled, her stonekin voice bouncing off the looming buildings loud enough to be heard in the back but not so loud that it carried to the troops encamped in the square a few blocks away. "The king's knights' base is just around the corner. You all saw what they did in the Founder's Square. Well, they're still doing that, and we're not going to stand for it!"

A wave of angry agreement swept through the crowd, and James's ears went flat. None of the fury was directed at him, but ever since the village, being in an angry crowd made him feel as if someone were going to bash him with a rock at any moment.

"They picked the wrong players to mess with!" Tina went on. "We're going to hit them like a hurricane. Smash their shit, free their prisoners, and head for the bank to regroup and fort up for whatever comes next. Now there're a lot of them out there, so I want everyone in the same formation we used for Grel'Darm. If you have questions, ask your class officer. They know all the specifics. Lowbies, you guys aren't fighting until we get you some better gear, so stay in the back with the casters, where you'll be safe. That's all there is to it. Now get to your groups!"

James winced while all the players around him cheered. The Roughneck officers immediately pulled their people together and started explaining the class-specific parts of the plan. Each group raised their weapons when they finished. When all arms were in the air, Tina drew her sword and waved the group toward the main road.

"James," Ar'Bati said frantically as the raid began to march. "We must not be part of this!"

"I don't intend to be," James said, turning to NekoBaby, who'd bopped back to their side. "We refuse to fight," he informed her. "Taser me all you want, but we're not helping."

"Umm, dude, no one *wants* you to help us," Neko said, looking James up and down. "You've got shit gear, and your pet NPC doesn't even rate. My orders are to keep you safe and out of Roxxy's hair. If you're not fighting, that just makes my job waaaay easier, so please feel free to do nothing at all."

"Oh," James said, shoulders sinking.

Neko patted him on the head one last time and sauntered back to her Naturalists, leaving him unsure if he felt better or worse.

63

After hours of walking through narrow, smoke-clogged streets, emerging onto the Royal Mile felt like stepping onto a stage. The blasting light of the noonday sun radiated down on the scarred flagstone highway, banishing the shadows. Now that there were no buildings blocking it, the wind from the knifelike green mountains beyond the city was free to blow the smoke away, leaving the corridor that bisected the city clear and bright.

Up the hill to the north, dead ahead, Tina saw the king's castle in all its glory. In stark contrast to the ruined city, the royal castle's gold-roofed towers gleamed as bright as torches behind the soaring outer walls. And in the middle, placed atop the tallest spire like a jewel in a scepter, was the Holy Bastion, the ancient magical artifact the city was named after.

She couldn't see the artifact itself from down in the street. Accessing the *actual* Bastion required a multistage questline in which one ran around discovering the history of Bastion the city and how it was related to Bastion the magical doohickey. Tina couldn't remember what the big sun crystal surrounded by alchemical machinery did, exactly--the Bastion Castle quests were for level thirties, which was a long time ago for her--but she vaguely remembered it was one of those super-weapon-against-evil things that were somehow never actually available when you needed them. It *was* pretty, though. Even from way down here, the Bastion's golden light poured through the white tower's stained-glass windows bright enough to rival the actual sun riding high in the blue sky above it.

But while the inner keep still looked like a fantasy king's enchanted sanctum, the outside of the castle told another story entirely. Now that they were closer, Tina could see that the castle's outer wall wasn't nearly as white as it had looked from far away. The smoke had gotten here, too, staining the giant stones a grimy, brackish gray. Even the golden gates looked dimmer, especially given what was growing in front of them.

Directly ahead, the extermination camp they'd spied on from the bakery was swarming like a kicked-over anthill. Now that she was on the road instead of looking in from above, Tina could no longer see over the ten-foot-high barricades of rubble, but the gap in the walls the wagons went through was directly in front of her, and that was where Tina was aiming.

"Right!" she said, lifting her sword. "Let's see how these cowards stand up to people who can fight back!"

The Roughnecks poured out of the side street and onto the Royal Mile behind her with a roar, shuffling and bumping each other as they moved into formation on the open road. As ordered, the Knights, Assassins, and Berserkers all moved to the front. The Sorcerers and Rangers fell in behind them, while the healers and lowbies shuffled around to the very back. Several feet to Tina's right, Frank jogged up to take the second spearhead position, closing his visor nervously since they were both now a good twelve feet out in front of anyone else.

Horns blared from the camp, sounding the alarm. Tina wasn't surprised and didn't care. Stealth was not her raid's forte. She'd kept them hidden in the backstreets for as long as she could, but there was no way to hide four-dozen raiders with giant glowing weapons once it came time to actually roll out. The shit-geared Royal Knights couldn't do squat against a raid like hers, anyway, so she just kept striding forward, trusting her people to stay in formation as she picked up the pace.

When they were less than five hundred feet from the front barricade, two heavy wagons were pushed together to close the entrance to the camp, and the plate-armored knights in red-and-gold tabards swarmed the rubble line, packing its ridge with their swords and interlocking shields. They'd moved the two ballistae she'd noticed earlier up as well, nestling the giant siege weapons into the stacked stones to hold them in place while crews cranked back the telephone pole-sized spear shafts, their two-foot-long arrow-headed tips pointed at the raid.

When the siege weapons were ready to fire, the tall elf captain with the graying black hair Tina had seen operating the gallows emerged to stand on top of the largest wagon being used for the blockade. Sneering at the approaching players, he raised a metal cone to his mouth.

"I am Captain Malakai of the Royal Knights!" he shouted, the simple megaphone boosting his already-booming voice to painful levels. "In the name of King Gregory, I command you to halt!"

Tina shrugged and raised her shield.

"The king has issued a decree!" Malakai went on, holding up a scroll of parchment bound with all kinds of official-looking ribbons and seals. "All players are to disarm and surrender themselves to be judged for crimes committed during and after the Nightmare."

Tina edged her shield higher. She was only two hundred feet away from the entrance to the camp now.

When it was clear she wasn't stopping, Malakai shoved the scroll into his assistant's arms, nearly knocking the much smaller man over. But rather than looking angry, as Tina expected, the captain's face was almost gleeful when he turned to yell at them again.

"This is your last warning!" he cried, his dark eyes bright with something that sent shivers up Tina's stone spine. "Lay down your weapons and surrender! Anything less, and we will slaughter you where you stand. Not even the vultures will want you after our vengeance is completed!"

Tina smiled in reply and swept her sword through the air until it rang. Behind her, a symphony of steel rose in reply as all the players readied their weapons, the air filling with power as spell casters gathered the beginnings of their magics, sending a hum like electricity through the raid.

"So be it," Malakai said, his thin lips curling in disgust as he turned to his knights. "*Open fire!*"

"Open fire!" Tina shouted at the same time, throwing up her shield. Frank did the same, dropping into his stance just in time as the ballistae on the barricades twanged, and two telephone pole-sized arrows launched toward the raid.

The massive bolt slammed into her bulwark with deafening force. Sparks flew from her metal boots as the impact pushed her down the cobbled street, but her enchanted shield had taken far worse than this. An arrow, even a giant one fired by a siege weapon, was nothing compared to the beating Grel had given her, and after pushing her several feet back, the bolt's massive barbed head broke into pieces, followed by the shaft. As metal shards and splinters exploded over her head, Tina glanced to the right to see that Frank had likewise stopped his bolt. She was taking a breath to tell him good job when the raid launched its attack.

A slim dozen glowing arrows flew over her head from the Roughneck ranks. Their tiny fusillade looked pathetic as it sprinkled down on the knight-covered barricade. The armored soldiers raised their shields in a tight formation to block the attack, but it didn't work at all. The magical arrows shot from enchanted weapons of legend punched straight through their mundane shields and armor and exploded, covering the barricade in a wave of fire and acid so bright, Tina was forced to look away.

Look away and *grin*. After all the hard two- and three-skull fights in the Deadlands, it felt so *good* to see what her raid could do against normal, at-level opponents. Men screamed as whole squads were immolated. Dozens more fell to the ground, thrashing as they were dissolved by the Rangers' Acid Shots. One arrow clipped Malakai himself, showering green acid all over the left half of the captain's body. Tina grinned in delight when he toppled off the wagon, screaming and clawing at his face as he went down.

"Melee to the sides of the road!" she shouted, breaking into a run now that they were now only fifty feet from the wagon-clogged entrance to the camp. "Sorcerers and Naturalists, fire at the entrance! Bust us in!"

The players in the front of the raid, her included, broke to the left and right of the wide road. This exposed the back line of spell casters but also gave them an open line of attack. Tina had barely gotten out of the way before fireballs the size of cars streaked past her while lightning flashed, striking the heavy wagons the knights had used to block the entrance to their camp.

The resulting explosion was so loud, it shattered the few windows that remained in the buildings surrounding the square. Metal and stone rocketed skyward. So did the knights who'd tried to use their shields or broken wall sections as cover. When the dust cleared, all that remained was an open, slightly molten hole through the center of the barricade, opening a clear path to the yard full of player-filled cage-wagons. What she did *not* see, however, was the expected army of armored men with shields on the other side.

"Roxxy!" Killbox yelled at her. "Are we charging in or what?"

She waved at him to be quiet and looked down at the tiny shadow under her feet. "SB! I need your eyes on the other side!"

"Got it," came the deadly whisper from her shadow. Then, a second later, his presence returned. "The enemy is grouped up in the tents on the side. They're going to try to flank us."

"*Melee back to the middle!*" she shouted. "Get through the gap, then break left for the tents!"

The melee fighters roared in reply and charged to the front. They were just in time too. As the raid began to pour through the burning hole the spell casters had opened, a rallying cry rose from the camp.

"*For the king!*"

With that, hundreds of plate-wearing knights leapt out at them from the tents that lined the camp's western edge. More jumped out from the shadow of the forward barricade, lunging at the raiders with their swords. "Death to the players!" they screamed. "Remember the Nightmare!"

"All forward!" Tina yelled, sending two knights flying with a sweep of her shield. "Stomp them down!"

It was a reckless thing to shout. Holding the line would have been a much better tactical decision, but shield wall-style fighting wasn't something the Roughnecks, or players in general, were good at. They were used to moving, chaotic raids and PVP brawls in which all they had to do was play their role. They weren't used to having to pay attention to the larger battle or keep up with multiple enemies who didn't follow the usual monster AI script. Even if they *had* been better prepared, the Roughnecks simply didn't have enough melee fighters to hold a line against an army this big. A full offensive push was the only thing they were really good at, so wrecking-ball assault was the plan, and Tina intended to hold up her end.

With a roar of fury, Tina ran into the oncoming wall of knights. Just before she crashed into them, she felt a twinge of doubt that maybe she couldn't take twenty guys by herself no matter the gear difference. But there was no backing out now. Her allies had already vanished beneath the wave of red-and-gold tabards and gleaming armor, so Tina gritted her marble teeth and plowed ahead, swinging her god-forged shield ahead of her.

Each swipe broke limbs like kindling. Swords burst into pieces when they landed on her, and men were sent flying. While her shield laid waste to her right, she used her sword to parry the men on her left, killing one by accident when her blade passed through his weapon like it wasn't there. He went down, grabbing her legs and cursing her name. Tina was still shaking him off when two elven knights circled past her shield to stab her in the back. But cries of victory turned into dismay as their swords slid off her glowing armor harmlessly. Grinning, Tina wheeled and slammed her shield into them, sending both men sailing over the barricade to crunch against the building a dozen feet behind it.

For all the knights she sent flying, though, the crowd around her didn't get any thinner. Enemies surrounded her on all sides, forcing her to wade through them as thought she were pushing through an armored marsh. It would have been really dangerous if killing them hadn't been so laughably easy. One swing of her blade was all it took to cut down a human knight straight through his shield, and she booted another so hard, his chest plate crumpled like a soda can. Someone smart threw a chain over her head to try to drag her down, but Tina caught the links in her teeth and bit right through then turned to bash the gaping soldier in the face with the edge of her shield.

Nearby, she could see Killbox towering over the normal-sized humans and elves. He was an island in a sea of red, ringed by shields, but for all their numbers, they couldn't touch him. His giant ax felled them in swaths like grass. A few mundane arrows sailed down from the castle's walls as long shots, but the broad-headed points couldn't even pierce Killbox's skin as he laughed and swung faster, carving a path of destruction toward the center of the camp.

Tina tried to follow, but despite how easy it was to defeat the knights, she was a tank, not a damage dealer. She simply couldn't take out as many people in one strike as Killbox did, and that slowed her down. Scowling, Tina swung her shield around to cover her side and stabbed the man in front of her through the chest, hurling his body into the oncoming crowd. The impact knocked three other knights flat, buying her a moment of space to jump onto a nearby cart to see how things were going.

The barricade was her biggest worry. The plan was for the Rangers, Naturalists, Clerics, and Sorcerers to take it over once the melee had pushed forward. She wanted them to be high up and out of the fight since they were impossible to protect in the bloody mosh pit of a battlefield, but again, players were horrible about falling victim to tunnel vision. Sure enough, the first caster she laid eyes on was a Cleric who hadn't stayed with the group because he was too busy winding up a big healing spell. A pair of towering Royal Knights leaped out from between the nearby tents and tackled him as she watched, shattering his building spell as they all went down in a pile.

70

Tina swore and leaped off her cart, but she was miles too slow. One of the knights had already pinned the Cleric and ripped his staff away, holding him prone on the ground while the other knight drew back his blade for the kill.

But then, seconds before the sword landed in the Cleric's chest, an arrow came screaming in at high velocity. It punched through the first knight's shoulder, came out the other side of him, and struck the second knight in the head. The force of the attack blew both bodies clear off the Roughneck Cleric, and then a jubatus Ranger leaped down from the barricade's rubble. He yanked the still-shocked Cleric to his feet, shoved the guy's staff back into his hands, and dragged him up to the group of Roughnecks standing on the high ground where Zen and KatanaFatale were shouting orders while firing off their own endless stream of attacks.

It was the most beautiful thing Tina had ever seen. She was just so awestruck by the sight of her officers actually following the plan that a group of knights almost managed to pull her down off the cart. She kicked them away absentmindedly, scanning the barricades to make sure everyone was in position, but for once, things actually seemed to be going right. As planned, the Roughneck casters now held the high ground for the entire southern sweep of the camp. They used the height to their advantage beautifully, raining arrows and spells over the melee's heads into the rear of the camp where the gallows were. Whenever a new group of knights gathered up to push forward and reinforce the men dying to the Roughneck's melee, a fireball or lightning bolt would descend on them, blowing them apart. On the far side of the camp, twelve men did manage to get together and charge a lone Berserker who'd waded in too deep, but just when they were about to swarm him, a bus-sized tornado of flame landed on their heads, melting their armor off them in a glowing river as they went down without even a cry.

Satisfied the battle was well in hand, Tina kicked away the next batch of knights trying to pull her down and starting scanning for the Assassins. They had the most important part of the plan, but as usual, they

71

were almost impossible to spot. She was about to give up when she saw ZeroDarkness appear in front of a cage-wagon full of players.

The jubatus Assassin stepped out of the shadows and sliced open the lock in the same motion. The players inside screamed in fright, but their shouts turned to joy when they realized the black-clad knife-wielding terror was on their side. The Assassin gave the cart a jaunty thumbs-up and pointed at Zen's Rangers on the barricade, then he vanished back into the shadows, leaving the door to the cage wide open as all the players inside rushed to freedom under the cover of Zen's arrows.

Just when Tina was starting to think they were going to pull this off without a hitch, she saw two of *her* Knights go flying through a tent. They rolled to their feet in unison, but they still looked shaken. Scowling, Tina looked around for what could have thrown such sturdy fighters and spotted a tight formation of Royal Knights emerging from the center of the battle. The group was formed up around the salt-and-pepper-haired Captain Malakai, his acid-burned face twisted in rage as he shouted commands to the rearguard of knights still trying to get past the arrows and fireballs to reinforce the front line.

All that changed when he caught sight of Tina.

"*There!*" he bellowed, pointing his sword at Tina. "I've got their leader! The rest of you, focus on the healers!"

With that, Malakai raised his shield to charge.

Knowing she'd need better footing than a cart, Tina leapt to the ground with an earth-shaking crunch. She didn't want to fight him near her people, though, so she charged forward and intercepted him in the open area in front of the cage wagons.

They connected with a crash that made her ears ring. Since they were both knights, they'd both charged in with their shields, but Malakai's guard was just standard metal. Tina's gleaming sun-metal bulwark sundered the captain's shield, leaving him with nothing to break his momentum as he slammed into her.

That should have given her the edge, but Tina had barely managed to get her footing before Malakai's sword swept out in a lightning-fast strike for her neck. But that weapon broke as well when Tina parried, her crimson-glowing blade cutting through the normal steel as if it were made of paper. Malakai's dark eyes burned with rage as he reeled back from the flying metal shrapnel, and Tina started to laugh.

"Kill the leader, huh?" she taunted, flashing a cocky smile at the enraged elf. "Not a bad idea. I'm thinking so goes the head, so goes the *snake.*"

She finished with a hard swing at the empty-handed captain's head. It wasn't a subtle attack, but with his sword and shield broken, there was nothing he could do to stop it. His only choices were lose his head or retreat, which was why Tina was shocked when her swing stopped cold.

She blinked, glancing up in surprise to see her glowing blade clutched in the elf's long-fingered hand. She'd sliced clean through his metal gauntlet, but the pale skin beneath was only nicked. She didn't even manage to see *how* nicked before Malakai pulled her forward with tremendous strength.

Tina was eight feet tall and half a ton of armored stone. She wasn't used to being knocked around by anything smaller than her, but Malakai's attack took her off her feet. She stumbled forward, catching herself on his chest only to end up staring at his bared teeth.

"I'm not a stupid guard trapped defending a drunken king anymore," he snarled in her face, his fingers biting down on her runed blade so hard the enchanted metal groaned. "This time will be different. This time, *you* will be the one who gets trampled under."

He sneered at her one last time, and then he punched her shield with his free hand. The force of the blow slammed Tina's shield back into her, throwing her off him. She landed staggering a few feet away, but at least he'd let go of her sword. She raised her blade and shield again, eying the captain with new caution. She was trying to figure out how the fuck he'd stopped her sword with just his hand when she remembered.

Captain Malakai wasn't just a ludicrously tall elf. He was a mini-boss. She'd only ever fought him during the Oktoberfest event, where he'd always gone down like a chump, but that was with a full raid at her back. He might not be a Dead Mountain level raid boss, but Malakai was still a level-eighty four-skull. His strength was balanced to challenge *ten* same-level players, and she was facing him alone.

"*Roughnecks on Roxxy!*" Tina bellowed, lifting her sword high so the others could see her through the smoke and the chaos. "*Anders*, get over here!"

Malakai looked at her in disgust. "Calling for help so soon, player?"

"Did I challenge you to a duel?" she said, lowering her blade again. "This ain't a fair fight, asshole. I'm here to kill you for all the players you've dicked over."

"Like you can--" Malakai started, but his back exploded in fire before he could get the words out. He screamed in pain, and Tina looked up to see KatanaFatale standing about ten feet behind the tall elf captain, staff already glowing for a second fireball.

Chest still heaving in pain, Malakai looked up at her and then whirled around, following her gaze to the Sorcerer. "Uh-uh," Tina said, smacking him with her shield. "Eyes on me, jerkoff."

He glowered at her, and Tina opened her guard, inviting him to attack her and ignore Katana. Now that she had a damage-dealer with her, it was time to teach this asshole the true meaning of tank-and-spank. But as she got ready to snatch her shield back up to block his hammer-like fists, Malakai turned his back on her and lunged at KatanaFatale.

"*Shit!*" Tina yelled, charging after him. "He's untauntable! Defensive, Katana! *Use a defensive!*"

Eyes wide in panic, KatanaFatale vanished in a flash of purple energy seconds before Malakai swung a devastating left hook through the empty air where the Sorcerer's head had been. Relieved at the narrow miss, Tina took a swing at Malakai's back, but he dodged at the last second then snatched a dropped sword off the ground and lobbed it over his shoulder.

It looked like a shit throw at first. The blade rocketed by her left side with a good foot to spare. But just as Tina was opening her mouth to taunt him for his crap aim, there was a gurgle of pain followed by a wet splash of blood. Stomach dropping, Tina looked over her shoulder just in time to see KatanaFatale drop to his knees, clutching the sword that had skewered him right through his throat.

"Short-range teleport skill," Malakai said as the Sorcerer's blood poured onto the grand square's flagstones. "Always goes fifty feet and always in the direction the Sorcerer is facing. Must obey line-of-sight. Eight-second cooldown so they can't 'spam' it."

Tina snatched her eyes off Katana to find the captain grinning evilly at her.

"After eighty years trapped watching your kind, you have nothing I haven't seen a thousand times."

"*Bastard!*" Tina snarled, stabbing at the captain.

He ducked and rolled at the last second, letting her sword slide through the empty air. Rage boiling in her chest, Tina followed up with a kick, catching Malakai in the face with her steel-covered foot. His head snapped back as she connected, blood spraying from his nose. Grateful to *finally* land some damage, Tina slashed at him again, but Malakai rolled away and kicked back at her in midair. She almost managed to dodge, but his boot caught the tip of her jaw, rattling her teeth. *Damn,* he hit hard. She was still making sure her teeth weren't broken when he rolled back to his feet with infuriating elven grace, sneering at her like he could do this all day. She was trying to come up with an attack he couldn't dodge when she heard a warbling voice behind her.

"Don't worry, Roxxy! I've got you!"

"Anders!" she barked, never taking her eyes off Malakai. "Forget me! Heal KatanaFatale *now!*"

"Okay!" came the panicked reply, then the fish-man yelped. "*Shit!* He's dead, Roxxy! He already bled out!"

The words hit harder than Malakai had. "Cast Raise Ally!" she ordered, glaring at the captain as if her hate could make him combust. "We've still got six minutes!"

"As if I'd let you," Malakai sneered.

"As if you could stop us," Tina snarled, charging him.

"So predictable," Malakai said, leaping to the side to avoid her. Tina slid to a halt where he'd been and whirled to face the captain again, but he wasn't even looking at her. He just leaned down and punched the flagstones, cracking the stone in half with his strength so he could grab a jagged chunk and hurl it at Anders.

Surrounded by golden symbols of floating power, Anders never saw it coming. The resurrection spell he'd been shaping shattered like golden glass as the gray stone smashed into the fish-man's face, but the Cleric himself didn't even make a sound. He just toppled backward, landing on the ground with a wet *thud*, out cold.

Blind with rage, Tina threw herself at Malakai's back, her sword clattering to the broken flagstones as she tackled him to the ground. "I'll kill you myself!" she roared, bearing down on top of him with Roxxy's full half ton of body weight as she wrapped both arms around the captain's neck and squeezed with all her strength.

Choking and gasping, Malakai clawed at the broken stones under his hands. Then, veins bulging in his neck, he started to get his feet back under him. Tina frantically increased the pressure on his neck, squeezing until her arms felt like they were going to pop out of their sockets, but it did no good. His face was purple, but he still managed to stand up, lifting her entire body off the ground as he did.

Counting on her metal bones, Tina hauled back and head-butted Malakai right in the top of his skull. Unable to roar or shout anymore, the dark-haired captain seized in pain, but he managed to get his hands up to grab her breastplate and belt, anyway. He was about to pull her off him, so even though her head was still swimming from the last one, Tina hauled back and head-butted him again, pounding her metal skull into his over and over until she saw stars.

But no matter how many times she hit him, Malakai refused to go down. He'd already gotten a grip on her armor at the shoulders, prying his neck out of her grip in a head-on battle of sheer strength. Tina cursed that his head was so small compared to her arms and that her bracers were slick with blood. No matter how she squeezed, she couldn't keep her hold, and eventually he slipped out of her grasp.

Gasping for breath, Malakai roared as he upended Tina, slamming her into the ground so hard, her back sundered an entire ten-foot section of flagstone. As she hit, something inside her--a metal rib, perhaps--*bent* instead of broke. Searing pain racked her side as the twisted metal poked into a vital organ, and Tina's arm went stiff, preventing her from getting her shield up fast enough. Seizing the opening, Malakai grabbed the bulwark in both hands and started trying to yank it off her arm. When it didn't slide off immediately, he pulled a dagger off his belt and stabbed her through the gap in her armor at the inside of her elbow.

Though not nearly as bad as the agony in her side, the new flash of pain still made Tina gasp. Far worse, the cut nicked the tendon that controlled her arm. Her silver blood was still trickling down the blade when her hand spasmed, and she lost her grip on her shield.

Crowing in triumph, Malakai yanked the bulwark off her and flung it behind him. The god-forged shield flashed golden in the smoky sunlight, sailing twenty feet before crashing like a meteor into the tent beyond the carts. Burned face pulling into a horrifying expression, the captain raised a boot to stomp her exposed head.

Tina saw it coming, but she couldn't seem to roll away. Her head was swimming, her arm was limp, and her side was a mass of agony. Lacking any other options, she crossed her arms over her face and yelled, "*Earthen Fortitude!*"

As she activated the stonekin's ultimate damage-reduction ability, Tina felt the kiss of the Bedrock Kings. Their power grew a mountain within her, turning her body, even her hair and her armor, into the hardest of stone as Malakai's boot crashed down.

The stomp smashed her several inches into the ground. Teeth bared like an animal, Malakai kept stomping her as hard as he could. Each blow drove her deeper into the crater and sent aftershocks vibrating down her metal bones, but the very stone that protected her kept her frozen in place, unable to move.

That was a serious problem, because Earthen Fortitude only lasted for eight seconds. Due to the industrial pounding Malakai was giving her, Tina's head was spinning too hard to think of a plan. By the time the mountain within her began to fade, she still hadn't figured out a way out of this, and Malakai definitely wasn't showing signs of stopping.

The last of her protection faded seconds after a stomp came down. As the power of the Bedrock Kings drained out of her, Tina stared at the raised metal boot with fatalistic calm. This next one was going to hurt, she knew, but there was nothing to do but take it. She couldn't move, couldn't even roll out of the crater he'd bashed them both into. All she could do was brace and wait, closing her eyes so she wouldn't have to see the hit that broke her skull.

But the blow never landed. Instead, there was a scream of pain as hot blood splashed across Tina's face. She opened her eyes in confusion just in time to see Malakai stagger back, and then something else was over her, something deadly and made of shadows that shouted at her in SilentBlayde's voice.

"*Tina!*"

She came back to herself with a gasp. Above her, Malakai was punching and swinging desperately at SilentBlayde, whose entire body was wrapped in living shadows. *Shadow Dance*, her stumbling mind informed her. It was the Assassins' big cooldown, their version of her Earthen

78

Fortitude. So long as it was up, SB was untouchable. The trouble was, it only lasted ten seconds.

He'd used his time well, at least. Much to Tina's gratification, Malakai now had a pair of sucking chest wounds from SB's swords. The injuries must have enraged him, because despite the fact that nothing was landing, he was still swinging at SB with fury. Wrapped in a cloak of shadow, her friend weaved around the blows with inhuman--in-*Elven*--flexibility. He even managed to counterattack, slashing Malakai whenever and wherever the captain left an opening. Every silver flash of his swords left a huge rent in the older elf's flesh, but as much damage as he was clearly doing, it wasn't going to be enough to take Malakai down in the ten seconds Shadow Dance lasted. Several of which were already gone.

Shit.

Body pounding in pain, Tina forced herself to get up. She had to get her shield back and turn this around. If she didn't get Malakai back under control in the next few seconds, he was going to kill SB, and it would be her fault.

That was enough to get her broken body moving. She scrambled to her feet and lurched forward. Since she was still in the crater, this meant she had to pass right by Malakai, but when he reached out to snatch her back down, SilentBlayde stabbed a gleaming silver sword straight through his upper arm.

Malakai released Tina with a howl of pain, and she scrambled away. The captain was already turning to chase after her when SB slashed a blade across the back of his neck.

"Show me your back if you dare, NPC," he snarled, stabbing Malakai again, in the ribs this time. "I do a lot more damage than she does. I will slice off any finger you lay on my Roxxy!"

Malakai turned away from Tina with a sneer. "You lack her health pool, Assassin," he said, eying the shadows that covered SilentBlayde's body. "When your ability ends, I will finish you in an instant."

SB probably had a witty retort to that, but Tina couldn't stick around to hear it. She was already sprinting toward the tents Malakai had thrown her shield into. She'd just dropped down to pry it out of the crater its impact had left in the ground when she found herself face-to-face with NekoBaby.

The jubatus healer was prowling on all fours through the tents. She squeaked when she saw Tina then slapped a hand over her mouth.

"*What are you doing?*" Tina whispered at the jubatus healer.

"I saw what happened to Anders," NekoBaby whispered back frantically, pointing through the gap in the tents, where Tina could see Malakai and SB were fighting. "Fuck if that's happening to me. I'm gonna heal from hiding."

"Good plan," Tina said, surprised despite herself.

"Want me to get you now?" the Naturalist offered.

Tina's whole body ached at the promise of healing, but she shook her head. "Cast Raise Ally on Katana first. He's almost out of time. When that's done, I want you to cast Verdant Glory. We'll bathe the whole battlefield in AOE and heal everyone in one go."

Neko bit her lip. "Are you sure? Big raid heals have a long cast time."

"SB and I will keep you safe," Tina promised. *This time,* she added to herself.

"I'm on it, boss," Neko said, bringing up her staff.

Tina slammed her shield on her arm and ran out of the tent, leaving Neko gathering up glowing green energies behind her. She got back to the battle just in time to see SilentBlayde's Shadow Dance end. As the darkness evaporated, his eellike flexibility vanished with it, and SilentBlayde finally had to parry an attack he couldn't dodge.

Malakai's fist crashed into the silvery sword in SB's right hand. Blood flew from the knight's knuckles at the impact, but the strike was still powerful enough to rip SilentBlayde's sword from his grasp. Blayde ducked the next attack and stabbed Malakai through the top of his foot on the way

80

down. He was on his way back up when Malakai lurched forward, driving a powerful knee into the Assassin's chest.

Tina went still as SB flew off his feet. He landed hard on his back in the wreckage of a cart. He kicked to his feet at once but then doubled back over as he started to cough up blood.

The sight made her whole body go cold, and then she turned on Malakai with new fury. It didn't matter what happened from here out. She could not let Malakai land a hit on anyone else. He was just too dangerous, too lethal. But even though she was running, she was still too far away to stop the dark-haired captain from closing in and taking another swing at SB.

That was the moment when Tina's heart stopped altogether. But then, just when she was certain--*certain*--she'd just witnessed Haruto's death again, SB managed to sway out of the way. He even got another hit in on Malakai in the process. It was a weak hit, barely enough to drive an inch of silver blade into his target, but it was more than Tina had managed. She was still staring in awe when Malakai grabbed SilentBlayde's outstretched arm and hurled the elven Assassin all the way back to the front of the camp.

There was no rolling to his feet this time. SB crashed into the piled stone barricade they'd come through in their first assault like a meteor. He hit so hard, he actually broke through the rubble, smashing through the stone to slide into the Royal Mile beyond. The air filled with new screams as the lowbies who'd been hiding back there scattered, and Tina held her breath.

Only to let it out again when she saw him move. He was still alive, thank god. His arm was bent back at an unnatural angle, broken in multiple places, but they could heal that. What mattered was that Malakai hadn't killed him. Not that that slowed Tina down in the least when she plowed her shield into Malakai's smug face at full speed.

There was a satisfying snapping sound as the captain's sneering expression met her wall of sun-metal with her entire weight behind it. He bounced gracelessly across the ground, sliding several feet before he managed to stop himself. That was much slower than he'd been before, but his whole body was riddled with cuts. His legs and knees especially were stabbed to bloody bits, and Tina felt a surge of pride. He'd only had ten seconds, but SB had *really* carved that asshole up, proving yet again that he wasn't the Roughnecks' number-one damage dealer for nothing.

Now she just had to keep the bastard occupied until Neko finished her spells. It would be hell to wait, but once Neko cast Verdant Glory, all of them would be returned to full health. Not only would she be fresh, but a fresh SB was going to join her as well, plus Anders and KatanaFatale. With that much firepower, they'd turn him into bloody, burned, knight-captain chunks.

All she had to do was hold out. *Just hold out,* she told herself as Malakai rose to his feet in fury, turning on her with fists clenched. *Hold out!*

Somehow...

Chapter 5

James

Five minutes prior, James was standing with the other healers on top of the camp's outer barricade, watching the spectacle of violence that was the Roughnecks' assault with bile in his throat.

He wasn't sure which part shocked him more: the power of players in top-tier equipment or the slaughter they were making of the Royal Knights. With Tina's raiders killing two men with every swing, it had only taken a few minutes for the front half of the camp to turn into a corpse-strewn bloodbath.

The back half of the camp was no better. The Rangers and spell casters had mercilessly rained down elemental destruction, leaving the once-elegant Grand Square a battlefield of charred flagstones and smashed stone. The air was choked with smoke from the burning tents, but on the few occasions it cleared, it was obvious that the bodies littering the ground were all wearing the king's red and gold.

As the enemy thinned out, so did the raiders. What had started as a melee at the front of the camp was now a free-for-all. Berserkers and Knights circled the edges of the camp, killing any knights they came across. It was just like a mob of players competing for monster kills in an over-populated zone back in the game, only this time the people who died screaming were real, their bodies breaking in a very messy, very not-video-game-fun sort of way.

Forced to look away as a Roughneck Berserker crushed a young knight's head like a ripe melon, James turned to Ar'Bati, who was standing very quietly beside him. "You okay?"

"No," Fangs said softly, his eyes wide and unfocused as he took in the carnage playing out in front of him. "This is your true power isn't it? The power of the players."

James nodded silently. Technically, the knights and the players were all level eighty. That should have made them equal, but unlike the knights with their mundane swords and regular metal armor, the Roughnecks were raiders. Every one of them was decked from head to toe in literal items of legend pried from the dead hands of the most powerful creatures in this world. They were unstoppable, untouchable demons of destruction. No wonder the people of this world feared them so much.

"That's right!" NekoBaby said beside them, her voice victorious. "Mess with the best, die like the rest! *Pow pow!*"

She mimed some playful punching motions, but just as James was about to snap at her that this was nothing to be happy about, his brother beat him to it.

"'To save us when we cannot save ourselves,'" Ar'Bati said, his grief-stricken voice cutting through Neko's mockery far better than anything James could have said. "That is the promise of Bastion."

He turned and pointed at the crimson-and-gold banners that still fluttered feebly from the lampposts. "Since I was a child, I was taught that the Holy King was our champion and our hero. He alone commands the power of the magical Bastion, artifact of the Sun and our only true shield against the Once King's undead and dark beings of the Lightless Realm. He also holds the debt of the ancient Bird Xthr, fourth born of the Unbounded Sky. If the need is great enough, he can call down these powers to defeat any foe. That is why he is called the *Holy* King, and his strength is why the Four Clans of the Savanna swore loyalty to Bastion. The same goes for the Sires of the Emerald Forest and the Schtumples of the Grand Mercantile. It's why all the lands around Bastion united into one kingdom rather than fighting amongst themselves. Despite our differences, we all rally around our king because we know that no matter what happens, no matter how bad things get, Bastion will *always* be here to defend us."

He turned back to Neko. "That is what Bastion means to us. For centuries, the Holy King and his Royal Knights have been our bulwark against everything that wants to destroy us. They are our shield, our light against the dark." He threw out his hand toward the bloody chaos of the battle below. "Do you even know what you are doing? You are slaying our saviors! The ones who are sworn to hold the line of peace and order in our world! That is a *tragedy*. How can you cheer for it?"

James's mouth was hanging open by the time he finished. He'd never heard Fangs in the Grass speak for so long or so passionately. The jubatus warrior was so close to Neko, he was practically in her face, his whole body shaking with the intensity of his feelings.

Unfortunately, NekoBaby wasn't nearly as impressed.

"Yeah, yeah," she said, rolling her eyes. "When this was a game, they were good. Now they're evil. Too bad for them."

"It was not them!" Ar'Bati cried desperately. "It was the Nightmare! They've been poisoned by it."

"Still no excuse," Neko said, shaking her head. "*Nothing* excuses what they've done."

"You have no idea what you're talking about," the cat warrior said, his voice trembling. "You don't know what it's like to watch your world end. To be enslaved without knowing why or how or if you'll ever get free. We had to exist in a dreamlike state, forced to live the same horrible day over and over and over. Nine out of ten of us *vanished*. We had no idea where our families were or if they were alive. We couldn't even talk to each other. We were trapped as puppets acting out whatever dramas the Nightmare needed us to perform. And if that wasn't hell enough, you players were always there to rub salt in our wounds. Your kind tortured us for decades for your petty vanities and childish glory. Of *course* this world hates you. You are worse monsters than the Once King's armies could ever be."

"Then why don't you join them then, Angry Cat?" Neko said, jabbing Ar'Bati in the stomach with a claw. "You're an NPC too. If you like them so much, why don't you go string up some lowbies in the gallows with your heroes, huh?"

"Never," Ar'Bati said fiercely. "What they have done here is dreadful, and I will never condone it. But I can understand why they turned to such acts, because I was like that too." He looked down at his shaking hands. "Being enslaved by the Nightmare filled me with hate and anger the likes of which you cannot comprehend. I spent every sleepless hour that I was trapped burning with the desire to make you players suffer as I had. I cursed your entire race every time the lich skinned me alive. Every day. Every month. Every *year* for eight decades, until I was no longer myself. I *became* my hate."

Ar'Bati flexed his claws. "If a player had been right in front of me at the exact moment when the Nightmare broke, there was nothing I wouldn't have done to them. I would have hurt that person in every possible way before killing them as I'd been killed. Then I would have found another and done it again. Over and over, as if all that death could heal me." He shook his head. "That I avoided such sin isn't because I am great. It's because of James. He stopped me before I did anything that could not be undone and helped me find an honorable revenge and proper reconciliation. I was spared the regrets of atrocities I would have committed in my madness if I'd been left on my own, and not a day passes where I don't realize anew how much I was saved by his kindness."

Ar'Bati said this like James wasn't standing right beside him. James felt his cheeks burning with embarrassment at the head warrior's words, suddenly envious of the Assassin's ability to vanish into the Lightless Realm. But while he was beyond grateful Ar'Bati's speech was over, Neko wasn't finished yet.

"So you didn't do anything bad, right?" Neko said. When he nodded, she smiled. "Then we're cool, Angry Cat. But these Royal Fuckers--"

"Deserve our pity," Ar'Bati said sharply. "It rends my heart to watch heroes trample upon their oaths and throw away their sacred honor, because I've stood on the precipice they're now falling from. I understand the regret and shame that awaits them when they come to their senses at

86

the bottom. They will *never* be able to face their families after this. The title of Sir is one that these men have worked for all their lives. Children barely strong enough to hold a sword swing it dreaming of being called a knight, and they're throwing it all away in their madness." He took a step away from Neko. "But you can't see that, can you? Those soldiers aren't broken men who need saving to you. They're just more NPCs for you to kill, troll, or loot, as your kind have *always* done to our world!"

James put a hand on his brother's shoulder as NekoBaby backed away. "Whoa there, Angry Cat," she said, gripping her staff. "Time for you to take a chill hairball."

Ar'Bati bared his teeth. "I will not--"

"Don't care," she said, turning her back on them. "I'm here to drop the heals, not argue with you. You can preach all you want, but we're still standing in an extermination camp. Killing these guys is justice."

"That's what they said of you players, too, I'm sure," Ar'Bati growled.

"Like I care what they say." The cat girl crossed her arms belligerently. "As far as I'm concerned, these guys are Nazis, which means we can do whatever we want to them." The cat-girl cupped her hands over her mouth to yell at a nearby Roughneck Knight fighting a patrol of men who'd joined the battle from the nearby city. "*Yeah! Rip his balls off, Frank!*"

She had other, even more creatively obscene suggestions, but James was no longer listening. He could feel the explosion building in Ar'Bati, and it was vital that he get Fangs away from here before his brother started something he couldn't finish. He put his arms around Ar'Bati's shaking shoulders and dragged him down the barricade, away from from NekoBaby.

"Please tell me you don't see this the same way, James," Fangs said as they picked their way down the rubble. "We're not just NPCs to you, right?"

"You are family to me, Fangs in the Grass," James said solemnly. "And for what it's worth, I think you're right. The Royal Knights are destroying themselves with this, and they're taking Bastion down with them. I want to stop it, but only the king himself can do that. They're his knights."

Everything was so wrong. James just didn't know what he could do about it. Rather, he knew *what* to do, which was to get into the castle and show jovial King Gregory what his men were up to in the hopes that the king would stop them. That was the only actual solution to their problem. It was the how to get there that had him stumped. He and Ar'Bati were effectively his sister's prisoners, and SilentBlayde had the letters that were his only proof. Without them, James had zero chance of getting into the castle as anything other than dead. Technically, they were still within his grasp, but the backpack of FFO's number-one Assassin might as well have been the moon for how little chance he had of getting there. He was getting good and depressed about that when he felt something enter his shadow.

There was no other way to describe it. One second, he and Fangs were picking their way down the rubble pile, away from the battle, and the next, there was something invisible and terrifying stepping into space that should have been only his. He felt Fangs jump as his body went stiff, then before either of them could do anything, SilentBlayde stepped out of the tiny scrap of shadow at James's feet.

"Holy crap, SB," James gasped, clutching his chest. "Don't do--"

The Assassin shoved James aside, knocking him to the ground as he hopped ten feet straight to the top of the barricade, where NekoBaby was throwing heals.

"Neko, get to Roxxy," he ordered in a sharp, very un-SB-like tone.

"What?" Neko asked, giving him a funny look. "Dude, I'm supposed to be back here guarding James and Angry Tacos. Roxxy has Anders. She'll be--"

"Anders is down," SB said in a voice that stopped her cold. "And KatanaFatale is dead. Tina's in trouble, and we need you *now*. Don't talk. Just go. I'll meet you there."

He vanished back into the shadows the moment he finished, leaving Neko in a panic.

"Shit, shit, shit, *shit*!" she said, scanning the battlefield. "SB never gives orders like that unless things are *serious*." She looked over her shoulder to give James and Ar'Bati the hairy eyeball. "You two *stay put*. I mean it! You're miles too short for this ride, so don't go out there and get killed like morons because--spoiler alert--Angry Cat ain't getting a raise. Now *don't move*!"

She put her staff in her mouth and scampered down the barricade on all fours in true jubatus fashion, vanishing into the chaos below.

The moment she was gone, Ar'Bati grabbed James's shoulders. "This is our chance."

"Our chance to do what?" James said frantically, climbing back up the barricade. "SB still has our bag of letters, and Tina might be dying!"

"Your sister is a monster. She can handle herself," Fangs argued, grabbing his belt to yank him back down. "We, however, might never get another chance! This is about more than just our honor. If we don't find a way to stop the knights, all of Bastion will bear their crimes for generations!"

"But I don't know what to do!" James cried.

"Gnoll shit!" Ar'Bati yelled back at him. "You always know what to do! You were four steps ahead of every corner in the Red Canyon. Do that again!"

James clenched his jaw with a curse and scrambled up the barricade to look at the battle again. The Roughnecks were scattered throughout the whole camp now. He couldn't see Tina in the chaos, but he could feel the ground shaking under his feet, which meant she was probably in the middle of combat. They were at the front of the camp. The fight here had been over for some time, so everyone had moved farther into the camp. Now that Neko had run off as well, the only players left back here were the low-level characters the Roughnecks had rescued, meaning he and Ar'Bati were effectively alone.

He tapped his claws on the rubble anxiously. Fangs was right. They'd probably never get a better chance to run, but what could they do without the letters? It was possible they could get into the castle just on the strength of being Claw Born, but they'd have nothing to use once they got inside. Having real, physical proof of the Once King's invasion had been the crux of his entire plan. Without that, all they had to convince the king was their word, and given the crazy state of the city, James didn't think that was worth much. He was still going over it in his head when someone tapped on his foot.

James jumped a foot in the air, tail fluffing in surprise. Ar'Bati--who'd been even farther up the wall--cursed as well, and the two of them looked down in unison to see a red-robed Sorcerer staring sheepishly back at them.

"Sorry," Flameboyant said. "Is this a bad time?"

"What are you doing here?" Ar'Bati demanded, sliding down the barricade. "You're supposed to be with the other low-level players."

"Yeah, but I saw you guys over here and thought you could use some assistance."

"Assistance with what?" Fangs asked suspiciously. "What do you think we're doing?"

"I don't know," the Sorcerer said with a shrug. "But I figured whatever it was, you'd go for it now that your watch-cat is gone, and I want to help."

That was a lovely thing to hear, but James had to ask, "Why?"

"Because I owe you guys my life," Flameboyant said, as if that should be obvious. "Also, this raid isn't exactly a happy place for me, if you get my drift."

James could see how traveling with the raid you'd attempted to commit suicide with wouldn't be ideal. Still. "I don't think you want to come where we're going."

"Sure I do," Flameboyant said. "You guys are the only people here who've been nice to me, and wherever you're going, it can't be worse than *that*." He tilted his head at the barricades, where the screams of the dying were still floating on the hot, smoky wind.

James and Ar'Bati looked at each other.

"It would be nice to have a Sorcerer," Fangs said.

It would, indeed. At level forty-five, Flameboyant was nowhere near the power of Tina's raiders, but then neither was he or Fangs, and it wasn't as if they had people lining up to come along. They were facing a desperate-enough situation as it was. If Flameboyant was offering to help, they couldn't really afford to turn him down, but James was still determined to make sure the Sorcerer knew what he was getting into before he made any promises he'd regret. He was explaining the situation with the Once King's invasion and the letters they'd taken from the Lich of Red Canyon when something crashed into the barricade beside them at high speed.

The makeshift wall of rubble exploded in a hail of stones. All three of them hit the dirt, covering their heads against the flying shrapnel. When James peeked up to see what had caused the explosion, though, it wasn't a giant spell or a ballista bolt. It was a person. Someone had been *thrown* through the ten-foot-high stone barricade and was now lying in a bloody heap twenty feet down the street behind them.

Given how the combat had gone up to this point, James's first thought was that it had to be a knight. The lower-level players--both the survivors from the massacre at Founder's Square and the new people the raid had freed from the camp here--must have come to the same conclusion, because they screamed in alarm and ran deeper into the shops on the Royal Mile, where Tina's officers had ordered them to hide. When the dust settled, though, James saw that was wrong. It wasn't a knight or even an NPC.

It was SilentBlayde.

"*Blayde!*"

James bolted forward, sprinting on all fours toward his fallen friend. He launched into a heal the moment he reached him, but as the green swirls of magic began to circle his fingers, James let them drop again.

SB was *very* injured. His arm was broken in two places, and his whole body was covered in wounds, but he wasn't actually in danger of dying. Any normal person would have been killed after being thrown through a foot-thick wall of piled rocks, but while the Assassin had a lot less stamina than a tank like Tina, he was still covered in legendary equipment, which meant it would take a lot more than this to kill him. He was already trying to push himself up, his good hand shoving feebly against the sooty flagstones. He'd almost managed a sitting position when his eyes opened.

"James," he whispered, the words barely making it past his bloody lips. "Thank goodness. Heal me, quick! I have to get back to Tina."

James bit his lip as his eyes darted down to the loosened top flap of the Assassin's backpack and the bag of letters still within. SilentBlayde's silver swords were nowhere to be seen, but the proof he and Ar'Bati had fought so hard for was *right there*, just a foot away. No one in Tina's raid believed the invasion was coming. They thought the undead were defeated, but there was no way the Once King would give up on such a massive and long-laid plan just because he'd lost one army, and there were *always* more undead. The invasion was still coming, and no matter what was going on with the Royal Knights, if they didn't warn the king, Bastion would be caught completely by surprise. If the capital fell, the continent would follow. The whole *world* could be lost if they screwed this up.

And we are never going to get a better chance.

"James!" SB said, looking at him worriedly with his one remaining good eye. "What are you waiting for?"

James smiled at his friend. "Sorry about this," he whispered.

And then he clubbed the Assassin over the head with his staff.

Even with its cloth binding, the Eclipsed Steel landed on SilentBlayde's skull with a painful-sounding *thwack*. Under normal circumstances, that blow wouldn't have been enough to make a geared Assassin anything but pissed, but SB was already on the very end of his last legs, and it was just enough. The elf lurched sideways, falling unconscious to the pavement. The moment he was out, James grabbed the bag of letters off his belt and shoved it into his own backpack.

"About time," Ar'Bati said as James stood up. "Let's go."

"Whoa," Flameboyant said, staring wide-eyed at the unconscious SB. "Isn't that your sister's boyfriend? Won't she be super mad?"

"She's going to be furious," James said. "Which is why we're leaving *now*." He smiled sadly at the Sorcerer. "Last chance to bail."

"No way," Flameboyant said fiercely. "I owe you big time, and I sure as hell don't want to stay around here. But is it okay to leave him like this?"

"SB is tougher than he looks," James said, sticking behind Ar'Bati as they made for the closest alley. "He'll be fine." Physically, at least. "But we do *not* want to be here when he wakes up, so let's run."

Flameboyant didn't wait to be asked twice. He just teleported ahead then reappeared in a poof of purple energy at the entrance to the alley fifty feet ahead. "It's clear," he whispered, waving them in.

Fangs darted past him, ears swiveling as his feet fell swiftly but silently on the cobbles. James couldn't quite match the warrior's natural stealth, but he managed not to make too much of a muddle of it as they vanished between the buildings, leaving the battle behind.

"What's the plan, James?" Ar'Bati asked when they were clear.

James glanced in the direction of the castle, which he could no longer see through all the buildings. "The front gates are a no go, so I say we head for the Diplomatic Quarter. It's a bit of a walk, but it's our best shot at a way into the castle that won't be guarded by insane Royal Knights." And since two of them were players, that was definitely a plus.

"Sounds good to me," Ar'Bati said, glancing up at the sun to orient himself before turning and starting down a road that led to the west. "This way."

Clutching his bag of precious letters to his chest, James hurried after him, motioning for Flameboyant to stay close as they jogged as quietly as they could through the warren of streets toward the castle and, hopefully, the victory that would make backstabbing one of his best friends and betraying his sister worth it.

Chapter 6

Tina

The fight with Malakai wasn't going as well as Tina had hoped.

Now that SB had sliced the bastard up, she'd been ready for a comeback. The battle for the camp was winding down, which meant backup would be arriving soon. But chasing down all the knights had left her Roughnecks scattered and separated, out of sight and yell distance from her position near the gallows in the camp's center. Which was bad.

"I'm going to kill you slowly," Malakai said, hunching down as he watched for an opening. "Then I'll have a healer raise you so my men can have a turn at torturing you. Or maybe I'll just break your neck and leave you unable to move. Force you to watch as we kill your companion, helpless and immobile, just as we were during the Nightmare."

"You need therapy," Tina said, keeping her shield up to hide how badly she was limping. Her whole body twitched to look at Neko and see how that heal was coming, but she didn't dare turn her head. The only reason Malakai hadn't gone for her yet was because he didn't know the Naturalist was hiding in the tent. If Tina gave her position away, it would be like Anders all over again. She had to buy time, and given how bad she was bleeding, talking was a lot safer than taking another hit.

"You know the Nightmare wasn't our fault, right?" she said, keeping her eyes on Malakai's feet. "We're as much innocent victims of this as you are. Up until three days ago, we thought this was all a game. I didn't even know magic existed until this shit fest went down."

"There is nothing innocent in you, *demon*!" Malakai snarled. "It wasn't enough to torture us while we were helpless. The moment the Nightmare broke, you *players* began to kill our people and ravage our city. You burned and raped and looted to your heart's content, using your power to crush those who were too weak to stand against you. But I am not weak! I will curse the Nightmare to my dying day, but I will use the power it gave me to kill every last one of you! I will make your kind pay in *blood* for what you did to us!"

"*Our* kind?" Tina cried. "Newsflash, dude, we're *all* human. These bodies are just characters we made for the game. Back in our world, we're just normal people. I'm sorry a bunch of dicks went nuts in your city, but that wasn't those level tens you've been indiscriminately hanging. You can't just kill all players because of the bad actions of a few!"

"It doesn't matter," he said, baring his teeth. "You are *all* guilty of something. The very nature of your 'game' turned my people into your targets and cannon fodder! Do you know how many of my knights were forced to die repeatedly every single day so you players could take your quests in safety? How many times *I* have died defending my king so you could win beer steins and ponies and other worthless *trash?*"

"Hey, King Gregory's Endless Beer Stein was *not* trash," Tina said. "And again, *not our fault.* We didn't know you were real!"

"Ignorance does not excuse the crime!" Malakai roared. "You will all pay for what you have done to us!"

He charged as he finished, launching himself into her guard with mad strength. Tina swore and ducked behind her shield for cover, wishing she'd had time to grab her sword as well. Sadly, the glowing red-runed blade lay a good dozen feet away in the crater filled with her silvery blood--way too far away for her to get to with Malakai pounding on her shield with his crushing fists. She'd just have to make do with her shield until Neko came through.

Tina hoped it was soon. She'd managed to stay on her feet so far, but her whole body ached from the hits she'd already taken. Malakai wasn't a building-destroying monster like Grel'Darm, but he was fast, small, and skilled, which was actually way harder to deal with. Grel's attacks had been easy to see coming, and he was so stupid it had been simple to position him wherever she wanted. Malakai was the exact opposite. He was impossible to control and didn't respond to taunts, and his punches were lightning fast and always changing up. She couldn't predict where he was going to

96

hit next, which was how his hits kept sneaking past her guard, battering her arms and shoulders.

He hadn't managed to land a finishing blow yet, but the damage was adding up. With every hit he landed, Tina slid a bit farther back, leaving a trail of silver blood on the ground. She tried to tell herself that was fine, that a little damage was to be expected when you tanked a four-skull boss solo, but her body was starting to feel dangerously numb. Cold stiffness like she'd never felt before was creeping up her stone limbs and turning her vision gray. She was focusing on avoiding as much damage as possible when she felt the first swell of NekoBaby's nature magic.

Relief hit Tina so hard, she felt like she'd been healed already. *Finally.* She wasn't sure how long it had been, but the six-minute window on KatanaFatale's resurrection had to be nearly closed. They'd cut it as close as possible, but if even a magic-deaf class like her could feel the spell, it had to be almost done. Once the rez went off, the heals would start dropping, and this whole fight would change. She just had to survive until then, but when she went to whack Malakai with her shield to make sure his attention stayed on her, the captain grabbed the top of the giant metal plate and shoved it down.

Tina let him, rolling with the blow instead of fighting it as he plunged the bottom lip of her shield into the stones. She was planning to use that as a brace for his next hit when Malakai put his boot on the flat of her bulwark and heaved himself over it, leaping over her head like she was a ramp.

Eyes wide with shock, Tina yanked her shield out of the ground and shot to her feet, cursing her stupidity as Malakai landed behind her and started sprinting toward the tent where NekoBaby was hiding. She was a moron. If she could feel Neko's magic, *of course* he could too. She should have gotten a hold on him the moment the spell started to build, but it was too late for that. Neko's tent was already overflowing with brightly glowing magical vines and flowers. She might as well have put up a sign that read Healer Here!

97

Tina's only chance was to get there before Malakai did, but the old elf was so fast, and she was so numb, her joints grinding together like old rocks. There was no way she could beat him. He was already yanking back the flap, hand shooting inside to grab Neko and break the spell that was their last chance to save KatanaFatale. Everything she'd bled to save was about to die, so Tina did the only thing she could think of and threw herself forward, dropping her shield to tackle the captain around the legs and bring them both down on top of the tent in a snarling heap.

The heavy white canvas tangled around them like water. Malakai rolled and twisted in her arms as she scrambled to pull him away from Neko with the last of her strength. His metal boot collided with her shoulder, sending a shock wave through her whole collarbone, but she refused to let go. Instead, she dug her fingers into the gaps in his breastplate, using the metal to hold him in place as she flopped her whole weight on top of him.

She was so focused on pinning him down, she didn't notice the scrape of steel as Malakai's flailing hand landed on some dead knight's sword until it was too late. His arm swept the blade toward her in a blur, but her hands were too busy holding him in place--and away from Neko-- to block it. Tina turned instead, hunching her shoulder up to catch the blow...only to realize what a bad move that was when the sword hacked into the side of her unarmored head.

There was a silvery chime and the familiar sound of breaking steel. Then pain exploded through her head, making the whole world spin and throb as silver blood started pouring down her face. She was still alive, though, so she gave the elf captain the most crushing bear hug should she could manage, overlapping the edges of her bracers to lock her arms behind his back to avoid him slipping loose like last time.

"*Cursed stonekin!*" Malakai choked out as he stabbed her with the broken hilt of his sword. Every hit sent the jagged inch of blade digging into her neck, but Tina barely felt the cuts. The world was getting fuzzy, and her body felt as if it was slowing down. She'd always heard that blood

98

loss made you weak, but her limbs seemed to be hardening into place, tightening around Malakai like cooling magma.

It was a terrifying feeling. Even against Grel, she didn't think she'd gotten this low on health. The captain was still smashing her in the head with his broken weapon, but even through the cooling fog in her head, she could hear him wheezing, and that gave her an idea.

It took several seconds to get her hardening muscles moving, but eventually, Tina managed to stand up. Since her hardened arms were still locked around Malakai, this meant she took him up with her, lifting his feet straight off the ground.

"Heh," she huffed as he struggled and cursed, kicking his legs wildly in the air. "You're big, but I'm bigger."

She locked her legs in place, using the support to squeeze him even tighter. The captain was struggling for breath now. His wild blows were still hammering her shoulders and head, but each one felt a little weaker than the last. Her vision was almost entirely black now, so Tina closed her eyes and just focused on squeezing, locking her arms down on him so tight, his breastplate crumpled like a tin can. She was working on squeezing hard enough to dent her breastplate next when she heard Killbox yelling her name.

"Hold on, Roxxy!"

The Berserker charged into the fight swinging his massive ax at Malakai's upper back. There was a wet *thwack* as it chopped into the captain, sending blood flying everywhere.

With no breath left to scream, the captain could only gape, eyes bulging as Killbox yanked his blade out and swung again, hacking at the elf like a post. His red blood flew in arcs to join Tina's silver pool on the ground, but even with her failing vision, she knew it wasn't going to be enough. The damn four-skull Malakai had a health pool meant for ten players to beat on, and Tina couldn't breathe anymore.

Her body was so stiff it felt like she was using Earthen Fortitude, but this wasn't the protection of the Bedrock Kings. This was something final, something cold and terrifying. She'd never thought too much about what death would feel like, but she recognized it now. Her body was closing around her like hardening concrete, burying her alive inside, but she had nothing left to fight it. Even though she was certain she could choke out the captain now--he seemed to need air regardless of health points--she knew there was no way she could do it before her health pool gave out. She also knew that if she let go, this guy was going to kill a lot of her people.

Gritting her bloody teeth, Tina held on. Malakai was still beating on her, ignoring Killbox's attack as he stabbed at her neck and shoulders in a furious attempt to get free, but she refused to let him. She ignored the pain and kept her arms as tight as a vise. She kept a shit-eating grin on her face, too, because if she was going to die locking this asshole in place, she was determined that grin was going to be the last thing he saw. Hell, they'd have to bury him with her.

That felt like a suitably hardcore death for the leader of the Roughnecks. Widening her grin, Tina steeled herself not to panic as her senses shut down one by one. The world went black, then her skin turned cold and numb. Next, her hearing filled with static, which slowly faded to nothing at all. She couldn't taste the blood in her mouth or smell the smoke of the city anymore. Soon, all that was left was crushing and the desperate vibrations made by Killbox's attacks on Malakai, then even that began to fade, leaving her sinking into the dark.

No, not sinking. She was being pulled, her soul tangled up in invisible coils as something reached up from the depths of the world to pull her down. But then, just before she lost hold of her grip on Roxxy entirely, Neko's ringing voice cut through the final silence.

"*Verdant Glory!*"

The shout was followed by a nuclear detonation of life magic. Vines, flowers, and translucent energy leaves burst into Tina's vision as the world around her exploded back into focus. Power and vitality flooded into Tina as glowing plants curled up her legs, banishing the cold and the numbness with an intoxicating rush of burning, vibrant life. Blinking in the new brightness, Tina realized she could see her silver blood running up from the ground and back into her, pouring through the cracks in her skin to resume its flow inside her. It was the weirdest, most uncomfortable sensation ever, but it was soon topped by the creaking inside her chest as all her metal bones bent themselves back into their proper places. She felt her severed copper hair regrowing, her joints unlocking as her flexibility returned. Malakai was still in her arms, though, so Tina didn't move them. She just stood there and kept squeezing, locked on her goal with tunnel vision until she felt familiar hands grab her shoulders.

"Roxxy! *Roxxy!*"

SilentBlayde's voice was loud and terrified in her ears. She blinked in surprise, turning her head to see her favorite Assassin standing beside her.

"It's done," he said, his tone growing gentle, like he was trying to talk her off a ledge. "Let him down. We need to go."

Confused, Tina looked at the black-and-gray-haired elf in her arms. Malakai's eyes were rolled back in his head, and his face was a terrifying dark purple. He looked so horrible, she couldn't understand how he was still twitching.

Then she realized it was her.

Dropping Malakai, Tina fell to her knees. Her body was shaking so violently, the overlapping plates of her armor clattered like metal bells. Even her teeth were knocking together, making it nearly impossible to form the question she desperately needed to ask.

"Katana," she got out at last. "Did we Raise Ally on Katana?"

NekoBaby shuffled into view, ears down. "He was gone halfway through my cast," she said in a tiny, frightened voice. "I'm so sorry, Roxxy. At least I saved you, though."

Tina felt as though the world had been yanked out from under her. She sagged to the ground though not from lack of strength. Neko's healing had repaired her body, but something deep inside her still felt broken. Stamped out. Lost forever.

"Tina," SB's voice was close and shaking as he tugged on her arm. "Tina, you have to get up. We have to leave."

Working together, SilentBlayde and Killbox hauled her back to her feet, sliding their shoulders under her arms to help her hobble away. The rest of the raid was already running past them, yelling something about reinforcements from the castle. Behind them, Tina could dimly hear the horns and the clatter of horses, but while a distant logical corner of her brain knew how much trouble that meant, she couldn't bring herself to care. All she could think about was how badly she'd failed Katana. He'd come when she'd needed him, and she'd gotten him killed. Now he was gone forever because of Malakai's stupid, pointless hate. Looking at the fleeing raid, Tina realized with a start that no one had even thought to grab Katana's body. He was still back there, forgotten with their enemies. Back there *alone*.

She started to cry then--quietly, secretly, because she was still the raid leader. If she went to pieces, everything else would, too, so though all she wanted was to bawl, Tina forced herself to keep it in, tilting her head down so that her copper dreadlocks fell to cover her face. In the end, the only one who saw her was SB, and he was polite enough to look away, his arm tight around her waist as they fled through the smashed barricades into the Royal Mile.

"Well," NekoBaby said when they made it to the shelter of the side streets where the lowbies were hiding. "At least we won. All the bad guys are dead, ZeroDarkness managed to free all the players in the cages, and you beat the boss! We're, like, heroes and stuff!"

The healer flashed her a sharp-toothed grin, but Tina just lowered her eyes. She didn't feel like they'd won. When the officers came over, Katana's absence was stark, a painful reminder of the cost of the risk she'd decided to take.

"Roxxy."

Tina looked up to find Zen staring at her, her face uncharacteristically soft. "We freed all the players," she reported. "Killed pretty much the whole camp and then some. We were about to start raiding their supplies, but the castle gates were opening, and you were down, so I gave the order to run. I know that should have been SB's call as your second, but he was knocked out too. By the time we got him healed up, the castle garrison was about to ride out. We were about to be overrun, so I told everyone to retreat." She bit her lip. "I'm sorry. I know we planned to arm and feed everyone on the knights' supplies, but we just couldn't make it."

"You made the right call," Tina said quietly, finally letting go of Killbox and SB to stand on her own. "Thank you for getting everyone out safely." It was more than she had managed.

"We only made it because you kept the boss busy," Killbox said, giving her a respectful look. "For what it's worth, what you did back there was the most hardcore thing I've ever seen."

"Thanks," Tina said with a weak smile. "I never want to do it again."

"*I* never want you to do it again," Neko agreed, shuddering. "You scared the nine lives out of me! I thought for sure I wasn't going to land that heal in time."

"Well, you did, and thank you," Tina said, looking around at the raid. Beyond the circle of her officers, everyone was watching her nervously, waiting for her to tell them where to go, what to do next. Normally, Tina relished that attention, but right now all she wanted to do was hide. If this had still been the game, she would have dumped herself out of VR right then and there. A few hours of barfing in her tiny bathroom from dumpshock sounded like paradise compared to taking even one more step through this horrible, hellish city. But this wasn't a game anymore, and she didn't have that luxury. Someone had to stand up and keep moving, and unless she was ready to give up her position as raid leader, that someone had to be her.

"All right," she said, pulling herself straight. "We didn't get everything we wanted, but we rescued our people, and that's what's most important. We've got a whole city to scavenge supplies from, so we're going to stick to the plan and make for the bank. They're already reinforcing the square behind us, which means we gotta move. Anyone who still needs healing, stay to the middle. Casters, you're cleared to heal as we march. Get everyone to full and stay on alert. We're still in enemy territory. Rangers and Assassins, you're our scouts. Keep an eye out for trouble and make sure we don't get lost. Everyone else stay in formation. I'm going to hang back and watch our rear since that's the most likely direction of attack. Zen, you're on point. Move out!"

Zen saluted and raced to the front of the raid as the players started to trundle forward.

When she was satisfied that everyone was paying attention and on the move, Tina turned to SB. "Sorry I didn't get to ask before," she said quietly. "But are you okay? Malakai hit you pretty hard."

"Not as hard as he hit you," SB replied, but though the words were typical flippant Blayde, Tina instantly knew that something was off. Though he was walking right beside her, he refused to meet her eyes, which made her more upset than if he'd yelled in her face.

"What's wrong?"

"We're missing some people," came the quiet reply.

Tina cursed under her breath, furious with herself for not doing a head count before starting the march. "Who's unaccounted for? KatanaFatale I know, but who else?" How many more of her friends had she gotten killed?

"No one else is dead," he said quickly. "It's just..."

He faded off, leaving Tina ready to gnaw through her armor in anxiety. "Just *what?*"

SB stopped with a sigh, and then he turned to face her at last. "James is gone."

104

Tina froze. "Gone?" she got out at last, then her hands curled into fists. "What do you mean, he's 'gone'?"

SilentBlayde looked down at his feet, tugging his mask up so high, it touched the bottom of his eyes. "He and Ar'Bati knocked me out and stole the bag of letters," he whispered. "I didn't wake up until one of the lowbie Clerics dumped her entire mana pool into me. By that point, they were long gone."

"Knocked you out?" she repeated, unbelieving. "How did *James* knock *you* out?"

"He got to me right after Malakai threw me through the barricade," SB explained, hunching lower and lower. "I thought he was coming to heal me. I never dreamed he'd whack me over the head! It wasn't even a real attack, but I was so low already, I couldn't take it." He wrapped his arms around his stomach. "I'm so sorry, Tina. I failed you. This is all my fault."

"No, it's not," Tina said emphatically. "It's James's fault."

It was *always* James's fault. She didn't want to believe he'd attack SB when he was nearly dead, but she should have known better than to trust her brother. He could make a mess out of anything. Now SilentBlayde was super upset, which was making *her* upset, and all she wanted to do was strangle her stupid brother for causing it all. Not even the drama vortex that was NekoBaby had been enough to counter his ability to wreck everything of Tina's that he got close to. When she got her hands on him again, she was going to hog-tie him with his own tail.

"I'm sorry, Tina," SB said, still not looking at her. "I couldn't save you from Malakai. I couldn't stop James. I couldn't do anything."

"Stop that," she ordered sharply. "For the last time, this is not your fault, and I don't blame you for any of it. And you *did* save me from Malakai. If you hadn't appeared when you did, he would have stomped me into Roxxy dust. I'm the one who should have kept him off you. I'm the tank."

"But you can't do it alone!" he cried, meeting her eyes at last. "You almost died! I'm the one who messed up. I shouldn't have let him hit me.

Should have been faster. If I'd been able to stay in the fight, we might have been able to save Katana, and you wouldn't have nearly..."

He looked back down at his feet, unable to finish, and Tina sighed.

"SB, come on," she said gently. "Look at me."

When he didn't lift his head, she moved a little closer. "Haruto--"

"Please don't call me by that name," he said in a hard, quiet voice. "Today is enough by itself without reminding me of my old life."

Tina smiled at him. "But I like Haruto. He's the best. I could never have made it to college without him, and we always had so much fun playing--"

"I'm not him," SB snarled, making her jump back. "Haruto is gone, and no one will miss him."

Tina blinked in surprise. She'd never heard SB sound so nasty before. She wanted to ask what part of what she'd said had made him so angry, but she was terrified to try. The one time she'd pushed him on this subject, it had almost ruined everything. Losing SB was a risk she'd sworn she'd never take again, but he just looked so hurt. She couldn't stand seeing him like that, not her SilentBlayde. So she took a shaky breath and eased forward again, speaking the words like she was easing her giant stonekin feet onto a sheet of thin ice.

"Want to talk about it?"

"No," came the sharp reply, making her flinch. When he saw it, SB sighed.

"Please, Tina," he said in a tiny voice. "Let it go. I will always give you everything SilentBlayde has, but I can never give you Haruto."

"But--"

"You don't want it, anyway," he said firmly, his blue eyes glittering above his mask. "Trust me. This is what's best for both of us."

Tina didn't believe that for a second. Almost from the first day he'd come up to her in Founder's Square, she'd known SB was hiding something. No matter how much time they spent together, he never told her anything about his real life. She'd always assumed he'd eventually trust her enough to tell her his troubles, but while he'd poured everything he had into the guild and their tanking video channel, giving her countless hours of his time while never asking for anything in return, he'd never given her that. Even here, in a totally different world, he wouldn't tell her.

And that hurt.

It actually hurt more now than it had the first time he'd shut her down, because they'd been through more. But while Tina wanted to yell at him that there was nothing he could say that would change how she felt about him, forcing this conversation would break their silent truce on this topic. That risked driving him away for good, and she had lost too many people today already.

"Fine," she said, putting her hands up in surrender.

SB let out a long breath. "Thank you."

Seeing how relieved he was not to tell her stung, but Tina forced herself to let it go. She had more pressing disasters to deal with right now, anyway. "I still need to ask you a big favor, though."

"What?"

"I need you to go find James," she said. "I'm sorry to ask. He's an idiot who doesn't deserve a rescue after knocking you out and running away, but he's still my brother. You heard how stuck he was on those stupid letters. I bet he's still trying to get them to the king, but we just kicked the hornet's nest big time back there, and if he starts trying to get into the castle, the Royal Knights will kill him for sure. He just doesn't understand how dangerous this place is! While we were fighting for everyone's lives in the Deadlands, he was chilling in a low-level zone, making friends with cats. I bet he thinks he can still solve this by completing a quest or some bullshit, but I can't turn the whole raid around to go and stop him. You're the only person I trust who can move through the city without being seen. I know he doesn't deserve it, but please, SB, save my stupid brother."

107

"Of course," SB said immediately, clutching his swords tight. "I was going to offer, anyway, since it's my fault he got away. I promise I'll bring him back to you safe and sound."

Tina hadn't realized how worried she'd been until he said that. "Thank you," she said, sagging in relief. "I don't care if you have to bind and gag him, and you don't have to rescue his pet NPC. Just get James back to me alive. That's all I ask."

"I'll bring him back to you, Tina," SilentBlayde swore. "Just keep moving toward the bank. I'll meet you there with James."

"Thank you," she said again. She felt stupid repeating the same words, but what else was there to say? James couldn't take care of himself, so as always, the responsibility fell to her, but she was bound to the raid, which meant SB had to pick up the slack. He was cleaning up her mess again, just as he always did, and yet again, she didn't know what she'd do without him.

"You're a life-saver, SB," she said, reaching down to squeeze his shoulder. "But please stay safe. If you die because of James's idiocy, I'll rip this whole damn city apart."

"I'll be fine," he said, pulling down his mask to flash her a dimmed version of his usual cocky smile. "I'm the best Assassin in FFO, remember? I'll have him back to you before you know it. Trust me."

Tina did. More than she was comfortable admitting. "See you at the bank, then."

SB pulled his mask back up and stepped into the shadows, vanishing without a trace. Tina stared at the spot where he'd been for several long moments, then she turned on her heel and started marching after her raid, sword drawn and shield up, ready to take out her frustrations on anyone who dared to try to stop her.

Chapter 7

James

In a narrow side street west of the Royal Mile, James crouched in the shadows behind a crate of empty jars, holding his bound staff close and his breath closer as he waited for a squad of Royal Knights to walk by. Above him, Ar'Bati clung flat to the underside of a shop awning while Flameboyant hid around the corner, crouching under a brown rug that was part of a pile of trash.

"Nice sword you got there, kid," one of the heavily armored knights said, smiling at the youngest member of his group, an elf who was staring at a yellow-glowing sword like it was his new darling.

"Thank you, Sir Roal!" the young elf said, holding up the weapon he'd been admiring. "I found it on the ground during my last patrol. It feel empty when I touch it though. Sir, you were in the Nightmare. Do you know how I get its 'stats'?"

"You gotta get it bound to you by a magic-user," another knight said in an annoyed tone. "Which you can't do because its owner is probably still alive. Didn't you pay attention to this morning's briefing? It's worthless to you as it is."

"Excuse me, sir, for wanting a sword that won't break!" the young knight said, lowering his luminescent weapon. "All the patrols who've died so far did so because they couldn't stop the player's weapons." He glowered down at his armor. "Why are we so poorly equipped? We're the king's own knights! We shouldn't have to scavenge for suitable arms. If I swing my sword, I want it to work."

The older knight, Sir Roal, stopped in his tracks. "Boy," he said in a tired voice. "You'd better hope you never have cause to swing any sword, player made or not. Swords are for killing. We're peacekeepers and defenders, not butchers. We've been lucky over here on the west side. All the players we've found were low-level and easily caged up."

"I heard Captain Malakai's units have seen a lot of action," the young knight said excitedly.

"Trust me, you don't want Malakai's brand of action," the older knight replied, patting his young friend on the shoulder. "Just be glad we're on loan to Captain Hightower of the Guard. Malakai..." He stopped, shaking his head. "That's all I'm going to say about that, and if you're smart, you'll say even less."

Some of the knights grumbled at the mention of Malakai's name, though whether they were grumbling because they disapproved of the Royal Knight's captain or Sir Roal's assessment of him was unclear. Either way, James was happy to see the back of them. The patrols had been getting thicker the closer they got to the castle. At this rate, they wouldn't get to the Diplomatic Quarter before midnight.

"James," Ar'Bati said, dropping back to the street as the guards vanished around the corner. "That man asks what I, too, have wondered. Why did the Nightmare give all the good non-players such bad weapons when you players and our enemies have such amazing ones?"

"It's the helpful NPC problem of game design," James said with a shrug. "FFO--at least the part of it that was actually a game--was designed to let the players be the heroes. The bad guys have to be strong, or they're no fun to fight, but allies can't be too useful or there'd be no need for player heroics. With the exception of plot-important hero NPCs like you, the normal guards and soldiers and such were deliberately weakened to make sure they'd need player help."

"Then we are in the worst situation possible!" the head warrior hissed. "Your stupid game made our allies powerless and turned our enemies into monsters none of us can fight! Bastion is out-matched in every way. I thought the Nightmare was the end of the world, but I'm starting to believe it was just the beginning of an even worse end, and it's all that damn game's fault!"

"I agree it's a raw deal," James said. "But the problem came packaged with the solution, and that's players. Yes, our enemies are powerful, but they're also balanced specifically so that players can beat them."

"Except the Once King," Flameboyant said, finally wiggling out of his hiding place and jogging after them. "No one's ever beaten him."

"Roxxy's Roughnecks almost did," James said proudly. "That's why it's so important that we all stop fighting each other. Like it or not, this world needs the players to beat what's coming."

Fangs's expression made it clear that he was firmly on the "or not" side of that, but he kept his mouth shut for once, motioning for James and Flameboyant to follow him as he snuck down the street the knight's patrol had just vacated. James followed as silently as he could, keeping his eyes on the lengthening afternoon shadows. He must have been doing it too well, because he walked straight into Ar'Bati's back, stepping on his tail in the process.

"What do you keep looking for?" his brother demanded angrily, rubbing his tail.

"Sorry," James said, moving over to make sure he was standing in sunlight. "But it's common sense to be cautious after you mug the best Assassin in FFO."

"You mean the elf you knocked unconscious with your staff?" Ar'Bati snorted. "You should not cower before him so much. It is dishonorable."

"It's smart," James replied, hustling them faster down the street. "We got lucky because SilentBlayde was already hurt, but make no mistake: dude is a monster. He's the number-one damage dealer in what was a top-five world-ranked FFO raiding guild. That makes him one of the most dangerous people in the world right now. Trust me. We do *not* want him to catch our trail."

"SilentBlayde, huh?" Flameboyant said, scratching his chin. "Isn't he the guy who wrote all those guides pinned to the top of the Assassin forums that everyone was always yelling at me to read when I tried the class?"

"That's him."

"Wow," the Sorcerer replied, looking impressed. "I didn't realize we were traveling with someone famous. Do you think he'll come after us?"

"Absolutely," James said. "I embarrassed him pretty bad in front of Tina, and he tends to take that personally. But their raid has bigger problems than us right now, so I'm hoping that if we just keep moving, we can get inside the castle before he catches us. The royal castle has shadow wards all over it that prevent people from entering the Lightless Realm, so it's pretty much the only place in the city that's safe."

Ar'Bati looked at him in disgust. "What was the point of getting free of your sister if you're still cowering before her dog?"

"Dude, did you see him while we were marching through the city?" James demanded. "SilentBlayde can step through shadows and stab you in the back before you know he's there. Of *course* I'm afraid of him!"

"If that's how you feel, why do you still call him friend?" Fangs growled back. "Seems to me a *friend* would help you in this crisis, not hunt you down."

James sighed. "It's complicated, okay? I've known SB for years now, and ninety-nine percent of the time, he's the nicest guy you'll meet. He's polite, funny, considerate, generous, honorable, honest--everything you could ask for in a friend. But he has one *horrible* problem."

"It's your sister, isn't it?" Flameboyant said. "I've seen how he looks at her. Dude's got it *bad*."

"'Bad' is an apt description," James said bitterly. "Like I said, SilentBlayde is normally a great person, but when Tina gets involved, his morals go completely out the window. There's literally nothing he won't do for her. He always feels horrible about it afterward, but that never stops him from doing it again, and it's only gotten worse since Tina went to college." James shook his head with a sigh. "That's one of the big reasons I avoid raiding with the Roughnecks. SB is cool but only so long as Tina's

112

nowhere near by. I swear he'd kill someone and hide the body if he thought it would make her happy. It's not a healthy relationship."

"You think he'll try to kill us?" Fangs asked as James hurried them into a sheltered alley--a nice, sunny one.

James winced. There was no sugarcoating this football, so he just spit it out.

"He won't kill *me*," he said as he walked briskly down the narrow backstreet. "That would hurt Tina, and SB would never do that. But I can't vouch for you guys. I'm afraid he'll murder both of you without thinking about it because it gets him to me faster. Especially you, Fangs, since he sees you as an NPC. So yeah, you're both in mortal peril, which is why I'm trying to *hurry*."

"Then we shall be careful," Ar'Bati said, marching out of the alley and into the open road.

James's heart leapt into his throat. "*Fangs!*" he hissed, running to the edge of the alley. "What are you doing? That is the *opposite* of careful!"

"I'm getting us allies," Fangs replied pompously. "As we should have done in the first place."

Panicked, James shot a glance back at Flameboyant, but it was already too late. Ar'Bati was walking straight toward a squad of eight Royal Knights, the same patrol they'd dodged earlier. As the tall warrior hailed them, the startled squad of knights scrambled to draw their blades. The youngest one even still had his glowing yellow sword out, which he immediately pointed at the jubatus warrior.

"Halt!" he cried, brandishing his enchanted blade. "The city is under martial law by decree of the king! Declare yourself!"

Ar'Bati strode forward fearlessly. "I am Fangs in the Grass, the Ar'Bati of Windy Lake, Son of Lord Rends Iron Hides, and Heir to the Claw Born clan of the Four Clans of the Savanna. I was charged by our elders to bring important news to the king, and I request your aid."

James held his breath, waiting for the violence, but Ar'Bati's approach seemed to be working.

"He's okay, sir," the young elven knight said as he lowered his glowing sword. "I think he's a quest-giver from the savanna zone. Lots of new players talk about him when they first visit the king."

"He's better than that," the officer said with a grin. "I remember you crazy cats from before the Nightmare. We used to have a Claw Born emissary before the game took her away." His look grew suspicious as he tapped his graying beard. "You'd know her, I'm sure. Her name was Emissary Thistle, right?"

"The emissary was *Acacia* Claw Born, and my *mother* is at Windy Lake," Ar'Bati said, turning up his nose in scorn at the knight's obvious trap.

"Ha!" the old knight laughed. "Good answer, Fangs! By the Sun, you aren't some little brat anymore, are you? Last time I saw you, you were a kitten. You wouldn't remember me, though. I'm Sir Roal. I've worked the Diplomatic Quarter for years." He put out his hand. "So glad to see you made it out alive."

Everyone was friendly after that. Swords were put up, shields lowered, and handshakes exchanged. But the good mood ground to a halt when James and Flameboyant stepped out from around the corner.

The other knights redrew their blades at once, but Sir Roal put up his hand. "So, Fangs of Claw Born," he said, his voice dangerously casual. "Mind explaining why you're running around with players? And why does one of them bear the mark of your clan?"

James could hear the disgust in the old knight's voice, but he held out his hand to Sir Roal, anyway. "I am James of Claw Born," he said, hoping that would explain everything. They'd been walking for a while now, and the shadows were getting longer. Standing out in the open like this, not to mention talking to Royal Knights, was enough to make James's back prickle with a thousand imagined daggers. They needed to get into the castle quickly, but Sir Roal was staring at his hand as though James had offered him a snake.

114

"Boy, how stupid do you think I am?" he asked, giving James a sneer. "I don't speak much of Wind and Grass, but I know 'James' isn't a clan name. If you think you can just name your character 'Whatever Claw Born' and expect to get a free pass--"

"Sir," Ar'Bati cut in, his voice as stuffy as it came. "James is my brother, rightfully adopted by Lord Rends Iron Hides. He might have started a player, but he is now one of us. You will treat him with respect."

Sir Roal's lantern jaw dropped open in shock. "You gotta be kidding me. How did that happen?"

Normally, James would have relished the chance to tell the story of how he and Ar'Bati had overcome prejudice and saved Windy Lake, but they were seriously running out of time. "I'll be happy to tell you everything once we're in the castle," he said quickly. "If you could just--"

"Absolutely not," Sir Roal said firmly. "I don't care who adopted you. We're under strict orders that no players are to be allowed in the castle for any reason."

"But this is an *emergency*," James pleaded, digging out his letters. "We have proof that the Once King is about to storm Bastion with the help of a corrupt portal keeper. You've been betrayed from the inside, and if we don't warn the king tonight, it could be too late. Please, you have to take us through!"

Sir Roal was a wall of disbelief, but the younger knight behind him went pale. "Sir," he whispered. "What he speaks of does match the plot from the latest expansion. It might behoove us to look over his proof at least."

"Ugh," Sir Roal groaned, tugging on his mustache. "You cats are always trouble, aren't you? Well, fine. This is officially too much crazy for the middle of the street. You can come with us, but I'm locking you up at the Diplomatic Quarter until we get this sorted out."

Going to jail sounded like a horrible plan to James, but if it would get them inside the castle wall--and more importantly, behind shadow wards--it was worth a shot. They did have an entire bag of proof. Surely someone there would be willing to listen. "I understand," he said, holding out his empty hands to be bound. "But can we go now, please?"

Sir Roal chuckled. "Never seen someone so eager to be arrested," he said, reaching for the well-worn coil of rope attached to his belt. "Just give me a second to get you secure, and we'll--"

There was a flash of silver in the dark, followed by gurgling screams as two of the knights fell to the ground, clutching their throats. James swore and grabbed a stream of floating magic, but he didn't even get the chance to start his healing spell before two more knights dropped, falling to their knees with a wet gasp as blood gushed from their necks. He kept gathering the magic, anyway, on the off chance they could be saved when something stepped into his shadow, and then a pair of gloved hands shot out to shove him to the ground, shattering his heal and sending him sprawling on the street.

"Son of a whore!" Sir Roal shouted, drawing his blade.

His remaining men did the same while Ar'Bati yanked James back to his feet.

"It's an Assassin! They've gotta come out of the Lightless Realm to attack. When he pops up again, grab him!"

James put his back to the knights and grabbed up fresh healing magics only to drop them again. The knights on the ground were already dead, and SB would never let him finish the long Raise Ally cast. Their only hope was to seize him the next time he came out of the shadows to attack. James was trying to look everywhere at once when a pair of throwing daggers came sailing down from the balcony above their heads, pegging two more knights right between the eyes.

"Fangs, back to back!" James yelled.

"What's the plan?" Ar'Bati demanded as his back slammed into James's.

"I don't know!" James said frantically, grabbing the still-bound Eclipsed Steel Staff off his back. "I've never beaten an Assassin as a healer before!"

"Light up the shadows!" Flameboyant yelled, his hands already burning bright with a fire spell as he dove for cover between them. "No shadows, no--"

The Sorcerer cut off with a gasp as the flickering form of SilentBlayde appeared just long enough to knee him in the stomach. James supposed he should have been grateful it was only a knee and not a knife, but Flameboyant still dropped like a stone, gasping and retching as he sprawled on the cobbles. When Ar'Bati moved forward to cover the downed Sorcerer, James heard a powdery *poof* sound, and the warrior yowled, dropping his sword to paw at his face as a cloud of dark-purple powder enveloped his head.

"He's only got one of those blinds!" Sir Roal yelled.

"Get your backs to a wall!" James cried, dragging the struggling Ar'Bati and the still-gagging Flameboyant to the edge of the street. "Don't give him an opening!"

Sir Roal and the youngest knight obeyed at once, slamming their backs beside James's against the cracked masonry wall of an abandoned wood working shop.

"Swords up!" Sir Roal ordered, holding his blade steady.

The younger knight obeyed, lifting his glowing sword in his shaking hands. "We're going to die!"

"Yes," replied a cold whisper. "You are."

"*No!*" James shouted, but it was too late. The young knight was already sliding down the wall, his rapidly glazing over eyes still wide in shock at the dagger sticking out of his heart. As he hit the ground, the Assassin emerged from the shadows at the mouth of the alley they'd come from, bloody silver swords gleaming darkly in his hands.

James had seen SilentBlayde step out of the shadows countless times, but he'd never realized how terrifying it could be until right now. The Assassin's black-and-red-runed set of armor shifted around him like living darkness as he stood at the edge of the Lightless Realm, and his face was completely hidden by his mask, leaving only his blue eyes to gleam like knives in the dark.

"'Blayde," James said, putting up his hand. "Just stop for a--"

"*For the king!*" Sir Roal bellowed as he charged.

"Wait!" James cried, but it was already too late. Given how he'd killed all the others, James expected SB to Shadow Step behind the knight the moment his back was exposed, but it turned out SilentBlayde didn't need stealth. All it took was a flick of his sword, and Sir Roal's throat split open, sending him to the ground in a waterfall of his own blood.

"There's nothing royal about knights who murder innocents," SB told him as he fell. "Die for your sins, and know that you deserve it."

Sir Roal gurgled and lay still, grasping SB's boot with the last of his strength. As the Assassin kicked the dead man out of his way, James dropped down beside Ar'Bati.

"Fangs," he whispered in the language of Wind and Grass. "Can you see yet?"

"The powder is starting to clear," Ar'Bati replied in kind, his voice no louder than a breeze in the grass. "What's the plan?"

"Pretend you're still blind and wait for your chance," James said, sliding back up the wall to his feet. "We're only going to get one chance."

Even as he said it, James knew he was being wildly optimistic as SilentBlayde slung the blood off his silver swords and started walking toward him.

"SB, buddy," James said, dropping his bound staff on the street so he could hold up his empty hands. "You need to turn down, because you're looking really scary right now." He glanced pointedly at the corpses the Assassin was stepping over. "I don't think you realize yet that you just murdered eight people."

"They're not people, James," SilentBlayde said angrily. "They're monsters. You saw what they did in the square." He kicked one of the dead knights with his boot. "This wasn't murder. It was justice."

"I don't know. Those guys seemed reasonable to me," James said, raising his empty hands higher. "One of them was a friend of my family, even. Not that you asked about that. You just *assumed* they were evil and slaughtered them, which is a problem, because from what I heard from them earlier, I don't think they'd done anything wrong."

"The NPCs never gave us the benefit of the doubt," SilentBlayde said, stalking closer. "Blaming us for the Nightmare. Summary executions without investigation or trial. Beatings and torture. They never asked if we were guilty. Why should I treat them any different?"

"But that's not what these guys were doing," James argued. "If you'd just listen--"

"Why should I listen to their excuses?" the Assassin demanded. "The knights have already shown us repeatedly who they are." He lifted his chin. "I know a monster when I see one, James, and I will not show mercy."

"*Can't you hear that you're using their words?*" James shouted, slamming his hands down in frustration. "Goddammit, Haruto! If you'd just stop for five seconds and *think*--"

"*Don't call me Haruto!*" SB roared, launching at him to pin his blade against James's neck. "I have power in this world that I never had back home, and I refuse to flatter beasts *ever* again."

James's hands flew back up the moment the sword edge touched his neck, but his scowl stayed put.

"*Are you even listening to yourself?*" he yelled in his friend's face. "Look at the blood on the street! Those men are *really* dead, and you're the one who killed them! But you're not actually an Assassin. You just *played* one in a game! You'd never do something like this in real life. Why can't you see that?"

"And why can't *you* see that everything in this world hates us?" SilentBlayde yelled back. "This place has done nothing but try to kill us from the moment we arrived. I have every right to fight back! But I don't care about the NPCs. I'm here because you betrayed me."

The ice in his voice at the end made James wince. "I'm sorry," he said. "I didn't want to hurt you, but I didn't have a choice. I had to do the right thing, and I knew that asking for your help was pointless because you never go against Tina. Not even when it's in your own best interest."

"I had to tell her I let you get away!" SB cried, eyes flashing in fury above his mask. "How could you do that to me? I thought we were friends!"

"We *are* friends!" James yelled furiously. "But you're being an idiot right now! You love FFO even more than I do, so why are you helping Tina destroy it? Don't you see? This could be a miracle for you. You're *in* FFO! You have magic and power and money and freedom and everything else you played the game to get! Everything you've ever claimed you wanted is right here in front of you, and you're shitting all over it! You're behaving just as badly as the knights in the camp, and while we're killing each other in alleys, the Once King is about to walk right in and take the greatest fortress in this world without a fight! You're dooming your own future, and you're too obsessed to see it!"

"You're the one who's obsessed," SB growled, finally removing his blade from James's neck so he could grab him by the collar. "I'm taking you back to Tina."

"Come on, dude. Don't do this!" James said, digging in his heels as the Assassin tried to drag him away. "You know Tina doesn't want to actually deal with me as her prisoner. She just wants me to be safe. Look, I'll make you a deal. Help me get to the castle, and then you can go back and tell her I'm safe with the king. I'll get where I'm trying to go, and you won't have to worry about me anymore. Everybody wins."

SilentBlayde shot him a chilling look. "How about I make *you* a deal? Stop making my life difficult, and I won't kill your pretend brother."

That was the final straw. Wrapping his hands in lightning as he'd seen NekoBaby do, James grabbed for SB's arm. The Assassin had been manhandling him because he'd assumed James couldn't fight back, but coming out of the shadows had been a bad move, because so long as

120

SilentBlayde was holding on to him, he couldn't vanish back into the Lightless Realm. If they could just keep him visible, they had a chance. But James underestimated SB's speed. He'd barely managed to brush the Assassin's armor before the elf released his hold on James's collar and melted back into the shadows. He'd almost vanished completely when Flameboyant suddenly sat up, hands glowing with flames as he pulled back to launch a fireball straight at SB's stomach.

It wasn't going to work. Even as he saw it building, James knew there was no way a level forty-five could land a hit on someone like SilentBlayde. But Flameboyant's valiant effort never even got to finish. Almost as soon as he sat up, the Assassin put him back down, stabbing him with daggers through both legs. The nascent fire spell shattered as Flameboyant went back down with a scream, and James whirled on the place where SB had been with new fury.

"You're gonna feel guilty when this is over, you know!"

"Why should I feel guilty?" floated the answer, the words jumping around him as the Assassin moved between the shadows. "You're the one who brought them out here. The lowbie will live, but your pet cat won't if you don't stop fighting and come quietly."

"Why are you acting this way?" James yelled at him, so angry he was having trouble being properly afraid. "I don't understand you at all! You're normally such a good guy, but you lose your damn mind every time Tina asks you to do something. Do you think she *wants* you to be like this? Murdering and threatening people like a villain?"

"Don't try to turn this back on me," SilentBlayde said with chilling viciousness. "This situation is *your* fault! You're the one who ran. All Tina wanted to do was keep you safe. Why won't you let her?"

"*Because I'm not hers to protect!*" James shouted at the top of his lungs. "I'm my own damn person, and I came here on a mission! If we don't warn King Gregory that the undead are coming, this whole world is toast! I'm willing to die to stop that from happening and that is *my* choice to make! Not Tina's, and not yours."

He was panting by the time he finished, but his only answer was silence. Gathering lightning around his hand again, James put his back toward Ar'Bati's, taking care to leave a good three feet of open room between them. As the head warrior leaned "blindly" on the alley wall behind him, James heard the soft scrape of his brother's claws against the brick as he readied to pounce. He held his breath and stepped forward again, leaving a bit more space, the perfect opening for an Assassin.

Sure enough, a heartbeat later, the smell of the open sky blossomed right behind him. James whirled the moment his jubatus nose caught the warning, lashing out with his lightning-covered hand. But even when he was falling for a trap, SilentBlayde was still too fast. James hadn't even gotten his hand halfway up before the pommel of a sword smashed into his temple, sending the whole world spinning. His lightning spell went haywire, blasting into the wall and sending a shower of bricks and dust flying. SB's hand was already closing around his throat when James heard Ar'Bati roar, and then two bodies crashed into him.

James, SilentBlayde, and Ar'Bati all went down together as the head warrior tackled the Assassin with all of his considerable might. True to his name, SilentBlayde didn't shout. James saw a foot sink back into shadows, but Ar'Bati grabbed the elf's cape and hauled him right back out. In response, SB flipped his blades back around in his hands and stabbed both of them into Ar'Bati's sides.

The sound of his brother's pained gasp knocked James back to his senses. Using the ground as leverage, James wrenched his body around and grabbed one of SilentBlayde's arms just as Ar'Bati's grip gave out. Years of martial arts practice took over from there, and he somehow managed to wrap his legs across the Assassin's chest and neck. SB immediately began to struggle, hammering on James's hold with his superior strength, but James just gritted his teeth and held on. If he let go, there was nothing stopping SilentBlayde from vanishing again.

When he realized he wouldn't be able to beat his way free, SB went to yank his swords out of Ar'Bati to turn them on James. When he tried to pull his blades out, though, the jubatus was already there.

"I won't die that easily!" Ar'Bati roared, grasping the silver swords that were still wedged into his sides with his hands. Then, as James and SilentBlayde writhed on the ground, the head warrior rolled away, taking his body--and the Assassin's swords still trapped inside it--out of SB's reach.

SilentBlayde *did* cry out then, screaming in rage as he lost his grip on the blood-slicked handles. But other than the blood, this was no different from all the other jujitsu matches James had been in, and he held tight. The Assassin twisted violently, trying to kick and elbow, but James just adjusted with him, keeping him at bad angles that rendered his superior strength useless. Anytime SB got out of one lock, James had already managed to worm himself around for a different hold, keeping him relentlessly trapped on the ground.

After five minutes of this, SB stopped trying to escape and started trying to kill him. His body turned hazy as he activated his Shadow Dance ability. With eellike flexibility, the Assassin was able to get a hand on the brace of daggers wrapped around his leg. The blades, which had been purely cosmetic back when this was a game, came out with a flash, sending James into a panic. He was trying to get on top of SilentBlayde to keep his arms pinned when the Assassin lurched up and knifed him in the ribs-- twice.

James yowled as hot pain shot through his side. But while it hurt like hell, the short dagger wasn't legendary like SB's silver swords, and despite his terrible gear, James was still level eighty. It took more than two hits from a mundane weapon to put him out. He'd already started working his way around for the next hold when the furious Assassin peppered him with two more stabs to the leg and a slash down his arm.

Bleeding and cursing, James still managed to get his knees around the shadow-wrapped elf's neck. Using his arms, he grabbed SB's right arm

123

and bent it nearly backward across his chest, cinching it in place with both of his.

As he started to apply the pressure that would cut off the Assassin's air, it occurred to James that he should probably offer SB a chance to surrender. He dismissed the idea just as fast. He couldn't trust SB right now, not one inch. The wild, murderous look in his friend's eyes through the living shadows proved it, so James clamped down on the Assassin's neck with all the strength in his legs, pulling on SB's right arm at the same time to crush him as hard as he could. He was praying the elf would pass out before he did when Shadow Dance ended, revealing SB's pale face as it started going purple, even as he jabbed James yet again with the tiny dagger in his free hand.

The worst pain yet exploded in James's right knee as SilentBlayde stabbed him straight through the kneecap. James screamed in agony, his grip loosening for a fraction of a second. Just long enough to hear SB gasp as he sucked in precious air.

Damn. I just lost.

He felt done for. The dagger was tiny, but SB still wielded it with the full might of his ultra-geared strength and speed, and the damage was adding up. James's only chance had been to choke him out before he lost the feeling in his arms, but now that SB had gotten a breath, that chance was slipping away. The Assassin had already managed to rip his arm free of James's blood-slicked grasp. One more limb, and the elf would be free. Then he'd kill Ar'Bati out of pure rage and drag James back to Tina by the bloody scruff of his neck. It was all over, but just as James was clenching his teeth for one final squeeze, his heard his brother say his name.

His head shot up. Fangs in Grass was only a few feet away, his hands still clutching SilentBlayde's silver swords in his chest, which was now black with his blood. But though pained, his orange eyes were clear when they locked on James's. "Brother," he panted, his eyes intent. "We die as Claw Born should."

He flicked his ears as he finished, and James clenched his sharp teeth with a hiss as he realized what Ar'Bati meant. He didn't want to do it, but there was more riding on this than just their lives, so James turned away from his brother and switched up his hold, yanking SilentBlayde's right arm up until the elf's wrist was right in front of his nose.

"With our fangs in the enemy," he growled, closing his eyes. "Sorry, SB."

His mouth flashed open, and then he sank his new fangs into the elf's wrist, biting straight through the gap in the Assassin's armored glove and into the artery beneath. Hot, salty blood exploded into James's mouth as SB tore his hand free but not before James had taken out a sizable chunk. There was a musical clatter as the little dagger SilentBlayde had been using to stab him hit the cobblestones next to his head, and then the elf's weight vanished from on top of him with a roar.

James's eyes shot open again, but SB hadn't gotten up for the kill. Ar'Bati had. In a last surge of strength, the warrior had launched off the ground and tackled the Assassin clear off James. They landed in a tangle in the middle of the bloody street with Ar'Bati on top. Frantic, SB grabbed for the silver swords that had been lodged in the warrior's chest, but Ar'Bati had already thrown them across the alley, leaving two gaping holes in his sides as he bit down like a lion on the thickest part of SilentBlayde's good arm.

The Assassin screamed in pain. Ar'Bati's eyes were already rolling back in his head as the blood loss hit, but he did not let go. Like a true wild cat, he clung to his kill, forcing SB to rip his arm free. Bleeding like a faucet, SilentBlayde fled for the shadows, but James caught his foot and dragged him back out. Tossing the elf into the middle of the sunlit street, James grabbed one of the silver swords Ar'Bati had thrown away earlier and raised it high over his head.

"James..." SB said fearfully, his blue eyes wide above his bloodstained mask.

"Think about your choices, Haruto," James said, and then he plunged the sword into SB's leg.

The supernaturally sharp silver blade went straight through the elf's flesh into the ground, splitting a cobblestone and stapling the Assassin to the road. SilentBlayde screamed as it hit, and then he cut off, his body slumping sideways as he finally passed out.

Panting, James collapsed beside him. He was dizzy and weak from blood loss, so he had to move carefully, rolling himself onto his knees to crawl across the street to the Eclipsed Steel Staff he'd dropped at the beginning of the fight. He knew he'd regret this later, but Ar'Bati and SilentBlayde were both bleeding to death in front of him, and Flameboyant didn't look much better. He needed full healing power, so he bit through the wards Gray Fang had placed around the head of his cursed staff, ripping through the white binding cloth to release its full potential.

The moment he set it free, the dark staff's nihilism roared back into his mind.

Kill them.

"Kind of hoping to do the opposite," James muttered as he started gathering up flows of life magic.

Petulant child, the staff scolded. *They are so close to peace already. This is your chance to end their suffering forever.*

James ignored it, focusing on his magic instead as he wove the flows into the Naturalist's big healing spell.

You wield mana so inflexibly, the staff said irritably. *Is this what you think magic is? Twelve narrowly defined spells?* The ghostly voice tsked in his head. *You are capable of so much more.* The black staff twitched in his grip. *Let me show you.*

"No, thanks," James said sharply, whacking the Eclipsed Steel Staff on the street. "I had more than enough of your 'help' back in Red Canyon. But I'm not the weak person I was then, so piss off."

Vulgar fool, the staff muttered, but James wasn't listening anymore. He just took the glowing flows of life he'd been weaving together and shoved them into his brother, dropping the biggest heal he had onto the unconscious Ar'Bati's head.

It was barely enough. Despite being level fifty, his brother was a two-skull with a mini-boss's health pool. He couldn't believe how much damage SB had done with that one stab. If they hadn't gotten his swords away at the start, James knew they'd all be dead. Tired and spending mana faster than he should, James sent heal after heal into Fangs in the Grass until, at last, his brother gasped and rolled over, hacking up blood as the air was forced back into his lungs.

James collapsed with a gasp as well, wiping the sweat from his clammy fur. Not for the first time, he wished he had more Intelligence gear to enhance his healing power, but he'd had to make a choice, and he'd chosen not to wear the smothering, leg-trapping healer's robes. That choice had saved their lives tonight since there was no way he could have gotten SB into all those holds while wearing a dress. He just hoped it didn't cost him everything now as he turned and spent the last of his sad mana on a spell for SilentBlayde.

Again, it was barely enough. James watched as the Assassin's wrist and leg closed up just enough to stop the bleeding. SB was still unconscious and slashed up, but he was alive, and that was what mattered.

He was about to lie down again when Ar'Bati grabbed him. The head warrior's eyes were still dilated from the healing high, but the fury in them was classic Fangs as he started shaking James like a rag doll. "What are you doing? Don't heal *him*! Heal yourself!"

"I'll live without healing," James said weakly, nodding at the unconscious elf. "He won't."

"So?" Ar'Bati bared his bloody fangs. "He tried to kill us!"

"He did," James said tiredly. "But he's still my friend, and Tina would kill me if I let him die."

The warrior cursed in of Wind and Grass and shot to his feet. "Don't move," he ordered, running into a nearby building. "I'm going to find something to bandage you with!"

Happy not to be getting yelled at anymore, James lay back down. Without much hope, he glanced at the dead knights, but the fight with SB had taken too long, and the life energy was long gone from their bodies. Sighing at the stupid, pointless waste, he glanced at the bloody Sorcerer next. "How you doing, Flame?"

"Not bad, all things considered," Flameboyant said, lifting his head. "He got me in the legs, but I don't think he was actually trying to kill me, or I'd be dead. I can probably walk if someone helps me." The elf flashed him a grin. ""Tis but a scratch!'"

James laughed at that then grimaced as the motion sent waves of pain through his ribs.

"Ouch," Flameboyant said with a wince when he saw the look on James's face. "Can I do anything to help you? I don't have heals, but..."

He trailed off with a shrug.

James frowned thoughtfully. "Actually, maybe you can. I don't suppose you have the Sun Writing spell, do you?"

"Of course I do," Flameboyant said proudly. "Maybe you haven't noticed yet, but fire is kind of my *thing*."

"Great," James said, forcing himself to sit up one last time. "I want to leave a message."

Five minutes later, a disgusted Ar'Bati came prowling back carrying a bolt of cloth. He tore it into strips and bound James's numerous stab wounds with rough strength. He bandaged Flameboyant's legs as well, his face dire. "There's no food," he said as he tied the Sorcerer's wounds tight. "This area has already been looted out. We need to get to actual safety."

When he was satisfied no one would bleed out, Fangs reached down to help his brother to his feet, but James shook his head. "Wait," he said. "We can't just leave SB in the street."

Ar'Bati recoiled with an open-mouthed hiss. "You *can't* be serious."

James looked at him pleadingly, and Fangs rolled his eyes. Walking over to snatch SilentBlayde out of the puddle his blood had made, he looked around for a moment, and then he shoved the Assassin into a nearby barrel.

"There," the warrior said, slapping the wooden lid down to hide SB's head. "Satisfied?"

"Yes, thank you," James said, holding out his arms for Ar'Bati to help him up.

Fangs hauled him onto his shoulder one-handed. He did the same to Flameboyant next, tossing the crimson elf over his other shoulder. "You sure did leave me with all the work here."

"Not my fault," James said, tucking his unwrapped staff under his arm so it wouldn't smack Ar'Bati in the face. "You have too much HP, bro. You took all my mana."

That earned him a snort as the head warrior set off down the alley, pausing only long enough to sneer at the glowing golden letters Flameboyant's Sun Writing spell had carved into the wall directly across from SilentBlayde's hiding spot.

Chapter 8

Tina

The only good thing Tina could say about the march to the bank was that at least she was too busy to worry about her brother and SilentBlayde.

Despite how easily they'd cut the Royal Knights down, the battle had taken its toll. Mana was low, which meant all her casters looked like college students the night after finals. The Rangers had refilled their ammo from their stores, but there wasn't enough left in the bags they'd brought with them from the Order's fortress to do it again. Food was short, water was running out, and there were more mouths to feed than ever.

Between the survivors of Founder's Square and the players they'd rescued from Malakai's slaughter camp, they'd added over a hundred people to their ranks. They now had more players under level forty than over. Since there wasn't enough room in the street for all of them to walk in a clump, her Roughnecks had to spread out along the column to make sure everyone was protected. But the added distance meant the players at the front were out of reach of the people at the back and the middle, which meant Tina now had to make sure her healers were evenly spaced out so that no section was left without support, and on and on and on.

It felt stupid even to think, but Tina literally could not believe that running an army could be this complicated. Every time she turned around, someone needed her to do something or answer a question or give an order. She was just grateful Zen was leading the way, because with all the running back and forth she'd had to do, Tina hadn't been paying attention to where they were going at all, which meant she was now totally lost. Since the buildings looked less expensive and the cobbles on the roads were more worn down, she presumed they'd already entered the less fashionable southern side of the city, but they could have been about to walk out the East Gate, for all she knew.

Even in the game, Bastion had been a large and confusing city. Now that everything was ten times bigger, the place had exploded into a warren. Other than the Royal Mile, which ran straight through the middle from the castle in the north to the South Gate, all the roads looked like they'd been made by people slapping down buildings wherever. Clearly, the concept of civic planning hadn't made it over to this world yet. As a huge, player-important building, the bank shouldn't have been *too* far from the castle, but with all the new distances, nothing was conveniently located anymore. Tina just hoped it wasn't too much farther and that Zen knew where she was going. It was already getting into the afternoon. People were starting to drag their feet, and Tina was never forcing a Deadlands-style death march ever again.

At least they hadn't had any more problems with the Royal Knights. There were no big armies or camps down here. Just small patrols that were easily killed from a distance by the Rangers, and even those thinned out the farther they got from the castle. Horns were still blowing from the hills behind them, but if there were reinforcements coming to chase them, they were being damn slow about it. She was just hoping their luck held out when the raid shuffled to a halt.

"Roxxy!"

Tina looked up to see one of Zen's Rangers waving her over. Getting a firm grip on her shield, Tina jogged to the front of the raid, where Zen was perched on top of a second-story balcony, scowling at something in the distance.

"What's up?"

"We've got movement," the Ranger said, pointing down the street.

Tina sighed. "Well, can you describe it?" She looked pointedly at the wooden balcony's flimsy supports and then down at her boulder of a body. "I don't think I'll fit up there."

Zen rolled her eyes and jumped down, landing the two-story drop with a graceful roll. "KillerKat's been going on about flashes of light for blocks now," she said, nodding at a jubatus Ranger, who looked painfully

131

smug. "I just saw it too. Looks like someone's spying on us with the Grand Schtump's Golden Binoculars."

Tina couldn't help but grin with amusement. The Grand Schtump's Golden Binoculars were a player-crafted item that let you see farther than the game's render distance usually allowed. They didn't have a level requirement, but they were stupidly expensive, difficult to make, and difficult to use, which meant whoever was up there wasn't a casual. The only ones who cared enough to spend that much gold on a few hundred feet of extra vision were serious players who knew FFO's mechanics and were stacking every advantage they could. Her sort of people, in other words.

"Looks like we've made a friend."

"I don't know if they're friendly," Killbox said, hefting his ax, which he'd clearly been holding the entire walk.

"Why wouldn't they be?" Tina asked. "We're all players. That puts us on the same side."

The Berserker snorted at her. "You don't PVP much, do you?"

"Nope," Tina said proudly. "I hated player versus player. Too stressful."

"And raiding isn't?"

"To each their own, dude," Tina said. "And I've experts like you on hand now, so tell me what's up with this situation."

The Berserker huffed, but the compliment worked. "When you wear your PVP tabard, you can attack and be attacked by anyone else wearing one," he explained. "That means you gotta look at everyone you meet as a threat, 'cause they're probably an asshole who'll kill you for the laughs if they think they can."

Tina chuckled. "Why do I get the impression *you* were that asshole, Killbox?"

"Hell yeah," Killbox said, flexing his giant biceps. "The strong pwn, the weak get owned. Nothing's better than stomping down people who think they're hot shit. Anyway, we're a pretty big group. Way too big to sneak around, so those guys have probably been watching us for a while. Since they haven't attacked yet, that means they don't think they can take us, or they're not sure if they should. Either way, the smart move is to keep their distance and watch for an opening."

"Well, that doesn't get us anywhere," Tina said, squinting at the place Zen had said the flash was coming from. "If there's an organized group of players out there, we need to be getting together, not playing chicken." She turned to Frank, who'd been staying up front just in case something needed tanking. "Hold the line here. I'm going ahead to talk to them."

"I don't think that's a good idea," Killbox said. "PVPers--"

"PVPers are still players," Tina said sharply. "Old habits may die hard, but surely no one's killing just for the lulz now that this isn't a game. They're clearly nervous about us, and why not? We're a freaking army. But if we don't talk, we're never going to get anywhere."

She started jogging ahead, and Killbox cursed. "Are you going out there *alone?*"

"I don't want to look threatening," she yelled back. "And what are they going to do to me? I'm the best tank left in the game."

"That doesn't mean you can't still die if you get outnumbered!" Killbox said angrily. "Didn't you learn *anything* from our duel?"

She remembered that she'd won. Pointing that out felt like needless antagonism, though, so Tina kept it to herself. "I'll be fine," she insisted. "And I don't want to cause an incident by bringing a big threatening group. Just wait there. I'll be right back."

She was picking up the pace when she heard heavy footsteps behind her, and then Killbox appeared at her side, his face grim.

"What part of 'wait there' did you not understand?"

"The part where I'm not going to cool my heels while you run out and die alone," the Berserker snapped, keeping his ax ready. "You might be a hotshot when it comes to raid bosses, but you're seriously going to get yourself murdered if you don't stop acting like such a goddamn Care Bear."

133

"Better they go for me than the others," she said, glancing nervously over her shoulder at the raid. "I don't know if you've noticed, but we've picked up a lot of liabilities, and players are a lot more dangerous than the Royal Knights were. If it does come to an attack, I feel a lot better tanking it out here away from the level twenties and thirties who could get killed by a stray hit."

"Still no reason to go out alone," Killbox said stubbornly. "Two isn't any more intimidating than one, but at least this way you'll have *some* backup."

He was still disobeying orders, but she had to smile at that. "Well, thanks for the support, then."

"Only smart move," Killbox replied. "Your elf boy would backstab the shit out of me if I let you run off and get killed."

"SB isn't my boyfriend," Tina said automatically.

Killbox started to snicker. "Who said anything about a boyfriend? Or SB? All I said was 'elf boy.' The boyfriend stuff was aaall you."

Face burning, Tina decided to ignore him after that, focusing on the quiet city around them instead as they ran down the road in the direction Zen had pointed. When they reached a square that Tina judged as both far enough from the raid and open enough for a good parley, she slowed to a halt, planting her boot on the edge of the crumbling, dried-out fountain in the middle.

"Hello up there!" she called up at the silent rooftops. "We know you're watching. We're not interested in fighting you, so how about you come down and talk? It's just the two of us."

Her words echoed between the empty buildings, and Tina held her breath. For all her talk of friends, Killbox now had her worried that they really would attack. Maybe these players had turned into bandits, pillaging and taking whatever they wanted. It wouldn't be hard, given how much power even a modestly geared max-level player had compared to everyone else, but Tina wasn't a soft target. Surely anyone savvy enough to invest in the Grand Schtump's Golden Binoculars would be able to recognize Dead

Mountain raid gear on sight and come out peaceably, but she still kept her shield ready, just in case.

They were still waiting when a piece of a white stone fronting broke free and clattered to the street behind them. In the quiet of the empty square, the sudden noise made her jump. Then she heard the soft scrape of steel on stone from the opposite side of the street, and she whirled around just in time to see magic light up the shadows.

In the darkness of a crumbling building, red-glowing staffs lit up the faces of two Sorcerers hiding behind a broken window. No sooner had she spotted them than Tina heard the creak of bowstrings from the roof above. Lots of them. The alleyways filled with shadows of heavy armor as people moved in from all sides to flank them.

Tina swore under her breath and yanked up her shield. She didn't know her player-versus-player gear as well as she knew her raid loot, but she saw two Berserkers who looked like Killbox clones, and one of the Rangers up top had the *Shadowkiller* bow that every Ranger in her guild had taken up PVPing to get last year. The pair of Knights cutting off their way back to the other Roughnecks were both dressed from head to toe in the wicked-looking black PVP plate set that Tina had let SB drag her into the arenas to try to earn just because it looked so cool. She hadn't made more than a few days, but it was painfully obvious that the players surrounding them were all serious player-versus-player fighters, and by the scars and grim looks on their faces, they'd already seen a lot of action here in Bastion.

"Well, shit," Killbox said, putting his back to hers as the circle tightened. "Nice knowing you, Roxxy."

"It's not over yet," Tina said, trying not to panic at just how fast everything had gone wrong. "Maybe we can just surrender. The Roughnecks aren't that far away."

"Still too far to help," he said, baring his teeth. "But I ain't going down like a punk."

135

Before Tina could ask what he meant by that, the Berserker stepped forward, pounded his chest with one fist while raising his ax with the other. "Listen up, assholes!" he shouted, his huge voice booming off the buildings. "You have us outnumbered, but know that I am Killbox! Grand Victor from Colosseum Seasons Two and Three and first in the world to earn the *'You've Killed How Many?!* achievement! You wanna fight us? I'm gonna kill half of you before I go down! So who's first?"

He finished with a wide swing of his ax and stepped back into position by Tina, who was staring at him in awe.

"Holy shit, dude," she whispered at him. "Are you for real? I didn't know you'd done all that stuff!"

"Fuck yeah, I'm a badass at my half of the game," Killbox replied with a grin. "Why else did you think I volunteered for suffering through a Dead Mountain raid? It was the only gear left in the game that was better than what I could earn in the arenas."

Tina shook her head in wonder. "How'd I beat you in that duel, then?"

He snorted. "You got lucky. I didn't know the new rules back then. If I'd understood we weren't limited to game mechanics, I would have smoked you."

Given how much damage she'd just seen him do to Malakai and the Royal Knights, Tina believed him. But any further conversation was cut off as an enemy Berserker stepped forward. He was a giant human with shoulders even bigger than Killbox's, wearing a suit of crimson plate armor decorated from head to toe with metal skulls. Instead of the Berserker's usual ax, he had a long-bladed spear that glowed a bloody red, which he pointed at Killbox's face. Behind him, a scrawny elf Assassin lurked with a pair of lightning maces that crackled and sparked, keeping his eyes on Tina. But while she was scrambling to remember the strategy SilentBlayde had taught her to use against Assassins, Killbox started to laugh.

Driving his ax into the dry fountain with a deafening clang, Killbox tossed his arms wide and ran straight at the crimson-armored Berserker. Tina's heart leaped into her throat as she braced for him to be impaled, but the enemy dropped his spear as well and grabbed Killbox in a huge bear hug.

"KB!"

"Cinco!" Killbox cried back, his voice sounding delighted.

Tina, still in fight-to-the-death mode, blinked in confusion. She had no idea what was going on, but the two giant men were hugging like long-lost brothers, grinning and crying manly tears of joy as they slapped each other on the back.

"Fuck, dude," the red-armored Berserker said when he could speak again. "I thought you were dead! You were raiding the Dead Mountain when this shit went down, so we all thought you were zombie food. Thank god you gave that boss speech, or we'd have slaughtered you. It's hell to recognize anyone without nameplates."

"Same to you, dude," Killbox said, wiping his eyes. "I didn't know your ugly face from anyone else's, but then I saw your spear. There's only one asshole left who's still hardcore enough to keep using the Blood Fang spear for three years running just because it has an attack speed exploit."

"Hell yeah, man!" his friend said proudly, tapping his glowing spear on the ground. "This beauty's saved my bacon a lot these last few days."

They both started laughing again at that, which would have been fine if the rest of the players weren't still ready to attack.

"Um, Killbox," Tina said, moving a little closer. "Mind introducing me to your friend?"

"Oh, right," Killbox said, grabbing her arm and pulling her forward. "Roxxy, these are my old gladiator pals! This is CincoDeMurder, current arena champion. And the Assassin behind him is Shankfest."

"Oh hell no," Shankfest said, jaw dropping as he lowered his lightning maces. "That's *Roxxy*?! Ooohhh shit, guys! We almost attacked the Roughnecks!" He whirled on CincoDeMurder. "I *told* you the female stonekin was weird, boss!"

"How the fuck was I supposed to know it was Roxxy!" Cinco shot back. "I heard everyone at Dead Mountain Fortress died!"

Tina grinned at that. "It's okay, guys," she said, sheathing her sword. "Times are crazy." She held out her gauntleted hand. "Roxxy of the Roughnecks."

"CincoDeMurder," the red Berserker replied, giving her a crushing handshake. "Guild leader of the Red Sands PVP guild."

"Weapons down, people!" Shankfest called to the players surrounding them. "We're cool!"

The other players obeyed at once.

Relieved, Tina let out a breath as staffs were extinguished, bows relaxed, and swords sheathed, but they weren't in the clear yet. "I'm happy you guys are reunited," she said. "But I have to know something before we can be friendly."

CincoDeMurder's toothy smile slid off his scarred face, replaced with flat-pressed lips. "Oh yeah? What?"

There was no nice way to put this, so Tina just spit it out. "Why were you about to attack us? If you guys are bandits and IRL player-killers, I'm not cool with that."

Shankfest butted in. "Yeah, well, we have to ask you the same question."

"The fuck does that mean?" Tina demanded.

"Our scout said you left Malakai's death camp escorting player prisoners," Cinco replied, square jaw set stubbornly. "We don't tolerate turncoat assholes."

"Then your scout must be blind, dude," Tina said with a snort. "We trashed the whole camp and freed everyone. Go take another look at my raid if you don't believe me. How many prisoners do you know who get to walk around carrying weapons and not wearing chains?"

Cinco and Shankfest exchanged a look of embarrassment. "Our Ranger is nearsighted, actually..."

"I told you letting him use my binoculars wouldn't fix it!" Shankfest said.

"Yeah, well, I couldn't let *you* scout anymore," Cinco snapped back. "Not after the incident."

Shankfest looked unrepentant. "Those legs were worth it."

"Yeah, well, we've got a whole damn army hot on our heels, so we have to keep moving," Tina said, getting them back on subject. "You guys seem pretty together. Want to join my guild? PVP and PVE are one and the same now, after all."

"Thanks, but no," Cinco said, shaking his head. "I'm not giving up my Red Sands, not even to the Roughnecks. But I *would* love to team up. It's been tough as hell surviving out here with just us."

"I can respect that," Tina said with a smirk. She was about to put out her hand to shake on it when Cinco turned to Killbox.

"What about you?"

"What about me?" Killbox asked, crossing his massive arms.

"You're a Red Sands man," Cinco said. "You should stop playing with the raider Care Bears and rejoin us."

"*Hey!*" Tina snarled. But before she could deliver sharp words about poaching her people, Killbox laughed in Cinco's face.

"Ha ha! Nice try, *Thomas,* but I'm an important officer 'n shit in the Roughnecks now. No way I'm going back to being your grunt."

"Damn," Cinco said. "Well, have fun with all that tanking-and-spanking there, *Star Symbol.*"

Tina choked. "Wait," she said, whirling on Killbox. "Your name is *Star Symbol?* Like, for real?"

Killbox glowered at Cinco. "Yeah, and not the words, either. My IRL name is the fucking keyboard symbol for a star." He turned up his nose. "See, this is why I don't want to work for you anymore, Cinco. Even when you're being nice, you're an asshole."

"Hey, you *star*-ted it," Cinco said, snickering.

"Wow, dude," Tina said, boggling. "No wonder you wanted to go by Killbox. Your parents were *dicks* to give you a name like that."

"Tell me about it," Killbox grumbled.

"Well," Tina said, slapping Killbox on his Atlas-sized shoulder. "Whoever you were before, you're Killbox, the Roughneck's mighty and terrifying Berserker officer to me now."

Killbox stood up straighter at that. "Damn right, I am."

Tina wasn't above giving Cinco a competitive smirk after that, and the other guildmaster huffed. He was still grumping about it when one of the Rangers on the roof, who was wearing a pair of golden binoculars around his neck, started gesturing frantically.

Cinco cleared his throat. "Yeah, well, now that we're cool and all, would you mind sending word to your people that you're not in danger? Your army is getting pretty close, and they look as trigger happy as all hell."

That was news to Tina since she'd specifically ordered them to wait, but sure enough, when she glanced down the street, Frank was only two blocks back with Zen and all the Roughneck's best ranged right beside him. It was bad form to be mad about well-timed backup, so Tina just grinned and waved her arms, motioning them forward with exaggerated "come here" gestures until they lowered their weapons.

When the Roughnecks reached them, Tina did a quick round of introductions. Several of her players seemed to recognize the Red Sands guild, but no one except Killbox actually looked happy to see them. Apparently, the PVP guild's reputation as griefers was widely known and well-earned, but they needed more max-level geared players too much to be picky, and in the end, no one complained about teaming up. At least, not out loud.

"Okay," Tina announced once introductions were over. "We've still got a bunch of pissed-off NPCs after us, so we need to keep moving toward the bank. Once we're safely forted up, we'll discuss what to do from there. Now everyone *march*!"

At her command, all the Roughnecks started forward. At Cinco's nod, his people started moving as well, merging into the main raid's column. After instructing Frank and Zen to keep watching the front, Tina hung back to resume her position at the rear, eying the smoky shadow of the castle high in the distance over the rooftops as she waited for everyone to shuffle by. When Cinco walked past, though, she caught the corner of his armor.

"I need to ask you something."

"Shoot," the other guildmaster said, giving her a cocky smile.

"Shankfest said everyone who was at the Dead Mountain Fortress dungeon died," Tina said, careful to keep her voice down so the passing raiders wouldn't overhear. "How do you know that if you were all in Bastion?"

"Because one guild got out," Cinco said. "*Richard's Ruin* was in the middle of the dungeon when things went down. So far as we know, they're the only ones who escaped."

"How?" Tina demanded.

"They'd downed a boss right before the wham-spin-wham, so they were alone in an empty room when it hit," he said. "Once they recovered, they shut the big-ass doors and sealed themselves in. They said they could hear the other raids dying outside."

Tina shuddered in horror. Now that he said it, she realized she'd actually heard the same thing. Right after she'd drunk the pan elixir to get herself out of the sensory overload, she remembered hearing screams drifting on the wind from the Once King's mountain fortress.

The memory made her feel terrible. She hadn't even thought of the other players then, hadn't considered how they would have been trapped and helpless in the Dead Mountain, surrounded by insurmountable odds. She'd just gathered her raid and run, leaving them all to their fate. But even as the guilt ate at her, she knew there was nothing she could have

141

done. They'd barely managed against Grel even with the Order fort. If they'd gone inside the Dead Mountain Fortress, all they would have done was die with the others.

But while that was slightly comforting, there was still a part of Cinco's story that didn't make sense. "If *Richard's Ruin* was trapped in DMF, how did they get out to tell you all this?"

"Pure stupid luck," Cinco said with a shrug. "You know how *Richard's Inferno* was the number-one guild in the world before the Once King fight broke them? Well, *Richard's Ruin* is what was left over. They didn't have enough people left to make progress on the dungeon anymore, so they just were focusing on doing achievements."

Now she understood. "They were trying for 'A Spell On The Wind,' weren't they?"

"Yup," he said. "You just have to beat the second boss, but you need twenty-five Sorcerers in your raid to make it work. So when the shit went down, they were trapped in a boss room with twenty five teleports, which turned out to be just enough mana to portal a raid back to Bastion."

"That's lucky as hell," Tina said with a whistle. "So where are they now? I assume you met them here."

A haunted look flitted across Cinco's face. "They're in my guild now. What's left of them, anyway. Lots of people found ways to portal into Bastion that first day, but the Royal Knights had the Room of Arrivals camped. Malakai and his assholes were killing everyone as soon as they popped through the portals. *Richard's Ruin* was the only serious raid to show up, so they managed to break out, but a bunch of them didn't make it. We attacked to help since it was the best chance we'd gotten to try to knock Malakai down, but we had to retreat. I only managed to save a few before we were forced to run."

That was grimmer news than Tina had hoped for. It also explained the extensive bloodstains she'd seen back at the portal room. "Glad we came through late," she said. "The Portal Keeper's Sanctum was empty by the time we got there."

142

"That's 'cause the portal keepers shut everything down *and* put up a ward against player portals. They magicked away the gibs, locked the place up tight, and moved on to deal with other problems." He looked at her with narrowed eyes. "How'd you manage to get here, anyway?"

Tina gave him the quick version how they'd narrowly avoided getting slaughtered all through the Deadlands, fighting Grel, and their subsequent deal with the Order of the Rising Sun to get back to Bastion.

"Damn, girl," Cinco said when she finished. "That's a hell of a tale. Y'all sound like some real-life heroes and shit. Glad we decided to be friends and not enemies."

Tina laughed. "Same here. I can't tell you how glad I am to have another group of well-equipped, max-level people around. All the folks we rescued are basically useless."

"So where to next?" Cinco asked. "I heard you mention the bank."

"You know somewhere better?"

"Can't say that I do," Cinco said, his face breaking into a grin. "Since our bags were all FUBAR, I hadn't even considered trying the bank, but that's a damn good idea."

"Thanks," Tina said proudly as the very last of her raiders went by. "If you're on board, what do you say we go make a withdrawal?"

Cinco's grin grew wider as he swept his arms in a comically elaborate bow.

"After you."

***

Unlike most other big player-important buildings, the Great Vault of the Schtumples was down by the river, well away from the castle on its hill in Bastion's lower city.

The buildings here were decidedly shorter and more practical than they'd been by the castle. This made the streets much less claustrophobic and canyon-like, but the cheap all-wood construction meant that the fires here had been burning unchecked for three days. Most of the houses and shops were now nothing more than smoldering piles of black logs, a far cry from the cheerful, airy, white-washed facades and colorful awnings that Tina remembered.

It was also more violent.

Aside from the camp by the castle, Tina and her raiders hadn't seen any patrols on their walk to the Royal Mile, probably because, with all the players there slaughtered and the Room of Arrivals supposedly locked down, Malakai and his knights considered that section of the city already secured. The farther they pressed into the southern part of the city by the river, though, the more patrols they ran into. Mostly they were Bastion City Guards, who were lower level than the Royal Knights and instantly recognizable due to their garish-yellow tabards.

They always ran when they saw the raid, and for the most part, Tina let them. It saved ammo and mana, and she felt sorry for the terrified level-sixties in their thin chain mail. Only one squad had held their ground, bravely defending a family of terrified NPCs from the players. Rolling her eyes, Tina ordered a pair of Berserkers to stand there and look menacing until the raid had passed before letting them go. But that was just for the guards. The Royal Knight patrols, they always killed on sight, shooting down the heavily armored men before they could raise the alarm.

They also picked up more players. Malakai's knights had used the transition to slaughter the players in the upper city, but they couldn't be everywhere at once. Most of the people down here seemed to have survived, and they were doing everything they could to keep it that way. They found a whole party of level-eighties when they triggered an ambush meant for the NPC guards and nearly got shot because of it.

Cinco was delighted when he saw how well they'd set it up--and how many rations they'd stolen from the City Guards--and instantly invited them to join his guild. Glad to no longer be alone, the new players had said yes without hesitation, making Tina wonder if she shouldn't also be trying to recruit since her Roughnecks were still ten short of being a full raid--eleven now, since KatanaFatale was dead. But as keen as she was for more firepower, she didn't want to grab just anyone off the street. Fighting with someone required a certain level of trust, and she wanted to get to know new members before she let them in, if only to make sure they weren't crazy or stupid, because she'd had enough of that.

But while each of these interruptions was small by itself, together they made for very slow going. The scattered groups of Royal Knights operating in the lower city seemed hell-bent on fucking with Tina's army at every turn. Once it became clear that they couldn't get near the raid on their own, squads started teaming up to stage hit-and-runs, often using captured players as bait for traps. Eager to help, lots of raiders broke rank and strayed from the main group straight into ambushes.

After almost losing several of her more aggressive members, Tina put Killbox in charge of a six-person task force to go and hunt the knights out before they could cause more problems. She got Cinco to do the same, deploying Shankfest and five other Red Sands guild members to watch the raid's flank. It was nerve-wracking to hear the clash of arms and roar of spells echo from nearby streets, but at least the ambushes stopped, and the army was finally able to make progress, grinding their way slowly toward the bank.

Then, just when Tina finally thought she could see the huge gray monolith of stone that marked the top of the Great Vault of the Schtumples, aka The Bank of Bastion, through the smoke, she felt something enter her shadow.

The sensation almost made her jump out of her stone skin. Her sword was out before she knew she'd drawn it, and she whirled around, nearly chopping ZeroDarkness in half in the process.

"Christ, dude," she exclaimed, lowering her blade as the jubatus Assassin threw his hands up in surrender. "Don't do that!"

"Sorry, Roxxy," Zero said, chest heaving as he panted. "SilentBlayde does it all the time, so I thought--"

"Yeah, well, that's because he's SB," she said grumpily. "I'm not used to other people, as you can see, so please pick another shadow next time." He nodded rapidly, and she sheathed her sword with a wince. "Sorry about that, by the way. Now, did you have something to report?"

The Assassin pointed down the road ahead of them. "Next intersection up, there's a big statue of the Buffoon King that's been toppled over. A bunch of people are waiting behind it in ambush."

Tina scowled. "Players, I assume?"

"Yeah," he said, looking around at the still-intact block of wooden houses and shops they were walking through. "I haven't seen a guard patrol in the last quarter mile, and all the side alleys in this area are loaded with traps. I think this is someone's territory."

"Right," Tina nodded. "Thanks, Zero."

The Assassin saluted and disappeared back into the shadows. When he was gone, Tina went to find Cinco, who was walking in the middle of the raid, flirting with Zen, who looked excessively annoyed.

"Any idea who this might be?" Tina asked as her lead Ranger bolted. "I thought you said you were the largest player faction in the city."

"It's not like we have a Facebook group for Bastion survivors," the red-plated Berserker replied with a shrug. "There's a lot of small, scrappy bands that have formed up over the past couple of days. They aren't guilds. I'd call them parties, but they're really more like gangs. Random people sticking together for survival."

"Right," Tina said, hefting her shield. "Well, I'm not making the same mistake twice. We roll in with everyone this time."

Pausing the march, Tina called in the anti-Royal Knight response teams before advancing. When they were all back together, she ordered everyone to keep their weapons down but stay ready for combat since they didn't know what was coming. When she was certain everyone understood and no one was going to be stupid, she gave the order to march forward.

Despite being at the head of an army that was now nearly three hundred players strong, Tina had to stiffen her back before stepping into the crossroads. As ZeroDarkness had said, it was a large square with a two-stories-tall granite statue of Bastion's King Gregory Heraldsford, affectionately known as "The Buffoon King." The statue was supposed to depict the gallant and handsome king holding the famous Dawnblade aloft, but someone had pulled it over, smashing off the king's head and turning his muscular body into a barricade that filled the entire length of the square. The square was also, so far as she could tell, empty.

"Where are they?" she whispered to ZeroDarkness, eying the quiet buildings and empty windows.

"Everywhere," he said from the shadows.

That wasn't reassuring, but whoever was here, there was no way they outnumbered the army that was now squishing itself into the square. Remembering Killbox's PVP rules, Tina climbed on top of the toppled statue to show them who were the strong ones here.

"We know you're there!" she bellowed at the empty buildings. "Come on out!"

When no one answered her, Tina scowled in frustration. Then she noticed that the barrel Frank was standing next to had a tail sticking out of it, and that gave her an idea.

"ZeroDarkness," she whispered. "Tell Frank to tackle that barrel and bring it to me."

She didn't know if the Assassin was listening or not, but a few seconds later, Frank jumped. The Knight shot her a baffled look, but Tina nodded and mimed a grabbing motion. Shrugging, Frank slung his shield onto his back and turned to grab the wooden barrel in a huge bear hug. There was a yowl of panic, and then a jubatus priest in tattered white robes jumped out of the barrel and tried to scamper away only to realize that she was surrounded.

"Bring her here," Tina ordered.

Several raiders jumped to obey, tackling the priest to the ground.

"Whoa, guys!" Tina said. "Bring her *nicely*, please. We're not a Mad Max--"

"They've got Jenna!" someone cried from the empty buildings around them. "Everyone out!"

The air was instantly filled with the sounds of weapons being drawn. Not just by her people, but by dozens and dozens of players emerging from every conceivable hiding place all around the square.

Tina moved a hand to her sword but stopped just short of pulling it. There were a *lot* of players, more than she'd thought those buildings could hold, but this was nothing like the terrifying ambush setup by CincoDeMurder. Many wore high-level armor, but no one seemed to have weapons beyond "rock" or "board with a nail in it." They were all dirty, ash smeared, and gaunt from lack of food. From the way they were shaking in fear, Tina guessed that a lot of them had been making do alone or in smaller, less resilient groups up till recently. But while they were clearly new at this, they stuck together admirably, forming a pretty nice formation around the square.

"Hold it, hold it," Tina called, waving her empty hands. "Everyone just chill. We don't want to fight."

The Roughnecks and Red Sands players didn't look like they necessarily agreed with that, but they lowered their weapons. Tina looked around at their pathetically armed attackers. Her glare intimidated one ichthyian player into to lowering his board-with-rusty-nails-in-it.

"Who's the leader here?"

"I am," someone with a smooth for-radio voice said.

Its owner, an elf with glittering gold hair, stepped out from a shadowy doorway a few moments later, and Tina's jaw fell open. The elf was dressed from head to toe in the most expensive vanity items in the game. Though they were filthy and ripped, there was no mistaking the Mountain Mist Gray Business Suit or the Elegant Top Hat, which, despite its lack of stats, was the most coveted headpiece in the whole game. He was also wearing a pair of smudged Ruby Shades--an item that could only be won through the Summer Fun Lottery--and carrying a solid-gold cane, which wasn't actually rare but so expensive to make that it might as well be. He still looked every bit as haggard as the group he claimed to lead--all except for his hair, which was perfect, giving more credence to Tina's belief that all elves possessed a secret racial ability called "Permanent Good Hair Day"--but he held himself with such arrogant poise that it didn't seem to matter. It was clear he considered such small matters as dirt and lack of food a temporary inconvenience, a category Tina apparently fit into as well, given the way he stared up his perfect nose at her.

"And who are you?" she asked, crossing her arms over her chest.

"Ladies first," he said with an arrogant half bow.

"Fine," Tina huffed, standing even straighter on top of the downed statue of the king. "I'm Roxxy, leader of the Roughnecks guild, world's first slayers of the Once King's Blood General during FFO." That last part wasn't technically true since she'd killed the Blood General with her *actual* Roughnecks, not the mishmash raid they'd had to cobble together after the game had turned real. But she'd liked Killbox's epitaphs earlier, and she wasn't about to be outdone by some snooty elf in a top hat, so she kept going. "We're also the people who defeated the Once King's army led by Grel'Darm the Colossal yesterday."

There were some serious *oohs* and *aahs* at that announcement, and the well-dressed elf clapped politely. "I know you, Roxxy," he said, pushing back his battered top hat to smile at her. "You and your guild have bought many of my pan elixirs and raiding supplies over the years. But I don't think you know me."

"Should I?" Tina asked. "Did we do business face-to-face?"

"Only through the auction house, I'm afraid," he said, leaning on his cane. "That was a very good introduction, but please--" He looked out at his people. "Won't someone tell her who I am?"

At that request, Tina saw a schtumple Knight--a diminutive, pug-eyed character who looked like a ball wearing plate armor--run out into the middle of the square, waving his stubby arms as he shouted in a game show announcer's voice, "He's the man who was once called the richest player ever! The FFO billionaire, the elven High Warlord of Economic PVP, the Earl of Elixirs, our glorious leader, guild master of the East Bastion Trade Company... *Assets*!"

The elf spread his arms dramatically while the crowd of ragged players he commanded dutifully hollered and cheered.

Down in Tina's army, CincoDeMurder rolled his eyes. "You mean the price-gouging dick?"

Tina recognized the name as well. "Wait!" she cried, suddenly furious. "I know you! You're the asshole who cornered the elixir market and jacked up all the prices! We've been paying through the nose for consumables all expansion because of you!"

"Guilty as charged," Assets said proudly, giving her a mocking grin. "I'm delighted to see that my reputation for being effective precedes me."

"How come you're in charge of all these other people?" Tina demanded. "Last I checked, you were level fifteen and your 'guild' consisted of you and your storage alts. Don't tell me you're paying them to follow you."

Assets stamped his golden cane down with a *ptack*. "Madame, *please*. No matter what the circumstance, a good businessman can always find assets to control and leverage to his advantage, hence my name. While most players keep worthless things like severed heads in their backpacks, mine contained nothing but valuables. Even after this unfortunate incident destroyed my inventory, I still had several stacks of potions to pull from, and potions are power." His shiny grin grew wider. "I could go into the tale of how many lives my elixirs have already saved, but I don't like to brag. As you can see, there are plenty who owe me their lives, so we should move on to more interesting topics, such as what *we* can do together."

Tina didn't want to dignify that with a response, but now that she knew who she was dealing with, it was impossible to brush the elf off. He wasn't on the world raiding charts as she had been, but Assets was a legend in his own way. She'd seen screen shots of his guild bank online. The dude had *thousands* of every crafting material, potion, magical food, and tradable legendary item in the game, and that was something she could use.

"All right," she said, putting her hands on her hips. "The Roughnecks are mercenaries now, so since you're a business guild, we should make a deal."

"I *love* making deals," Assets said, his tone loaded with innuendo, which Tina ignored.

"I know you've got maximum stacks of everything useful, plus a literal mountain of gold--"

"One-point-five *billion* gold, to be precise," Assets said, preening. "But you were saying?"

"I was *saying*," Tina continued, flashing the elf a smirk of her own, "you're famous for having all this wealth, but you can't get to it, can you?" She nodded at his hungry and threadbare troops. "You've gathered a pretty good group with what you had in your bags, but if you could get to your vaults, you'd all be fat, happy, and decked in gold. You'd also be forted up inside the bank, and not out here hiding in empty buildings. Since this isn't the case, I'm betting you can't get in, can you?"

"Alas, we cannot," Assets admitted with a helpless shrug. "The Schtumple Bank is no longer welcoming to anyone, even such an esteemed client as myself."

"Well, we're about to change that," Tina said, waving at her army before nodding at the bank, which she could now see just a block away. "We're gonna crack that sucker open and take back what's in our vaults. You have a hundred times more crafting materials than the next ten wealthiest players put together, even the Roughnecks' own guild vault. Promise us thirty percent of that, and we'll make sure the rest of your wealth is returned to you after we've conquered the bank."

"Outrageous!" Assets shouted, his ethereally handsome face turning scarlet. "You want thirty percent to 'give' me back what is rightfully mine? That's no deal. It's robbery!"

151

"You have zero percent right now, pal," Tina reminded him. "And one-third is cheap for hiring the best--and *only*--people in the world who can get it back for you."

Assets's face pulled into a scowl, and then he chuckled. "That's the most mercenary line of thinking I've ever heard," he said with a sigh. "I only wish I'd thought of it myself. But I'm afraid this whole discussion is moot."

"Oh?" Tina said.

Assets pointed over his shoulder at the bank. Thanks to all the smoke, it was still hard to see through the haze even this close, but if she squinted, Tina could just make out the familiar five-story gray monolith of ancient stone that marked its face, its surface reinforced with magic that prevented any cracks or seams. The only way inside were two doors made from the same indestructible sun-metal as her armor and shield. But while that much matched what she remembered, the towering army of golden golems standing in front of it was new.

"Holy shit," Tina said, jerking back. "Are those the ones that are normally inside?"

"The same plus friends, I'm afraid," Assets said sadly. "Now you see our dilemma."

Tina did. Back in the game, the schtumples who ran the bank had been guarded by three-skull, level-eighty-one golems loaded with area-of-effect weapons and anti-swarm abilities. They were mostly there for color since no one was stupid enough to start shit in the bank, but on the rare occasion when a player got too exuberant spamming spells and clipped one, the golems would aggro and turn that player into paste in under three seconds flat. They were supposed to be some of the hardest-hitting NPCs in the game, not that Tina had ever been crazy enough to try one out for herself, but she'd never heard of them leaving the bank before. Apparently, that was off now. There were a full dozen standing guard in front of the bank's door, and that was a serious problem.

"Oh, it gets worse," Assets said when he saw the horror on her face. "You remember the five-skull schtumple racial leader, the Grand Schtump? Well, his roundness arrived on day zero to throw all of us players out on the street and lock the bank down tight. In addition to the golems you see there, there's a second army of level eighty-one, two-skull golems inside along with the legendary Black Golds Legion, the Grand Schtump's personal bodyguards." He shook his head. "Not even the Buffoon King himself could force his way in now, I'm afraid."

"Damn," Tina said. She was even less familiar with the schtumple part of FFO's lore than she was with the rest of it, but it all sounded bad. If SB had been here, he could have filled her in on all the details Assets was undoubtedly leaving out, but it sounded like the bank was a no go, which meant they were screwed. She'd been counting on those vaults to reload everyone's supplies and keep the raid functional. Without them, they'd be out of food by tonight, and they'd have nowhere safe to sleep.

She wasn't the only one upset by this, either. The whole raid was pissed off, yelling at Assets's players as though this were their fault.

"But that's *our* stuff! They can't lock up *our* stuff!"

"My mounts! My pets! Do you know how long I worked to collect them?"

"We're gonna have to march and fight to the death *again*, aren't we?"

"I want to go home!"

"Can we leave? Bastion is too hard! Let's go conquer a low-level zone!"

"*Quiet down!*" Tina shouted, banging her shield until everyone shut up. "We're still in a standoff here!"

"I'm sorry to be the bearer of bad tidings," Assets said, motioning for his people to lower their weapons. "But while your plans appear to be in ruins, Roxxy of the Roughnecks, I am still most curious as to what you will do now. Depending on the answer, we may deign to join you."

153

He looked at her, then, and so did his guild. Everyone did. As if by some silent agreement, all three *hundred* players crowding into the square turned in unison to stare at Tina, hungrily, tiredly, their armor bashed and their shoulders slumped. Even CincoDeMurder and his Red Sands were looking to her, waiting for her to announce what they were going to do now.

Part of her, the Tina part, didn't understand why people did this. Didn't they know that she was just as lost as they were? That she was only ever one step ahead of complete failure? The Roughnecks were still gun-shy of her, cringing whenever she yelled, yet they too looked at no one else when it came time to pick the direction. Just her. *Always* her.

But while the Tina part felt overwhelmed by that, the Roxxy part of her knew what to do. Roxxy the guild leader knew that they needed supplies and shelter, and if they couldn't get it from the castle or the bank, they'd just go somewhere else. The only question was where, but the more she thought about that, the more she realized there was only one answer left.

"Okay," she announced, standing taller to make sure everyone could see when she pointed to the south. "The bank's a wash. We'll figure out how to get our stuff later, but right now, we're changing course for the Trainers' Hall!"

"You mean the Isle of Newbs?" Cinco shouted back. "Why?"

Assets, however, burst into delighted laughter. "A splendid idea!" he said, clapping his manicured hands together. "We shall join you if you'll have us."

"Happy to," Tina said, hopping down off the fallen statue of the king to start them marching down the road toward the south. "Everyone, follow me."

Everyone did. There was some muttering, especially from Cinco's group, but in the end, every single player fell in behind her, marching down the road toward the river and the city's southern wall.

154

∗∗∗

"Assets gets it, but I don't," CincoDeMurder said, running to catch up with her at the front of the raid after they'd been walking for a good five minutes. "Why the Trainers' Hall, Roxxy? It's supposed to be for new players to learn professions, but it's still a giant compound full of high-level NPCs and class trainers. It's gonna be a stiff fight if they're still there. Not that I'm afraid of them or anything," he added with a flex of his bulky shoulders. "But why *there?*"

Tina glanced at him. "What's your crafting profession, Cinco?"

"Blacksmith."

"Same here," she said. "Did you grind it up to max level at the city's main forge?"

Cinco scoffed. "Fuck, no. I leveled it at the Trainers' Hall because it has everything you need to make stuff in one--" Cinco's blue eyes suddenly lit up. "*Oh!*"

"Now you get it," Tina said with a grin. "The Trainers' Hall is the only place in the city that has facilities for every crafting profession. They've got forges, ovens, alchemy tables, supply vendors: everything we need to outfit an army. It's also the only free-standing structure left in the city that's big enough to house us all, *and* it's isolated on its own island in the middle of the Herald's River. The walls might not be as thick as the bank's, but it's still everything we need in a base."

Cinco gave her an impressed look. "I like it," he said. "But now we've three guilds together, what do you think about just bailing from Bastion?"

Tina glanced over her shoulder at the royal castle, which was now little more than a glint of gold high on the hills behind them through the smoke. "Afraid of what's coming after us?"

"Hell no," the Red Sands leader said stubbornly. "But this place is *wrecked.* I'm not afraid of the knights or the king. I just don't see the point of fighting to the death over somewhere that's still on fire. Bastion was our

155

only option when we were all alone, but we've got a legit army now. We could go somewhere else. Someone mentioned conquering a zone, which isn't actually a bad idea. All the places around Bastion are pretty low-level. If we wanted to, we could go out to one of the smaller cities, take it over, and make all those NPCs work for us."

He finished with a grin, but Tina shook her head, copper dreadlocks swaying. "Nah, I don't like it. I don't want to rule some medieval village, and what we need is here in Bastion." She banged a gauntlet on her chest piece, which was still dented from where she'd crushed Malakai, and from Grel's beating the day before that. "I need sun metal and earth-imbued steel to fix my gear. My armor's the best in the world, but even it can't take unlimited punishment. Another boss fight, and it'll probably fall right off me. The rest of the Roughnecks have similar needs for their weapons and armor. We've been riding high because we're better geared than everyone else, but if we lose our stuff, our ability to kick ass will go down enormously."

"Yeah, good point," the Berserker said, rubbing his own armor, which was looking pretty banged up between the skulls. "If we don't keep our gear advantage, the knights will win on numbers alone."

"Exactly," Tina said. "But even more importantly, I don't *want* to stay here. Even if we did take over somewhere where we could live like lords, we'd still be trapped in this stupid world. But the king of Bastion has a dimensional adviser who's an expert in all things portals. He might know why we all got stuck here in the first place, and even better, he might know how to send us *back*."

"That would be nice," Cinco said, mopping the sweat from his brow. "I like my new body a lot, but fuck do I miss air conditioning." He sighed. "Guess we gotta stay and fight, don't we?"

Tina nodded. "This is our best chance. If we run, the king will restore order to the city, beef up his army, and probably come after us cause we're a giant threat. If we stay, though, we keep the city under siege and the king under pressure. If we can regroup, resupply, and gather more people, we might even be able to beat him and take the castle. Then he'd *have* to help us."

"He'll probably want us to go home even more than we do at that point," Cinco agreed. "But we'd definitely need a boot on his neck, 'cause I ain't begging. Not after the shit he and his knights have done."

"Damn straight," Tina agreed, cracking her knuckles. "Payback is definitely overdue, and we still don't know how many players he's got captured in the castle. We're the strongest around. That makes us their only hope."

Cinco whistled. "Damn, girl, you think big. And here I was just trying to survive." He gave her an appreciative look. "I can see why you're still the leader of the Roughnecks. You're tough *and* smart."

Tina stumbled at the unexpected praise. "Thanks?"

"So do you still want to go by Roxxy?" he asked, walking a little closer. "It's a pretty name, but I'm guessing it's not your real one. What are you actually called?"

Tina was getting less comfortable with this conversation by the second. But as awkward as Cinco's blatant flirting was, it was still nice to have a fellow guild leader to chat with, and it wasn't like her real name was a secret. "It's Tina," she told him with a shrug. "I don't really care which people use, to be honest." She glanced at him. "What about you? Do you want me to keep calling you CincoDeMurder?"

Cinco threw his head back with a laugh. "Of course! My name is *awesome*. And who ever heard of the great and terrible leader of the Red Sands, *Thomas* the Berserker?" He shuddered. "I have my reputation to think of."

Tina couldn't help but laugh at that. "Well, I'm counting on you to live up to that rep when fighting time comes, 'cause I've got a feeling we're in for it."

Her shoulder was suddenly heavy as Cinco clapped a hand on it. "Babe, you ain't seen nothing yet."

Before she could decide on how to react, he let her go and walked off whistling. Tina was staring at his back in confusion when a brilliant light flashed behind her.

It looked like a lightning bolt, but the evening sky was cloudless above the haze of smoke. Also, the light was the wrong color. Lightning, at least the sort she knew, was usually bluish white, but this flash had been pure gold, like the sun glinting off a mirror.

Bracing for horrors, Tina whirled around, but the city looked mostly the same. The only difference was that the golden light that always shone from the Bastion's tower top of the castle was now *way* brighter. Even at this distance, the glare was almost too much to look at. And it was *growing*, the golden shimmer expanding over their heads as she watched to cover the entire city in a glowing golden dome.

"What. The. Fuck," Tina said, craning back her neck to follow the golden light as it passed over their heads. Then she turned to her Roughnecks. "*Anders!* Lore me!"

The fish-man Cleric pushed his way forward. "It's the Resplendent Aegis of the Bastion!" he cried, gills wiggling excitedly. "The king's activated the ancient artifact!"

That didn't sound good. "What does it do?"

"All kinds of neat stuff," Anders said, lifting his webbed fingers to tick off the benefits. "It stops the undead, blocks necromancy, and it seals off the--"

Without warning, ZeroDarkness stumbled into view right in front of them, falling out of the shadow beneath a covered porch as though he'd been kicked out.

"--Lightless Realm," Anders finished, looking around as all the other Assassins in the raid popped into view. "Which means no stealth."

Tina's stomach shrank into a ball. She looked at Zero, who was gasping as if he'd just been dunked in ice water, and then back at the city. The burning, dangerous city, where SB was still out *alone*.

158

Her mouth opened to call for a rescue team before she knew what she was doing, but she closed it just as fast. Even if she could put together a crack force, she had no idea where SilentBlayde was. She'd sent him off to look for James back at the Royal Mile, which meant he could be anywhere. If she sent a team after him, they'd have to go back into the area where the knights were patrolling, which meant she might just be sending more people to their deaths. She couldn't justify that, especially not when they were so close to safety. She could already smell the river, which meant the Trainers' Hall should be just around the corner.

"Roxxy?" Anders said, clutching his staff nervously. "Are you okay?"

"I'm fine," she lied, turning her back on the city. "Keep moving."

She'd send people out later, she promised herself, after they were secure. SB was the quickest person on his feet she knew. He was clever, deadly, and brilliant under pressure, and he knew this world better than any of them. He was also an elf, which meant he didn't stand out like she did. If anyone had a chance of surviving in Bastion alone, it was him. Hell, he was probably looking for her at the bank right now. He'd only need one glimpse to understand the situation and one more to spot their trail. It wasn't hard to follow an army, after all. He'd probably be here any minute with James in tow, which meant it was up to Tina to make sure they had somewhere safe to come back to.

With that, she picked up the pace, marching the raid down to the river bank and across the fishing docks toward the wide stone bridge that led to the Trainers' Hall.

It had been a while since Tina had been down here to grind her professions. Laying eyes on the building again, Tina liked it even more than she remembered. Bastion's verdant mountains ran diagonally from southwest to northeast. Here, in the southwesternmost corner of the city, the steep foothills opened up to form a valley where the Heraldsford River emerged from the mountains, pouring into the city and down a series of canals before spreading out into a wide, branching waterway that

159

completely surrounded a hill at its center, forming a large island where the Trainers' Hall rose like a citadel.

As the name suggested, the main building was a large hall made of rough stone blocks sitting at the very top of the hill. It was quite large because it had to hold stalls for all the beginning-armor vendors as well as trainers for all of FFO's six classes, but it still wasn't big enough. Around the stone building, smaller structures had been constructed for all of FFO's crafting professions, forming a hub of trainers and supplies. Bridges connected the island back to the city on three sides, but otherwise it was completely cut off by the river, which ran down from the mountains. Since the water entered the city on the western side, it hadn't yet been polluted by the ash from the fires, leaving it clear, swift, and deep, acting as both a water source and a protective moat. It was truly a perfect little fortress, and Tina was determined to make it theirs.

"Roughnecks on me," she called, stepping onto the stone bridge that led across the water.

Her raid obeyed at once, hurrying into what was now their standard formation--tanks up front, melee on the edges, healers and casters in the middle. A few moments later, Cinco and his people stepped up to join the formation as well. Swelling with pride at how fast everyone had come together, Tina drew her sword and marched them forward. She'd only made it half-way across the bridge when the heavy wooden doors of the main Trainers' Hall flew open, and a motley army poured out.

Even by her new low standards, it was a sad showing. Despite their scavenged helmets and crossbows, it was immediately obvious that most of the "soldiers" were kids. They ranged from lanky eight-year-olds to burlier teenagers, which matched what Tina remembered of the apprentices that were always running around the crafting areas. In the whole group, there were only six adults, and only one of them was actually armed. It was the Knight trainer, a statuesque human woman wearing the thickest plate armor Tina had ever seen who stepped forward to meet the raid as they left the bridge and started up the grassy hill.

"I am Dame Fiona Steelwall!" she yelled, striking a defensive stance in the doorway as Tina marched forward. "Master of the Knightly Arts! Who are you to so brazenly approach the Island of Dawn's Hope?"

Tina and CincoDeMurder stepped forward. A few seconds later, Assets ran up from the rear of the raid to join them, striking a pose that would have been impressive if he hadn't looked so threadbare. There was a pause while the three of them exchanged glances, and then, since no one else was doing it, Tina stepped forward.

"We do," she announced loudly, keeping her sword out but down. "We are the leaders of this army, and we have chosen the Trainers' Hall as our new base."

"We will not suffer your abuse willingly," Fiona said, keeping her own weapon up. "Know that I was level eighty-one and three-skull during the Nightmare. I have every knightly skill in your game and many more you have never seen. The other five masters arrayed behind me are no less powerful. You face obliteration if you proceed!"

That was too much for Tina to take with a straight face. "*Ha!*" she barked, pointing her sword at the shaking wall of children. "Is that why you gave all your apprentices crossbows? You must be really confident in your ability to wreck us."

The Knight trainer waved a dismissive hand. "We work together, live together, and fight together. That is the bond of master and apprentice."

"Lady," Tina said, "it's gonna be 'die together' if you don't stand down. I've *three* full raids of players here. That's two more than I need to take this place. You don't have a chance."

"Is that so, *player?*" the Knight spat, raising her hand. "You leave us no choice. *Present barrels!*"

At her cry, the line of apprentices shifted, and a squad of teens wearing blacksmiths' aprons rolled out a wagon full of barrels banded in white-painted iron. Tina recognized the color coding at once. So did the other players, causing the whole raid to jump backward.

161

"Wind-fire powder?" Tina cried, glaring at the Knight NPC. "What the hell are you? Suicidal? You light even one of those and we're all gonna die in a firestorm! I thought you wanted to live!"

"We will not surrender to be enslaved and defiled by you monsters," replied Dame Steelwall, sheathing her sword to accept a burning brand from the girl behind her. "We are prepared to die as heroes here if it means taking you filth down with us!" She reached the smoking, tar-covered brand back toward the barrels as she finished.

Tina jumped forward. "Wait, wait!" she said, throwing down her sword and shield and then waving her hands to show that they were empty. The action caused the Knight trainer to pause, giving Tina hope that the woman wasn't actually crazy enough to blow up herself and all her students just to spite a few players. But while her display worked on Dame Steelwall, it didn't work on everyone. At the back of the wagon, a vengeful young man with hate burning in his eyes kicked a white-banded barrel off the top of the stack. It bounced down the grassy hill toward the raid, and Tina froze in horror.

Wind-Fire powder was the most volatile magical substance in FFO. It didn't even technically need fire to go off. A good blast of air would do it, which meant if that barrel ruptured, they were all going to be consumed in a fire tornado that would burn open the other barrels behind it. One blast would hurt enough, but there was enough Wind-Fire powder in that wagon to torch the whole city to slag.

Every bounce the barrel made down the hill, Tina swore it was going to spill. Wind-fire powder was heavy, and the barrel seemed to be packed to bursting with the deadly stuff. Thankfully, the soft, grassy hill alone wasn't enough to break it, but the old sword-sharpening rock between her and the bouncing barrel would. One hit--that was all it would take, and everything she'd fought so hard for would go up in flames.

That was more unfairness than Tina could take. Leaving her weapons in the grass, she charged forward, hoping that no one followed her. As the bouncing barrel launched out of a dip in the hill and flew toward the waist-high sharpening stone, Tina dashed forward to put herself between the barrel and the stone. She made it just in time to catch the flying oak container before it crashed, but Tina's body wasn't any softer than the stone she was trying to protect it against. Frantic to avoid causing the disaster she'd been trying to avoid, she twisted and let the barrel's momentum take her to the ground, plunging her body into the soft dirt. She was starting to think she'd done it when her body hit a buried rock she hadn't noticed in the tall grass, and a cracking noise sounded in her ears.

The sound had barely finished before her entire right side erupted in flames. Tina roared in pain, but she didn't let go of the barrel. If she released it, the bindings would snap completely, releasing the burning powder into the wind to spread out of control. If that happened, they were all toast, so Tina gritted her teeth against the pain and shoved her hand into the gap, stopping the powder that was pouring out with her own fingers.

It mostly worked. The leak stopped, but her metal gauntlet started heating up. With great effort, Tina stood the barrel on its end, taking great care to keep her hand wedged into the hole. A few of her raiders ran forward to help, but Tina shoved her free hand at them. "No one move!" she bellowed, sending her reinforcements screeching to a halt, and then she turned on the trainers who were still standing frozen in the hall's doorway.

"You didn't let me finish," she said through clenched teeth. "I said we wanted your *base*, not you! You got some crazy high opinions of yourselves, thinking we'd want *you* for anything. Our demands are simple: *get out*. Just take your little bullshit army and walk away, and we won't touch a hair on your heads."

Her hand was a mass of pain now. The Wind-Fire powder that had gotten out earlier had coated her side, filling every crack in her armor with smoldering fire. The urge to stop, drop, and roll while screaming for heals was nearly overwhelming, but Tina forced herself to stay put, glaring at the NPCs until, at last, Dame Stonewall lowered her head.

"Very well," the Knight said. "We will make for the castle, then."

Protests erupted from the masters behind her, but the Knight trainer waved them down. "We must keep ourselves alive so we can serve the king!" she cried. "These buildings are not special. Let the demons have them. The sacred Bastion already shines in the sky! Surely the king's justice will fall upon them before long."

With that, the trainers started down the hill. The moment the adults started walking, the apprentice army bolted for the opposite bridge, leaving the cart full of Wind-Fire powder where it stood in the doorway. Tina watched them as long as she could, trying to make sure they were all actually going before she gave out. Unfortunately, that turned out to be more than her body could handle. The NPCs had barely made it to the far bridge before she sank back to the grass in agony.

As the building flames started to engulf her she saw people breaking ranks and running her way.

"Water magic! Purge and smother!" NekoBaby yelled as the cat-girl and other Naturalists surrounded Tina.

Tina was starting to lose feeling in her right arm, which was even more alarming than the burning had been. Then, out of nowhere, water poured into her gasping mouth.

When she looked up, she and the barrel were both trapped inside a gigantic sphere of pure-blue water. She couldn't breathe, but that felt like a small price to pay as the flames on her right side began to smother and die. Her armor--super heated by the fire she'd been holding back--turned the water white as it boiled it away, but Neko and the others must have been adding more, because the sphere surrounding Tina only got bigger.

When the burning in her right side was gone and her armor was no longer instantly boiling everything around it, Tina decided it was time to leave. Since her right arm didn't work anymore, she turned her shoulder to pull her fingers out of the barrel, abandoning it in the water as she slogged away to look for an exit. The magical bubble of water should have been easy to leave, but its swirling eddies and churning bubbles messed with her sense of direction. Being a rock, she didn't float, so at least she knew which way was down, but the orb's shimmering outer surface distorted the sunlight, filling the water with dancing glimmers that made it impossible to tell which direction was out.

After about a minute of confusion, Tina realized that she was being stupid. It was a sphere. Any direction would do.

Still holding her breath, Tina plowed forward. Pushing through the water was hard, but she wasn't actually in a hurry. She'd been under for a good two minutes now, but her lungs weren't even pained, making her realize just how long stonekin could hold their breath. Filing that tidbit away for later, Tina put her head down and focused on plowing through the water, forcing her giant body against the magical currents until she finally broke the surface, walking out of what had to be a twenty-foot-wide sphere of floating, undulating blue water.

NekoBaby rushed her at once and started throwing glowing green magic all over her. Flowers bloomed at Tina's feet as the euphoric feeling of the healing washed away her pain and trauma. When the life-magic high faded, she flexed her right arm to make sure it still worked, sighing in relief when her fingers wiggled as usual.

"Good job, Neko. Thanks for the save."

"No problemo, boss," the healer said with a salute, then she turned back to the giant drop of water they'd made on the riverbank. "So, um... what do we do with the barrel?"

***

"Home sweet home," Tina said thirty minutes later.

As promised, all the trainers and their apprentices had evacuated the compound. The giant drop of water was gone, and the leaking barrel of Wind-Fire powder was now sitting in the grass, surrounded by a water-magic seal to keep it contained. The rest of the barrels had been less magically--but no less securely--taken care of with rope and canvas, tied down to the wagon, and wheeled back inside the Trainers' Hall, which was now *theirs*.

Tina and her raids now completely controlled the stone hall and the island it sat on. After being on the run all day, it didn't feel real that they could finally stop. But with guards at all the bridges and surrounded by a river too wide to easily shoot over, they were as close to safe as it was possible to be in Bastion. The squat hall and surrounding stone sheds weren't fancy or elegant, but they were sturdy, easy to protect, and packed full of forges and looms and stocked to the ceiling with piles of vendor trade-goods, which made them better than any castle, in Tina's estimation. She wasn't even sure what they were going to do with it all yet.

With that, Tina's eyes moved to the mob spilling all over the green hill. The sight of over three hundred players milling around in a rainbow of glowing weapons and armor was more intimidating than she'd expected, because now that she'd gotten them here, she had no idea what came next. Other than the Roughnecks, no one had food other than what was in their pockets. She didn't know everyone's levels or professions, and the Red Sands were the only other well-armed group. How the hell was she going to equip and protect them? More importantly, how was she ever going to retake the city? She'd called them an army all day, but the crowd in front of her looked more like a mob. What was she going to do with this?

She was being crushed under the weight of that question when she suddenly remembered Killbox's plan for taking out Malakai's camp. His suggestion to kill the guards, free the prisoners, arm them with the enemy's weapons, feed them with the enemy's food, burn fifteen tents, and so forth hadn't actually worked in practice, but it had been strangely on the money-- because it was a format all of them had instantly understood. She had no more experience running an army than any of the people out there had being in one, but they *all* knew how to play FFO.

166

Seen from that angle, Bastion wasn't any different from any other gone-to-hell zone they'd quested through a hundred times back when this was a game. Tina already knew the recipe for taming places like this. Everyone here did, which was why the moment the idea entered her head, Tina jumped on it.

"Listen up, everyone!" she bellowed, silencing the whispering crowd as all the eyes snapped to her. "This place belongs to us now, so we're not calling it the Trainers' Hall anymore. I hereby officially rename this island as Camp Comeback, and it's going to be our official *quest hub* for Bastion city!"

A confused murmur went up at that, but Tina wasn't finished.

"Since this base was taken by our combined efforts, everything in these buildings--all the crafting goods and food and bandages and everything else--belongs to the Roughnecks, Red Sands, and East Bastion Trade Company guilds!"

That caused a lot of angry shouting among the lowbies, but she was having none of it. "You don't like it?" she bellowed at the crowd. "Too bad! You want our protection, that's the price, but that doesn't mean you can't get yours. There will be quests! And work! There's plenty here for everyone of all levels to do, and I guarantee that you'll be paid and fed for your efforts."

"What kind of quests?" someone yelled from the crowd.

"You'll see," Tina said coyly, mostly because she hadn't thought them through yet. "But what's most important is that, starting here, we're going to carve out a chunk of this world for *us*. There are still a lot of players trapped in the city. We going to save them! There're still a lot of asshole Royal Knights out there killing people. We're going to stop them! There's a lot of food and supplies hiding out there in the city. We're going to find it! It's a big list, but if I've learned anything from years of FFO, it's that there's nothing more persistent, more destructive, and more effective than a bunch of players all grinding quests together!"

167

This earned her many proud laughs from the crowd, and Tina raised her fists high. "We're going to be a scourge on this goddamn city, but the *good* kind. We're gonna shut down the fighting and the abuse. We're going to find food and water for everyone. We're going to put this whole damn city on *our* terms. *Are you with me?*"

The crowd responded in an ecstatic roar as hundreds of players shouted back their approval. Tina swayed with the heady rush of rallying such a large crowd. She still wasn't used to being in front of so many people, let alone being able to move them. As the applause rained down on her, she thought she'd float right out of her armor. When it finally died out, Tina took a shaky breath and waved CincoDeMurder and Assets over.

"We need to get organized fast," she said, keeping her voice down so the energized crowd wouldn't know she hadn't actually put anything together yet.

Assets polished his ruby sunglasses. "What do you have in mind?"

"I was thinking we'd play to our strengths," Tina replied, turning to Cinco. "Our first and most dangerous issue comes from ourselves. Internal threats are all player versus player, so that makes Cinco and the Red Sands perfect cops. Set up guards and patrols inside these buildings and halls. No one *but* you is allowed to PVP. That means no killing but also no abuse, stealing, griefing, et cetera. If someone starts shit or tries to take what isn't theirs, shut them down."

Cinco gave her a red-armored thumbs-up. "Can do."

"Second, Assets."

The elf looked up with a sharp-eyed smile. "Yes?"

"This place is loaded with loot," Tina said, pointing at the former crafting hall full of crates, barrels, and stacks of metal that had all been just art assets in the game. Now, though, all of that stuff was real, and it was theirs for the taking. "You're used to managing lots of goods. Go seize all those supplies and make us an inventory. From here out, you're in charge of logistics. We'll divide up the valuables later when we actually know what we have, but we need to get everything on lockdown ASAP. Got me?"

The gold-haired elf's eyes twinkled with delight. "I'll have a manifest ready for you before nightfall."

"What about the Roughnecks?" CincoDeMurder asked.

Tina pointed back toward the city. Thanks to the river and all the open space it provided, they had a clear view north straight up the city to the royal castle, where the Bastion still gleamed like a spotlight through the haze of the smoke.

"Our external threats are all NPCs," she said. "So the Roughnecks are going to be outer security. I'll establish patrols and scouts so that nothing from the city surprises us. We'll be the first to intercept any outside attack. Also, since I've got the majority of the geared healers and my Ranger Officer is a legit nurse, my guild will handle medical as well."

"And the quests?" Assets asked.

Tina shrugged. "I'm still working out the specifics, but for now we'll just make 'em up as people ask. Just make sure to keep the exchange rate quest-like. You know, pay someone one loaf of bread to go find fifteen loaves of bread, that kind of thing. We're all so used to it that hopefully no one will notice they're being ripped off until we've gathered enough supplies to pay them better."

"And they called *me* mercenary," Assets said with an evil chuckle. "That is devilishly one-sided. I couldn't love it more."

Tina grinned back. "Desperate times, desperate measures. We've gotta turn this little something of ours into a *big* something before we're starved out or overrun. Clock's ticking, so let's get moving."

The other leaders nodded and broke apart before walking back to their guilds to explain the new way of things to their seconds. For Tina, though, she was left alone. Despite it being nearly sundown, SB still hadn't shown up. She didn't know if that was because he was being cautious or because he was in trouble, but there was nothing she could do. Already, Roughnecks were coming up to her for patrol orders, peppering her with so many questions, she didn't even have time to look at the burning city as the sun sank below the western walls.

Chapter 9

Haurto

SilentBlayde woke up in a barrel.

It was a new experience, that was for certain. With his numb legs crammed up against his chest, it was also a very unpleasant one. Moving as best he could, he started rocking in hopes of tipping the container over so he could get out, grateful that James had at least stashed him out of sight after...

He stopped rocking, head flopping down to rest his forehead against his knees. The smell of dried blood filled his oaken hiding hole with a metallic reminder of what he'd done. What he'd *been*.

SB squeezed his eyes tight as a hot wave of shame overwhelmed him. He'd nursed his failures and anger all through the city in pursuit of James. Then, when he'd caught up at last, he'd gone nuts. He'd acted like an animal, stabbing James not just once but dozens of times. He particularly remembered driving the small dagger into his friend's kneecap, a pain he was sure James wouldn't forget any time soon.

Covering his face with his hands, SilentBlayde replayed the entire fight in his head, hoping that maybe he hadn't actually been as detestable as he remembered. No luck. All he could see was James trying to save lives while he stepped out of the shadows to take them. He'd hunted them like a beast, lashing out at anyone who dared to anger him.

This apple didn't fall far from the tree, did it?

At least he'd been winning until that damn NPC of James's had tackled him. As he'd learned during the fight on the frozen hill in the Deadlands, he only had so much speed before his body gave out, and he'd foolishly used up most of it killing the knights. He'd been so caught up in ending things quickly so that he could get James back to Tina, he'd played his cards too early, leaving him unable to exploit the split-second pause before Ar'Bati had clinched him. He'd still gotten a good stab in, but Angry

Cat had been more resilient than he'd given him credit for, and the distraction had allowed James to get a hold.

It was humiliating to remember. SB was faster, stronger, and better geared than James had ever been, but Tina's brother had shown him how little that mattered now that this was no longer a game. Every time he'd twisted out of one lock, James was already putting him into the next, always forcing him into positions in which SB's superior strength and gear were useless. And when he'd finally run out of cooldowns, speed, and breath, James's legs had been around his neck.

That was when things had gotten *really* bad. SilentBlayde hadn't felt that helpless since that horrible night at the Sakura Festival when he was eight. The connection to the memory had driven him into a wild panic, sending his hands to the knives he hadn't even realized came out of his set until he'd pulled one. He'd completely lost control, stabbing James over and over like a maniac, but the *worst* was the look on his friend's face right before James had torn out his artery.

With our fangs in the enemy.

"We are enemies now, aren't we, James?" SB asked his bloodstained knees. He had to apologize for this, but what could he say that James would believe? He couldn't count how many times he'd had to make amends to Tina's brother for something he'd done, but this was the worst by far. Just thinking about how he'd acted made him want to stay in the barrel forever, because James was right. He never did learn, did he?

SilentBlayde was sinking deeper into his regret when a sudden flash of light blasted in through the cork hole in the barrel's top. Something inside him lurched at the same time, making him gasp. He couldn't explain what had just happened, but the shadows in the barrel with him--the darkness that had always beckoned so invitingly--now felt like a door that had been shut in his face.

Suddenly terrified, he resumed rocking the barrel frantically and finally tipped over his hiding spot and spilled out into the street. His legs were a mass of pins and needles when they unfolded, so he pushed up on his elbows instead, reaching out a hand to a nearby shadow...

Only to have his fingers land on rough cobblestones. There was no feeling of sinking in, no welcome or safety. The Lightless Realm was completely cut off.

It was a Shadow Ward, he realized, snatching his shaking hand back. The bane of all Assassins' existence. But what could have possibly have made a Shadow Ward this big? Wards were normally small circles cast by Clerics, no more than a few meters wide. Certain important holy NPCs such as the High Priest of the Sun could cast larger ones, but the only thing in the game capable of creating a Shadow Ward big enough to cover a whole city was...

His thoughts trailed off as he finally noticed the strange golden light filling the alley. He'd thought it was just the glow of the afternoon sun, but when he looked up, the sky itself was covered in a glowing golden barrier he'd never seen before but recognized instantly.

The Resplendent Aegis of Bastion!

The ancient artifact from which the capital city drew both its founding and its name. For the king to activate such a magically expensive device meant that he considered Bastion to be in critical danger, and SilentBlayde feared the Roughnecks were the cause. They *had* just wiped out a major camp and killed Captain Malakai, the city's second most powerful raid boss after the king himself. He had to get back to Tina and warn her, even if it meant telling her he'd failed again.

Gritting his teeth against the pain in his legs, which were now on fire as the blood began to flow again, SB pushed himself to his feet. A rush of dizziness hit him as he came up, and he almost passed out again, falling to his knees. He barely managed to catch himself on the wall opposite where his barrel had been. He was still trying to catch his breath when he saw dimly glowing letters from an almost spent Sun Writing spell scrawled onto limestone--letters written in *English*.

I won't tell Tina.

SB began to shake. The message wasn't signed, but that didn't matter. He knew who it was from, and seeing it made him more ashamed than ever. Even after everything he'd done, James had given him a second chance. Tina would never find out how badly he'd acted today, which meant he hadn't ruined everything after all. Tears pricked at his eyes as he realized how lucky he'd just gotten.

"Thank you, James," he whispered to the wall, rubbing his arm across the stone to scuff out the last of the Sun Writing spell's magic. When it was gone, he straightened up with new resolve and took stock of his situation.

The street he'd killed the guards in was bloody but empty. Someone must have come by to collect the bodies while he'd been unconscious. SB wasn't sure how he felt about that. He didn't regret killing the knights who'd slaughtered his fellow players, but the memory of how brutally he'd executed them made him feel dirty. Again, it seemed, James had been right. He wasn't actually a killer. He'd just played one in the game. Now that the game was real, though, where did that leave him? These were the skills he had. If they weren't him, what was?

That was too big a question for him to handle right now, so SB moved on to his physical state, which was no less messy but a lot easier to work with. His armor wasn't too damaged since the fight had been mostly grapples, but the black leather was stiff with clammy blood, and his wrist still had a ragged gash from James's fangs under his glove. The wound was a deep, angry purple, but at least it wasn't bleeding. Neither was his thigh where James had stabbed him. Since there was no way his body could have repaired so much damage on its own in one afternoon, that left only one explanation.

James had healed him

The realization made SB's eyes cloud up all over again. To heal someone like him, after everything he'd done... He didn't deserve such generosity. He *had* to make it right.

Head still swimming, SB grabbed the wall and hauled himself to his feet. After a bit of hunting, he found his swords on the ground where they'd fallen out of the barrel with him. Bending down to grab them sent a spike of pain through his injured leg, but he was reasonably sure he could walk so long as he had something to balance against.

Bracing his shoulder against the wall, he sheathed his silver blades, then he started limping down the road. From the street signs nailed to the buildings, he figured out that he was in the northwestern part of the city, near the Diplomatic Quarter. That was far too close to the castle and a long way from the Royal Mile, where he'd started. Since she was heading for the bank, Tina would be even farther away.

If he'd had the Lightless Realm to hide in, it wouldn't have been so bad, but the thought of limping all the way across Bastion on a bum leg in the *open* felt impossible. It was the only way to get back to Tina, though, so SB gritted his teeth and sucked it up, limping along the wall as he went over his mental map of Bastion to try to work out a path south that would keep him to the side streets and hopefully well out of the way of any patrols.

After less than one block, he was forced to stop and fashion a crutch from a long, narrow plank. The wood was noisy and got in the way, but at least it let him take his weight off his leg, which felt so fragile now he was worried it'd burst open if he continued to push it. He still stuck to the shadows, hiding himself in a mundane manner, but it was hard to sneak with the bulky crutch clacking and banging with every step. Even so, no one came out to see what was making all the racket, and the crutch did let him go a little bit faster. He was starting to think this might not be so bad after all when the side street he'd been following suddenly ended, and he found himself just around the corner from the Royal Mile.

SB shoved himself into the doorway of a busted-up storefront, peeking around the edge at the swarming main street of Bastion. He'd come out almost on top of the camp the Roughnecks had demolished earlier, but you'd never know it had been a victory, looking at it now. Armored knights in red-and-gold tabards filled the destroyed square, marching ten abreast down the wide Royal Mile. The cavalry had mobilized as well, riding out in swift patrols down the major streets toward the south. Most intimidating of all, the giant front gates of the royal castle were now open, the huge doors vomiting rank upon rank of soldiers out into the city. Most didn't move past Malakai's destroyed camp, but they were transporting supplies from the castle at a terrifying rate, building a new camp even larger than the one the Roughnecks had destroyed.

Flinching, SB ducked back into the dark shop. Clearly, crossing the Royal Mile here was a no go. He'd have to sneak down and try again farther south, where the soldiers were thinner, but he wasn't sure if that was a good option, either. Watching the soldiers, he realized the only reason he hadn't had trouble yet was because he'd been so close to the castle. The knights weren't patrolling up here because they considered these streets already secured. They were moving in force farther down the city, though, which was exactly where he had to go. Even if he stuck to the side streets, things were only going to get more dangerous the farther south he went, and he didn't think he could defeat another full patrol of knights with a wounded leg and no Lightless Realm to hide in.

His breaths started coming faster as he realized just how bad his position was. He was trapped on the other side of a net that was closing around Tina and the player threat in the south. He couldn't fight, couldn't hide, couldn't run, and couldn't even walk without help. How was he going to get back to her? How was he going to get *anywhere* like this?

Fighting down the panic, SB took a deep breath and looked around for something he could use--anything to give himself an edge. The building he'd dived into for cover was so dark, it took him several moments to realize he was standing in the rear entrance of the Sunburst Tailoring shop, the one that fronted onto the Royal Mile and sold high-end thread and fabrics to master-level crafters. Like every other shop he'd seen so far in the city, the place had been looted out, all the expensive textiles stolen or burned. There was still a box of scraps in the corner behind the tailor's workbench, though, and that gave him an idea.

Ducking down so the soldiers outside wouldn't see movement through the cracked front windows, SB hobbled as quickly as he could along the back wall of the shop toward the workbench. Crouching behind it, he pulled the box of scraps over and started digging through it. Most of the strips of fabric were too small to use, but there were some tunics, pants, and cloaks set aside for mending that were still more or less in one piece. As he pulled out all the usable pieces, SB breathed a sigh of relief that a large chunk of Bastion's population was elven. Human shoulders were too wide, their arms too short, and their torsos too stocky for his frame, and he didn't want his disguise to look like a disguise.

When he'd assembled a full set that looked as if it would fit, SB stripped out of his armor. Peeling off the form-fitting leather was both a relief and a pain. He'd lived in his raiding set for days straight now. It was filthy and bloodstained and smelled horrific, but that didn't stop him from missing it the moment it was off. It wasn't just the magical boost the legendary set provided. The black armor with its red-glowing runes was SilentBlayde in his mind. Without it, he felt naked and vulnerable, but full Assassin's armor was utterly incompatible with the short-sleeved green tunic, linen breeches, and sturdy work shoes he'd scavenged, so he forced himself to remove it all and shoved his body into the new clothes as fast as he could.

All that speed stopped, though, when he got to his face wrap.

He froze, body trembling. The vulnerable feeling of being without armor was nothing compared to the thought of walking around with his face bare. But there was no way this was going to work if he kept his mask.

177

Fingers shaking, SilentBlayde pulled off his wrapped helmet one layer at a time, reminding himself with each turn that his father wasn't in this world. He had a different face here, one that bore no sins. In this place, he was just another elf. No one here would ever know who or what he really was. Even Tina didn't know his family name. He'd left his shame with his real body back in Japan. He was SilentBlayde now, not Haruto. It would be okay.

That was enough to make him finally remove his helmet. He pulled off his ninja mask next, tucking them both into his backpack with shaking hands. Then, face bare, he stood up and turned to look himself over in broken mirror that was still hanging in the tailor shop's fitting area.

The shop was so dark, he had to hobble closer to see. Pressing as near to the cracked glass as he could without getting sliced, SB ran a delicate finger down his smooth, razor-straight elven jaw. The bones underneath had no bumps or ridges, no flaws his fingers could detect. Freed from his helmet at last, his long golden hair hung down to frame his face, which was symmetrical and straight, his nose and brows sharp and finely wrought.

It was the same face he'd seen every time he'd logged in for the last six years, but he'd never seen it in such detail before--never seen it as *his*. He reached up to brush his hair away, turning his head this way and that, but no matter which way he moved, SilentBlayde was flawless.

He smiled at the broken mirror with a shuddering, giddy breath. No father, no whispering neighbors, and a perfect face. James was right. This *was* a miracle.

As happy as that realization was, it brought the rest of what James had said into sharp relief. Back at the Order Fortress, he'd told Tina that he wanted to live in this world as SilentBlayde because it had come naturally and because she'd needed to hear it. Now that the reality of his new liberation was actually sinking in, though, the ash smudging his perfect face served as a reminder that the world he wanted to live in was very much still on fire. Not all of that was their fault, of course, but James had been correct when he'd said that if they wanted to stay here, they had to stop breaking things. SB wasn't sure how they'd do that, but one thing was absolutely certain.

"I have to get back to Tina," he told the elf in the broken mirror. "Mere survival isn't enough anymore." They had to look beyond just themselves and their next day. They had to do better.

Clenching his fists with new resolve, SB turned away from the mirror and covered himself in a large, patched cloak. He strapped his sheathed blades underneath it, crossing them over his back so the hilts wouldn't be visible from the front. It was extremely uncomfortable and he'd never pass a pat-down, but going unarmed wasn't an option. It would have to do.

He picked up his crutch again then pulled his new hood low over his face and hobbled out of the shop. The new camp in front of the castle had only gotten bigger while he'd worked on his disguise. Patrols now stood at both ends of the street, blocking his exits. Sneaking was no longer an option, so he took a deep breath and stepped out into plain sight, limping toward the Royal Mile while he frantically practiced his cover story under his breath.

SilentBlayde had always been good at lying. He didn't know if was a natural talent or if he'd just gotten good because he'd been breathing lies since he was eight, but it was a skill he relied on every day, and playing online games had only made him better.

The internet was the one place where no one knew or cared who Haruto Watanabe was. With every game he'd tried, he'd plastered over the ugly truth of his real life with new, easily worn personalities. In TrinityTimeVR, he'd been Sato, a studious middle schooler who always made top marks. Then, in Guns Galore Arena, he'd become Kaito, a class rep blowing off steam. He'd learned from each role, and when FFO had come to Japan with much fanfare, he'd known the highly social game would require his best persona yet. Since playing the highly responsible

Kaito had been exhausting, he'd planned for SilentBlayde's "real" player to be a laid-back high schooler with a cool hint of delinquency named Asahi.

All of that had gone out the window when he'd met Tina. She'd been his first real friend in Forever Fantasy Online, and he'd quickly discovered she was also the first person he couldn't bring himself to lie to. To stay with her, he'd abandoned his other faces and played FFO as Haruto, living as himself despite the doom he courted by doing so.

But while he'd accepted that terrible decision as the price of staying in Tina's life, the knights were not her. Lying to them was as easy as breathing, and by the time he reached the end of the street, SilentBlayde had already come up with all the details of his new identity, waving his hands at the cluster of armed men marching down the Royal Mile with perfect frantic eagerness.

"Good knights!" he cried, rushing toward them before they could start questioning him. "You are a sight for sore eyes! Pray tell me, is the Royal Mile safe to travel?"

All the knights had gone for their swords the moment they'd seen him. As he spoke, though, all their hands had drifted away except for one. Their leader, a grizzled veteran even taller than him, kept a hold on his weapon, looming over SilentBlayde with hate in his cold blue eyes.

"Depends on who is asking," he sneered, looking SB's carefully mimicked hunch up and down. "Declare yourself or be slain, elf."

SB cowered quite convincingly, sinking nearly to the ground. "Please, Sir Knight! M-My name is Sky of Highcloud--" It was the most stereotypically elf name he could think of. "And I am but a humble leather worker seeking his family!"

He finished with more cowering, lowering his head meekly while he went over what he'd just said again in his head to make sure he hadn't messed anything up. Faking a persona online was one thing, but aping FFO's archaic manner of speech took things to a whole other level. *Don't use any slang,* he reminded himself. *No modern words. Talk like an NPC.* Maybe he should offer them a quest.

180

The knight glanced at his fellows and then released his weapon to grab SB's arm in a steel grip. "Where were you during the Nightmare?" he demanded, pulling SilentBlayde's hunched body straight in an effort to look at his face. "I remember no one in Bastion by your name."

SilentBlayde stammered to buy time. Bastion had been the largest city in FFO, but the number of NPCs here during the Nightmare couldn't have been more than one or two hundred. It was no surprise they'd all know each other, by name if not by face since they couldn't move much. He was trying to think of an area in the city Mr. Highcloud could have come from that this man wouldn't be able to call bullshit on when one of the other knights--a very young man who looked barely out of his teens-- stepped forward.

"Sir Dan," the young knight said, his voice pitying. "This poor man is clearly not a player. You shouldn't treat him so harshly."

The leader, Sir Dan, growled at that, but his anger just seemed to make the younger knight more determined. Looking at his kindly face, SB recalled what he'd seen at the Order Fortress, how not all of the NPCs had been present in FFO. Just like the land had expanded when this had ceased to be a game, nine out of ten citizens of this world hadn't been trapped in the "Nightmare." They'd been somewhere else. Where, he had no idea, but it gave him his out.

"Wha-What is this 'Nightmare' you speak of, Sir Knight?" he said, making sure his voice cracked at the most pathetic moment. "Is that what brought the player demons to destroy our city?"

He was proud of that one, but the hand crushing his arm only tightened. "If you weren't in the Nightmare, then why are you in Bastion?" Sir Dan demanded. "I know of no Highcloud shop or business."

"I-I travel, sir!" SB improvised quickly. "I sell leathers. I came down to Bastion with yeti hides from the Winter Nation."

"And where are these hides?" the knight demanded, squeezing him tighter.

"With my family," he said, no longer having to fake being in pain. Why did the bastard have to grab his injured wrist? "Please, sir, you are hurting me! I only wish to return to my wife and children! They are staying in an inn to the south. If the Royal Mile is safe, please let me pass so I may return to them!"

SilentBlayde thought that was a very convincing sob story, but the older knight just sneered. "I don't believe you," Sir Dan said, wrenching SB to the ground. "If you're really just an elf from the north, why do you have a player's face?"

SB winced, hoping the knight would mistake it for pain. He'd forgotten that all players had the same dozen faces available during character creation, but it was too late to improve his disguise. All he could do now was to stick to his role. Since this man clearly hated players, he decided to roll with that. If Mr. Highcloud had been on the receiving end of player brutality, that would explain his injuries as well.

"Please, sir, have mercy!" he cried, turning his arm in the knight's grip to show him the wound James's bite had left. "A player attacked me! He beat me cruelly and stole my food and my money. I have been hiding in basements for days, hearing sounds of battle. I don't know if my family is safe or how to find them again in all this chaos. All I want is to pass so that I may be reunited with them. Please help me!"

The lies came out naturally, rolling off his tongue like the thousands before. It wasn't until he finished that SB realized just how believable his words were. A grain of truth was the best salt for a lie, which was why he'd chosen this story over the other possibilities. Now it was out, though, he realized with a shock that there were probably lots of people in the city right now who could have told the same tale honestly. He'd certainly seen enough dead shopkeepers when he'd been scouting for Tina. But while the tale was so believable even he was starting to buy it, the mask of vengeance on Sir Dan's face did not change.

"Sorry, peasant," the knight said. "I don't know who you really are, but you have the same face as the thousands of player-possessed elves I've had to stare at for the last eighty years. That's too bad for you, because a living player is a risk we will no longer tolerate."

With that, the knight pulled his sword and raised it high. As the weapon went up, SilentBlayde slid his free hand under his cloak to grasp the handle of one of his swords. He was already planning how he'd stab the knight through the chest and then, hopefully, move on to the rest of the patrol before they realized they'd been tricked when the young knight who'd spoken up before reached out to grab Sir Dan's arm.

"Sir Dan, stop!" he cried, wrestling the bigger knight's weapon away from SB. "This is murder! Can you not see that he is injured? He wears no player armor and carries no weapons. He is an innocent man, one of the vulnerable citizens we are sworn to protect! Think of your honor!"

The two knights struggled for a terrifying moment, and then Sir Dan shoved the younger man away, but he did not turn his blade back to SB. Instead, he shoved the sword with Bastion's sunburst crest on its hilt back into his sheath.

"Damn new recruit!" he yelled, not so much releasing SB's arm as throwing it the direction of the ground. "You like him so much, you deal with him."

The young knight's eyes went wide. "Me, sir?"

"Aye, you," Sir Dan said, sneering at SB, who was focusing on looking convincingly terrified. "If you care so damn much about honor, you can take him to his blasted family. But know this!" He shoved his gauntleted finger in SB's face. "This creature is a player. I can smell it! He lies through his teeth, but he'll show his true nature in the end, and when he does, that blood will be on *your* hands!"

"I have faith that this is the right decision," the young knight replied, standing up straight even though his voice was shaking. Sir Dan spat on the ground at his feet, turned his back on them, and marched back to the other knights waiting in the Royal Mile. The rest of the squad followed, glaring over their shoulders. When they were gone, the young human knight kneeled down to offer SB his hand.

"My apologies, Master Sky," he said, flashing SilentBlayde an apologetic smile. "I wasn't in the Nightmare, either, so I don't comprehend what has happened to Sir Dan and the others to make them act this way. Please know that they were honorable men once and will be again. They're just mad with anger right now, so please don't judge them too harshly. Meanwhile, I will help you find your family."

"Thank you for saving me," SB said, the wobble in his voice in no way faked. "What should I call you, Sir knight?"

"My name is Sir Jamie Tillerson," the young man replied proudly. "You may call me Sir Jamie."

"Sir Jamie, then," SilentBlayde said, moving closer to his rescuer in case one of the crazier knights changed his mind and came back. "May we travel by the Royal Mile? It looks to be under the king's protection--long may he reign--and would be the safest way to reach my family. I left them in an inn by the bank. If they have not been forced to flee, I hope to find them there."

The young man shook his head, his too-large helmet sliding against his brown hair as he did so. "I'm sorry, but the Royal Mile is closed to all but the king's soldiers, and the south of the city is off limits as well. According to our reports, the player army that destroyed Captain Malakai's outpost has taken over the Trainers' Hall. For their own safety, no civilians are to be allowed near it."

SB barely caught his grin in time. That was a priceless piece of information. He didn't know why Tina hadn't gone for the bank as planned, but the Trainers' Hall was an inspired second choice. With its defensible positions and piles of supplies, they could hold out there for days. Now he just had to reach her.

"But I *have* to go south," he begged, hiding his eagerness behind a not wholly feigned mask of worry. "My family--"

184

"I know you wish to reach them," the young man said sadly. "But I cannot let you put yourself in danger." He thought for a moment, and then his eyes lit up. "I know! We'll be moving against the players' camp soon, so I will be in that part of the city. If you tell me where your family was staying, I promise I will search for them for you. In the meanwhile, I'll take you to the Diplomatic Quarter. That's where all the other citizens of Bastion are waiting while the peace is restored. You'll be quite safe there, and maybe you'll meet someone who knows of your relatives."

It took all of SilentBlayde's discipline not to curse in the boy's face. The Diplomatic Quarter was right next to the castle, practically hugging the walls. Going back in that direction was the last thing he wanted. He supposed he could let the young knight lead him off and then kill him the moment they were alone, but while he would have had no problem gutting Sir Dan, doing the same to Sir Jamie--who'd stood up to his superior officer to save SB's fake life--felt like one sin too many.

"Oh no, I have troubled you too much already," SB said, frantic to find another way out. "Your offer is most generous, but I cannot hide behind walls while my wife and children are in peril. If I can't go south down the Royal Mile, I'll just find another--"

"Absolutely not," Sir Jamie said firmly, grabbing hold of "Master Sky's" good arm. "I insist on escorting you to safety. On my honor as a knight, I'll take you to the Diplomatic Quarter and see that your injuries are cared for."

SB tried to come up with a reason he couldn't go, but he'd lied himself into a corner. Sir Dan was still watching from the road, too, which meant he couldn't even fight back as Sir Jamie pulled him his feet and began escorting him back the way he'd just come.

***

"And that's why my brother, Mist, had to wear a yeti-hide dress all Winter Solstice," SB finished, struggling to keep his voice jovial and steady.

They'd been walking for nearly two hours. Even with Bastion's new expanded size, the journey between the Royal Mile and the Diplomatic Quarter in the city's northwestern corner shouldn't have taken more than thirty minutes, but between SB's leg and the constant challenges issued to them by every patrol they passed, their progress was slower than a crawl. The real challenge, though, was dealing with Sir Jamie.

The young knight had been nothing but polite and helpful, but his presence still ground SilentBlayde's nerves raw. Not only did he have to constantly shift his body to keep him from discovering the swords hidden under his cloak, but Sir Jamie insisted on *talking*, forcing SB to weave an increasingly complicated life history for Sky of Highcloud. It had taken all his knowledge of FFO's Winter Nation zones to keep things believable. He'd never been so glad of the weeks he'd spent on the Unciatus faction grind.

But as frustrating as it was, Sir Jamie's company was worth every thin-ice lie. The young knight's assurances had gotten them past nine patrols, several of which had had the eyes of true player haters. That was eight packs of knights more than SB was confident he could beat while wounded and without his gear, but leaning on the shoulder of a Royal Knight was as good as a free pass. The patrols still stopped and harassed him, but they always let them go in the end. One squad of City Guards even offered to take SB off Sir Jamie's hands so he could return to the front, but the young knight had refused, claiming he'd been ordered to take responsibility for the injured citizen personally, and he meant to do just that.

"You have quite the sense of duty, sir," SB said as the guard patrol walked away. "Sir Dan would never know if you took help."

"But *I* would know," Sir Jamie said sternly. "A knight's honor is more important than his life. Sir Dan may have meant it as a punishment,

186

but this task was given to me, and I will see it through. I owe my dear father and mother that much at least. They sacrificed much so that I could pursue the knighthood, and I always swore I would never let them down."

SB looked down at his feet to hide his grimace. Honor. *That* was a luxury he'd been born without. But while he didn't envy the knight his shackles of duty, the rest of what Sir Jamie had said filled SilentBlayde with bitter, shameful jealousy. Sir Jamie *Tillerson* clearly hadn't come from a rich or powerful family--just a loving one.

They shuffled in silence after that. Sir Jamie was busy watching the now-dark streets for player attacks, and "Sky of Highcloud" claimed exhaustion, which wasn't a lie at all. Between the pain and the blood loss and the long, shuffling walk, SB was so tired he was having trouble keeping his act up.

He was sticking to safer silence when they finally reached a hilltop that had a long, eight-foot-high terrace cut into it. The top of the terrace was crowned with an attractive--but still highly defensible--fieldstone wall that had been hastily augmented with converted-wagon archer boxes and a makeshift barricade of sharpened wooden posts blocking off the cut-in stairs.

"Who goes?" came a call from the top.

"I am Sir Jamie Tillerson, in his Majesty's service!" Sir Jamie called back. "I have a man here who needs help!"

A pair of City Guards in yellow tabards and flimsy chain appeared at the top of the steps. "Well met, Sir Knight!" they said, hurrying to drag the barricade out of the way. "Come in, come in."

Tiptoeing between the spikes, SB and Sir Jamie climbed the steps to what had once been an expansive flagstone plaza. SilentBlayde remembered the front of the Diplomatic Quarter as a novelty vendor area designed to look like a slightly anachronistic shopping mall, complete with food court. Now, though, the noodle stands and fried sweets counters were shuttered, and the umbrella-covered tables were gone. In their place, a sea of canvas army tents filled the square from edge to edge, and every one of them was packed with people.

SilentBlayde's eyes went wide at the sight. Well, this explained where the population of Bastion had gone. The Diplomatic Quarter was packed full of refugees. As they walked farther in, he saw that the tent city extended beyond the square as well, filling the boulevards and courtyards behind it. Everywhere there was space, ragged people with fearful eyes and ash-smudged faces had crammed themselves in. Mothers attempted to bathe hungry babies in small wooden tubs. Fathers waited in lines for food and water rations with their children in tow. Others just sat on the ground, staring at nothing. They were all NPCs wearing the standard Bastion town clothes, but seeing them like this, SB found it hard to draw the usual lines. They just looked like people--hungry, terrified people trying to survive.

"Lieutenant," Sir Jamie said as the City Guards closed the barricade behind them. "This man has been injured by players. He needs healing at once. Where do I take him?"

The guard simply pointed across the square at a long tent in the very back. Nodding, Sir Jamie started leading SB toward it, but the closer they got, the slower SilentBlayde walked. They weren't even inside yet, but he could already smell the stench of rotten blood and bad wounds. When Sir Jamie pushed aside the door flap at last, the inside was even worse.

The medical tent was nothing but the wounded lying on wooden and canvas cots that were packed in so tight, you couldn't walk between them. Nurses in various uniforms rushed around, but there didn't seem to be any medicine to dispense. Behind a sheet in the back, someone was screaming for mercy while a man in doctor's robes readied a bloodstained hacksaw. He didn't even wash it before going in, and SB turned away in horror.

"You there," Sir Jamie said, snagging the sleeve of a harried-looking Cleric as he ran by. "This man is on death's door. He needs healing."

The Cleric, a short jubatus with dark-brown fur and bloodstained robes, gave SB a single look before turning away again. "He's already been magically healed," he said brusquely.

Sir Jamie frowned, and then he looked at SilentBlayde. "Why did you not tell me you had been healed already?"

"I-I-I did not know," SB improvised, covering up his panic with a look of confusion. "It must have happened while I was passed out on the street. Maybe some kindly Cleric or Naturalist took pity on me."

That sounded weak even to him, but before Sir Jamie could ask any more awkward questions, the busy Cleric pointed at a wooden cot in the center of the tent. "We don't have mana to spare, but he won't die tonight. Just put him over there, and we'll get to him when we can."

SB wanted nothing more than to get away from this place, but he was too tired and too deep in the lies to fight as Sir Jamie gently led him to the cot the Cleric had indicated. His hidden swords dug into his back as he lay down, but he couldn't possibly take them off without revealing what he was to the whole tent, so he gritted his teeth and bore it, hoping the pained expression would add a sense of verisimilitude.

"Well, Master Sky," Sir Jamie said when SB was finally down. "I have delivered you to safety, as promised. I must return to my unit now, but I swear I will look out for your family when we go south to crush the player rebellion. Stay in this camp, and I will send them to you when I find them. Meanwhile, be sure to get your rest. Your family will need you healed up and strong when you are reunited."

"Thank you, Sir Jamie," SB said, and he meant it. "I will always remember your kindness."

The young knight shook his hand and left the tent, and SilentBlayde let out a sigh of relief. Sir Jamie was a good kid, but he was still so glad to be out of the knight's presence at last. Lying down felt good too. Coming into the tent, all he'd wanted was to run away, but now that he was flat, his body felt as heavy as lead. He knew he needed to get up and get back to Tina, but the lumpy cot had a gravity he couldn't fight. Before he could even start on a plan to sneak away, he nodded off, his eyes falling shut.

And dreamed of Tina.

* * *

"Thanks for watching, and mash the subscribe button for more!" Tina and SB said at the same time, holding the excited tone until the red Recording dot clicked off.

SilentBlayde let out his breath. He was back in FFO--the game version, not the terrifying new reality. He was in VR again, wearing the body of SilentBlayde the character and standing outside an instance portal in one of the forest zones. *Which* portal and *which* zone, he wasn't entirely sure, mostly because he wasn't paying attention. He was too busy watching the video feed that floated in the corner of his vision, where Tina--the *real* Tina--was sitting in her computer chair in her bedroom at her parents' house and smiling at him like he was the best thing in her world.

He wasn't on camera, of course. He only ever appeared in their videos as his character. Tina had been the same at first, but then she'd read that videos with real people's faces in them got more hits, so she'd bought a used camera and a program that let her play FFO in third person from her computer and started appearing in their videos as herself.

It had worked like a charm too. Tina never believed him when he said she was pretty, but the world clearly agreed with him, because the moment she'd started putting her real face in their videos, views had gone through the roof. The only bad part was that people had started demanding to see his face as well, but saying no to random internet commenters was a small price to pay for the privilege of getting to look at Tina in real life.

And *oh*, was she something to look at. As always when they were filming, Tina had gotten "all gussied up." SB wasn't sure about that particular piece of English slang, but it seemed to mean "comb hair and put

190

on makeup." She complained every time that she was plastering her face, but his mother put on twice as much just to go outside, so he didn't understand. Maybe it was an American thing.

Makeup or no makeup, though, SB loved getting to actually *see* her as Tina, not Roxxy. She had long, exotic wavy brown hair that poofed out like a soft cloud around her lovely face with its fragile, delicate features. Her skin was pale in the winter and freckled in the summer, and her large amber-brown eyes lit up with excitement whenever she talked. Or at least, whenever she talked to *him*. Her mouth was small and perfect, too, especially when she was smiling, as she was now.

And she was so *small*. SB wasn't sure how tall she actually was, but she had to sit on a box to keep her chair from swallowing her during filming. SB knew better than to comment on it--that way lay death--but he secretly thought it was adorable. *All* of her was. Filming with her like this was his favorite thing to do because it let him look at her as much as he wanted without feeling self-conscious. He'd already blatantly stopped piloting his character so he could just stand there and drink her in. He was watching the way the tips of her curls slipped over her shoulders to nestle in the crook of her collarbone when he realized Tina was talking to him.

"Sorry?"

"I said I've got some good news," she repeated, tucking her hair nervously behind her ears, which was so cute he lost his train of thought all over again.

"What's that?" he managed at last.

A huge smile lit up her face as she grabbed a piece of paper with the Seattle University logo off her desk and waved it at the camera. "I got in! Number-two library sciences school in the USA, baby!"

"Congratulations!" he said excitedly, grinning as she started bouncing in her chair.

"It's all thanks to you, dude!"

SB shook his head, his character mimicking the motion in the game. "All I did was play FFO. You're the one who aced all your AP classes last year."

"It *is* thanks to you," she said stubbornly as her cheeks turned the most perfect shade of pink. "You're the one who does all the editing that makes our videos not suck. With the revenue from our channel, I should have just enough to make tuition and rent for the first year. I'm gonna be living in a three-bedroom apartment with six people, but I *made* it! Hell, if we keep adding subscribers like we have been, I might be able to pay for all four years without a penny of debt!"

As genuinely happy as he was to hear all that, SB's real joy was for himself. Getting into her first choice college meant she'd need to keep playing FFO and making videos with him for at least four more years. Better still, he'd discovered that becoming a librarian in the US required a masters degree, which meant another two years, if not more. Hell, if he got *really* lucky, maybe she'd go for a PhD. Those took *forever* to get. If he played his cards right, he might be able to keep her in his life for another decade.

"Anyway," she went on, pushing her hair away from her face again. "I have to take a foreign language for my degree, and I can't think of anything I'd like to learn more than Japanese."

"It's a wonderful language," he said. "I'll be happy to send you all the manga you..."

She was smirking at him. It was the same look he usually saw on Roxxy's face right before she gave the order to do something she thought was *really* clever. "Taking Japanese comes with an added bonus."

"What's that?"

"The JET program!" she said excitedly. "I have to get my bachelors first, so it's still four years away, but after that I can go to Japan! Isn't that awesome?"

SB froze. JET was a program that sent American college graduates to Japan to teach English, which meant there'd no longer be an ocean between her and the tragedy that was his real life.

"B-But won't that be really expensive?" he stammered at last, desperately trying to keep the panic out of his voice. "It's not cheap to live here. Can you afford it?"

"That's just it, dude," she said with a grin. "JET is a *job*. Your country pays me to come over to teach, and that kind of cultural exchange stuff is right in line with my major. Libraries are *all* about community building. Having JET on my resume will totally help me get accepted into the master's program when I come back, and I'll get to visit you! It's a win-win!"

The light in her eyes got brighter and brighter as she talked. Normally, he loved Tina's enthusiasm for adventure, but now it felt like she was a train plowing exuberantly toward a broken bridge. Panic rising, he wondered if he should fake a disconnect.

"Just think!" she barreled on, oblivious. "I'd be over there for a whole year. They might send me to work in the ass-end of nowhere, but Japan has amazing trains. We could finally hang out IRL! Wouldn't that be awesome?"

She grinned beautifully at him, making him shiver and panic at the same time. Now was absolutely the time to disconnect. He had a macro that would crash his client. The dump shock would make him barf, but it'd be worth it. Anything to put off this conversation. But while he was scrambling for his macro library, his panic must have made it to his character's face, because Tina's delighted smile faded into a frown.

"What's wrong, Blayde?" she asked. "I thought you'd be really excited about this. You look like I just said I'd killed your cat."

"I- I..." he stuttered.

Her frown deepened. "Don't you want to meet up in real life?"

There was no right answer to that question. When he failed to reply, her face pinched, driving his panic even higher. He knew that look.

That was how her face got right before her temper blew up. Wincing, SB braced for impact, but something even worse happened. Tina started to cry.

She tried to hide it, turning away from the camera and using her hair to cover her face. Unlike him, though, Tina wasn't a good liar. She couldn't cover up anything, and her attempts just made the reality hurt even more.

"Does it have to do with why you refuse to tell me your full name?" she asked at last, voice cracking. "Or why you've never shown me what you really look like?"

SB cursed silently. Of course she'd caught on that there was something, but that didn't change that he still had to hide it.

"Yes."

"Why?" she asked, still not looking at him.

"I can't tell you." The words were knives across his tongue.

"Why not?" she demanded, her temper finally kicking in as she whirled on him. "I don't understand. You've *always* been here for me. You work three times as hard on our video channel as I do, but you've never asked for a share of the money or anything in return. We're always together in FFO. Hell, people joke that we're married." She dropped her eyes again, and her voice began to wobble again. "I'm not asking for a commitment or anything like that. I just want to meet you. You know, the *real* you."

That was the single most terrifying thing she could say. "I'm sorry, Tina," he said, flicking his hand behind his back to bring up James's GTFO macro. "But that's impossible."

"Why?" she asked. "Are you in a coma? Is that why you're online so much? Are you quadriplegic? 'Cause I'll still come. I'll wheelchair you all over Japan if that's it."

The "yes" was on the tip of his tongue. She'd just handed him an out that would solve this problem forever, but he still couldn't bring himself to lie to her. Not to his beloved Tina.

"No, that's not it."

She stared straight into the camera. "Is it me?"

"No!" he said quickly. "I--"

"I know I'm not what American girls are supposed to look like," she said, getting more upset with each word. "I'm as short as a kid, no boobs, no butt, frizzy hair. I'm not anything like what a--"

"It's not any of that!" he said sharply. "You're lovely! Far better than someone like me deserves to be around."

"Then why?" she demanded, glaring at him with red-rimmed eyes. "You're the most important person in my life. If there's something wrong, I want to know. I want to help you." Her small hands clenched on her desk. "I-I want to *be* with you. Please, just tell me--"

"I can't," SB said desperately. "I can't meet you. Ever. And I can't tell you why. That's just how my life is. It's not something anyone can fix."

With that, he flicked his hand and activated the crash macro. Its script divided by zero, and the game crashed, leaving him spinning away into the darkness.

When he worked up the courage to log back in two days later, Tina wasn't there.

She didn't come back online for two weeks, didn't answer his texts, and didn't talk to him at all. It was like she'd fallen off the face of the earth. Then, just when he was sure he'd ruined everything, she logged in for their Saturday raid like nothing had happened. When he'd desperately opened a private chat, she informed him she'd gotten the flu but that she was better now and ready to raid.

It was a terrible lie, but he'd embraced it with open arms. They'd had a great raid, and when it was over, he and Tina had gone out to farm reagents together, just like always.

And neither of them ever mentioned what had happened again.

***

SilentBlayde woke with a gasp, his whole body churning from the vivid memory of anxiety and nausea from the dump shock. The medical tent was darker now, lit by glowing white rocks that had been hung on strings from the tent poles. Other than that, it was all the same rush of injured people and doctors trying to keep them alive.

No one seemed to have gotten to him yet, but his leg hurt noticeably less, a testament to player-character regeneration rates. Doing the math in his head, SB estimated that if it took two hours for him to heal to full in-game without aid, it probably took at least twenty now, assuming he rested the whole time. That was amazing by normal human standards, but he didn't have twenty hours to lie here. He had to get back. He'd just started to push up from his cot when a bandaged hand landed on his arm.

"You might not want to do that, boy."

SB jumped. The hand turned out to belong to the heavily injured older man wearing a soldier's padded surcoat in the cot next to him. When he saw SB looking, the old soldier let go of his arm and lifted a bandaged finger to his lips. "Cover yerself. Quick."

Confused but too wary to ignore a warning, SB grabbed the wool blanket he'd been issued and pulled it up to his chin. Then, for good measure, he pulled his hood down over his head, as if he were blocking the light to sleep.

It was damn good that he did, because a few seconds later, Malakai, the four-skull captain of the Royal Knights, stalked into the tent.

SB choked under his hood, eyes going wide. No. There had to be some mistake. Malakai was *dead*. He'd had to coax Tina into dropping the captain's lifeless body. There was no *way* he could be--

"*Captain!*" The shout cut through the moans and groans of the medical tent as an aide wearing the knight's red and gold rushed through the flap after Malakai. "Sir, *please* return to base! It's only been six hours since your resurrection, and you are still healing. The Clerics--"

"The Clerics have done enough," Malakai said, scanning the tent with his sharp eyes. "I will sleep when my work is done, but I cannot rest knowing that--*Ah ha!*"

The elven captain strode down the rows of cots and plunged his hand into a nest of blankets, dragging an ichthyian out by his head-fin.

"*Gotcha!*" Malakai said savagely. "I knew there would be more players hiding in here!"

"Waaa!" cried the green-scaled fish-man, flapping his gills in panic as he writhed in Malakai's grip. "I'm sorry! Please don't hurt me! I just wanna go home! I'll never play again! I want my mommy! I--"

Malakai silenced the sobbing ichthyian with a savage shake. "You want your mommy?" he repeated with a sneer. "You're not even a man yet, are you? You're just a *child* possessing that body."

The player started sobbing even harder at that. The captain shook his head in disgust and tossed him to his assistant, who scrambled to catch the slippery fish-man. "It seems the rumor of demon children is true. Add him to the hostages, and make sure his wagon is first in line when we move on the rebel's camp. The sobs of their young will surely cut their hearts open."

"Yes, sir," the aide said wearily, dragging the crying ichthyian off to hand him over to the knights waiting outside. Meanwhile, Malakai turned back to the tent, his eyes scanning the cots. "I wonder if there are any more."

SilentBlayde sank deeper under his blanket. Malakai picking up that the players were vulnerable to hostages was a bad development, but right now, SB was far more concerned with the fact that bosses could apparently be *rezzed* like players. He'd never heard of anything like that back in the game, but there were plenty of NPC Clerics. Hell, three of them were in the medical tent right now. Why wouldn't they have the same Raise Ally spell as the players? They had everything else.

He steeled his body to keep it from shaking. This was bad. Tina and the others thought Malakai was dead. If he reappeared out of

197

nowhere, he'd catch them completely by surprise. Add in hostages, and the Roughnecks would be left in a terrible position. He *had* to warn Tina, but he didn't dare move. His swords were still pressing into his back, but there was no way he could kill Malakai in the ten seconds before Shadow Dance ran out, assuming his shadow-based abilities even worked while the Bastion was active, or that he'd be able to damage him at all. He'd barely managed to knock a chunk out of the captain's health when he'd at been full health and wearing all his gear. As injured and stripped as he was, he didn't stand a chance, so as much as it stung, SB forced himself to lie still and breathe normally, pretending to be just another poor casualty of war until, at last, Malakai turned and marched out of the tent, yelling for his troops to fan out and check the other refugees again.

When he was certain the captain was gone, SB shook his hood off and turned to thank his savior. As he rolled over, though, the words died on his tongue. There was a stack of bloody armor lying under the old soldier's cot--bloody plate armor very similar to Roxxy's, bearing the sunburst sigil of the Bastion's Holy King.

The wounded knight chuckled when he saw the fear flash over SB's face. "Don't worry, kid. I'm not gonna rat you out."

"How'd you know?" SB asked quietly.

The knight started to answer, but a hacking cough cut him off. He covered his mouth with a bandaged hand and lay back, clutching his side, which SB could now see was wrapped in cloth that had been stained nearly black with old, dried blood.

"You talk in yer sleep," the knight said when the coughing finally passed. "I picked up some of your languages while I was trapped in the Nightmare. I don't know much Japanese, but I'm pretty sure *kawaii* means cute." He winked the eye that wasn't covered in bandages at SB. "You dreaming 'bout a girl?"

SilentBlayde felt his checks heat to roughly the same temperature as the sun while the old knight laughed at him. "There's no shame in it," he chided, and then he leaned closer. "Was it a good dream?"

"*She* was good," SB said quietly, looking anywhere but the old man as he scrambled to change the subject. "If you were trapped in the Nightmare, why didn't you turn me in?"

There was a long silence while the knight considered the question. "Don't know, to be honest," he said at last, sinking back into his cot. "I came out of the Nightmare full of more piss 'n' vinegar than all my life before. The first players I saw were doing some real shitty stuff, and I had no problem taking my rage out on 'em."

His face fell. "They were lowbies. Didn't stand a chance against me. They screamed for mercy, 'o course. 'I thought this was a dream!' and 'I didn't know it was real!' But I didn't listen. All I could think about was the cross-dressing Valentine's Day zapper or the flaming bag of poop achievement or all the raids against His Majesty that I died in for nothing. It all got to me, like a mad buzzin' in my head. So I cut 'em right down, but when it was over, I felt differently."

"Your remorse won't bring their lives back," SB said fiercely.

"You think I don't know that?" the old knight snapped. "Why do you think I didn't toss you to the captain?"

SilentBlayde snapped his mouth shut, and the old knight sighed. "It wasn't that I didn't want my vengeance, but for all that time I spent hating you in the Nightmare, I never actually realized who you were until I cut you down. You're not demons. You're just a bunch of scared kids whose wooden swords got swapped with real ones."

He sank deeper into his cot, wincing when the movement hurt his wounds. "There just comes a point when you get tired of all the death, you know? It's easy to kill a man when you're mad and he's right in front of you, but suffering never stops there. However this shakes out, I'm still gonna have to make the rounds telling widows how their husbands died and finding new homes for orphans. Assuming I get out of this at all."

He flashed a morbid smile, and SilentBlayde winced as James's accusations that he was killing innocent men came back to him. Had he made a widow today? Or orphaned a child? If Sir Jamie had been in that group, SB would have cut him down without a thought, and then someone would have to go and tell his loving parents that their dutiful son was never coming home. That he'd died doing his duty, and SB was the monster who'd killed him.

He had to roll away after that, staring up at the tent's green canvas ceiling as he tried to remember the horror of Founder's Square and Malakai's camp. He needed that anger, that certainty he was doing right, but it didn't come. When he looked back at the memories, all he saw was death. This whole city was full to the brim with it, and no matter how SB tried to justify his part in that, all he saw was James's horrified face and the blood that he--Haruto--had spilled on the ground.

"We're all wrong, aren't we?" he whispered at the ceiling.

"Some are right, some are wrong," the knight replied stoically. "But we're past that mattering anymore." He dragged his bandaged hand over his face, and then he started to laugh. "Shit, who am I kidding about making rounds? I ain't ever leaving this tent."

SB opened his mouth to say that was nonsense, but the old man cut him off with a glare, pushing up on one arm so he could look down on the elf properly.

"Listen, boy," he said, his breaths wheezing as if it was taking everything he had to stay up. "And listen sharp, 'cause this might the last good I do in this world. We are *all* at fault for this mess. Some of us more than others, but that don't matter right now. I know it's tempting to mete out punishment, but what's the point of justice if you have to burn the whole world to get it? All these people huddled here--these normal folks and families and people who weren't even in the Nightmare--they ain't got nothing to do with any of this. There's innocents on both sides getting trampled on account of us shitheads, and someone's gotta make it *stop*."

He stabbed his bandaged finger in SB's face. "I'm tellin' you this cause I know you're something special. You got one of them legendary rings on your left hand. You've tried your best to hide it, but I know you've got power, and your regrets are as plain as day. So take it from an

200

old soldier who knows: if you ever wanna look yourself in the mirror again, you'll use that power to stop this madness. 'Cause we're headin' for a war. All this hell you see right now, it's just the start. It can still get a lot worse for everyone, and it absolutely will if no one puts their foot down and says, 'No more.'"

The knight's strength must have given out after that, because he collapsed back to his pillow, panting and coughing up blood. When the attack passed, SB reached out a trembling hand to tap him on the arm.

"Sir knight?"

Nothing.

Frantic, SB reached up to check the knight's neck, slumping in relief when he felt a heartbeat--barely there but still moving.

"Doctor! Cleric!" SilentBlayde shouted, leaping out of his cot. "*Anyone!*"

At his ruckus, a tired and blood-splattered Cleric came over. "What?"

"This knight is dying!" SB said, crouching beside the old man. "He needs healing now*!*"

The jubatus Cleric's tired, empty eyes barely moved at SilentBlayde's panic. He simply shrugged and leaned over, prying open the old knight's eyes. "I'm afraid he's too far gone," the Cleric said wearily as he straightened up. "And he's level eighty, which means there's not enough mana left in this whole tent to save him. Sorry, son."

"A resurrection, then," SB pleaded. "He doesn't deserve this!"

"*None* of us deserves this!" the Cleric yelled back at him, suddenly furious. "You think we *like* watching people die? But we only have so much mana to go around, and Raise Ally takes most of it! Even if I did have the magic left, bringing him back means twenty other people would have to go without healing that could save their lives. Do *they* deserve that?"

"No," Blayde said feebly. "No, they don't."

The Cleric gave him a sharp nod and stalked away, muttering under his breath. SB flopped back down on his cot, listening to the old knight's breath as it grew shallower and shallower. "What is your name?" he whispered. "Please, give me that at least."

But the knight never spoke again. He died a few minutes later, leaving SB sitting alone. The Cleric came back to move the body soon after, saying something about needing the beds, but SilentBlayde didn't hear him. He just lay on his back, staring at the ceiling without seeing it until sleep took him again.

There were no dreams this time. When he opened his eyes again, the tent was gray with the first light of the false dawn. There was a new body huddled under blankets on the old knight's cot, but SB didn't look at him. He just stood up and tested his leg, putting as much of his weight on it as he could. It still twinged, but he was able to walk several steps without a crutch, which would have to be good enough.

The overworked Clerics didn't even question him when he gathered his things and left the tent. The guards at the barricade were a bit more trouble, but their job was to keep players out, not citizens in. They did their due diligence and informed him of the danger, but when "Master Sky" insisted he was leaving to find his family, they didn't lift a finger to stop him as he climbed over the barricade and hurried down the stairs, limping down the street as fast as he could go.

The moment he was out of sight, SB slipped into an abandoned house and changed back into his armor. It was still clammy with blood, but the augmented strength and power made him feel a million times better. The first step on his injured leg was a pointed reminder that he still had to take it easy, though, so kept his short cloak and face wrap in his bag and donned his NPC disguise over his armor. It wouldn't hold up to more than a casual glance, but he felt he could handle some unwanted attention now, and speed was of the essence. He wasn't sure if Malakai's attack would come today or tomorrow, but he was certain it would be soon, and he needed to warn Tina as soon as possible. Thankfully, he knew where she

202

was now, so he wrapped Master Sky's tattered cloak tight around his body and started walking as fast as he could south through the wrecked city toward the island of Dawn's Hope.

Chapter 10

James

James must have passed out after they put SB in the barrel. One minute, he was bouncing through the streets on Ar'Bati's hard shoulder, and the next, he was waking up to the glorious rush of magical healing.

His eyes snapped open, and he instinctively tried to sit up. But his head was euphoric *and* dizzy, so he ended up going right back down, blinking in confusion. He was still trying to figure out where he was when a delicate, feminine, feline face appeared above him.

"I think I got the worst of it," the jubatus woman said, her pretty voice twanging with a distinct New Jersey accent. "He's still pretty low, but I'm only level twenty-three, and he's probably eighty at least. That's the best I can do."

"It's fine," replied the gruff voice of Fangs in the Grass. "He's awake now. You are dismissed."

The jubatus player, whom James could now see was dressed in the bright-pink robes and blue bracers of a low-level Cleric, turned up her nose and stalked away. Wincing at his brother's rudeness, James pushed himself up groggily.

They were in a cage--a big, metal cage, which explained the stripes he'd seen earlier. The floor was lined with dirty blankets, and there was a large, smelly bucket in one corner, but other than being incarcerated, the handful of players locked inside looked unharmed. They were also--with the exception of Flameboyant, who was sitting against the bars near James's feet--all jubatus, which struck him as odd. Sitting up further, he saw that their cage was one of many set up in the middle of an elegant flagstone street.

They were all full of players divided by race, but when he looked around at the lantern-lit buildings, he understood why. They were on Embassy Row, the street in the Diplomatic Quarter where all the different racial factions in the game had their Bastion headquarters. Their cage--and the other three cages filled with jubatus players--was in front of a large yurt bearing the sigils of the Four Clans of the Savanna. A short distance away, two cages stuffed full of scaly fish-men and fish-women had been set up in front of the fishbowl-like ichthyian embassy, and so on down the road. What caught James's attention the most, though, was how *not* on fire everything was.

With the exception of the new open-air jail, Embassy Row looked exactly as it had in-game. There were no broken windows or smashed-in doors or blood on cobblestones. The lamps were lit and burning merrily, filling the dark street with cheerful golden light. He couldn't see past the large, ornate embassy buildings into the main part of the Diplomatic Quarter, so maybe that was where all the crazy improvised fortifications and wreckage lived, but it looked as if this place had at least escaped the chaos, probably because Embassy Row was nestled right up against the towering outer wall of the royal castle, which meant they were closer to the king than they'd ever been.

Grinning at the prospect, James turned to face his brother. "Thanks for finding me heals," he said, nodding gratefully to the jubatus Cleric, who rolled her cat-eyes. "Looks like we made it to the Diplomatic Quarter."

"Yup," Flameboyant said cheerfully. "Your brother carried us both the whole way and yelled at the City Guards until they let us in. He's one tough mofo!"

"I did what I had to do," Fangs said, though James didn't miss the way he puffed up at the praise. "But we are still imprisoned despite my efforts, and Flam-boy-ant cannot yet walk."

"I figured you needed it more," Flameboyant explained. "We couldn't wake you after you conked out on Ar'Bati's shoulder."

"I intended to take you to one of our Naturalists at the Embassy," Ar'Bati continued. "But *idiots* refused to listen to reason, and now we are here."

205

"I'm not surprised they stuck us in a cage," James said. "A mini-boss from Windy Lake coming in with two wounded players on his shoulders probably did look hella suspicious."

"*I* am surprised!" his brother hissed at him. "Use your eyes!"

James blinked and turned to look again. He saw the other players cowering from Ar'Bati. He saw the embassies and the guards assigned to cage duty. His eyes had already moved on farther down the street when they suddenly snapped back. The men guarding them weren't Royal Knights. They weren't Bastion's City Guard, either, or human at all. They were tan-furred jubatus warriors whose shields and armor bore the sigils of the Four Clans of the Savanna.

"Wait," James said, turning back to Fangs. "Are we being held in here by *your* warriors?"

Ar'Bati punched the dirty ground. "We are. Filthy traitors! They've always resented me since it is in some ways true that our father purchased my position. Now that I've shown up with players in tow, they're acting as if I'm a turncoat. They refuse to believe that you are the son of Rend himself and speak of nothing but their loyalty to the king of Bastion and how they must wait for orders from the castle."

James sighed. He'd forgotten about the embassy guards. There were only a handful of quests that took place in the Diplomatic Quarter, and those were mostly low-level, intro-to-the-world stuff. But though it had been a very under-utilized part of the world, it was still a part of Bastion near the castle. That meant all the peacekeeper, guard-style NPCs had been level eighty just like the Royal Knights, including the jubatus warriors.

"I can't believe we've been imprisoned by those who are supposed to follow *my* orders as Head Warrior!" Ar'Bati hissed, bearing his fangs at the jubatus outside, who ignored him. "This is rank betrayal!"

"There is a bright side, though," James said with a smile. "These guys are max level."

"That only makes our situation even more difficult!"

206

"Right now," James said. "But you were worried about the clans being too low-level to fight back. Now we've discovered you have an entire contingent of high-level warriors. That's a huge find! Just think how happy your dad will be when he hears the news. When we get out of this, we'll send word to your mother, Acacia. She was the ambassador here, so they'll listen to her."

Ar'Bati's face, which he had scrunched up in fury at the words "low-level," fell into shocked awe. "James," he said, clapping a hand on James's shoulder. "I am so glad you are my brother!"

"Eyes on the prize," James replied with a grin.

"I like that player saying," Fangs said with a sharp nod. Then he frowned. "But how are we getting out of here? The warriors will not listen to anything I say, and the City Guard has taken over the rest of the Diplomatic Quarter to serve as a refugee camp for the displaced citizens of Bastion. Everyone here sees players as the enemy. Even if we were to read the lich's letters aloud, no one would believe us."

That was a problem. James frowned, staring down the cage-filled street as he turned the situation over in his head. He was still looking for an angle they could use when he spotted another tent a few buildings down the road. It looked a little bit like the Savanna clans' giant yurt, but unlike Windy Lake's smooth-shaved white hide, this one was made from thick pelts and giant tusks and guarded by a pair of fearsome-looking cat warriors with fluffy snow-white fur.

"Fangs," James said, pointing at the white cats. "How are our relations with the Winter Nation?"

"You mean the Unciatus?" Ar'Bati scowled. "Distant. We share a physical likeness but little else. Why?"

"Cause I think I've got a trick we haven't tried yet," James said, grabbing the bars and pulling himself to his feet. "Help me get their attention."

Before Ar'Bati could ask what he meant by that, James took a deep breath and yelled at the top of his lungs. "Unciatus of the Winter Nation! The son of Rends Iron Hides wishes to speak with your ambassador!"

Every player in the cage jumped at his shout. Ar'Bati jumped as well, tail bristling. "What are you doing?" he snapped, grabbing James by the shoulders. "You can't just *bellow* down the street like an animal!"

"We're not getting anywhere being quiet," James pointed out. "No one else is listening to us, and jubatus of the Savanna don't even have an ambassador in Bastion anymore since the Nightmare sent your mother back to Windy Lake."

"That still doesn't explain why you're yelling at the Unciatus!" Ar'Bati snapped, glaring through the bars at the white-furred guards, who were looking at James with a mixture of curiosity and amusement. "You think that just because both of our peoples resemble *cats* that the Winter Nation is automatically our ally? We don't even have relations with them!"

"I didn't choose them because of their race," James said confidently. "I chose them because I've done every quest in the royal castle there is. Every. Single. One. I've delivered every secret note and fetched every cask of rare wine for every stupid noble in that place, including Lady Siku, the Unciatus's ambassador. *Trust* me, if she's a tenth as ambitious now as she was back in the game, she'll come out."

Ar'Bati didn't seem to know what to make of that, so James just flashed him a fanged grin and turned to yell again. "*Hello!* We have vital diplomatic information Lady Siku needs to hear! This is a once-in-a-lifetime opportunity to gain the king's favor!"

He kept this up for a good twenty minutes. From the pain on his face, Ar'Bati clearly hated every second of it, but he didn't say another word. James was beginning to worry his voice would give out when one of the white-furred Unciatus guards left his post and jogged across the street to the heavily fortified side entrance into the royal castle. After a quick conversation, the Royal Knights guarding the door let him pass, and the Unciatus warrior vanished into the castle.

After another long wait, he reemerged, only this time, he wasn't alone. There was a whole squad of white-furred cat warriors coming out through the door with him. James assumed that their fur-lined blue-dyed armor and whalebone spears were traditional garb, because he couldn't believe that anyone would choose to wear such warm clothing in the sweltering, tropical heat of Bastion, but the real prize went to the tall Unciatus woman walking at the center of the group.

She was dressed from head to toe in heavy white silk robes tied at the waist with a stiff, obi-like leather belt depicting ivory-beaded Unciatus whalers spearing one of the great beasts that lived in FFO's deep seas. Her long, fluffy fur was pure white marked with the crispest, darkest of black spots, and her protruding fangs were as sharp as swords. Even in this hot, dusty place, James could smell the scent of fresh snow coming off her as she approached their cage, her lovely face set in the cat-person version of an aristocratic sneer as her ice-blue eyes took in the filthy, cowering players and the bloody state of James and Ar'Bati's armor.

"Lady Siku," James said quickly, determined to get the first word in since he was negotiating from inside a cage and needed every edge he could get. "Your fame precedes you. Thanks for coming."

"It was not as though I had anything better to do," the Unciatus lady replied in a crisp, condescending voice. "The king has confined all the ambassadors to the castle during this unpleasantness, so all business has ground to a halt." She looked James up and down. "I don't normally respond to summonses, especially not those shouted on the street. You said you had something important for me, player. Speak it quickly, and mind your tongue. I'll not tolerate impudence from filthy strays."

Ar'Bati bared his teeth at that. "You are the one who should mind how she speaks," he snarled. "I am Fangs in Grass, Ar'Bati of the Clans of the Savanna and heir to the Claw Born. This is my adopted brother, James of Claw Born and hero of the Savanna."

"Hero?" Lady Siku chuckled. "I suppose it's not hard to be heroic in such a low-level zone, though I am shocked to hear the heir of Claw Born call a player *brother*. Did Rends Iron Hides finally take one too many hits to the head?"

Ar'Bati clenched his fists. "We have just met, but already you dismiss my brother's deeds and insult my family? On my honor, I could demand a duel for either!"

"Nonsense," Lady Siku said with a coy smile. "I was only asking questions, not making claims. Don't be so prickly." Her blue eyes lit up. "Wait. Aren't you the one they call Angry Cat?"

If Fangs had been angry before, he was nuclear now. James grabbed his shoulder to remind him of their mission, but his brother shrugged him off, grabbing the bars that separated them from Lady Siku, who was clearly loving this reaction. But as James braced for the explosion, his brother surprised him.

"I refuse to answer that question because it has nothing to do with why we are here," Ar'Bati said through clenched fangs. "We are here on a matter of great import to Bastion and all the world. These *fools*"--he looked pointedly at the jubatus warriors, who were blatantly gawking at Lady Siku--"will not listen, but my brother, James, believes you might. So if you are done wasting our time on insults, we must discuss information critical to Bastion's survival."

"I'll be the judge of what counts as important," Lady Siku replied, turning to James, who flinched. The jubatus lady was lovely, but she had the hardest, coldest eyes he'd ever seen, like chips of blue ice. For all her haughtiness, though, she was still here, which meant she'd already listened more than anyone else. That was an opportunity he couldn't waste, so he rushed to say what he'd been trying to say since they'd stepped through the portal in the grasslands.

"The Once King's armies are readying to invade Bastion," he told her, grabbing his bag full of letters. "We have intercepted enemy communications that prove a conspiracy to sabotage the city's defenses. The undead armies are already massing in every zone. When the traitors act, they will teleport into Bastion and attack us from the inside. It could already be happening. We must notify the king and stop the Once King's agents before it is too late!"

He was panting by the time he finished, but instead of freaking out as he'd expected, Lady Siku just gave him a weighing look. "That is an interesting claim," she said at last, drawing a silk fan from her wide sleeve to wave the evening heat away from her face. "But what does a player know of the Once King? The undead cannot invade. We are safe inside the Bastion."

"Did you not hear me?" James said angrily. "They have a traitor inside the city! One of the portal keepers who has betrayed the king is going to teleport the Once King's armies into the center of the city. The city walls will do nothing to--"

"I'm not talking about the *walls*," she said condescendingly. When James looked at her in confusion, she snapped her fan closed and pointed at the sky.

More confused than ever, James looked up through the cage bars, and his eyes went wide. All this time, he'd assumed the golden glow lighting up the city night came from the lanterns that lined the wealthy Embassy Row, but that wasn't it at all. The night sky itself was glowing, the stars dim behind a golden shield of shimmering, watery sunlight. He'd never seen anything like it, but he knew what it was, and he understood what Lady Siku meant now. She hadn't been talking about the city of Bastion. She'd meant they were safe behind *the* Bastion, the Holy King's sacred barrier against undeath.

"Now do you understand?" Lady Siku said primly, sliding her fan back open to resume the breeze to her face. "Your threats of Armageddon have already been neutralized. There is no force, undead or player, that can beat the Bastion. We are perfectly safe."

"But for how long?" James asked, snapping his head down. "The Bastion is mighty, but the king can't keep it up indefinitely, and the Once King isn't going to just give up. So long as the traitors remain undiscovered and in position, he can just bide his time and attack the

211

moment the barrier goes down. Even worse, the Bastion will already be exhausted, which means we'll be caught without our greatest weapon. If anything, the fact that the Bastion is already up only makes this situation even direr. You *have* to warn the king!"

"I don't *have* to do anything," Lady Siku said, but her blue eyes strayed to the bag of letters. "You said you had proof of betrayal? Give it to me, and I will judge."

James's fingers tightened around the sack. "Not until you get us out of this cage and into the castle." That way, at least they could find a way to get to the king even if this white cat betrayed them.

Lady Siku shrugged. "I could just order my guards to take them from you."

He froze, suddenly very aware that he was still at less than a third health and staring at five level-eighty NPCs. If she made good on that threat, he'd be at a severe disadvantage. But brute force had never been one of his tools, and James wasn't nearly out of tricks yet.

"You could rob me," he said, lifting his chin. "But then you'd never get the benefit of everything else I know. This invasion is just the most pressing crisis. I have other secrets that could bring the powers of this world to their knees."

Lady Siku arched a fluffy white eyebrow. "Such as?"

"Nothing I'd be stupid enough to speak on the street," James assured her. "But you know I'm telling the truth. During the game, I earned the 'Upstairs-Downstairs' achievement. You were a quest giver in the castle during the Nightmare, so you know what that entails. I know over a hundred quests' worth of Bastion's political secrets. I could be convinced to tell them to you... *if* you help us."

That was a seriously shaky limb to go out on. It had been years since James had done the Bastion-castle-intrigue quests, and he had no idea how many of those situations were based on real events and how many had been invented by the developers. For all he knew, the whole thing was worthless. From the gleam in Lady Siku's hard eyes, though,

212

some of the info must have been worth the risk, because she turned to the guards with a greedy smile.

"Let them out."

"B-But, my lady," the jubatus guard stammered. "Captain Malakai gave us all strict orders that no players were to be--"

"I don't obey Captain Malakai," the white feline hissed. "The only orders I take in Bastion are those of the king himself, and *he* has granted me full autonomy to act in the best interest of our two nations. I have listened to this player and judged his knowledge vital to Bastion's defense, and I will be taking him into custody immediately. If you have a problem with that, you can take it to the king."

From the looks on the guards' faces, that was the last thing either of them wanted to do. After a final nervous look at the castle wall above them, the taller of the two removed the keys from his belt and unlocked the cage, waving James, Ar'Bati, and Flameboyant out into the street, where they were immediately surrounded by Lady Siku's towering Unciatus guards.

"Don't make me regret this," the Unciatus lady whispered to James, giving him a final piercing look from above her fan before turning on her heel and marching back toward the castle. Her guards followed at once, closing ranks to make a ring around the three prisoners as they walked past the Royal Knights Lady Siku had already pacified, through the heavy, ancient doors and the dark tunnel that ran through the thick outer wall, and into the royal castle at last.

James almost tripped over his feet when the main palace finally came into view. He'd been to the castle countless times in-game. The giant fortress had been a nexus of quests for all levels and a clearinghouse of faction reputation-reward vendors for all the game's more eccentric groups such as the cursed schtumples, who lived in lava, or the ichthyian rebels, whose base was inside a perpetual maelstrom. But while he knew this place inside and out, being here "in person" was a hundred times more impressive.

Surrounded on all sides by towering walls, the Holy King's castle was a tall fortress of brilliant white limestone and golden roofs glittering in the reflected light of the Bastion above. The layout consisted of four elegantly curving five-story buildings arranged in a ring around an absolutely massive keep in the center. Towers had been stuck everywhere they'd fit, making it look as if the whole fortress were reaching for the sky. At the highest peak of the giant tower crowning the central keep, the Bastion shone like a spotlight, creating a golden beam that ran straight up into the starry sky and lighting up the stained-glass windows in the tower that surrounded it so bright, the pictures they depicted--a mural that told the story of how the Sun had gifted the Bastion to the first Holy King and its subsequent use to drive back the Birds and later the undead--were projected onto the paving stones below, making it look like they were wading through a lake of color as Lady Siku led them toward one of the outer buildings.

"This is incredible," Ar'Bati whispered, his eyes wide as he drank it in. "My mother told me tales of the castle, but this is even grander than she described."

"It is pretty dope," Flameboyant agreed, arching his neck back to stare at the sky. "But why is the Bastion already on? You don't think we're too late, do you?"

James shook his head. "If the undead were invading, I think we'd know. Armies of skeletons aren't exactly quiet." He dropped his voice. "I'm worried it's on because of us."

Ar'Bati's face grew grim. "If this is the result of your sister's rash actions against the knights, then she has doomed us all. If the Bastion is not at full strength when the invasion arrives, we will be left helpless."

"I know, I know," James said frantically. "But there's nothing we can do about it now except keep pushing forward and hope that the Holy King's as big a badass as the game lore makes him out to be."

No one looked happy with that answer. James wasn't, either, but he didn't know what they could have done better. He was just happy the real Lady Siku seemed to be just as power hungry and reckless as her character had been in the game.

Every time anyone--knights, guards, minor officials--tried to stop her from bringing James and the others anywhere, she stomped all over them, barging her way across the open court that surrounded the palace complex, into one of the buildings that surrounded the main keep, up several flights of elaborately decorated stairs, through a set of double doors bearing the white paw of the Unciatus Winter Nation, and into an elegant, lofty hallway decorated in furs. But then, just as James started to get excited about actually making progress, Lady Siku turned and unlocked a wooden door banded in heavy iron.

Inside was a luxurious three-room suite complete with a king-sized bed laden in downy-soft furs, a spacious fireplace, a dining table for four, and what appeared to be an entire room for taking baths. But while the decorations were the height of luxury, the narrow, arrow-slit windows had iron bars behind their glass panes, and the walls were solid stone.

"There," Lady Siku said when they are all inside. "I have brought you to the castle, as requested. Now." She held out her elegant hand. "Give me the proof of this supposed treachery and invasion. I'll go through it and determine if it is worth his majesty's attention."

James clutched the bag of letters to his chest. "With respect, lady, we brought these letters for the king him--"

"Do you really think the Holy King of Bastion will give an audience to two ratty players and a quest-giver from the grass cats? And in the middle of the night?" Lady Siku pointed at the night sky through the barred window, and then she laughed. "Absolutely not. I am your only friend in this place. The rest of the palace sees players as demons. It is by my grace alone that the Royal Knights aren't already here to turn you into a bloody mess on my carpet. Now, I have done my part. You are in the castle, as requested. Now you will uphold *your* end of the bargain and hand over proof of this invasion. If I deem it worthy, I will take the news to the king."

215

James gritted his teeth. "We don't have time for--"

"So long as the Bastion is up, we have all the time we need," Lady Siku said, snapping her fingers impatiently. "The hour is too late for this ridiculousness. Hand over what you have now, or go back to your cage in the street."

James looked down at his sack of letters. He *really* didn't want to surrender his only proof to anyone but the king himself. At the same time, though, they'd been incredibly lucky to get this far. Lady Siku was an ambassador and a high-ranking noblewoman in her own right. He was a stranger and an enemy, but she was part of King Gregory's court, which meant she probably talked to him all the time. It might not be as direct as he'd wanted, but surely she'd bring this to the king's attention, because everyone lost if Bastion fell to the undead. That put her on their side, right?

His logic didn't fill him with confidence, but in the end, there wasn't much of a choice. If they went back to the cage in the street, they'd either be slaughtered by the knights or stuck until the undead came. Either way, they'd be dead, and their mission would be a failure. That was a failure James could not accept, so he reluctantly handed the letters over, wincing as Lady Siku snatched the bag from his hand.

"Finally," she said, peering into the bag with a curious scowl before handing it to one of her guards. "You will wait here. When I've looked over these letters and determined the validity of their contents, I'll be back to discuss what else you can give me. In the meanwhile, enjoy your comfortable new accommodations. You might be in them for some time."

She flashed them a lovely smile and walked out, leaving the guards to shut the reinforced door behind her.

As the heavy iron lock clicked into place, Flameboyant flopped down on the bed. "Well," he said optimistically. "At least we're in the castle. That's something, right?"

"Don't be a fool," Ar'Bati growled, glaring at the barred windows. "We've merely upgraded our cell."

216

Chapter 11

Tina

Their first night as an encamped army was nothing like Tina expected.

She'd thought there'd be fights, but no one wanted to start trouble with the PVP all-stars of the Red Sands guild walking around like they were just waiting for someone to give them an excuse. She'd thought there'd be thievery since there were loads of desperate folks, but Assets had gotten everything truly valuable under lock and key with world-class efficiency. The self-proclaimed High Warlord of Economic PVP seemed to possess a nearly psychic ability to spot and foil any embezzling or graft that wasn't his. He had their stores accounted for down to the kernel of corn and the fletching of each arrow by midnight, and anyone who tried to filch so much as a molecule more than their appointed ration was reported to the Red Sands police and forced to dig latrines next to a sign that read Food Thieves Club.

The Royal Knights hadn't been a problem yet, either. Tina had thought for sure they'd be in for a fight tonight, but though her scouts reported lots of movement on the Royal Mile, no serious threats emerged, leaving the Roughnecks free to help Zen set up a mini-hospital in the former first aid trainer's hut to take care of all the cuts, bruises, and scrapes that were too minor to waste healing on but still dragged down battle capability. The whole camp was running incredibly smoothly, actually, which *sucked*, because Tina had been counting on a constant stream of disasters to keep her mind off SilentBlayde.

He still hadn't come back. She'd thought for sure he'd pop in after the sun went down and it was easier to sneak through the city, but while new players had been pouring into Camp Comeback all evening, drawn out of their hiding places in the city by word of a safe haven, SB hadn't been among them. Neither had James. By the time midnight rolled around, she'd given up even the pretense of being in charge and started pacing the bridges, questioning everyone who came through about whether they'd seen an elf Assassin in raid gear or a jubatus Naturalist traveling with a stupid NPC, but no one knew anything.

The anxiety was so bad, Tina found herself wishing for an attack so she could do something with all the horrible, nervous energy building up inside her, but the night stayed infuriatingly peaceful. There was no clank of armor or creak of siege weapons being rolled into position, just the gurgle of the river and the wind blowing down the mountains, which was infuriating in its own way because the peaceful noises did nothing to cover up the moans and grunts emanating from the camp behind her.

Of all the annoying problems Tina had anticipated from gathering a giant army of players together, *rampant sex* hadn't been one of them. Again, though, Camp Comeback had surprised her. Every time she walked around a corner, opened a closet, dug behind a pile of crates, or went anywhere that wasn't in direct line of public sight, she'd caught naked or half-naked people in the act. Now that she was alerted to the problem, Tina couldn't *not* hear covert noises of pleasure wherever she went. They were even out by the water, furiously pawing at each other on the grassy riverbank just out of range of the bridge's torches.

Tina hated every second of it. She couldn't technically complain since people were still doing their work--guards were at their posts, watches were being kept, and so forth--but aside from being *really* embarrassing, the reckless screwing was a serious logistical problem. Even assuming their new bodies were clean of whatever STDs existed in this world, characters in FFO didn't come in forms other than young and maximumly healthy, which meant they were in for major baby-daddy drama a few months down the road if people didn't knock this shit off.

She was already planning to ask Zen about checking to see if this world had some kind of contraceptive potion or spell or whatever. For now, though, there was nowhere in the base that didn't feel like being off camera at a porno shoot. Tina ended up spending the entire night pacing the base's three bridges while alternating between crippling panic over SilentBlayde and her brother and rage over the irresponsibility going on behind her. The only positive note so far as she was concerned was that at least she had time to think up all the quests she needed people to do.

When dawn broke at last, she stomped up from the bridge into the main hall to drag the large table from the alchemy classroom into the open yard between the clustered buildings. She grabbed paper and a quill from the scribe's workshop and struggled to use the stupid feather and inkpot to make a list of all the tasks she'd come up with. She worked fast because she assumed people would be eager to get to work. After all, quests were the only way any of them were getting new equipment or vital survival items like potions. *Surely* everyone would be in a rush to get their hands on the good stuff before it was all snatched up, but by the time she finished her list, the only one who'd emerged was Frank.

"Morning, Roxxy," her fellow tank said cheerfully, fastening his dented breastplate back onto his muscular torso. "Sleep well?"

"I slept great," she lied, glaring over his shoulder at the grassy slope under the trees where bodies still lay nestled together under cloaks despite the bright light of the rising sun. "Please tell me we're not the only ones up."

Frank chuckled. "Well, people were pretty busy last night. Lots of horizontal tangos going down, if you get my drift."

Tina dragged her hands over her face. "This is *ridiculous*. I didn't bring all these people here so we could have an orgy!"

"Aww, don't be too hard on them," Frank said, flexing his biceps at her. "We're all so young and good-lookin'. Add in the mortal peril and away-from-home parts, and I'm not surprised one bit that folks are all over each other. We're just like a bunch of sailors at port."

She looked at him in horror. "*We?* Have you been in on this too?" The words were barely out of Tina's mouth before she realized how rude she was being.

Thankfully, Frank just grinned. "Naw," he said, not even blushing. "Don't get me wrong. I was something in my wilder days, but as young as this new body is, I'm not interested in flings. I like my women like I like my whiskey: mature and complicated."

Tina could only groan at that. "I'm going go kick over some blankets and make people get clothes on." she muttered, standing up. "The sun's getting high, and we don't have time for this bullshit."

But as she turned toward the part of the camp she'd started thinking of as "Inappropriate Sex Hill," Frank grabbed her arm. "That's not what's really bothering you, is it?"

She gave him a warning glare, but as always, it rolled right off him. "Maybe I'm out of line here," the old tank said gently. "But you're not normally the kind who gets flustered by the small stuff."

Tina did *not* consider three hundred people screwing and sleeping in when they could be attacked at any moment "small stuff," but that wasn't what Frank was asking.

"You're missing your fella, ain't ya?"

"SB's not my 'fella,'" she said bitterly. "And of *course* I'm worried. I sent him out alone to get James yesterday, but he's still not back, and now the Bastion's up, which means he can't stealth. He could be trapped or captured or *dead* or--"

"You know he ain't none of that," Frank chided. "Not being able to sneak around like usual might slow him down a bit, but your Blayde's a bright boy with a silver tongue that could sell milk to cows. I'm sure he'll clever his way back to your side soon enough. Meanwhile, you should try relaxing a bit as well. We're finally safe, and no offense, but you look like your rock's been wound too tight. It ain't like an army's gonna pop out of the river. Why don't you take a page from everyone else's books and relax. Go get some breakfast from the kitchen or something."

Tina's mouth was already open to tell him she couldn't possibly relax when she processed the last thing he'd said. "Wait, kitchen? Since when do we have a *kitchen?*"

"I don't know," Frank said with a shrug. "But it's real popular. Everyone who's not still asleep is in there--"

Tina whirled and stomped toward the buildings. "Watch my table!"

"Watch it do what?" Frank yelled, but Tina was already inside, stomping through the auditorium-sized main hall and out the back toward the good cooking she could now smell on the wind.

Her body didn't even react. As a stonekin, Tina had no interest in real food. She was fueled by magical rocks, and she didn't even seem to need one of those every day. As such, she hadn't even thought about breakfast, which was kind of nice in an efficient, no-need-to-worry-about-pesky-biology sort of way. For the fleshy members of her raid, though, breakfast seemed to be as important as screwing, because when she reached the Cooking Trainer's hut, the place was overrun. The crowd was so thick, she couldn't even get through the door. She was still trying when she spotted Killbox coming out with something golden and delicate-looking clutched in his giant hands.

"Morning, boss!" he said cheerfully.

Tina reached out to grab his shoulder, pointing at the thing in his palm, which couldn't possibly be what it looked like. "What is that?"

"French croissant," he said, taking a giant bite of the crustiest, flakiest, most buttery pastry Tina had ever seen.

"Where in the hell did we get croissants?"

"I dunno," Killbox said. "But there're plenty more if you want one."

Roxxy didn't care. Tina, however, had never wanted something more in her life. She pushed past the still-eating Berserker into the kitchen. The moment she walked inside, the smell of freshly baked bread filled her senses. Dozens of players were packed into hastily arranged tables, eating folded omelets, croissants, and entire loaves of fresh bread with butter. Others were eating sausages and grits topped with a sweet vinegar-reduction sauce and caramelized onions. One table at the back was yelling something about more crème brûlée, and a fire-spec Sorcerer in the

222

kitchen laughed as he said he could only cast so fast. She was still staring at it all in dumbstruck wonder when NekoBaby grabbed her arm.

"Roxxy! Come sit with me!"

Tina let herself be pulled over to a heavy-duty stool.

The cat-girl sat down next to her with a giant plate heaped full of bacon and sausage. "Chai tea latte?" she asked, offering Tina her mug.

Tina took it dumbly, staring at the adorable image of a happy cat someone had drawn on the surface with foam art. "Neko," she said when her brain finally started working again. "What in the world is going on? Where did all this amazing food come from?"

"Ish--mmph..." The jubatus paused to swallow a mouthful of bacon. "It's coming from awesome town, that's what! Get this: profession skills are *legit* now. If you've maxxed out cooking, that means you're a world-class chef! We found that out this morning when JordanRamsey over there volunteered to cook. Dude just grabbed a pan and started churning out soufflés. Then the herbalists figured out which local plants matched which herbs from back home and booyah! Welcome to Camp Comeback's gourmet cafeteria. Here, try some!"

The cat-girl grabbed a piece of thick-cut bacon and pointed it at Tina's face like a weapon. The smell of the perfectly cooked smoked pork filled her senses like a promise. Looking at it, she already knew that the texture would be both succulent and crispy. She thought about how good it would taste, how the perfectly rendered fat would melt on her tongue. How it wasn't a fucking magical rock.

But as wonderful as her human memory told her the bacon would be, her body didn't want it. It didn't want any of this amazing food--not the warm mug of tea in her hands or even a coffee. It didn't care about sex, didn't want to be kissed or touched. It was a fucking stone robot that ran on air, water, and magical goddamn rocks.

Staring at the perfect piece of bacon she wasn't ever going to eat, Tina didn't know if she wanted to laugh, cry, or kill something. After her horrible night, violence almost won. She could already see herself leaping

223

to her feet in rage and flipping the table over, cursing the whole irresponsible room right out the door. But as righteous as that would make her feel, it was just being the monster again--a giant child throwing a tantrum because everyone else had food and sex and knew where their loved ones were, and she didn't.

But Tina was determined not to be that person anymore. It didn't matter if she had to drag herself kicking and screaming to get there. She was going to be a goddamn raid leader, a *good* one who didn't flip tables. So, instead of screaming, Tina put NekoBaby's chai tea latte down on the table and stood up to face the crowd. They'd been watching her, too, proof that everyone still saw her as a threat, because they all went quiet as she rose.

"What do you think you're doing?"

The whole room looked down at their plates, fidgeting under her disapproving gaze like kids with their hands caught in the cookie jar.

"I know it's tempting to slack off now that we're no longer on the run," she said. "But there's an army out there getting ready to attack us, and most of you don't have weapons or armor yet. There are still players out there hiding like rats to avoid being captured and tortured. Some of you were those players just yesterday, and yet you're in here making latte art and baking pastries. I told you last night that we'd be giving out quests so that everyone could pitch in and make sure we all don't die. I was there this morning, but you were all too busy *fucking* and eating fancy food to show up."

People winced at that, but unlike back in the Room of Arrivals, Tina was glad to see it, because they weren't wincing at her. They were cringing in shame, which meant she had a hope of derailing this hedonism train without having to be an ogre about it.

"Mealtime's over," she said, pointing at the chefs, who instantly scattered. "The kitchen's closed until tonight. If you want to eat, you'll have to work for it, so wipe your mouths, grab whatever gear you have, and meet me in the courtyard to get your quests."

With that, she turned on her heel and stormed out, finally giving in to her rage as she stomped back to her table in the courtyard. Frank wisely said nothing when she appeared, just brushed off her seat so Tina could sit back down. She was restacking the notes she'd made when the first of the players scuttled into the courtyard and started forming a line in front of her.

***

The quests idea worked even better than she'd hoped.

From the moment she'd closed down the kitchen, her table had been crowded with a steady stream of players patiently waiting for work. Part of Tina wanted to stay belligerently angry, but that was just her grief over bacon and croissants talking. It was hard to be actually mad when everyone who came up seemed to eager to help out, but she kept up the gruff exterior, anyway. It kept the line moving better.

"Name, level, class, and professions, please," she said to the ichthyian in front of her.

"Julia, level thirty-five, Assassin," the skinny fish-girl replied at once. "I'm only halfway through leatherworking, though."

Tina eyed her ratty leather armor and lack of weapons and made a note on her list. "I can't give you a combat quest because of the Bastion and your lack of weapons, but we have lots of medium-armor classes with broken gear. Go to the leather workers' hut and craft ten suits of level-thirty Dustwalker armor. Do that, and you'll get a set of Dustwalker Blades."

The girl's fish eyes lit up at the mention of new weapons, and Tina bit back a grin. Not five minutes ago, she'd given another player a job to make a batch Dustwalker Blades in exchange for a suit of Dustwalker Armor. When both jobs were finished, they'd both be rewarded, and she'd still have nine extra of each. This quest-giver deal was *such* a scam. She just wished it wasn't costing her an entire base's worth of crafting supplies to

225

run it. Even with the materials cost, though, it was totally worth it. Everyone stayed busy, her army was gearing up, and once they all had weapons, she had plenty more work that needed to be done. And speaking of.

"Here's your quest," Tina said, handing the girl a paper with the basics--name, level, make ten sets of this armor, get this sword as reward-- scrawled across it. "Once you're armed, combat quests will be available if you want them. Now scoot on over to Frank, and he'll put you on the master list so we know where you are and what you're doing. Once that's taken care of, you can get to work."

The blue-scaled girl gave Tina one of those horrible, piranha-mouthed ichthyian smiles. "Thanks, Roxxy!" she said as she hurried over to the line in front of Frank.

"Welcome," Tina said, turning to the next person. "State your--"

"BouncyMako," the male jubatus said excitedly. "Level sixty, Ranger, bowyer, herbalist. Ready to fight!"

"So I see," Tina said, checking him over. "You have a decent weapon, and level sixty's high enough." She nodded and looked him in the face. "We have an unknown number of Royal Knight patrols in our immediate area. Not enough to attack us directly, but they're still watching our movements and harassing the lower-level players who are out scavenging. There are several level-eighty groups already in the city, doing kill quests for knights, but they need help. Get up to the rooftops, and tell them where the targets are. Assist in the elimination of five Royal Knight patrols, and you'll get..."

The Ranger had functional weapons and armor, which meant she couldn't offer gear, but they had almost no money to give out, and "experience points" weren't a thing anymore. Then she noticed the cat-man's boots were an awful mustard color, which usually meant they were a shit loot drop from below level sixty.

"And you'll get a rare set of level-sixty boots," she finished.

"Upgrade! Rock on!" BouncyMako said with a fist pump.

226

Smiling at her cleverness, Tina sent him off to Frank. "*Next!*"

"Next" was a timid-looking level-twenty Knight. He was one of those players who were too low-level to be of any use in combat, and he had no crafting professions at all. That was fine, though. Tina still had something he could do.

"Take a sack from the pile behind me and fill it with food any way that you can," she ordered. "You can use fishing, hunting, looting the nearby city, whatever. Just don't use any food you find here in the base, and if you go into the city, watch out for Royal Knights. We have scouts and killer-teams out there running sweeps, so if you get in trouble, just call for help. If you complete this quest, you will be rewarded with Camp Comeback faction points."

The Knight's shoulders slumped. "Just faction points? Not gear?"

He wasn't high-level enough to be worth making gear for, but there was no good in telling him that, so Tina went for another angle. "Faction points are vital," she said. "If you don't get some points every day, you don't eat. Don't get any for two days, and it gets even less pleasant. There will be rare food items and easier work opportunities as your points increase, so it's worth it. Just keep at it."

The lowbie knight grabbed his sack and grumbled his way over to Frank.

When she was sure he wasn't going to cause a stink, Tina moved on to the next person. And the next. And the next and the next. She sent people out for food, lumber, cloth, scrap metal, stone, and more. Anything they could possibly use that someone could carry, she sent players out to collect.

Sometimes, people even volunteered real-life skills they thought might be useful. Tina almost jumped for joy when she got a senior civil engineer from Chicago. "CraftyJohn" was quickly put in charge of building fortifications around the completely open field that surrounded Camp Comeback. After getting a list of everything he'd need, Tina sent out a whole new round of collections. She also started assigning human

227

bulldozers--i.e. Knights and Berserkers--to do whatever he told them for a set period of time. Even low-level strength classes were ten times stronger than a normal human. Tina had no problem making them into living construction equipment.

But while CraftyJohn was a great find, the best part of the entire morning arrived in the form of a tall human Sorcerer wearing a crown of living flames atop his short-cropped black hair.

"Whoa," Tina said, leaning back on her anvil-seat. "Are you wearing the *Prometheus's Fire* movie-promo-event crown?"

It was a *super* rare item. The last time she'd checked, it had been selling online for over three thousand real-world dollars and not just because it looked totally boss. Even though it wasn't technically a level-eighty piece of gear, its chance to add extra fire damage every time you cast was so overpowered that some high-end raiders still wore it. Now that she was looking, the rest of the guy's gear was equally impressive. She didn't know caster stuff nearly as well as her plate and swords, but she was certain his gorgeous robes came from the Dead Mountain. She was trying to place his impressive golden staff when the tall Sorcerer cleared his throat.

"Richard," he said crisply. "Sorcerer. Level eighty. Tailoring and Artificer professions. And I'd like to join your guild, if I may."

Tina had to put her hands on the table to steady herself after that. "Wait," she said slowly, eyes darting from one piece of amazing legendary gear to the next. "You aren't just some random Richard, are you?"

"I am formerly the guild master of *Richard's Inferno*," Richard replied in a steady, almost monotone voice devoid of sarcasm or humor. "We were the number-one-ranked guild in the world until our implosion. I was also the leader the of late *Richard's Ruin*, though that name ultimately proved to be too ironic even for my tastes. Currently, I'm a member of the Red Sands guild, but I'd like to change that."

He said all of this like it was nothing, but as he spoke, the people waiting in line behind him started freaking out.

"Holy shit, that's *Richard*!"

"Guys! Guys! Richard's still alive!"

"I'm using his spec right now!"

Tina wasn't quite at the random shouting point, but inside she was jumping up and down. Poaching someone as geared and elite as *the* Richard--FFO's number-one Sorcerer--from CincoDeMurder would be the coup of the century. There was no way she was saying no, but since this was a coalition, she still had to ask.

"You're absolutely welcome in the Roughnecks," she told him, standing up to offer him her hand. "But before you join, I have to know-- why do you want to switch guilds? Is there drama with Red Sands that I need to go resolve?"

Richard shook his head, moving it beneath the floating crown of flames, which didn't even wobble. "No drama. I'm just tired of being called a Care Bear all the time. I'd like to be with a guild who appreciates that PVP isn't the only worthwhile way to play FFO."

"Well, hells yeah, you're hired!" Tina said, grabbing his hand and shaking it. "Welcome to the Roughnecks! Go talk to Anders or Zen. They're in medical and easy to find. They'll tell you all the rules of the guild and get you set up."

He nodded. "And what is my quest?"

It took Tina several seconds to remember what he'd originally been in line for. "Oh, right." She grinned. "A hard worker! I like that. Since you're so geared, you're on patrol killing duty. After you get set up in our guild, talk to Killbox to join a Roughneck kill squad."

"Accepted," Richard said in his weirdly flat manner. "Thank you, Roxxy."

"No problem! Happy to have you!" She beamed as the tall Sorcerer walked away, rubbing her hands together with glee.

"He famous or something?" Frank whispered as she sat back down on her anvil.

"He's a legend," Tina replied. "Dude's played FFO since *alpha*. How else do you think he scored 'Richard' as his character name? He's been a world-ranked raider since the very first raid boss came out. I don't even play casters anymore, and even I've heard about his Sorcerer guides."

"Well, glad to have him aboard, then," Frank said, getting back to his job.

"Glad" didn't begin to cover it. If she hadn't still been so worried about SB and James, Tina would have floated away. But even the joy of nabbing the world's greatest Sorcerer couldn't banish the fear gnawing at her insides as the sun crept higher and higher into the sky. Every time she had to give a quest to a high-level player, she was tempted to send them on a rescue mission, but it was just too dangerous. She didn't even know what part of the city SB was in anymore. Any team she sent out after him would have to include a who's who of her best people, and she just couldn't justify it. She had too many people here to protect.

Tina didn't have to like it, though. She consoled herself by assigning several groups to nearby search-and-rescue quests. Players had been arriving in a steady stream since last night, but there were probably still plenty out there who were hiding in basements and didn't know yet that there was safety to be had. The more players she could gather, the stronger they'd be and the better everyone's chances got. But while the rescue missions helped a bit, nothing could make her smile by the time the line in front of her finally petered out.

"Hoo-*ee*," Frank said, stretching his arms over his head. "That was some mighty delegation! These here quests are the weirdest way to assign work I've ever seen, though. I don't know how you came up with so many off the top of your head like that."

Tina shrugged. "It's not that hard. Quests have a pattern to them, and we've all done thousands. I'm just happy it worked. You'll notice that no one had serious objections even when they got nothing but faction points. That never would have flown if I'd invented my own system, but we're all so used to it being this way in-game, nobody thought to protest."

230

"So what's next?" Frank asked.

Tina thought a moment. "You used to be a chemical plant manager, right?"

"Yup," he said. "Before I retired, I was in charge of over fifteen hundred--"

"Great!" She clapped Frank on the armored shoulder. "You hang here and manage all the random problems people are sure to come back with. If you don't know the answer, send them to me."

"Can do," Frank said. "Where will you be?"

Tina took a longing look at the city, where SB was still missing, then she sighed and waved a hand down at her armor. "Maintenance."

"Complete Rebuild" might have been more accurate. Her once-amazing suit of sun-metal plate was dented and warped almost beyond recognition. Every piece had gashes or outright holes, and the padding inside was stiff with dried blood, both hers and her enemies'. There was blood on the exterior, as well, plus dust from the Deadlands and ash from the burning city. With a little makeup on her face, she could have made a very authentic zombie.

"I'm gonna visit Assets for a portable mana-anvil and some materials to repair my baby," she said, rising from her seat. "I'll be on the north side of the camp by the river if you need me."

Leaving Frank to kick his feet up on the table like a boss, Tina went in search of the East Bastion Trade Company guild leader. Fortunately, Assets was easy to find. The dapper elf had taken over a large stone building in the rear of the complex and stuffed it full of supplies. A train of Trade Company players, all of whom were somehow now wearing green-and-gold tabards, streamed in and out constantly as they filled requests. Assets himself was standing on top of a tall crate in the middle, wearing what looked like a brand-new Armani suit and checking each order against the list on his improvised clipboard.

Tina came over with a raised eyebrow. "Where'd you get the new duds?"

231

"Hello to you too, Roxxy," Assets replied without looking up. "The East Bastion Trade Company has several players with maximum Tailoring skill. When all this is over, I'd love to start a fashion revolution on the side. Robes! Pssh! We can do so much better than that. Spell-casters the world over will want to wear my collections."

"Well, just don't waste too much magical cloth."

"That's my line," the golden elf said, frowning down at her. "You are being extremely liberal with our very limited supplies. At this rate of consumption, we won't last long."

Tina shrugged. "Bricks of metal don't win wars unless we make them into swords. Think of it as an investment in our army."

"An army that has sworn no loyalty and is not formally assembled," Assets snapped, brandishing his clipboard at her. "These people can leave with their shiny new gear any time they like while we're left holding the empty bag."

"And where are they going to go?" Tina asked. "We're the only show in town."

"Never expect a population to act rationally, Roxxy. That's the crux of modern economics." He sighed. "But that's not why you came here, is it?"

"Nope," she said, handing him her own "quest." "I need to fix my armor, or I'll be no good on the front lines."

Assets' perfectly trim eyebrows shot up as he looked at her list. "These are some *very* expensive ingredients. Also rare. I'm not even sure if we have some of them."

Looking at the incredibly detailed list on his clipboard, Tina found that hard to believe. "This is mission critical. I'm the only tank here who can handle anything above a level eighty four-skull. Frank would be the other, but he's still too green to handle a serious threat on his own. I don't feel it's bragging to say that my gear is a strategically important asset. If it cracks, we're fucked."

"Fair enough," the elf said with a sigh, checking things off his list. "We only have enough for one round of repairs, though. You'll have to make it last."

"I'll do my best," Tina promised.

Assets snapped his fingers, and a crew of Trade Company workers loaded Tina up with a portable magic anvil and three crates of shining metal that smelled like warm sunlight. She thanked Assets and, arms piled high, trotted off to the north side of the island.

It was a surprisingly nice place to set up shop. To the north, a waterfall poured down the green mountains into the high foothills before tumbling into the city, where it flowed south, eventually splitting around Camp Comeback's hill. The swiftly running water had been clear and blue last night, but the wind must have shifted, because today the flow was murky with ash. Tina saw dozens of players, not to be discouraged in their quests, spread out along the river's banks. Armed with makeshift fishing poles, they doggedly tried to fill their quest sacks with as many fish as possible.

It was a bright, idyllic scene. The fires must be burning themselves out at last, because the haze of smoke was no longer blocking the sky, leaving the noonday sun to shine bright and warm as she sat down in the thick grass to begin removing her armor.

It took some doing. The silver elven runes that held her suit together were hidden in hard-to-reach places. She had to bend herself into a pretzel, but eventually she got her chest plate, leg plates, and so on to unlock.

As each piece came off, Tina sighed in relief. It hadn't felt like it, but she'd been in this suit for days now. Other than her boots, she hadn't removed any of it since before the transition. When all dozen or so pieces were removed, her whole body felt as light as a feather. Even with the strength the armor gave her, there was no denying how murderously heavy the stuff was, or how disgusting. The inside looked worse than the outside.

Apologizing to her precious suit, Tina knelt in the grass by the river and started scrubbing each piece of her gear with the large brush from the blacksmithing crate Assets had given her. When it was all clean and lying in the sun behind her, Tina looked down to discover that *she* was every bit as gross.

Since clothes provided no ability bonuses, Tina had never bothered equipping Roxxy with a shirt or pants. She didn't even have underwear, though on closer inspection, she found she didn't need it. Her stone body had none of the things underwear was designed to cover: no nipples or orifices of any sort other than her mouth. Everything else was just smooth curved stone, like a statue.

Noticing that creeped Tina out more than anything else had so far. Even her diet of magical rocks didn't feel as weird and dehumanizing as discovering there was literally nothing between her legs. Now that she thought about it, she realized she hadn't had to pee since the transition. She drank water, but it was like topping off the fluids in a car. She was just replacing what she'd lost to evaporation and blood loss, not keeping cells alive.

None of this should have surprised her since stonekin were magical amalgams created by the Bedrock Kings to fight the undead, but knowing that you were a magical rock monster was very different from actually seeing the proof. Tina must have stood on the riverbank for a good five minutes, poking and prodding her stone body, which, since she was naked by human standards, definitely got her some weird looks from the nearby fishers. But though she could feel the sun's warmth on every inch of her, Tina didn't feel exposed. She just felt like a rock. A super *cut* rock.

"Damn," she said, running a hand over her literally chiseled abs. Her legs and arms were blocks of muscle as well, which made sense considering she wore six hundred pounds of plate armor all day every day. She still didn't understand why a stonekin needed boobs or shapely hips or a perky butt, but it was comforting to know she still had something human left. Ironically, Roxxy's sexless statuesque body actually had more curves than Tina's real one, which was just unfair. Especially since she no longer seemed to care if anyone noticed.

Sighing at that depressing thought, Tina dunked herself into the water. As expected from a mountain river, the Heraldsford was shockingly cold, but other than a mental preference for warmth, her stonekin body didn't seem to care about temperature. She scrubbed her granite skin with the same coarse brush she'd used on her armor, taking advantage of her newly discovered ability to hold her breath for crazy-long periods of time to dunk her head and wash each of her copper dreadlocks one by one.

When she was clean from head to toe, Tina hauled herself out of the river and got out the enchanted anvil, a freestanding hunk of fire-enchanted iron the size of a car engine, and put her battered breastplate on it. She wasn't entirely sure how the thing worked, but just like her Knight class abilities, the knowledge from her max-level blacksmithing skill came the moment she reached for it. A few test hits with the hammer, and she was quickly removing dents and warped bits like a pro. When she reached for the box of sun-metal, though, all she could say was, "Ooo."

While not a lore buff like SilentBlayde and James, Tina still knew that sun-metal was primal stuff. The ancient celestial elves had had a method for capturing the first rays of the Sun every morning and turning them solid. That primordial light had been made into many things, metal being just one of them. But while that knowledge was long lost, there were still elves alive--or at least, there had been in the game--who could make sun-metal using alchemical contraptions, which was probably where this box had come from.

Even with that, though, the metal was super rare and expensive. And pretty. *Oh,* so pretty. It felt like steel, but it shone the same yellow-white as the sun did the very first moment it came over the horizon. It was warm to the touch and had an inner light that gleamed even in total blackness. It was a real shame she had to alloy it with earth-imbued steel, but her blacksmithing skills told her that pure sun-metal was vulnerable to cold and cold-based attacks. Sighing in disappointment, Tina beat the

235

metals together with her magical hammer, turning the lovely golden bricks into much more sturdy yellow-tinged steel. When it came time to beat it into her breastplate, though, that was when Tina finally came to understand what "forged by the gods" really meant.

As a top-level blacksmith, she could make some amazing armor, but none of it compared to this. She didn't understand how the layers of alloys could be so thin or so numerous or how the wave pattern on the inside worked at all. Maybe it reinforced kinetic distribution. She had no idea. The armor she'd won from the Dead Mountain was advanced far beyond her understanding, ringing under her blows with literal divine harmony.

Wiping her brow, Tina looked up at the sun gleaming in the sky. Anders had told her once that he could feel the presence of the divine Sun whenever he cast spells. She'd thought it was just his nerves at the time, but when she hammered the holy metal, Tina could have sworn she could feel divine eyes looking down on her, guiding the metal as it bent and re-formed itself beneath her hammer until, not fifteen minutes later, she proudly held up her whole, flawless breastplate.

It gleamed beautifully in the sunlight, making her yearn to brush and polish it even more. Her precious armor deserved no less, but she was getting worried about Frank, so she sighed and picked up the next piece, her poor mangled arm guard.

After that, she fell into a sort of divine meditative state as she worked. With the Sun guiding her hammer, her mind was free to worry about SilentBlayde. For the millionth time, she kicked herself for letting him go alone. She should have sent a team, should have turned the whole goddamn raid around. If she'd been wiser, less cocky, he'd be here with her.

She missed him. She missed his cheerfulness and the way he could always make her laugh. She missed his constant comforting presence in her shadow. She even missed his bad puns. Most of all, though, Tina missed having someone to talk to. She didn't really have any other real friends here. David was dead, Neko was a pain, DarkKnight was Frank now, and the other four Roughneck healers were all B-string raiders she saw once a week at best. She didn't know any of them half as well as they knew each other, and when they did speak to her, it was always as their raid leader, not as her.

Good and depressed, Tina pounded her hammer on a particularly large dent in her shield. Caught up in her work and her moping, she didn't notice the fisher-players pointing at the city until Killbox's shout made her jump. When she whirled around, one of the Roughnecks' kill patrols was running across Camp Comeback's northern bridge with their weapons drawn. On the other side, a rag-covered NPC was sprinting out of the city straight toward the incoming players. He didn't look like much of a threat to Tina, who was gearless anyway, so she just stood there and watched as Killbox's patrol moved in to intercept.

But Killbox didn't swing at the beggar. He and the other Roughnecks ran right past him, sprinting off the bridge toward the pack of Royal Knights who were chasing right on the beggar's heels.

Swearing loudly, Tina grabbed her weapons off the grass and ran in to cut the beggar off herself. Killbox and the others were still pursuing the knights, who'd turned right back around and started sprinting in the other direction the moment they saw the players, but she wasn't about to let some random NPC use *her* patrols as cover to sneak into *her* camp. She'd almost made it to the bridge when the fleeing NPC tore off his ratty cloak, revealing long golden hair and a dirty, tired elven face. It was the same face as a dozen other elves in the camp behind her, but Tina recognized the way he looked at her instantly, even without his mask.

"Blayde!"

Her sword and shield hit the ground as she sprinted forward, and she snatched him up in a huge bear hug. "I'm so glad you're alive!" she cried, burying her face in his sooty hair. "I was so worried!"

SB patted his hands against her shoulders, softly at first, then harder, his chest spasming as he choked. "Mercy, Roxxy! Mercy!"

237

She let go at once, and he dropped to the ground gracefully. But though she'd only been squeezing him for a few seconds, his face was still beet red, and he was panting hard.

"I'm so sorry," she said, kneeling down so she could look at his face. "Did I hurt you?"

SilentBlayde shook his head and looked determinedly at his feet. "I'm not... that is..." His face got even redder. "What happened to your *clothes*?"

Tina blinked and looked down, realizing far too late that she was still naked. She paused, waiting for the mortification to kick in, but just like earlier when she'd noticed the players gawking at her by the river, it didn't come.

That was slightly alarming. Just a few days ago, the thought of being naked in front of SB would have had her climbing the walls. Now it barely even fazed her. She was far more concerned with how pale he was around the blush, how tired and bloody and *wounded.*

"Oh shit, dude," she said, reaching out to steady him. "You need heals! What happened?"

"It's a long story," he said weakly. "But I... I couldn't get James. I'm so sorry."

Tina's breath caught, and then she shook her head. "It'll be what it'll be," she said firmly. "He's the one who decided to run. He can fend for himself for a bit. I'm just happy you're alive, and speaking of."

She grabbed a low-level Cleric--who had been fishing nearby--and ordered him to dump as much healing as he could spare into SB. It wasn't enough to get him back to full, but he still looked worlds better when it was over. The healing euphoria left him weaving drunkenly, so Tina helped him down the hill to the grassy stretch by the river where she'd been working.

"Sit," she ordered.

SB flopped down in the grass by her anvil, leaning toward the magically warmed steel as if it were a cozy fire. Tina sat down beside him, smiling like an idiot when their hands met seemingly of their own accord.

"I really missed you," she said, squeezing his fingers gently so she wouldn't hurt him again. "I can't say how happy I am that you're back safe."

"I missed you, too, Tina," he whispered, leaning his head against her shoulder.

Tina breathed in deeply. Even when it was sweaty and dirty, she could still smell the scent of the clear sky drifting up from his golden-yellow hair. The scent fogged her brain and sent it spinning. Her body remained annoyingly inert, but it was so nice to feel *something*, Tina didn't even care that it was turning her into an idiot.

"It wasn't the same around here without you," she said when she regained the ability to use words. "No puns at all."

He chuckled weakly. "Things too square, then?"

"More like a rhombus of insanity," she tossed back.

"Good thing I'm back. I've got an *angle* on the problem."

"I appreciate your *acute* help."

"I take it everyone else has been *obtuse*?"

Tina couldn't take it anymore. She threw her head back with a groan that turned into a laugh. SilentBlayde joined her, both of them falling backward to lie on their backs in the warm grass.

"God, I missed you," she said, sighing, and smiled at the blue sky. "It's been awful not having you around. I was a wreck. You don't even know."

He wiggled happily at her words. "You seem to have done all right for a supposed wreck," he said, pushing up on his elbow to look around at the busy base. "This place is incredible! I can't believe you slapped all of this together in one night and a morning."

"Never underestimate the power of players in large numbers," Tina told him proudly. "And I didn't do it alone. We've got a multi-guild coalition thing going with the East Bastion Trade Company and Red Sands. CincoDeMurder in particular has been super useful. And surprisingly politic."

SB's blue eyes flashed with an emotion Tina didn't recognize. For a stupid, crazy moment, she hoped it was jealousy. Whatever it was, it vanished instantly, replaced by polite interest.

"Cinco's here?" he said casually. "I'm not surprised he survived. That guy is a combat monster in game and out. I used to merc for Red Sands whenever they were short for guild-versus-guild battles. They're good players." He tilted his head at her. "How did you end up working together?"

She told him the story of what had happened after she'd sent him after James. As she talked, SB stretched back out in the grass beside her, which only made everything better. She couldn't remember being happier than she was right now, lying in the sun while SilentBlayde rested next to her, their arms touching. Then he tilted his head to rest it on her shoulder, and things got even better. The surge of joy she felt was so strong, she got lost in the middle of explaining of the quest system, which was fine since SB didn't seem to be listening anymore, anyway. He just lay there beside her, staring at the sky, breathing slowly, like he wanted to stretch each breath out.

Since he wasn't looking at her, Tina took the rare opportunity to study him. For all the changes being trapped in FFO had brought, SB had always been her constant. She'd only ever known him as the elf Assassin, SilentBlayde, and other than things being real now, he didn't look or act any differently now than he had before the transition. If anything, being sucked into FFO had just made him feel even more... *him.*

Tina took a moment to consider that. Before she'd stupidly sent him after her idiot brother, Blayde had said he couldn't give her anything of Haruto, his real self. His secrets had always been a huge problem--not because she was worried about what he was hiding but because he was hiding them from *her.* No matter how close they got or how much she let

240

him in, he'd never trusted her enough to do the same, which kind of made any hopes she had for a long-term relationship back home impossible. Now, though, Tina had to wonder if she really needed to know. They were here, in another world, *together*. Whatever he was hiding back home couldn't reach them in this place. Maybe she should just let her worries go and grab the happiness that was in front of her. Everyone else in camp seemed to be doing so with reckless abandon. Why not them?

Just the possibility was enough to make her giddy. Her stonekin body's complete disinterest in fleshy concerns--and lack of compatible parts--would be a problem, but Tina bet she could make it work. Would he be willing to do the same, though? Part of her readily believed he'd give them a try, at least, but another, much more gun-shy part remembered how badly things had gone when she'd tried to get closer to him by suggesting the JET program. What if SilentBlayde's big secret was that he only liked her as a friend and couldn't bring himself to tell her?

Tina squirmed uncomfortably. Maybe she *wasn't* ready to throw caution to the wind just yet. She was about to get up and get back to business when SB rolled over to hug her arm.

She froze. Without her armor, she could feel every inch of his warm, solid chest. When her head stopped spinning, she looked down to see that his eyes were closed. She wasn't sure if he was asleep or just resting against her, but she didn't move a muscle. She just lay there, as still as the stone she resembled, barely daring to breathe until, far too soon, he pushed himself up again.

"Sorry," he said, his face flushed. "I'm sure you have stuff to get back to."

"No, no, it's fine," Tina said in a rush. "Though you should probably go to the hospital. Those heals got you off death's door, but you still look like you could use a lot more."

He blinked in surprise. "We have a hospital?"

Tina nodded proudly. "I had Zen set one up in the former first aid building. We're totes professional and shit now."

SB laughed. "I'll have to go and see it, then," he said, but he still didn't move. Tina didn't, either, and not just because she didn't want this to end. Talking about how injured SB had been reminded her of the other giant worry that had weighed her down all night and day. The one she couldn't keep putting off.

"I'm sorry if you don't want to talk about this," she said quietly, clenching her fists in the grass. "But I need to know what happened on your mission. Where's James? Is he still..."

She couldn't finish. Her brother had been a thorn in her side since they were kids, but that didn't mean she didn't love him. It was *because* she loved him that his antics made her so angry. James never seemed to understand how much he could hurt her. If he'd run away and died out there alone, she would never forgive him, or herself for letting it happen.

When SB didn't answer at once, a lump the size of a softball formed in Tina's throat. She was about to beg him to just spit it out when SilentBlayde said, "He defeated me."

She couldn't have heard that right.

"Wait," Tina said, shaking her head to make sure there wasn't still water in her ears. "What do you mean, '*defeated*'?"

"He beat me," SilentBlayde clarified, staring at the grass like he wanted to sink into it.

Tina gaped at him. "*How?* You're--"

"I know," he said, dragging his hands through his golden hair. "There was no way it should have happened. If this was still the game, it never could have, but your brother is a multiple black belt in real life. You and me and everyone else, we just played at being Knights and Assassins, but James has practiced fighting for years. He's the real deal, and when things got real, he was just better than me. In a lot of ways."

If it had been anyone except SB, Tina never would have believed it. It didn't seem possible that her weak, spoiled, easily discouraged brother-- the kid who'd dropped out of college and gotten their family into hundreds of thousands in debt for *nothing* rather than fail a few classes--was the same person Blayde was describing. She knew James was good at martial arts--she still had the kink in her arm where he'd broken it by accident trying to teach her a throw--but fights in this world weren't like sparring on a padded mat. They were real and terrifying and do-or-die, all the things the brother she knew couldn't handle. The whole thing just sounded crazy, but SilentBlayde had never lied to her before, and he certainly had no reason to lie about this.

"So where is he now?"

"I don't know," Blade said, shoulders slumping. "I was almost dead when our fight was over, so--"

Tina jumped. "Wait, James tried to *kill* you?"

"It was self-defense," SB said quickly, looking more ashamed than ever. "Things got... I let things get out of hand. Anyway, James defeated me and ran, and then the Bastion went up, so I couldn't follow. Last I heard, he was still headed for the castle, but I don't know more than that." He slumped over, wrapping his arms around his stomach. "I'm sorry, Tina. I failed you."

"No," Tina said firmly, putting a giant stone hand on his shoulder. "*I'm* sorry. I should never have sent you alone. I was cocky. I underestimated James, both his danger and his stubbornness, and I underestimated how dangerous the city was. I made the wrong call on every count. This is my fault."

He shook his head frantically, but Tina didn't even let him say it. "My. Fault," she repeated firmly. "I never should have involved you in my family drama. If James is that determined to go do his bullshit, fuck it. I'm tired of trying to mom him, anyway. He can deal with the consequences of his actions on his own for once. I'm just glad to have you back."

She'd hoped that would make him smile, but SB only looked grimmer. "There's more," he said quietly, meeting her eyes at last. "Malakai's alive."

"No, he's not," Tina said. "I killed him."

"You did," SB confirmed. "And then the Clerics at the castle rezzed him."

Tina's mouth fell open, and then she shot to her feet in fury. "Those cheating *fuckers*! Bosses don't get to rez!"

"Well, no one told him that, because he's up and on the warpath," SilentBlayde went on, speaking quickly and carefully, like he was trying his hardest to get this right. "He's still hunting players, but he doesn't seem to be hanging them anymore. He's taking hostages, and I'm pretty sure he means to use them against us. He knows about this base, and he's rallying all the knights plus a ton of other soldiers to attack. I don't know when, but it won't be long. They're already massing on the Royal Mile."

Tina's scouts had seen that much already, but this was still bad news. "Well, when he comes, we'll be ready," she promised, looking around at the progress CraftyJohn had already made improving the island's defenses. "This won't be like the extermination camp. We've got an army, too, and I know how Malakai fights now. He won't catch me unprepared again, and when I kill him this time, I'm going to make sure he *stays* dead."

She flashed SB a bloodthirsty grin, but he didn't return it. He just pushed himself shakily to his feet. "I think I'd better get to that hospital. If we're going to be in for a war, I can't afford to be walking around at low health."

"You shouldn't be, anyway," Tina said, bending over to collect the armor she'd finished repairing and then forgotten about in her joy. "Give me a second to put my stuff back on, and I'll take you over."

He nodded weakly and politely turned away while Tina strapped her armor back onto her sun-warmed stone body.

***

"Hey, hey, GabbyBlayde is back!"

Tina had barely led SB up the hill before NekoBaby shot out of nowhere, tackling the elf in her enthusiasm. "Did you staple-gun anyone good?"

Before he could answer, a bunch of the other Roughnecks ran over, surrounding SB in hugs, back pats, and teasing while NekoBaby doused him in green light and glowing flowers. When the heals were done, Neko led the whole crowd toward the kitchen, shouting something about mandatory victory pizza. The last thing Tina heard was SB's silvery laugh as their guild dragged him inside. Smiling at the happy chaos, Tina turned and went in search of Frank, who was still exactly where she'd left him.

"Hey there, boss," Frank said, taking his boots off the table. "Did I hear SilentBlayde was back?"

"He is," she said, lowering her voice. "But we've got trouble. What's our status?"

Frank nodded and pulled out the list he'd been keeping all morning, tracking every player's location and quest progress including the number of armaments made, tons of food acquired, the progress of the fortifications, the number of Royal Knight patrols killed, and so on. Just that would have made for quite an impressive list, but Frank had saved the best for the big dramatic finish: the number of players rescued.

"Wait," Tina said, grabbing the paper from him so she could see it for herself. "Two *thousand*? We've added two thousand lowbies?"

"Numbers don't lie," Frank replied with a grin.

Tina whistled in appreciation. She'd seen people streaming in all night and day but never counted them. "Where'd you put them all?"

"Main hall and some of the empty supply buildings. Most are below level fifty, and a scary number ain't even twenty yet. There's also some non-players mixed in as well."

"NPCs?" She scowled. "Who let them in?"

"I did," Frank said, looking her in the eyes. "They had kids with 'em. I can't say no to kids."

Tina smiled. "You're a good man, Frank."

Frank pshawed and waved the compliment away, but Tina was already bent over his list again. "I think our luck might finally be turning around," she said excitedly. "This quest thing worked a lot better than I thought it would, and now we've got even more people to send out. A few more days at this rate, and we'd *own* this town."

"But we don't have a few days, do we?" Frank asked, glancing nervously across the river toward the city. "Scouts keep coming back with reports of a big army massing at the castle. You don't get that many people together unless there's something you want to crush, and we're the only other show in town."

"It gets worse than that," Tina said, straightening up. "Leave the quests for now. I need you to find CincoDeMurder and Assets and have them meet me in the main hall. Tell 'em to bring their officers as well. We've gotta make a plan."

"Yes, ma'am," Frank said, giving her a salute before jogging off. Meanwhile, Tina turned around and walked back toward the kitchen, where every Roughneck in the base seemed to have gathered to watch NekoBaby trying to make SilentBlayde eat a pile of food bigger than he was. The crowd went silent when she walked in, smiles falling off their faces when they caught sight of hers.

"Officers, get yourselves together and meet me in the main building in five minutes."

Neko and the others got up reluctantly.

"What's going on, Roxxy?" Killbox asked.

"Fighting time is coming sooner than we'd like," she answered, turning to address the whole room. "I need all of you here to go out and spread the word. Everyone in the city needs to come back before dark. No one goes back out."

This declaration was met with looks of alarm and fear but no hustle.

"Move it, people," Tina ordered, clapping her hands.

The crowd broke up and ran off in different directions while the officers picked up their weapons and started toward the main building. Satisfied everyone was on task, Tina marched off to find the only Roughneck who hadn't shown up to Neko's impromptu 'Welcome back, SB!" party, who also happened to be the one she most wanted to talk to.

Despite hearing a lot about it, she hadn't actually been inside the temporary hospital Zen had set up in the medic trainers' hut. It turned out it looked a lot like a World War II–style field hospital. The building-- which was really more like a large shed--was filled with neat rows of cots and tons of cabinets stuffed full of supplies against the building's only wall. Most of the beds were occupied, but Tina didn't see many wounded. The majority of the people in here seemed to just be exhausted, starved players from the city.

Zen looked up when Tina barged in, her face instantly serious. "What's wrong?"

Glancing at the players watching them nervously, Tina walked over to Zen and leaned down to whisper in her ear. "I need you to take a handful of our best Rangers and go scout the Royal Mile."

"Okay, but why me?" she asked. "You've plenty of scouts."

"Because I need you to be *fast*, and you're the only one I trust to make sure no one overdoes it with the godly speed," Tina explained. "I also need someone who can look at a possible emergency situation and not freak out."

The former ER nurse nodded grimly and set down the plate of bread and water she'd been carrying. "I'll get right on it."

"Thanks," Tina said, but the Ranger had already shot out the door, moving so fast she looked like an electric-green blur.

Tina hurried after her before the players in the hospital could bombard her with questions. Everyone would find out soon enough. First, she had to make sure she had good answers, so she marched her way over to the island's main building.

The former Trainers' Hall was an open two-story stone-barn of a building. The inside was a massive circle ringed with six alcoves, one for each class in FFO. CincoDeMurder and Shankfest were already there, dragging Tina's quest-giving table into the middle of the room so they'd have somewhere to meet. Assets and his two attractive assistants showed up next. As Tina was piling paper and charcoal writing sticks onto the table, her officers started showing up. A lot of other players wanted to come in as well to find out what the ruckus was about, but Cinco, as on the ball as always, had stationed his PVP squads at both doors to keep this from becoming a circus. Even so, three guildmasters plus their officers made quite the crowd. There wasn't room for everyone at the table, so only Tina, Cinco, and Assets sat down while their officers stood behind them. When everyone was assembled, Tina straightened up and cleared her throat.

"All right, everyone," she said. "We've got fresh intel that says the Royal Knights are massing for an attack sooner rather than later. Also, Captain Malakai, their level eighty-one four-skull boss, is back in action."

Assets arched a golden eyebrow. "Was he out?"

"We killed him yesterday," Tina explained. "But it looks like NPCs can cast Raise Ally as well, because he's back up and leading the charge. We should expect big guns and a lot of troops."

"How many troops?" Cinco asked, scratching his newly shaved face.

Tina shook her head. "Not sure yet. Zen is scouting now, though, so we'll know soon."

"Should we wait for her?" Assets asked, tapping his clipboard nervously.

"No. We've lots to do before she gets back," Tina said, pulling out the list she'd borrowed from Frank. "My Knight officer has been keeping a tally of our numbers as we get new arrivals. Counting the three guilds we already had, we should now be able to field six full raids of level-fifty-and-over players. That's a lot of ass-whoop, but we've still got too many people without proper weapons and armor, so I think equipment needs to be our first priority. We should empty the warehouse into the forges and get our army geared."

Assets made a strangled noise at the word *empty*. "And what, pray tell, will we do for replenishment and materials *after* this battle is over?"

"This is the king's big push against us," Tina replied. "If we rout his army, he may not be able to hold the city anymore, which means this whole place could fall to us. That opens a lot of options for new supplies, including a siege on the bank. All the stuff in there is ours, anyway."

The elf's golden eyes gleamed with greed. "I do have a *great* deal of investments I'd like to reclaim."

"I'm more interested in deployment," Cinco said, grabbing one of the charcoal writing sticks Tina had brought to draw a quick, very rough map of Camp Comeback. "The Herald's River is deep and fast, which makes a water assault hard but not impossible. We've got three bridges here, here, and here." He drew three lines sticking out of the island north, east, and south. "Those are the obvious routes of attack. How are we covering them?"

"Seems obvious to me," Tina said, leaning in with her own pencil to draw a circle on each bridge. "Three bridges, three guilds. We'll each make a raid of our best people and take a bridge to hold. The other three raids are full of randoms who haven't worked together before, so we'll station them between us on the shore, where their lack of discipline and experience won't matter as much. That way, they'll only have to fight the guys who are willing to wade through deep water, and they'll be close enough to run over and reinforce any of the main bridge groups, should we need it."

"Sounds like a plan," Cinco said. "But why are we still using raids? There's no interface anymore telling us that we have to have fifty people. We could field specialized units: melee-only, ranged-only, spellcasters, that sort of thing."

"That would be great if we had more time to practice," Tina said. "But things are already hard enough without us having to learn an entirely new way of fighting together. Raids are what everyone's used to. Do you really want to add to our difficulties right now?"

"Good points," Cinco grumbled, scowling. "Fine, raids, it is."

"Glad you agree," Tina said. "Because I need your help. You used to put together big PVP mash-up groups all the time, so I want you to organize the non-guilded raids. You know, fill them with people, balance out high and low levels, assign chains of command, get them working together as a team, that sort of stuff."

"Can do," Cinco said, cracking his knuckles. "You wouldn't believe the randos I whipped into shape during pickup battleground season, and they were usually stoned. Organizing sober people fighting for their lives should be no problem at all."

"What about the players who are too low-level to fight?" Assets asked. "We have a *lot* of them now."

"There's going to be a lot more to this than just the front lines," Tina said. "We need fire-fighters, people to drag away the injured and dead, people to bring whatever food, weapons, potions, lumber, et cetera we might need during the battle. Messengers too. Most importantly, though, even low-level healers still have the crap version of Raise Ally, which can save lives if we're quick enough with it. The Royal Knights outnumber us, but that'll change fast if they're taking fatalities and we aren't."

"Sounds like you want a support raid," Assets said, scribbling notes on his clipboard. "I'll handle that. Have everyone too low to fight report to me, and I'll make sure our back end is covered."

Tina grinned. "That's what I'd hoped you would say."

With the main plan decided, everyone dug down into the details. There was a lot of talk about raid balances and supplies deployment. Intelligence characters did calculations in their heads to determine how many healers would be needed and how fast they should cast which spells to ensure maximum efficiency. Tina and Cinco were shoulder to shoulder over their map, plotting out the best arrangement for the melee on each bridge, when the chatter in the room suddenly died out.

Tina popped her head up to see Zen striding past the guards at the doors. She hadn't seen the Ranger look this grim--or dirty--since the battle against Grel'Darm, and she gripped the table, bracing for the worst.

"How bad is it?"

"Bad," Zen said, grabbing one of the sheets of paper and a writing stick. "It's not just the Royal Knights," she said, drawing two straight lines to represent the Royal Mile and then filling the space between with precise symbols in neat rows. "Each of these marks is a different unit. They've got archers, heavy cavalry, and garrison troops. Oh, and siege weapons."

She added several large boxes to the space between the lines that represented the Royal Mile, which was already so crammed full of marks, Tina couldn't count them all. "How many soldiers are in a unit?"

"They're all different depending on the sort," Zen replied, her already-grim face growing grimmer. "But we counted as many as we could, and our best estimate is there are ten thousand soldiers camped out on the mile already. Maybe more."

The already-quiet room grew deathly silent as everyone took that in.

"That's a lot of fucking guys," Cinco said at last, running a red-gauntleted hand through his short dark hair.

"It gets worse," Zen said.

"How can it get worse than being outnumbered thirty to one?" Assets demanded.

"They have players in cages," Zen replied, leaning down to draw a line of circles with the letter P in them. "A lot of them. I don't know what they're planning to do with them, but Malakai's moving the cages around the same way he does the siege weapons." She glanced up. "He's back, by the way."

251

"I heard," Tina said grimly, looking down at the map in dismay. Then she forced herself to straighten up. "Makes no difference, though. Big or small, a crap army is still a crap army. Let them come. They'll just break on us like everything else."

That set the crowd around the table whispering, and Assets rolled his eyes. "Not that I don't appreciate the can-do attitude, but we're talking about ten *thousand* soldiers ranging between level sixty and level eighty who are being led by a raid boss. We only have three hundred people over level fifty, and no raid boss. That's not good math."

"It's not about the numbers," Tina repeated with maximum bravado. "You played FFO from the auction house, so you haven't seen what a good raid can really do. The Roughnecks were trapped in the Deadlands after the game went down. We had to fight the Once King's *entire army* at the Order of the Golden Sun's fortress. Including Grel'Darm the Colossal, who could stomp Malakai into pretty-boy elf paste. We didn't even have a full raid, but we still won, and we can win here too."

Her heart was pounding, but Tina ignored it, standing up so she could face the entire group with her biggest shit-eating grin. "We've got three guilds here and six raids. That's more players fighting together than we ever had in FFO. We'll catch whatever the king throws at us and kick it back so hard he'll curse the day he decided to fuck with us. They thought FFO was a Nightmare? They ain't seen shit."

The others looked at each other nervously as she finished. SB in particular looked upset, but Cinco just grinned.

"Well, I'm sold," he said. "It ain't like we can surrender, and if we run, all that ass-whoop will just chase us across the zones, picking us off a few at a time. Much better to stand and fight here where we can control the battle. I always was the die-on-my-feet type."

"Well, *I'm* the type who'd rather not die at all," Assets said angrily. "This doesn't have to be an all-or-nothing deal. We haven't tried negotiating yet."

"You can't negotiate with these people," Tina said. "They hate us so much they have player death camps, and they outnumber us by a ludicrous amount. They're not going to listen to anything we say."

"Maybe not at first," the elf said. "But while I don't share your suicidal determination to fight to the last breath, I'm certain we can put up a bloody good showing, emphasis on the *bloody*. The king's on the warpath right now, but he might be convinced to sing a different tune and come to the table once half his army is floating facedown in the river. Especially if we employ some leverage."

Tina and Cinco shared confused looks. "What leverage do we have?"

Assets flashed them a sly smile and flipped his clipboard around to show them the base's inventory, tapping a delicate finger on a line in the middle. Frowning, Tina leaned closer, squinting to read the entry written in Assets's meticulous, clear handwriting.

Wind-Fire Powder, it read. *Twelve Barrels. One slightly cracked.*

Since they had finally made it inside the castle, James's plans involved strategizing and investigating avenues of possible escape from their luxurious new prison cell. But after a long day of traveling through the war-torn city as his sister's prisoner, fighting a duel to the near-death, and losing half his blood, his reality was passing out the moment he lay down on something that wasn't the ground. Even Ar'Bati must have succumbed to exhaustion, because when James awoke at last, the cat warrior was snoring in a padded armchair while Flameboyant was passed out next to him on the sofa with a fluffy white fur pillow over his face.

Squinting at the bright sunlight pouring in through the barred window, James sat up in the bed. His whole body still ached but not nearly as much as he'd expected. Thanking his lucky stars for player-character regeneration rates, he slid out from under the covers and tiptoed over to the window to see what they were in for.

War seemed to be the answer. The paved yard between the castle itself and the outer wall was packed full of soldiers. Large units of Royal Knights, City Guard, and even cavalry were marching toward the front gates while logistics troops followed them with wagons full of ammunition, weapons, armor, tar, and other terrifying things. The Bastion's golden shield was harder to see now that the sun was high, but it was definitely still there, glittering against the bright-blue sky.

The sight made him wince. He wasn't sure when exactly they'd been locked in here last night, but it had to be close to noon now. If Lady Siku had actually kept her promise and delivered those letters to the king this morning, surely someone would have come for them, but no one had. They hadn't even gotten breakfast, which could only mean one thing.

They were being ignored.

"Good morning, James," Flameboyant said, sitting up with a yawn.

His voice caused Ar'Bati to wake with a snort, and then the warrior shot to his feet. "Has the white she-devil returned?"

"Not yet," James said.

"Then there is nothing *good* about it," Fangs snarled, stalking over to the window to tug on the bars. But they were set deep in the stone, too much for even Ar'Bati's strength to move. "We are still prisoners."

"Hey, I'll take this cell over being locked up on the street any day," Flameboyant said, looking around at the beautifully decorated room. Then he spied the tiled bathing area, and his eyes lit up. "I'm going to take a bath!"

"How can you think of baths at a time like this?" Ar'Bati demanded.

Flameboyant shrugged. "How can you not? Have you smelled us lately?" He lifted a long finger. "This is a *tactical* bath, gentlemen. The king's much more likely to take us seriously if we don't reek like old gym socks."

That wasn't a bad point, actually. Given the way things were going, James wasn't optimistic about their chances of actually getting to King Gregory, but it couldn't hurt to clean up, and he definitely needed it. His armor and fur were caked in blood and soot--not exactly confidence inspiring.

"You seem awfully cheerful for someone who was ready to take his own life this time yesterday," Ar'Bati growled, glaring over his shoulder at the Sorcerer. "Are you certain you fully comprehend the seriousness of our situation?"

"'Course I do," Flame replied as he walked into the bathing area and started working the hand pump to fill the copper tub. "But that's the thing about hitting rock bottom: there's nowhere to go but up. Yesterday I was alone and thought I was crazy. Today I'm locked up with you guys in the fantasy equivalent of the Ritz-Carlton. That's a pretty big upgrade, from my perspective."

Ar'Bati harrumphed and turned back to the window, but James smiled. "I'll take the tub when you're done."

Flameboyant saluted and got back to pumping water. While he worked, James resumed his anxious gazing out the window.

"What do you make of all that?" he asked Ar'Bati, quietly, nodding down at the soldiers.

"I think rallying the army is a wise move," Ar'Bati replied. "The king will need all of his forces should our warning fail."

"I don't think that army's for the Once King," James said, stomach clenching. "If Lady Siku had kept her promise and showed the king our letters, we wouldn't be locked up in here. That's probably for Tina." He shook his head at the siege weapons being rolled toward the gate by teams of daft horses. "This is going to end in tragedy. If the king and the players beat each other bloody, there'll be no one left to fight the real enemy when the invasion arrives."

"Then we must make sure it does not," Ar'Bati growled, marching over to the locked doors. "*Hey!*" he bellowed, banging on the steel-reinforced wood. "We must speak with Siku!"

"*Shut up!*" yelled the guard outside. "The king's called an emergency war council. *Lady* Siku is currently at court, awaiting the results. She'll speak with you when she's ready."

Ar'Bati banged both fists on the door with a roar, but just like the barred windows, it didn't budge.

"Can we get breakfast, at least?" James called.

The guards laughed at that, and James sighed. "Worth a try."

Fangs snorted and started stalking around the room. Still not entirely healed, James went back to sit on the bed. He was contemplating going back to sleep--as they said in the army, rest when you could--when he became aware of a cold presence emanating from the floor beside him.

Wincing, James leaned over the edge of the bed to grab the Eclipsed Steel Staff off the carpet where he'd dropped it last night. Even with the late-morning sunlight streaming through the windows, the cursed weapon was a shadow across his hands, reflecting nothing. Its handle felt oily and unpleasant against his skin, and the twisted metal ornamentation at its top was unsettling to look at, like an optical illusion gone wrong. He supposed he should be grateful Lady Siku was arrogant enough to leave them their weapons, but he almost wish she'd taken the staff away. Just holding it made him feel uneasy, like something terrible was about to happen. He was looking around to see if there was a closet he could shove it into when the cold voice whispered in his mind.

You cannot deny the living their release.

"I should never have unwrapped you," James muttered, turning around on the bed so that Ar'Bati wouldn't see him talking to no one.

But you need me, the staff replied, its whispering voice strangely sympathetic, almost kind. *You suffer just as they do. I can help you end the pain. Yours and theirs.*

"No, thanks," James said angrily. "I don't want to kill anyone, least of all myself. I'm very against suicide. But feel free to shut yourself up."

I cannot die, it replied sadly. *Not until all the living have been freed of the torment of their existence. I owe them that mercy at least.*

James rolled his eyes at the staff's repetition of the undead party line. He was about to shove it under the furs so he wouldn't have to look at it anymore when he realized he was wasting an opportunity. They'd been fighting tooth and nail to get ahead of the Once King's plans, but the Eclipsed Steel Staff was a relic of the Dead Mountain. According to the Lich of Red Canyon, the cursed weapon had been made by the Once King himself. If it could *actually* talk--as in have a conversation beyond just trying to convince James to kill himself--maybe he could get it to drop some usable intel.

"So, staff," he said, changing his tone as he leaned closer over the weapon's slick black surface. "Do you know who I am?"

I know you are alive, the weapon replied. *But I will remedy that soon. Do not worry.*

That wasn't a threat. The weapon sounded legitimately concerned that James was trapped as one of the living, which he found interesting.

"But I like being alive," James said. "Most living things do. Why can't the Once King just accept that and let us be?"

A cracked gem wishes not to break further, the staff replied poetically. *But what has been shattered can never again be truly whole. You* think *you are happy because you are ignorant of what you have lost. You see this sad, ruined shadow and call it life because you have known nothing else. But* I *know. I remember the paradise that was, and I will not abide what you have become.*

"I suppose it makes sense that corrupted sun-metal would feel that way," James replied, tapping his fingers on the cold surface of the Eclipsed Steel. "Do you yearn to return to the days when you were pure and holy?"

More than you could ever know.

The sadness of those words made James want to cry. There was no more question of if the staff was intelligent. It took a certain depth of mind to feel that level of suffering. He was also intrigued by what the weapon claimed to remember. "So just how old are you?"

I am the oldest save for the Sun, the Moon, the Wind, the Water, and Zthr.

"Whoa," James said, shocked. "You're talking about back when you were a sun-metal staff, right? Because Zthr was the first Bird. If you're next after him, that would make you as old as the Age of Skies, and way before the Ghostfire or Necromancy." He frowned harder. "Also, what's the moon doing in that list? I know the Sun, the Wind, and the Water are all gods in this world, but FFO has no moon. Did it used to?"

Silence.

"Hey," James said, tapping the black metal with his finger, but though he could feel the cold radiating off it more strongly than ever, the staff didn't speak again. Since it wasn't trying to get him to kill himself or his friends, James couldn't exactly complain, but that didn't stop him from sighing. It wasn't every day you discovered your weapon was an intelligent magical item from primordial times. What else did it know about the history of this world? Did it have a previous owner? Or a name besides "Eclipsed Steel Staff?"

He was desperate to know, but before he could get the weapon to wake up again, the door to the bathroom burst open with a fragrant blast of stream.

"*Ahh,*" Flameboyant said, strolling out with his damp crimson robes over his arm, a fluffy towel wrapped around his waist, and a cloth binding his wet crimson hair high on his head. "I feel *so* much better. Who wants to go next? I left the tub heated."

Ar'Bati harrumphed, but James looked up in surprise. "How did you heat the tub?"

"With fire magic," the Sorcerer said proudly. "Putting fire straight into water just turned it into steam, so I shoved the tendrils of magic into the tub instead. Worked great! The whole thing heated up like a big copper kettle. There should be enough residual heat left for at least one more bath, but I'll probably have to pump it up again after that."

By the time he finished, James's jaw was on the floor. "Wait," he said, putting up his hands. "Wait, wait, *wait*. You're saying you just *put magic*--as in no spell, just raw magic--into the tub, and it *worked*?"

"Pretty much," the Sorcerer said, pointing up at the multicolored ribbons of magic that were always floating in the air. "The red streamers always burn when I grab them to cast my spells, so I figured why not just use that? The real trick was not getting the metal *too* hot. There might be a corner of the tub that's a bit melted now, just FYI."

As a Naturalist, James didn't use fire magic, so he couldn't see the "red streamers" the Sorcerer was referring to, but he'd grabbed enough water, lightning, earth, and life to get the general idea. What he couldn't believe was that he'd never thought of that. This whole time, he'd only ever grabbed magic to cast the spells he'd learned from the game. He'd modified them a little, like when he'd copied NekoBaby's trick of wrapping lightning around her palm to make a Taser hand, but it had never occurred to him to just use *raw* magic.

"Flame," he said, grinning, "you're a genius!"

259

The Sorcerer blushed. "Ah, naw. I wasn't trying to be fancy. Cold baths are just the devil, and necessity *is* the mother of invention."

"The mother of *brilliance*," James said, his mind racing as he stared at the magic floating all around them. Looking at how the streams twirled together, he suddenly remembered how his staff had criticized the healing spells he'd cast on Ar'Bati and SB last night as childish and clumsy. At the time, he'd thought the cursed weapon was just trying to put him down like usual. Now, though, he realized the staff was just telling him the truth. This whole time, James had been casting his spells as if he were still a Naturalist in a game, but there was no more action bar full of preset, class-specific abilities. It was all just magic--*his* magic in *his* hands, waiting to be woven together in different ways to create different effects.

James began to bounce in excitement. If Flameboyant could shove fire into a copper tub to make it hot, what new creations could he create out of the power floating above their heads? Could he make a lightning storm? Move the stone of the castle itself? Maybe if he blended all the magics together, he could invent something entirely new, a whole new spell that had never existed before he thought of it. He was about to grab some magic and start trying things out when the lock on the reinforced doors clicked, and Lady Siku swept into the room.

Just like last night, she was dressed in fine white silk. This time, though, the long fall of her wrapped grown was wrinkled at the hem, as though she'd spent the whole morning pacing. Her face was similarly annoyed, ice-blue eyes glaring impatiently at James as she walked in and dumped the lich's letters out on the low table in front of the sofa.

"Half of these are in English," she announced imperially. "The rest are in Old Elven, neither of which I read. You will translate them for me."

A guard placed a stack of paper, a quill, and an inkpot down on the table beside the letters, but James barely spared it a glance.

"Why are you only doing this *now*?" he demanded, glaring at the white cat-woman with shaking fury. "I gave you those letters last night. It's already midday. I thought I made it clear that this was an *emergency*."

"I've been busy," Lady Siku snarled back, nodding at the sunny window where the troops were still marching out the gates. "In case you haven't noticed, we're dealing with an emergency of our own. The king has been in a war meeting since dawn, strategizing with his generals about how to deal with the player threat in the south of the city. I deemed it politically inadvisable to interrupt him with your crisis, especially since any potential undead invasion couldn't even occur so long as the Bastion remains active."

"'*Politically inadvisable?*'" James repeated, voice getting louder. "We're talking about the *Once King*! Creator of the Ghostfire and the force who wants to destroy *all life* in this world! One look at those letters was all you needed to know you couldn't read them. Why didn't you ask me to translate last night? I told you yesterday that he has traitors inside this castle, helping him open a backdoor through your defenses. Bastion or no Bastion, those spies are still working." He stabbed his finger at the pile of letters. "Their names are *right there.* All you have to do is tell the king to arrest them! Why haven't you?"

"You do not tell me how to conduct my affairs, *player*," Lady Siku said icily. "Need I remind you that you are only alive through *my* good graces. I can throw you back to Captain Malakai's men any time I choose, so watch your tongue."

"Do you *want* to die?" James yelled at her. "If the king and the players kill each other, there will be no one left to stand against the Once King's armies! You should be banging down the king's door to bring him this information so we can all start working together against the *actual* threat. Not wasting everyone's time while Malakai fills him with hate!"

"That's *Captain* Malakai," Lady Siku snapped. "And his hate is deserved! The stonekin leading the rebellion in the south killed him yesterday, you know. It's a miracle of the Blessed Sun that the Clerics were able to resurrect him in time, but death has only strengthened his resolve. He will crush the players and return order to Bastion. If you don't want to die with the rest of your kind, you will shut your mouth and *do as I say.*"

261

Ar'Bati growled low in his throat at that, but James just sighed. "If I translate the letters, will you take them straight to the king?"

"Of course not," Lady Siku said. "Weren't you listening? I'm not stupid enough to get in Malakai's way. There will be nothing said about the undead until all other operations are complete and the city is retaken. At that point, we can discuss possible traitors. Until then, I'm the only thing keeping you alive, so it's in your best interests to keep me happy. I'd hate for Captain Malakai to put *you* in his kindling wagons."

James didn't know what she meant by that, but the way she said it made him shudder. "This is ridiculous," he said through clenched teeth. "We have to--"

"*We* don't have to do anything," she said, pointing at the paper and ink on the table. "*You* need to do as you're told. Translate the letters now, and I'll use them when I judge the moment to be politically advantageous. Meanwhile, you can go ahead and tell me the secrets you promised last night."

James blinked. "The what?"

"The secrets," she said, snapping her fingers impatiently. "You said if I got you into the castle, you'd tell me all the palace courtiers' dirty laundry you learned from doing quests. The letters can wait, but I need that information before one of my enemies gets wise and finds a player of their own. I've kept my end of the bargain. Now it's your turn. Speak, and then I'll see about getting you food."

She sat down on the couch, tail twitching impatiently as she waited for him to start reciting quest details, but James couldn't say a word. Lady Siku's political ruthlessness was the very thing he'd gambled on to get them inside the palace in the first place, but this was insane. How could *anyone* hear that the Once King was coming and decide that petty gossip was more important?

He was already opening his mouth to try explaining again--because there was no way a rational person would act like this if she actually understood the threat--when one of her white-furred guards walked over and shoved the quill into his fingers. He was forcing James's hand down to the paper when James finally accepted the truth.

This wasn't going to work.

Not only was Lady Siku not going to take his letters to the king as she'd promised, she was actively working against the idea. She didn't care about Bastion. All she cared about was getting more power inside her own little sphere, so what if the rest of the world burned. No matter what James did or how much he gave her, she was never going to hold up her end of things until it was *politically advantageous*. And in the meanwhile, Tina and the knights would fight, everyone would die, the Bastion would eventually go down, and this whole continent would be consumed by the Once King's Ghostfire.

A happy ending, his staff whispered in his mind, its cold voice giddy with anticipation. *You should do as she says.*

"No," James said.

"What was that?" Lady Siku snapped.

"No," James said again, snapping the quill and throwing it down as he shot to his feet. "I'm not wasting any more time on this nonsense! I didn't betray my sister to sit here and play your games. I came--I *fought* to get here so that I could warn the king and save Bastion, and that's exactly what I mean to do."

"You can do nothing if you're dangling from a noose!" Lady Siku hissed, jumping to her feet as well. "Sit back down and do as I say, or I'll throw you all to the--"

She cut off with a strangled grasp. The moment she'd started talking, James had grabbed a fistful of earth magic and shoved it into the stones at her feet, bending the magic into his Stone Grasp spell but not the usual version. Back in the game, the giant stone hand had been a crowd-control spell meant to keep monsters and hostile players off him for no more than twelve seconds. But Flameboyant had taught him yet again that this wasn't the game. There was no reason Stone Grasp had to be twelve seconds long other than that was the number written in the spell text.

Now that he was actually looking at the magic he was casting as *magic*--not a game mechanic--James saw zero actual reason the stone hand couldn't last for as long as he was willing to keep feeding power into it. So that was what he did, channeling the amber flows of power through the castle's stone floor and into a giant hand that grabbed Lady Siku's entire body and squeezed her tight, shutting off her threats like a switch.

The room rang with the sound of her bodyguards drawing their swords. James snatched up his staff from the floor beside him and used it to send a wave of earth magic forward. The guards barely made it three feet before he'd wrapped every white cat in the room in a collar of living, squeezing stone.

"What now?" Ar'Bati demanded, stepping up beside them. "They're all level eighty, but if you release them one by one, we might be able to--"

"Screw fighting," James said, sweat pouring through his fur as he fought to keep so many Stone Grasps in place. "We're going to do what we came here to do. We're going to the king!"

Fangs's cat eyes turned round. "The king?" he repeated, horrified. "We can't just barge our way in on the king! He's the *king*!"

"Normally, yes, but I think we abandoned protocol," James said, nodding at the letters Lady Siku had dumped on the table. "Grab our proof and get it back in the bag. Meanwhile, Flame, I need you to start pumping fire into the window bars. Get them melty just like you did the bathtub."

"Okay," Flameboyant said nervously, scrambling to get his robes back on over his wet body. "But I don't know if it'll work. Iron is a lot denser than copper."

"Just do your best," James said as Ar'Bati swept the letters into his bag.

The temperature in the room rose as Flameboyant began stuffing fire magic into the bars that kept them trapped. James was dying to watch, but he didn't dare take his eyes off the people he was keeping trapped in his Stone Grasps for more than a glance. If his hold slipped, one of them could slip out and attack or raise the alarm. Either was inevitable eventually, but James was determined not to be caught with a wall at his back. Unfortunately, though the room was getting quite hot, he didn't hear any molten bars falling to the ground.

"It's no good!" Flameboyant cried after almost a minute. "I've put all the fire I can into them, but they're still not melting!"

"You got them red hot, though, right?" James said, arms shaking with the strain of holding three level eighties captive. "That means they're weak. Ar'Bati!"

"On it," his brother said, marching into the bathroom. For a moment, James had no idea why, then he heard the sound of breaking tile and wrenching metal as his brother yanked the copper tub off its foundation. "If we must be criminals to bring warning to the king, then we shall be effective ones!"

With that, the warrior threw the entire copper tub at the barred window. The heavy glass, already cracked by the heat, shattered completely, and the molten red bars bulged outward, but only one actually snapped. The others took multiple hits, bending further and further as Ar'Bati hammered on them with the rapidly crumpling copper tub. Finally, when the bathtub had been bashed into a malformed copper ball, the last bar gave way, leaving the window open to the castle outside.

"Time to go," James said as Ar'Bati hurled what was left of the tub at the guards gawking below.

"But it's a sheer wall!" Flameboyant cried. "And a thirty-foot drop! How are we going to--"

He cut off with a yelp as Ar'Bati grabbed him around the waist and swung outside, clambering up the building's rough-hewn stone wall just as fast as he'd climbed trees back in the savanna. Alone in the room now, James walked backward toward the window and climbed onto the ledge, taking great care not to step on any of the molten spikes left from the broken bars. When he was finally in position, he let the earth magic go.

265

The giant stone hands of the Stone Grasp spell crumbled seconds later, giving him one last look at Lady Siku's furious face as she began to scream. *"Guards! Knights! The players have escaped!'*

There was a lot more than that, but James didn't bother to listen. He'd already stuck his staff into his mouth and started to climb, doing his best to follow Ar'Bati's path up the wall. But whereas the head warrior had made this look easy, James hadn't grown up climbing trees and cliffs in the savanna. Or as a cat, for that matter. The moment he left the relative safety and easy footholds of the chunky window ledge, he froze, completely unsure of where to put his feet or hands on the wall, which now looked as smooth as a marble column.

"Hurry!" Ar'Bati called down to him.

Staff stuck in his mouth, James could only glance down at the dizzying drop and the soldiers that were rushing around below.

"This was *your* idea!"

He wanted to tell his brother that he didn't know how. It was not like scaling trees, cliffs, or buildings were things he had any real experiences doing. Instead, he shot a pleading look up at Fangs in the Grass.

Hanging by one arm from the wall twenty feet above, Ar'Bati looked down to give him a superior scowl. "Don't be shameful! You are jubatus, and a Claw Born at that!" He lifted his free hand to show James the small, sharp claws he was using like crampons to pull himself up the wall. "Your body knows what to do! Stop messing it up with thinking and *climb*!"

Shaking, James stopped looking at the sheer wall and the drop below and forced himself to stare at the stone in front of him. As with all rock, he could feel the magic inside it, but that wasn't actually what he used this time. Instead, he followed the flows to the points where his claws could find purchase, giving him a handhold where there seemed to be none.

266

After that, he made progress more and more quickly. Sometimes he'd screw himself up by looking down and panicking, but Ar'Bati was right. If he shut his mind up and trusted his body, it knew what to do. It was just like when they'd run across the grasslands. If he tried to control it, nothing worked, but if he surrendered to his instincts, his balance and body took care of themselves, taking him all the way up the castle's white wall to where Ar'Bati was waiting.

"Good job," the warrior said, grabbing James by the tunic to haul him up the last few feet to the castle's slick golden roof--or rather, *one* of its slick golden roofs. The royal castle was made up of several buildings surrounding a central keep. Lady Siku's apartments had been in one of the smaller buildings in the back, so though they were high, they were still well below the towering central keep crowned with the circular tower where the activated Bastion was gleaming like a searchlight.

"So what now?" Ar'Bati demanded as James shielded his eyes against the magical supernova shining above them. "We are free and inside the castle at last, but we do not know where the king is, and the guards are rallying."

He was right. The paved yard--which had been swarming with soldiers since they'd woken up--was now packed with armed men pointing up at them. A few arrows flew past as James watched, clattering off the stone below them and forcing them farther up the sloped roof.

"Oh snap, they're shooting at us," Flameboyant said fearfully.

"Of course they are," Ar'Bati said, his voice grim. "We are fugitives and believed enemies of the crown. But all will be resolved once we speak with the king and become the saviors of Bastion. We just have to reach him."

"How are we going to do that?" the Sorcerer asked.

Ar'Bati pointed at James. "My brother is always the one with plans. He has a demon's mind for wiggling out of seemingly hopeless situations. I have seen him turn defeat into victory many times, and I know he would not have sent us out the window if he didn't have a fiendishly good plan."

"Great!" Flameboyant said, turning to James. "How are we getting out of this?"

James began to sweat. He appreciated his brother's vote of confidence, but honestly, this escape had been one of his *least* thought-out endeavors. He was honestly impressed they'd made it this far. Fortunately, the plan from here was pretty straightforward: get to the king and get the letters in his hands by any means necessary.

He even had a pretty good idea of where he was. Back in the game, King Gregory had never left his position in the throne room unless he was off getting drunk for the Oktoberfest event. Normally, then, the throne room would be the obvious choice, but Lady Siku had specifically said the king was in a meeting. The throne room was a giant hall meant to hold hundreds, not the sort of place you held planning sessions. But the council chamber--a still-grand but much smaller hall at the top of the War Fortress on the palace's western side--was perfect. It had broad tables and a full map of the city. Not that those had ever been used by anyone during the game, but James was ready to bet they were being put to work now. It *also* had a giant stained-glass window to let in the sunlight, which solved the next problem of how they were going to get in.

"All right," James said, reaching out to take the bag of letters from Ar'Bati and tie them to his own belt. "We tried for an audience, and we failed. Now, we're just going to have to crash in on King Gregory and hope for the best."

"And how will we avoid being executed on the spot?" Ar'Bati asked skeptically.

"I'm... not entirely sure," James admitted. "But I can't think of another way to get his attention. It's clear no one's going to let us get close to the king. If we're to have a prayer of stopping this stupid war before we do the Once King's work for him, we have to take matters into our own hands. But I think we've got a shot. I talked to King Gregory several times back when this was a game. He's a good person and a kind one. You don't get nicknamed 'the Buffoon King' for ruthlessly executing your enemies on

268

sight, after all. I can't guarantee this won't be a suicide mission, but if anyone in this place will give us the benefit of the doubt, it's him."

"Very well, brother," Ar'Bati said, his face deathly serious as he clapped a clawed hand on James's shoulder. "Death before dishonor. We will save this continent from the Once King, no matter the cost."

"No matter the cost," James agreed, patting Fangs's hand before turning to Flameboyant, who was watching all of this in horror. "You don't have to come, Flame," he said quietly. "This is a lot more than you signed up for when you ran with us, and I don't blame you if you want out. If you want, we can tie you up here, and then you can fake-betray us to buy your own safety when the knights come."

"Absolutely not," the elf said, shaking his head so violently, the water from his still-damp crimson hair flew out in stinging needles. "I owe you my life, remember? I'm going to repay you, and given what you're planning to do, this might be my last chance. No way I'm bailing."

His determination sent James into a panic. "Dude, I appreciate your dedication, but you *really* don't have to do this. You've already paid me back more than enough, and I didn't save your life just so you could come with us and..."

He couldn't finish, but though his face was pale, Flameboyant did not back down. "I'm tired of hiding while other people die," the elf said, voice shaking. "From the moment I woke up in this place, I've done nothing but hide and watch while others killed or got killed or did horrible things. I didn't help anyone, I didn't do anything but try to stay alive, and I hated myself for it. That's why I threw myself at your raid. I wasn't even brave enough to take my own life. I had to make you all do it, but you gave me another chance."

Flameboyant stopped for a shaking breath, and then he looked James in the eyes. "What do I have to be afraid of? I already died once. And if this *does* work, we'll save everyone. That's what you keep saying: that this is going to save the world. I don't know if those lives will be enough to balance out all the people I didn't lift a finger to save during my first days

269

here, but at least this time I can go out as a hero instead of a suicide bomber. That's worth a shot, I think. So are we doing this or what?"

James didn't trust his voice enough to answer. Flameboyant was always so jovial and happy to go along, it was easy to forget that he'd been through hell just like the rest of them. This whole world had been put through the wringer, and it was only going to get worse unless they stopped it, which meant Flameboyant was right: it *was* worth a shot. Compared to the lives those letters could save in the king's hands, the three of them were nothing. Win or lose, the very act of trying would make the world better. James could think of no worthier cause to spend his life on and no better people to do so with.

"Glad to have you aboard," he said, reaching out to squeeze the Sorcerer's shoulder. "Here's the plan: we're going to bust into the Council Chamber and find the king. I haven't seen a single griffin rider since the game became real, so if we stick to the roofs and out of sight of archers on the ground, we should be okay. Once we get in, we get these letters into the king's hands by any means necessary. Got it?"

Fangs in the Grass and Flameboyant both nodded, eyes set hard.

"Good," James said, turning west, but he couldn't even see the War Fortress through the castle's main keep, which was both bigger than the building they were on and separated by a good eighty feet of empty space. "We need to get to the other side of the castle complex," he said quickly, pointing at the main keep. "It'll take too long to go around the outer buildings, so I think we should go straight over the top. That should also give us a good vantage point of the council chamber on the other side. The only part I don't know is how we're going to make the jump."

"I've got an idea," Ar'Bati said, scrambling up the golden roof a bit farther to grab the weather-worn rope that was holding up a line of fluttering flags in the king's crimson and gold. Keeping low, he undid the knots and pulled the line out of the metal rings that kept it in place, then he returned to James with a long coil.

270

"Good thinking," James said with a grin. "But how do we get the end across?"

"I can handle that part," Flameboyant said, squinting across the gap at the keep on the other side. "See that window?" He pointed at a narrow, stone-encased window almost exactly like the one they'd broken out of, only without the bars. "Teleport goes fifty feet in a straight line. If Ar'Bati throws me, I can teleport the final distance. Once I get there, I'll tie the rope to something, and you can both climb across."

"While being shot at from below," Ar'Bati said dryly.

Flameboyant shrugged. "Climb quickly?"

"They have to shoot way up, and it's windy today," James said, peeking over the edge at the archers below. "We can make it. We'll be two cats on a wire."

"*I* can make it," Ar'Bati said, leaning down to tie the end of their rope to one of the metal hoops he'd just removed it from. "You might have a problem. You're still not very good at being jubatus."

"Well, I'll have to learn fast, because those archers aren't going to stay on the ground." James nodded at the runners shouting the alarm all over the castle. "This place is going on high alert. It's only a matter of time before we have soldiers up here as well, and then we'll be cornered." He turned to Flameboyant. "Do it. We'll make it work."

The Sorcerer nodded, grabbed the other end of Ar'Bati's rope, and tied it around his wrist. "Okay," he said when it was tight. "Throw me before I chicken out."

James held his breath as Ar'Bati picked up the elf. He knew firsthand just how strong the warrior was, but it was still a fifty-foot drop to the pavement, and falling damage was no joke. A drop like this could kill a max-level player, and Flameboyant was only level forty-five. If they screwed this up, he'd splat, but there was no turning back. Ar'Bati had already launched the Sorcerer into the air, throwing him across the gap with all his strength.

The elf windmilled his arms as he flew up in an arc. Arrows shot past him, nicking his fluttering crimson robes, but Flameboyant didn't even seem to notice. His attention was locked on the target window, and he watched it like a falcon as he started to fall. Then, just when James was sure something had gone wrong and they'd just thrown their friend to his death, the Sorcerer vanished in a puff of purple energy then reappeared a second later two feet on the windowsill.

Then he promptly crashed right through the window.

James winced as the glass shattered. Apparently, teleportation didn't cancel out momentum. Fortunately, the room he'd crashed into must have been empty, because Flameboyant reappeared a few seconds later, scratched up but very alive as he wrapped the rope around a table leg inside and pulled it tight.

"That's our cue," Ar'Bati said, glaring down at the archers, who were already nocking a new volley. "Ready?"

James was not, but he didn't have much of a choice. It was now or never, so he took a deep breath and charged ahead, keeping his eyes determinedly on the rope and not the drop below it as he ran on all fours across the single-line bridge Flameboyant had made for them. Ar'Bati ran right behind him, making the rope bounce and sway. The motion made James's brain spin, but as promised, his jubatus body handled it. So long as he kept his human-centric expectations out of the way, he was able to trot right across using his tail to balance. If he hadn't been so terrified, it would have been amazing, but it was hard to enjoy the spectacular feats this new form was capable of when arrows were flying past your head, so James just focused on getting across as fast as possible, racing across the rope to fall into a panting heap at Flameboyant's feet.

"*Don't stop!*" Ar'Bati hissed.

Before James could ask why he couldn't have two seconds to catch his breath, he heard the sound of boots in the hallway. Flameboyant had crashed into a sitting room very much like the one Lady Siku had locked them inside, except this one hadn't been modified to double as a fancy prison. The doors were plain wood, good quality but nothing that could stop a Royal Knight, much less the dozen his sharp ears could hear pounding toward them.

"Hoo boy," Flameboyant said, untying the rope from his wrist. "Better move."

Ar'Bati nodded and hooked James by the collar to yank him up. When he was back on his feet, the warrior grabbed Flameboyant around the waist and swung back outside, dodging left just in time to avoid the arrow that shattered on the wall right next to his head. Flameboyant yelped and curled himself into a red ball around the warrior's arm, which would have thrown James off balance. Again, though, his brother was a two-skull. He didn't even wobble. He just kept climbing one-handed, scaling the vertical stone wall as nimbly as a monkey.

With a final look at the door, James scrambled after them, getting his body out the window just in time as a squad of armored knights burst into the room. They were shouting at each other to draw bows when James grabbed a passing ribbon of earth magic and slapped it against the wall. He didn't have a plan, exactly, but he didn't really need one. He just shoved power into the stone until he felt something move. Seconds later, the ornamental slab above the window broke from its mortar and fell, crashing down into the opening to block their way.

Grinning at his cleverness, James shook his stinging hand and kept climbing. Between the extra-long stone-grasp spells he'd used on Siku and her guards and that move just now, he could tell his mana was getting low. His new spells didn't seem to take any more magic than the ones he'd learned from the game, but he'd been casting a lot, and he wasn't wearing healing gear. His leather armor was all Agility and Strength: great for climbing and martial arts, not so good for battle casting. He couldn't have everything, though. He resolved to save the rest of his magic for healing, using his enhanced agility to scoot past Fangs and make it to the top first.

They came out on a steep golden roof directly below the main keep's central tower. They were *very* high now, easily a hundred feet off the ground. Above their heads, the Bastion shone like a miniature sun, heating the air and making James's fur stand on end. He'd never been close to magic this powerful before, at least not when he could actually feel it, but the only word he could think of to describe it was *divine*. He was still gawking at it in wonder when Ar'Bati grabbed his shoulder.

"*James!*"

James blinked and turned to his brother, who was looking grimmer than James had ever seen him.

"If we're going to do this, it has to be now."

For a second, James didn't understand what Ar'Bati meant. Then he heard it. There were boots clanging on the gold-plated roof--heavy, armored boots, coming in their direction. A second later, he saw the first of the Royal Knights round the bend of the Bastion tower's base, swords already drawn.

"*Run!*"

The three of them bolted, scrambling along the tilted, slippery metal roof.

"The council room should be right in front of us!" James yelled as they ran, wishing yet again that he had more intellect gear as his brain scrambled to remember the War Fortress's interior layout. "Middle floor, I think. It should be the only room with a giant window."

"But how do we get to it?" Flameboyant cried, huffing and puffing and occasionally teleporting forward as he struggled to keep up with the long-legged jubatus. "I can teleport, but I can't carry both of you. Also, I'll just be crashing through a window again, and I don't think this one's going to be as friendly a landing."

James wasn't sure. He had to think of something, though, because the end of the roof was approaching fast. He could already see the fortified peak of the War Fortress rising above the edge of the gold-metal sheeting. But it was so far away, and the knights were right behind them.

"We need to buy some time!" James yelled. "Let's try to--"

He hadn't even finished before Flameboyant spun around and unleashed a torrent of fire. The giant swirls of orange fire were so big and bright, they overpowered even the Bastion's light. They crashed into the knights chasing them like glowing waves, washing the soldiers under in a flood of smoke and flame. The men fell screaming, batting at their hair and their red-and-gold tabards and everything else flammable as the fire spread. They were still rolling on the roof when James whirled on their Sorcerer.

"*What was that?*"

"How could you kill the *Royal Knights?*" Ar'Bati demanded at the same time.

"Fire Tornado," Flameboyant said proudly before turning to glare at the head warrior. "And I didn't kill them. I'm level forty-five, remember? They're level eighty. The most I can do is give them some burns, but it still makes a good distraction. Even if you know it won't kill you, there's nothing more important than not being on fire."

Ar'Bati snorted, but James was still sputtering. "B-But Fire Tornado is a big PVP-area spell!" he said at last. "You can't even get into the rated battlegrounds until level fifty. Why do *you* know how to cast it?"

"I saved up my skill points to buy the spell early," the Sorcerer said proudly, drawing himself up to his full height with a toss of his crimson hair. "The great and powerful *Flameboyant* uses only the most spectacular of fire spells!"

"Right," James said, giving the guards, who were still rolling on the ground, one last look. "Um, good work. Now let's see what we're in for."

With that, all three of them stepped up to the edge and looked down.

Just as James remembered, the Bastion War Fortress was a sturdy old fort of a building. Unlike the rest of the palace, it had no soaring towers or pretty windows--just thick walls, arrow slits, battlements, and smokestacks for the forges. Back in the game, it had been where the Royal Knights had their headquarters, and that still seemed to be the case. The whole place was swarming with soldiers and workers churning out materials for the coming battle.

The only part of the five-story building that wasn't heavy stone, steel, and flame was the giant circular stained-glass picture window depicting the founding of the knighthood by Bastion's first king in the middle of its front face. The glass was the highest quality, big and clear enough for James to see their goal. Through the jewellike hues, the council chamber looked exactly as he remembered, only now there was a huge chair at the head of the long table, and sitting in it was a huge red-headed figure.

James's heart sped up so fast it made him light-headed. He couldn't see the man's face from so far away, but no other human in Bastion was eight feet tall and covered in sun-metal plate armor. It *had* to be King Gregory. Unfortunately, he wasn't alone. In hindsight, James wasn't sure why that came as a shock. Obviously, a war meeting would have to include other people, but he hadn't stopped to think about just *who* those people would be. Now, though, he could see the truth clearly, and it made his hammering heart slow right back down to nothing.

The room was a who's who of Bastion's most powerful and deadly. In addition to the king--who himself was a five-skull raid boss--James saw the captain of the City Guard, the captain of the castle garrison, the high priest of the Sun, the arch-sorcerer, and worst of all, Captain Malakai of the Royal Knights.

It was a lineup even Tina's crew would have had trouble with. Fortunately, the captains didn't seem aware of the disturbance outside. They were all listening to Malakai, who was sitting directly across from His Majesty, hammering his fist on the table like he was trying to make a point. No one was looking at the window or the figures on the central keep's roof above it, but James didn't think that would make a difference when they came crashing through.

"Um, guys?" he said, voice shaking as he reached down to grab the packet of letters. "Remember when I said I couldn't guarantee this

276

wouldn't be a suicide mission? I'm going to have to revise that to 'definitely.' Going in that window is a one-way ticket, and I won't think less of either of you if you decide to--*ow!*"

Ar'Bati had smacked the back of his head.

"What kind of attitude is that to start a battle?" his brother snarled. "Did we not already prove we were prepared to die?" He bared his teeth. "We just broke out of prison and set knights on fire. If we do not complete our mission, the Claw Born will be branded as traitors. *Incompetent* traitors!" He shook his head. "I will not allow it. I'd rather die than face our father as things are now. We came to Bastion to give letters to the king, and we shall do so. Death before dishonor!"

"Hell yeah!" Flameboyant said, lifting his fists. "But I think you're being too down on our chances. Sure, that's a room full of badasses, but the high priest and the arch-sorcerer are both caster types. If we bust in on their heads, they're going to have to wind up their spells before they kill us. That gives us three seconds at least to get that bag to the king."

"What about Malakai?" James asked. "He's a four skull. I'm not sure how his fight with Tina ended since we left early, but you felt the ground shaking. If he gave her trouble, he's going to make cat-burgers out of us."

"Where is your honor?" Ar'Bati demanded. "If the priest and the sorcerer have to wait to cast, then the captains are the only true barriers between us and the king. We might be only three, but we have the element of surprise and our backs to the wall. That's a lot in our favor. Now tell me, can a four-skull survive falling three stories?"

"I think so," James said. "But--"

"Good," Ar'Bati said, clenching his fists. "Then you can leave two of the captains to me."

"I have some dirty Sorcerer tricks as well," Flameboyant said proudly. "I can keep a captain busy for ten seconds or so. No promises after that, though."

"If we live more than ten seconds, we'll figure it out from there," Ar'Bati said confidently. "You and I will take the captains, and James will handle the letters. I've been on the receiving end of his damnably inescapable arguments too many times to doubt his skill with words. If anyone can make the king listen, it is him."

"Well, if we're going, we should do it soon," Flameboyant said. "'Cause the tin cans are twitching."

The knights behind them were indeed starting to shake off the last of Flameboyant's flamboyant fire attack. Wincing, James turned back to the window, pulled his staff, and clutched it in his free hand. "We're going to have to make a big jump, and we can't miss," he said, looking at Ar'Bati. "Remember how we got into the lich's laboratory back in Red Canyon?"

"I do," Ar'Bati said with a grin. "Are we flying again?"

"We're going to try," James said, gathering the streams of wind magic into his hands. "Grab hold of my arms, guys, and get ready to jump on my mark. And in case I don't get to say this later, it's been a pleasure and an honor knowing both of--"

"No," Ar'Bati said firmly, locking his arm through James's. "No goodbyes. They curse victories. We will save all of Bastion today and be welcomed home as heroes."

"I like the sound of being a hero," Flameboyant said, grabbing onto James's other arm.

"Then let's do it," James said, winding up the last of his spell. "On three, two, *one!*"

He released the Gust spell he'd been building, blasting the three of them off the roof with a wall of wind. They jumped at the same time, adding their strength to the magical wind as they flew across the gaping chasm of empty air between the castle's main keep and the War Fortress. Below them, in the rallying square, squads of knights and guardsmen looked up in surprise at the three bodies soaring over their heads like birds to crash straight through the middle of the fortress's stained-glass window.

They burst through the colored glass like cannonballs, sending shards flying over the men gathered below. For one terrifying, almost comical moment, the greatest warriors and sorcerers of Bastion looked up in baffled confusion, their mouths falling open. Then the council room erupted into chaos as Ar'Bati folded his body, turning his fall into a flying elbow that landed straight in the face of the captain of the City Guard.

The unprepared human was flattened instantly as Ar'Bati crashed into him. After rolling right back to his feet like a true cat, Ar'Bati grabbed the astonished captain by the metal yoke of his armor and hurled him straight back the way they had come, using his monstrous strength to toss the stocky mini-boss right out the broken window before the man could come to his senses.

It was an absolutely marvelous move, but James barely caught more than a glimpse of it. He was too busy trying not to crash as he hurtled toward the middle of the war table. In the end, his jubatus body saved him again, flipping him at the last second to land on his feet. But while the two cats had it in the bag, Flameboyant was an elf. He had no supernatural instinct to assist in his landing, and he was going down fast. James was scrambling to work up another wind spell to give him something to land on when the Sorcerer vanished in a poof of purple energy then reappeared on his feet at the back of the room just in time for the two remaining captains to draw their swords and turn on him.

The captain of the castle garrison had barely gotten his weapon out of its sheath before Ar'Bati turned and tackled him, but Captain Malakai didn't even pause as his compatriot went down. He just lunged and swung, slicing Flameboyant in half with one stroke of his sword.

James cried out then stopped. There was no blood, no screaming. The bisected elf he'd been staring at just vanished like a mirage, and then Flameboyant--the *real* one--appeared behind Malakai with his empty backpack ready in his hands. The knight captain was cursing the Sorcerer's illusionary double when the elf jumped up and shoved the burlap bag over Malakai's head, yanked the drawstrings tight, and hung on with white knuckles.

"Go, James!" he yelled frantically. "Do it!"

James nodded and turned around to face the very confused--and very alarmed--looking king.

He was quite the sight. King Gregory had been big in the game--all bosses were, even supposedly human ones--but in real life he was absolutely massive, even bigger than Tina's stonekin. His sun-metal armor gleamed as golden as the Bastion itself, making him look like a truly *holy* king, and for a moment, James was struck dumb by something that could only be described as awe. Then he came to his senses, dropping to his knees on the table in front of the king before he wasted any more of the precious time his friends had sacrificed to buy him.

"Your majesty," he said, speaking as fast as he could. "You are being betrayed from within. We have proof that the Once King is planning to invade--"

He was drowned out by a cry of anguish from Ar'Bati, and then the smell of blood filled the room. The Arch-Sorcerer, whom James had ignored up to this point, finished his casting at the same time, and James heard Flameboyant gasp in surprise as the temple-bell-like sound of a Temporal Prison went off with a flash of purple energy. Moments later, Malakai's muffled cursing gained clarity as the tall elven captain ripped the backpack off his head and whirled around, his furious black eyes locking on James.

Realizing time was up, James abandoned words and lunged at King Gregory, upending his bag of letters into the surprised monarch's lap. "*The undead are coming!*"

That was all he managed to shout before searing pain erupted in his chest. Looking down, James saw a sword blade sticking him to the table--most likely through a lung, if his shortness of breath was any indication. But though his blood was now gushing out at an alarming rate, James wasn't done.

"Please..." he gurgled, ignoring the blood filling his lungs as he reached out his hand to the king. "Please read... We gave our lives to get these to you. *Please--*"

280

He fell with a gasp as the sword was whipped out of him, landing facedown on the table. He'd barely hit when a steel-gauntleted hand grabbed his shoulder and whipped him onto his back, and James found himself staring down the blade of a sword and into the hateful eyes of Captain Malakai. But as the captain braced to finish the kill, a deep, trembling voice said, "Hold."

"*Hold?*" Malakai snarled, his eyes flicking over James's head to the king behind him. "With respect, your majesty, this just proves what I've been saying all along. The players are mad! They've even breached this fortress. How many more defeats must we suffer before you allow me to exterminate--"

"You dare to *lecture* your king, Malakai?" someone said in a raspy voice James didn't recognize. The speaker sounded close, but James couldn't see him. He had no idea how much Malakai hit for, but it must have been a lot, because his vision was already going dark.

"If you weren't so blinded by your bloodthirst," the raspy voice went on, "you'd see that two of them bear the mark of Lord Rend of the Claw Born. I don't actually think they're players, but even if they are, we can't just kill them outright."

"Save your damn compassion, priest," the knight captain snarled. "Your insistence on *waiting* and *chances* is the reason the player problem has spiraled out of control! That *Claw Born* over there threw Captain Hightower through a fourth-story window! They mean to kill us all!"

Ahh, James thought. The raspy voice must be the High Sun Priest Raffestain, the old elf Cleric who was basically the pope of Bastion--and clearly every bit as wise and compassionate as the game had made him out to be, bless his sacred heart.

"By the authority of the Sun, I declare you shall not kill them!" Raffestain said furiously.

Malakai responded in elven with what was clearly profanity. The Sun priest responded in kind, and then James felt warm sunlight on his skin. No, it was greater than that. The light had a weight and a movement

281

to it, as though it were the breath of a living thing. The feeling left him trembling in awe as life flooded back into his body.

The warmth and euphoria of the high priest's healing magic filled him to bursting. The pain vanished, the hole in his chest shut, and the bleeding stopped. But before he could take his first non-perforated breath, a metal boot landed on his ribs.

The strength of the kick hurled him off the table and through a line of chairs. When he hit the ground, James got his head up just in time to see Malakai's hand shoot forward to grab him. He instinctively counter-grabbed the towering captain's arm for a lock only to discover he couldn't twist it at all. The damn elf's arm was as strong as an iron girder. James's move didn't even slow him down as Malakai's hand closed around his throat like a vise, lifting James out of the wrecked chairs and up until his feet were dangling a good six inches off the floor.

"Stop this now, Malakai!" shouted Raffestain. "The king ordered you to hold!"

"And hold I did," the captain replied, squeezing tighter. "You were the one who healed without orders! But why don't we let his majesty decide?" Malakai gave James a final sneer and turned around, holding him out like a caught fish to the king. "How would you have me dispose of this trash, your highness?"

"Do not involve his majesty!" the high priest cried. "You know he has not the temperament for such grisly matters!"

"You were the one who brought him in, old man," Malakai said, lifting James higher. "One word from his majesty, and I will gut all three of them for daring to show their demon faces here."

Twisting in Malakai's hold, James tried to turn to get a look at the king. He caught a glimpse of the High Priest, a straight-backed elf dressed in white-and-gold robes sewn of the high clouds themselves, but the king was hidden behind him, crouched low in his throne like a child being scolded, which struck James as a very odd way for an all-powerful monarch to behave.

"Your *Majesty*," the captain said impatiently. "How shall these intruders be killed? If you wish me to decide, I will happily--"

"Don't listen to him, your highness," Raffestain said angrily, turning to face the king as well. "He'll just butcher them like he did all the others, and we'll never know why they did this. We can always execute them later. For now, we should keep them for questioning."

The room was filled with the clank of armor as the king shifted anxiously in his chair. Then he fiddled with the letters, stacking them neatly on his giant knees. Then, *finally*, King Gregory spoke.

"I, um, that is--" His deep voice wobbled with uncertainty, and then he nodded his crowned head. "If you think we should question them, Raffestain, that is what we will do. I am curious about why they attacked me with a bag of letters. These papers do not appear to be of a deadly sort."

"An excellent choice, your highness," the high priest replied with a bow. Then he turned to glare at the knight captain. "You heard your king, Malakai! Release that player at once."

James had never seen a storm of conflicted emotions like the one that rose in Malakai's dark eyes at that. Loyalty and murderous hate, anger and duty, rage and discipline--they were all there, shifting and flickering as each warred for dominance. For several horrible moments, James feared the captain was incapable of *not* killing him. But as great as his hate was, Malakai was still a knight, and in the end, he let James go, dropping him on the floor of the council room like a discarded rag.

It took James several seconds to get his breath back and to find his friends. As he'd heard, Flameboyant was trapped in the Arch-Sorcerer's Temporal Prism, which looked like a giant purple bubble with an elf frozen inside it like a prize from a toy machine. On the floor beside him, the captain of the castle garrison had his sword on Ar'Bati's neck. The warrior was bleeding, but he didn't look seriously injured, just stubborn and determined, glaring at James with an unspoken demand that he make this right. James felt the same way, so he forced himself to his feet.

Ignoring his screaming instincts, he turned his back on Malakai and knelt before the king.

"Your Majesty," he said, speaking each word like it might be his last. "I am most sorry for the manner of our entrance, but there was no other way to reach you in time. Please know that we are not your enemies."

The king's gray eyes flicked nervously to Raffestain. When the high priest didn't answer for him, Gregory opened his mouth, closed it, then licked his dry lips. James watched with growing uncertainty. The king hadn't been like this when he'd met him before, but that was back in the game when all he could say was his scripted dialogue. He'd fully expected King Gregory to be a bit different now that he could choose his own words, but of all the reactions James had expected from the eight-foot-tall five-skull raid boss who ruled Bastion, barely concealed panic at being directly addressed was not one of them.

The king was still fiddling with his fingers when Raffestain came to his rescue. Without asking permission, the Sun priest snatched a scroll directly from King Gregory's lap. "You chose a very violent method of contact," he said, flicking a drop of James's blood from the paper before unrolling it. "Let's see what was so important you'd jump through a window to bring it to us."

The "us" part of that made James wince. Before this point, he'd assumed the kingdom was run by its monarch. In the game, Bastion's ruler was very active, certainly not a figurehead. Looking at the dynamic now, though, James wasn't sure if he was trying to convince the king or the king's council. Unsure what else to do, James focused on the king anyway since Raffestain was taking forever to read.

"Your Majesty," he said respectfully, "we tried several times to bring this information to you legitimately, but no one was willing to listen because of our status. Even though I was formally adopted by the Claw Born, I am still a player, and that was all some needed to name me enemy."

He shot a pointed look at Malakai.

"But I am also someone who lives in this world," he went on, nodding at his companions. "We all are. That's why we risked everything to speak with you. Getting Your Majesty's attention is the last chance Bastion has. The undead are planning an invasion, and if nothing is done, they will be successful. We crashed through your window hoping that, if nothing else, this incident would prompt *someone* to read those missives. They prove what we say is true, and it's still not too late to act on them."

"*Lies!*" Malakai shouted from right behind James's head. "They came to assassinate you! All players want is destruction!"

"His Majesty is buried in the proof of our good intent," James said angrily. "Just read the damn--I mean, please peruse the documents we've brought to you at great risk to ourselves. They were taken from the desk of one of the Once King's oldest lich-lords."

To James's continued shock, the King looked at the High Priest again.

"Go ahead, Your Majesty," Raffestain said, placing the scroll in his hands like a mother handing her child a spoon. "I sense no harmful magics, and they are quite the read."

The people in the room waited in unbearably tense silence while the king started to read. When he was done with that letter, he reached for another, his bushy red eyebrows drawing more closely together with each word. Finally, when he'd read the whole stack, the towering king rose from his oversized chair, placing the pile of letters in the seat he'd just vacated to keep them away from the pool of James's blood, which was still congealing on the table.

"Raffestain," the king said, his voice filled with new urgency.

"Yes, my lord?"

"You are skilled at the oldest forms of elven. Do these letters say what they seem to say?"

"I believe they do, my lord," the priest replied. "But your command of elven is excellent for a human, and you read English better than I do, so

I'm sure you did not make a mistake. But I would be happy to read them again if you wish. Just to be certain."

The king considered that offer carefully, but the deadliness of this situation must *finally* have been getting through, because he shook his head. Clearly relieved at being let off the translating hook, Raffestain turned back around to look down his nose at James.

"What is your name?"

"James Anderson of Claw Born, sir."

"James Anderson," the high priest repeated, speaking the name slowly, as though he was testing it. "How did you get these letters?"

"The Ar'Bati of Windy Lake and I slew the lich of Red Canyon," James replied. "We found those in his desk."

"And how did you manage that?" the priest demanded, looking him over. "I can see from your armor that you are low-level. Though the Ar'Bati of Windy Lake is a sub-boss, I very much doubt the two of you could have killed that lich alone."

"We were not alone, sir," James said stubbornly. "We fought alongside the gnolls to defeat the lich and free all the Savanna from the Once King's terror."

That statement earned James a raised eyebrow. "You must think us fools," the high priest rasped. "You would have us believe that the jubatus of the Savanna worked *together* with their greatest ancestral enemy?"

"It is true!" Ar'Bati cried, ignoring the captain of the castle garrison, who swore and pressed his sword even harder against the warrior's throat. "James convinced us to work with the gnolls, and now the Once King's plans in the Savanna are vanquished! The gnolls have been freed from the curse of undeath, and our peoples now work together in unity to face the coming invasion."

Behind him, James could feel Malakai practically vibrating by the time Fangs finished. "My king," he said through clenched teeth. "This story is so *obviously* false--"

"And the 'of Claw Born' part of this James's story?" the high priest said over him.

"It is also true," Fangs in the Grass said proudly. "James is my brother by adoption, and I am proud to fight by his side, today and all days."

That proclamation was met with silence, and then the high priest burst out laughing. "Old Rends Iron Hides never misses an opportunity, does he?" he said, wiping his eyes. "That wild old cat, adopting a player! I'm going to have to invite him to the capital to hear the whole tale when this is over. How did Acacia take it?"

"I doubt he could have done it without my mother's approval, sir," Ar'Bati replied. "She reappeared at Windy Lake when the Nightmare broke."

"That is welcome news, indeed," Raffestain said. "We worried greatly for her when she could not be found in Bastion." He smiled at Ar'Bati before turning back to the king. "I can't help but believe their story, Your Majesty. I know better than to question the famously prickly honor of the four clans' Ar'Bati. If he would stake his pride on this, it must be so."

James almost fell over in relief. Across the room, his brother's grin grew even wider despite the sword at his throat. Their joy didn't last for long, though, because now that the old elf claimed he believed their tale, he was staring at the letters piled on the king's empty throne in new alarm.

"By the Sun!" he exclaimed, whirling on the king, which caused the timid monarch to jump back. "We're in big trouble, Gregory! I must go to the Bastion immediately and add more Clerics."

He turned toward the doors, where a whole contingent of soldiers was waiting awkwardly for someone to tell them what to do. "You there," the priest said, snapping his elegant fingers. "Go tell Captain Hightower to stop rallying troops for his majesty's rescue and take a squadron to secure the Room of Arrivals. Malakai, I want you to go arrest Portal Keeper Star Fall immediately. Dead or alive, it doesn't matter. He must not be allowed to activate the portals!"

An animallike growl issued from Malakai's throat. "I only take orders from his majesty."

Raffestain rolled his eyes and turned back to the king. "King Gregory, if you agree with me on this course of *very urgent* action, could you *please* give the order to make your knight captain do his job?"

Even though the old priest was on his side now, the way he said that made James wince. He was talking to the king the same way a parent would say, "Eat your peas, little boy." Even between old friends, it was painfully disrespectful, but no one called him on it. The king didn't even scowl. He just hunched his big shoulders and said in a quiet voice, "Do as Raffestain says."

As impossible as it seemed, Captain Malakai's face grew even more murderous. "I will not be--"

"You heard your king," the priest said with a superior sneer. "*Go.*"

Gregory winced at the obvious antagonism and backed away from his knight captain, covering the obvious retreat up by bending over to write something down on a bloodstained piece of paper from the table, which he then handed to the captain of the castle garrison.

"Please arrest everyone on this list," the king said timidly. "They are all spies and saboteurs of the Once King. Most have, I fear, already carried out their plans, but do try to get whatever information you can from them so we may attempt to repair the damage."

The human captain of the garrison yanked Ar'Bati to his feet and marched over, keeping his sword on the warrior's neck even as he accepted the paper.

"And please release the head warrior of Windy Lake," Raffestain added.

The captain scowled and glanced at the king. When Gregory nodded, he let Ar'Bati go, bowed, and stomped out, bellowing orders at the waiting soldiers before the doors were even closed. When he was gone, James began to rise to his feet as well, but he only made it halfway before he realized Malakai was still glaring at his back like he was trying to put a knife in it through sheer will.

"*Malakai*," the old priest said sharply, "snap out of it, man! We have a crisis on our hands. Stop glaring at the young Claw Born and go help us fix this problem!"

"Yes, Malakai," added the arch-sorcerer, speaking in the same calm, soothing voice used to talk down a growling dog. "The king has spent the last four hours listening to your excessively bloody and frankly barbaric plan to crush the player encampment in the south and given it his blessing. Surely that will be enough blood even for you. Now go arrest Portal Keeper Star Fall so we don't get backstabbed the moment the Bastion goes down, and you can get right back to plotting how to kill every player in the city."

"Do not speak so lightly of my work, magician," Malakai growled. "While you talk and hide in the castle, scuttling after imagined threats, my knights and I are out there *dying* to defend Bastion from the real demons that are already in our midst!"

"Yes, yes," Raffestain said impatiently. "We've heard the story of your heroic death *several* times now. But this is--"

"You are fools to take this demon at his word!" the captain snarled, reaching down to grab James by the scruff of his neck. "But you were so caught up in the 'Claw Born' part of his introduction, you missed the part that was actually important." Malakai yanked James around, putting them face to face again. "What did you say your name was, player?"

"James Anderson of Claw Born," James repeated meekly.

The captain's eyes flashed. "James *Anderson*. Any relation to Christina Anderson?"

James went still.

"Who's Christina Anderson?" Raffestain demanded. "And why should we care? Sounds like a little girl."

"She's no little girl," Malakai growled, the hate in his eyes burning brighter than ever. "After my resurrection, I interrogated many players to discover more about the stonekin who killed me. Turns out, this 'Roxxy' was quite famous in their realm, a military scholar who taught others the art of combat on something called the 'YouTube.' But like all of them, she is merely a demon inhabiting a stonekin's body, and her *real* name is Christina Anderson." He tilted his head at James. "How interesting that the only player to make it into the king's presence would share a name with our greatest enemy and leader of the rebellion that even now threatens the throne."

"Come, man," Raffestain said dismissively. "A common name is no proof. There's a thousand elves named Highcloud, and no one would say they're all related. Rends Iron Hides is an honorable old cat who is unquestionably loyal to Bastion. There's no way he'd adopt a son who was related to a rebel leader." The priest turned to James. "Right?"

James swallowed, sweating bullets. This would be the perfect time to say he'd never heard of Roxxy, but denying his sister felt too much like betrayal, and it would undoubtedly come back to bite him later when the truth came out. Everyone in the Roughnecks' raid knew that he was Tina's brother. If Malakai was interrogating players, it was just a matter of time before he found someone who could prove James and Tina's relation. If he lied now and got found out, everything else he'd said would also be thrown into question, including the letters they'd nearly died to bring here. He couldn't let that happen, so with a wince, James told them.

"Christina Anderson is my sister."

"*I knew it!*" Malakai shouted, shaking James at the king. "Do you see their plot now? He's in league with them! This 'invasion' is nothing but a ploy by Roxxy and her rebels to distract our attention so they can buy time to build up their power and steal your throne!"

"No, it's *not!*" James cried, reaching up to pry futilely at Malakai's impossibly strong grip on the back of his neck. "Tina is my sister, but we've been separated for most of our time here! She was stuck in the Deadlands, fighting the Once King's armies, while I was in the Savanna, defending Windy Lake. I only found her again when we teleported into

290

Bastion yesterday, and even then, I wasn't part of her raid. I was her prisoner, as were Ar'Bati and Flameboyant. We're *not* working together! I actually tried to stop her from attacking your camp because I didn't want to be party to rebellion against the king!"

"Such lies," Malakai scoffed. "You really expect us to believe that you, a *player*, would side with the king against your own blood?"

"*Yes!*" James shouted. "Because I'm *not* lying!" He turned desperately to the king, who was watching all of this in shock. "The undead are coming, Your Majesty! And Tina doesn't want your throne. She's only fighting the knights because they were killing players. This whole war is a giant misunderstanding, and it's going to get us all killed when the Once King's army arrives and finds us in chaos. I tried to tell my sister, but she wouldn't listen, so the three of us escaped from her to warn you in person. My companions and I went through many perils to bring these letters to you, including defeating the Assassin my sister sent after us."

James hated how that sounded. He was helping Malakai paint Tina as a villain when her only real crime was being too hotheaded and heavy-handed. But there was no room for gray areas or complicated family histories here. He *had* to make the king believe. "I swear all of this is true," he said earnestly. "The Ar'Bati does as well. We are *not* your enemies!"

The king and Raffestain exchanged looks, and then the old priest sighed. "This does complicate matters," he said, picking the stack of letters up off the throne again. "But no matter the source, this threat is too dire not to act upon. I suggest we lock the player and his companions up until we've investigated everything thoroughly."

"If that's how you feel, then I agree," the king said, looking relieved. "We'll proceed with the arrests of the accused traitors. Meanwhile, these players and the Ar'Bati shall be locked in the dungeon until this is sorted out. Will that satisfy you, Captain Malakai?"

"No, it will not," the captain said sharply. "You are allowing Raffestain's weakness to cloud your judgment. We have the brother of our most dangerous enemy in our possession! This is an unprecedented opportunity." He tightened his grip on James's neck. "Let me keep James Anderson, your majesty. I'll make him howl such that his demon sister will crawl out of her camp on her--"

"*No,*" the king said, making everyone jump. He hadn't shouted, but his deep voice was suddenly deafening, filling the room until the stones shook. The noise made Gregory jump, too, and then he dragged a hand over his face. "We'll not torture one sibling to lure out another," he said, quietly now. "Such acts stain the honor of Bastion."

"But this is war," Malakai argued. "We can't ignore such a powerful--"

"No, Malakai," the king said, his eyes tired. "I've already given you my armies and my siege weapons and everything else you've asked for to deal with the player threat. But this goes too far. We can't torture the player whose warning might well be our salvation."

The captain's grip began to shake on James's neck. "You can't possibly--"

"The king has spoken," Raffestain said sharply. "Let him go, Malakai. He can do us no harm locked in a dungeon, and we might need him later should we have questions."

"Yes, questions, quite right," the king agreed, nodding quickly. "Take all three of them to the dungeon. Gently, please."

The guards waiting outside the door looked at each other nervously, but they didn't actually obey until Raffestain waved them in. With a growl that would have done a jubatus proud, Malakai released James at last, dropping him to the floor, where he landed on his feet and immediately put his hands out for the guards to bind, doing his best to look as docile and nonthreatening as possible. After a few pointed looks, Ar'Bati did the same, though he looked decidedly sourer about the iron bands being slapped around his wrists.

"You will regret this," Malakai promised the king as the guards started easing Flameboyant out of the arch-sorcerer's bubble. "Players do nothing but destroy what we have built. You are making a terrible mistake trusting this one."

Raffestain rolled his eyes at that, but the king looked deeply troubled, and James stepped forward. "If I may ask a boon," he said gently. "I'd like to request an audience with His Majesty to prove we mean Bastion nothing but good. It can be through cell bars. I just want a chance to talk."

The king looked baffled by this request, but when he looked at Raffestain, the old elf shrugged. "I see no danger in the request. If His Majesty wills it, it makes no difference to me."

The king's lips twitched in the hint of a smile. "Then I will consider the request," he said, nodding at James.

James beamed back, giving the king his most earnest smile as the guards dragged him away.

Chapter 13

Tina

After the frantic battle-planning session for Camp Comeback broke up, Tina got everyone present to agree to keep the wind-fire powder, aka plan B, hush-hush. They didn't require much convincing. All the guild leaders and officers understood that wind-fire powder was a weapon of mass destruction and therefore not something to be used lightly. Tina didn't want to think she was the kind of person who would seriously consider engulfing the world's largest city in a nuclear-grade firestorm just to win, but she had people to protect, and their backs were to the wall. It was definitely a last resort, but there was no point in making a threat if you weren't prepared to use it. If they were cornered and push came to shove, she was prepared to shove with all they had.

When everything was decided and everyone was on the same page, CincoDeMurder ordered his PVPers to let everyone in to hear the plan. The players, who'd been waiting outside for an hour now, crammed themselves into the former training hall's giant stone building. With so many people, Tina expected chaos, but the crowd was grim and silent, listening without so much as a peep as she, Cinco, and Assets explained what was coming and the plan they'd worked out to beat it.

"I'm not going to lie," Tina said once everything had been explained. "The odds are hella against us. But we've got a good position, a plan, and a whole bunch of badasses of our own. The Roughnecks have already proven that we can munch through Royal Knights like popcorn. We've got no problem doing so again, but this fight is too big for just one raid. It's going to take all of us--low levels, max levels, healers, crafters, *everyone*--working together to survive, so I want everyone to go back out into the yard and organize yourselves by level and class. Also, if you have a max-level crafting skill, get together in front of the Blacksmithing Hut.

The guild leaders, officers, and CraftyJohn, our new civic engineer and master base builder, will be out shortly to give everyone new quests."

The crowd slumped a bit at the mention of quests. Tina didn't blame them. It was already afternoon. Most of the players in front of her had been working since dawn, and that was on top of yesterday's harrowing march. Many of them were still injured and exhausted from hiding in the city, but there was nothing for it.

"I know you're tired," she said gently. "I'm tired too. But this is our big stand. Remember: we're the survivors. We all worked our asses off to make it this far. Like hell are we going down now. So get out there and get yourselves ready. We'll be out to get this thing started shortly."

The players nodded and started walking back out into the yard to organize themselves into the groups Tina had described. When she was sure everyone was on task, she turned back to the gathered leaders and CraftyJohn, who'd left the larger player mass to join them.

"You guys know the drill," she said. "Assets, you're on logistics, so all the lower-level players and crafters are yours. Cinco, you're training battle teams. Anyone out there who's geared and over level sixty is all yours. CraftyJohn, you're in charge of base defense. Grab all the muscle you need from the other groups, and don't be afraid to rip stones out of buildings if that's what it takes to get our borders secured. My Roughnecks will handle heals and any boss fights as well as contributing to general defense."

"What about quest rewards?" Assets asked. "People won't work if they're not motivated."

"Their motivation is not dying," Tina said firmly. "If we survive this, everyone who contributed gets max-level faction status with Camp Comeback. People understand what that means now."

"And no one's going to slack when their asses are on the line," Cinco finished.

"Exactly," Tina said, looking around at her fellow leaders. "Everyone know what to do?"

They all nodded and started toward the doors. Cinco started bellowing for fighters to come to him before he was even outside, while Assets had his assistants rounding up the low-level players for him like sheepdogs, sending all the burly-strength classes over to CraftyJohn. Satisfied that everything was running smoothly, Tina went out to round up her Roughnecks, only to find they were already together and waiting for her.

The sight made her grin. She wasn't sure when exactly things had changed, but the group in front of her looked entirely different from the grudging crowd she'd addressed in the Room of Arrivals. They were still quiet and grim, but it was a determined sort of silence now, all of them gripping their weapons as Tina hopped up on a rock to address them.

"Roughnecks," she said proudly, "we're the only real raid here, so we've got the toughest job of all. We're going to be holding the north bridge, which is the largest and most likely the main avenue of attack. We've got the best gear in this whole place, so if you haven't already, I want everyone to stop by Assets and his crafters and make sure your equipment is in top shape. But as powerful as it is, our gear is only part of our advantage. Our real strength is our ability to fight together. As I mentioned earlier, Malakai's alive again, and there's also the king to worry about. That's at least one, possibly two bosses, but raid bosses are our thing. As soon as one appears, I'll give the signal, and we'll all group up to take them down just like we did Grel."

"But we don't have walls to collapse this time," Zen pointed out.

"Our enemy's also not the size of a building," Tina replied, leaving out the part where that actually made them harder to fight. Grel, at least she could position. She hadn't been able to control Malakai at all. The king would probably be even worse, but there was nothing she could do about that. She'd just have to cross her fingers and hope that a raid could still kill a raid boss, even an intelligent one.

"This isn't like the Deadlands," she said firmly. "Grel'Darm was a boss from the Dead Mountain, the hardest instance in the game. The king

296

and Malakai are normal-world bosses. They're tough, and they hit hard, but they don't have any fancy mechanics or ghost fire. This is a classic tank 'n' spank. All we have to do is keep them controlled and burn them down. Easy peasy."

"Maybe we'll even get loot!" Neko said excitedly.

"Maybe," Tina said with a smile. "But we all know how to do our parts already, so after you take care of your gear, I want all the damage dealers helping Cinco train up the others. We're also in charge of healing, so Naturalists and Clerics, you're going to be organizing the lowbies into healing raids. Anders, you're on point for that."

The fish-man Cleric lifted his staff in agreement while Neko glared murder at him. Tina wasn't happy about that dynamic, but there was no way she was putting *NekoBaby* in charge of other people. If she left Neko under Anders, though, there were sure to be problems, so she came up with a quick solution instead.

"NekoBaby, you're helping Zen expand the hospital to get it ready to receive non-critical wounded. Other Rangers, you're on scout duty. I want to know every move the enemy makes."

The Rangers saluted and immediately grouped up to start organizing shifts. Zen rolled her eyes at being given Neko duty, but she didn't object, which was good enough for Tina.

"That's it except for Sorcerers. You guys come to me. I've got a special job for you. Everyone else, get to work."

The raid saluted and split, everyone hurrying off to their assignments except for the Sorcerers and SB, who stayed stubbornly by her side.

"Don't want to go help Cinco?" she asked him quietly as everyone else moved off.

"He doesn't need me," SB said, shaking his head. "There's not much I can offer so long as the Bastion's up, and anyway, I just got back. I'd like to stay by you, if that's all right."

Tina's heart began to pound at that. If she'd still had real blood or flesh, she was sure her face would be burning. Thankfully for her pride, stone didn't reveal anything, leaving her looking only slightly off kilter as the Sorcerers came forward, chattering excitedly.

"*Roxxy!*" cried an exuberant jubatus Sorcerer with red-streaked fur. "Did you know that *Richard* joined the Roughnecks?"

"Um, I'm the guildmaster, so yes," she replied dryly, turning to give the tall, black-haired human Sorcerer of mention a smile. "Liking it so far?"

"No one has made fun of me yet for my lack of PVP Arena titles, so yes. I am enjoying it very much," Richard replied flatly. Then his gaze flicked past her to SB. "You're an elf Assassin standing next to Roxxy. I don't suppose you're *the* SilentBlayde, are you?"

"I am," SB said, stepping up to offer his hand. "Hi, Richard. It's an honor to finally meet you."

For the first time, Richard's ever-serious face burst into a smile as he lurched forward to shake SB's hand. "The honor is mine, I assure you. Your gearing spreadsheet comparing the optimal DPS output for all endgame Assassin armor was genius. I made all of my raiders use it before we fell apart."

SilentBlayde blushed. "I got the idea from your famous Mega-Sorcerer Math post a few years ago. But I'm so happy you survived! Welcome to the Roughnecks, by the way."

"I was most thankful to be admitted," Richard said. "It is a relief to be back among civilized people who appreciate the execution challenge of raiding."

"No argument there," Tina said with a cocky grin before turning to the other Sorcerers, who were still talking excitedly about getting to play with *the* Richard. "All right, folks, serious-pants time. I called you over here because I've got a secret mission for you."

"*Really?*" one of the Sorcerers gasped.

"Legit," Tina confirmed. "As in you can't spill the fucking beans on this 'cause it might get us all killed. The Sorcerers didn't have an officer in the meeting earlier because--"

Because KatanaFatale died was what Tina had intended to say, but her throat was still having trouble with those words, and they weren't necessary, anyway. She knew from the way everyone's shoulders fell that they felt the loss as much as she did. "Anyway, someone needs to be in charge. Which one of you wants to be the new officer?"

All the Sorcerers turned to look at Richard, who looked slightly abashed.

"Actually, they've already chosen me."

Tina gaped at him. "For real?" He nodded, but she still didn't believe it. "No offense, Richard, but you just joined this morning. How are you an officer already?"

"Duh, because he's *Richard*," an ichthyian Sorcerer informed her scornfully. "He wrote the FFORaiders-dot-com Sorcerer Guide! Most of us are using the fire-talent build *he* invented. Hell, it's even called Richard-spec. It wouldn't be right if he wasn't our rep."

All the other Sorcerers nodded as though that should have been obvious. Beside her, SB was struggling to smother his laughter, while Richard just looked uncomfortable. He didn't try to argue down the praise, though, so Tina just shrugged.

"Right on, then," she said. "If you're sure he's the one you want..."

"Definitely," the Sorcerers said, patting Richard on the back, which only made him look even more uncomfortable.

When the hubbub finally died down, Richard cleared his throat and turned to face Tina. "So what was it you wanted us to do, Roxxy?"

Tina leaned in closer, lowering her voice. "You're familiar with wind-fire powder, right?"

"Of course," Richard said. "It was heavily used in the Ember Valley questlines as a transparent metaphor for nuclear weapons."

"Yeah, well, we've got some," Tina said. "Enough to consume this entire city if need be. I don't intend to use it, but if this goes bad and we get cornered, wind-fire powder is the only weapon big enough to force the king to negotiate. There's no point in making a threat if you can't actually carry it through, though, so I need a way to make sure we can set the wind-fire powder off without torching ourselves in the process."

Richard frowned. "What sort of way?"

"I was hoping you could tell me," she replied with a shrug. "I've seen NekoBaby and a few of the other casters doing new things with their magic that they couldn't do back in the game. Sorcerers are masters of fire, and NPCs are always casting wards and barriers. Can we do something like that?"

"You mean a ward against fire?" Richard said thoughtfully.

Tina nodded. "Ward, barrier, counter-spell--I don't care what it is so long as it can protect us from the wind-fire powder's inferno."

The Sorcerer frowned thoughtfully, standing so quiet and so still that Tina started to worry.

"Um, Richard? Did you hear me?"

Richard blinked as if she'd startled him. "Yes, sorry. I heard you, but there are a lot of variables to consider before I can answer. For example, the tremendous surface area of any sphere large enough to encompass two thousand people, which has an exponential impact on the ratio of barrier strength to compounding mana requirements. Also, does it need to be a full sphere? All wards in the game are spherical, but is that an absolute requirement? Could we save on the power requirement by making a pyramid or dome? And how much power would be required of each Sorcerer to--"

"Okay, okay, I get the idea," Tina said, holding her up hands. "You guys work on that and let me know when you figure it out."

Richard nodded and lapsed back into silence, completely ignoring the other Sorcerers, who broke into instant arguments behind him. Shaking her head, Tina left them to it, confident they'd figure it out eventually. She'd already seen the miracles Intelligence gear could work, and Sorcerers had the most of any class. Also, they had Richard, the most skilled Sorcerer in FFO. The dude had figured out how to exploit every damage-increasing hack in the game. *Surely* he could do the same with actual magic. Tina just hoped he'd be able to explain it to the others.

Watching him stand in silence while everyone else talked around him, she was starting to understand why his old guild had fallen apart. Richard was clearly a genius, but he was also one of those people who were so analytical it made normal social interaction difficult. Tina couldn't imagine what had driven him to be a guild leader. Even the best-run guilds were constant drama engines. It must have been hell for the poor guy, but he was clearly a glutton for punishment, because he'd accepted the position of officer here. Tina would just have to trust him to do it well.

With that, she left them to their work, walking back into the middle of the now-empty stretch of grass in front of Trainers' Hall. Everyone else was already off, frantically working on their jobs under the guidance of the other leaders. The efficiency should have made her happy, but as the chattering clump of Sorcerers dragged the still silently thinking Richard into the storage house to get a look at the wind-fire powder, all Tina felt was a cold lump growing in her stomach.

"You okay?" SB whispered beside her.

"I'm fine."

He gave her a skeptical look, and Tina sighed.

"Just feeling the pressure," she admitted quietly, turning to gaze up at the Bastion gleaming in the distance. "Everyone's doing everything I could ask, but we're still in a really tight spot. I mean, I just talked to a bunch of Sorcerers about making us a magical bunker to hide in while we torch a city. That's heavy stuff. Even if everything goes right, people are probably going to die, and..."

And she was afraid. It was easy to be brave in front of a crowd, but now that everything was in motion, the impossibility of what they were trying to do felt like a rope tightening around her neck.

301

"I don't want to make the wrong choice," she said at last. "My screwups have already gotten enough people killed. That Sorcerer who died at the Dead Mountain on day zero, David on the hill in the Deadlands, KatanaFatale yesterday... It's my fault they're gone. *I'm* the one who messed up and made a stupid call, but they had to pay for it. I don't want that to happen again."

"It won't," SB said, pulling down his mask to give her a smile. "CincoDeMurder and Shankfest won the international FFOCon 2v2 tournament last year, and Assets is the only billionaire in FFO history. As for Richard, well, you've seen yourself how famous he is. What I'm trying to say is that we're up to our necks in world-class players, so there's no reason everything has to fall on you. All you have to do is what you've already done: keep everyone together and pointed in the right direction. I know you can do it. You're one of the best tanks in FFO history. So long as you're at the front, that army won't stand a chance. If we're lucky, it might not even come to a fight. Don't forget--those soldiers aren't mindless NPCs anymore. They're people, which means they can get scared just like us." His grin grew wider. "I bet they'll take one look at what you've built here and break."

"I hope you're right," Tina said, but her heart wasn't in it. She'd seen the hate in Malakai and his knights. That sort of irrational anger didn't just go away because you were facing a tough opponent. They'd already proven they would fight the players to the last breath. Tina knew her people would do the same, mostly because they had no other option. That was the trouble with "do or die"--it didn't leave a lot of room for compromise. But she appreciated the sentiment nonetheless.

"Thanks for the vote of confidence, 'Blayde," she said, giving him a smile back. "I'm one of our only max-level blacksmiths, so I have to get to the forge and help with armor. What do you want to do?"

SB shrugged. "Normally I'd say scout, but I'm pretty useless thanks to the Bastion. I am a max-level leather worker, though."

"We actually have plenty of those," Tina said, thinking it over. Then she spotted a beleaguered Frank sitting behind the quest table, dealing with a flock of players Assets had "delegated" back over, and her face lit up.

"Hey, 'Blayde," she said with a grin. "Ever wanted to be a quest giver?"

He glanced at the table, and a delighted look spread over his face before he replaced his mask.

"Totally."

***

The rest of the afternoon passed in a blur. Tina spent most of it in the forges, banging out armor and swords for the seemingly endless stream of Knights and Berserkers who were missing key pieces of gear. Assets grumbled constantly about how much of their metal she was using, but Tina paid him no attention. They'd worry about resupply *after* they survived. Right now, she was armoring their front line, and if that wasn't worth every bit of iron on the island, nothing was.

Everyone else seemed to be working just as hard. She could hear Cinco drilling units just outside, and the Rangers checked in constantly with reports on the king's army, which seemed to be busy with some kind of crisis in the castle. That was fine with her. Maybe they'd get lucky and some ambitious lord would try for a coup. Anything that kept the NPCs at each other's throats and away from hers.

She was on her way back to Assets's supply pile to pick up another load of metal when she spotted a fluffy jubatus tail twitching from around a corner. The butt of its owner was unfortunately known to her, so Tina sighed and walked around the bend to see what was going on.

Sure enough, NekoBaby was standing on a stacked pile of teetering crates, using the height to peek through the back window of one of the smaller huts surrounding the main hall. Tina couldn't remember which trainer had used that particular space, but the free-standing building was lovely: a small, tall, circular structure with an airy dome on top, sunburst details painted across its whitewashed sides, and a ring of tiny stained-glass windows around the top that Neko was holding herself up by the claws to look through.

"What are you doing?"

Neko jumped at her voice, then she turned around with a hiss, pressing a finger against her lips. "*Shhh!*" she said, pulling herself back up to the window. "Can't you see I'm spying?"

"Which is why I'm calling you out," Tina replied, crossing her arms over her chest. "You're supposed to be helping Zen."

Neko snorted. "Grumpy Mom doesn't need help from me. She could run that hospital with her eyes closed. That place is like an episode of *ER* minus the drama. This is way more important." She squinted through the window. "Anders is up to something *weird.*"

"As long as it's consensual and his work is getting done, I don't care what he's doing," Tina said irritably. "And it's none of your business, anyway, Neko. We have more important things to..." She trailed off, eyes going wide. "Wait, what are you *wearing?*"

She'd been so focused on Neko's behavior, she hadn't realized the cat-girl's outfit was equally as bizarre until just now. In addition to Frank's giant shapeless undershirt, which she'd been wearing belted over her torn robes since the Deadlands, Neko had added bulky leather shoulder pads *under* the cloth. It made her look like a football player, and the leather bra-band-thing she'd wrapped around her chest only added to the effect. The straps were pulled so tight over the cat-girl's prodigious bosom, Tina felt short of breath just looking at her, but the weirdest part of all of this was that none of it was necessary. She'd seen to it personally that Neko's robes, ripped days ago by Anders during the delusional start of things, had been mended by Camp Comeback's tailors. She should be totally back to normal now, so Tina couldn't comprehend why she was wearing such insanity.

"Holy crap, Neko," Tina blurted. "What are you doing with all that? This stuff isn't even magical."

"Stuff..." Neko said, ears drooping as she looked down.

Tina was so shocked she took a physical step back. A demure and dissembling NekoBaby? Forget weird behavior. Something had to be *seriously* wrong.

"Neko, are you okay?" she whispered, moving closer so she was eye to eye with the cat on the crates. "I'm your friend. You can tell me."

The cat-girl rolled her eyes. "Gah, don't go all counselor on me," she grumbled, looking everywhere but Tina. "This isn't a cry for help. I just hate how I look, okay?"

"Believe me, I feel ya," Tina said, pulling some of her copper metal-not-metal hair forward. "Being nonhuman is pretty damn unsettling. You should see how I look under the armor."

The cat-girl snorted. "Everyone got a look at *that*, Miss Nudist-by-the-River. But it's not the cat stuff I mind. That part's actually pretty cool, but this girl shit is the pits! My body just feels so *wrong*."

"Not getting used to it?" Tina asked. She knew that most players were adjusting to their new bodies whether they liked it or not. Her own distancing from "fleshy" concerns was a prime example, but maybe the change was different when it came to gender. After all, there were plenty of normal humans back home who felt like they'd been born into the wrong bodies, and she'd never tell them to just "get used to it."

"No, I'm not fucking adjusting, and I don't want to!" snapped Neko. "So many people here won the fucking lottery. Look at SB! He looks like Legolas modeling for a shampoo commercial. Why didn't I roll an elf? Or even a normal jubatus? I'd be totally cool as a tall, burly cat-dude, but this... I *never* feel right, Roxxy! I have hooters. I have this dainty fucking body. I have new parts down below to deal with. It's not me, it's *wrong*, and it's *all the time*! I can't live like this!"

"And that's why you're binding your chest flat and wearing shoulder pads?" Tina asked. "To look more manlike?"

"It's a start," the cat-girl said, tiny hands balled into fists. "I know they look stupid, but it's the best I could think of. I was no athlete back home. Hell, I was a shut-in. I admit it. I hated how I looked back then, too, but I would give anything to be in my old body again now. *Anything!*"

That last cry was so desperate, it made Tina's heart ache. She reached forward awkwardly and pulled NekoBaby into a hug. The Naturalist tensed at first but didn't fight her, so Tina held on, patting NekoBaby on the back while the cat-girl trembled.

"It'll be okay," she whispered into Neko's fur. "This is only temporary. We'll find a way out of here, and everything will be fixed. For both of us."

NekoBaby held on for another few seconds, then she buried her face in the crook of Tina's shoulder plate with a sob. "I just want to go home."

"I'll get you home," Tina said quietly. "I promise."

They stayed that way for about a minute, Tina letting NekoBaby cry softly on her armored shoulder. Then NekoBaby pushed away from her, her face flushed with embarrassment beneath her damp fur. "Can we not talk about this ever again?"

"Never again," Tina promised, crossing her heart--or where her heart would have been if she'd still been human. "Now please go back to the medical tent. I know Zen's super-competent, but she's not a magical healer. I need you to make sure she doesn't get veteran-nurse-seen-it-all tunnel vision and forget that things are different here."

"Okay," Neko said, wiping her nose. "But who's going to keep an eye on fish-boy? 'Cause he's being *super* weird, and I don't just say that because I hate him." She scowled. "I'm still planning to poison him, by the way."

"I know," Tina said bitterly, wondering how she was ever going to resolve what had happened between Neko and Anders or if she even could. Leylia's or no, he'd done something unforgivable, and Tina had no idea what to do about that except make sure it never happened again.

"Leave Anders to me," she said. "You get to Zen. Remember: you healers are the most important part of this fight. If we go down to Bastion's army, you'll never get to poison anyone."

NekoBaby huffed. "I guess so," she muttered, climbing down from the crates at last. "Thanks, Roxxy."

Tina knew better than to ask what that thanks was referring to. She just shooed the healer off and walked around the circular building to see what Anders was doing to freak Neko out.

What she discovered was not what she'd expected. The white circular building turned out to be a small temple to the Sun. This must have been where the Cleric trainer stood, she realized belatedly, poking her head through the curtained entrance. Now that she was looking at it, she vaguely remembered coming here as ClaraSpell years ago. The place was pretty small--just a single circular room below a domed ceiling with a ring of stained-glass windows that transformed the sunlight into a rainbow of color--but it was lovely and surprisingly holy feeling, especially since Anders was kneeling on the worn golden rune at its center, bowing his head to the east as his fish lips murmured silent words.

He stopped when she came in, and Tina immediately felt guilty, as though she'd interrupted something important. She raised her hands in silent apology and started to slip back out again when Anders said, "It's okay."

"I didn't mean to interrupt you," Tina said, tilting her head curiously. "Were you praying?"

Anders sighed. "I was trying to." He glanced nervously at her. "Do you think that's strange?"

Tina remembered the enigmatic presence she'd felt looking down on them when Anders had cast his cleansing spell in the Deadlands, not to mention the unseen power that had guided her hammer during her sun-metal smithing earlier, and shook her head. "Absolutely not. There are *definitely* higher powers in this world." She leaned forward excitedly. "So did anyone answer you?"

Anders's fish-face grew sad. "Sort of. I wasn't asking for anything, though. I was apologizing."

He certainly had a lot to apologize for. Anders had tried to rape the unconscious NekoBaby back when they'd first transitioned from game to real FFO, before he'd known things were not a dream brought on by his Leylia's disease. Tina had stopped him before he'd done the deed, but that didn't mean the damage hadn't been done to all involved.

"Seeking atonement from a higher power is a good start," Tina said. "But the one you should really be apologizing to is NekoBaby. He's the one you hurt." Since Anders knew the cat-girl's secret and they were alone, Tina felt okay using NekoBaby's true gender.

"I have apologized," Anders said. "Many times. But he won't accept it. That wasn't what I was asking the gods for forgiveness for, though."

Tina winced. "What new infraction do you need to pray for?"

Anders held up his glittering staff, turning the crystal at its peak to catch the light of the afternoon sun until the whole temple glowed bright gold with the light that was unique to FFO Clerics.

"For this," he said, flashing the light a few more times before he set his staff down on the ground. "I'm a Cleric *class*, Roxxy. I use the holy power of the Sun every time I cast a spell, but you and I both know I'm not an actual, ordained Sun priest. I didn't earn any of these holy powers through humility or goodness of heart. Fate just handed them to me because I rolled the class. Stop and think about the theological implications of that for a minute, and you'll see why I felt the need to apologize."

"Holy shit," Tina said, taking a step back. "Are you stealing power from a *god*? Is it mad?" Because she didn't think she could tank the Sun if it became a problem.

"I am definitely stealing," Anders said. "All player Clerics are, but I think saying sorry helped. At least, I know the Sun isn't mad at *me*."

"You're blowing my mind, Anders," Tina said, shaking her head. "You actually talked to a god? As in legit greater being?"

"Talk isn't the right word," Anders said with a shrug. "I just get feelings, one of which is that we are as unfathomable to the Sun as it is to us. It doesn't seem to understand why mortals act as we do. I tried to ask about players specifically, but all I could get was that our relationship falls into the 'it's complicated' category."

"That's good to hear," Tina said with a relieved breath. "Complicated is a lot better than furious. So are the other gods friendly? Can we talk to them too?"

Anders looked down, the feathery gills on his neck wiggling as he considered the question. "I'm pretty sure the Naturalists talk to the Wind and the Water on a daily basis without knowing it," he said at last. "They're basically nature priests, if you want to get technical about it. So yes, I'd say we can clearly talk to gods. Whether they'll listen or care is another matter."

"What about the Bedrock Kings?" Tina asked excitedly. "Can I pray to them? Because I have some questions about Stonekin 101 that need explaining."

That earned her a burbling laugh. "As each stonekin is supposedly handcrafted by the Bedrock Kings, I wouldn't be surprised if you could talk to them," he said. "I've no idea how, though, since they're not gods. According to the Wiki, the Bedrock Kings were celestial elves who turned their backs on the Sun and made a kingdom deep underground, hence their name."

Tina looked around the Sun temple nervously. "That sounds dark. I'm not on bad terms with the Sun god here, am I?"

The ichthyian Cleric looked at the Sun coming in through the western windows, and his fish eyes grew distant, like he'd stepped out of his body. It was super creepy to see, and Tina was about to tell him to forget it when he suddenly came back.

"You're in the 'it's complicated' category too, it seems," he told her with a smile. "The Sun is very..." He trailed off, searching for the word.

"Mature," he said at last. "But I guess that's one of the benefits of being an eternal greater being. You always get to take the long view."

"I'm okay with complicated," Tina said, giving him a smile. "Thanks for checking. If you're done conversing with gods, though, I need you to get back to work. As I just told Neko, heals are the most important part of this operation. We're outnumbered enough as it is. We can't take any more people going down. I'm trusting all of you to figure out how to keep everyone up on limited mana."

"Of course, Roxxy," Anders said. "I was just letting the others have a break. The new healers especially aren't used to casting for long periods of time. I was letting them recover before we trained again."

"Sounds great," Tina said. "Thanks for the hard work, Anders." She started to walk out but stopped. "I hate to keep bringing this up," she said with a sigh. "But if Neko tries something on you, don't react. Just bring it to me, and I'll handle it. I don't want the situation between you two to deteriorate any further."

Anders gave her a determined look. "Neko could stab me, and I wouldn't lay a finger on him. Never again."

"But I would have to," Tina said sadly. "I know it sounds callous, but the two of you are the best geared and most experienced healers we've got. I can't afford to lose either of you, so let's just keep things separate, okay?"

Anders nodded. Tina nodded back and left the temple, wondering if she'd ever have a conversation with Anders that didn't cause her an existential crisis.

***

By sunset, Tina had used up all the metal Assets had allotted her. On the one hand, this was great because it meant she was still able to forge armor at speeds close to what she'd managed in the game. On the other hand, it was a pain because now she was going to have to ask the stingy elf for more. At least she was on the lower-level suits now. Those took far fewer materials but still more than what she had left, so Tina sucked it up and marched across the now-dark grass toward the storage area of Camp Comeback.

The camp had changed a lot while she'd been working. Even in the dark, she could see that the once-open riverbank was now lined with walls and stone chunks that could act as charge breakers. It was a phenomenal amount of work considering how little time they'd had, and she made a mental note to reward CraftyJohn if they survived this. But while some of the changes were great, others were more concerning.

As she made her way toward Assets's domain, Tina was shocked by all the new clusters of low-level players huddled on the grass or sleeping under overhangs of the less useful buildings. Frank had said two thousand earlier, but the reality of that number was something else. Looking around in the dark, Tina felt like they'd been flooded by a sea of hungry people. They were all alarmingly dirty and gaunt, but what really threw her for a loop was that some of them were children.

Since there were no underage player character models, Tina realized with a jolt that these must be the NPC families Frank had been talking about. Most ran when they saw her coming, but a few watched her curiously, staring at her with that trademark child's lack of self-awareness as she walked past.

Tina stared back. She had no idea what could have inspired NPCs to come here, but other than their ages, they didn't look that different from the huddled players. They were just more scared, desperate people looking to her for protection, just like everyone else.

She missed a step as the staggering weight of that responsibility sank in. Holy shit, how was she going to do this? How was she going to keep so many people safe? How was she going to keep them all from starving? This whole island was about to become a battleground. Where would they go when the fighting started? She couldn't assign kids jobs as she could players, but what was she going to do with them all? In the game, kids had been untargetable, but the girl trailing curiously behind her looked solid and terrifyingly vulnerable. How was Tina going to keep her from dying to a stray arrow?

It was a horrifying thought and one she didn't have an answer to. She'd already put in motion every plan she could think of. There was nothing else to do except push on, so Tina forced her growing panic down and marched into the well-lit storage building draped in the green and gold of the East Bastion Trade Company.

Stepping inside was a new form of depressing. The once-packed-to-bursting storage hall was now looking empty. To one side of the door, players were lined up to make supplies requests from a low-level Sorcerer wearing a Trade Company tabard and armed with a clipboard. Assets himself, however, was nowhere to be seen. Tina was looking around for him when she spotted a schtumple setting up shop just outside of the massive doorway.

That was strange enough to make her pause. Schtumples were an even less popular player class than stonekin, so you never saw many of them, and those you did were usually one-off joke characters. This one wasn't dressed in armor like a player, though. Tina wasn't sure what it was, actually. Since they were all as round as balls, schtumple gender was hard to tell, but this one was handsomely dressed in brown breeches and a green linen shirt pulled comically tight across its spherical body. It had thrown a blanket over a pair of crates to form a table in the grassy area just beyond the doorway and was setting out common items like boots, daggers, and such. All suspiciously close to the storage warehouse.

Tina stomped over and glared down at the schtumple. "Those had better not be from the warehouse, or we're gonna have a problem."

The schtumple jumped at her sudden voice and rolled back behind its table to look up at her in pug-eyed terror. "My ladyship, please, let me assure you that these goods were scavenged by myself and my lord from the city in days prior. Can I not set up a shop here?"

312

"*Ladyship?*" Tina repeated, even more suspicious now. "You're an NPC, aren't you? What's your name? And who gave you permission to sell things here?"

A bead of sweat trickled down the schtumple's furry lump of a head as it stammered for an answer. Tina gritted her teeth, wondering how many other infiltrators and thieves Frank's altruism had let in. At least the "goods" laid out on the blanket were suitably ash-covered, suggesting that they had indeed come from the city, but the rest of this felt as fishy as hell, especially the whole selling-things-to-refugees angle, given that they were all supposed to be working together. She was about to tell the schtumple to get out when she heard someone running over from inside the warehouse.

"Wait!" Assets cried, running out of the warehouse at a faster clip than Tina had ever seen the elegant elf manage. "He's okay, Roxxy!"

Tina crossed her arms over her chest as Assets finally made it over, panting from exertion while his ever-present pair of attractive assistants fanned him with stacks of inventory lists.

"Please," he gasped. "Don't harass... Master Goldcaller. He's a friend."

Tina glared back down at the schtumple, who flashed her a nervous, round-toothed smile. "*You're* friends with an NPC? How did that happen?"

Assets adjusted his ruby shades and straightened up. "He was one of the schtumples who ran the auction house during Forever Fantasy Online. I've spent countless hours, the bulk of my play time, really, standing in front of him, buying and selling the goods that made my fortune. He's the one who saved me after the wham-spin-wham by dragging me behind his counter while I was incapacitated. The first person I saw when I woke up was Master Goldcaller asking if I was all right."

"Yes, yes," the schtumple, Master Goldcaller, added emphatically. "Assets is a long-time customer and friend. I was very concerned for him when he fell over at the Nightmare's end."

313

Tina stared at the little round ball of an auctioneer in amazement. Apparently, there was at least one NPC in the world who didn't hate or fear them, and she'd been about to kick him out. "Wow, okay, sorry about that, Mr. Goldcaller. You're cool to stay and set up your shop, but if I may ask, why did you decide to stick with Assets? I didn't think the citizens of Bastion liked players very much."

The schtumple's pug eyes squished with disdain. "We're in the same pot, then. The Royal Knights tried to kill me too. Called me a dirty, thieving schtumple! I tried to go to the bank for help, but it's sealed and I cannot get in. This is a very big problem for me since the auction house is also shut down. Assets understands my plight and has given me a *job*. How could I not follow him?"

He said the word *job* as Tina would have said *cake* or *college tuition*, and she tilted her head. "What's so great about a job?"

Master Goldcaller gasped, stumpy arms flying up to cover his mouth with his round hands.

"Jobs are very important to schtumples," Assets clarified when it was clear Master Goldcaller was too shocked to speak. "They don't have mana like we do. Instead, they seem to use some sort of racially created money-based magic. I don't entirely understand how it works, but I get the distinct impression that not having a job places Master Goldcaller here in grave peril."

"Much peril," Master Goldcaller said, nodding frantically. "Schtumples need jobs and gold to live."

"And I was happy to provide," Assets said with a grin. "I needed to rebuild my fortunes, anyway, so I've taken him on as my personal employee. No one knows the auction house better, and he's very precise."

"Good accounting is a holy act," Master Goldcaller agreed, smiling at Tina. "You are one of Assets's business partners, yes? If you have questions about how to schtump, I will happily answer them for a discounted fee. I've noticed you have several schtumple players among your tanks. I would not want them to suffer as I have."

Tina harrumphed. "If you don't want them to suffer, why not just tell us?"

"That would be giving something away for *free*," Master Goldcaller said, looking at Tina as though she'd just blasphemed. "No schtumple could ever do such a thing."

"I'll pay his fees," Assets said quickly. "This seems to be a legitimate issue that needs to be addressed. I'd noticed that schtumple players were suffering from a depression much more acute than the others. I'd thought it was due to going from human to, you know"--he moved his hands in the shape of a circle--"but now I suspect the problem might be more metaphysical. I'd been meaning to ask Master Goldcaller about it, but I just hadn't found the time. Now that you're here, though, this is a great opportunity. You have schtumple players, too, right?"

None of the Roughnecks were schtumples, but there were several among the refugees they'd picked up. Now that Assets mentioned it, Tina had noticed schtumple players seemed more down and listless than other races. Like Assets, though, she'd just assumed that was because they were stuck as schtumples. Not that being a stonekin was a picnic, but at least she wasn't three feet tall and perfectly round. And addicted to gold and work, apparently.

"So schtumples need gold to live?" she asked as Assets handed the coins over.

"No, no," Master Goldcaller said, happy to talk now that he'd pocketed his fee. "Gold *is* life. It's our magic, the reason we're born. Schtumples don't have mothers and fathers like humans and elves. We're born only when a job becomes available. The job is our purpose, how we earn our gold. Without it..." He shook his head. "No job, no purpose, no gold. No gold, no life. I was facing doom when the auction house closed down, but Assets saved me by giving me a job. Now do you understand why I was so happy to follow him?"

"Sort of," Tina said, trying to wrap her head around all that. "So if I give the schtumple players jobs and cash, they'll perk up again?"

Master Goldcaller looked at Assets, who handed him another coin. "It cannot hurt," he said, fingering the gold lovingly. "Player or not, we are all bound by gold. It is our life, our strength, our magic, and our pride. Without it, we are nothing."

Tina blew out a breath. And here she'd always thought schtumples were just FFO's token greedy race. Apparently, it ran a lot deeper than that. She couldn't say she understood it, but she wasn't a schtumple, so she didn't have to. If Master Goldcaller was willing to explain this to the players and keep them from wasting away, that was good enough for her.

"Can a schtumple have two jobs?"

Master Goldcaller didn't even ask for a coin for that one. "Absolutely!" he said excitedly. "Two jobs means we are twice as important." His pug eyes grew cunning. "Did you have a job for me?"

"I do," Tina said. "We've got gold in the stores. Not much, but it's not like there's anything to buy with it right now. I'll pay that to you if you teach players how to--" She frowned. "How did you put it?"

"Schtump," the schtumple replied.

"Schtump," Tina said. "Just explain to them what you told me in a way they can understand, and I'll consider the job done."

"I accept," Master Goldcaller said at once, holding out his pudgy little hand. "Thank you very much, Guild Leader Roxxy."

Tina shook his little hand carefully and turned back to Assets, who looked very positive despite Tina giving away all their gold. "You're not going to yell at me?"

"Money is only worthwhile if you have something to spend it on," the elf said with a shrug. "No one's selling us supplies out here, but if Master Goldcaller can turn our schtumple population back into functioning members of society, I count it as money well spent."

"Glad we finally agree," Tina said, happy that the problem was easily taken care of. Now she just needed to find a real stonekin who could teach her how to live, and they'd be all set. "How are supplies looking?"

316

"Terrible," Assets said with a sigh, waving her inside. "But you're the one using up all our iron, so you knew that. Lumber and food are in short supply as well."

"Limiting the fancy cooking will save on food," Tina said. "And we only need to make it a bit longer. Once this fight is over, we should be able to scavenge freely." Or they'd all be dead or cowering in a magical bubble while the city burned in a wind-fire inferno. Either way, food would be a secondary problem.

"I certainly hope so," Assets said, flipping through his clipboard to show her a wall of figures. "By our calculations, Camp Comeback consumes, on average, two pounds of food per person per day. Combat characters need more. Mana users especially can eat up to five meals per day if they cast a lot. I've already been informed that more than that isn't practical due to stomach capacity reasons, so don't expect infinite mana if given infinite food. But as a whole, given the amount of combat we've already seen, we need about five thousand pounds per day to feed our entire population."

Tina gaped at him. "*Five thousand?*"

"Now you see why we're running short," Assets said grimly. "The amount of food we can fish up and scavenge is grossly insufficient to meet our needs, and there's diminishing returns on looting supplies from the city since we quickly eat up everything around us and therefore must go farther each day. At current rates--and my skills at doing paper-only math are rusty, keep in mind--I estimate we can last two, maybe three more days before I have to stop feeding the non-combat characters. I've already placed everyone below level fifty on half rations to slow our burn, but we're coming up on some very hard choices."

Tina swallowed. No wonder the lowbies outside looked so hungry. "What about the city stores? Bastion's supposed to be a city of over a hundred thousand people, right? Surely we can find enough to keep two thousand going."

"In a healthy city, yes," Assets said. "But Bastion is a city under siege. It's early summer already, but you'll notice that no one is coming in from the farms with produce and animals to sell, and not just because Bastion's in a state of war. I've talked to several of the NPCs who came to us for shelter, and it seems that *all* of the surrounding zones are under attack by local quest lines run amok." He shook his head. "Even if we survive this, I fear we're in for a bad famine. This is still an agrarian society. There's no global market ready to fill in the gaps from local supply-chain disturbances. If the farms around Bastion don't start producing, there won't be food for anyone."

"Damn," Tina said, looking back at the glowing light of Bastion above the dark city. "Good thing we're going home, then, 'cause it sounds like this place is going to hell in a handbasket."

That all seemed pretty obvious to her, so Tina was surprised when Assets ripped off his ruby shades. "*Miss* Anderson," he said sharply. "Please step over here with me for a moment, if you will."

Caught off guard by the teacher-like tone, Tina let Assets pull her behind a nearby stack of crates. When they were out of earshot, Assets demanded, "Do you *know* who I am?"

"The Earl of Elixirs...?" Tina offered, wondering what the fuck she'd just stepped in.

"*No*," Assets said, flipping his hair in an overly feminine fashion. "The FFO Billionaire is just a character I play. I'm actually Bridget Walsh, CFO for a company whose name would not be on the S&P 500 without me. I sit on the boards of three other multinational firms as well, so I hope you understand how much it means when I tell you that I *don't want to go home*." The elf finished with a stomp of his foot.

Tina could only gape. "You're a *girl*?" she blurted out. "*And* you're like some kinda real life bigwig?" When Assets nodded, Tina's jaw dropped farther. "Why the hell do you want to stay here, trapped as a low-level character? Don't you have better things to do, like go home and be rich?"

"Because money is the only score I've ever cared about," Assets replied haughtily. "And there's more of that to be made here than I could ever get at home. If we can survive to exploit them, this is a land rich in economic conquest. They're still on a gold standard! They don't even have the concept of a central bank or business loans or corporate taxes. Do you know how much money I could make here? I could be this world's Rockefeller!" The elf clenched his fists. "Don't you see? The fact that I'm the wrong gender is insignificant compared to the fact that I'm young, beautiful, healthy, and have a lifetime's worth of economic knowledge no one in this world has even encountered before. Every old trick is new again, and they're all mine to exploit. I understand that going home is what keeps us players together as a united front, but there are many here-- myself included--who intend to stay. Probably more than you realize, so I'd appreciate if you weren't so quick to throw this world under the bus, because after you're gone, *we* will be calling it home."

"What about plan B?" Tina demanded angrily. "I don't mind if you want to stay--that's your business--but I won't endanger everyone else's chances because you want to stay here and play Monopoly. *You* were the one who suggested using wind-fire powder."

"As a lever to get the king to the table," Assets snapped. "Not literally!"

"A lever you can't use is just a stick," Tina snapped back. "I'm all for bluffing, but if the bluff fails and we get cornered, I need to know if you're going to have a problem pulling that trigger and burning Bastion to the ground if that's what it takes to save ourselves."

"I'll do what it takes to survive this mess so that I can one day climb to the top," Assets said coldly, putting his shades back on to hide his golden eyes. "Have no fear of that. My main problem is not being recognized or protected by the law. I can't do business properly without the law on my side. If we bring the king to his knees or conquer Bastion for ourselves, that will change. It is the first and most essential step for my plans.

Abusing the absence of modern economic theories and regulatory laws will be the second."

That statement didn't make Tina feel much better. In fact, this whole conversation was making her wonder if she was nurturing a future supervillain. But for now at least, Assets was *her* supervillain, and she had people to save.

"So long as we're still on the same page about what has to be done, we have no quarrel," Tina said firmly. "Once we find a way home, you're free to do whatever you want, but until that point, we do whatever it takes to keep this crazy train on the tracks and full steam ahead. Agreed?"

"Agreed," the elf said.

Tina nodded. "Good, and on that note, I need more metal."

Assets made a face. "I'm not made of iron, you know. Other people also need--"

"Those other people can use other metals," Tina said sharply. "I'm making the armor that's going to keep our front lines alive. I'll be at the forge all night if I have to, but I can't work without materials, and we can't survive if our front line folds."

"Then I suppose I'd better tell my people to start scavenging for lost nails," Assets said bitterly. "Because that's what we're down to."

"If I can melt it, I can use it," Tina said with a grin. "Just have them get it together and bring it to the forge. I'll take care of the rest. Oh, and try to get everyone some food tonight at least. Malakai didn't attack today, but that just means he's probably going to attack tonight or tomorrow, and I want everyone at full power."

Assets grimaced again. "I'll see what I can do."

"I know you can handle it," Tina said, walking out into the night. "You're the best."

"Flattery will get you nowhere," the elf called after her, but Tina didn't miss the smirk on his handsome face as he turned and started hustling his people into the corners for scrap metal.

Since she couldn't work until Assets got her more supplies, Tina took the opportunity to check on Cinco. It was now well after dark, but the training going on in the flat stretch of grass on the island's southern side showed no sign of stopping. Lit by giant bonfires, three whole raids of players were working in groups, attacking lines of dummies made from hay bales while CincoDeMurder, Shankfest, and other Red Sands guild members screamed at them.

"For the last time, *morons*, stop attacking his chest!" Cinco bellowed. "The chest is the most heavily armored part of the target! It's also the part his weapon is *guarding*. This isn't a game anymore! You can't just swing for whatever and knock off hit points. On a real body, you need to go for the instant kill or a disable. That means the head, the throat, the knees, or the elbows. Everywhere else is a waste of time, so stop being lazy and kill that fucker! Now *go again!*"

The players winced and started whacking dummies, their wooden practice swords landing slightly closer to the head.

Cinco was sucking in breath for another yell when he saw Tina coming over. Grinning, he waved at her and elbowed Shankfest. "Hey, watch these idiots for me for a sec. If anyone goes for a chest shot again, stab them where it counts. Maybe they'll learn that way."

Tina winced at the violent joke, then she noticed how much blood was splattered on the grass, as well as the line of Red Sands healers relaxing nearby, their places surrounded by plates of food from where they'd clearly been replenishing their mana from *lots* of healing.

"Holy shit, Cinco," Tina said as the other guild leader jogged over. "You're being a bit brutal, aren't you?"

"Hi to you, too, Tina," the red-armored Berserker said, taking off his helmet to give her a wink. "And the brutality is part of the program. We don't have time to instill proper discipline in these kids. Pain is the quickest teacher I've got, so that's what I'm using."

"I understand that," Tina said, shifting her feet on the bloody grass. "But this feels... excessive."

"It might be," Cinco said. "But they'll be dying if they fuck this up tomorrow, so I think some excess is in order."

Tina sighed. "Just don't break anyone, okay? We don't have that many people over level fifty."

"Better they break here than on the battlefield," Cinco said grimly, then he flashed her a grin. "But I don't think we'll have any dropouts. No one survives this long post-transition without getting blood on their hands. Even this mishmash of idiots has a lot of guts. No aim, but guts."

Tina still didn't like it, but she decided to let it go. Cinco wasn't entirely wrong. She didn't want people to run screaming when the enemy came at them, either, and if his methods kept them from dying, well, it was only for one more night.

"So what brings you over here?" Cinco asked, grinning at her with his hands on his belt. "Need some instruction in fighting too? FYI, I'm duke-ranked with the long sword and spear by two HEMA associations back home. We're pretty busy, but I don't mind giving you some of my personal time. You know, one guild leader to another."

He leaned in as he finished, getting uncomfortably close, but Tina knew better than to back away. She'd been dealing with macho dudes since she started gaming, and playing Roxxy only made things easier.

"Not today, thanks," she said, using the distance he'd closed as an opening to give him a friendly--but not soft--punch on the pauldron. "I just came over to check on your progress. Are we going to get gibbed?"

Cinco rubbed his arm. "Individually, they're mostly good enough. As a unit?" He shrugged. "We've gotten past the stabbing-each-other stage, but it takes at least one big battle to gel a raid's teamwork. It's a pity we can't get that before we need it."

That was not what Tina had hoped to hear. Maybe she'd taken for granted just how well the Roughnecks had pulled together on the march through the Deadlands. Still, she heard a "but" hanging in Cinco's voice. "But?"

"But," Cinco continued with a smirk, "we have a lot of real mad-dog killer types in the mix in here."

"That doesn't sound like a good thing," Tina said in alarm, remembering all the bodies they'd seen on the march through Bastion. "*Please* tell me you aren't talking about actual murderers."

"Surviving in Bastion is for the strong and the savage," Cinco replied nonchalantly. "I don't ask how people did it because I don't want to have to deal with any checkered pasts. But 'mad-dog killer' is just PvP slang. It means we have people who are really good at fighting solo on a chaotic battlefield. They're called mad dogs because, while they're great at taking out the enemy, they get carried away with it, which makes them suck at teamwork."

That was a relief to hear. Tina really didn't want to deal with crime-and-punishment issues yet. But lack of teamwork was going to be a problem.

"Don't worry, Tina," Cinco said, giving her a wink. "I've whipped worse groups than this into winners during the public war events. These folks are actually really good material because no one's dicking around like they would in-game. Everyone understands we're screwed for real this time, and that does wonders for discipline. If they can survive this battle and get a bit more training, we'll have some crack troops."

"Then let's do our best to get them through," Tina said, pointing back at the forge. "I've finished most of the high-level armor if you want to start sending people up. Start with the lowest geared. They'll get the most benefit."

"Will do," Cinco said. Then he moved in close again. "And that offer for private lessons is always good. I also do MMA grappling, in armor and out, if you're looking for someone who can take you."

He gave her a long once-over, and Tina clenched her teeth. She didn't want to have to train this raid herself, though, so she swallowed her sharp comeback, waved for him to carry on, and headed back up to her smithy to see if Assets had found her metal yet.

And behind her, glowing in the dark across the city, the Bastion flickered.

Chapter 14

James

The dungeon beneath Bastion's royal castle seemed to be the only part of FFO that *hadn't* gotten bigger when the game became real. James supposed that made sense. After all, the old prison had been an entire instance with seven floors, five bosses, rats the size of Labradors, and zero actual functioning cells. The *real* prison was a far more practical single hallway below the central keep, with thick stone walls and two rows of cells separated by arm-thick iron bars.

The wooden bunks and straw-strewn floor weren't as posh as Lady Siku's prison, but there was plenty of room to move around, and nothing was truly filthy. The wards on the walls cut off the natural flow of magic, leaving the air empty of the colored streams he used to cast, but James wasn't supposed to be using spells, anyway. They were in here to be model prisoners, and that was exactly what he meant to be.

"Hooray for not dying!" Flameboyant said as he flopped onto his cot. "Most successful unsuccessful suicide mission in history!"

"I'd prefer if we were not in prison again," Ar'Bati grumbled, pacing the length of the large cell he and James had been locked in together. "But I agree it was a victory. We delivered the letters, and action is being taken to stop the Once King's attack. Our honor is still in question, but I'm certain we will be vindicated when the true traitors are brought to justice."

"Yeah," James said, staring glumly through the bars at their weapons, which the guards had piled in the corner by the door a good twenty feet away. "We got the mission done, guys. Let's be proud of that."

"You don't sound like you're proud," Flameboyant pointed out. "What gives, man? We *won*! The king listened to you."

"He did," James admitted, putting his head in his hands. "But only after I threw my sister under the bus. I was talking to the *king*! It was the perfect time to explain her side of things, but I was too focused on the Once King to even think about it. I made her sound like a villain just so they'd believe me!"

"You cannot save her from her own actions," Ar'Bati said in disgust. "She *did* attack the Royal Knights. She *did* imprison us. She *did* send an Assassin to stop you. If she sounds like a villain, it's because she's acted villainously."

"But you know she only did all of that stuff to protect her people and me!" James said angrily. "I'm worse than SilentBlayde. At least he only screws people over out of love. I threw Tina to Malakai just to get an edge in an argument!"

Sharp pain exploded across the back of his skull as Ar'Bati smacked him. "Stop eating your own tail," his brother scolded. "You're nothing like that pitiful Assassin. He threw away his honor for a woman who doesn't even look at him. You did what needed to be done to save us all. If your sister has an ounce of sense, she'll understand that."

"Maybe she will eventually, but..." James slumped down to the straw-covered floor with a full-body sigh. "You don't know our childhood. Tina didn't just wake up one day and decide I was an incompetent idiot who couldn't be trusted. I did that. I... I used to push her around a lot when we were kids. I broke her arm once by accident, testing out a new hold. I knew I had no business trying a move like that on an untrained person, but I was in such a rush to get my first black belt that I did it anyway, and she paid the price. She *always* pays for my mistakes. FFO was supposed to be different. I'm supposed to be *good* here, but I'm still just... me."

There was a whole world in that word that James didn't want to think about. He was trying to push all the guilt and anger and self-loathing back into its box before his evil staff sensed it when Ar'Bati smacked him upside the head again.

"*Ow,*" James said irritably, rubbing his skull. "Would you stop that?"

"No," Ar'Bati snapped, tail lashing. "Not when you are being so ridiculous."

James looked away with a glower. "Not in the mood for the tough straight-talk routine right now, Fangs."

"Too bad," his brother said, reaching down to grab James around the waist.

Depression turned into alarm as James was hauled up off the floor and thrown into the opposite wall of the cell. He smashed against the iron bars hard enough to set his head spinning. By the time he was back on his feet, Ar'Bati was stalking in front of him, his slitted eyes gleaming in the dark like a tiger's.

"Listen to yourself," he snarled at James. "You are the general who won the battle for Red Canyon! Your bravery and cleverness saved Windy Lake from gnolls, undead, and Lilac's turning, and your compassion saved me from dishonor. For all these reasons, you were adopted as a son of Rends Iron Hides, one of the four lords of the Savanna. How dare you disparage yourself? Do you know how hard I've had to work just to keep up with you?"

James froze in confusion. "What?"

"You are the hero of the entire Savanna!" Fangs yelled. "We achieved complete and total victory over our enemies because of *your* actions, while I did nothing but try to tear you down. But you did not hate me for it. You accepted my hate and welcomed me as your friend. It is because of you that I did not become a monster willing to slaughter women and children in pursuit of revenge. When I look at Captain Malakai, I see what I could easily have been if you had not stopped me. You are my savior, my *brother.* So stop saying that you are a bad person!"

"Just because I did good by you doesn't mean I was always that way!" James cried. "You don't understand. The me you know now isn't how I used to be. I've been a terrible brother to Tina my whole life, and I just keep doing it! I got our family into debt. I ruined her chance to get a loan for college. I--"

327

"You haven't senselessly beaten her in a rage," Fangs said. "You never stabbed her or tried to murder her *twice*." The warrior shook his head. "If I can come back from those depths, you can come back from whatever wrongs you've done your sister. She must care about you, or she wouldn't have sent her best Assassin to bring you back when you ran."

"She *does* care," James said bleakly, looking down at the ground. "No matter what I did or how mad she got, Tina never stopped caring and worrying about me. I know that, and I *still* served her up to Malakai on a platter. What kind of person does that make me?"

"One who would choose the good of a kingdom over his own," Fangs said in a surprisingly understanding voice. "But our duty is done. The king has been warned. You are free now to be the brother she deserves."

James shook his head. "She won't want me."

"Then you must prove to her that she is wrong," Ar'Bati said. "You must find a way to earn back her respect and trust. Only then will she understand why you did what you had to do. Maybe it will happen when your warnings are proven right and the Once King's army arrives. Maybe it will take more. Your sister is as stubborn as the rock she's made of, but if you prove her wrong enough times, even she will have no choice but to acknowledge that you are not a coward who needs her protection. But nothing can be done while you insist on beating yourself up and acting like the self-hating, incompetent fool she considers you to be."

James didn't know what to say. As usual, Fangs saw things from a totally different angle than he did. James wasn't sure it was the *right* one, but it helped put his tattered relationship with his sister into a fresh perspective, and that made him feel a lot more hopeful than he'd expected.

"Thank you, brother," he said quietly.

"You're welcome," Fangs replied, giving him a final punch in the arm. "That's all that needs to be said, then."

James had nothing else he *could* say. Fortunately, Flameboyant seemed more than eager to fill the awkward silence.

"Well," the elf said cheerfully, "if you guys are done throwing each other around, I'm going to try to catch some sleep. All that casting and almost dying on an empty stomach wore me out."

"We should all sleep," agreed Ar'Bati. "Evening is already here, and it sounds as though Captain Malakai means to march at dawn. There's a good chance we'll remain imprisoned and unable to act, but we should still ready ourselves for battle. Just in case."

With that, the warrior grabbed the top bunk and swung himself up. Still silent, James slipped into the hard bed on the bottom and stared at the tick marks carved into the stone wall beside him, wondering if it was too late. For what, he didn't even know. There didn't seem to be a good outcome to any of this. Whoever won this war, lives would be lost, the city would be weakened, and relations between players and the people of Bastion would get even worse. No matter what Ar'Bati said, James couldn't help but feel that he'd let a once-in-a-lifetime opportunity slip through his fingers in the council room. There had to have been something he could say, some argument he could make to convince the king--or apparently more importantly, Raffestain--that the players were not their enemies. That they *needed* each other.

Restless and angry, he rolled over in the dark, repeating the conversations in his mind to try to figure out what he could have done better, how he could fix this. No matter which way he looked at it, though, all he saw was betrayal.

This led his brain to start rehashing every time he'd done Tina wrong, and *boy*, were there a lot. Other than those few happy months when she'd been leveling Roxxy and they'd played FFO together as though it were the only thing in the world, James couldn't actually remember a time when they hadn't been at odds. He tried to focus on the happy memories, like their first run through Red Canyon back when Roxxy had been two levels too low and SilentBlayde could still only communicate via the in-game translator. It had been one of the worst dungeons James had ever suffered through, but he still remembered it fondly because it was one of the only times he could recall Tina being happy. Every time they wiped, she'd thanked him over and over again for staying in and healing them even though he didn't need the loot. It had made James feel like a hero, like a good brother.

That would be the *only* time. As he'd told Fangs, Tina hadn't gotten her low opinion of him from nowhere. Outside of FFO, all of his memories were of him treating her like trash, like how he'd selfishly squandered all of their family's money on his failed degree or the year he'd guilted their parents into taking their whole family out of state to watch his first national competition on her tenth birthday. He even stole a slice of her cake before they lit the candles because he'd been hungry and he'd felt that he'd earned it since he won his match.

Now, of course, he knew that he'd been a horrible, spoiled little brat. But by the time he'd gotten smacked around enough by life to wake up and realize the damage he was doing, it was too late. Even his apologies were just more sticks on the fire because he'd broken faith with Tina too many times for words to mean anything. He didn't know how to make her see that he was different now. He'd never gotten up the courage to tell her about the horrible event that had started the spiral that led to him flunking out of college.

He'd tried to. If there was anyone who deserved an explanation for his behavior during that terrible, terrible summer, it was Tina. But every time he tried to talk to her about it, he ended up saying something that screwed things up even more. It was all just so *broken*, and now he was doing it again. It didn't matter that it had been for a good reason. He'd thrown Tina to the wolves to save himself in this world just like he had back home. How could Ar'Bati say he was a hero? He couldn't even do right by the one person who most deserved it.

On and on it went. His body was exhausted from his wounds and all the mana he'd spent, but his brain just wouldn't shut up. He had no idea how long he lay awake in the dark, bashing himself bloody on a lifetime of wrongs. It must have been hours, because when he heard the scrape of the cellblock door opening, his balled-up body was too stiff to jump. By the time he managed to unwind enough to stand up, the person was already coming down the hall.

James's ears twitched. Whoever was coming, they didn't clink as a guard would. It was very dark in the cellblock, but his jubatus eyes could still pick out the strangely giant shape of a man in a cloak feeling his way down the hall. He stopped when he reached James's cell and fumbled in the dark to fit keys into the lock. When he saw James staring, he lifted a finger to his lips. James nodded and said nothing then looked nervously over his shoulder at Ar'Bati as the king--for there was no one else the eight-foot-tall stranger could be--unlocked the cell and stood back, making room for James to dart through the open iron door.

When he was in the hall, the king lifted his finger to his lips again then motioned for James to follow him. James nodded silently and obeyed, padding down the stone hall behind him, which was an experience. Now that he was no longer kneeling, he was finally realizing just how *big* the holy king of Bastion was. Even out of his armor, he was bigger than Roxxy, so tall that he had to hunch over to keep his cloaked head from banging on the high ceiling. It struck him as ludicrous that a living human could be so large, but the king with him now was the same size he'd been back when FFO was a game. Malakai was oversized as well, which led James to think the towering stature was a legacy of being a raid boss.

Either way, King Gregory moved very quietly for a giant. His leather shoes made no sound at all as he led James past the empty prison cells, up the stairs, and into the guard room, which was the only way in or out of the dungeon area. There were no guards inside, though, just a table with a lantern on it and some chairs in an empty, windowless stone room.

"Sit," the king said, taking a seat on a sturdy oak stool.

James obeyed at once, sitting down across from the king and placing his hands on the table where the monarch could see them. King Gregory smiled and reached into the saddle-bag-sized leather satchel he carried under his enormous cloak to pull out two jugs of wine and a stack

331

of something that looked like playing cards. He also pulled out a silver wine cup, which looked comically small in his giant hands. He set it carefully on the table and filled it from the jug, pouring the wine with extreme slowness before sliding the cup across the table to James.

"Please."

James smiled nervously and took a sip. He was no expert on wine-- he mostly stuck to beer and tequila--so he had no idea if it was good or not. Honestly, he found the taste unpleasantly sour, but he made a show of enjoying it nonetheless, savoring his mouthful before placing the cup down to get to business.

"Your Majesty--"

"Just Gregory, please," the king said, waving down at the plain white shirt he wore below his cloak. "I get 'your majesty-ed' enough upstairs."

"Gregory, then," James said nervously. "Thank you for the wine and for coming. I really appreciate it."

"I appreciate the opportunity to have a real conversation with a player," the king said, giving him a smile. "Your kind talked to me day and night during the Nightmare, but I never got to talk back, at least not in my own words." He pushed the stack of playing cards he'd brought across the table. "I was hoping you could show me how to play this Pokémon game I've heard so much about. After eighty years, I'm dreadfully curious."

That request was so out of left field, James didn't know if he should laugh or panic. He covered his shock by reaching for the card deck. The gold-embossed cards were a royally nice version of the same four-suite set used in the FFO Carnival mini-games. They weren't that different from standard playing card decks back home, which unfortunately made them utterly unsuitable for the king's request.

"I'm sorry, but these aren't Pokémon cards," James said. When the king's face fell, he scrambled to add, "but I can use them to teach you poker. Would that be okay?"

"Yes, please," Gregory said with renewed enthusiasm. "Can you show me how to 'hold 'em' as they do in Texas?"

James swallowed a snort before it looked like he was laughing at the king. "I can try. We'll need something to wager, though."

The king promptly dumped out his coin purse on the table. James split the pile, making sure that His Majesty's stack was larger than his own, and started dealing. After several hands, the king started memorizing the combinations of what beat what. Since James was unsure of what Bastion's monarch really wanted, he kept the conversation to the game and waited. When no questions of real substance emerged after half an hour, though, James decided it was time to press.

"Did you come down here just to play cards with me, or is there something else you'd like to talk about?"

Gregory shuffled the playing cards in his enormous hands nervously, then he put them down with a sigh. "I'm not trying to mislead you," he said carefully. "I just thought a game would break the ice. You players always seemed obsessed with them, even referring to yourselves as 'gamers.' I thought it would get us started on the right foot."

James boggled at that for a moment. "But... you're the king," he said at last. "Any foot you choose is the right one."

"Not always," Gregory said quietly, tilting his giant head to study James in the lamplight. "But since you ask, there is something I must know. Why did you risk your life to bring us news of the undead?"

"Because if I didn't, all of Bastion would fall," James replied.

"But you're not a citizen," the king pressed. "You're not even from this world. Why would you put yourself in such danger to save us?"

"Well," James said thoughtfully, "there's the obvious motive of self-preservation. I'm stuck in this world, too, now, and I'd rather not become an undead slave to the Once King. On a personal level, though, I think it's because I'd rather die doing the right thing than run away and let the world burn just to save my own hide. I've been a failure long enough in my world to know that it's no way to live, and since I've gotten a chance to start over again here, I thought I'd try to get it right this time."

James thought that was a very good answer. In hindsight, he knew he'd thrown himself through that stained-glass window for the same reason he'd jumped into that pit with Gore Maul: because it was the only way he could keep living with himself. But the king just looked confused.

"But you are level eighty, are you not?" Gregory said. "I learned during the Nightmare that that was the greatest accomplishment players could achieve. How could one such as you consider himself a failure?"

James batted self-consciously at one of his tufted ears. "Actually, being level eighty isn't something people in my world care about if they don't play Forever Fantasy Online. Back home, I'm just a college dropout who's buried in debt. I'm kinda the shame of my family."

"I can sympathize with that feeling," the king said sadly. "I am well aware that, outside of this castle, I am known far and wide as 'The Buffoon King.'"

"I think it's meant affectionately," James said quickly, but the king gave him a cutting look.

"I'm not *actually* a fool," he said hotly, then his face fell. "But I am unqualified to rule. I was the third son. No one thought that I would ever take the throne, especially not me. But then my father and brothers died in the Forgiven War, and the crown landed on my head. I tried to be a good king, but everything I touched ended up in disaster. My advisers always had to step in and fix my messes. Sometimes, I thought it would be better for everyone to just shorten the process and just let them handle things from the start, but I wasn't willing to give up on my responsibilities just yet. I thought I was starting to make a little progress when the Nightmare hit. After that, well, everything just became impossible. I'm lucky they let me enter the council chamber as I am now."

James frowned. That attitude explained why the king let Raffestain and the others treat him like a child, but he still didn't understand. "Why would the Nightmare make it impossible for you to be king?"

The king stared at him as if he were insane. "How can you ask that?" He spread his giant arms. "*Look* at me. I'm a monster! The Nightmare filled me with so much strength that I break everything I touch. It wasn't so bad when I was stuck in the throne room, unable to do anything except repeat the same lines over and over to players, but now I have to actually live around other people like this, and I just can't. I can kill anyone less than level eighty with a careless gesture, and I *have*. The whole castle is terrified of me, and rightly so. I'm a nightmare."

Gregory clenched his giant fists on the table. "If I had an heir, I'd abdicate at once. The only reason I'm still king is because someone has to wield the Dawnblade and control the Bastion. But I can't rule like this, not that I was any good at it, anyway." He shook his head firmly. "No, it's better for everyone if I keep to my rooms and stay out of my advisers' way. It's taken me all the days since the Nightmare ended just to learn how to pick up a wine jug without crushing it. How can a man like me possibly be Bastion's king? It's absurd. My country's better off without me."

The king's words were heartbreakingly sad, but they filled James with hope. If King Gregory had spent all the time since the Nightmare hiding in his rooms while he learned to deal with the strength that came from being a five-skull raid boss, then maybe he *didn't* know about the atrocities his knights were committing in the city. That would resolve the paradox of how a famously good man--and after that confession, James was certain the king sitting in front of him was a *good* man--could be behind Malakai's rampage. Maybe he wasn't out of chances to save Tina yet.

Terrified excitement rose in James's stomach as he leaned forward, bringing his hands down on the table with a *thunk*. "I disagree with all of that."

Gregory's head shot up at the vehemence in his voice, but James wasn't finished. "You may not be the most experienced king," he said, "but there is no mistake in judgment you could possibly make that would be worse than the colossal disaster Captain Malakai is leading Bastion into at this very moment."

"What do you mean?" Gregory demanded, his face showing his confusion. "Malakai has been the captain of the Royal Knights since my father's reign. He is passionate, certainly, but he's an honorable and loyal man who is more than qualified to lead our armies to victory."

"If you'd seen what he was actually doing out there in your name, you wouldn't say that," James said, picking his words carefully. "What has he told you about my sister, Tina?"

"That's she's what we've feared most," the king said quietly, staring at his cards so he wouldn't have to look at James. "A top-tier raider in charge of a large, functional guild that seems well supplied and well coordinated. We still don't know how she managed to get into the city when all player portal magic was supposed to be warded off, but she's been both destructive and unstoppable since her arrival. Her soldiers have killed an enormous number of our patrols, and her raid slaughtered Malakai's player containment camp to a man before the castle garrison could sally forth. She even killed Malakai herself. It's a miracle the Clerics were able to get there in time to revive him. If they'd been even a minute slower, it would have been too late.

"Now they tell me she's gathered all the toughest player factions into an army on the island of Dawn's Hope. Thankfully, all of the trainers made it out alive, but my prayers that she would pass through Bastion and leave us be have not been granted. There's no reason she would take over one of the last functional crafting facilities in the city unless she was readying for an attack. Malakai believes she intends to sack the castle and take my crown. That's why I turned on the Bastion at his request and why I've given him command of the army. Even I know that no one gains power faster than players. Malakai says the only way to stop her is to strike first and destroy her before she destroys us, and I believe him."

James sat quietly while the king talked. Gregory must have been making those same arguments to himself for some time, because the words spilled out of him in a swift, practiced torrent. When he finally fell silent, James put his hands flat on the table with a sigh.

"I can see why you're scared of her," he said gently. "Things do look pretty bad from your side. In hindsight, though, I think I asked the wrong question. I'd like to try again, if that's all right."

When the king nodded, James said, "Who do *you* think Tina is?"

Again, Gregory's eyes slid down to lock on the table, and James smiled. "I won't be offended if you have a poor opinion of her," he promised. "I just need to know your honest thoughts so I can help you deal with her."

The king's head snapped back up. "You would help me against your own blood?"

"I want to stop a war," James said firmly. "That's the best way to help everyone, *especially* my sister. So please, tell me what you think."

Gregory frowned, drumming his huge hands on the table. "Honestly?" he said at last. "I think she's a monster. I know how that sounds coming from, you know..." He waved his hands at his giant form. "But you can't deny she's like something out of a Hallow's Eve tale. She appeared from nowhere with an unbeatable army and immediately started killing my knights, who were already sacrificing themselves trying to save the people of Bastion from the players who were running amok. She attacks without provocation, kills indiscriminately, and takes whatever she wants. Malakai says she's even joined forces with the infamous Red Sands murderers who were the single greatest cause of death in the city before she came. That she would accept such people into her company proves her villainy." The king shook his head. "I'm sorry to speak ill of your kin, James, but you have been honest with me, and so I must be honest with you. Your sister is a terror, and I feel that we are right to fear her."

As unsurprising as Gregory's terrible opinion of Tina was, hearing it still made James wince. "Thank you for being honest. I understand why you see things that way, but there's an important point on which you are misinformed. One that changes the whole situation."

"What's that?"

James looked him in the eye. "Tina did not do any of these things *without provocation.*"

"Are you saying she's being misled?" Gregory asked excitedly. "If that's the case, then maybe we could--"

James shook his head, killing the king's hopeful expression. "She's not misled. She thinks she's a hero who's standing up to a blood-drenched tyrant." He nodded. "You."

Gregory recoiled in horror. "*Me?*" he squeaked. "But I've done nothing to her! I've been merciful to a fault, given the situation. My father would have ordered a purge of the city the moment the Nightmare ended, but I've insisted that every player deserves a trial just like any other soul in Bastion. That's why I've had Malakai making arrests instead of killing on sight. Your sister's the one attacking the law keepers. *She* is the tyrant, not me."

"She has killed knights," James admitted. "No one denies that. But what you need to understand is that she thought she was in the right. Tina's actually a very moral person who'll do anything to protect the people who depend on her. Do you know how she managed to portal into Bastion then?"

"That should have been impossible, so no. I don't know."

James flashed him a wide smile. "She got the portal because two days ago, Tina and her Roughnecks helped the Order of the Golden Sun defeat an undead army led by Grel'Darm the Colossal. It's because she and the other players stepped up that the western continent isn't falling to the Once King as we speak. In gratitude for their bravery, Commander Garrond commanded his mages to make her a portal to Bastion. That's why the wards against player magic didn't stop it, because it wasn't a *player* portal. It was Commander Garrond's, the man entrusted by all the unified kingdoms to keep the Once King bottled up in the Deadlands." James leaned forward. "Do you believe that someone as honorable and dedicated

338

to the safety of this world as *Garrond* would allow Tina into Bastion if she was actually the monster you describe?"

The king frowned deeply, giving that question careful thought. "No," he said at last. "I have met Commander Garrond before, and I think he would have fought her to the death before he allowed her into Bastion if she was not worthy."

"And did you know," James went on eagerly, his jubatus side excited to make the kill, "that when she first arrived in Bastion, Tina's original plan was to come work for you and help defend the city? She *wanted* to be on your side from the very beginning. Because she's a player and Bastion has always been the *good* guys."

"So what changed?" the king asked desperately. "Is she possessed? Did the Once King corrupt her? For the person you describe sounds like who you players used to be: selfless, brave heroes who threw themselves in the way of danger for the sake of others. Why is she now our enemy?"

"It was your knights that did it," James said bitterly. "I told you I was her prisoner back in the throne room, and that's true, but not because she's a villain. It was my fault. My sister thinks I'm an impulsive fool who can't take care of himself. She thought I'd do something crazy to get the letters to you and put me under guard for my own protection. Considering I threw myself through your window, I can't say she was wrong, but I traveled with her Roughnecks for our first hours here in Bastion as we tried to get to the castle. All along the way, we kept finding the bodies of our fellow players. Players who'd been murdered in cold blood by your knights."

"Murdered?" the king asked, voice shaking. "No. They must have fought the knights and--"

"There was no fighting," James said coldly. "Founder's Square is full of players whose throats were slit while they were down during the transition from the Nightmare. They couldn't fight back. They couldn't even *move*. Naturally, Tina was furious. Those were our people. Many of her raiders recognized the bodies in the square as friends and family. Many

339

of the raiders wanted to get revenge, but I managed to convince them that you, the good King Gregory of Bastion, would never sanction such a slaughter. Tina agreed and ordered her players to continue to the castle so we could meet you and find out why this had happened. That was when we discovered Malakai's extermination camp, and everything broke down."

"It was not an *extermination* camp," Gregory said angrily. "I ordered Malakai to round up players so that they could stand trial. They were just being held!"

James sighed. "Have you been out into the city, Your Majesty?" Gregory shook his head.

"Well, I have. I saw the whole thing, and I can tell you, there were no trials. Any player high enough level to give the knights trouble was killed outright, and those low enough to bully were beaten, abused, and eventually hung without quarter or mercy. *That* was the scene Tina saw, and it's why she decided to attack."

By the time he finished, Gregory was shaking. "And you saw this?" he demanded. "Saw it yourself?"

"With my own eyes," James said, nodding. "The Ar'Bati of Windy Lake saw it, too, as did hundreds more of your own people. This was not a secret operation. It was going on in broad daylight directly in front of your castle door."

"I can't believe it."

"That doesn't matter," James said angrily. "Whether you believe or not, it happened. I didn't agree with my sister's decision to slaughter the Royal Knights, but I was completely on her side that the lawless genocide and torture of players had to be stopped. That's why Tina is fighting. She's not a monster who's been magically corrupted. She's someone who came face to face with injustice and decided she wasn't going to tolerate it. And since the ones doing the killing were *your* knights, she decided *you* must be responsible for their actions. That's why *you* have an army out there calling for your blood. You aren't the Buffoon King outside these walls

340

anymore. You're the oppressor, the tyrant, the face attached to all the atrocities we players have suffered. The rebellion at Dawn's Hope isn't growing just because Tina's a good leader. It's swelling because Malakai and his knights--*your* knights--have made it abundantly clear that the people of this world want to murder us all, and if we want to keep living, our only choice is to fight back."

With that, James sat back in his chair. He knew he'd just rolled hard on Gregory, but the king seemed to be a timid man. James was hoping the shock of perspective would knock him out of his castle and into action. To his surprise, though, Gregory didn't look blown over by these sudden revelations. He looked *furious.*

"My knights would never engage in such conduct!" he cried, slamming his fist down on the table so hard, the six-inch-thick oak split. "They are sworn to uphold the law and sanctity of the Holy Throne! Each one of them is carefully selected for their virtue and honor. They train for years and are purified by the Sun itself before they are given the title of Sir. You *must* be mistaken. Malakai tells me every day of the players he's arrested and sent to the mines behind the castle to work while they await trial. He has only killed those who have been in open rebellion to me!"

"If that's what he's said, then he's *lying* to you," James snapped back, too angry to be polite. "I've been in his camp. I've *seen* the gallows made for twenty and the piles of player corpses beneath them. Did you know that many players are children? We all look like adults, but there were kids as young as ten playing FFO. How guilty is a ten-year-old child?"

The king shot to his feet, filling the room and making James cower as he suddenly remembered that this "timid man" was also a five-skull raid boss.

"Do not besmirch Captain Malakai's name!" Gregory cried, voice booming. "He has selflessly served Bastion for over thirty years! He lost his own family in the Forgiven War because he chose to stay at his post instead of rushing to their aid. He's given *everything* to protect this city and what it represents. I have seen his anger and his bloodlust, but considering

341

what you players have done to his knights, I don't think it is undeserved. Still, he could *never* be the demon you describe."

"But I was there," James said. "I saw him--"

"You players are the ones running rampant!" the king shouted over him. "I have endless reports of your thievery, brutality, and barbarism! My citizens cower in a fortified camp because you players have rampaged across our city. Can you deny your crimes?"

James locked his fangs in frustration. He'd seen the evidence of player wrongdoing in the bodies of families and shopkeepers strewn all through the city, and Flameboyant had even seen the worst firsthand. Even so...

"Some players have acted badly. I can't deny that, but you can't accuse players of atrocities while turning a blind eye to the same actions by your knights. Both sides shoulder blame for the current situation. That's why you need to believe me and take control of your men! Your knights are confusing revenge with justice, and they've committed heinous acts in your name, which is why you have a rebellion!"

"That's enough, James," said the king in a terrifying voice.

Panic rose at those words, bringing back the king's stories of his lack of control. But though he was perilously close to becoming a stain on the stone floor, James didn't back down. This might be his last chance to stop Malakai's war. Tina's life depended on him here and now. He refused to let her down again.

"I can prove what I say is true!" he yelled, shooting to his feet so fast, his chair fell over. "Walk *ten feet* outside of this castle, and you will see the gallows. Go to Founder's Square, and you will see the Royal Knights' victims lying in *mountains*. Malakai's sins carpet this city! Look anywhere, and you will see that I am right, but you cannot call yourself king while you hide inside walls and ignore your--"

"*Enough!*"

The king's bellow was a physical force that slammed James into the wall. When he picked himself up again, the king was staring at him in horror, his whole body trembling.

"I should never have come down here," Gregory said, sweeping up the cups and cards. "I should never have gotten my foolish hopes up."

"What hopes?" James demanded, lurching forward to grab the king's sleeve. It was a suicidal move. Even though James was level eighty, the five-skull king could kill him with a backhand, but he didn't let go. He couldn't let it end like this, not when he'd gotten so close. "Why did you come down here, Your Majesty? I'm the one who brought up Tina. If you weren't here to collect information on the enemy, then why? What did you hope to learn?"

The king's shoulders slumped, the terrifying anger draining out of him like water, leaving only sadness behind. "I came because I wanted to know why you--you alone, out of all the players--were still acting like a hero," Gregory said quietly. "I spent eighty years watching you players fight for Bastion with peerless bravery. The tasks I was forced to give you--dungeon and raid quests, you used to call them--were nearly impossible, but you always came through. I know now that it was a game to you, but that doesn't change the fact that you fought and died for Bastion. That's why, just as I cannot believe what you say of Malakai, I couldn't believe his tales of you, either. I'd hoped that you all were under a curse, that there was some evil driving you to commit these acts of selfish barbarism. Since you, James, seemed unaffected, I was hoping there was something in you we could use to cure the others. Some spell or knowledge I could take to Raffestain to purify the madness from your fellows. But I see now that it was just another fool's errand. There is no magic, no curse, no easy solution. You are nothing more than what you seem, and neither am I." Gregory sighed. "I truly am the Buffoon King."

"No, you're not," James said earnestly. "You came down here looking for something with which to save your enemies. I think that makes you a *great* king. No one else I've met has thought to ask why the

343

players are causing so much trouble. Even if it wasn't what you hoped, I find the fact that you cared enough to investigate very admirable."

"Yes, well, your faith in me is poorly placed, I'm afraid," Gregory said bitterly. "Tomorrow morning, Malakai will ride out to put down your sister's rebellion, and Bastion's player problem will be solved. You needn't worry about yourself, at least. I've already forgiven your assault on my council as the genuine act of heroism that it was and given you all a full pardon. Since you are a Claw Born, I will summon Rend to the capital to collect you and your companions after we've repelled the Once King's invasion."

The way he said that made James shudder. "Your Majesty," he said, feeling a sense of déjà vu. "I don't think that's a fight you can win on your own. If the numbers in those letters are even close to accurate, you could be facing multiple undead armies, including several raid bosses. Even if we succeed in stopping the traitor Star Fall from opening a portal and letting them in, the Once King isn't just going to just give up and go away. The enemy will still be out there, and even if your army was fresh and not about to fight Tina's, I'm not at all confident Bastion can beat them back without player help."

"I know that," the king said tiredly. "But there's nothing we can do. There's simply no way to repair our relationship with the players now. Too much damage has been done, which is why I've called in Bastion's greatest favor."

That statement stopped James cold. "You--you're not talking about Xthr, are you? *Please* tell me you didn't burn Bastion's greatest promise over *this*!"

"I had no choice," the king said angrily. "As you just reminded me, I have a player army about to slaughter all of my men! With Xthr's help, I can end the player rebellion before it begins and save countless lives. He owes my bloodline a service from long ago. It is only to be used in a time of greatest need, but I can't think of a peril greater than what we face now.

I only pray that the kings who come after me feel the same, assuming we still have kings when this is all over."

James put his head in his hands. Just when he'd thought things couldn't get any worse. Xthr wasn't just a name from FFO's lore. He was a primordial Bird from the Age of Skies and a world boss who only appeared in special cut scenes. Players hadn't even been allowed to attack him because his stats were balanced for future expansions, which meant even the current world's best gear wouldn't be good enough to fight him. If Malakai had a beast like that for backup, Tina didn't stand a chance.

"Have faith that your sister will surrender when faced with an unwinnable battle," King Gregory said quietly. "I swear that she will get a fair trial if she does. They all will. That much, at least, I can promise you."

"Thank you, Your Majesty." The words dropped from James's mouth automatically.

"It's the most this royal idiot can do," the king replied, opening the door to let the terrified prison guards back in. "Thank you for the game."

James couldn't do anything but sigh at that, putting up his arms as the guards shuffled him back to his cell.

Chapter 15

Tina

Tina spent all night at her anvil. She would have liked to take a break, but weapons were what they needed most, and as one of the few max-level blacksmiths in the camp, her skills were in high demand. Fortunately, stonekin didn't seem to need rest any more than they needed warmth or food, so even though this was her second all-nighter in a row, she made it through.

The rest of Camp Comeback wasn't so tireless. While Tina just kept going, the rest of her people worked in shifts. Frank, Anders, and Zen took turns managing the production areas to make sure that all the weapons and armor people needed got made as night turned into dawn. More helpers, random low-level people, mostly, ran as gofers between Assets's warehouse and the various workshops, delivering goods and keeping all the crafters stocked. As new goods came off the line, Sorcerers and Naturalists worked in shifts to bind the new equipment for the classes who couldn't see magic.

It was brutal, tiring work. Everyone moved with frantic purpose that bordered on panic, but while Tina could no longer make a magical sword in thirty-five seconds as she had in the game, twenty minutes to make a superior-quality level-eighty weapon was still incredible. By the time the sun rose, she and the other smiths had armed everyone in the combat raids with the best gear available.

While she worked in the forges, the other raid leaders did their parts as well. Cinco kept his raids training late into the night, while Assets oversaw logistics, keeping an entire party of top-level chefs cooking late, preparing all manner of packaged meals for the combat groups, particularly the healers and casters, who'd been eating like freaks to keep their mana up. People joked that they'd made the first *haute cuisine* MREs in history, but Tina was just happy that no one on the front lines was going to be caught without food.

By the time the sun peeked over the city walls, all that could be made had been. The warehouses were empty, so Tina sent the rest of the lower-level smiths to the kitchen for breakfast and went off in search of SilentBlayde.

He'd been popping in on her all night, at least until she barked at him to get back to work. It wasn't that she didn't cherish his company, but SB was now Camp Comeback's main quest giver. If they were going to be ready, she needed him making sure every player was doing their part, not hovering over her. Now, though, everything was done, which meant she was finally free to give him the attention she'd desperately wanted to earlier.

It took a while to find him. The whole camp was busy getting food and preparing for the day, but no one in the kitchens had seen him. He wasn't in the sleeping areas, catching a last-minute nap, either, or at the quest-giving table, where Frank was snoozing. She was starting to panic when she finally spotted a lone slim figure swimming through the long shadows in the river on the island's north side.

Tina broke into a grin and jogged down the grassy hill toward the riverbank. She was about to shout his name when SilentBlayde came out of the water, and Tina lost her ability to speak.

He must have been bathing, because he was naked except for his linen shorts when he walked out of the water. She'd seen the male-elf model body before, of course, but never like this. Never for real. He was dripping wet, his golden hair and skin practically glittering as he shook himself off. She could see every line of his lean body and the graceful arc of his back as he bent over to wring the water out of his hair. He looked like an ethereal creature, which she supposed she should have expected from an elf, but none of the other elf players had ever looked half as wondrous to her as SB did right now, stretching his arms over his head in the pink-gold glow of the warm dawn.

The moment fell apart when SilentBlayde turned and spotted her. His face instantly turned bright red, then he dove for his clothes and put his mask on first before shoving his legs and arms into his armor with less than his usual grace.

A better friend would have looked away to spare him the embarrassment, but Tina was too busy cursing her stonekin's indifference to the male perfection on display in front of her. If she dug down to her old self, she could still appreciate how his linen shirt clung to his wet chest or the way his leather armor encased his long legs, but it was only in her mind. Now that the initial shock of seeing him was over, her body was quickly reverting to its usual stony indifference, and that made her want to cry. She was *finally* here in real life with Haruto, and she couldn't be more than an armored rock. She'd never felt so robbed. She was fighting not to break something when SB finished dressing and walked up the bank.

"Sorry about that," he said, his face still flushed above his mask. "I wasn't trying to put on a show. I just figured I'd sneak in a bath while everyone was at breakfast."

"It's okay," Tina said, turning her attention to the water so she wouldn't have to look into his blue eyes and feel nothing. "It's been a gross few days. A bath is definitely in order."

"This is actually my second," SB said self-consciously. "I washed off last night, too, but I still didn't feel clean, so I decided to try again." He chuckled weakly. "I think being an elf has turned me into a neat freak."

Tina laughed at him. "What are you talking about? You've always been that way. I mean, you clean your bathtub after *every use.* Who does that?"

"People who don't want gross bathrooms, of course," he replied, then his eyes widened with horror. "Wait, do you have a scary American bathroom of doom?"

"Hey, we clean it occasionally," Tina said defensively. "But I share an apartment with three other girls. Our bathroom is so covered in hair-care-product bottles there's no room for dirt to settle."

348

SB made a hand gesture to ward off evil. The motion knocked a damp strand of golden hair down into his face. Without thinking, Tina reached out and brushed the silky-smooth strands back into place. It was a tiny, simple thing, but by the time she finished, SilentBlayde had gone stock-still.

"Sorry," Tina said, snatching her hand away. "I was just... that is..." She shrugged helplessly. "I'm not used to you looking disheveled, you know?"

"I should probably brush it or something," he said, running a gloved hand through his unbound hair. "I've never had hair this long. I don't know what to do with it."

"I bet it dries perfect all on its own," Tina replied with a smirk. "From what I've seen, 'Eternal Good Hair Day' seems to be a secret elven racial ability. I'd be envious, but Roxxy's copper dreads don't even tangle, which is a miracle compared to the rat's nest my real hair used to be, so I guess I can't complain."

"Your hair was never a rat's nest."

Tina had to laugh at that one. "Dude, have you *seen* my hair? It has a mind of its own. I used to break hairbrushes every month. Not flimsy ones, either. I'm talking about the big plastic bastards."

"Well, *I* liked it," SilentBlayde said stubbornly. "It looked soft."

If stonekin were able to blush, the gentle way he said that would have made Tina's face catch fire. "It was pretty soft, I guess," she mumbled, looking down at her giant feet in the grass. "But at least I don't have to deal with it anymore. Nothing about me is soft or fluffy now. Just stone and metal all the way through."

She clanged her metal glove against her stone temple for emphasis, and SB looked up curiously.

"What's it like?" he asked. "Being a stonekin, I mean. I just realized I never asked you."

Tina thought about that for a moment. "Pretty great, most of the time. Being so much bigger than everyone else is a little inconvenient, but the power is amazing. I'm huge, I'm tough, and I barely need sleep anymore or--get this--air. Being able to feel the hum of the ground is also pretty cool when I have time to focus on it."

She tried her best to keep her voice upbeat, but she'd forgotten how well SB knew her, because she'd barely finished before he said, "But?"

Tina sighed. "But it can be dehumanizing. I can't eat real food or sleep in normal beds. I try to be careful with my strength, but I still mangle so much stuff by accident, like doorknobs. If a doorknob around here doesn't work, that was probably me. And being in close quarters with the lowbies is nerve-wracking as shit. All it would take is me turning around too fast, and I could kill someone with an elbow to the face."

She leaned down with a sigh and grabbed a rock to toss into the river. "If I'm honest, I miss being human so much it hurts sometimes. I'd give anything at this point just to drink coffee again. Or break a brush on my stupid hair."

"We'll find a way to get you back," SB promised. "I'm sure we can."

"I wish I shared your optimism," Tina muttered, chucking another rock into the river's blue depths. "The cozy-up-to-the-king plan went out the window the moment we attacked Malakai's camp, which means all the portal keepers, sages, and everything else we need is locked behind castle walls and an enemy army. Even if we win, I don't know if we'll ever be able to get their help after all the bad blood."

"That's probably true," he said sadly. "But we still did the right thing saving the others."

"I'm not saying I regret it," Tina said quickly. "But I can't help feeling as if everything we've done has made things worse. We're facing a huge battle, one I don't know if we can win. Even if we do pull it off, there's bound to be losses, and I just..." She trailed off, chucking the next rock so hard, she threw it clear over the river. "People always accuse me of treating them like soldiers, but I know damn well that they aren't. I don't want to lose anyone. If there was a way we could bail out of this, I'd do it in a heartbeat."

"But we can't," SB said, looking up at dawn-lit city with the Bastion glowing at its peak.

"Nope," she agreed. "We're an honest-to-god rebel army now. No ruler's going to tolerate something like that. Even if we decided to say fuck it all and leave, there's nowhere to go. This whole world is nothing but monsters and NPCs who hate our guts."

"It's not all bad," SilentBlayde said, putting a hand on her arm. "There's places I'd love to go with you when this is over. We could visit the Sea Under the Sea or the High Clouds. Remember how we used to hang out under the Gem-Water Cascade to do video editing? I bet it's *amazing* now that everything is real. And while all the player housing is gone, I can think of a lot of places in FFO that'd be nice to live in."

He sounded so hopeful, but every word that came out of his mouth felt like a stone settling in Tina's stomach. She knew SB wanted to stay. He'd said as much straight out back at the Order Fortress. The trouble was, Tina didn't. She was sick of this world and its constant problems, sick of being an unfeeling hunk of rock. All she wanted was to get back to her real life with pizza and internet and normal problems like being broke, not having to fight for her life every damn day. Like Neko, she just wanted to go home, but if she went and he didn't, she'd never see SilentBlayde again.

Just thinking about that made the weight in her stomach double. She knew frustratingly little about Haruto's real-life situation, but the bits she had managed to pick up were enough to understand that it sucked utterly. She couldn't blame him for not wanting to go back to that. He was a gorgeous elf here, young and powerful and in perfect health. If they managed not to die today, he could probably make a great life in this world, maybe even marry a pretty elf girl and have a whole baseball team of impossibly cute elf kids. Meanwhile, she'd be a rock--a big, tough, uncaring rock who never aged or ate or *felt*.

Tina was reeling back to chuck another rock good and hard at the water when she spotted a flash of bright green running toward them from the city. Squinting in the morning light, she realized it was Zen. The

Ranger was sprinting down the road at full speed. She slowed down a tiny bit when she reached the bridge, but Killbox and the other guards just stepped aside to let her through, leaving her clear to race straight to Tina, kicking up a cloud of dust in the process.

"Whoa," Tina said, stepping aside to give the green-haired Ranger space as she skidded to a halt. "You just got off shift. Aren't you supposed to be sleeping?"

"I... was... sleeping," Zen panted, doubling over as she fought to catch her breath. "But then one of my Rangers came in with a report, and I figured I'd better check for myself."

"That fast?" SB said, his voice showing his worry. "You know that--"

"I *know*," she cut him off. "The super speed was just for the way back, but this was worth the risk." She took one last breath and straightened up, her face pinched and fearful when it met Tina's. "Malakai's on the move. His army's marching toward us as we speak. I give it thirty minutes, an hour tops before they're on our doorstep."

"Well, crap," Tina said, looking over her shoulder at the camp, which was still recovering from their all-nighter. "I'd hoped we'd have more time, but at least now I don't feel bad for making everyone work through the night."

"I just hope we can fight on lack of sleep," Zen said, giving Tina a tired smile. "We're not all stone machines like you."

It was clearly meant to be a compliment, but in the current context, the good-natured words felt more like barbs. There was no time for wallowing in self-pity, though. They had a war to win, so Tina turned and pointed up the hill.

"Go up and tell people it's game time," she ordered. "Everyone needs to finish breakfast and get into position pronto. This is not a drill."

Zen nodded and vanished, racing up the hill so fast, she looked like a green streak. When she was gone, SB pulled down his mask to give Tina a smile. "We'll make it through this."

"I hope so," she said, pulling her shield onto her arm. "Ready for another day of dancing with the devil?"

SB gave her a thumbs-up. "We'll give them hell. And some high water too."

His voice was as nonchalant as always, but Tina could hear the doubt beneath it. She knew hers was no better, so she kept her mouth shut, jogging up the hill toward the camp, which Zen had already thrown into a frenzy.

***

Fifteen minutes later, the whole island looked like a kicked-over anthill. Everyone was up and scrambling into their new gear while shoving food into their mouths as quickly as possible. After making a quick circuit of the camp to make sure no one was shirking, Tina walked into the main yard to find Cinco and Assets waiting as requested, breakfast still in hand.

"Tina," Cinco said around a mouthful of biscuit.

"Roxxy," Assets said, nodding her way while sipping his tea latte.

"Gentlemen," Tina said, moving in to close their triangle. "We ready for this?"

"Not in the least," Assets replied, glaring pointedly at the chaos surrounding them. "We gave it a good go, but it's simply not possible to make a functional army in a day. This is going to be a disaster."

"The fancy-pants elf is right," Cinco said and shoved the rest of his biscuit into his mouth then washed it down with an entire tankard of something that smelled almost but not quite like coffee. "I pushed them as hard as I could, but the random raids are still a mess. They're basically just dangerous mobs. If they hold their position in any form, I'll be amazed."

"That's why we're putting them in places where they can't retreat," Tina said with a grim smile. "Even the worst pull together when you put their backs to the wall." The other two raid leaders shared a sideways look, and Tina crossed her arms over her chest. "No complaining now, guys.

353

This is the army we have, and the war is coming to us. It's too late for second guesses."

"We're not second guessing," Assets said angrily. "But just because we picked the best of bad options doesn't mean it wasn't still *really* bad. Even if we manage to survive, our future is very short. The warehouses are empty, which means no repairs, and there's only three days of food left. Five if I cut rations to the bone."

"We'll cross that bridge when we get there," Tina said. "I'm used to the future being measured in hours. Days are a luxury. I can change the whole world in three days. All I care about is 'Can we fight *now*?'"

The elf shrugged. "Maybe? We're as good as we're going to get, but I still don't think it'll be enough to--"

"'As good as we're going to get' is good enough for me," Tina said firmly. "The scouts are saying that Malakai's cavalry is already sweeping through the streets east of us, so I want everyone fed and in position behind CraftyJohn's barricades ASAP. You guys gather your groups. I'll get the Roughnecks."

"Right," Cinco said, giving her a nod. "Let's do this."

The three raid leaders broke apart, each going to rally their parts of the plan. Tina went to the central area, where her giant desk was, where most of the Roughnecks had already gathered. Tina sent SB and Neko out to round up the rest, then she pulled Richard to the side.

"How's the fire-ward plan coming?" she whispered.

The tall, thin Sorcerer pulled a thick packet of papers out of his bag. "We started by running some single-Sorcerer test wards versus our own attacks to pin down preliminary formulas as concerns ward-based mana efficiency versus magical thermal energies," he said. "From there, we progressed to more specific experimentation involving small amounts of wind-fire powder. From this, we discovered that the powder's explosive properties rely on reaching an ignition threshold based on the size of air magic it--"

Tina held up a hand to interrupt him. "I'm sorry, Richard. I actually find this fascinating--I mean, you guys are doing magical science, which is amazing--but I don't have time to listen to your report. If we survive this, you and I are going to get a beer and go over the whole thing in detail, but right now, all I need to know is can you do it, and what do you need from me?"

The cutoff didn't seem to bother Richard in the slightest. He just flipped to the last page of the thick packet he was holding and turned it around for Tina to see.

"The ward you requested is quite possible," he said. "But it requires twenty Sorcerers in Dead Mountain Fortress-level gear. Since players of that caliber are needed for battle, they won't have the mana needed to deploy the ward on call. To solve this problem, I have assembled five dozen mid-level Sorcerers to serve as mana pumps. I spent all night laying as much groundwork as possible within the bounds of secrecy, but it will still take thirty minutes to reach the required critical magical mass. If you can give me that, though, we can surround this island in a fire ward so powerful, not even wind-fire powder will be able to pierce it."

He finished with a proud smile, but while Tina was very impressed with his work, she wasn't sure if she was happy or not that the wind-fire-powder plan was a go. Ace in the hole or not, a magical nuke was still a nuke, and not once in history had the use of weapons of mass destruction resulted in a happy victory. That said, she wasn't in a position to turn down any chance at victory, so she forced a smile onto her face and gave Richard a thumbs-up.

"Good job. Thanks for putting everything together so far. I don't think anyone else could have done it."

To her surprise, Richard smiled back, the first real emotion Tina had ever seen him show. "Thank you, Roxxy," he said earnestly, reaching out to shake her hand. "This was the most fascinating project I've ever worked on. I intend to devote much of my time to additional study in the days ahead."

355

"I'm looking forward to seeing what you find out," Tina said, grinning back. "Now, let's make sure we get to see more days."

"We are ready," Richard promised. "The Roughneck Sorcerers are a talented and dedicated group. We will not let you down."

"I know you won't," Tina said, hoping silently that the same could be said of her.

***

Fifteen minutes later, Tina was standing on top of her table, looking down at the nearly four hundred players who'd be fighting today. Asset's support raiders, who were all sporting white headbands, had already herded the low-level players and NPC refugees into the stone storage buildings for safety, which meant only the fighters remained. They didn't look much like an army, but overall, Tina was pleased with how clean and well-fed everyone looked. Weapons were sharp--or brand new-- and armor gleamed. Holes had been patched, and everyone's backpacks were full of ammo, water, and food. It was as good as they were ever going to get, so Tina banged her shield to get their attention, standing straighter as six full raids' worth of eyes locked on her.

"Listen up," she said, speaking slowly to make sure she didn't flub the speech she'd come up with for this. "Today's the day the tyrant will try to put us down. The king and his knights have already tried to exterminate every player in this city. Now they're coming for us, but we're not helpless victims taken down by the transition, who'll lie still while our throats are cut. We're fighters, survivors, but even more than that, we're *gamers*. Before any of this happened, all of us spent hundreds of hours in these bodies, fighting desperate battles against way scarier odds. People always told me I was wasting my life playing FFO, but the fact that we're all still standing here alive today is proof that that's bullshit. Every one of you is a badass motherfucker who's already overcome the worst of what this world can dish out. We're the few, the proud, the *hard-core*! We are the last things standing between those murderers and the thousand terrified people huddled in the buildings behind us. The only ones who can get justice for all the friends, family, guildmates, and comrades that the knights have already killed. We are the *final* line, but we are the greatest. We're *players*, and together, we're going to show those NPCs what it means to mess with us!"

A roar went up from the crowd. Tina answered it, drawing her red-glowing sword and stabbing it into the air above her head.

"This isn't just about survival," she reminded them. "If we beat the king today, we're going to take him for everything he's got. The castle, the portal keepers, the magical library--it'll all be ours! For those who want to go home, this is the first step. For those who want to stay, this is the fight to show we won't be pushed around. But stay or go, none of us have a future if we don't win now, so put on your game faces and get into position, because today's the day we teach this world not to fuck with us."

She jabbed her sword higher into the sky, and the whole field yelled back. Players brandished their glowing weapons, and a few fireballs shot into the air. Tina let them go on for another half a minute, then she sheathed her blade and waved at everyone to get moving. When she was satisfied everyone was going where they should, she jumped down to the grass where the Roughnecks were already gathered.

"Okay, everyone," she said to them. "We've got the toughest spot: the north bridge. It's the widest, and it faces the plaza, which means we're the first troops they're going to see and we've got the most ground to cover. But it doesn't matter how many knights Malakai throws at us. We've already faced an army, and these guys today are nothing on Grel or the Once King. We're gonna own this."

The Roughnecks responded with cheers and high fives. Tina grinned back, hoping their bravado was more genuine than hers. It was easy to talk big, but while the knights weren't as geared as her people, they also weren't mindless like the undead, which meant they weren't predictable. They'd stomped them hard at the death camp by the castle, but there was no way Malakai would let that happen again. He'd be prepared this time. Tina just hoped they were too.

Keeping a determined expression on her face, Tina led her raid into position on the north bridge. As they arranged themselves on the Camp Comeback side of the river, she wished she'd thought to make herself a helmet while she was cranking out armor for everyone else. Something to cover her head would have been a relief as she took her position in the middle of the bridge's ten-foot-wide stone span. There was no cover between the squat stone railings, and it was only thirty feet to the other bank, well within bow shot, which meant she'd have to be fast with her shield. It would be just her luck if she took an arrow to the eye because she'd been too busy to make herself some head protection. But it was too late to fix now, so Tina twisted her copper dreadlocks into a bun on top of her head and looked around to see how the rest of her army was doing.

"Pretty good" seemed to be the answer. CraftyJohn had lived up to his name, lining their bank of the river in nine-foot-tall hunks of iron-banded stone he called "tank breakers." Due to time constraints, the massive X-shaped barricades only covered the banks along the shallow parts of the river. The deep sections by the bridges weren't protected, but the Herald's River ran so fast and swift there, Tina was counting on no knights being suicidal enough to try to swim across in their armor.

Even with the gaps, it was still a damn impressive sight, given how fast they'd had to throw it all together, and the tank breakers provided good cover for the non-guild combat raids, aka the people who needed it the most. They still looked uncomfortably like a mob, but at least they were all armed and facing the right direction. The Red Sands raid looked much more impressive holding the eastern bridge, and while she couldn't see the south bridge combat team from where she was standing, Tina trusted them to be in position after all of Cinco's drilling. Assets's people were definitely ready. They were all in neat formation at the top of the hill, ready to do whatever the combat raids needed. Assets himself was getting the low-level healing teams into final position, placing each one where their spells could reach the most people without forcing the vulnerable casters to leave cover.

"Defenses are looking good," she said, glancing back at Killbox. "How's our offense?"

"Ready to rock and roll," Killbox said, giving her two big thumbs up. "Fuckers won't know what hit them."

"We moved all the rocks into position behind the bridge before sunrise," Frank added, pushing up his visor to give her a grin. "Physics is going to be on our side this time!"

Tina flashed them a huge grin and turned back around. But when she looked down to see if SB was as ready for this as she was, he was staring at the ground.

"Hey," she said quietly. "You okay?"

"I'm fine," he said quietly, hunching his shoulders. "Just nervous."

"About what?" Because she couldn't believe he was afraid of the knights. He'd carved those bastards up like paper at the camp.

"Everything," he said, wrapping his long arms around his middle. "It's just... I just wish we didn't have to fight. We've done really well for what we had, but I don't think this battle is going to end well for anyone."

"Real battles never do," Tina said. "But Malakai and the king have made it clear what they think of us. Maybe they'll change their tune after we kill half their army, but until then, we have to fight. It's that or be exterminated."

SB nodded, but he still wasn't meeting her eyes. "I know we don't have a choice," he said. "But this isn't like fighting the undead. Those knights are people just like us. This isn't like the extermination camp. We saw *those* knights killing innocent players, but this army is coming to put down a rebellion. In their eyes, I'm sure they think they're saving their home. I don't mind killing murderers, but a lot of the people we'll be fighting today are probably just good men fighting for their king."

"Oh my *god*," Tina said, running her hands over her face. "James was talking to you, wasn't he?"

359

SB's silence was answer enough, and Tina turned to face him. "Listen," she said, putting her hands on his shoulders. "We're the good guys, not them. Maybe not every single one of the people we'll be fighting today has personally killed a player, but they're all still soldiers who hate our guts and work for a king who's a genocidal maniac. I don't know what my idiot brother told you, but I guarantee you it's one hundred percent wrong. He's got it stuck in his head that we can reason with the NPCs, but if that were true, then this wouldn't be happening. Never forget: they're the ones coming for *us*. We weren't doing shit down here except trying to survive while the king sent Malakai and his army to crush us. I refuse to feel guilty for defending ourselves and the people who rely on us, and neither should you."

"I know that," he said quietly. "But--"

"No," she said forcefully. "There is no 'but.' These are the same bastards who massacred Founder's Square and every player they've met since. They don't deserve your mercy. I'm not asking you to be happy about killing--none of us are--but I need you here with us, Blayde." She smiled at him. "You're my second-in-command. I can't do this without you."

He nodded and straightened up, hands falling to his swords at last. "I won't let you down," he promised.

"You never do," she said, leaning down to give him one last wink before turning her attention back to the opposite shore.

Just in time. She hadn't heard them over the gurgle of the swiftly running river, but riders were starting to enter the wide stone plaza at the end of their bridge. It wasn't a few men on armored horses, either. Rows and rows of cavaliers in the royal red and gold were pouring into the square from every street, their raised lances creating a forest of spikes over their heads. Alarms rang out behind her as the rest of Camp Comeback spotted the enemy, but when Zen and her archers nocked their arrows, Tina held up her fist.

360

The riders weren't alone. Once the cavaliers had secured the square, foot soldiers started marching in. Soon, the entire plaza and all the streets leading into it were packed with spearmen wearing the red surcoat of Bastion's army over their chain mail. Even the city guards had been drafted. The poor low-level bastards were mixed in with the rest, easily identifiable by their yellow tabards and expressions of pure terror.

Tina wasn't worried about the city guards, but the force in front of her was still terrifyingly huge. There were so many enemies packed into the square, she couldn't begin to count them, and this was just what was in front of the Roughnecks. From the clatter of armor and the curses coming from the raids behind her, she knew the other bridges were equally bad. But as many of them as there were, none of the soldiers looked particularly dangerous, and Tina was starting to think this might not be as bad as it looked when the Royal Knights appeared.

They came in like a crimson wave, forcing the other soldiers out of the way as they marched to the front in units of no fewer than a hundred each. Mobs of archers came in behind them, followed by wooden catapults. There were so many, even the flagstone plaza built to hold Bastion's epic festivals couldn't contain them all. By the time they were all arranged, the lesser soldiers had been forced out onto the docks that bordered the river.

It was a horrifying sight, but of everything pointed at them, Tina was most concerned about the siege weapons. Arrows, she could handle, but if one of the storage buildings housing the refugees took a boulder, the whole thing could collapse. She was kicking herself for not asking Richard for a ward against flying rocks when the wall of troops across the river shifted, and Malakai himself came into view.

The absurdly tall captain was standing on the seat of a huge wagon drawn by two sturdy draft horses. The bed of the wagon was filled with what appeared to be damp wood arranged in a pile around a central pole with a crying ichthyian wearing the mismatched cloth robes of a low-level caster tied to its base.

361

The fish-man was sobbing so loudly, Tina could hear him clear across the water, and he wasn't alone. Behind Malakai, more carts were coming in, each with a player prisoner. Some of the posts had multiple people tied to them. Every race was represented, and they were all low-level. Squinting across the river, Tina didn't see a single piece of gear above level fifteen. She also saw that the wood at their feet wasn't just wet. The way the air shimmered above the piled logs told her they were soaked in oil, which meant the carts weren't just for drama. They were rolling pyres, a whole line of them pulling right up to the edge of the river.

Tina's stomach clenched with rage. She'd known Malakai would have hostages, but she'd thought they'd be in cages like before. The pyres were an unexpected twist, one Malakai intended to use quickly, given the burning torches the knights escorting the wagons held perilously close to the oil-soaked wood. She was still working out how they were going to handle it when the elven captain hopped off his wagon and walked to the mouth of her bridge, sneering down the stone span straight at her.

"I am Captain Malakai of the Royal Knights!" he cried, his booming voice echoing off the buildings behind her. "In the name of King Gregory Heraldsford, I command you to cease your treasonous acts and surrender. Anything less, and we will bring the justice of our swords down upon you!"

Tina answered that by spitting on the stone at her feet. "Yeah, well, I'm Roxxy, leader of the Roughnecks Guild!" she yelled back. "I speak for everyone on this island, and we're not surrendering shit. We've seen what you do to players. You're murderous thugs who kidnap and kill anyone too weak to fight back, and we're having none of it. You think we're scared of you? My raid has already defeated the Once King's entire army! Attack us, and we will stomp you into the ground!"

Even from thirty feet away, Tina saw Malakai's eye twitch at her defiance. "*So be it!*" he roared back. "Let none say that you were not warned! If you will not yield, then I have no choice but to show you what happens to those who rebel against the Holy King!"

362

With that, the tall elf turned on his heel and marched back to his wagon, grabbing a torch from his knights as he went. He didn't even pause to threaten Tina again. He just plunged the fire into the oil-soaked wood, grinning in delight as the whole wagon went up in a blaze.

Tina jumped back as the fire flared. She hadn't expected the killing to start so quickly. The entire point of hostages was to threaten your enemy into doing what you said, but Malakai hadn't even done that much. He'd just started burning them like that was what he'd wanted to do all along.

"Roxxy, what do we do?" shouted NekoBaby behind her as Malakai started toward the next cart. "He's going to barbecue all of them!"

Tina had no idea. The whole point of fighting at the bridge was to limit the enemy's numbers. If they charged across to rescue the burning player, the Roughnecks would be alone and surrounded in the middle of the enemy army. They'd also open a hole in Camp Comeback's defensive line, allowing Malakai to send his cavalry behind them for a perfect flanking attack on the other raids. Any way she looked at it, going in was the worst decision possible, but she couldn't just stand there and watch someone burn to death.

"Zen!" she shouted, never taking her eyes off the panicking ichthyian. "Can you hit from him here?"

"I can shoot Malakai, sure," the Ranger said, running up beside her. "But it won't do any good. I don't do enough damage to take down a--"

"Not Malakai," Tina said. "*Him.*" She pointed at the player, whose robes were now starting to smoke, and Zen's dark face grew ashen.

"You want me to *shoot* the lowbie?" she cried, horrified. "But that will kill him!"

"Can't be worse than burning to death," Tina said grimly. "But I'm not talking about a mercy kill. We can't charge across to save him without risking everything, but we can sure as shit plant a Grapple Arrow in his chest and yank him over. It'll suck, but we can rez him once he gets here, and it beats letting Malakai roast him."

The player's screams of pain were getting quite horrible now, but Zen still shook her head. "I'm not shooting a hostage in the chest."

"But--"

"I'll shoot the pole he's tied to instead," Zen finished, nocking an arrow with a rope tied to the end into her bow. "Honestly, Roxxy, do you even know how to Ranger?"

Before Tina could reply to that, Zen aimed, pulled, and loosed her shot in one liquid motion. The Grapple Arrow flew down the bridge, streaking over the surprised Malakai's head to sink deep into wooden pole the player was tied to. Zen gave the rope a quick test tug to make sure it was stuck, then she tossed it at Tina. "*Pull!*"

Tina didn't wait to be asked twice. She grabbed the rope and pulled as hard as she could, using her stonekin's weight and enormous strength to rip the pole straight out of the burning cart. The fire had already weakened the wagon's bed, so it wasn't even that hard. One yank was all it took to send the player flying past the captain to land at their feet. Green-glowing magic started falling even before he landed, bathing the still-screaming player in magical healing as Tina reeled him the last few feet to the Roughnecks' line. SB cut him free of the pole the moment he was in reach and handed the dazed and gasping ichthyian back through the raid toward the support area. Tina watched until she was sure he was safe, then she turned back to Malakai with a smug grin on her face.

"You were saying, asshole?"

The elf captain's face was a mask of rage. "Move the carts back!" he bellowed, never taking his eyes off Tina. "I swear, I will make you listen to each and every one of their screams before this is over. And when I crush this rebellion, the rest of you shall share the same fate. You will *all* burn for what you have done to us!"

Tina just shrugged and waved her hand forward. At the command, a volley of arrows erupted from the Roughneck ranks, cutting down the knights who were trying to move the hostage wagons farther back into the plaza. As the shots rained down, three Rangers in Dead Mountain Fortress

364

gear pushed past Tina to plunk oversized arrows with huge, barbed heads and ropes tied their ends into the remaining hostage poles. They fired one after the other, tossing each rope to the front line of Knights and Berserkers the moment it was locked down. Once they got the ropes, the melee classes used their monstrous strength to follow Tina's example and yanked the poles free.

Malakai's face turned an even deeper shade of reddish-purple as his hostages went flying past one by one. He was drawing his blade to cut the ropes and stop them when Zen hopped up on the bridge's stone railing and started firing at the captain like an elven machine gun.

For a second, Tina hoped it would be that easy. Malakai was out in front and alone, a painfully easy target as Zen's arrows began to fill him like a pincushion. She managed to put two in his legs, one in his arm, and three in his chest before the four-skull captain leaped backward like a rocket, spoiling the next two shots while cutting the third out of the air with his sword. Zen kept firing, but he'd already scrambled back behind the cover of the knights, who sheltered him behind their enormous shields. From so great a distance, even Zen's deadly arrows bounced off the metal, and she lowered her bow with a scowl.

"He's too far," she said, hopping down off the railing. "I'm just wasting ammo."

"You did good enough for me," Tina said joyfully, grinning down at the hostages the Roughnecks were hauling in and cutting free as fast as they could.

As a final insult, some devilish Ranger had the great idea of sending fire arrows into the empty wagons, burning them anyway in a giant blast of fire that sent the knights scattering.

It was a gorgeous sight, and Tina took a moment to breathe in the smoky air before turning to grin at her raid. "Good job, guys! That was perfect."

Zen saluted her back, and Tina turned around again, cupping her hands over her mouth to yell more insults at Malakai. Before she could think of something suitably scathing, though, the catapults in the back of the plaza bucked. Then the air was filled with the whistle of flying rocks as a volley of boulders launched into the air.

"Shit." Tina dropped her hands to yank her shield up over her head. "*Incoming!*" she shouted, lifting her already booming voice to a roar as the rocks soared over them toward the other raids. "Naturalists! Externals!"

"Circle of Thorns!" rose the call-out from Naturalists all over the island. Staffs of every level flared with green light, and massive ironwood vines erupted from the ground around each raid and grew rapidly into a dome-shaped hedge of impenetrable wood.

They'd barely finished before the deadly rocks flung by the catapults crashed into the densely packed thickets, shattering the foot-thick vines. Hiding in the darkness of the hedge, Tina flinched as she was peppered with splinters, but despite the cracks, nothing got through. But while the Roughnecks were safe, the same couldn't be said for everyone else.

All around the island, screams of pain erupted from the non-guild raids where inexperienced players hadn't been in position to get under the Circles of Thorns in time. As the shroud of thorns over her vanished, Tina saw the massive craters in the dirt where rocks had plowed into her players, crushing people under their weight. A few more Circles of Thorns sprang up as she watched, way too late to block anything but wasting precious defensive cooldowns nonetheless.

Tina grimaced at the waste but didn't say anything. Everyone who'd fucked up already knew it, which meant yelling would be pointless. She was much more interested in all the heals and Raise Ally spells that were already going off as the raids picked themselves up. The fast response was exactly what she'd wanted, but the sight of all that mana usage still had her slightly panicked. This was just the opening of a very long battle. If they were burning this fast already, they were going to run out.

By this point, all the Circles of Thorns that had gone up were starting to fall away, dropping the boulders they'd caught harmlessly to the ground around them. Most fell into the river, but a few landed in the grass directly behind the raid. One smooth-sanded stone plopped onto the bridge just a few feet in front of her, and Tina's face broke into an enormous grin.

"Well, well," she said, making sure her voice was loud enough for all the knights to hear as she reached down to run her gloved hands over the painstakingly crafted catapult ammunition. "Thanks for the ammo, jerks!" She grinned one last time and stepped back, turning slightly to yell over her shoulder. "Team Shot Put, you're up!"

"Oh yeah," Killbox said, cracking his knuckles as he led the rest of the strength-based classes forward. "Time to lay the smack down."

Tina dutifully got out of the way as the Berserker sauntered up to the boulder that had landed on the bridge in front of them.

Flexing arms that would give canned hams envy, he picked up the beach-ball-sized hunk of granite as if it weighed nothing. "Ready, boss?"

"Fire at will," Tina said smugly.

"Hooah!" Killbox ran a few feet down the bridge, hopped the last step, then hurled the catapult stone back toward the enemy army. People whistled in appreciation as the rock sailed through the midmorning sunlight like an artillery shot, arcing nearly fifty feet into the air before crashing down right on top of the catapult line.

The resulting crash of wood and stone was deafening. Splinters flew so high into the air, Tina had to lift her shield to protect her face. But the attack wasn't over. Behind them, the rest of Team Shot Put was grabbing the not-quite-as-round-or-as-large-but-still-deadly rocks Frank and the others had piled behind the bridge. Hefting the stones like softballs, the massively strong Berserkers hurled them across the river and into the enemy ranks, taking out knights and carts and catapults in a hail of stones. A few enterprising members even ran back to snatch more catapult stones from where they'd landed by the other raids then ran back onto the

367

bridge to hurl them as Killbox had, pummeling Malakai's army under a meteor storm of flying rocks.

"Whooee!" Killbox shouted as the rocks flew over their heads. "And they used to say I was no good at baseball!"

"I know, right?" Tina agreed. "Who needs siege weapons? You guys are the most destructive bastards around."

She gave Killbox a high five that left her hand stinging and turned back to Malakai, who'd been forced to take cover in one of the far buildings as the last of Team Shot Put's attacks rained down. "What do you think of us now, Captain Loser?" she taunted. "Got anything else you want to try, or are you ready to take your own advice and surrender? Personally, I'd recommend giving up now. This isn't exactly going your way, and we ain't even gotten to the real ass-kicking yet. If you and your Buffoon King want to get out of this with any army left, you'd better call it quits, 'cause we can do this all damn day."

She couldn't even see Malakai anymore through the chaos of broken catapults and injured soldiers, but that was fine. As much as Tina hated the captain, her taunts weren't actually for him. They were aimed at the normal soldiers, the men that--as SB had said--were just following orders. Malakai's hate was such that he'd fight them until he could no longer stand, but normal people weren't half as hard-core. If she could break the enemy's morale, she could end this without having to take another attack. That was her hope, anyway, but the Bastion Army must have been very well trained, because no one broke ranks as Malakai forced his way out of the house he'd sheltered in and started ordering his men forward.

Shaking her head at the stupidity of it all, Tina lifted her shield. "Get ready for incoming!"

While the raid got into position behind her, Tina set her stance at the front, shifting her shield nervously as Malakai's soldiers started grabbing debris out of the ruined plaza. Some of the broken beams were so heavy, they had to be carried by ten men. Tina watched in confusion as

Malakai waved his hand forward, sending his spearmen and archers rushing out of the safety of the rear streets, across the cratered square, and straight toward the riverbank itself with their armfuls of salvage.

"What are they doing?" SB whispered.

Tina had no idea. It looked like they were about to charge her bridge with a bunch of random garbage. Before she could figure out how to deal with that, though, the enemy stopped just short of the river and started throwing down the debris they'd picked up. Broken catapults and hunks of stone were piled on top of each other in crisscross stacks, forming a wall of cover for the archers to squeeze between as they started firing at the players on the bridge.

"Crap," Tina said, hunkering down behind her shield. "Arrows incoming! Get to cover!"

The others were running before she'd finished, sprinting toward the makeshift walls at the Camp Comeback end of the bridge just in time as the shots started raining down. Of everything the enemy might bring, archers had been the most predictable, so she'd had CraftyJohn build them a shelter. The piled stone walls made a hefty barricade, but the splashes of golden-and-green light showed that too many arrows were still getting through. She'd wanted to save their limited ammunition and mana for the inevitable bridge fight, but the healers would run themselves dry long before the enemy ran out of arrows at this rate, so Tina set her jaw and gave the order everyone had been waiting for.

"Ranged attack, go!"

A cheer rose up from behind the makeshift wall, then spells and glowing arrows began to pour around the edges of the barricade as the Roughnecks' Rangers and Sorcerers unloaded. Tina and Frank--the only two players with shields that could protect them from the arrows and thus the only two who'd stayed on the bridge--were forced to hit the deck as fireballs and acid shots screamed over their heads to explode along the enemy line.

369

It wasn't anything Tina hadn't seen before, but it was still a damn glorious sight. The Roughnecks' ranged smashed through Malakai's makeshift barricade like a boot through tissue, blasting it apart and crushing the soldiers cowering behind it. Men screamed as poison arrows dissolved their flesh, and still more were sent running as the Sorcerers' fireballs caught clothing and wooden debris. The smell of charred flesh drifted back on the wind as the other side of the river turned into a raging inferno. When all the enemy arrows had stopped falling, Tina lowered her shield with a whoop.

"*Yeah!*" she shouted, stabbing her sword into the air. "That's how it's done! Everyone back into position!"

Cheers rose as the Roughnecks rushed back onto the bridge to obey. Seeing them running to get back into position made Tina want to cry. It was so different from the Deadlands. Everyone was listening and doing their part, obeying her orders without backtalk. *This* was what a raid was supposed to be, and they were going to crush anything that got in their way.

"Should we charge them?" Killbox asked as he got back into place behind her. "They look pretty toasted."

The opposite riverbank was indeed a sea of fire and broken bows. Wounded and dead archers littered the ground, while terrified spearmen tried to drag the injured to safety. It was the perfect chance to push the line, but Tina shook her head.

"We can't abandon our spot," she said quietly. "We're badasses, but most of the other raids are still just barely coordinated mobs. If we move out, we'll roll what's in front of us, but Malakai will send men in behind to take out our allies. We have to hold."

"We've held like bosses so far," NekoBaby said happily. "Let them keep trying. They have to get tired of banging their heads against the Roughnecks sometime."

That was in fact the plan, but though they'd wrecked everything Malakai had tried so far, it wasn't a fraction of what he'd brought with him. The black-and-gray-haired elf was already back on his feet and calling in reinforcements from the side streets, waving his arms toward their bridge in violent gestures as the cavalry moved forward.

"Here come the ponies," Tina muttered, glaring over the edge of her shield as the armored riders formed up on the other side of the bridge for a charge. "Listen up!" she shouted, standing up straight. "I want Rangers on the riverbank to the left of our bridge. Sorcerers, you're on the other side. Make sure you have a clear shot at the enemy's half of the bridge. Frank, you're with me. Melee, get behind us. Pack it in!"

Frank hurried to her side as the rest of the raid scrambled to rearrange itself. Tina noted that her fellow tank had a few arrows stuck in his armor, but otherwise, he looked all right--slightly terrified, but that was pretty normal for him.

"Ever thought you'd have to stop a cavalry charge, Frank?" she asked with a grin.

"Can't say it's crossed my mind," Frank replied nervously, peering over his shield at the wall of armored mounts that was about to launch at them. "Um, do we even have the mass to stop horses? They got a lotta force on their side."

"Well, I weigh as much as a horse, so maybe?" Tina shrugged. "Won't know until we try."

Frank did not look reassured by that. "Anything I should know before this starts?"

"Yeah," Tina said. "Keep your head *below* your shield. They're going to be coming in high. If you put your head up, you're liable to get a lance through your face, so stay down."

"If I'm not looking, how will I know when to brace?"

"You won't," Tina said. "But it's better than getting speared through the head. Just try not to get knocked over. Our job is just to stop the horses. The others will handle the rest."

"R-Right," he stuttered, bracing his shield in front of him.

"It'll be fine," Tina said, reaching out to grab his metal shoulder. "These guys aren't any scarier than what we fought at the concentration camp."

"That was pretty scary," Frank said, putting his visor down. "I ain't sorry we did it, but it's not an event I'm eager to repeat. Maybe it don't bother stone people like yourself, but I've never seen so much blood in my life."

"Yeah, *their* blood," Tina reminded him pointedly. "We were all fine until--"

A thunderous noise cut her off. On the other side of the bridge, the enormous unit of cavaliers had finished forming its two-rider-wide column and was starting the charge. The clatter of hundreds of hooves on stone was louder than anything Tina had ever heard, shaking the bridge under her feet. The movement brought Frank's force comment back to mind, and Tina suddenly was no longer so sure she could stop a charging horse on her own after all--or at least not a hundred horses.

"Change of plan!" she yelled, hunkering down behind her shield. "Melee, move in to brace the tanks!"

She wasn't sure if they'd heard her over the roar until she felt Killbox's iron-gloved hands land on her back. Reassured he had her back-- literally--Tina shifted into a lunge stance: right leg forward, back leg wedged against the Berserker's massive boot. When she was lodged in place, she sheathed her blade and put both hands behind her shield. Next to her, Frank did the same, leaning so close, his tower shield bumped into hers. Behind them, all the other melee did the same, hunkering down against the tank line's backs as they all braced for impact.

The wait was one of the most harrowing things Tina had ever experienced. She kept telling herself that this couldn't possibly be worse than Grel, but blindly hiding behind her shield while hundreds of armored riders thundered toward her had to be one of the most intimidating moments of her tanking career. Not knowing when she'd be struck was the worst part. The bridge was only thirty feet long, and the horses were moving at a full gallop, yet it still felt like years before the first hoof landed on her shield, almost knocking her over despite the wall of muscle braced against her back.

"*Steady Ground!*" she yelled, turning the bridge beneath her feet into solid bedrock.

She landed the ability just in time. No sooner were the words out of her mouth than a tremendous weight landed on her shield, banging the edge of it into her forehead. The tip of a lance passed through the copper dreadlocks on the back of her head a second later. Tina could feel its edge like a razor sliding over her scalp, but it did not pierce her stone flesh, and she did not fall.

More horses crashed into her, their iron-shod hooves clattering on the wall of her shield as their weight came down. Riders were sent flying as their momentum suddenly stopped, launching over her head into the melee behind her, where they were quickly hacked to bits. But the charge didn't stop. Since she didn't dare look over her shield, Tina had no idea how many horses had crashed into her, but the sheer mass of them was piling up her shield. The sunlight vanished as armored knights and kicking horses were pushed over her by the sheer force of the charging men behind them.

Tina spluttered as hot blood poured over her, struggling not to fall to her knees. This was nothing like Grel's attack. His blows had been powerful, but at least they'd been fast. This felt like she was being slowly crushed, and it just kept coming. By the time her Steady Ground faded, Tina couldn't see a thing. There had to be thousands of pounds of men and metal piled on top of her, making her armor groan. Screams of pain and the sounds of weapons clashing were the only signs she had that the fight was still going. Then Killbox's hands vanished from her shoulders, and the weight on top of her got even heavier, the whole mass moving in bursts and shakes, as if the Roughnecks were climbing over it.

Then just when Tina was sure she was going to be crushed under the combined weight of every horse in Bastion, someone roared in fury. It sounded like a Berserker, but it was *ahead* of her, not behind, which was all wrong. As the tank, Tina was always supposed to be the front line. If someone was out ahead of her, that meant she was failing her job.

The fury over that thought brought a burst of new strength. With a roar of her own, Tina heaved against the pile weighing her down, pushing up with her shaking legs until the mass started to slide. Tipping sideways, she crashed into the bridge's stone railing and clung to it for balance as the whole mess slid off her shield with a wet, sticky sound. As the light returned, Tina had never been gladder to be a stonekin. If she'd been human, she would have lost every lunch she'd ever eaten as a dozen crushed knights slid off her block into the river below.

As it was, the sight of so many defeated enemies just made her shake with triumph. The charge had stopped. All of the enemy's momentum was spent, leaving just a bunch of knights on horses facing off against her melee line--Killbox and Frank specifically since the bridge's narrow span bottled the Roughnecks just as much as it did the knights. None of the other close-quarters-combat fighters could get past the front line without risking losing a limb, but while that was definitely a problem, it was also the entire point of this plan.

"Good job, guys!" Tina yelled, throwing the last knight off her shield into the bloody water below. "Keep them there!"

Killbox nodded and swept his ax through the knight he was fighting on the bridge. Satisfied the line would hold, Tina turned to wave her arms at the Rangers and Sorcerers she'd sent to the riverbanks. While hand-to-hand fighters couldn't go more than two abreast down the stone bridge, the ranged damage dealers didn't have that problem. From their position on the sides, her Rangers and Sorcerers had a clear view of the knights piled up on the bridge, exactly as planned.

"Open fire!" Tina yelled, pointing at the opposite side of the bridge. "Concentrate on the back lines! Don't hit our people!"

The rest of the Roughnecks waved back, then the whistle-*thunk* of arrows filled the air once more. The roar of flames followed, dousing the knights' back line in an explosion of orange fire. But while the ranged had clearly gotten the "*Attack!*" part of her orders, they seemed to be having trouble with the rest. Tina was forced to duck as an arrow sailed right past her face to land in the chest of the knight Frank was currently hacking at. When another shot almost pierced her fellow tank's head, Tina decided to shield up behind them so the front-line fighters didn't get one in the back.

The rest of the players on the bridge hit the ground as the close shots came in, and just in time. The ranged were getting caught up in the bloodlust now, turning the knights' half of the bridge into an inferno. Packed in so close together, the enemy didn't even have a chance to retreat before they were shot to bits or burned to cinders. It got so thick that even Frank and Killbox were forced to stop swinging and hit the dirt. Tina took that as a chance to reclaim her place at the front, but by the time she'd squat-walked past Killbox, nothing on the bridge in front of her was moving. The whole span all the way back to Malakai's side of the river was now a singed wasteland of blood and burned body parts. It was so horrific, even her stonekin stomach turned, forcing her to swallow as she lifted her arm in the air.

"Cease fire!"

The barrage of arrows and fire puttered to a stop, leaving her standing in the deathly quiet of the slaughtered bridge. "Well," she said happily, "so far, so good."

"Says you," Frank muttered, looking down at his gory armor. "I think I'm gonna barf."

Tina was pretty bloody as well. Her newly cleaned armor was now soaked in blood. Man or horse, she didn't know, but it didn't bother her as it seemed to bother everyone else, and she used that to her advantage. "Take a break, everyone," she ordered. "We've broken all their toys, so now we wait and see what's up next. I've got the bridge. You guys take five and mana up."

The others made grateful noises and shuffled away from the horrifying bridge as fast as possible. Even SB left, covering his eyes as if he couldn't stand the sight of it. Grateful there was something good about being a stonekin, Tina strode out into the middle of the blood-soaked span and lifted her hand to her face, shielding her eyes against the high sun as she studied her enemy.

It wasn't a good view. Despite the carnage they'd unleashed, it looked like they'd barely made a dent in the army's numbers. Malakai was already yelling for the next unit to move forward, but while the knights obeyed without hesitation, Tina was happy to see that the common soldiers no longer seemed so eager to listen. The spearmen and archers were especially leery of entering the front half of the plaza, which was within player bow range, and the yellow-coated city guards seemed to be in open revolt. Malakai turned to scream at their commander as Tina watched, stomping his feet and even throwing things at the poor man.

But just as she started to think the enemy was cracking at last, Malakai turned his back on the city guards and yelled something to his knights. Tina was too far to hear what, but lots of mounted knights started moving into position for what appeared to be another bridge assault. Given how the last one had gone, she was amazed they'd try something so suicidal again, but then Malakai started moving his spearmen toward the riverbank, spreading them out in a line along the water with archers stationed behind them.

She shifted her feet, fighting the urge to call the Roughnecks back. She was dying to attack while the enemy was still getting into position, but it hadn't been the promised five minutes yet. If she didn't give her casters time to eat and drink their mana back, they were going to fold fast, so she sucked it up and waited, watching Malakai move his pieces into position with increasingly frenzied gestures. Then, at last, the captain himself drew his sword, and Tina knew they'd run out of time.

"Everyone back in position!" she yelled. "Here they come!"

The raid must have been watching the gathering soldiers as well, because they jumped to obey. Tina had barely gotten herself braced behind her shield before Killbox had her back again, bracing her with his weight and strength. They were going to need it too. The second cavalry charge was even bigger than the first. Thanks to her stonekin senses, Tina had the "bonus" sensation of the ground itself quivering with the rush of the oncoming army, and it wasn't just horses this time. Whole squads of spearmen were plunging straight into the shallower parts of the river, plowing through the chest-high water with their spears held over their heads. Behind them, the archers started firing with wild abandon, peppering the bridge with arrows Tina's forces could no longer afford to hide from.

"Shields up!" she shouted, forcing down the fear that was clawing up her throat at the thought of being buried alive again. "Ranged, fire at will! Everyone else, keep your heads down!"

Behind her, the melee obeyed, curling themselves into balls as the arrows started to fall. Beside her, Frank stamped his stance down and lodged his shield with hers. Fireballs and arrows flew from their side of the riverbanks and hit the riders at the back of the bridge. But even as the front line went down, the knights behind them kept up the charge, pounding down the bridge like a hoofed freight train.

Head down behind her shield, Tina saw the spear units reach her side of the river through the bridge railing. As intended, the random raids met them with a storm of arrows and spells, but she didn't have the time to watch and see if Cinco's hard-core training had worked. She could *feel* the horses riding at her through the stone, and she braced for impact, hunkering down behind her shield for the wall of force--which never came.

Tina blinked in surprise, looking up just in time to see the rider of the horse she'd braced against jump *over* her shield to land on top of Killbox behind her.

"For the king!" the rider cried, stabbing his spear into the Berserker's massive shoulder. He was still screaming when the next knight jumped off his horse as well, clearing Tina's shield by inches to crash into the knight behind Frank.

"*Shit!*"

Tina surged to her feet, bringing her shield up with her to smack the next jumping rider out of the air, but it was too late. It had *looked* like a repeat of the first charge, but in fact, only a third of the knights had attacked their shield wall. The rest had plunged their mounts into the river on either side of the bridge. Tina hadn't thought horses could swim through such deep water, but though they were clearly having trouble, enough were getting through, charging past her position on the bridge into the shallows near where her ranged camps were still shooting blindly at the knights on the bridge.

"*Zen!*" Tina bellowed at max volume as she brought her sword down on the back of the knight who was still stabbing Killbox. "*Richard! The water! Shoot at the water!*"

She had no idea if they'd heard her, but someone must have noticed, because the arrows and spells stopped coming at the bridge and started sailing out over the river. The deep-blue water turned red as the knights went down under the onslaught, but there were just so damned many of them. Even with the wall of fire coming at them, they were eventually going to make it to the banks by sheer numbers.

If that happened, they were done. The casters and Rangers were powerful, but they couldn't hold up against hundreds of mounted knights. If they got overrun, the knights might actually be able to kill them. Ranger special attacks often wouldn't work on targets closer than six feet away, and casters couldn't cast if their hands were busy defending. All the knights had to do was get on top of them, and the whole defense would crumble. Not good.

"*SB!*" she shouted, turning to hack at the knights in front of them now that she'd killed the ones attacking Killbox and the other knights. "Frank and I have the bridge. Take all the melee to the riverbank to defend the casters and Rangers! *Go, go, go!*"

She reached back and lugged Killbox to his feet as she finished. The bloody Berserker looked woozy, but he saluted and ran off. SB was slower to obey, casting her a very worried look before he hopped onto the bridge railing and started running back toward Camp Comeback, yelling at the rest of the Berserkers and Knights and ZeroDarkness to follow him. As they left, Frank moved closer to her. "Are you *sure* we've got the bridge?"

Tina stabbed the knight who'd been trying to attack her through the chest. "We have to," she said. "If we go down, everyone gets flanked. It's a tank's job to be the wall. Nothing gets past the two of us."

Frank nodded, but his face was pale below his visor. Tina didn't blame him. The bridge in front of them was covered in dead bodies, and more were still coming. Many of the knights were actually dismounting to climb over the corpses of their comrades to attack, eyes burning with hatred as they drew their swords.

Tina clanged her sword against her shield in defiance. "Come get some!" she yelled. "We'll take you all!"

Beside her, Frank gulped nervously, but it was too late to rein in the bravado. The knights were already charging, their boots sliding in the blood of their dead as they crashed into the two tanks holding the bridge alone.

Chapter 16

James

Early that morning, before the battle at Camp Comeback commenced, James was sitting in his cell, frantically explaining the king's late-night visit to Ar'Bati.

"Let me be sure I have this correct," the warrior said slowly once James had told him everything. "The Holy King of Bastion came down to talk to you *himself*, and you're upset?"

"Of course I'm upset!" James cried. "The king still doesn't believe that Malakai's cracked. Worse, he's called in the ancient favor with the Great Bird Xthr to help take out the players. This whole thing is spinning out of control, and *everyone's* going to die if we can't find a way to stop it!"

"It's not as bad as all that," Fangs said with infuriating calm. "Your sister started a rebellion. Of course it's come back to bite her in the tail. But I think the king was wise to call in the great favor. They say Xthr has power that hasn't been seen since the world's creation. Even your monster of a sister will take one look at him and know that she has no chance. She'll *have* to surrender."

"Tina won't surrender," James said, shaking his head frantically. "If she thinks she's in the right, she'll fight to the last breath no matter what. Trust me. I've seen her do it. Also, while he was never actually attackable, Xthr was part of FFO just like everything else here. That means he still has hit points, and as Tina always liked to say: if it has HP, we can kill it. I wouldn't put it past her to think she can take out an ancient Bird. She's always wanted a big world first."

"Then she is a fool," Ar'Bati snapped. "But you can't stop her from cutting off her own head, James. You've already done more for her than she deserves. If your sister doesn't see that, then she is blind. But you keep skipping over the most important part of this."

James blinked. "What?"

His brother flashed him a fanged grin. "We've been pardoned. The king forgave our crimes and cleared our names! We're still in prison, but that's merely a formality."

"But Tina--"

"You think too much on Tina!" Fangs snapped. "Think of yourself for once. You *did* it! You got the letters to the king and made him believe you. Bastion is now warned of the Once King's attack. Once the traitors listed in the lich's letters are found and stopped, the undead's invasion will be foiled."

He reached out to grab James by the shoulders. "Don't you see? We've saved the whole world! Songs will be written of our exploits! Other than your sister getting what she deserves for rebelling against the king, which is *not* your fault, this mission has been a total success! We will return to the savanna as heroes. When the other clans hear of our actions, we'll be drowning in marriage offers of the highest quality. I'm already in line to inherit the Claw Born, but if we both choose wisely, we can make powerful alliances and position ourselves to be the leaders of Windy Lake. Together, we will shape the destiny of the Four Clans for decades to come, ruling as brothers surrounded by our plentiful and powerful families! You speak constantly of finding a way home, but what could your world offer that is better than this?"

James gritted his teeth. Political marriages notwithstanding, Ar'Bati painted quite a glorious picture, but he couldn't embrace it. "It's not that I *want* to go home," he said. "I *have* to. If I vanish forever, my debt will fall on my parents. I can't betray them like that, and I won't abandon my sister. You shouldn't be so fast to kick her under the bus, either. Bastion needs the players if it's going to survive. If Tina dies fighting Malakai or Xthr or the king himself, there'll be no one left to stand with us when the Once King comes."

"I think you underestimate us," Fangs said. "But I understand your loyalty to your sister. She is your family, as I am, which is why I will help you save her from her own stupidity. But I will *not* fight against the king.

No matter how the knights are acting, so long as they are the *Royal Knights*, fighting them is treason, and I will not, nor will I allow you to, risk the Claw Born's honor for Roxxy."

That was fair enough. James had no idea how they were going to stop this war, anyway. He couldn't see what time it was thanks to the lack of windows, but the army had to be marching out by now. Also, they were still in prison. He was wracking his brain to find a way out of this when Flameboyant, who'd been quietly listening this whole time from his cell across the way, suddenly stood up.

"Heads up, guys," the Sorcerer whispered, grabbing the bars. "I think someone big is coming."

James and Ar'Bati both moved to the front of their cell just in time to hear the prison's outer door open at the end of the hall. James couldn't see what was coming from where he was standing, but his sensitive ears picked up the jingle of multiple armored men coming their way. Sure enough, a few seconds later, a four-squad of Royal Knights marched down the hall between their cells. But though they wore the same red and gold, these knights didn't look like the ones Tina's people had slaughtered. Their heavy armor was much more ornate, and their chests were decorated with medals denoting brave service to the throne.

The four knights didn't look at the prisoners. They simply walked in and positioned themselves in front of the cells, creating a protective square. When they were all in position, the prison door clanked again, and King Gregory Heraldsford himself entered the dungeon.

The eight-foot-tall king looked very different from how he had looked last night. He was wearing his full suit of sun-metal armor, and there was a golden-hilted sword on his hip that filled the dark dungeon with gentle sunlight as he came closer. As well it should. James hadn't seen it in person since the game, but there was no way he wouldn't recognize the Dawnblade. It was one of the most sacred relics of Bastion's royal line, a sword that had supposedly fallen from the sky, a gift to the Holy Kings from the Sun itself. According to the Wiki, it was made of solidified solar-

382

fire, not just sunlight as normal sun metal was. James didn't know if that was all still true, but he was certain the Dawnblade's presence was a huge deal. It was an ace the kings of Bastion only brought out for the most dangerous of times. During the game, it had only appeared during the big cinematic cut-scenes.

Seeing it for real now, with his own eyes, was as terrifying as it was impressive. He was still staring at it in awe when the king said his name.

"James Anderson of the Claw Born."

James jumped at the sudden boom of his voice and belatedly dropped to a knee. "Your Majesty."

Gregory waved him impatiently back to his feet. "I know how this looks," he said angrily. "But we've no time for formalities. Your words last night have gnawed at me, so I did as you requested and inquired about the fate of the players at Founder's Square."

James's heart leaped into his throat. "And?"

"And I have been met with vague answers and uncharacteristic evasion," the king snapped, his eyes flashing with rage. "All of my men, even Raffestain, have refused to give me a straight reply! I even sought to question Captain Malakai directly, but when I ordered him to appear, I was informed that he'd already left the castle to begin his campaign against your sister, which is cause for great concern as he was *supposed* to request final approval before marching out. When I investigated further, I found that Malakai also ignored my order to capture Portal Keeper Star Fall, who--much to my dread--I've just discovered is missing from the castle grounds."

"Then we have to find him!" James cried, grabbing the bars. "Star Fall is the one who's supposed to open the portal for the Once King's armies at the Room of Arrivals! If he's successful, the undead will pour into the city!"

"I *know*," the king said angrily, reaching up to pinch the bridge of his nose with an armored hand. "It seems I have been more foolish than

383

even I believed. All of my orders appear to have been ignored, and I would be unawares even now had you not urged me to question."

He sighed and dropped his hand, looking down at James with beseeching eyes. "Of everyone in this fortress, you are the only one who has been truthful with me. You tried to tell me what was going on outside my walls, even when I did not want to hear it. That makes you my most loyal subject at the moment, so I have come to ask you and your companions to join me as I ride out to see for myself what has happened to my kingdom since I can trust none of my advisers to tell me. I will witness what is wrong, and right it with my own hands if I must."

James glanced at Ar'Bati, who was grinning from ear to ear. "Of course we will go with Your Highness," he said, fighting to keep the smug smile off his face. "It would be our honor."

More than an honor. Going into the city *with* the king was better than any outcome James had dared to hope for. There was no way Malakai could clean up the evidence of his genocide in one night. All they'd have to do was ride out the front gate, and King Gregory would instantly see that everything James had said was true. Add in Malakai's dereliction of duty over Star Fall, and he'd never had a better chance to convince Gregory that his captain was cracked. After that, all he would have to do was convince the king to talk to Tina instead of trying to crush her, and he could save everything.

But while James was desperate to get the king to his sister, Portal Keeper Star Fall's disappearance was the more immediate problem. He had faith Tina could hold against Malakai for a while, but if the traitor managed to open a portal, they were all dead. He was about to suggest to the king that they take care of that first when Gregory beat him to it.

"I've already sent Captain Hightower and all of my honor guard except the four you see here to the Room of Arrivals," the king said. "Malakai may have failed me, but they will not. If the traitor Star Fall attempts anything, my men will stop him. But saving Bastion from the undead means nothing if we can't save it from ourselves. I beg you, James, please come with me. I cannot call myself a king if I don't ride out and face what I have allowed to happen through my inaction."

Just hearing that made James's heart soar. "I can think of nothing I'd like more."

The king nodded and waved for his knights to open the doors. A few minutes later, James, Ar'Bati, and Flameboyant were all free, armed, and on their way out of the castle's main keep. There were horses waiting for them in the eerily empty courtyard. Now that the army had marched out, the castle felt hollow and fragile, making James more nervous than ever as he scrambled onto the bay horse the stable boy held steady for him. Even so, the animal almost threw him when James's Eclipsed Steel Staff touched its flank. He yanked the weapon up and tied it high on his back to make sure the cursed metal didn't touch his mount again as the king mounted up beside him.

Since Gregory was a king, James had expected him to have the classic white stallion or something similarly regal. As huge as he was now, though, the only animal capable of carrying King Gregory was an enormous, placid-looking draft horse with hooves the size of dinner plates. It was so big, there didn't seem to be a saddle that fit it, leaving Gregory with nothing but a blanket for padding as he eased his weight onto the animal's back.

When they were all mounted, the veteran Royal Knights formed a protective square around the party, and they all started toward the front gate. The king grew decidedly more agitated as they drew closer to the castle's entrance, fidgeting nervously on his giant horse as the giant gates began to creak open, only to go perfectly still when he saw what lay beyond.

The plaza in front of the castle was a wasteland of craters and bloodstains. The holes Tina and her crew had put in the ground were all still there, but the gallows, metal cage wagons, and tents for the knights were gone. The barricade of rubble was still there, but all other signs of the player concentration camp had been removed.

385

"Sir Townsend," the king said, turning to the Royal Knight beside him. "This was where Malakai's player containment camp was, correct? What happened to it?"

"It was decommissioned, my king," the knight replied, keeping his eyes carefully away from James. "Captain Malakai deemed its resources necessary for the counterattack on the player rebellion. All the players held here were moved to the mines instead to await trial."

The king's shoulders slumped in relief at that, but James gripped his reins tighter. "That's convenient," he said, moving his horse around to glare at the old knight before turning back to the king. "You should ask him what was done with the bodies. There had to be hundreds of them. They made that giant bloodstain over there."

He pointed at an absolutely massive stain that was so layered on, it had turned the stones black. The king winced and turned back to his knight, but Sir Townsend only shrugged.

"The reports said nothing of body disposal, my lord, but there could not have been that many." The knight's eyes slid over to James. "If I may be so bold, perhaps your player guide has been exaggerating out of desperation to save his sister."

James's ears went flat at that, and King Gregory sighed. "I can't pretend I'm not relieved to discover the front of my castle isn't a charnel house," he said, flicking his reins to start his giant horse moving again. "But this does not bode well for you, James. I pray to the Sun that you have not lied to me as well."

"I have told you nothing but the truth," James said fiercely, shooting the old knight a murderous look. "If you want proof, we should go to Founder's Square. I doubt anyone has had the time or manpower to clean that up."

Gregory cast a longing look down the Royal Mile toward the south. "It's a bit out of our way..." He thought a moment longer, then he shook his head. "I must know," he said, turning his horse off the wide road toward the narrower street that led to Founder's Square. "Let's go quickly, though I must admit, I hope that you are wrong."

James said nothing. He just followed the king into the shadowed canyon-like road between the tall, burned-out buildings that he and Tina had followed just a few days before on their trek to the palace. As they went, James couldn't help but notice how empty the city felt now. There were no more knight patrols, no people at all. Even the rats were gone, leaving the streets uncannily still as they rode in silence toward the square.

"I can't believe how much destruction there is," the king muttered, his face pale as he stared up at the blackened buildings. "Who started these fires?"

"Players did, my lord," Sir Townsend said at once. "I heard that the knights and guards in the city tried to extinguish the flames, but they had to focus on getting the people to safety, and they were under constant attack from the players."

The king glanced back at James, clearly expecting him to contradict this, but James could only shake his head. "I was in the savanna zone during the first three days, so I don't know--"

"I was here," Flameboyant said suddenly.

The king turned to look at him, and the elf flinched on his saddle, but he didn't stop.

"He's not wrong that players did some awful stuff, Your, um, Your Kingship. But if I can speak plainly, everyone was being a dick. Knights were killing players, players were killing knights, normal people were just trying to get out, and meanwhile, the whole city was going up in smoke. It was hell, plain and simple. Nothing else to call it."

Ar'Bati looked mortally offended at Flameboyant's use of crude language in the presence of royalty, but Gregory just looked sadder than ever, staring bleakly at the once-beautiful buildings of Bastion's most expensive quarter, which were now slumping piles of rubble. Most of the bodies had been cleaned off the street, but the bloodstains still remained, as did the smell of death. The stench was inescapable, hanging like an oppressive cloud in the warm, still morning air. It got so bad, James ended up putting his shirt over his face to protect his sensitive nose. Ar'Bati did the same, but the king seemed to be in too much shock to notice. He just sat on his horse, eyes wide as he took in block after block after block of destruction.

"How did it come to this?" he whispered at last, reaching out to touch the burned stump of what had been an old-growth decorative palm tree. "I saw all the reports, but they just said things like 'abandoned bakery' and 'fire-damaged fountain.' I didn't know, didn't realize that it could be..." He stopped, fists tightening on his reins. "I should have known," he said angrily. "I should have been there for my people, been out here helping. But I wasn't. I was sitting safe in my castle, reading sterilized reports in blissful ignorance while my kingdom burned down around me. I came out here to save Bastion, but what of Bastion is left to save? I could empty my coffers to the floors, and it wouldn't be enough to repair even the blocks we've passed. How am I going to make this right? Who will live in this desolation?"

"You don't have to fix it all yourself," James said, riding up beside him. "The monarchy didn't build every building in Bastion, and it won't rebuild them, either. This is your people's city. All you need to do is be there to help them."

"My efforts are always the opposite of help," Gregory said, looking furious with himself. "Raffestain was the one who set up a safe zone for people in the Diplomatic Quarter, and Captain Hightower of the City Guard is the one who's kept it safe."

"Because those are their jobs," James said quickly. "Not yours. The king can't do everything."

"But I did *nothing*!" Gregory cried, shamefaced. "You know what my big plan was? I wanted to throw an end-of-the-Nightmare celebration. I thought it would put people in a good mood and help improve morale. My advisers humored me, but I could tell they thought it was stupid. Now, I see how right they were."

388

"*You* weren't stupid," James said. "You didn't know because no one told you. It's not your fault your advisers hid vital--"

"It is my fault," Gregory said. "My fault for being a fool. My fault for being the sort of person they didn't believe could handle the truth. Had I been better, braver, anything but what I am, everything might have been different."

Before James could answer that, a noise broke the stillness, shaking the heavy air with a distant roar. As loud as it was, though, James was having trouble placing it. It almost sounded like a storm or maybe an avalanche, some sort of enormous disaster. James was flicking his ears to try to pin it down when Ar'Bati spoke. "It's the sound of battle," he said gravely, pointing south toward Trainers' Hall. "The fighting has begun."

"Then we have no more time to waste," the king said angrily, kicking his horse. "I will not fail my knights as I failed my people. I must go to the front lines myself and--"

"Wait, please!" James cried. "Please, Your Majesty, you must see Founder's Square! It will prove I'm telling the truth!"

"There is no time," the king said desperately. "My men are dying as we speak. They need their king! I'm Bastion's only five-skull raid boss. Instead of cowering in my rooms, I should be down there using the power the Nightmare gave me to do some good for once." He smiled at James. "Even if there's been no evidence of your claims, I still have reason to thank you. Your words were what spurred me to action. If not for you, I'd still be hiding in the palace, and for that I will be forever grateful, even if you did falsely claim that my knights were--"

"It's not false!" James cried. "I wasn't lying, Your Majesty, and I can prove it! If you'll just follow me one more block to--"

He cut off with a choke as Sir Townsend moved his horse between him and the king. "Remember your place, *player*," he snarled. "You will not speak to the Holy King in such a familiar fashion."

"I'm sorry, James," King Gregory said. "But I have to go support my knights. I've let all of this go much too far. Malakai and my people have had to shoulder far too much. Hopefully Roxxy has the sense to surrender, but even if I must fight her myself, I will end this with my own hands before any more of my subjects get hurt, as a king should."

He turned away as he finished, sitting tall and straight on his giant horse. He was lifting his heels to kick off into a gallop when James lurched forward. "If you're going to fight the players, then start with me!"

The king whirled around in his saddle. Ar'Bati and Flameboyant jumped too, but James didn't dare look away from the king. "I was the one who told you Malakai's sins littered the city," he said desperately, moving his horse closer to the king's. "If you think that's a lie, then cut off my head. Execute me for misleading you, because there's no other way I'm letting you leave before I've shown you the truth."

The king jerked back so fast, he nearly fell off his horse. "*No!*" he said, horrified. "I'm not going to--"

"Then come with me to Founder's Square," James growled, leaning forward in his saddle until he was staring the king down.

"I just told you there's no time," King Gregory said, growing angry. "Even if you were exaggerating Captain Malakai's involvement, you were right about everything else. I can't afford to waste any more--"

"We didn't risk everything trying to save Bastion so you could put it in even greater danger!"

That was not the way one spoke to a king. Ar'Bati gasped behind him, and Sir Townsend drew his blade, but the king just looked shocked, and James took his opening before someone called his bluff and really did cut his head off.

"I'm relieved you're finally ready to fight for your kingdom, Your Majesty," he said, politely this time. "But you've drawn the wrong conclusion. Captain Malakai didn't go to the player camp to fight for Bastion. He's fighting for himself. You heard him in the war meeting. He and his knights are hell-bent on revenge. I've seen proof of their madness with my own eyes. Ride one block farther, and you'll see it for yourself. I'm not saying the players are innocent, but I *am* saying that you owe it to your

390

people--*all* of your people, not just your knights--to learn the whole truth of what happened when the Nightmare broke. If Founder's Square is empty, I will let Sir Townsend kill me for misleading you. I won't even fight back."

"*James!*" Ar'Bati hissed.

"No," James said fiercely, reaching out to grab the king's massive arm. "This is worth my life. That's how much I believe in it. If you go down there and fight at Malakai's side, you won't just be killing players. You'll be killing Bastion's best chance at survival. If we let hate and misunderstanding turn us against each other, we might as well open the portal ourselves and let the undead come. That's why I can't let go. I refuse to let you do the Once King's killing for him. I will not let you doom this world."

That was a touch overdramatic, but if there was ever a time for drama, it was now. James was clutching the king's armored arm with all his strength, grabbing the warm sun metal so hard his fingers ached. Not that that would matter if the king decided to leave--as a five-skull, Gregory could flick him into a building without breaking a sweat--but James was ready to bet that no one had dared to manhandle a king, and he needed the edge that shock gave him. If nothing else, at least he knew the king was listening. James just hoped his gamble paid off, because Gregory's knights were already moving in. Sir Townsend especially looked eager to hold James to his promises. But as the old knight lifted his sword to cut James's hand off the king's arm, Gregory put up his hands.

"Enough," he said, his voice slightly panicked as he motioned his knights away from James. "You win, James. I'll ride one more block. Just please stop this."

Shaking with relief, James pried his hand off Gregory's arm. "One more block is all I ask."

Still eying James as if he were insane, the king turned his horse back toward Founder's Square again. His knights moved into tight formation around him, leaving James to Ar'Bati, who smacked him upside the head.

"What were you thinking?" Fangs demanded. "You could have gotten yourself killed!"

"If I was worried about being killed, I wouldn't have jumped through a window onto the king's conference table," James reminded him, urging his horse after the king's. "Death before dishonor."

"You almost had both!" his brother snarled, riding after him with a pale-faced Flameboyant in tow. "Any one of those rude sentences could have been your last! Do you not have kings in your world?"

"Not where I'm from."

Ar'Bati dragged a hand over his face, muttering under his breath about eternal shame, but James couldn't stick around to listen. Gregory was nearly to the crossroads where the street they'd been following met Founder's Square. He held his breath as the king turned the corner, terrified that Malakai had worked a miracle and somehow managed to hide the proof of his crimes, but he needn't have worried. By the time he caught up with the king--who'd gone stone still on his horse--the stench had already told him everything he needed to know.

Aside from two more days spent rotting in the hot Bastion sun, the scene at Founder's Square was exactly as James remembered. The once-lovely plaza was still a mass grave with corpses piled high. The air was thick with flies and the chatter of scavengers, and the smell was so bad James had to fight not to vomit. Even the king's veteran knights were forced to look away lest they lose their stomachs. The only one who didn't turn was Gregory himself. He just sat on top of his giant horse, staring at the scene in the square as though he hoped it would vanish if he just looked at it hard enough.

"By the Sun..." he said at last, closing his eyes. "This was done by my knights?"

"Yes," James answered quietly, swallowing against the bile that wouldn't stay out of his throat. "My sister's raid stumbled on this scene

392

two days ago when they first arrived in Bastion. When we investigated, we found torn cloth from the Royal Knights' tabards clutched in the victims' hands. Witnesses rescued from that building there"--James pointed at the ripped-open inn where the only survivors had been hiding--"confirmed that the Royal Knights slit the higher-level players' throats while everyone was still incapacitated post-Nightmare. The lower-level ones were captured, beaten, and taken to the camp in front of the castle for execution without trial. *This* was the scene my sister saw, and it's why she decided to fight the knights."

Gregory took a shaky breath. "I still..." He paused to swallow. "I've seen your proof now, James," he said, striving for calm. "But this is still hard to believe. You must understand. I've known Malakai since I was young. He simply isn't the sort of man who would do something like this. I would have said that none of my knights were, but the Nightmare did terrible things to us all. Still, even if some were driven mad, surely Malakai would not have hidden the truth from me." His face brightened. "Maybe he didn't know. He was in the palace with me when the Nightmare broke. Founder's Square *is* a good distance from there. Maybe he was unaware of the full extent of--"

"Oh, he knew," Flameboyant said angrily, tearing his eyes away from the dead to glare at the king. "I was here on day zero. I was scavenging for food when I spotted Captain Malakai at the Room of Arrivals. There's no way to get to the portals from the palace without riding through here. Hell, he would have had to have ridden over the bodies to get there. So yeah, he saw *all* of this. He just chose not to tell you."

The king turned to his knights. "Is this true?"

Sir Townsend shifted uncomfortably in his saddle. "I did not know of this, my king," he said at last. "I knew the captain and his knights had killed many players, but I was told as you were that it was in self-defense."

"*Self-defense?*" Flameboyant cried, stabbing his finger at a dead Sorcerer who looked very much like him. "Their throats were cut while they were unconscious!"

"If wrong was done, it would have been Malakai's job to handle it," Sir Townsend snapped back. "Disciplining the knights is the captain's duty! He would have been right to handle it internally and not burden His Majesty."

"He wasn't 'handling it internally,'" James said angrily. "He was *covering it up* because he was part of it!" He turned back to the king. "You have to believe us. These things *did* happen. Why else would my sister-- who's done nothing but fight the undead in Bastion's name--turn on Bastion? It just doesn't make sense unless Malakai turned on her first."

"You can't turn on a demon," Sir Townsend snarled. "This is player propaganda, Your Majesty. He is saying anything he can to protect his rebel of a sister. Give me the word, and I will silence him at once."

"No," King Gregory said, closing his eyes with a deep breath. When he opened them again, he fixed them on James. "I have seen what you asked, but it is still not proof. All we have here is a field of dead and your word that my knights are the ones who killed them. Such an accusation goes against everything the knighthood stands for, but I cannot ignore that someone killed all of these people. It is clear there was no battle here. These people did not fight back, and since players *always* fight back, I have to believe they were killed while they could not."

He thought about that for a moment, and his face grew grim. "Since players were the only ones incapacitated by the Nightmare's end, that means these murders could only have been done by someone from our world." His eyes flicked back to the copious dead. "A *lot* of someones, acting in coordination. Since the Royal Knights were in charge of policing Founder's Square, that corroborates your story, but I still can't..." He shook his head. "It's not enough. I cannot turn on my own Knight Captain for this alone. I must have the story from Malakai himself before I condemn him."

That wasn't the complete turnaround James had been hoping for, but considering the king had been ready to ride to Malakai's aid just three minutes ago, he was ready to take it. "That's fair enough, Your Majesty," he said. "Everyone deserves the chance to defend themselves, but I am confident he cannot. If you talk to the players, you'll find hundreds whose stories match ours. Malakai wasn't secretive. We *all* saw what he did. If you question your own knights, I'm sure you'll find men there who'll back us up as well, because we're telling you the truth."

"We will see," the king said tiredly, turning his horse away from the carnage in the square. "I've never wished so hard that I was being played for a fool, but we will see."

With that, he kicked his horse into a gallop. His veterans fell into formation around him a few seconds later, spurring their mounts to catch up with their king. With a final worried look at Ar'Bati and Flameboyant, James scrambled after him, clinging to his horse as they charged south down the empty streets toward the growing roar of battle.

***

By the time they reached the streets surrounding Trainers' Hall, the din had become deafening. The once too-quiet city was now a cacophony of screaming men and horses punctuated by the clash of steel. When they spotted the mass of support troops that formed the army's rear, the king reined in his charging horse. But before he could speak-- before the support troops they'd come up behind could even turn around-- a pack of mounted knights burst in from a side street, nearly riding the king over.

"Out of the way, idiot!" the lead knight shouted as his horse reared. "This street is supposed to be kept clear at all times for--"

The knight went silent, his ash-streaked face turning ghostly pale as he recognized the giant and unmistakable man he'd almost run over.

395

"Your Majesty!" he cried, jumping off his horse to prostrate himself on the ground. "Forgive me! I did not know you would be here!"

King Gregory didn't answer. He was too busy staring at the bloody jubatus girl the knight had been carrying tied up over the back of his saddle. All of the royal entourage was, for every one of the horses the riders had abandoned to bow before their king had a shabby-looking prisoner tied up on the back of their horse. *Player* prisoners, as made clear by the way many of them were yelling for help in English.

"Who are these players?" the king asked in a low voice.

The lead knight pressed his forehead even harder against the dirty street. "Criminals, my lord! We're taking them to the front on Captain Malakai's orders."

"To the front?" The king scowled. "My orders were that all player prisoners were to be held in the mines to the north while they awaited trial. Why does Malakai need them here?"

The knight's eyes went round at the question, and he began to stammer.

When it was clear that no straight answer would be forthcoming, the king's look turned sharp. "What is your name?"

"Samuel Gardner, my king."

"Sir Samuel," King Gregory said, sliding off his giant horse so that he could better see the man cowering on the ground. "Answer the question. Why did Captain Malakai order you to bring these prisoners here?"

The knight said nothing. He just stood there shaking slightly.

The king clenched his fists. "What is it that steals your voice?" Gregory asked.

"My shame does, sire!" the knight cried desperately, clenching his eyes shut.

"There is no greater shame than disobeying your king!" Sir Townsend snarled, his face scarlet. "Answer His Majesty's question, knave!"

"I wish nothing more than to obey!" Sir Samuel said frantically. "But I cannot." He slammed his head down on the pavement. "Forgive me, my liege!"

King Gregory sighed and pulled his sword. The Dawnblade rang like a silver bell as it cleared the sheath, and James held his breath. But the king did not strike the shaking knight down. Instead, he gently lowered his golden blade to the cowering man's shoulders and tapped Sir Samuel once on each side.

"As Holy King, I hereby absolve you of your sins, Sir Samuel Gardner," King Gregory said. "Rise now a new man, and tell me what is going on."

He sheathed his sword as he finished, but Sir Samuel didn't get off the ground. If anything, he sank even lower, his shoulders shaking with sobs. "How could you forgive me?" He hiccupped. "You don't know what I've done."

"I don't," the king agreed, reaching down to take the sobbing man by the arm and gently pull him up. "But I'm giving you absolution anyway because I have to know what's happening, and I'd rather let one guilty man go free than risk the fates of thousands. The Sun has burned away your sins, Sir Samuel. If shame held your tongue, let it be dissolved, and tell me what these prisoners are for."

Sir Samuel wiped his eyes one last time, then he began to speak in a rush. "They are hostages. We had others, but the rebels rescued them before we could leverage them properly. Captain Malakai sent my unit to raid the Diplomatic Quarter for more."

The king recoiled. "The Diplomatic Quarter?" He looked up at the dozen pathetic-looking players lashed to the backs of the knights' saddles. "You mean these were not criminals but players who'd already surrendered and been handed over to their embassies?"

Despite the promise that his part in this had been burned away, Sir Samuel's face still turned red with shame. "Yes, Your Majesty."

"Why?" the king demanded. "What does Malakai intend to do with them?"

The knight looked down. "He means to use them against the players. The captain says the enemy loses discipline when their weakest members are in danger, so he sent us to fetch more. Captain Malakai was going to torture them in front of the bridges to lure the rebels out of their stronghold."

James's stomach clenched with every word. Given the absolute nature of Malakai's hatred, he could only imagine what the captain had in store, but imagination wasn't necessary when Sir Samuel continued, describing Malakai's original plan to burn the players alive. When that had failed, he'd sent back for more to carve up instead. He'd even ordered Sir Samuel to look specifically for players who were children because they'd be more effective. By the time the knight finished, bile was burning in James's throat, and from the expression on the king's face, he knew he wasn't alone.

"I see now why guilt stopped your tongue," Gregory said quietly, his huge hands clenching into fists. "But why would Captain Malakai do such a thing? I gave him my army, everything he asked for. He should have more than enough men here to subdue the player threat without sinking to such dishonorable acts. Why would he commit such crimes?"

"*Because they deserve it!*"

The sudden shout made everyone jump.

At the back of the group, one of the knights shot to his feet, his bloody face white with rage. "This is your fault!" he screamed at the king.

"Sir Dan!" Sir Samuel screamed. "Contain yourself!"

"Why should I?" the furious knight, Sir Dan, yelled back, pointing at the king with a look of pure rage. "He's supposed to be the Holy King! Chosen by the Sun itself! But if he had all that power, why did he let the Nightmare take us?" His burning eyes flicked to James. "We had to be their playthings for eighty years! They humiliated and insulted us, pillaging our world for their childish *game*. And when the Nightmare ended, they just became worse, killing and taking whatever they wanted!" He bared his teeth. "The players deserve whatever we do to them! My only regret is that we didn't kill more. They're greater demons than the Once King's undead, and you're no king of mine if you side with them!"

King Gregory staggered back as the knight finished, eyes wide with shock. Then his own rage took over. "So you *did* kill them?" he cried. "Not just here but in Founder's Square and the camp in front of my castle! Is it true you slaughtered them without trial?"

Sir Dan lifted his chin stubbornly. "Death is the only justice for the likes of them."

"But what of your oaths?" King Gregory cried, pointing at the player prisoners. "You were going to torture *children*!"

"You know *nothing* of our oaths!" Sir Dan roared. "You're the royal idiot who drinks all day in the castle while we're dying in the streets! Captain Malakai is the only one who understands. That's why he's been fighting on the front lines himself while you cowered inside your walls. You're a five-skull raid boss! If you cared to, you could have come out and saved us when the player army destroyed our camp. But you didn't. You left us to *die,* and you dare speak of *oaths*!"

He ended his tirade by spitting directly on King Gregory's metal boot. The other knights leaped to their feet in panic, grabbing Sir Dan and wrestling him away while Sir Samuel fell back to his knees.

"Please forgive his insubordination, Your Highness!" he cried, pressing his forehead into the ground. "Many of our comrades have perished today. He is out of his mind with grief. He doesn't mean it!"

"I meant every word!" Sir Dan screamed from where the others were holding him down. "The Buffoon King's a coward and a traitor and a sham--"

Someone punched him in the face to shut him up, but the king just lowered his head. "Take him away. And return the players safely to the Diplomatic Quarter."

The knights nodded and started dragging Sir Dan down the street. He left, screaming profanity and cursing the king's name.

Flinching at every insult, Gregory slowly turned to James. "You were right," he whispered, looking down at his hands. "About Malakai. About my knights." He shook his head. "I've made a mess of everything, and now it's too late."

"It's *not* too late," James said firmly, looking down the street toward the bridges, where he could still see players holding form. "The fight's not over yet. We can still put a stop to this."

"How?" Gregory demanded. "You saw Sir Dan. Even if I pardoned everyone's crimes, that hatred and anger isn't going to go away. Everyone would just keep fighting, and who am I to say they shouldn't? They went too far pursuing it, but my knights still deserve justice for what the players have done to them. But the players deserve justice as well, and I..." He shook his head hopelessly. "What can I do, James? I know now that I was wrong to stay out of this for so long, but even if I'm ready to do whatever it takes, I don't know what that is. There have been so many wrongs on every side. How can we ever make peace?"

It was a devil of a question. Even for a Holy King with legitimate divine powers, blood didn't wash out easily. The players and the knights had been killing each other for days. There was no magic fix to make them all forget and forgive. It was the same sort of thorny post-war situation he'd studied for his International Politics classes back when he'd actually paid attention in school. Lots of actual diplomats had wrestled with exactly this same problem, trying to resolve the bitterness left behind by civil wars and blood feuds. James was wracking his brain for historical examples he could steal from when he realized something important.

"Peace is the goal," James said. "But it's not the solution." He looked at the king. "Do you think you can make everyone stop fighting for a moment?"

"Not alone," Gregory said. "I've been killed by raids many times before, but I don't have to do it on my own." He pointed at the sky. "It looks as if my help has arrived."

Confused, James tilted his head back, but all he saw was the shimmering golden dome of the Bastion covering the sky. Then the barrier flickered, and he saw it. There was a winged shape as big as the castle itself flying just beyond the Bastion's shield. Even with all his lore knowledge, James had only seen it once before, but it wasn't the sort of thing you forgot.

"That should do it," James said, smiling grimly. "Let's go stop a war."

Chapter 17

Tina

Tina didn't know anymore how long she'd stood on the bridge next to Frank. She didn't know how many knights they'd killed or how the fight on the riverbank was going behind them. There was no space for any of that, no room in her mind for anything except the knights charging down the bridge, their eyes blazing with hate under the shadows of their helmets as they swung their swords at her head.

Tina slammed her shield up in reply, breaking their swords before cutting them down with her own. Beside her, Frank swung his shield like he was opening a door, sending the men on his half of the bridge flying into the river. She didn't even wait to see them splash down before she was back in position, yelling at Frank to get his shield up as the next wave of knights charged in.

As she struck for what felt like the millionth time today, slicing the knight who'd attacked her nearly in half, Tina grimaced at the blood that coated everything. There was so much of it that even her sword's red glow was lost in the mess. Frank looked as though he'd been swimming in the stuff, and Tina knew she was even worse. She could feel the blood in every crack and crevice of her armor, feel it in her hair and on her face and down her neck. If she'd been human, it would have been the stuff of nightmares. Frank certainly had a thousand-yard stare going. But Tina wasn't human. She was Roxxy, and she fought like a machine, picking up Frank's slack whenever he hesitated as they methodically slaughtered another five men. She was shoving their bodies over the railing into the river so they wouldn't get in her way when a horn sounded from the enemy's bank of the river in a pattern she hadn't heard before, and the knights she'd been bracing to take on suddenly started to fall back.

"Finally," Frank panted, his voice shaking like a leaf. "Did we win?"

"I don't think so," Tina said, nodding at the army that was still waiting across the water. Given how many they'd killed, she'd hoped she'd be able to see a decrease, but it didn't look like they'd made a dent. Ten thousand men, it seemed, was a lot more than she'd realized.

"They're probably re-forming to try something new," she said, raising her bloody sword high. "Roughnecks, back to the bridge! Rally on Roxxy!"

Her order rang out across the island, but nothing answered it. Suddenly terrified a disaster had happened while she'd been focused on the bridge, Tina looked over her shoulder, but it was fine. Her people were all coming. They just weren't making noise. They were very bloody, but they didn't seem injured. Like her and Frank, the blood on their armor had come from other people, but you wouldn't have known it from their faces. Despite being physically whole, the raid that formed behind her on the bridge had the same terrifying thousand-yard stare Frank was wearing, and though her stonekin's indifference kept Tina from feeling it, it wasn't hard to guess why.

The island behind them was almost as bloody as her bridge. Knights and soldiers had been hacked to bits in the grass, and the river was so choked with bodies that the usually swift water ran sluggish and red. Almost all of the dead seemed to be knights, which made her happy, but she was the only one. Everyone else looked like they were fighting not to vomit as they picked their way down the bloody bridge to get back into formation behind her.

"Good job protecting our flank," she told them, smiling to try to dispel the heaviness. "How did it go?"

"Not too bad," SilentBlayde reported, though his drooping ears told a different story. "We only had five people go down in total."

Tina froze. "*Five dead?*"

"We got the Raise Ally spells off in time," the Assassin assured her. "But they came back too weak to fight, so I had the support teams haul them inside."

That was a relief. "Thanks, Blayde," she said, turning back to the raid. "Good job, everyone! Looks like the enemy's giving us a break, so I want everyone to eat and drink while they can."

"I never want to eat again," someone said in a sick voice.

"I know it was rough," Tina said, doing her best to sound reassuring. "But you all made it work! I'm proud of you, but we can't quit yet. The enemy's still kicking, so I need everyone to eat, even if you don't want to. We've still got a lot of guys to chew through, and it's important that everyone keeps their--"

"I don't want to chew through any more guys!" yelled a Ranger, shoving his way forward. "This isn't like fighting the undead. Those were just skeletons and zombies. These are *people*." He held up his bloody hands. "I don't even know how many people I've killed this morning! It's mass murder. I don't want to do it anymore!"

"None of us want to do this," Tina said firmly. "We didn't ask to be stuck in this world. We're the victims here! We shouldn't have to bear these idiots' hatred or fight for our survival, but *we do* so *we will*."

"We didn't have to attack the king!" someone in the back called out. "That's what started all of this! We should have run when we had the chance."

A chorus of "yeah!" rang out, and Tina stomped her foot. "Should have run, huh?" she said angrily, glaring at them. "Fine. Raise your hand if you'd rather we left all those players in Malakai's camp. Tell me again how you were cool with leaving our fellow players to die."

The whole raid looked at their feet, and Tina nodded sharply. "That's right," she said. "We did what we knew was right. I'm not going to call anyone a coward for having regrets. We've all been through the shit today, and it ain't over yet. But never forget that this is happening because we were the only people brave enough to do the right thing! We're not murderers. We're the goddamn heroes! We're the best damn raid on this whole island. That's why I need all of you to eat your goddamn gourmet

404

sandwiches and truffle butter croissants, because if we don't keep it together, it's all going to fall apart."

Tina thought that painted a pretty clear picture, and sure enough, people started to eat. She was silently congratulating herself on finally learning to manage her raid when a hand went up in the middle.

"What about plan B?"

Tina cursed under her breath as the whole raid began to nod. She'd thought she'd done a good job keeping their wind-fire ace in the hole secret, but apparently she hadn't given the grapevine enough credit, because no one looked surprised.

"Plan B is only for emergencies," she informed them. "It's not something we can just roll out."

"Isn't this an emergency, though?" one of the Sorcerers in the front asked. "I don't know what plan B actually is, but we just had five people *die*. Surely that's cause enough to roll out the big guns."

Many players nodded, and Tina winced.

"This is a *really* big gun," she told them. "If we pull this trigger, all of Bastion is going to get blown away. You guys are upset about killing a few hundred knights who were trying to kill *you*. I know you're tired of fighting, but trust me when I say that plan B is not the better option. Hopefully, we won't have to use it at all."

"But will you use it?" SilentBlayde asked suddenly, looking at her.

"If I have to, absolutely," Tina said, speaking fast so no one would hear her voice shake. "If those assholes put our backs to the wall, I'm not afraid to give them the middle finger of God in return. But we've got a long way before we're in last-stand territory, so I want everyone to keep giving it their best, okay?"

The raid grumbled, but food was going into mouths, which was enough to make Tina happy. The horns coming out of the knights' camp, however, did not.

"Damn," she muttered, shielding her eyes against the sun as the knights across the water re-formed into squads for a fresh attack on the bridges. "Here we go again. I don't suppose you know how the other teams are holding up?"

"Worse than we are," SB reported, his voice bleak. "Cinco's group is a machine, but they've still got less gear and fewer veterans than the Roughnecks, and Assets's team on south bridge was always a weak link. I saw their healers cast Raise Ally on their main tank twice during the last assault. Even healed to full, that's a lot of damage for one player. I don't know if he can take another run."

"Well, shit," Tina said, glancing back at the looming stone fortress behind them. "All that talk, and we might end up using plan B soon, anyway."

"We might not have to," SB said hopefully. "They could try to siege us out. They have the supplies for it, and they have to be sick of this by now." His voice wavered slightly. "*We* sure are."

"It *is* pretty gross," Tina agreed, looking down at the bloody river with a wince. "But I don't think they're going to stop. Have you seen what Malakai's been doing?"

"No," SB said, squinting across the river. "I haven't seen him since after the hostages, actually."

"Well," Tina said, straightening up. "I'm a bit taller than you are, and I could see him just fine. He spent the whole last attack screaming at his men from on top of his wagons. The dude didn't even look like he was giving orders. He was just yelling at them to kill us. He can't stand that we're alive, which means he's not going to do something as smart as a siege."

"Is he still there now?"

Tina got up on her tiptoes, but the overturned wagon where the captain usually stood was empty. "Not right now," she said. "But it doesn't matter. Even if he wised up and ordered them to back off, every knight over there has been whipped into a damn froth. They're not going to stop hammering us until we break or they do."

SB's face was pale when she finished. Tina hated that she was the one who'd made him look that way, but the truth was the truth. The knights weren't going to stop, and if the raiders were going to avoid using the wind-fire powder, they had to be just as dedicated.

"Looks like they're going to try for the water again," she said as the knights across the river spread out along the bank. "Frank and I will keep holding the bridge. You take the rest of the raid and get back to the riverbanks. Don't let the our sides fall."

"We won't," he promised. "But what if you get overrun? If you send us all back to the main island, you'll have no backup here."

"I'll signal for help if it gets bad," Tina promised.

"I'll watch for it," he said, his blue eyes gleaming above his mask. "I've got your back, Tina." He always did.

"Thank you," she whispered.

SB pulled down his mask just long enough to flash her a smile before calling for the rest of the raid to get back to their previous positions in the grass. As they shoved the last of their food into their mouths and shuffled after him, Tina turned to Frank.

"You okay for one more?"

"Not really," her fellow tank muttered, lifting his visor to push his blood-stiff hair out of his eyes. "But it seems we ain't got much of a choice. Here they come."

The knights were indeed gathering at the end of their bridge. Tina hadn't counted how many had come at them last time, but this felt like more.

"How many of these bastards *are* there?" she snapped, getting her shield up again. "I thought knighthood was supposed to be a rare honor."

"It *is* for a whole kingdom," Frank said, popping his visor back down. "Not much point in having a military if you don't field a big one."

As if they'd been waiting to prove him right, the knights chose that moment to start their charge. The sound of horns rang through the air, followed by shouts as the next attack plunged their horses into the gory river. On the bridges, the mounted knights began their charge, making Tina's knees rattle as the horses thundered toward them.

"Here we go again," Tina said, ducking behind her shield. "Frank, lock in!"

Frank dutifully locked his shield against hers as the horses came closer. Just like before, the trained war mounts leaped at their riders' command, flying into the air to come down directly on top of Tina's shield. With no one to brace against this time, Tina had no choice but to dig her boots into the stone of the bridge itself, planting her knee on the ground as she activated her cooldown.

"Steady Ground!"

Next to her, Frank called out his ability as well, and the two of them locked into place just in time as the mass of armored men and horses crashed down. It was the same as before, a bloody mass of riders smashing to a halt against their defense as the force of their momentum met the immovable wall of the tanks' defense, but with one horrible exception.

As the charge hit, the lead rider leaped high off his mount. He flew up so high, Tina saw his shadow flash over her head before he flipped over in midair and landed with flawless elven grace on the bridge behind them, all while wearing full plate armor and with four swords strapped to his back, no less.

"Someone's spry," Tina grumbled, thrusting her shield to knock the other knights off them. "Back to back, Frank! I'll take the front. You handle Sir Du Soleil back there!"

Frank grunted a reply, hauled himself up, and whirled around so that his back was against Tina's and his shield was facing the knight who'd jumped over their defenses. Left to guard the rest of the bridge alone, Tina planted herself wide, swinging with her sword and shield out to stop any who tried to pass.

Frank's armored back banged into hers as they faced off against their respective opponents. It was a pretty big stretch, but most of the men in front of Tina had been injured in the crash, which took the edge off a bit. She blocked a thrown lance, sliced open the knight who charged her on the left, and shield-bashed two more off the bridge and into the water. She was repositioning herself at the center of the bridge when Frank vanished from her back.

She jumped at his sudden absence, whirling around just in time to see her fellow knight flying through the air toward Camp Comeback. He landed nearly a hundred feet away, plowing a line of dirt and rocks before cratering into the stone side of the smithy. She was still trying to figure out what the fuck had just happened when the knight who'd leaped over their defense took off his helmet and threw it aside, shaking out his long gray-streaked black hair with a twisted sneer of hate.

"Time to die, Roxxy."

"*Shit!*" Tina snapped her shield around to block Malakai, which left her back open to the knight who'd been trying to attack her before. Not willing to take her eyes off the four-skull captain for a second, she head-butted backward, crushing the charging knight's face through his helmet. He went down with a scream of pain, but the bridge behind her was still crowded with knights, and with Frank gone, there was no one left to stop them. It was just her with Malakai in front and the knights at her back, trapping her in the middle of the bridge, well out of range of the rest of her raiders on the riverbank.

"Shit, shit, *shit.*" Tina spun with her back to the stone railing while stabbing the knight who'd been going for her back. She didn't have a plan for this. She could bail into the water, but then there'd be no one to stop Malakai and his men from charging straight into Camp Comeback. If she stayed, though, she'd be facing Malakai alone. That hadn't gone well for her last time, and she was pre-injured this time. None of the knights had gotten a serious hit on her yet, but all the little scrapes added up, as did the exhaustion from a full morning of fighting. Facing him here was a *terrible* idea, but she couldn't let him get to the shore.

Still swearing under her breath, Tina pushed off the railing and turned to face Malakai. After dropping the broken swords he must have smashed on Frank's shield, the dark-haired captain charged her barehanded. That seemed like a stupid thing to do until Tina remembered how crap the knights' gear was, and how hard Malakai's fists could hit. The four-skull's blows hammered her shield like cannon shots, pushing her right back to the railing. She was trying to steady herself when he grabbed her shield.

Tina was at least ready for that part. Keeping her sword hidden behind the massive tower shield, she let him pull her defense down, and she slashed at his face the moment her bulwark was out of the way. Malakai shrieked and staggered backward, clutching his bleeding face, but two more knights surged into the gap. Tina's second attack was spoiled as one man grabbed her sword arm, so she turned and drove the edge of her shield into his neck, crumpling his throat. As he fell, she hooked the other knight with her now-free sword arm and slung him at Malakai.

The armored knight crashed into the captain like a catapult shot, and they both went down in a blood-slicked pile. Grinning at the destruction she'd caused, Tina used the chaos to take out a few more of the knights who'd followed Malakai onto the bridge. She was cutting them down as fast as she could to buy herself some breathing room when Malakai suddenly appeared right beside her.

She'd been so focused on clearing the bridge, she hadn't even noticed him getting up until he was in her face. His fist collided with her jaw as he decked her on the chin, snapping her head back so hard she was amazed her neck didn't crack. She was still trying to get her head back down when Malakai grabbed a broken lance off the bloody ground and drove it through the chain armor covering the gap in her knee plates.

Pain exploded through Tina's leg. Malakai's iron lance had pierced all the way through her knee and out the bottom to crack the bridge itself. Silver blood was pouring out of her, adding to the swimming feeling his punch had left in her head. The world began to dim as she tilted sideways, her huge weight carrying her over the railing toward the foul water below.
No.

With a roar, Tina grabbed the bridge, her huge hands crumbling the stone railing as she pushed back to her feet. She couldn't go down here. There was no one else to stop Malakai, no one else to take the hits. If she failed, she'd let all of Camp Comeback down, so she forced herself to stand again, ripping the lance out of her leg with a bloody snarl. Malakai snarled back and swung for her head. She saw the punch coming this time, though, and managed to duck, swinging her shield low as she did to slam the sharp metal edge into the side of the captain's knee. She was rewarded with a roar of pain as the captain lost his feet and fell over, landing on his back on the bloody bridge.

Frantic to make it count, Tina shot back up and slammed her boot down on the captain's chest as hard as she could. A knight's sword broke against her exposed back as she did, but Tina ignored the attack, stomping down again with her full weight on the captain. She stabbed him at the same time, plunging her red-runed sword through his armor and into his shoulder.

Again and again, she hit him. Weapons bounced and broke off her armored back as the other knights tried to stop her, but Tina paid them no mind. Her whole world was focused on Malakai, stomping and slicing the captain until he was as bloody as the ground she'd trapped him on. She was working on cutting through his neck when one of the knights from behind leaped onto her back and got his arms around her head, covering her eyes.

Swearing, Tina halted her assault to reach up and rip the idiot off. It was only for a second, but it proved to be a second too many. The moment she let up on the pressure, Malakai grabbed the foot she still had planted on his chest and pushed up with all his strength.

Tina gasped as her feet went over her head. The knight she'd been tearing off her face let go with a cry, then everyone went down in a heap on the blood-slicked bridge. Tina and Malakai made it back to their feet at the same time, but despite her best efforts, the captain had no serious injuries at all. He was bloody, and his armor was shredded, but below the sundered metal, the cuts on his body were depressingly shallow--a fact that Malakai was only too happy to rub in her face.

"How's it feel to be on the receiving end of your Nightmare?" the captain asked, pulling down his slashed-up breastplate to show her his chest, which her stomping hadn't even bruised. "I have too much HP for any one player to kill, especially a tanking-geared class like yourself. Give up and die. You can't beat me."

"Fuck that," Tina snarled back. "I already killed you once before. I'll do it again."

Malakai laughed in her face. "Don't flatter yourself. The only reason you were able to do anything last time was because you had two healers and an Assassin helping you, but you're alone now." He flashed her a bloody grin. "Today, you will die by my hand, *monster*."

Tina's answer to that was to throw her shield at Malakai's head. He ducked it easily, but she hadn't actually been aiming for him. Her goal was the giant crash her shield made as it bounced off a rock on the Camp Comeback side of the bridge--a crash loud enough to get SB's attention. The Assassin finished off the knight he'd been dueling and raised his sword in acknowledgment. Satisfied, Tina nodded and turned back to Malakai, who was staring at her warily.

"Throwing away your best defense?" He shook his head. "I didn't think you, of all players, would give up so easily."

"I'm not giving up anything," Tina said, sheathing her sword so she could face Malakai with open, empty hands. "Just taking the gloves off."

Malakai sneered at that and waved at his knights, who were still clumped up on the bridge behind Tina, waiting for their chance.

"*Attack!*"

At his command, the whole bridge charged Tina as one. Tina responded in kind, lunging forward to tackle Malakai off his feet as the knights crashed into her back. They all went down together in a stabbing, kicking heap, but while Tina wasn't stronger than the four-skull captain, she *was* heavier. Her stonekin body, wrapped in metal, hit him like a freight train, and she used the chance to wrap her arms around his body, getting Malakai in a bear hug just as she'd ended their fight with last time.

"I knew you'd do this," he gasped as she locked her arms behind his back and started to squeeze. "But it won't... work twice..."

He was right. The other knights were piled on top of them, stabbing her with their swords. With her arms locked around Malakai, she couldn't defend, and the damage was already piling up. If choking him out had been her plan, it was going very badly, but that wasn't Tina's intention at all. She'd known from the moment she'd thrown her shield that this wasn't a battle she could win. The best she could do was take Malakai out of the equation, so she held on just long enough for SB to reach the bridge. The moment she saw him running toward her, she left the rest to him and rolled sideways, taking Malakai with her as she crashed through the bridge's stone railing and off the edge.

For a moment, there was nothing but air. Malakai was squirming like a fish in her arms, punching and stabbing at her head with his broken swords. Tina didn't even try to stop him. She just focused on holding on, crushing the captain's body against hers as they splashed into the gore-filled river.

The light vanished as soon as they hit. Blinded by the muck, Tina quickly lost sight of which way was up. Vile, bloody water poured into her mouth and nostrils as they sank, while the swift current pushed slimy, unidentifiable chunks into her armor. If she hadn't been made of stone, she would have barfed her guts out, but she was. She was a rock--the same inert, unfeeling stone she'd cursed this morning. Right now, though, she'd never been happier to be a stonekin, and not just because it saved her from the trauma of the bloody river. She was happy because she was a rock and Malakai was not, and as they sank into the depths, that made all the difference.

Malakai realized he was in trouble the moment they hit the water. He squirmed and thrashed in her grip, churning the water and knocking them around. But as strong as he was, even Malakai couldn't punch

413

properly underwater. His blows still hurt, but they were nothing compared to what they'd been before. As the seconds ticked by, they grew weaker still, until finally the captain stopped attacking her altogether and focused everything on trying to escape.

Grinning in the bloody depths, Tina just hugged him tighter. As she'd learned during the Wind-Fire-barrel incident, she could hold her breath a long-ass time, much longer than any fleshy critter could hope to. Malakai might have the advantage in every other category, but when it came to this, Tina had him beat. All she had to do was hold on, wrapping her stone limbs around him like an octopus as he struggled desperately in the dark, bloody, heavy cold of the river bottom.

After thirty seconds of this, Malakai started to panic. She could feel the shift in his movements as he stopped struggling and started really trying to kill her. She couldn't see what he was doing in the dark, but she felt the knife in his hands when he started stabbing it into the gap in the armor around her neck, cutting into her windpipe with all his strength.

The feel of blood flowing freely out of her sundered throat made Tina panic. She almost fucked everything up by letting go of Malakai, but she got ahold herself at the last second, forcing her arms to stay locked as she closed her eyes and pulled on the stone inside her.

Earthen Fortitude.

The embrace of the Bedrock Kings came up through the muddy river bottom like a blessing, hardening her flesh against Malakai's attack and turning her into even more of a boat anchor. As the spreading stone snapped Malakai's knife in her neck, Tina was gladder than ever that she'd saved her ace in the hole. For six beautiful seconds, she truly was a stone prison binding him to the ground. Then the gift of the Bedrock Kings started to fade, taking Tina's good feelings with it.

It felt like she'd been drained. As the magical protection left, her body went from rock solid to stiff and crumbly. That last one in particular was a bad sign. Crumbly meant that she'd lost too much blood again, probably from the hole in her neck, which was now bleeding freely again.

She needed to get back to the surface and get some heals, but damn, Malakai was still kicking. If she let him go, he'd get his air back, and this would all be for nothing, so Tina dug her feet into the mud and held on, ignoring the silver blood she could taste floating by her in her dark current.

It took forever. Years seemed to pass while the captain struggled and she bled. It was too dark at the bottom of the river already to see her vision darkening, but Tina knew from the growing stillness in her head that she was getting closer to the point of no return. There were healing potions on her belt, but she couldn't reach them without letting go of Malakai, and she couldn't drink them underwater, anyway. A heal would have solved everything, but there was no way any of the Roughneck casters could see her through all the muck. She had to do something, though. Her body was hardening faster than Malakai was drowning. If they didn't stop this soon, she really would end up being his tombstone.

When she got the first hint of the falling-out-of-her-body feeling, Tina decided to take a chance. Moving slowly, she transferred Malakai from a bear hug to a one-armed headlock. The captain's struggles doubled when she unwrapped her arms from his middle, but she wasn't the only one on her last legs, and it wasn't enough for him to break free. Satisfied Malakai was still on lockdown, Tina tightened her arm around his neck and started walking up the slant of the riverbed toward the shore. She hoped it was the *right* shore.

Popping and cracking like rocks in a mine, Tina trudged her way up the river bottom. Her feet sank deep into the soft mud, making every step a challenge, but at least Malakai wasn't fighting her anymore. She didn't know if he was dead or just conserving his strength for the next opening, but a dead weight was a lot easier to haul than a fighting one. Tina just wished she knew where she was hauling it. She felt like she'd been walking for ages, but she still hadn't spotted the river's surface. She couldn't even see the sun through the gore, which was a problem, because her breath was finally starting to run out.

415

Fighting not to panic, Tina kept trudging up the bank, telling herself over and over that the river wasn't that wide. It *had* to end sometime. Had to.

The blackness around her broke like lightning. Thanks to the gore flowing into it, the surface of the river was covered in a layer of scum, blocking all the light. She hadn't even noticed it before she'd broken through, her head bursting into the glare of sunlight and the roar of battle.

Tina opened her mouth with a gasp. The dank air tasted better than anything before in her life. She sucked in a huge gulp before going back down to make sure Malakai was still secure, but the captain wasn't moving at all. Satisfied, Tina grabbed a healing potion off her belt with her free hand and broke the surface again to dump the healing liquid into her mouth.

She drank all three of her potions in rapid succession. The euphoria of magical healing surged down her throat and spread to her limbs, washing the terrifying crumbling feeling away. Her flexibility returned, as did her strength, making her feel like she could jump straight out of the water--which, if she hadn't still been holding Malakai under, she would have.

"Ick, ick, *ick!*" Tina cried, gagging as a wave washed the disgusting river water into her open mouth. She spat it out and slammed her trap shut, keeping her lips pressed together as she looked around to see she was on the wrong side of the river.

At least that explained why the walk out had taken so long. She was standing in the shallows near the opposite side of the bridge, facing the plaza where the knights were still rallying. A shout went up as she was spotted, and Tina was forced to duck back under as a volley of spears flew into the water. She was bracing to walk all the way back across to her side when she realized Malakai was floating in her grip, completely still. He wasn't quite dead yet, but he was definitely unconscious, and that gave her an idea.

Grinning under the water, Tina surged back up, using her new strength to march up the riverbed straight into the enemy. The knights formed a ring as she emerged from the water, but they held back when they saw Captain Malakai dangling from her arm like a wet blanket. Widening her grin, Tina grabbed the elf by his soggy hair and held him aloft, shaking him at his men until the bloody water from his clothes splattered at their feet.

"That's right, assholes," she said as they scuttled back. "Your captain *lost*. He's not dead yet, but I can change that anytime I want, so why don't we make a deal?"

"We don't deal with *players*," spat a stern-looking blond man with a gold rope on his shoulder.

Tina shrugged. "Then I guess you don't care about your captain."

She wrapped her hand around the captain's throat as she finished, and the officer went still.

"That's more like it," Tina said smugly. "Here's what we're going to do. You're going to let me walk down that bridge, and I won't rip Malakai's head off."

"Why should we agree?" the officer demanded. "You'll just kill him when you reach the other side."

Tina scoffed. "I'd never be so wasteful. I know how much Terminator Elf here is worth to you." She shook Malakai at them one more time before tucking him back under her arm. "Maybe you haven't heard yet, but I'm a mercenary. I'll be happy to sell Malakai back to you at an extremely inflated price after we win, but if you don't want him to die in front of you, you'd best back off before I decide he's more trouble than he's worth. Just make it quick. He's almost gone. It'd be a real shame if he croaks by accident while you were busy making threats you can't back up."

The knights began whispering together in hushed voices as she finished. Tina could hear them assuring each other they'd free Malakai after they won, but she didn't really care. All she wanted was to get back to her side of the river without having to fight her way through an army, so she let them talk until, at last, the knights moved out of her way.

Tina wasn't above swaggering her way out of the water, nor did she deny herself the joy of dragging Malakai behind her by his hair. But as satisfying as it was to rub her victory in the knights' faces, she stopped caring about them the moment she saw her bridge.

The span the Roughnecks had guarded all morning looked even worse than it had when she'd thrown herself off it. Mounted knights were everywhere, but to her surprise, they all seemed to be in retreat. Quickening her pace, Tina pushed through them to see what the hell was going on. She was terrified the bridge had fallen and these were actually soldiers retreating from the battle on the banks. When she finally made it past the fleeing soldiers to the halfway point, though, fear transformed into relief--then pride.

The last ten feet of the bridge was a blood-soaked scene of slaughter. There were no bodies on the ground, but there were arms, limbs, and broken weapons, and standing in the middle of it all was SilentBlayde. He was dirty and panting, but his silver swords were gleaming through a thick coating of crimson. Most important of all, not a single gib of Bastion's knights had made it to the island behind him.

"Tina," he gasped, his tired face lighting up when he saw her. "You're all right!"

"And you held the bridge!" she cried, running toward him.

His mask hid his face, but Tina knew he was grinning. "I told you I had your back."

He did. He *always* did, and she'd never loved him more for it. If she hadn't been so disgusting, she would have picked him up and whirled him around. But she didn't think he'd appreciate being hugged by someone who looked like she'd crawled out of a blood-based oil spill, and there was still Malakai to deal with.

"Whoa," SB said when he saw the captain under her arm. "Is he still alive, or did you just take a trophy?"

He was so still, Tina had to hold her fingers under his nose, but sure enough, she felt his breath, faint but there. "He's alive," she said, sliding the captain back onto her shoulder. "But he probably needs CPR to stay that way."

SB looked confused. "*Do* we want him to stay that way?"

Tina nodded. "Hell yeah. We've scored ourselves a legit prisoner of war. Maybe we can use him as leverage to get out of this mess."

As SB knelt down to thump the water out of Malakai's lungs, Tina hopped up on what was left of the railing to look over the battlefield.

The knights were still giving Tina space, so their bridge was clear, but down on the riverbank, the other Roughnecks were up to their eyeballs in spearmen. The defense was still holding, but everyone she saw was drenched crimson, and the other bridges looked even worse. Cinco's front was solid, but Assets's line had been pushed almost back to the grass, and the random raids were awash with cavalry fighting tooth and nail for a hold on the beach. Behind them all, the grassy hill was streaked by trails of red from all the casualties who'd been dragged off to medical.

"Damn," Tina said, hopping down again. "We're holding on by the skin of our teeth. We gotta end this somehow."

She glanced back at SB, but he was still busy giving the elf captain mouth to mouth. A few seconds later, Malakai coughed and choked, causing SilentBlayde to jump away like he'd kissed a nuclear weapon. Tina had her sword out before she realized the dark-haired elf was still unconscious.

"He's gonna need a healer," SB said, wiping his mouth on the back of his hand. "I think he might have been under for too long."

Tina nodded and waved over a squad of white-headband-wearing players. After giving them firm orders to "chain him up like Superman" and "only give him enough healing to keep him alive," she let the support team haul Malakai off and moved on to other problems.

"Where's Frank?"

"In medical," SB said grimly. "The fall broke his neck clean through. The healers were able to save him, but they couldn't get him back up to fighting shape. We're almost out of healing on all fronts, so Zen said to put him in a bed and don't let him move until we get more mana."

"Damn," Tina said, scowling. She was well aware that would have been her, too, if she hadn't weighed so much, but it was still shit luck being down a tank. She was about to tell SB to return to the fight and leave the bridge to her when a shout split the air.

"*Stop!*"

The baritone command boomed across the battlefield. It was so loud Tina felt it in her chest, and she wasn't the only one. Every combatant--player or NPC--jumped at the sound, then the whole battlefield turned to the opposite side of the river, where an enormous man was sitting astride an even bigger draft horse. He was as tall as Tina and covered in glorious sun-metal plate armor. His chest and arms were draped in the royal red and gold, and the sword he'd lifted above his head glittered like condensed sunlight in his massive hand, lighting up the riverbank.

"Crap," Tina muttered.

"Tina," SB said at the same time. "That's--"

"The king," she finished angrily. "The goddamn *king*. He *would* show up when we're all worn out."

"*This battle is over,*" the king said in a voice that shook the ground. "*Armies of Bastion, I order you to retreat.*"

For a moment, the whole battlefield stood dumbstruck at that, then the enemy turned and fled. Spears were cast down as soldiers abandoned the gore-drenched river fortifications. Some retreated across the bridges. Cinco's group took the opportunity to kill a few more, but Tina was happy to step aside and let them run. When they were gone, all the player raids flopped to the ground. People dragged themselves away from the bloody shores to fall on the first clean spot of grass they reached. Only the support players kept moving, dragging the wounded back toward the medical area as fast as they could before things started again.

"I wonder what he's up to," Tina said quietly as she and SB watched the soldiers scramble back to the other side of the river. "The Buffoon King's not a hard fight, but he's still a five-skull. We were barely holding together as it was. If he'd come in, he could have turned the whole battle. He has to know that, so why order everyone to fall back?"

"Maybe he's tired of losing people," SB said, his face slightly green as he looked down at the bloody river. "I would be."

"Yeah, but you're a good guy," Tina said. "I bet they've got something else up their sleeve now that they know we're not just gonna fold. But we've got options too. We've got Malakai, and we've got plan B. If they come at us again, I think we should roll out the big..."

Now that his armies were in retreat, the king was riding toward the Roughnecks' bridge, and he wasn't alone. There was another figure beside him, a tall jubatus wearing weirdly mismatched armor and carrying a black staff--a very *familiar* jubatus.

"Are you fucking kidding me?"

It was James. Her *brother* was riding at the goddamn *king*'s side. His pet NPC and the suicide mage were there as well, but James was all Tina could see--that and a very dangerous wash of red tingeing her vision. SB was frantically saying something beside her, but Tina couldn't hear him over the rage that her brother had gone and fucked everything up *again*. He'd run off and ended up a fucking hostage, and as always, she was the one who was going to have to pay.

"Tina," SB said, grabbing her arm. "Tina, please, you're scaring me."

"He's the one who should be scared," Tina growled back, yanking her arm out of his grasp. "I'll deal with this. You go and tell them to bring Malakai back out. They're not the only ones with hostages."

SilentBlayde didn't look happy with that order, but he obeyed, flashing away so fast, he was little more than a blip in the sunlight. Alone on the bloody bridge again, Tina marched forward to meet her enemy. She'd just about made it to the midpoint when golden light flashed in the sky.

Tina froze, eyes going wide. The Bastion, the golden shield that had been hanging over their heads in the sky for two days now, was flickering like an old lightbulb. It pulsed several times in rapid succession, then with a final flash, it died, leaving the sky clear and pure blue again. But that wasn't why Tina kept staring. She barely noticed the Bastion's fall, because she was too busy looking at the thing waiting behind it.

It was almost as big as the sky itself, a monster of shadow and flame with claws the size of telephone poles and wings that blotted out the sun. It landed as she watched, sliding through the space where the Bastion had been to dig its claws into a line of sturdy limestone buildings just up the hill. The giant stone blocks cracked when the creature's weight hit them, but it still didn't seem wholly real. Even sitting in direct sunlight, its body was wreathed in shadows much like SB's was when he activated his Shadow Dance cooldown. She was still staring at it in dumbstruck horror when SilentBlayde leaped out of her shadow.

"*Tina!*"

"The fuck is that?" she demanded, too panicked to notice shadow-walking was apparently back on now that the Bastion was down. "Since when does this game have a shadow dragon?"

"It's not a shadow dragon," SB panted, his face pale. "That's a Bird."

Tina went still. "A Bird," she repeated quietly, glancing down at him with round eyes. "As in capital B *Bird?*"

The Assassin nodded. "I felt it lurking in the Lightless Realm right before the barrier went down. That's Xthr, Fourth Born. The Great Bird who owes a debt to Bastion."

A debt the king had clearly just called in.

"Fuck," Tina swore, stomping her foot so hard the bridge shook. "Fuck, fuck, *fuck!*" As if James and a five-skull king weren't bad enough, now they had a raid boss no one in the game had ever fought before. Tina

422

didn't know if they could have handled all of that fresh. Wounded and out of mana, they didn't stand a chance. But the king was still coming. They had to do something, so Tina did what she did best.

She acted like a raid leader.

"SB!" she shouted, making the elf jump. "We're about to have serious incoming. I want all the Roughnecks healed and mana'ed up to full. *Especially* Frank. I don't care if we have to drain Camp Comeback dry. I want every raider filled up and in position at the end of this bridge *stat*. *Go!*"

The Assassin saluted and vanished into the shadows. Satisfied that was at least going as planned, Tina turned and ran back across the bridge to reclaim her shield from where she'd thrown it. Across the grass, the other two guild leaders broke ranks and hurried toward her.

"What the hell is going on?" Cinco yelled. "Why is there a goddamn *space dragon?*"

"And the king," Assets added, his already-pale face ashen. "What's the plan?"

"The new plan's the old plan," Tina said firmly, slamming her shield onto her arm. "Everyone who's not in Dead Mountain Fortress gear needs to get inside the warded buildings. Cinco, don't let anyone panic. Break arms if you have to, but you keep everyone inside and in position. Assets, make sure the wind-fire powder is ready to go."

Assets nodded, but Cinco crossed his arms over his chest. "What are you going to do?"

Tina looked over her shoulder at the giant shape darkening the northern sky. "If I'm lucky, bluff like hell and see if we can't negotiate. If I'm not..." She sighed. "Just get ready to hunker down."

The other guild leaders nodded, and they broke. By the time Tina made it back to her bridge, the Roughnecks were waiting for her. Heals were still going off to get everyone to full, but the whole raid was on its feet--including Frank, which was a relief.

"How's your neck?" Tina asked. "Sorry you got thrown."

"I'm sorry I let him throw me," Frank said, tilting his head gingerly as if he were afraid it would fall off. "He had quite the arm for such a scrawny fella. Glad you whupped him."

"Whuppin' is what I do," Tina said with far more bravado than she felt. "And we've got a lot more to go."

"You say that as though 'whuppin" is even on the table," Richard said, wiggling his way through the crowd to point frantically at the battleship-sized winged creature of shadow and claws sitting casually on Bastion's skyline. "That is *Xthr*! The Last Great Bird! He wasn't supposed to be a combatable boss until the next expansion. I don't even know if he has stats! How can we kill something that doesn't have *stats*?"

"The same way we kill everything else," Tina snapped, banging on her shield to get her raid's attention. "Everyone, get in formation! Casters and ranged in the middle, melee to the front. Anders, you're healing me. Neko, you watch Frank. All other healers are on the raid. Don't let anyone die! I want everyone on their A-game. We do not have leeway to fuck this up!"

The whole raid leaped to obey, rushing into position with a speed that would have made Tina cry if she'd had room for such soft emotions. As it was, she just stomped up and took her position beside Frank in the grass, watching the end of the bloody bridge they'd held all morning as the king's procession slowly rode over it. They stopped at the end, then like he was the one leading this farce, James climbed down from his horse and walked out alone, striding across the trampled, bloody grass with a scroll clutched tight in his hands.

Chapter 18

James and Tina

Fifteen minutes earlier.

"**I**'m glad you keep parchment and quill in your saddlebags, Sir Townsend," James said as he wrote out yet another copy of the treaty he and the king had just hastily drafted.

"I would be unworthy to travel with His Majesty if I did not carry such minimal necessities," the old knight replied stiffly. "A knight is always prepared to serve with honor."

He said that last bit with a stern glare at Sir Dan, who was now bound, gagged, and under guard. They were at the rear of Malakai's battle force, tucked away in an alley behind the plaza the knights were using as a staging ground. King Gregory had wanted to push forward, but James had begged him to hold back. They'd only get one shot at defusing this situation, and he meant to do it right, reading over the agreements he and Gregory had put forth over and over until he was certain he'd missed nothing.

"That should do it," he said, blowing on the ink to help it dry.

"Finally," the king said, lifting his pale face to the sound of battle going on only a block away. "I was worried I wasn't going to have any subjects left if we waited much more."

"It'll be worth it," James promised. "Neither the players nor the knights are monsters. They're all just angry people who've been pushed too far. But even angry people don't want to throw their lives away for nothing. If we offer both sides a path out of this mess where they get to keep their pride and their lives, I'm sure they'll take it. It'll be just like the gnolls and Windy Lake."

Ar'Bati grunted at that, but he didn't contradict as James rolled up the scrolls he'd written and handed one to the king. The second one, however, was another matter. "So," James said awkwardly, looking down

425

at the scroll that was still in his hands. "Who wants to be our liaison to the players?"

"Don't look at me," Fangs in the Grass growled. "I'm Angry Cat. I'll just eat their tacos."

"I can't do it," Flameboyant said, shaking his head. "They all still think I'm a mad-bomber psycho, remember? They'd probably just shoot me again if I came over from the knights' side."

"Why are you even asking this?" Ar'Bati demanded, glaring at James. "You're the one with the Great Stone General for a sister. Clearly, it has to be you."

"Oh no," James said, waving his hands frantically. "No, no, no. I am the *worst* person to bring anything to Tina. She still thinks I'm a giant screwup. Just looking at me puts her in a bad mood. If I bring this treaty to her, she'll reject it without even reading. We'd be better off if King Gregory took them both."

"It cannot be me," the king said solemnly. "I am the enemy. Anything I bring her will be seen as a trap. You are the only one here she will listen to."

"You obviously haven't seen me and my sister together," James said sadly. "'Listening' isn't her usual reaction."

"Then you must make her," Ar'Bati snapped, turning to face James head on. "You have done nothing but cower before your sister since we came to this city. No wonder she sees you as a failure. It's the only attitude you ever show her! But we no longer have the luxury of licking old wounds. It's time to decide, James--what is it you wish to be to her? The screwup who always runs away or the older brother who's there when it matters?" He pointed at the scroll in James's hands. "This is your plan. Have faith in it! You were brave and strong before the elders at Windy Lake. Be that person again now. Stand up and show your sister that you're no longer who she thinks you are. All of Bastion depends on it."

"I *know*," James said desperately, his voice cracking as all the old fears came back. "I know how important this is. I wrote the treaty! But you

426

don't understand. I deserve everything Tina thinks about me. I *was* a screwup. I *did* run away and leave her with a giant mess she's still digging out of. What am I supposed to do? Walk out there and tell her all of that doesn't matter?"

"I never said it didn't matter," his brother snarled. "But you can't keep being a coward! Whatever happened in your past, she'll never change her mind about you unless you show her that you're different *now*. Fight, spit, claw, curse--it doesn't matter what you do. Just don't run away. If you get in her face and refuse to back down, she'll *have* to listen."

If James got in Tina's face, he was pretty sure she'd pummel him into the dirt. But as terrified as that made him, Ar'Bati was right. His entire plan hinged on getting both sides to talk. That included him. All the treaties in the world wouldn't do squat if he didn't have the guts to talk to his own family. If he meant a word of anything he'd said about not letting Tina down, he had to do this. He just hoped it didn't end up with his *actual* guts on the ground.

"This is going to end in tears," he muttered, clutching the scroll in his hands.

"So long as it doesn't end in blood," Gregory said bitterly. "Are we ready?"

With a deep breath, James nodded.

The king nodded back. "Then let's go stop the fighting."

With that, the group moved out. They rode in tight formation, moving through the bloody streets as quietly as ghosts. No one noticed as they passed. All of the knights and support forces were too busy with their own tragedies and furies to look up and see the enormous man riding past. They made it all the way to the river before anyone even thought to challenge them, and even then, they only had to stop because of the massive knot of knights gathered at the edge of the northern bridge.

"What is going on?" Gregory demanded.

All the knights jumped. Even when he was speaking softly, the king's voice was a presence. It rumbled through the air, making the armored men whirl around. Their eyes widened as they realized who they were looking at, then they dropped to the ground, falling off their horses in their rush to get to kneel before their king.

"Y-Your Majesty," one of the knights, a blond man with a gold braid on his shoulder, stuttered. "What are you doing here?"

"I asked you first," the king said, his lips tugging up in a hint of a smile before growing serious again. "What is the state of the battle? Where is Captain Malakai?"

The blond knight began to shake. "He has been captured, my king."

Gregory's face grew pale behind his red beard. "Captured?"

"The player leader, the stonekin, drowned him in the river," the knight reported. "He lives still, but the enemy has him in their possession. We were discussing how best to conduct a rescue when you arrived."

James winced. If Tina had captured Malakai, it was definitely time to step in. Even though he'd been driven mad, the loyalty Malakai commanded from his knights was serious business. If he hadn't been so crazy and vengeful and dangerous, it would have been touching, but taking Malakai prisoner was the worst thing Tina could have done from a de-escalation standpoint. His knights would crawl over broken glass to get him back, which meant the pressure was on more than ever. If James couldn't get both sides to listen, they'd be killing each other until no one was left standing.

"Your Majesty," the knight officer said, looking hopefully at his king. "Please help us. You have the strength of the Nightmare still. You could go in there and rescue the captain. The players wouldn't stand a chance!"

The other knights nodded at this, gripping their weapons in readiness, but the king shook his head. "I fully intend to reclaim Captain Malakai, but not by arms." His blue eyes went to the horrifying river, and the king's face paled. "There has been enough blood spilled already. I will not lose any more of my people to this senselessness. This war ends now."

The blond officer scowled. "But sire--"

He reached out, but the king had already stepped forward, raising his voice like a trumpet. "*Stop!*"

The command echoed across the city. On the other side of the bloody river, the chaotic battle froze. James could almost feel the recognition spreading through the crowd as knights and players turned to look at the giant man standing at the river's edge.

"*This battle is over.*" The king's voice shook the ground. "*Armies of Bastion, I order you to retreat.*"

For several moments, nothing moved, then like a tide, all of the soldiers turned and fled. They must have been desperate for a chance to run, James thought as he watched them. No one even stopped to finish off the wounded as they retreated. They just ran, surging across the bridges and through the bloody river to hide behind their king.

"There's the first part done," Gregory said with a deep breath, glancing nervously at the golden glowing sky. "But I can only command my soldiers. The rest will be up to you. And him."

He looked up at the dark shape hidden behind the glittering shell of the Bastion, and James clutched his treaty tightly.

"Let's do it."

The king nodded and drew his sword, making James shiver. The moment the Dawnblade left its sheath, all the tendrils of magic in the air began to spiral around it like moths to a flame. James didn't know if the king could see the magic or not, but his sword didn't cut any of the streamers as he raised the ancient sword high above his head.

"I'm lowering the Bastion now."

Those words made him start to sweat. Other than him having to talk to Tina, this was the part of the plan James liked the least. The Bastion was their only wall against the undead. The king had assured him many times that his knights had taken care of the rogue Portal Keeper Star Fall, but lowering it while the Once King's invasion was still a possibility felt like a very bad idea. It had to come down sometime, though. King Gregory had admitted to him when they were hashing everything out that the holy power that kept the barrier up was almost depleted and would need to recharge, anyway. Taking it down now meant they'd still have a little juice left to put it back up again later if they needed to, and if the Bastion didn't come down, then Xthr couldn't come in.

The Great Bird had actually arrived some time ago, but as a creature of the Lightless Realm, he'd been trapped on the other side of the Bastion. Normally, that was how the shield was supposed to work, but the Bird was on their side this time. As a lore nerd, James was dying to know what the first king of Bastion had done to get one of the oldest monsters in the world in his debt, but his curiosity would have to wait. He just hoped Xthr was as serious about keeping his word as Gregory seemed to think, or they wouldn't have to worry about Tina, because the Great Bird would eat them all.

As the Bastion vanished, James wasn't sure that wouldn't happen anyway. He'd seen Xthr before in cut scenes, but watching CG and seeing the reality were worlds apart. He'd known the Bird was waiting because the king had told him, but none of the monarch's words could have prepared him for how *big* the ancient monster was, or how terrifying. The closest thing James had to compare it to was a dragon--a sky-darkening, reptilian monster with wings that flickered like burning shadows. The multiple claws on each of its four feet were the size of buses, and the wedge-shaped horned head at the end of its thick, snaking neck was as big as a building.

And if sheer size wasn't advantage enough, Xthr had clearly arrived ready for war. James had no idea where giant monsters got armor, but the Bird's shadow-wreathed body was covered in what were clearly worked metal plates fastened to it by blazing arcs of crackling purple magic latticed across the bulk of its body. As a Naturalist, James couldn't actually see the streams of dark magic pouring off the Bird, but he could feel the power to his bones, making all of his fur stand on end as the giant boss turned its glittering, geometric, crystalline eyes on the king.

Gregory lifted the Dawnblade in response. His giant body trembled as he did, but for all his claims of being a bad king, Gregory clearly understood when not to show weakness. His face was firm and stern as he stared the giant Bird down. James could have sworn Xthr smiled at that, his giant jaws curling up before the Bird turned to face the rest of the figures on the island, settling his giant body on several buildings at the crest of the nearest hill so he could loom over the island more comfortably.

When it was clear the monster wasn't going to move again, Gregory lowered his sword with a shaky sigh. "It is done," he said, turning to James. "Shall we go?"

James wanted desperately to say no. He wanted to get away from the shadow monster in the sky. He wanted the reassuring golden glow of the Bastion back. He *desperately* wanted not to have to march across that river and face his sister, but it was too late for all of that. He'd already spotted Tina standing on the crest of the bridge in front of them with SB. She looked more like a bloodkin than a stonekin with her crimson-stained armor--a true demon.

The king clearly thought so. Gregory, who'd stayed rock steady in front of the Bird, actually flinched when he saw Tina staring down at him, turning to give James a worried look. "Are you sure you can do this?"

"No," James said honestly. "But I have to." If Tina didn't stop fighting, the war would never end. He wasn't just doing this for Bastion. He was doing it for her. How he would make her see that, James had no idea, but he owed it to her to try, so he rode forward with the king, crossing the bridge Tina had just vacated to find her raid waiting for them on the other side.

"She certainly does move fast," the king whispered.

James nodded. The island, which had been a raging battlefield just a few minutes earlier, was now almost entirely empty. All the players-- high level, low level, healers, damage dealers, wounded, and able bodied-- had been moved inside the big stone Trainers' Hall at the top of the island's main hill. James could still see a big Berserker in crimson armor herding them inside and being none too gentle about it. This left only the raiders to face the king, which was a smart move. The Roughnecks could down King Gregory no problem, and far more easily if they didn't have to worry about hitting less-geared people. If it had just been the king, James was sure Tina would have already attacked, but it looked like even Roxxy's Roughnecks weren't crazy enough to charge a five-skull while Xthr watched, which meant stage one of the plan had worked. Now he just had to pull off the rest.

"We have your back if you need us," Ar'Bati assured him quietly, squeezing his shoulder. "Good luck."

"Thanks, Fangs," James whispered back, giving his brother what he hoped was a confident smile as he slid down off his mount, then he started across the bloody grass toward Tina's army.

***

"Isn't that your brother?" Zen asked, shading her eyes against the bright sun as James walked forward. "The one who ran away?"

Tina nodded, her jaw too clenched to speak.

"Glad to see he's all right," Frank said with genuine happiness. "But I don't like that he's coming out alone. I've seen movies. The only time they let the hostage walk out alone is when it's a trap."

"Dude, what kind of trap could it be?" Neko demanded. "There's a freaking purple laser dragon hanging out on the high-rises! I don't think it's going to matter what Roxxy does. That birdy can barbecue this whole island in one pass."

"Well, he must want *something*," Killbox said, pointing at the paper in James's hand. "He brought a note."

"Maybe it's a surrender," Anders said hopefully. "It was pretty common in medieval wars to release hostages in the hopes of buttering up the enemy before a treaty. Maybe that's what's going on here."

"I don't care what he wants," Tina growled, sheathing her sword so she'd have a free hand. "I'm going out there and grabbing him. You guys wait here. I'll be right back."

"Tina, no," SB said quickly, grabbing her wrist. He let go again when he saw the look on her face, but he didn't give up. "Look at the enemy," he pleaded, pointing at the towering king, who was still waiting on the bridge. "No one's attacking. Xthr could have burned us all by now, but he's just sitting there waiting. Don't you see? This is a parley. They probably sent James out to negotiate since he's your brother. It was probably his idea."

"Just because he wants to talk doesn't mean I have to listen," Tina snapped. "They've got a Bird, but we have Malakai and plan B. I don't know what James has gotten himself into, but it's obvious he's in over his head. *Everything* hard is over James's head." She bared her teeth. "If they want to negotiate, we'll do it with the king. You know, the guy who *actually* has power. But I'm not going to miss what might be my last chance to save my brother."

"I get that," SilentBlayde said desperately. "But if you grab the messenger and carry him back over your shoulder, it's going to look like an attack. This is a delicate situation. If they misunderstand what you're doing, you could bring Xthr down on us, then we'll lose everything we've fought for."

Tina cursed under her breath. She hated that SB was right, but not as much as she hated the fact that it was James. Any other representative, she would have been fine with. Hell, she actually kind of liked the idea of parleying with a king. That sounded cool and important. This was just obnoxious. Dealing with all this complicated political shit would be hard enough without her brother poking at old wounds, which he *absolutely* would. Even when he was trying to be nice, James couldn't go two minutes without finding some new way to piss her off. If things hadn't been so serious, she would have sent one of the other Roughnecks to spare herself the aggravation. But things *were* that serious, so Tina sucked it up and stepped forward.

"Don't agree to anything without consulting us first!" Zen called after her. "Whatever deal the king's sent over, the officers still need to vote on it."

"Yeah, yeah," Tina grumbled. "Just make sure plan B is ready to go, 'cause I might have to come back quickly."

"We are ready," Richard said as the other Sorcerers nodded. "All you have to do is say the word."

That made Tina feel a little better as she strode across the bloody, trampled grass toward her brother.

He was waiting for her at the edge of the dirt furrow Frank had plowed in the grass when Malakai had thrown him. Tina stopped on the other side of the ditch, staring at her brother with a surprisingly varied mix of emotions. Twenty seconds ago, she'd have said she was just angry. Now that she was standing in front of him, though, Tina wasn't sure how she felt. Rage was there, of course, but so was relief at seeing him unharmed. There was love for her brother, who, despite everything, was still the only family she had in this place, but also resentment because he'd made everything into such a mess, especially her. He was right there, practically in arm's reach, and Tina still couldn't save him. Truly, no one could screw things up like James could.

"Tina," he said, breaking the heavy silence at last. "I'm glad you're all right."

"Doing better than you," she said, glancing at his hands, which were surprisingly not tied. "Why am I not surprised you managed to get yourself made into a hostage?"

"I'm not a hostage," James said quickly. "I'm working with the king. We want to stop the--"

"Working *with* the king?" she cried, suddenly furious. "The dude who wants to kill us?" She threw her hands in the air. "Seriously, James, how do you always manage to find a way to screw me over?"

434

"I'm not trying to screw you over!" he yelled back at her. "I'm trying to *save* you!"

"What sort of fucked-up James-logic figures working with my enemy counts as saving me?" Tina demanded. "If you wanted to help, you should have listened to what I actually said! I had *one thing* I needed you to do, and that was to stay put and not cause trouble. But in true James fashion, you went and did the *exact opposite*. Now we have a fucking Bird breathing down our necks, and you want me to believe this is your idea of helping?" She clenched her fists. "*Do you even know what that word means?*"

"It's not that simple!" James cried. "You're the one who didn't listen when I tried to tell you how serious things are. You just wanted me to shut up and follow orders, but I'm not one of your raiders! I'm your *brother*, and I told you I had a job to do here. I didn't escape to hurt you. I ran away because someone had to warn the king about the undead invasion, and unlike you, he believed me! Now I've brought him here for *your* sake, and before you say that's not helping, whose order do you think stopped the fighting?"

Tina snapped her mouth shut. That...was a fair point, actually. But that didn't mean she liked it. "So are you responsible for Xthr too?" she demanded. "Great save, bro. Stop the fight by putting us over a barrel. And for the record, we were *winning*."

"No one was winning, Tina," James said bitterly, his inhuman cat-eyes moving over her bloody armor. "Look at yourself. You look like a murderer."

"Because they made me one!" Tina cried. "Your king-buddy's knights wanted to exterminate us! I will *not* apologize for defending my people!"

"What the knights did was wrong," James admitted. "But that doesn't make slaughtering them back *right*. I know you never paid attention to FFO's plot, but have you seriously forgotten everything that happened over our last seven years of gaming? This is *Bastion*! City of light and sunshine, whose name literally means 'protection.' Malakai's hate might have dinged your faith in that, but that doesn't change the fact that we've always been on Bastion's side. The Once King certainly sees it that way. You can claim the game plot doesn't matter anymore, but you've been to the Deadlands. You *know* the Once King still wants to kill all the living, but at this rate, he won't have to, because you'll have done it *for* him!"

"What do you want me to do?" Tina demanded. "Roll over and let Malakai kill us?"

"I want you *both* to stop," James said, thrusting the scroll he was carrying at her. "Just read this."

"What is it?"

"A peace treaty," her brother explained.

Tina arched a copper eyebrow. "Does it include the enemy's unconditional surrender and an apology for the trouble they've caused us?"

"Of course not, but--"

"Then no dice," she snapped. "I know you're Mr. Both-Sides, James, but this isn't a shades-of-gray issue. Malakai was running a *death camp*. He wants to exterminate us. I'm not making peace with Nazis."

"They're not Nazis!" James cried. "At least not all of them. Malakai and his knights will pay for their crimes, but the majority of Bastion just wants this to *stop*."

"If that's true, why did the king let this happen?" Tina demanded, pointing at the mass of people across the bloody river. "Whose army do you think that is?"

James flinched. "It's Bastion's," he admitted. "But you have to understand, King Gregory didn't know what Malakai was really doing. He was ignorant of--"

"What do you mean, 'didn't know'?" she cried. "We kicked down a hangman's scaffold on his *front door*. There's no way he didn't see that, so either he's lying and you're stupid enough to believe him, or he really is a Buffoon King. Either way, I'm not making a deal. Someone who's that stupid or that deceitful isn't someone I'm dumb enough to trust."

"Can you at least *read* the treaty before you reject it?" James pleaded, opening the scroll to show it to her.

Tina scowled at the familiar handwriting. "You wrote this, didn't you?"

"Yes," James said proudly, which was all she needed to know.

"Then I'm *definitely* not going to read it."

"But--"

"No," she said firmly, glaring him down. "You've wasted enough of our time already. I swear to God, James, you'd let Hitler off the hook if he told you a good-enough sob story. But unlike you, I'm not a fuckup. I actually understand the concept of saving someone, which is why you're going to turn around, give the king a little wave, then come back with me. When we reach the raid, we'll make a break for the hall. The fire ward is already set up, and the wind-fire powder should be in position. All I have to do is give the word, and this war will *really* be over. No treaty needed."

James's eyes were wide by the time she finished. "Wind-fire powder?"

Tina gave him a superior look. "I told you I don't fuck around. We were planning to wear the king's army down then use the wind-fire powder as leverage to negotiate Bastion's surrender, but now that the king's brought a Bird into play, that's all off the table. No one rolls out a super-weapon like that unless they're ready to use it, which means we have to use ours first. Now signal the king so he doesn't shoot at us, and let's move."

"*No!*" James said. "Would you just listen to me for once in your--"

"Why should I listen to you?" Tina yelled at him. "You never once realized the seriousness of the situation I'm in! While you were off playing diplomat to the idiot king like this is still a fucking *game*, I was fighting through the city saving *actual* people from his murderers. There are thousands of players on this island depending on my raiders to protect them, and you're still wasting time on bullshit!"

437

"It's not bullshit!" James yelled back. "I'm risking my life to save people, too, starting with you! You're my little sister! I love you, and I'll do whatever it takes to save you!"

Those words hit Tina straight in the gut. She wasn't sure what hurt more--how long she'd been waiting to hear her brother say that, or the fact that she was stupid enough to believe him. Not the loving-her part. She'd always known James loved her. It just never made a difference. Loving her hadn't stopped him from breaking her arm when they were kids or eating her birthday cake before she'd even gotten to open the box. It hadn't kept him from using up the college fund that was supposed to be for both of them and leaving her with nothing.

Tina was sure he'd loved her when he'd knocked out SB and run away, leaving her to worry and clean up his mess. That was how James's love worked: he did whatever he wanted, and Tina was just expected to accept it. She was supposed to *listen* and *understand*, even though he never did the same for her, because James was *special*. James was the important one, the one whose ideas she was always supposed to go along with no matter how fucking stupid they were. And when his plans inevitably blew up, Tina was always the one who had to clean up the mess. James never suffered for his actions. Never paid.

Even when they were stranded in another world, he was the one standing with the king, telling her to eat her losses and pain for the greater good. *His* good. Never hers. James didn't even think to ask if she wanted to be saved. He just showed up and expected her to drop everything and go along with what he wanted. Even when he was standing right in front of her, Tina was still the one left waiting in the rain, still the one who was expected to give up her good for his. And she was sick of it.

"No."

"Tina--"

"Don't 'Tina' me!" she roared, clenching her giant stone fists. "I'm so *fucking* tired of you telling me what I'm supposed to do! But I'm not letting you fuck this up like you've fucked up everything else. This time, you're doing things *my* way. Now *come on.*"

She grabbed him by the wrist, her stonekin's giant hand engulfing his entire forearm. She was about to yank him off his feet when a bolt of blue-white lightning exploded between them.

Gasping in pain and surprise, Tina stumbled back. "*What was that?*"

"Something to make you listen," James said, planting his feet in the grass.

She gaped at him. "You *fucking* tased me!"

"Because you were trying to drag me away!" James cried. "But I'm not letting you push me around anymore. I know I've given you little reason to respect me, but this is too important to let you ignore just because I'm the one saying it." He pulled his black staff off his back and stabbed it in the ground like a spike. "I am *not* moving from this spot until you read the agreement I've worked out with the king!"

For a terrible, furious moment, Tina was tempted to leave him-- just walk away and let him burn along with all the rest of this horrible city, but she couldn't. No matter how many times he let her down, James was still her brother, and like an *idiot*, she loved him. That was what made everything so hard, because no matter how badly he treated her, she'd never been able to turn her back on him, and this time was no different.

She wasn't above manhandling him, though. But when she reached out to grab him by the scruff of his neck, James danced away from her hand, lightning arcing from his fingers as he readied another spell like she was his goddamn enemy.

"What the hell are you doing?"

"What I said," James replied firmly, his eyes dancing in the white crackle of his lightning. "I'm not going with you. Not until you listen."

"That's not a choice you get to make," she said, grabbing for him again. "We're going *now.* End of discussion."

He shoved out his hand at her as she came in, shocking her with enough lightning to make her wince. When she glared murder at him for it, James glared right back, showing her his sharp, feline fangs as he hissed.

"Make me."

Chapter 19

James

"**M**ake me."

The words felt like hot rocks leaving his mouth, but James didn't take them back. There were only two options when Tina got this angry: surrender or attack. Surrender was usually the easier choice, which was why it was always the one he'd taken. This time, though, the stakes were simply too high. He *had* to make her take him seriously, even if it meant his life.

That wasn't melodrama. It was hard to put into words just how terrifying his sister looked right now. Her stonekin towered over him, an eight-foot-tall, half-ton monolith of blood-soaked armor and shaking fury, all of which was directed at him. Tanks weren't known for their damage, but James was dead certain she could turn him into paste.

Challenging her alone like this was a *colossally* bad idea, but even though the king, Ar'Bati, and Flameboyant were just a few dozen feet behind him, it didn't even cross James's mind to call for help. If he got others involved, the war they'd risked everything to stop would just start right back up again, and anyway, this whole thing was his fault. The reason Tina didn't trust anything he said was because he'd always let her down. He'd failed her so many times he couldn't begin to count them. He didn't know if standing up to her now would make a dent in all that bad blood, but he couldn't afford not to try. If he let her drag him off now, everything he'd sacrificed to achieve would be lost, and not just him. Fangs, Flameboyant, the king, the gnolls, Windy Lake, the kingdom of Bastion itself--they would *all* be in danger if he failed again.

He'd rather die than let that happen. His only hope now was to prove that this once--this *one* time--he wasn't the same old James. If he could just get her to see him as a worthy opponent instead of a screwup brother, she might just hear him out. It was a long shot, but it was the only

441

shot James had left, so he held his ground, clutching the Eclipsed Steel Staff firmly in his hands as he faced off against his sister.

"Are you really going to do this?" Tina sneered, looking down on him with emerald eyes as cold and hard as the stones they were made from. "You know you don't stand a chance, right? You're not even wearing real Naturalist armor."

She grabbed for him as she finished. Not slowly as she had before, but fast, her giant arm flying at him like a stone bat. For a terrifying moment, his whole body clenched in fear as the half ton of magical rock coated in legendary armor came hurtling toward him. Then a decade of martial arts practice took over, and James moved without thinking, ducking under her incoming arm and sliding the unbreakable length of his Eclipsed Steel Staff between her knees. When it was in position, he turned sideways, levering the weapon like a bar to knock her off balance.

Or rather, he tried to. The moment the staff hit her legs, it rebounded as if he'd stuck it into a moving car tire rather than a person, smashing him in the chest. The force took him clear off his feet, and he crashed to the ground a few feet away. Panicked, he scrambled back to his feet in the bloody grass, but Tina wasn't on top of him as he'd expected. She was still standing where he'd just tried to trip her, her face pressed into the palm of her stone hand.

"J, please stop," she begged. "This is super embarrassing. You're just making yourself look bad. I wouldn't care about that, except you're also making SB look bad since you supposedly beat him."

Remembering the promise he'd had Flameboyant write in the alley, James swallowed a retort about his fight with SilentBlayde. The Assassin was standing at the front of the Roughnecks' raid fifty feet up the grassy hill, talking with great animation to the other Roughneck officers while keeping a worried eye on Tina. But while James was relieved to see that SB had made it back safely, he knew he'd get no help from that quarter. No one was as bad as SB when it came to slavish devotion, but the other Roughnecks were also still loyal to Tina. If she said fuck it, they'd follow, then he'd lose everyone. This was the most important fight of his life, so when Tina gestured at him to stand down, James clutched his jaw and shook his head no.

"Dude, really?" Tina demanded. "You know I'm going to kick your ass. I don't want to have to hurt you. Stop being stupid."

"It's not stupid to fight for what you believe in," he said firmly, tucking the treaty into his backpack before turning to face her head on. "You say I always give up, but I'm not running this time, and I'm not coming with you. If you want me to go, you're going to have to force me. If I win, though, you have to promise to read my treaty and take it seriously."

Tina rolled her eyes so hard it looked painful. "Fine," she groaned. "But remember: you asked for this. Don't cry when I drag you out of here by your tail."

She cracked her giant stone knuckles as she finished, and nervous sweat began to bead behind James's pointed ears. She was so much bigger than he was--bigger and stronger and covered in armor even more magnificent than the king's. Every instinct he had was screaming at him to bolt back to Ar'Bati before she turned him into another bloody stain on the grass. If he left this battlefield without her, though, James knew he'd never see her again.

That was even more unacceptable than the shame of running away. He'd rather be beaten to a pulp than lose her yet again, so before she could get into position--before she'd even stopped rolling her eyes--James dropped into a crouch and sprang, using his catlike reflexes to launch himself straight at her face.

Her emerald eyes widened with surprise, but her tanking instincts were too sharp for such cheap tricks. A split second after he jumped at her, her shield was in position, covering her body in a metal wall. He couldn't even see her behind the door-sized slab of sun metal. But the giant shield meant she couldn't see him, either, and he used that to his advantage, landing lightly on the sun-metal wall on all fours before grabbing the top of Tina's shield and launching clear over it.

Feet flying over his head, James flipped over Tina in a perfect arc. It was a move his human body could never have pulled off, but jubatus were as agile as the cats they resembled, and the Agility gear he'd chosen to wear instead of heavy caster robes only made it easier. He was completely in control as he flew, grabbing her head in his hands as he passed over. When he had a firm grip, he twisted in midair, wrenching her head to the left. He wasn't trying to break her neck--even if he'd been willing to, he didn't have enough force to crack that much stone--but the sudden turn forced her to step sideways to keep her balance. The moment she moved, James turned again, throwing all of his weight and momentum to the left in an effort to knock her to the ground.

Even though his Strength and Agility were nothing like hers, James was sure he could've rolled a bus with this move. There was just no way she could balance all that weight on one unsteady foot. But though he'd executed the move perfectly, he'd underestimated Tina's tanking skills. Though Roxxy stumbled, she did not go down, leaving him scrambling on the wrong side of the throw as he crashed into her armored back.

It felt like slamming into a wall. James lost his grip on her head and dropped onto the ground with a grunt. He was already rolling to get out of the way, but Tina was too fast. It was almost unfair how such a giant stonekin could move like lightning, whirling around to slam her shield down on top of him, pinning him on his back in the bloody grass.

"Hah!" she crowed as James struggled. "Ready to stop yet?"

James ignored her and pushed with all his limbs, but the difference between them was just too great. All the strength in his body wasn't enough to budge the shield she held down with one arm. If he was going to have a prayer of keeping the fight going, he'd need to use magic. His Stone Grasp spell was powerful enough to punch her shield away, but if he summoned the stone hand beneath him, he'd wind up caught in its grasp, which would be comically bad.

He could alter the spell. He'd already done so once when he'd summoned up stone hands to grab Lady Siku and her guards. That time, though, he'd just been holding the normal spell longer than it was supposed to last. For this situation, he'd have to change the way the hand itself worked--tweaking it to push instead of grab. That was a big change for a spell called Stone Grasp, *and* he'd have to do it on the fly. Tina was already leaning her weight on her shield to slowly increase the pressure, clearly hoping to flatten him into submission. If he was going to get out, it had to be *now*, so James decided to give it a go, releasing the shield to grip his staff as he wove the orange-and-golden flows of earth together.

It was a *lot* harder than he'd anticipated. The Naturalist spells he'd learned from the game were part of his muscle memory. He didn't even have to think about how they went together. It just happened like habit, his body going through the motions automatically. Now, though, he felt like he was trying to knit a 3-D shape out of taffy while simultaneously doing long division. Even knowing exactly what he wanted, actually getting the magic into that shape was one of the hardest mental exercises James had ever had to do. If he hadn't had the giant extra Intellect boost from his staff, he could never have kept it all in his head. He still wasn't sure how he actually managed it, but the quickly escalating force of Tina's weight on his chest was a powerful motivator. Somehow, it all came together, and the moment it did, James thrust the magic upward, holding his breath as Tina's shield pressed his body into the soft earth.

A heartbeat later, the ground around him exploded. Four mighty stone fingers thrust up from the grass like pistons, striking Tina's shield and forcing it skyward. It happened so fast, his sister nearly lost her grip, shooting to her feet as she struggled to snatch her shield back before the rocketing stone ripped it off her arm. Suddenly free, James kicked to his feet, but he'd barely gotten upright before he was forced to dive out of the way as Tina smashed the still-rising stone fingers to rubble.

Shards of rock flew past as James rolled through the grass. Tina's gauntlet flashed by his head as she made a grab for his shoulder. Her armored hand missed by the thinnest distance as James dodged right, and he came up panting several feet away with his Eclipsed Steel Staff ready in his hands.

"Dammit, James!" Tina yelled at him as she got her shield back on her arm. "You're really pissing me off!"

"We can stop anytime you're ready," he told her, grabbing a fresh handful of earth magic out of the air. "All you have to do is agree to read the treaty I brought and--"

He cut off as Tina started to charge. Leaping to the side, James hurled the magic he'd gathered at her chest, folding the ribbons of power into a copy of the spell he'd used to pin down Lady Siku. The moment the magic touched her, stone hands burst from the ground to grab Tina's legs. But unlike the white jubatus noble lady and her guards, who'd been sitting down, Tina had momentum on her side, and she was a lot bigger. The stone hands barely managed to get around her before she kicked them free, stomping the rock into magically bound rubble as she charged James like a freight train.

Clearly, trying to stop a half ton of stone with more stone wasn't going to work. Swearing under his breath, James launched himself out of Tina's path, trusting his Jubatus instincts to land him on his feet as he changed tactics and started grabbing up streams of water and life, frantically tying the magics together until he had something that looked like a backward version of the Cleansing Spell. It was like nothing he'd ever tried before, but it felt terrifyingly close to the corruption and poison spells necromancers used. *So* close, in fact, that James fully expected his cursed staff to wake up and start purring, but it didn't. Now that he was paying attention, the weapon actually felt oddly empty, as if the presence that usually inhabited it was gone.

That seemed significant, but James had no time to investigate. He was already launching his experimental spell at Tina, who'd stopped on a dime and turned to charge him again, sword swinging to cut his staff in half.

James got the black metal out of the way just in time, snatching it to his stomach as the twisted life and water magics exploded in his sister's face. Her charge staggered to a halt as she started coughing, and James's hopes soared. Unfortunately, aside from that initial stumble, not being able to breathe didn't seem to slow her down at all. The smile had barely made it to his face before Tina lurched forward again and plowed into him.

Smashing into her shield felt like falling face first onto pavement. The front of James's body exploded in pain as he flew backward. As always, his instincts came to his rescue, landing James on all fours in the bloody grass, but his head was still ringing like a gong, and blood was pouring from his nose. The world was spinning so fast, James had no idea which direction Tina was in or how close she was, but he could feel the ground shaking under his feet. Taking that as a sign, James picked a direction at random and rolled, getting out of the way just in time as the giant stonekin trampled through where he'd been.

Scrambling to his feet, James hurled a sloppy healing spell onto himself. It didn't fix much, but the euphoria blocked the pain from his ribs and chest, clearing his head just in time to see Tina turn and leap for him yet again.

So overpowered! James dove for safety, cursing the unfairness of it all. Even poisoned and having to contend with the physics of moving hundreds of pounds of stone, Roxxy was still more agile, faster, and quicker to react than he could ever hope to be. He didn't know if it was just their gear difference or if stonekin had a natural advantage now that the balance mechanisms from the game were no longer in play, but he was in a seriously bad position. Magic was the only edge he had, but she kept coming at him so fast, he never had a chance to work up a really big spell. He needed to buy himself some time, and when she backed him up toward the river, James got an idea as to how.

447

Flinging out his arm, James grabbed as much water magic as he could. There were tons of it moving in waves above the swiftly flowing river, so he didn't even have to shape it that much before throwing it at his sister. The result was a geyser of water that hit her in the chest like a blast from a fire hose. It wasn't enough to stop her, but the water's pressure and the mud slick it was creating in the grass under her feet did slow her down enough for James to stop running and start building the spell he actually wanted, sweeping his staff in giant arcs across the sky as he pulled down ream after ream of bright-white air magic. He piled it up as long as he could, wrapping the magic around itself while Tina struggled in the mud. Finally, when she was almost in grabbing distance and her face looked furious enough to crush his skull with her anger alone, James unleashed the power he'd been piling up, striking her in the chest with the brightest, biggest bolt of lightning he'd ever seen.

The resulting explosion threw them both across the field. Soaked and covered in conductive metal, Tina took the worst of it. James was only slightly singed when he pushed himself up again, but his sister's whole body spasmed as the electricity flooded through her into the ground. It went on for so long that James began to sweat. He knew she had tons of health, but it still felt wrong to straight-out blast her. He was hoping the electrocution would at least have temporary paralytic effect and buy him some breathing room to heal up, but that dream died as Tina planted her sword in the ground and pushed up, electricity still crackling from her armor as her enraged eyes locked on him.

"*James!*"

His name came out in a roar, and James flinched back. He'd never seen her this angry, including the day he told her he'd dropped out of college. She was literally steaming from the overheated water as she bent down and grabbed a basketball-sized rock to hurl at his head.

"You are *dead!*"

He dodged the rock by the breadth of his whiskers, but the second one hit him dead in the leg, snapping his bone like a twig. Pain exploded through his entire body as he dropped to the soggy grass, gasping and heaving as the nausea of the intense agony hit home. He knew from the shaking ground that Tina was almost on top of him, so he grabbed the first magic that came to hand, which turned out to be water and earth. He had no idea what he was going to do with that combo, but if his sister reached him, it was over, so he bundled the magic together and threw it, hoping for something useful. What he got was a miracle.

The moment the magic touched it, the riverbank, still sodden from his earlier water geyser, began to slide. Turned into sludge by the flood, the rich river dirt ripped free of the net of the grass's roots and gave way in sheets, and Tina's charge only made it worse. Between her pounding feet and massive weight, the ground simply couldn't hold. Even her godlike strength and agility weren't enough to keep her on her feet as the mudslide took hold, sending her careening like a tractor-trailer on ice down the hill toward the bloody river.

James stared after her in shock for several heartbeats before he realized how stupid he was being. Grabbing his staff, James greedily swept together the biggest healing spell he could hold. It dropped into him with a magical high that made his head feel like it was floating away. Normally, James hated the feeling of being that high, but he was desperately glad of the euphoria now, because the spell also popped his leg back together, repairing the shattered bone with a stomach-churning *crunch*. His skin was still closing back over the former compound fracture when James staggered to his feet, but while the pain was nonexistent now, his whole body felt exhausted, a sure sign that he was running low on mana. He was using it up too fast like this, but James had no idea what else to do. Martial arts were out. Tina was way too big to take down with the grapple he'd used on SB, and she wouldn't even feel a punch.

He was still searching for a solution when he spotted Tina clawing her way back up the mudslide. She was down on all fours, using her sword and shield to dig into the soft, sliding earth and pull herself up hand over hand. From the fury on her face, James knew better than to let her reach him, but he had no idea beyond that. He couldn't run, couldn't fight her hand to hand, and his magic was almost gone. Whatever spell he cast next would probably be his last. If he didn't figure out how to win in the next move, he'd lose everything--including Tina. She'd never respect him if she had to drag him back to her raid, and James would never forgive himself if he let her go through with whatever horrors she was plotting with wind-fire powder. No, for everyone's sake, no matter the cost, he had to end this *now*.

With that, James steeled his resolve and dropped low, clutching his staff to his chest. Across the destroyed slope, Tina finished her crawl up the landslide and turned on him again, her muddy face murderous. It was a look that would make anything with a brain want to run, but James stubbornly stayed put, holding his ground as she started to charge with her shield up and her sword behind it so he wouldn't know what angle she was striking from until it was too late.

If he'd still been fighting, that would have been a real problem, because she moved too fast to dodge at close range. But James wasn't fighting anymore. This was now do-or-die, so he let her get right up on him, crouching low on the shaking ground as she got closer and closer, sword finally snaking out to attack his left side.

When the red-runed blade was close enough to kiss his painted leather armor, James leaped up with all his strength. His body uncurled like a spring, launching him high into the air. Glaring at him, Tina shifted automatically, swinging her shield up to protect her head from another grab like the one he'd tried at the start, but James knew better than to bother. Instead, he planted his feet directly on her rising shield and jumped off it, using her own strength to launch himself up and away.

When he was high enough to see Xthr looking at him curiously from across the rooftops, he straightened up and looked down at his sister, far below in the sundered field. There was no chance of a safe landing from this height, but he was fairly certain even Tina's monstrous strength couldn't get her stonekin up this high. For the next few seconds at least, he was safely out of her reach, and that gave him the chance for an attack that was impossible on the ground.

Feeling slightly crazy, James threw out his arm to grab one of the truly enormous streams of air magic that floated high above the ground, the ones he normally never touched. Grabbing it gave him all the lightning he could ever want, plus a lot more he didn't, but he knew it was all or nothing. He grabbed as much as he could, ignoring the smell of burning fur as he wound the magic into a bolt the size of an old-growth tree and hurled it down at the stonekin standing directly below.

The whole island blazed white as lightning arced from his staff into Tina. It had to be enough electricity to power a city block, but James still knew one bolt wasn't enough to take his sister down. He needed more, so he transferred his staff to his right hand and started yanking in magic with his left, feeding the torrent and burning all the mana he had left as he funneled more and more lightning down the spell until his vision whited out and the whole sky smelled of ozone. Then with a jolt that ran from the tips of his toes to the core of his soul, James's mana suddenly ran dry.

As fast as it had come, the blinding light vanished. A heartbeat later, the ground met him with a wet crunch. Since he'd fallen from so high, even James's jubatus instincts couldn't do a thing to save him. He cratered into the mud with enough force to crush a normal person like a tin can. But as undergeared as he was, James was still a level-eighty player. Lots of things broke, leaving his body a ball of pain, but he didn't die on impact. He was trying to feel happy about that when he realized he couldn't see Tina.

Coughing and gasping, James forced his body up, looking around frantically until he spotted his sister kneeling in a smoking crater ten feet away. She was absolutely still, frozen in a defensive position with her sword and shield crossed above her head. She didn't even seem to be breathing.

For a horrifying second, James thought he'd gone too far. Stonekin turned back into stone when they died, and he'd never seen Roxxy look

451

more like a rock than she did now. Even her copper hair was gray and still where it had fallen over her face, making him panic. He was trying to crawl toward her when the monochrome grayness covering her body began to fade away.

Shuddering like an old engine, Tina shook her head and lowered her arms. The color of her armor, hair, and eyes blossomed back as she rose out of her crouch. Still sizzling slightly, she wiped the blackened soot off her face and turned on James.

He lurched back. His sister looked as mad as a bear woken in winter. The ground trembled as she roared and charged at him, but he couldn't get out of the way. He'd broken his leg again in the fall, and he had nothing left for a spell. No more deep-blue mana resided within him. All he could do was scoot backward across the ground pathetically as she skidded to stop in front of him, sword already coming down to skewer him through the chest.

Panicking, James threw his arms over his face in terror, but the pain he'd been waiting on never came. Instead, there was a metallic clang and a crunch as the blade sank into the churned-up dirt beside him. Then Tina's massive gauntlet seized him by his leather armor and hoisted him high into the air.

"What is *wrong* with you?" she bellowed, lifting him up until they were at eye level. "You made me use Earthen Fortitude, you jackass!"

His response was to raise his one good, shaking hand and punch her in the face. Fresh pain exploded up his arm as his broken fingers hit stone. The hit slid off Tina's cheek without even making her blink. It was the weakest punch he'd ever thrown bar none, but it was all he had left. He was working up the nerve to do it again when Tina dropped her head.

Her shoulders began to shake. James couldn't blame her. If he hadn't been the one hurting, he'd probably have laughed himself sick at that sad little punch too. A few seconds later, though, James realized his little sister wasn't laughing at how pathetic he was. She was crying.

"Why?" Tina whispered, her stone fist shaking against his neck where she held him up. "Why are you fighting me so hard? Do you hate me that much?" she demanded. "I was just trying to keep you safe! Why is it that every time I try to help you, you blow it up in my face?" Her stone voice dissolved into sobs, making her sound very much like the old Tina again. "Why are you always against me?"

The tears in her voice hurt worse than the broken rib poking his left lung, but as bad as the pain was, it gave James hope. If she was crying instead of killing him, that meant she still cared. And if she cared enough to ask those questions, maybe she'd actually hear him this time when he answered.

"I don't hate you, Tina," he said, leaning into her grasp. "I *love* you and I'm doing this to save you. I'm sorry I was such a jerk to you when we were kids. I'm sorry I broke your arm and ate your cake. I'm sorry I spent all our family's money then flunked out of school anyway. I'm sorry I ran away to FFO. I left our family with a giant debt and ruined credit, and I didn't even stay at home to help. I just worked a crappy job and made minimum payments and played FFO, and meanwhile, I left you--a teenager--to deal with the fallout all by yourself. It's my fault you had to make an FFO video channel to pay for college. My fault Mom and Dad had to constantly work overtime and were never home for you. It's *all* my fault, and I'm sorry. I'm so, so sorry, Tina."

There was nothing in that outpouring that James hadn't said to her before, but it wasn't until this moment that he realized how hollow his earlier apologies must have sounded. It was easy to say "I'm sorry" when you weren't doing anything to fix the problem. With the exception of playing FFO with her, James had never actually spent time making things right with his sister. Hell, even in FFO, he'd only helped her with the activities that amused *him*. When she asked for his help with raids or dungeons--things Tina actually cared about--he'd always found excuses not to go. Because *he* didn't want to. Because he'd rather zone out and have fun than spend a few hours helping his sister. No wonder she'd thrown all of his offers to "do anything to make it up to her" back in his face. Because whenever she *did* ask him for something, he flaked. He *always* let her down.

Well, no more. James was a different person than he'd been five days ago. A *better* person, and he was determined to prove it. He'd kill himself being the brother Tina deserved if that was what she wanted. Before he could figure out a way to make her believe that, though, Tina's head shot back up.

"If you're so sorry, why are you *still doing it?*" she demanded. "You say you're sorry, but you're *still* not on my side. You ran from me to go join forces with the guy who wants to kill us all!"

"But he doesn't," James said frantically. "That's what I've been trying to tell you! King Gregory--"

"*I don't care!*" Tina roared. "You know what I care about? I care that my own brother cares more about the damn NPCs than he does about me! You spend more time worrying about your made-up *cat brother* than you do about how we're going to get home or stay alive. It's just like back home! You get so caught up in what's important to *you*, you don't even notice when it stomps all over what's important to *me*. But I'm not that helpless little girl, waiting in the rain for someone to remember her, anymore! I'm *Roxxy*, leader of the Roughnecks, and I am getting us out of this mess."

She was shaking by the time she finished. James was shaking, too, but not out of fear. He was shaking with fury at himself for not seeing the truth sooner. Tina wasn't bullying him because she thought he was an idiot who couldn't be trusted. She was rolling over him because that was the only way she knew to make herself heard. Back home, no one listened to her. While he'd been a constant source of drama with his endless competitions, Tina had always been the quiet, responsible one. He couldn't remember the last time she'd made a suggestion anyone in their family had actually heeded. It was always "oh, Tina can take care of herself" or "Tina's tough. She'll get over it."

454

Even he'd thought that way because Tina was always so self-sufficient. It was easy to see her as a machine, but she was just human, and she was only twenty-one. She was barely out of high school, and she was having to lead an army and fight to the death to save the lives of people who depended on her. No wonder she'd reacted badly when he'd walked up and told her she was wrong. She'd built this entire camp to protect herself from Bastion. For all he knew, she'd lost friends in this battle, people who were never coming back. Of *course* she'd blown up when he'd walked out here and demanded she drop everything and do what he wanted. He hadn't even asked what she'd been through.

Just thinking about that made James want to bang his head against a wall. No wonder he'd flunked his international politics class. Relations between nations were always about understanding the situation from the other person's side, but he couldn't even manage that with his own sister. He was supposed to be bringing her a peace treaty, but he was the one who'd come out ready for a fight. All Tina had wanted was for him to come inside with her where it was safe because she didn't trust the king and had no reason to. He was just another boss to her, another enemy. James hadn't even taken the time to explain why that was false. He'd just demanded she take his solution, completely ignoring the fact that, from her perspective, she was winning a battle against a genocidal tyrant. Who the hell would just smile and accept a truce out of *that*?

Stupid, stupid, *stupid*. But while James could now see he'd made a mess of everything, he still had no idea how to fix it. He'd achieved his goal, he'd gotten his sister to listen, but he no longer knew what to say. But then, maybe that was where he'd always gone wrong. He'd always tried to talk his way out of his troubles with Tina, but what she really needed--what she'd always needed--was for him to *do*.

Ignoring the pleas of his battered body, James reached out and wrapped his one good arm around Tina's massive shoulders and pulled her into a hug. Or more accurately, he pulled himself in since moving Roxxy was impossible, but it still seemed to work. The moment he rested his head against her cheek, Tina grabbed him back, her huge stone body shaking with silent sobs as she hugged him back.

"I'm sorry too," she said, her voice gravelly. "I said some really unforgivable stuff, but I was just so *mad*. I'm sorry I hurt you and called you names and sicced NekoBaby on you. It was petty and mean and immature, and I'm sorry. You're my brother, and I love you. I'm sorry for how I've treated you since we found each other again, and I promise I'll be better, just please don't run away again."

"I won't," James promised, hugging her as hard as he could. "I swear, I won't ever abandon you again, Tina. Not here, not back home, not anywhere. I know I don't always explain myself well, but even when it doesn't look like it, I'm *always* on your side. All I want is for everyone to get out of this safe and whole, especially you. You're my baby sister, and I love you."

Tina really started crying after that. She kept apologizing for it and wiping her face, but James had never been happier to see her bawl her eyes out. For the first time since they were kids, maybe the first time *ever,* he felt like they actually understood each other. There was a lot more to go, starting with the two armies they were having this breakdown in between, but James felt more hopeful about the future than he had in a long, long time.

"Okay, I swear, I really am stopping this time," Tina said, finally letting him go with a long sniff. "I guess I should read your treaty now, huh?"

James blinked at her. "You will? I mean, I'd love that, but I didn't win."

Tina snorted. "You delivered the final blow. That makes you the winner in my eyes. But this whole fight was stupid, anyway. Let's just forget it happened and get you to a healer, because oh-em-gee, dude, you look like you're about to die."

James did feel as if he were about to die, but he was too happy Tina was going to read his treaty to care. He was very quickly explaining to her again that Malakai had been the one who brought the army down and that the king hadn't known anything and was the one who wanted to stop the fighting the most as she carried him back toward her raid when James heard the rasp of a sword being drawn.

They both froze, then James looked over Tina's shoulder to see the king was off his horse with his sword drawn. Ar'Bati's weapon was out as well, which was when James realized just how bad this must look. He'd challenged her to a fight and gone down. Now Tina was carrying his battered body away. They probably thought he was being taken prisoner again.

"Just a sec, T," James said, lifting up his one good arm to cup his hand around his mouth. "I'm okay!" he shouted at the king. "Send Fangs over, please!"

King Gregory did not look convinced, but he nodded to Ar'Bati, who raced out onto the battlefield on all fours. He stopped just short of Tina's reach, and she rolled her eyes.

"Do you want to go back to your Taco Cat now?"

"Just for a moment," James said. "I have to make sure they know everything's okay. You should do the same. SB looks like he's going to have a heart attack."

The Assassin was, in fact, already on his way over with NekoBaby in tow. Given how things had gone last time, James wasn't particularly eager to see either of them again, so he scooted back to Fangs. "I'll take care of things on the Bastion side," he assured Tina. "You need to read over the treaty, anyway."

"It's not just me," Tina said, finally looking down at the scroll. "My officers and I need to discuss this before we make any kind of decision. We'll go over the details and get back to you with our answer."

Just hearing her say that made James grin. He hated how she'd ended up here, but his sister really was a damn fine leader. She was already showing his scroll to SB while Neko strolled over to James, dropped a massive heal that refilled his entire health pool, then flipped him off.

Weaving drunkenly in the healing euphoria, James waved at the Naturalist's back as she flounced over to join Tina, then he turned to Fangs. "Did you see?" he asked his brother excitedly. "I did it!"

"I'm happy to hear that," Ar'Bati said, glaring at the circle of Roughnecks that was quickly expanding to include all of Tina's officers. "Because from where we stood, it looked like she was crushing you to death."

"No, no, we're good now," James said. "Or, at least, we're better than we were. But she's reading the treaty, which is a huge step!" His face broke into a massive grin. "We may get out of this in one piece yet."

Ar'Bati glowered at Tina's back one last time then offered James his arm. James took it gladly, letting his brother haul him back to his feet. Even fully healed, the damage he'd done to his body still left him weak and woozy feeling, and his mana was still at zero, which meant he was so tired he could barely stand up. Fortunately, Fangs was strong enough for both of them, practically carrying James back to the king to deliver the good news.

Chapter 20

Tina

Tina watched James limp back to the king, taking deep breath after deep breath as she waited for the jumble of emotions to settle in her chest. Feeling upended was pretty normal after a blowup with James, but the fact that most of the swirling emotions were good ones was a new development--a great one.

James had really changed. She didn't know if it was from getting trapped in FFO or if he'd been different for a while and she'd just been too pigheaded to see it, but she was glad they'd finally made something like peace. For the first time since she could remember, Tina felt as if she had a real brother, one she wouldn't have to corral or mitigate anymore. Maybe when they finally found their way home, she and James could go out for a drink or something--a cheap one since they were both still as broke as shit, but anything would be great. She just wanted to know what it was like to be able to talk with her brother and not have it be a crisis, which definitely excluded their current situation.

"All right," she said, leaning on her tower shield as she turned back to her officers. "What are we dealing with?"

"Whoa, there, cowgirl," Neko said, swirling her staff to build up her green magic. "First, we gotta top you off. Your brother took a chunk out of you! Not as big as the one he took out of himself, but still."

"I'm amazed he was able to come up with new spells on the fly like that," Anders said from the other side of the group. "We've all experimented a bit with casting, but I've never seen anyone take it that far."

"It was very impressive," Richard agreed, eying James greedily. "Can you make him tell us exactly how he did it?"

Tina chuckled. "James doesn't exactly follow my orders, but I'm sure he'd be happy to tell you whatever you want if you ask him. I'm not surprised he had something like that up his sleeve, though. James has always been a hell of a fighter."

SB's shoulders drooped at that. Tina was trying to catch his eye to give him a reassuring smile when Killbox slapped her on the back.

"Well, it was a great fight to watch!" the Berserker said cheerfully. "So does the talent for violence run in the family? You two must have some crazy parents is all I'm saying. Like total Viking-warrior shit, right?"

"No way," Tina said, laughing. "Our parents are former corporate wage–slaves. They held out until I went to college, then they moved to California to become organic hemp growers. They're part of that whole New Hippie movement thing now. I don't think they even get sober anymore."

"I did not see that coming," Killbox confessed.

Tina shrugged and clapped her hands. "Business, people. Business! We all know about plan B, but James might have just brought us a Plan C. Blayde's the only one who's actually read the whole thing so far, so I'm going to hand this over to him to tell us what we're looking at."

"It's pretty clever, actually," the Assassin said, holding up the scroll James had given her. "The treaty is based on an idea from Earth, actually. It's called the Forlorn Hope."

Tina scowled. "That's not an encouraging name."

"It wasn't encouraging back then, either," SilentBlayde said. "My military history isn't as good as James's, but I'm pretty sure the idea originated in Europe. Whenever an army needed soldiers for a particularly deadly operation like charging a wall, they would build up a unit of conscripts, usually criminals, to take the losses in place of their usual soldiers. In return for doing the dirty work, all the Forlorn Hope soldiers would be promised wild rewards if they survived, including pardons for all their crimes."

"Gotcha," NekoBaby said as she finished healing Tina to full. "So it's bribery, then."

SB nodded. "Basically." He pointed at a paragraph in James's neat handwriting halfway down the scroll. "The deal the king is offering follows those same lines. First, both sides agree to cease all hostilities immediately. Second, all combat-capable players are to be drafted into a new battle group called the Forlorn Hope, which will then be dispatched by the king to kill off the Once King's armies before they can attack Bastion."

"That sucks," Killbox said. "Not that we can't take them, but why are we the ones who have to die?"

"I'm not finished," SB said with a sharp look. "As part of this treaty, the Royal Knights will *also* be stripped of their titles and forced to join the Forlorn Hope as well."

Tina chuckled. "That'll suck a lot more for them. They don't have gear like we do, the poor bastards."

Several players grinned at that while SilentBlayde kept reading. "In return for our service," he went on, "all players will be pardoned for their crimes and granted citizenship within the kingdom of Bastion. The same goes for any surviving knights." He squinted at the page. "It doesn't say if the knights will get their titles back, though. I think those might just be lost forever."

"Good," Tina said vengefully. "Is that all?"

"More or less," SB said, rolling the scroll back up. "There's a lot of corollaries for specific cases such as what to do with knights who weren't stationed in Bastion when all of this went down, but the main idea is we fight for the king, and all of this goes away."

"Hmmm," Tina said, crossing her arms in front of her. "That's actually a lot better than I was expecting. Too bad it doesn't solve any of our problems. We want to get *home*, not fight an endless line of suicide missions for the king. I don't mind fighting, but picking our contracts as mercenaries is a far cry from being King Gregory's throwaway troops. If he decided to use us as suicide bombers against the Dead Mountain

461

Fortress, we'd just be right back in this situation, except we wouldn't have a fortress, an army, or plan B to back us up anymore."

Tina thought a moment longer, then she shook her head. *Sorry, James.* "I can't support this," she said firmly. "It's clear this treaty's trying to please everyone, but I have to look after *us*, and from that angle, this is not a good deal. We've been damn lucky not to lose any Roughnecks in the fighting today, but that'll change fast if we sign up to be shock troops. I don't want to spend months rubbing elbows with possibly backstabbing Royal Knights who hate our guts while stomping down every skeleton and zombie on the continent before we even earn the right to find a way home. I say we keep our upper hand and demand better."

NekoBaby bit her lip. "But what about the giant dragon, yo? I don't think wind-fire powder will bother him."

"The Bird isn't a problem," Tina said firmly. "Remember the Bastion Castle quests? Xthr's only here because he owes the king of Bastion a favor. If we blow the wind-fire powder, there'll be no more Bastion and no more king, which means no more favor. I don't think an ancient Bird's going to risk himself to keep promises posthumously."

She thought that made perfect sense, but the rest of her officers were strangely silent, staring at the ground.

"What about James?" SB asked in a small voice.

"Don't worry. I'm not leaving anyone behind," Tina said quickly. "We'll just tell James the other raid leaders have questions about the treaty. We'll also tell him that we need the king to release all of Malakai's player hostages as a sign of goodwill. The king seems to be in deep with my brother, so I bet we can make it happen. Once we get everyone over here, we'll all go inside the buildings to 'talk.' The moment we're inside, Richard will activate the fire wards, and *bam.* War's over, we win. Sound good?"

Once again, everyone was quiet, and Tina began to shift nervously. "What's wrong, guys? Why the long faces?"

Neko looked up at her, ears flat. "We were talking earlier," she said in a small voice. "And we kind of don't want to do the wind-fire-powder plan anymore."

Tina stared at her, uncomprehending. "Why not?"

"Because it's horrifying," Anders said angrily. "This isn't an attack that only kills our enemies. *All* of Bastion will be consumed, including innocents. Including other *players*. There were still refugees coming in as late as this morning. You know there have to be more out there. If we do this, we might live, but they'll all die."

"Why are you bringing this up *now*?" Tina demanded, looking around at the group. "You were all in the room when we came up with plan B. You were fine with it then!"

"Yeah, because it was only ever supposed to be a *threat*," Neko reminded her. "The plan was to kill the king's army, threaten him with wind-fire, and collect winnings. *Actually* burning everything to the ground was never part of the deal!"

"The deal changed when the king brought in a *Bird*," Tina growled. "We can't fight that thing! I don't like this any more than you do, but we're backed into a corner. Our only path to freedom is to fort up, blow the place, and see if we can make something out of the ashes."

"Or we could take the king's offer," Anders said. "It's a gamble, but if we can pull it off, the rewards are exceedingly generous."

The others all nodded, and Tina stared at them, slack-jawed. "Are you serious?" she said at last. "The rewards are only generous because we're not expected to survive! Do you *want* to be part of Operation Meat Shield?"

"We're pretty good at fighting the undead," Killbox pointed out. "And I know this will sound weird coming from me, but I'm as sick as fuck of killing actual people."

"Me too," drawled Frank, his face pale. "I chopped the legs off this one guy on the bridge, and damned if his friend didn't risk his life to drag him out. Poor bastard still died, of course, but not before he pressed some

463

badge into his friend's hand, tellin' him to 'take this to my son' while his friend cried over him and swore never to forget him. It was just like in the movies, only it was real." He shook his head. "It doesn't matter that I had good reason to do it. I killed some little boy's papa today. I don't want to do that ever again."

"I never want to do *any* of this again," Killbox said, his voice showing his disgust. "Pwning noobs in the arenas was one thing, but these last few days have been the grossest and most depressing of my life. If signing up with the king means I never have to kill a real-live person ever again, then Hail Bastion."

"The same goes for me," Zen said sternly, her dark face drawn and tired. "I'm a nurse. I'm supposed to be making people better, not shooting them full of holes." She looked at Tina. "I was the one who encouraged you to attack Malakai's camp, and I don't regret that, but if the king's offering us a way out without more killing, I want to take it."

"I can't believe I'm hearing this," Tina said, looking around the circle. "Did you guys not hear SB's history lesson? It's called the *Forlorn Hope*, not the Actually-Going-to-Happen Hope. The only reason the king's dangling pardons and citizenship in front of our faces is because he doesn't think we'll survive to collect. He doesn't want player citizens. His whole country hates us, remember? And even if we *do* survive, we're still right back where we started. The king will have conscripted himself an army of the biggest badasses in the world. You think he's going to just let us talk to his portal keepers and find a way home after that? Of course not. That's *stupid*. He's never going to let us go, which means we'll be right back to fighting him."

She grabbed the scroll out of SB's hands and shook it at them. "There is literally nothing in this deal that's good for us long term. I appreciate that you're all tired of killing. I'm tired, too, but we have to keep our eyes on the prize. We can't sell out everyone's futures for a cease-fire today."

"If it's *everyone's* futures, then we can't decide anything without Cinco and Assets," Anders pointed out. "This affects them, as well."

Tina's eyes widened. Anders was absolutely right, but if they brought this treaty to the rest of the players, everything would dissolve into chaos.

"We should vote on it first," she said quickly, stalling for time. "I'm not going in there unless the Roughnecks are a unified front."

As always, Zen's eyes widened in surprise when *Tina* suggested a vote, but Tina had this council thing down now. The only way the officers could override her decision as guildmaster was with a unanimous vote, and that was never going to happen because SilentBlayde was the Assassin leader, and he always had her back. He would vote with her no matter what, which meant Plan Wind-Fire was as good as go. She'd still have to convince the other guild leaders to go along, but she had no doubt Cinco would be all for burning this shithole to the ground. Assets wouldn't, but he'd be outvoted, so his opinion didn't matter.

Thinking it through that way, Tina didn't even know why she'd wasted time arguing. She should have just called the vote at the beginning and avoided all this drama. But late was better than never, so she turned to face her officers, careful to keep her face concerned to maintain the illusion that this wasn't just going through the motions.

"Okay," she said. "If you want to take the king's Forlorn Hope deal, raise your hand. If not, leave your hand down, and we'll go with the Wind-Fire powder instead."

Killbox's hand shot up, as did Frank's. Zen's went up next, followed by Richard's and Anders's. After a moment's hesitation and a nervous look at Tina, NekoBaby put her hand up as well. Tina was about to call the vote there when SilentBlayde slowly lifted his hand into the air.

Tina felt like someone had kicked the world out from under her. The other officers started chattering in happy relief the moment they realized the vote had passed, but Tina couldn't parse what they said. She was entirely focused on SilentBlayde as he slowly put his hand back down, his blue eyes locked on the ground at his feet.

Tina's hands curled into fists. "Why?" she whispered.

SB flinched from the quiet question as if it were a blow. "Because just looking out for ourselves isn't good enough anymore," he said, voice shaking. "We're part of this world too. I know you're only trying to save people, but we can't just kill everyone to get our way."

"*This is not our fault!*" she cried. "We were just defending ourselves! The NPCs started this! They should be the ones who burn for it, not us!"

"They aren't NPCs, Tina!" SB yelled back, lifting his eyes at last. "They're people, and they *aren't all bad*!"

"They *hate* us!" she reminded him. "I know! I had Malakai screaming his hate in my *face*! You think that's going to change just because we agree to be the king's stooges? You think every single one of those knights won't stab us in the back the moment we're weak?"

Tina didn't realize she was screaming until she heard the silence after she stopped. All the other officers were watching her and SB with wide eyes, backing away slowly as if they were afraid it was going to come to blows. Neko had even started a healing spell, which hurt way more than Tina had been prepared for, but *nothing* stabbed deeper than the hurt in SB's eyes as he stared back at her.

"If they hate us, it's because we taught them to," he pleaded. "Only one in ten of these people were in the Nightmare. The other nine learned to hate us the normal way: because we killed them. Or savaged them. Or stole from them. They hate us because we call them NPCs and treat them like they're not human, and they're not wrong!" He threw out his hand at the city behind her. "Our backup plan was to burn the biggest city in this world to the ground to save ourselves! Are you really surprised they see us as villains?"

"Don't you *dare* try to make us the bad guys here," Tina snarled. "We're the victims! We're defending an island of refugees from an army, for fuck's sake!"

"Refugee isn't the same thing as innocent," SB said, shaking his head. "You're not blind, Tina. You saw the dead townspeople in the streets on our way here. The knights didn't do that. You have to know we're protecting some players who've done utterly terrible things."

"Name one," Tina challenged.

"*Me*," SB said, pulling his ninja mask down to show his full face. Tina took a step back.

"Maybe your hands are clean," he said desperately. "But mine aren't. I killed good people because I thought like you do. I told myself they were all just evil NPCs, and that meant killing them was okay, but they're not, and it wasn't. They're *people*. Yes, there are psychos like Malakai, and yes, we should fight them, but most of the people on both sides of this war are *good*. We should be working to save *them*, not locking ourselves in a hole while everything else burns." He clenched his gloved hands tight. "I'm sorry, Tina, but I can't do this. I've killed too many already, made too many mistakes that can never be taken back. I need to atone for those crimes, not commit more. How am I supposed to live in this world when you're chomping at the bit to destroy it?"

Every word he said felt like a knife in her gut. What the hell had happened to SB while he'd been out in the city? Whatever it was, she desperately needed to fix it, stomp it down, and make sure it never bothered him again. She couldn't stand to see him this upset, but it was what he said at the end that cut deepest of all.

"You want to live here?"

SB froze, eyes wide. "I-I..."

Tina's fists clenched tighter. This wasn't exactly a surprise. He'd already said he wanted to stay once before back at the Order Fortress. *She'd* already been over all of this in her mind while she'd been tying herself into knots over him. But hearing SilentBlayde say it again now, in front of everyone... that made it real, and Tina didn't know how to take that.

"What about me?" she said in a small voice. "I can't stay here." She held up her massive hands. "I'm a giant rock monster! I don't eat, I don't

467

sleep, I don't feel, and every day, it gets worse! I can't live like this. I just want to go home and be human again. Not be stuck in this world with no indoor plumbing, where everyone hates our guts!"

"We'll find you a way home," he promised. "Taking the king's treaty doesn't mean we stop looking for a way back. Deciding *not* to destroy the city actually helps that because we'll still have the--"

"But you want to stay," she said again, the words coming out like knives. "Even if I don't."

SilentBlayde's eyes fell back to his feet. "I-I..." He stopped, body shaking. "I can't go back," he said at last. "Even if you burn this place to the ground, I can't go back."

Tina took a hitching breath. Honestly, that wasn't a surprise, either, but hearing it still made her feel like she was falling apart.

"Can you..." She stopped to swallow. "Can you at least tell me why?"

He shook his head, and Tina's free-falling despair did a U-turn right back into rage. "This is the same reason why me visiting you on JET was a no-go, isn't it?"

He nodded.

"And you're still not going to tell me," she said, fists clenching tighter and tighter. "Even here, in a different world you've already said you're never coming back from, you *still* don't trust me enough to tell me the truth."

"I can't. I'm sorry," SB said in a small voice. "Even here, the reasons why haven't changed. I just... I can't tell you."

Tina began to curse. She cursed loudly, and she cursed for a long time in every language she knew. It was a terrible, immature way to react, but she couldn't seem to stop. She just felt like such a fucking idiot. Nothing had changed. Three damn years of pretending she wasn't hurt, that they were still just friends and everything was fine, and *nothing* had changed. The whole damn world was new, and she was still an idiot girl mooning over a boy who didn't want to be with her, who'd rather live in the *ashes* of a world rather than go home with her. He'd even tried to warn her. Two days ago, he'd told her to her face that she could have everything of SB but nothing of Haruto, and she'd *still* deluded herself into thinking there was something between them. She was such a fucking idiot.

"Well," she said in the terrible silence after her profane tirade finally ended. "Guess I can't argue with that. You've made it obvious that you don't want me to know the real you. And you're not going back no matter what I say or do. *And* you're not going to tell me anything that might let me fix the problem or even understand why you're stabbing me in the fucking heart. I get it, but just so we're *perfectly clear*, I gotta ask, what am I to you?"

SB was ghostly pale by the time she finished. He stared at her with eyes full of desperation. For what, Tina had no idea. Probably to get out of this conversation, but she wasn't letting him off the hook this time. There was no game client to crash here. If he was going to hurt her like this again and refuse to even tell her why, then goddamn it, Tina was going to have one answer at least.

"I need to know," she said, her voice cold and hard as the deep bedrock. "Because all this time, I was thinking one thing, but it's clear now that that was wrong. So help me understand, Blayde, because I *clearly* can't get it by myself. What am I?"

She let the question hang, and SilentBlayde swallowed. "You're the most important person in the world to me."

Tina clenched her teeth until they creaked. "Bull. *Shit.* If I were important, you'd act like it. You'd let me in, let me help you, but you never do. You give and you give and you *give*, but you never want anything of mine in return. Do you know how much that hurts? How worthless it makes me feel?"

Her voice cracked then, and Tina turned away. "Well," she said bitterly, staring at the torn-up ground. "At least you can stop lying now, because I've finally figured it out. I'm your fucking charity case. I'm the poor, desperate girl you log on as SilentBlayde to go play rescuer for and feel better about yourself."

"That's not it!" he cried, reaching for her. "I--"

Tina slapped his hand away, hard.

"It was a great setup," she went on. "You got me whenever you wanted, and when you didn't, you could just log off, and I went away. No wonder you kept me out of your real life. Can't have me getting out of my lane, right?"

"That's not how it was!" SB said desperately.

"Well whatever *it* was, you won't tell me. So *I'm done*," Tina snarled. "I'll find a way to repay the money I owe you. I guess that means gold since you'll be staying here, but that actually makes things easier. Unlike Tina, Roxxy's rich, and I don't think I'll ever be playing FFO again."

"Tina, no," SB choked out. "Just let me--"

"Nope," she said, turning her back on him. She had to, or else she'd cry. "I can't think of a single thing that's left to say, except screw you."

She glanced at the other Roughneck officers, who'd been watching this whole thing play out in horrified silence. "Drama's over," she announced. "And the vote's been cast. Looks like we're done here."

"What about the other guild leaders?" Anders asked nervously.

Tina shrugged. "What about them? Cinco will want to burn it all, and Assets will want to take the king's out. That makes me the deciding vote, but you've already decided for me, so deal's done." She shoved the treaty's scroll into Zen's chest. "Take this back to the king and tell him we accept, but anyone below level fifty has to be exempt from combat. By fucking God, I'll stand on that bridge and tank you all myself before I let anyone throw the lowbies off this cliff."

"No call for that," Zen said, taken aback. "I absolutely agree that lowbies should be excluded, but what are you going to do?"

Tina pointed at the rest of the Roughnecks, who were still waiting with weapons drawn in front of the fire-warded stone building where every other player in Camp Comeback was hiding and counting on them.

"I'm going to go tell everyone else what we've done. And for the record, I hope you're all right and I'm wrong, 'cause we're gonna regret the hell out of this if you aren't. But the die's been cast. This is how the Roughnecks work, so I've got no choice. If we're screwed, we're just gonna have to make it work."

With that, she stormed off. SB tried to stop her, but she put her hand out inches from his face.

"Don't talk to me."

He jumped back like she'd taken a swing at him. Trying not to feel like she'd been punched herself, Tina kept going, shaking the ground with her steps as she marched up the hill toward the stone shelters.

Chapter 21

James

James did not like what he was seeing.

He'd come back to the king full of hope for the future, but his soaring good mood had started crashing as he'd watched Tina and her officers. Standing on the bridge, he was too far away to hear what they were saying, but from the way Tina was stomping the ground, it did *not* look good.

"She is truly terrifying," King Gregory said quietly, staring across the ruined riverbank at Roxxy before dropping his eyes to the gore-covered bridge and the corpse-choked river underneath. "They all are. I heard the players bragging of their prowess when I was trapped during the Nightmare, but I thought it was only that: bragging. I never imagined the truth would be greater than the stories."

"This is extreme," James assured him quickly. "You're seeing what happens when raid-geared players run up against normal people. The power difference the Nightmare created is monstrous. You've seen the evidence of that in your own body, but that's exactly why we needed peace. Even if the Once King weren't coming, the players have to be peacefully integrated into society and given a stake in this world. Anything less will just lead to more tragedy."

"Then let us hope they take your treaty," the king replied, looking nervously back at Roxxy, who was screaming what sounded like a stream of random profanity. "I must admit, it does not look promising."

"My sister will do the right thing," James said firmly. "Tina's a good person who takes care of her people, and her fellow Roughnecks are the same. We've offered them a fair deal that's in everyone's best interest. They'll take it."

The king looked reassured by that, but Ar'Bati's tail was lashing harder than ever. "Are you sure? For someone made of stone, your sister is surprisingly unstable."

"She wasn't born a stonekin," James reminded him. "She's human. We all are, or were. Anyway, she'll come around. I know it."

Flameboyant and Ar'Bati shared a skeptical look, but they didn't say anything else. James was glad of it. It wasn't easy to defend his sister as someone who valued peace when he was standing in the evidence of her fury. The bridge beneath them reeked of death, and the river smelled even worse. He was also concerned that none of the players had come out of the island's stone buildings, which he now suspected were fire shelters after hearing Tina talk about wind-fire powder. He'd done his best both to convince his sister and give the players a fair deal, but it really did look as if Tina's raiders were still planning to launch their attack. His suspicions turned to dread when Tina suddenly stomped off, shoving her hand in SB's face as she walked up the hill toward the sealed stone Trainers' Hall.

"Oh dear," the king said.

"It's not over yet," James said quickly. "Look!" He pointed at the rest of the group, who were coming in their direction. "Those are the Roughnecks' officers." And the Ranger in front--Zen, he believed her name was--had his scroll. "They must be coming to talk!"

"*Only* to talk, I hope," Fangs growled, hand going back to his sword. "That's a lot of magical equipment coming our way."

The players approaching them *were* armed to the teeth with the best weapons in the game. It was pretty terrifying to see in the current context, but James just shook his head and motioned for everyone to let go of their weapons.

"We can't talk peace if we look like we're going to fight!" he hissed at them.

The veteran knights gave him the stink eye, but Gregory nodded.

"Weapons down," he ordered, straightening up on his massive horse. "If this comes to violence, we shall not be the ones to start it."

Gritting their teeth, the four veteran knights released their sword hilts as the player group stepped onto the bridge.

Now that they were close, James was starting to panic. He still didn't know what his sister had decided, but SilentBlayde looked as if someone had just killed his family in front of him. That could *not* be good. James desperately wanted to run forward and ask what had happened before the group reached the king, but he was the one who'd written a treaty and made this into a formal situation, so he stayed put at the king's side, waiting nervously as the knot of players came to a stop at the zenith of the bridge five feet away.

For several heartbeats, no one said a word, then James realized that, as the connection between the players and the king, he was the one who needed to start things off.

"Um, Your Majesty," he said, gesturing at Zen, who was standing in front. "This is Zen, the Roughnecks' Ranger officer. She--"

"Actually," Zen said, pushing her emerald-green hair away from her face, "my real name is Kayla Johnson. Roxxy sent us to tell you that, on behalf of Camp Comeback, we accept your offer of peace but only if players below level fifty are exempt from combat."

James closed his eyes with a shudder of relief. The king sighed as well, though James was probably the only one close enough to notice.

"I am most happy to hear it," Gregory said, smiling. "I agree to your demand whole-heartedly. Thank you, Ranger Kayla. I cannot say how glad I am that sense has prevailed this day. Please accept my apologies for the conduct of my knights. I promise they will be held accountable, and I look forward to working with you and all players as Bastion's allies once again."

He held out his hand as he finished. Then his face turned slightly red as he realized that being an eight-foot-tall man sitting on the back of a massive draft horse, he was far too high for even the remarkably tall Ranger to reach. Shaking his head in frustration, Gregory quickly slid off his horse to the ground. He still towered over Zen, but at least she could take his hand now. She did so without hesitation, grabbing the king's massive palm and shaking it firmly.

"Just so there is no confusion," the king said as they shook, "you speak for *all* the players, yes? Not that I doubt your word, but I was under the impression that Roxxy commanded the forces here."

"Roxxy is the guild leader," Zen explained. "But the Roughneck officers vote on all important decisions, and we voted for this." She smirked. "We're not a monarchy."

That was a gutsy thing to say to a king, but Gregory actually looked relieved. James, however, did not like what he was reading between the lines. "Did Tina vote for the treaty?"

"She *voted*," Zen said, her lovely face a steely mask. "But she lost. This is what *we've* decided." She nodded at her fellow officers. "Roxxy's going to have to learn to live with it."

James shuddered, fur standing on end. No wonder his sister had been swearing up a storm. He still wasn't entirely certain how the Roughnecks' leadership structure worked, but he knew it took a unanimous vote by *all* of the class officers to override Tina. That meant SB had voted against her, too, which explained why the Assassin looked so gutted. That was good, though. SilentBlayde needed to stand up to Tina, especially since it seemed she'd voted *against* peace. That was a pretty horrific realization to have about one's sister, and James wasn't the only one who picked up on it.

"So Roxxy did not want to join the new Forlorn Hope?" the king said nervously. "You forced it on her?"

"Roxxy is stubborn," Zen said with a shrug. "But she keeps her promises."

The king shifted nervously on the bloody bridge. "Are you certain of that?"

For a moment, James didn't know what Gregory was talking about. Then it dawned on him. While they'd been talking here, Tina had gathered all the other Roughnecks and taken them inside the stone

Trainers' Hall. This meant that, with the exception of James and the Roughneck officers, all of the players were now inside the buildings--the *warded* buildings.

"James," Ar'Bati whispered, "didn't you say your sister was planning something with wind-fire powder?"

James nodded slowly. Then he shook his head. "She wouldn't do that."

"Are you sure?" Fangs growled. "I know you must defend her because she is your family, but we've all seen her savagery. She is not one who tolerates defiance. Now she's in there with her army while everyone who defied her is out here. Are you *certain* we can trust her?"

James's mouth went dry. He wanted to say yes, of *course* they could trust Tina, but that was just his gut, his emotions. The cold, hard reality of the situation was that she'd voted against his offer of peace. James had no idea why, but it meant he couldn't ignore what Fangs was saying or how bad a position they were in if his brother was right. He wanted to believe in Tina, but she had a very bad habit of making rash decisions when she was angry, and he'd never seen her angrier than she'd been today. It felt like betrayal, but there was too much riding on this not to be sure. He *had* to ask.

"Um," he said, clearing his throat. "I'm sure Tina will come out in just a second, but on the off-off chance she doesn't, what's the situation in there? Like, if she were to give an order, would the other players obey?"

The Roughneck officers shared a nervous look.

"There are two other guild leaders," the ichthyian Cleric, Anders, said slowly. "Technically, she'd need to get them on her side before any course of action could be decided, but honestly, that would only be a formality. CincoDeMurder and Assets command their own guilds, but Roxxy's always been the leader of Camp Comeback. Most of the players inside that building owe their lives to her. If she gave an order, I doubt they'd disobey. Especially since they know nothing of what's happened outside."

A horrible silence fell over the bridge as the fish-man's words sank in. Tina was inside a warded building with two thousand players who didn't know that peace was on the table. She was their hero, their great general. She could tell them *anything*, and they'd believe her.

"She wouldn't do it," SB said, but his voice was shaking.

Zen's was not. "She won't do it," the Ranger said firmly. "I've butted heads with Roxxy plenty of times. She's stubborn and reckless, and she needs to work on her temper, but she's not a liar. She already said she'd accepted our decision, and I believe her. She's just in there telling the others what's happened, exactly as she said she was going to. She'll come out when she's done. I know it."

The certainty in her voice made James feel like a horrible brother. He should have been the first to defend Tina, not the first to doubt her. He was about to throw his voice in with Zen's when Trainers' Hall's enormous doors opened, and Tina stepped into the sunlight. She was flanked by two other players, a tall human Berserker in bloodred armor and a golden-haired elf wearing what appeared to be a designer suit. These must be the other guild leaders, James realized, and they were not alone. Players of all levels were now streaming out into the sunlight, grinning and laughing and cheering in relief as they stepped out into the open air.

"See?" Zen said, lifting her chin at the king. "I told you."

"And I am ashamed to have doubted," Gregory replied.

So was James. He was almost dizzy with relief at the sight of Tina leading the others across the sundered battlefield. She still looked terrifyingly angry, but her weapons were sheathed, and more importantly, she was *here*. She was out in the open, coming toward him with the others in peace, which meant he'd done it.

"We stopped the war," he said breathlessly.

"We did it!" Fangs cheered at the same time, grabbing James in a bruising hug. "Wait until our father learns of this!"

James was grinning so hard his face hurt. He even gave the king a thumbs-up, which the monarch returned enthusiastically. The

Roughnecks were cheering as well, waving excitedly to the rest of their guild as the player group surged onto the bridge. The only one who didn't look over the moon was SB, but James would find out what had happened to him later. Right now, his focus was on his sister as she strode up the hill.

The jubilant crowd parted before her as she stepped onto the bridge, their happy shouts falling silent. Even the king shifted nervously as Roxxy approached, pulling himself straight to look her in the eyes, which was probably the only time Gregory had ever had to do so. James tried to smile at her, but his sister's face was a stony mask as she lifted her hand and dropped something at the king's feet.

It took James a horribly long time to realize the bloody cylinder of metal was a man. Not just any man. It was Captain Malakai. The tall elf was wrapped up like a mummy with chains that ran from his nose to his toes. He seemed to be conscious, but he couldn't move or speak through all the metal the players had lashed around him. He was still giving it his best try, wiggling like a caught fish on the bloody stones, when Tina planted her massive boot on his chest and flattened him back onto the ground.

"I believe this belongs to you."

King Gregory's eyes widened with horror. "I..." He stopped to clear his throat. "Thank you for not killing him. Despite his present crimes, Captain Malakai has long been a loyal servant of Bastion. What will it take to convince you to return him to us?"

That was a dangerously open-ended question. James fully expected Tina to go for the throat and demand the moon, but Tina didn't even seem interested in the king. She just looked tired and ready to be done with all of this.

"I want unfettered access to a living portal keeper," she said wearily. "Also, keep this asshole away from us. I'm not fighting him again."

She stomped on Malakai as she finished, causing the elf captain to scream what was obviously profanity through his multiple gags.

Wincing at the display, King Gregory nodded. "A fair request. I agree to it. I shall see to it personally that my portal keepers are made available to you as soon as is safe."

Tina nodded back and kicked Malakai forward, rolling him across the bloody pavement to the king's feet. The captain stopped with another muffled scream of rage, but his voice fell silent when he saw King Gregory looming over him.

"Captain Malakai," the king said, his voice shaking with anger and sadness. "You stand accused of conspiracy to conceal the massacre of innocents at Founder's Square, of disobeying sovereign orders, of conducting unlawful executions in the name of Bastion, of attempting to murder and torture children, of carrying out unjust punishments, and of leading the Royal Knights down a path of dishonor and degradation. What do you have to say for yourself?"

He reached down to yank the chains away from Malakai's face. The captain glared at him the whole time, practically spitting in rage as the king removed the gags from his mouth.

"I have only sought to protect the people of Bastion!" he snarled when he could speak again. "To slay evil and to punish the wicked is my duty as a knight. If I disobeyed you, it was only because you were too weak and cowardly to do what must be done. I would have saved this city."

"Your hate has done more damage to Bastion than the players ever could," the king said furiously. "Your actions today have opened wounds that will take lifetimes to heal! Your quest for personal vengeance led my knights down a path of vengeance and blood no atonement can ever wash clean."

"I led them to *justice*," Malakai hissed. "We fought for Bastion. While you cowered in the palace, we died fighting the player demons! How *dare* you call yourself king?"

Gregory closed his eyes with a sad sigh. "I'm sorry, Malakai," he said quietly. "You are right. I *was* cowering, and in my weakness, I allowed you to do this. I permitted this sickness of hate to consume you all, and our country has paid the price. But I will not let my people down any longer." He shook his head and looked back at his knights. "Take him away, Sir Townsend."

Malakai began to shout curses as the leader of the king's veteran knights leaned down and grabbed him by the chains around his chest. The other knights hurried to help, shoving the gag back into Malakai's mouth to stop the mad captain's stream of abuse as they dragged him away.

With a heavy sigh, Gregory turned and followed. James did, too, as did Tina and everyone else. They crowded onto the bridge a few steps behind the king as Gregory marched back across the water to the plaza on the other side, where all the knights--those who were still alive, anyway-- had gathered.

The army watched in silence as their captain was dragged away. Several of the men looked angry as he passed, but far more looked ashamed, staring stricken at their boots as the king stepped up to stand in front of them.

"You all know what has happened today," the king said, his booming voice heavy and sad as it echoed across the silent plaza. "Though you were following Captain Malakai's orders, you have all acted in a manner that flies in the face of everything it means to be a knight. By harming the innocent and killing for personal vendettas in Bastion's name, you have brought shame on our kingdom and violated your sacred oaths. Nothing can undo the damage that was done this day, but these crimes must have an answer. Therefore, it is with a heavy heart that I hereby strip every man here of his title and position. If you wish to reclaim your honor as a citizen of Bastion, you may serve alongside the players fighting the undead in the new Forlorn Hope, but never again shall you be knights. The title of 'sir' is reserved only for those whose honor and valor are incorruptible. I, too, share the shame of this, and I promise to help you fight and protect Bastion until a new generation of knights can rise to take up the burden we are no longer worthy of carrying."

The silence that followed that pronouncement was so heavy, James worried they would all be crushed. No one said a word as, one by one, the solders reached up and ripped the golden medals bearing the sunburst of Bastion--the seal of knighthood--from their tabards. These were passed forward and eventually gathered in buckets by the officers. When every knight had given up his insignia, the final pot was brought to the king by Sir Samuel Gardner, the soldier who'd nearly run the king over when they'd arrived and the first to confess the Royal Knights' crimes to the king.

"Sir Samuel," the king said, looking with surprise at the bare spot on the knight's chest where his insignia should have been. "I already absolved you of your sins in return for your truthful statements. You may keep your title."

"Thank you, Your Majesty," Sir Samuel said solemnly. "But I cannot. Not even the Sun can burn away the guilt I feel over how I've behaved these last few days. I wish to join my comrades in the Forlorn Hope, if you will allow it."

Gregory's shoulders slumped. "As you wish," he said. "I'll not deny a man his honor."

Sir Samuel bowed his head. Then to James's astonishment, the former knight turned to Tina.

It took her a second to notice. Despite standing directly behind the king, she hadn't actually been paying attention. She'd been standing with her head down, staring at the back of her shield like she was trying to burn a hole through it. She only looked up when Zen elbowed her, raising a copper eyebrow in confusion as the former Sir Samuel dropped to his knees.

"I cannot speak for my fellows," Samuel said to the ground in front of her. "But I wish to say for my own sake how sorry I am for how we have acted. We were slaves to our anger, but nothing justifies the cruelty we've inflicted. I cannot apologize to the dead, but as the leader of the players in Bastion, I hope you will hear me in their stead."

He said that with his heart in his throat. Behind him in the plaza, many of the other disgraced knights nodded, their faces pinched as they fought not to cry. But as much as Tina clearly wanted to tell them to go fuck themselves, she wasn't *actually* made of stone, and in the end, all she could do was sigh. "Yeah, well, we got a little out of hand too," she confessed, running a gauntleted hand through her bloody copper hair. "Um, consider it heard, and good luck to all of us in the Forlorn Hope."

James let out a tense breath as Samuel ducked his head before her one last time and rose to return to the mass of former knights. He was hoping that would be that when someone shoved his way out of the crowd and started marching toward the king--several someones. A whole segment of the knights had broken away from the others and was marching forward, and at their head was a man James recognized. It was Sir Dan, the knight who'd yelled at the king earlier, and his badge was still on his chest.

"You have no right to take the knighthood from us, you coward king!" he yelled, ripping his badge off and throwing it at Gregory's feet. "We *quit*! We swore our oaths to Bastion, and we'll never serve a man who would allow those demons to live among us!"

Gregory flinched as the tiny brass disk bounced off his boot, and James's hand went to his staff. Many of the former knights were reaching for their weapons as well, but the king held up his hand.

"The airing of grievances is the sacred right of every citizen of Bastion," Gregory said slowly. "Does this mean you will not be participating in the Forlorn Hope, Mr. Dan?"

Dan bared his teeth with a snarl. "Not on your life."

"What about the rest of you?" the king asked, looking out over the men who'd followed Dan up. "Do you agree?"

The others nodded, their faces curled in snarls, and Gregory shook his head. "Then you are all exiled instead," he announced firmly. "Every knight who fought here today shares the same guilt. If you will not fight to obtain forgiveness, then you must leave. Bastion's protection is only for those who honor the law."

"We wouldn't want to live in a kingdom that lets them be citizens," Dan spat, glaring at Tina and James before turning around with a wave of his hand. "Let's go, everyone."

Gregory scowled as the former knight led his group away, his face growing more and more dire with every man who peeled off the group to join them. In the end, there were almost a hundred who chose to follow Dan into exile rather than stay and fight alongside players. It was only a fraction of the whole, but it was still a lot more than James had expected.

"I fear that we'll meet them again as bandits," Gregory said quietly as the men filed out of the plaza. "Execution would have been more prudent, but I couldn't bring myself to kill them. It's my fault this happened. I was the one who let things get so out of control."

"It's not your fault," James said firmly. "They're not children, Your Majesty. 'Just following orders' isn't an excuse in my world, either. These men made these decisions themselves. It's their responsibility to pay the price for their actions."

The king sighed. "You say that, but we were all so abused by the Nightmare. If I'd come out on that first day instead of hiding, how different would things be? I didn't hate the players. I could have stopped this."

"'Would' and 'could' are a quick way to drive yourself crazy," James said. "Believe me. I know. I've been there. But we can't--"

The world lurched sideways.

Scrambling to keep his feet, James quickly realized that wasn't actually what had happened. The ground was still where it had always been, but the force pulling him toward it was swinging crazily in all directions. He could actually feel gravity moving through him in chaotic waves, and he wasn't the only one. Everyone else--the king, the players, the soldiers--looked just as confused and nauseous, frantically grabbing the bridge, the lampposts, each other, or *anything* that might be stable as they tried to fight the unnatural forces crashing through them.

"What the hell is that?"

"*Your Majesty!*" someone yelled in a booming voice. James's head snapped up just in time to see the stocky captain of the city guard ride hell-bent into the plaza. Armored men dove out of the way as the captain thundered past, pulled to a stop in front of the bridge, and dismounted so fast he practically threw himself at the ground at the king's feet.

"Speak, Captain Hightower," Gregory said, gripping the bridge railing to keep himself upright.

"Your Highness!" the captain cried, his face showing his desperation. "I led your soldiers to the Room of Arrivals to arrest Portal Keeper Star Fall as you ordered, but we could not get inside! The traitorous elf had already turned our barrier against player portals into a ward against the living. We tried to breach it, but the magic was too strong, and now I fear we are too late!"

A chill went down James's spine. "That feeling just now," he gasped, lurching toward the captain. "That wasn't gravity going nuts. That was a portal being opened! A *big* one!"

As if it had been waiting for him to give the cue, the whole city began to shake. Stone crashed in the distance as buildings collapsed, then the bright, sunny air was split by a gut-wrenching metal-on-metal screech. It was a noise anyone who'd raided the Dead Mountain Fortress knew by heart, even James. That was the sound the Once King's elite skeletons made when they spotted a player.

"Shit!" Tina swore behind him.

"*Well, well,*" said a voice in his mind. "*Would you look at that.*"

James jumped into the air with a yelp. For a terrifying second, he was convinced that the Once King was speaking inside his head. Then an enormous shadow passed over their heads, and James realized that wasn't it at all. The words didn't come from the undead. They came from Xthr.

The massive Bird flew over them like a supertanker, the wind from his wings blasting the men in the plaza to the ground before it swept over the river to land on the roof of Trainers' Hall. The giant beams split as the monster's claws dug in, and for a second, James thought the whole place was going to collapse under the Bird's weight. But Tina had chosen her fortress well. The stone hall creaked and groaned, but it held, serving as a perch for Xthr as the ancient Bird extended his long neck until his bus-sized head was hovering in the air just above the king.

"Fate, it seems, is not without a sense of irony." Xthr chuckled, his glittering crystal eyes flicking toward the north of the city. *"The Once King has saved you, Gregory Heraldsford. When you first called me here, I thought I was going to get out of this without having to do more than endure the hateful light of the sun. Now, though, it appears you haven't wasted your line's ancient favor after all."* The Bird flashed them a sharp-toothed, shadow-wreathed smile. *"I'm sad to say that you* won't *go down as the most foolish king in Bastion's history, though you may still be known as its last."*

"Can you not save us from this?" King Gregory cried.

Xthr lifted his massive head to peer over the city toward the plumes of dust James could now see rising from the northern side. *"I'm afraid not. As the fourth born of* all *creation, I am greater than any one sent against you but not all of them together."*

"All?" James shouted. "How many is *all?*"

The Bird swiveled its huge head back down to give him a scathing look, then an image shoved its way into his head. James gasped as his vision vanished, replaced by an enormously wide-angle view so terrifyingly high above the city, it could only have come from the Bird itself.

"Behold," Xthr whispered, *"your enemy."*

James stared in horror. From this high, he could see all of Bastion laid out beneath him like a tapestry, including the stately dome of the Room of Arrivals, which had been blown wide open. Sitting on the broken stone were two Birds. They were smaller than Xthr but still enormous--

enormous and *wrong*. Their giant, reptilian bodies were rotting beneath the swirling shadows, and their crystalline eyes burned with the haunting blue-white light of the ghostfire.

There was quite a lot of ghostfire, actually. Beneath the zombie Birds, the exploded shell of the Room of Arrivals was full of movement. There was so much of it, James's first thought was that it was some kind of attack, a spell to flood the room and burn out the enemy, but that wasn't it at all. As he stared at the blue-white flames, James realized he was looking at a portal--one *giant* ghostfire portal that took up the massive building's entire floor.

He was still trying to wrap his head around that when dozens more portals--normal-sized ones cast by the same sort of portal scroll James and Ar'Bati had taken from the lich and used to get to Bastion--opened all around what was left of the Room of Arrivals. His stomach churned with each new gateway, but the constant feeling of gravity flipping out from under him was nothing compared to the terror that clenched him from ears to tail as the river of undead began to flow through.

Armored skeletons, unarmored zombies, plague dogs, and archers shambled forward by the legion. With them came packs of giant undead war boars and wolves, their rotting flesh held together by metal plates and their empty eyes filled with the ghostfire. Whole *armies* of the Dead Mountain Fortress's two-skull skeleton knights were climbing out of the giant ghostfire portal in the floor, and behind them came even more horrific enemies: packs of three-skull dungeon patrols and undead bats the size of cars. Every undead enemy in the game seemed to be crawling over itself to flood out of the Room of Arrivals into Bastion, but the most terrifying thing of all was the giant skeletal hand that reached out of the massive ghostfire portal in the floor, gripping the floor to pull the body upright before Xthr took his vision back.

"*And now you know your death,*" the Bird said, shaking his huge head sadly. "*Pray to your Sun that the King himself does not take the field. I fought him many times when the sky was still warm but never more than to a draw.*"

486

"Then all is lost?" Gregory said, despairing.

The Bird answered with a roar that shook the stone. Even the undead stopped as the deep, primal bellow echoed through the city, then Xthr spread his wings and took to the sky. "*All has been lost many times, but still we fly on!*"

The Bird roared again, and across the city, two more ghostly cries rose in answer. "*My brothers cry to be set free,*" Xthr said, looking down on them from high above. "*Draw your Dawnblade, foolish king! This will be a fight more desperate than even Heraldsford itself! Now is the time to make good on the promise of your sacred line. Raise the shield of the Bastion, and let us fly once more to war!*"

With that, the Bird took off with a scream, streaking across the sky to intercept his undead brothers, who were already flying in with claws ready. There was a screech of tearing metal as they crashed together, but James didn't have time to see how the fight turned out. He was already turning to the king.

"Raise the Bastion!"

"I... I don't know if I can!" Gregory said, his face ghostly pale. "I already used up most of its power keeping it up for two days!"

James cursed under his breath. He'd known that would come back to bite them, but there was no point in I-told-you-sos. The screams of the undead were clear from all the way across the city. If they didn't get moving to stop them, there'd be no Bastion left to save.

"But how?" the king asked when James told him this. "You saw the Bird's vision! There are *armies* of undead, creatures from the Dead Mountain itself. How can we fight that?"

James was opening his mouth to answer when Tina beat him to it.

"With an army of your own, duh."

Gregory and James both whirled around to see the stonekin staring them down, a defiant sneer on her perfectly carved face. "Have you forgotten your own deal already?" Tina taunted, lifting her chin. "The whole point of the Forlorn Hope was to have players fight the undead in

Bastion's name. Well, the undead are here, which means I guess I owe you an apology, James."

James nodded shakily. "Can you fight them?"

Tina gave him the cockiest look he'd ever seen. "Who the hell do you think we are? We're the Roughnecks. We chew up Dead Mountain monsters for breakfast." She turned back to the king. "It's time for you to see the top-shelf quality of what you've bought. All you have to do is give the word, and we'll get your city back for you. But when it's done, we're free. Deal?"

She stuck her hand out in a stabbing motion, and Gregory grabbed it.

"Deal," he said, shaking frantically. "Save Bastion from the undead, and I will count your duty to the Forlorn Hope fulfilled."

"Good enough for me," Tina said, dropping his hand as she raised her voice to a deafening bellow. "*Roughnecks, on me! We got work to do!*"

Players scrambled to obey as Tina led them off the bridge, her face set in a mask of determination James recognized from her raiding days. That terrified him, because unlike raiding, there were no second chances here. A wipe in this situation meant death. *Worse* than death--with all that ghostfire flying around, dying in this fight could mean losing your soul to the Once King. If those blue-white sparks got into a player's body, they'd rise again as undead. James couldn't let his sister face that alone, so with a final look at Gregory, James left the king's side and raced to hers, sprinting with the rest of the Roughnecks as the city filled with the clatter of bone.

Chapter 22

Tina

Tina ran through the bloody streets toward the sound of battle. Behind her, she could hear the rest of the Roughnecks shouting at each other to keep up, but only one person actually did.

"What's the plan, T?" James asked, running up jubatus-style on all fours beside her.

"Find the undead. Beat them until they stop moving."

"That's not a plan!" James scolded her. "That's just angry fighting."

Tina rolled her eyes. "Fine, plan me, then."

Her brother stumbled in surprise at the request and fell behind for a second before racing back to her side. "O-Okay, then," he said, frowning as he thought the situation through.

Tina was happy to let him do the work. Her mind wasn't a happy place right now. The less time she spent using it, the better off she'd be. She just wanted to beat something into tiny, tiny pieces so she wouldn't have to notice how empty her shadow felt without SB inside it.

"The Once King's been planning this invasion since the Deadlands opened," James said at last. "And he's only gotten more freedom since the game became real, so I think it's safe to assume that he's sent all his big guns. The royal castle is the only place in the city that's defensible against the really big bosses, so I say we fort up there. Most of the civilian population and all the player prisoners Malakai didn't bring down here are already in the Diplomatic Quarter right next door, so it shouldn't take long at all to move them, but we'll need to evacuate all of your people from Camp Comeback. I think the best way to do that is to use the Royal Mile. It goes straight through the city to the castle, and it's got the most room to fight while still being narrow enough to keep the enemy from attacking us all at once. Once we get everyone inside, King Gregory can reactivate the Bastion to protect us."

Tina snorted. "*Can* he reactivate the Bastion?"

"There should be some power left," James said, though he didn't sound certain to her. "But the castle's a huge fortress with only a few key doors to defend. Even without the Bastion, we should be able to hold out there for a little while. Either way, it's the best plan I've got. We just need the Roughnecks to keep the undead back long enough to get everyone inside."

"We'll do that," Tina said, looking down at her brother. "Now get off the front lines. You're out of mana, and there's no time to recover."

She expected James to balk at that, but he just nodded. "I'll be with the king!" he called as he peeled off. "Come find me later at the castle!"

Tina waved at her brother as he vanished into the stream of players. The moment he was gone from her side, CincoDeMurder stepped up to take his place.

"All right, Tina," the Berserker said, puffing with the effort of keeping up with her huge strides. "What are we doing?"

"Roughnecks will take the big bosses," Tina replied. "You guys keep the small fry off of us. We'll take and hold the Royal Mile to make a safe corridor for everyone to evacuate to the castle."

"Got it," he said. "I like simple plans. Though you might want to add 'don't die' to the list. Might be kind of important."

He grinned at his own joke, but Tina didn't grin back. It wasn't that she didn't appreciate the gallows humor. She just didn't feel much like smiling or worrying about staying alive. Honestly, it all just felt like too much work right now. If it wouldn't have made her a quitter, she'd have charged right into the thickest part of the undead and gone out in a blaze of glory. That image fit her current dark mood nicely, but if she went down, there would be no good tanks left, and Tina was too much of a raid leader to tolerate that.

"Just make sure we don't get swarmed," she told Cinco. "I know all of the Dead Mountain bosses by heart, but a lot of them have stupid, complicated fight mechanics, and we're not in their normal rooms. We're going to have to pay extra attention if we don't want to get creamed, and we can't do that if a bunch of crappy zombies are gnawing on our healers. Just keep us clear. We'll handle the rest."

Cinco saluted and blew her a kiss before falling back to the rest of his Red Sands. Satisfied the Berserker would do his part, Tina turned back to the road and kept running--alone. The high sun overhead turned her shadow into a black pool at her feet, but nothing was inside it. She was reminding herself that was a good thing when the road she'd been sprinting down opened into a plaza, and the bank came into view.

The giant stone building still had its golden doors locked tight, only now they'd been reinforced with a shimmering golden raid-level ward. The army of level-eighty-one two-skull golems that had been standing out front the first time Tina's raid had passed by was nowhere to be seen, probably because the bank schtumples had pulled them all back inside, which was a shitty thing to do. The schtumples might not like the players, but they were all against the Once King, and an elite golem army would have been really freaking useful right now.

"*Cowards!*" she yelled at the sealed golden doors as she ran past. "You think you're safe in there? Come out and join the fight!"

As always, nothing answered. Sneering in disgust, Tina kept running, following the roads that wound through the sprawling city like roots until she reached the Royal Mile, the wide road that cut north and south through Bastion like a highway. Looking up it, Tina could see all the way to the castle gates. The Bastion was still flickering at the top of its highest tower, but the magical artifact's glow was much dimmer than the first time Tina had stepped out onto the Royal Mile a few days ago, and that made her nervous. Forting up in the castle wouldn't do much good if the king didn't have enough oomph left to keep the undead off them after they got in.

"Fucking Malakai," she muttered under her breath as she led her players around the bend onto the Royal Mile, which was still scattered with debris from the army's march on Camp Comeback. "Fucking waste of fucking magical artifacts on fucking *bullshit*."

Discordant shrieks tore through the air above her, and Tina instinctively lifted her shield to cover her head as the two undead Birds swept by like jetliners, bathing the elegant limestone buildings that fronted the Royal Mile in purple fire. They roared in triumph, their empty ghostfire eyes dancing as the three-block swath of the city to Tina's left erupted into shadowy flames. They were coming around for another pass when the whole sky darkened, and Xthr came in like a storm front, blasting them with dark fire of his own. Smoking, rotting scales fell from the sky like car-sized, blade-sharp hail as the attack sent the lesser Birds screeching and tumbling.

One of the falling scales almost ran Tina through, forcing her to jump to the side before she was crushed. "Goddamn space dragons!" she yelled, shaking her fist at the Birds as the aerial battle moved off. She was looking back to make sure no one else had gotten hit when she heard something crash on the road ahead of her.

Tina whirled around, shield up, then she skidded to a stop. A few hundred feet up the Royal Mile, something was kicking its way through the buildings the undead Birds had just flamed. A giant club bashed the corner off a shadow-flame-covered tavern as she watched, then a twenty-foot-tall skeleton emerged from a side street. Stomping down the rubble with its massive boots, it turned its ghostfire eyes on Tina and screamed, breaking what little glass remained with an earsplitting--and eerily familiar--roar.

"Holy Toledo!" Frank said, his metal boots throwing up sparks as he skidded to a halt beside Tina. "Grel'Darm's back?"

"That's not Grel'Darm," Tina said, nodding at the skeleton's head, which was only as tall as the rooftops. "Grel was eighty feet tall. That's his mini version, Prototype-GD. He was a special boss event during the Deadlands' opening. He's ten levels lower than Grel and only a four-skull."

Frank's hunched shoulders relaxed. "Oh, well, that don't sound too bad."

"He still sucks," Tina said. "He's weaker, but he still has all the same abilities Grel had, and he's got friends."

Sure enough, smaller undead were already pouring through the hole Prototype-GD had left in the burning buildings. The skeletal archers started shooting at the raiders as soon as they came around the corner, forcing Tina and Frank to put their shields up. She was about to yell for Zen to put the small fry down when a whole group of players thundered past with CincoDeMurder in the lead.

"Red Sands, hooo!" Cinco yelled, brandishing his spear as he crashed into the first line of zombies. The rest of his guild followed suit, bashing and smashing the smaller undead into bone chips while their casters and Rangers rained down death on the undead that were still trying to get out of the side street. Prototype-GD watched them in dumb confusion for several seconds before his ghostfire eyes flared, and he lifted his club. He was about to bash Cinco on the head when Tina pegged him square in the jaw with a broken paving stone, knocking out a tooth.

"Hey, Ugly!" she bellowed. "Your fight's over here!"

With a roar that shook the street, Prototype-GD forgot all about Cinco and started toward her, his giant boots cracking the street as he lumbered forward.

So grateful to have properly stupid enemies that responded to taunts again, Tina lifted her sword. "Roughnecks, *charge!*"

She pounded forward as she finished, bracing her shield in front of her like the cattle guard on a train as she closed the final distance between her and the boss. Screeching like a band saw, the twenty-foot giant raised its club over its head with both hands, its ghostfire eyes blazing.

"Roxxy!" Frank yelled frantically behind her. "Isn't that Howling Strike?"

It was, but unlike the mountain of Grel'Darm--whose Howling Strike attack could and had pounded her into a stonekin-pancake--

493

Prototype-GD wasn't even level eighty. He was only twice her height, his club only as long as a tree branch rather than an entire tree. Charging him head on was still a stupid, reckless thing to do, but Tina was feeling stupid and reckless and way too ready to punch something, so she ignored the attack signals and threw herself at the boss like a stone wrecking ball.

Prototype-GD's Howling Strike landed as she came in. Tina swerved at the last second, avoiding the tree-limb-sized club by less than an inch as she leaped forward to tackle the monster around its bony knees. The sudden impact was enough to make the monster stumble, but the real magic didn't happen until Tina took a page from James's book and twisted, throwing her weight to the side just as her brother had done during their fight.

Her spin wasn't nearly as well executed as his had been, but the weight difference between her and the mini-Grel was a lot smaller than it had been for her and James, so it still worked, spinning them both so that they landed on the cobblestone street with her on top. The moment they hit, SilentBlayde and ZeroDarkness leaped from the skeleton's shadow, their flashing blades sending clouds of bone chips into the air. The other Roughneck Berserkers and Knights arrived a heartbeat later, adding their weight to Tina's as they swarmed the giant skeleton and started hacking it to bits.

"Grab the other leg, Frank!" Tina yelled over the deafening ring of steel on bone. "Hold it down!"

Holding one kicking leg each, the two tanks kept the skeleton from kicking its way off its back or kicking anyone into the nearby buildings. They were still struggling to hold it still when the ghostfire in its eyes flashed.

"Chain Fire incoming!" Tina yelled as the heat began to build. "Healers--"

"*On it!*" NekoBaby yelled from surprisingly close by.

Startled, Tina looked up to see the jubatus standing right behind her, holding a massive ball of water over the melee's heads. Even more surprising, Anders was next to her, feeding golden holy magic into the Naturalist's water spell. The end result looked a bit like a giant water disco ball, but before Tina could ask what they hell they were doing, the skeleton screamed, and the Chain Fire began. Screams filled the air as raiders erupted in blue-white ghostfire. Tina was struck as well, her body exploding in fire even as her mind was engulfed with hatred for the living. She was struggling to hold it together when NekoBaby's voice shouted in her ear.

"*Holy Water Shutdown!*"

Tina braced for the relief of the heal, but the Naturalist's spell didn't fly at her. Instead, NekoBaby swung her glowing staff like a bat, slamming the ball of glittering golden water straight up the skeleton's nose. Prototype-GD shrieked as golden light and aqua energy blasted from every crack in its body. The ghostfire searing through Tina vanished a second later, taking the unnatural hate with it as the boss's Chain Fire snuffed out.

"Oh yeah!" Neko said, preening. "Who's got two thumbs and just shut down an uninterruptable attack? *This* girl!"

"You were supposed to be healing," Tina said but not angrily. It was hard to be mad at someone who'd found a way to short out a boss's most painful attack before it hit more than a handful of people. Heals were already coming in from the Roughnecks' other casters, in any case, soothing her burned stone and filling her with euphoria as the Roughnecks continued hacking the skeleton boss to pieces. When it was small enough that Tina no longer needed to hold it down, she pushed up and turned to the casters.

"Good job."

Neko beamed. Anders smiled as well, though the happiness vanished when Neko shot him a nasty look and dragged her finger across her neck. Clearly, their team-up had been a temporary truce. Tina was just happy it had worked so well. These fights were going to be a *lot* easier if they weren't stuck with the same old spells and mechanics from the game.

495

They were going to need it. In the few minutes it had taken them to take down Prototype-GD, the northern half of the Royal Mile had filled with undead. Packs of zombies and undead hounds were swarming in from the west, pouring into the Royal Mile from every street that connected this part of the city with the Room of Arrivals. It was hard to tell since they were stuffed in between buildings instead of spread over a battlefield, but Tina estimated that the army here was already at least as big as the one that had attacked the Order's fortress--possibly larger.

The only good part was that these zombies seemed to be much lower level than the ones they'd faced in the Deadlands. Cinco's group was chopping them down by the dozens, which was why the Roughnecks hadn't already been overwhelmed, but it wouldn't last. Already, the sheer size of the horde was forcing the Red Sands to spread themselves perilously thin, and the enemy was still coming, pouring into the Royal Mile from every alley and shop window. If this kept up, they were going to be surrounded on all sides.

"We need a bigger push!" Tina yelled, leaving her guild to finish off Prototype-GD to look for another option.

She found it in the form of Assets. The elf was right behind her, leading the main mass of players from Camp Comeback from the back of a white warhorse that looked suspiciously like the one Captain Malakai had been riding when he'd first come in. But while the players behind him were all lower-level fighters from the random and support raids, they were all armed with new, at-level equipment thanks to the quests they'd completed, and that gave Tina an idea.

"We need to secure the Royal Mile so people can get to the castle," she told Assets. "Can your people back up Cinco and push the line?"

"We can do far better than that," Assets said, straightening up on his saddle as he lifted his diamond-tipped cane into the air. "*Shields forward!*"

At his command, dozens of lower-level Knight players carrying pilfered tower shields from the Royal Knights marched forward in a line.

496

Zombies crashed into their ranks, but while the Royal Knights' equipment hadn't held for beans against the raiders' end-game weapons, they did just fine against low-level undead. Locked together in formation, the players' shield wall didn't even wobble as the Once King's shock troops smashed themselves into it, and the surprises weren't over yet.

"Cavalry!" Assets yelled again, waving his cane over his head like a saber. "Attack!"

Tina's jaw dropped as dozens of Trade Company Sorcerers and Rangers--all mounted on horses just like Assets'--rode past to take up position behind the shield wall. The height advantage of the horses gave them a clear shot over the Knights, and they used it ruthlessly, pouring fire down on the zombies who were scrabbling helplessly against the smooth steel of the stolen shields. When those were down, they fired into the undead's back lines, painting the street with arrows and fire and opening up clear ground for the shield wall to move forward in a line.

"Where the hell did you get the horses?" Tina asked when she got over her shock.

Assets smirked at her from the back of his armored steed. "The Royal Knights were suffering from an over-supply of horses and an under-supply of riders. I merely took advantage of the imbalance."

Tina arched an eyebrow. "Isn't that stealing? I thought we were supposed to be obeying the law now."

"No, no," he said. "On the way out of Camp Comeback, I managed to nab a copy of that contract--which I'm quite upset you agreed to without consulting us, by the way--from the Naturalist working with the king, and the language was very clear that our crimes don't get washed away until *after* this battle. Until then, what's a little horse theft on top of rebellion?"

Tina couldn't argue with that, especially given how effective Assets's horse thieving seemed to be. The Trade Company's shield wall had already reached Cinco's position, joining up with the hard-core killers of Red Sands to push the front even harder. But as the legions of crappy zombies fell, they cleared the way for more dangerous enemies, one of which Tina could already see coming down the Royal Mile toward them.

"*Roxxy!*" Neko yelled.

"I see it!"

Leaving Assets to keep the others moving, Tina ran back to her raiders, who were clustered on top of the pile of bone chips that had been Prototype-GD. NekoBaby pointed down the Royal Mile when she arrived, and Tina set her jaw. Through the sea of clambering zombies, about one block beyond the players' shield wall, two large mounds were crawling toward them. One was a literal moving hill made of dead bodies, its countless torsos and writhing limbs savaging anything that got close. The other was a towering ogre-like creature made from sewn-together bodies that left a river of caustic red slime in its wake.

"Crap," Killbox muttered. "They called in all the B-listers, didn't they?"

Tina nodded. The monsters crawling toward the player line were Corpse Legion and Dreadpool, the final two bosses of Ghostfire Bay, a ghost-pirate-themed--and *extremely* disgusting--raid that was only two tiers below the Dead Mountain. Normally, raiders could choose which boss they fought first, but this time they were both together, moving down the Royal Mile in formation like a pair of corpse-slugs on parade, and that was going to be a problem.

"Could Cinco's group keep one busy for a while?" Anders asked, his fish-face grim. "I don't know if two at once is doable."

Tina shook her head. "Cinco's busy," she said firmly, readying her shield. "Bosses are our job. Doable or not, we're gonna do it."

The other Roughnecks started shaking at that, but Tina didn't have time for this bullshit. "You're the ones who wanted to fight for the king," she reminded them angrily. "Put up or shut up."

With that, she turned and started jogging toward the Trade Company's shield wall. "Open the line!"

498

The lower-level players jumped at her bellow, then they got out of the way. A stream of zombies poured through the moment the shields parted, but Tina just bashed them aside, flinging zombies into the air with her shield as she stormed her way toward the double boss pull.

"Roxxy!" Frank called, running up behind her. "You sure you want to do this so far out in front?" He whacked a skeleton's head off with his sword hilt. "Looks a little dense."

"Hell no, I don't want to fight them out here," Tina snarled back. "But we don't have a choice. That shield wall's only holding because the majority of these are crappy zombies brought in from lower-level zones. Corpse Legion and Dreadpool are legit end-game raid bosses from the current expansion. If they touch Assets's baby players, our main line's going evaporate."

"Well, hell," Frank said, his face pale. "Guess we're in for it, then." He whacked a few more zombies out of the way to get a better look at the two monsters they were hacking their way toward. From the look on his face, though, he clearly wished we hadn't.

"Please tell me we can tank these guys without having to touch them."

"No such luck," Tina said bitterly, pointing her sword at the pile of bodies that was crawling over the zombies in front of it on a bed of severed arms and legs like some kind of horrifying human millipede. "That's Corpse Legion. It's a sentient mound of bodies that has to be tanked in a retreating circle. If you stop moving or it gets too close, it'll absorb the tank, which is certain death, so I'll tank him. You tank Dreadpool, the giant made of stitched-together corpses on the right. He's your standard tank-and-spank except for when he Liquefies. When he starts to shake, get the hell out, because he's about to turn himself into a bottomless pool of bodies. If you fall into that pool, it's certain death yet again, so make sure you stay out of the way."

"I'm hearing a lot of certain death," Frank said nervously.

"It's not too hard to avoid," Tina said. "Just make sure you keep Dreadpool off to the side and out of my way so I don't fall into the pool while I'm leading Corpse Legion around backward."

Frank sighed and whacked another zombie. "This sure sounds complicated."

"Welcome to raiding," Tina said cheerfully. "Though, to be fair, we normally fight these guys one at a time. Doing them together's going to be a dance, but just think of it like an achievement run. Just, you know, one we have to ace on our first attempt, or we all die."

That was supposed to be a joke, but Frank didn't even look like he'd heard her. He was too busy staring at the big corpse giant and muttering under his breath about cooldowns and not fucking things up.

"You'll be fine, Frank," she said gently. "You're with us. Everyone here has done a lot of raiding, and these guys are old bosses. We got this in the bag."

She said that a lot more confidently than she felt, but at least the lie helped Frank shake a little less. When she was sure he wouldn't fall apart, Tina picked up one of the zombies trying to bite her arm and hurled it at Corpse Legion.

"Hey, trash heap!" she bellowed as the flying body bounced off the corpse mound's side with a dull, fleshy *squish*. "Remember me? I farmed your gross ass for a year running! But I'm gonna be your last dance this time, motherfucker!"

It was a good thing that Tina was still so mad. If rage hadn't been pounding through her, there was no way she could have weathered the flood of fear that came when the giant corpse mountain--which looked and smelled so, *so* much worse than it had back in the game--turned and screamed at her, its mass opening in a black, bloody mouth made of hands to show a throat full of wiggling fingers as it started to charge, flinging zombies out of its way in its rush to run her down.

"Frank, go grab Dreadpool," she ordered, readying her shield for the pickup. "Everyone else, watch your feet and stay out of the tanks' way. All damage on Corpse Legion!"

The rest of her raid shouted their acknowledgment, but Tina could barely hear it over the wet *thud-thud-thud-thud* staccato of Corpse Legion's thousands of rotting hands and feet hitting the ground as it rushed her. Keeping her shield directly in front of her, Tina sliced wildly at the dozens of incoming arms reaching around her defenses to try to grab her. The sun vanished as the giant monster loomed over her head like a crashing wave about to break. Taking her cue, Tina jumped backward, getting out of the way just in time before a metric ton of mangled bodies collapsed on the spot where she'd been.

Struggling to find her rhythm, Tina kept backing up, using her sword to cut off all the hands, legs, arms, fingers, and teeth the monster tried to slip around her shield. Back in the game, Corpse Legion had come at a fixed rate. Now, though, all the bodies in the pile seemed to be going for her at their own speed, forcing Tina to move in fits and starts as she struggled to balance not getting buried under the constantly collapsing corpses and not getting so far out in front that the boss lost interest in her and went for someone else.

Walking in the right direction was also a challenge. Richard and the Sorcerers had cleared the area immediately around them of undead using their big-area spells, but with so many enemies, there was only so much space they could keep open while still attacking the boss. This meant Tina only had a tight circle to lead Corpse Legion around that didn't have her bumping into the other players or wandering into the space where Frank was hopefully tanking Dreadpool.

Not that she could see the other tank while walking backward. She couldn't even see if the Roughnecks were doing damage over the giant pile of bodies in front of her. All she could see were the bodies that were constantly collapsing toward her head, and even that was almost more than she could handle.

Corpse Legion might not have been as strong as something like Grel'Darm, but all the little hits mattered. For every three limbs Tina hacked away, one or two got through, and all that damage was quickly adding up. By the time Tina started her second lap around the circle, she was bruised and battered. Heals landed on her every now and again when things got a bit too bad, but she could tell her healers were conserving their mana, which was smart. Even after they defeated these two, they were in for a long fight. It made sense not to over-heal small damage, and honestly, Tina kind of liked the pain. It kept her focused on the fight and off the pair of flickering silver swords she could see hacking huge chunks out of Corpse Legion's corpse pile in the corner of her vision.

By the time she started her third lap, the Roughnecks had managed to hack the boss down to half its starting size. She was starting to think this might not be so bad when a shout went up behind her.

"He's shaking!" Frank yelled, his voice surprisingly close. "Scatter, people, scatter!"

"*Tina!*" SB yelled at the same time.

Jumping at his voice, Tina looked over her shoulder to see that she was not where she'd thought she was. She'd thought she was still walking backward in her circle, but she must have drifted a bit, because she was actually much closer to the little fountain courtyard Frank had been tanking Dreadpool against than she'd realized. Frank was actually running straight past her, his face a mask of terror as he realized what their positions meant.

Tina realized the truth at the same time, which turned out to be far, far too late. Dreadpool had already shaken himself into a growing pool of angry red slime, the edge of which was already touching the heel of Tina's boot. If she kept going backward, she'd walk right into it. If she stopped, though, Corpse Legion would collapse on top of her.

Stuck between two certain deaths, Tina did the only thing she could think of. She hunkered down, making herself as small as possible behind her shield as she popped all her cooldowns.

502

"Steady Ground! Earthen Fortitude!"

Her feet rooted to the ground, and the embrace of the Bedrock Kings rushed up to grab her a split second before the wave of screeching zombies crashed down on her head. All light vanished as the corpses consumed her, their hungry hands and mouths clawing and biting her from every angle. Blood and bile from thousands of leaking, rotting bodies poured down into her armor, nearly making her gag even though her stomach was as stony as the rest of her right now.

Unable to close her eyes due to her body's hardening, Tina stared into the dark of the grasping bodies, consoling herself that if she had to fuck up, at least she'd gotten eaten by Corpse Legion instead falling into Dreadpool. Her raid had already hacked the corpse pile down. Maybe they could finish killing it before her cooldowns ran out.

It was a desperate hope and a foolish one. As Earthen Fortitude faded and her flexibility returned, Tina still couldn't see any light through the sea of mouths and hands surrounding her, but the pain rocketed up as the pressure of all those bodies started to dent her armor. With no more Steady Ground to anchor her, the endless grasping hands pulled her off her feet, moving her farther into the monster's endless maw. As the pain mounted and the blackness grew darker, Tina realized with a start that this actually might be it. She couldn't even move her sword to try to cut her way free as the thousands of hands locked her down, locking her in place as the monster started to pull her body apart.

Then just when she was about to go to pieces, an arc of golden light flashed in the bloody dark above her face, carving off the top of the pile of zombies trying to eat her. A massive armored hand appeared next, reaching through the freshly cut chasm of clean-severed body parts to grab her by her breastplate collar, then an unstoppable strength ripped her up and out, pulling her free from Corpse Legion's maw to set her down at King Gregory's feet.

"Are you all right, General Roxxy?" the king asked, his sword flashing as bright as the morning sun as he slashed away the tendrils of arms and legs Corpse Legion was still sending after its prey.

"I'm--" Tina stopped, clenching her fists to hide her shaking. "Thanks for the save," she said when she could speak again. "I didn't think we'd see you until we got to the castle."

"I cannot lead from the rear anymore," the king replied, holding the pile of corpses--which was now only a quarter of its original size--back with the Dawnblade while the rest of the Roughnecks hacked it to bits. "And I didn't send you out here to die."

That was a welcome surprise. "Glad to hear it," Tina said, sighing in relief as a heal landed on top of her. "Where's James?"

The king turned and pointed back toward Camp Comeback. "Your brother said he was still 'too short for raid bosses,' so he stayed behind to make sure all the players got out, and to gather some kind of weapon. I'm not entirely sure what, but he asked me to go to the front and help you."

Tina snorted. "That sounds like James."

"He is most brave," the king agreed. "I am glad he stayed to see to the rear, because we have our hands full on all fronts." He pointed north, and Tina turned to see what was left of Bastion's army joining the Trade Company shield wall for a push. Between the two of them, they'd made it a good distance toward the castle, but the forward momentum seemed to be stalled.

"If we can just get to the castle, we can secure this road and use it as a pipeline to move everyone inside," the king went on. "The Diplomatic Quarter is right next to the castle, so it should already be evacuating. Once the players from your island are safely within the walls, all the noncombatants left in the city should be accounted for. After that, we can collapse this front and activate the Bastion. If it only has to cover the castle, then I think it will work."

"Sounds like a plan," Tina said, glancing at her raid, which had just finished hacking what was left of Corpse Legion to pieces and was now turning to Dreadpool, which Frank was still keeping cornered in the courtyard of what had once been a very fancy inn. "We'll keep doing our thing here. You go push that front."

"Are you certain?" Gregory asked. "You still have one more monster to defeat."

Tina shook her head stubbornly. "You paid for raiders. You're going to get raiders. Leave the bosses to us. You just focus on pushing to the castle. The sooner we get everyone inside, the sooner we can end this and write off our debt."

"Then I will go," the king said, smiling at her. "Good luck, Roxxy, and may the Sun be with you."

"May the Force be with you too," Tina said, flicking the blood off her armor.

The king turned and jogged back to his draft horse, which his veteran knights were holding for him a good distance away. "To the gates!" he ordered, sweeping his golden Dawnblade toward the castle. "For the Sun! For Bastion!"

The ground trembled as a thousand armored knights on a thousand armored horses yelled in reply and charged up the hill. The Trade Company's shield line scattered out of their way as the mass of riders trampled the squishy zombies and shattered fragile skeletons on their way to the castle gates. The level-eighty-knights' lances went through low-level undead like they were tissue, and King Gregory's Dawnblade turned a dozen zombies to ash with every stroke.

For a soaring moment, it looked as if the king's charge was going to make it the whole way in one go, but then the army of former knights crashed to a halt as they ran into the glut of undead besieging the castle's gates. Horses reared, and men shouted, hacking and slashing at the undead. Some were pulled screaming from their mounts by the ravenous hordes. Others were taken down by the enemy's archers. King Gregory himself took out an undead catapult, picking up the whole siege engine, wagon and all, and tossing it into the main body of the undead's army, sending zombies flying.

"Nice!" Killbox said, his face splitting into a grin. "Now that's what a raid boss of your own is for!"

"Hey, guys?" Frank shouted, his panic evident in his voice. "The big pool guy is still up!"

"Right," Tina said, dragging her eyes off the desperate fight at the gates and back to their own battle. "Back to work, everyone!"

Frank had been tanking Dreadpool the whole time she'd been dealing with Corpse Legion, and while he'd done a pretty good job for a guy who'd never tanked until last week, he was looking pretty rough. Freshly healed up from her near swallowing, Tina lifted her shield and charged the lumbering giant made of stitched bodies, taking its attention from Frank with one good shield bash to the seams that held its leg together. The giant roared and dissolved again almost instantly, forcing them all to scramble back to avoid its deadly well of blood.

Dreadpool lived up to its name three more times before they managed to take it down. The Roughnecks erupted into a cheer of victory when the stitched corpse giant finally fell over into a perfectly normal pool of blood. Tina let the celebration go on for a minute before yelling at everyone to shut up and get their mana back. While the casters ate and drank, she looked down the road to see how the king's battle was doing.

"Mixed" seemed to be the answer. The king and his men had cleared the force at the gates, but they were now pinned in by countless smaller bosses. There were death-infused elementals, corrupted walking trees, and even a giant rotting panther, and that was just what Tina could see from where she was standing. There were more waiting down the castle walls, filling the air with magics and special attacks as they pounded the king's army against his own castle walls.

"Holy crap!" Killbox said, coming up beside her. "How many *are* there?"

"The game has eight expansions, plus vanilla," replied Richard between bites of the choux bun he was eating as fast as possible. "Each expansion had an average of twelve dungeons, nearly all of which involved the undead in some form or fashion since the Once King was FFO's major plot enemy even before he was introduced as a killable raid boss. Dungeons generally contain between five and eight bosses, so do the math, and that's over three hundred potential enemies with a three-skull rating or higher. And that's not even counting all the special-world and quest-event bosses. Of course, the majority of those should be under level eighty, but I don't think that's going to help much given the sheer numbers we're facing."

"It's FUBAR is what it is," NekoBaby said around the apple fritter she'd shoved into her mouth. "This is worse than those dungeon speed-run challenges, and they don't even drop any loot!" She kicked the hacked corpse of Dreadpool. "Stingy bastard!"

"No complaining," Tina warned. "You all voted for this, so if you're mana'ed up enough to yack, let's fucking fight."

Neko cringed at her tone, but Tina didn't care. She was already charging down the Royal Mile toward the rear of the army surrounding the king's forces. Carving her way through lesser zombies, she picked the first actual boss she laid eyes on--a giant snake wreathed in ghostfire that she vaguely remembered from one of the desert temples. She couldn't remember exactly what it did, but she knew it was only a level forty, so she didn't stop to find out. She just swung her sword and chopped off its tail then leaped back into the air as the boss's blood became lines of spinning flame as they hit the ground.

The Roughnecks had to jump rope as they hacked the creature apart. More blood meant more spinning blades, turning jump rope into double Dutch. But as complicated as the mechanics turned out to be, forty levels was still too much of a difference, and the boss went down a minute later.

The flame spinners were still sputtering out when a lightning-infused undead boar turned and charged them. Tina and Frank caught one tusk each, then together, they hurled the entire animal into a boss made of swamp water and rotten plants. Steam and squealing erupted as the two collided, their magics misfiring as the Roughnecks ripped them apart.

After that, things quickly dissolved into chaos. A griffin boss covered in poison tried to attack from above, only to go down with ten of Zen's arrows in its wings. The giant slime that tried to suck them into its toxic sludge was turned into a cloud of noxious fumes by the Sorcerers' fireballs. The giant shadow panther split into seven smaller panthers that all went for healers, but the two Assassins took them all down first, killing each cat in one hit before the casters even realized they were under attack.

Since they were almost all under-leveled and made for three- to five-man groups, no one boss was particularly hard. The trouble came from the fact that it was never just one boss. They came in waves of fives and tens with no break in between. Each one had its own special considerations and mechanics. Some had attacks that could instantly kill even a level-eighty player if they didn't do things just right. Others were invulnerable to damage until certain conditions had been met.

It was the same old jump-through-the-hoops ridiculousness that had made dungeon fights so fun back when FFO had been a game. It was a lot less fun now that it was actually deadly and all happening at once, but this was the stuff that had gotten Tina hooked on FFO and raiding to begin with. She'd tanked *all* of this before, and she knew--or at least very quickly remembered--every single enemy they faced, and she kept that knowledge flowing to her raid.

"It's HarveyDangerGnoll! Grab blue orbs and avoid red ones! Here comes the Halloween boss! Catch his head when he throws it! It's the Ghostfire Ghost! It has to eat a priest before we can kill it! Anders, get in its belly!"

They danced through purple laser beams, slid on sheets of ice, and held their breaths through clouds of poison. Tina was burned by acid, doused in magical napalm, and at one point, eaten by a giant undead clam. Twice, she had to crack Frank out of a crystal iron maiden, and she nearly bit it herself when she slipped in the remains of a death-water slime and fell straight into the path of a massive zombie crocodile. It was only SilentBlayde's miraculous appearance that saved her arm from being bitten off. He stabbed out both of the boss's eyes in a single attack, killing the boss before its jaw could finish closing. As Tina pried herself free, he cast her a quick, sad glance before vanishing back into the Lightless Realm.

On and on it went. While the Roughnecks battled bosses, Cinco and the other Red Sands members shielded them from being flanked by the still-rising hordes of lesser undead, while Assets and his newly armored and mounted Trade Company kept the masses off the refugees and lowbies, who were still waiting to get into the castle. On the other side of the boss army, the king and his men were fighting a brutal battle to hold the castle's front gate.

Stuck in the middle of it, Tina wasn't even aware of the passing of time. Her whole world had shrunk to enemies and mechanics: hitting this not that, don't stand in fire, *do* stand in the blue stuff, smash the crystals, pick up the orbs, on and on forever. Then with almost jarring suddenness, she found herself facing a wall of former knights. Behind them, King Gregory was panting on his horse, looking almost as confused as she was. They were so caught up in the battle lust, it took both of them several seconds to realize what the fact that they were seeing each other--and not an endless wall of bosses--meant.

"Did..." She stopped to swallow against her dry throat. "Is it done? Did we kill them?"

"I think we did," the king replied, looking around.

They all looked around in awe, but sure enough, while the waves of zombies Cinco and Assets's groups were holding back were still going strong, the boss-filled square in front of the castle was now empty.

"Holy crap," NekoBaby said, her eyes huge. "We just killed, like, every boss in the game! There has to be an achievement for that!"

509

"The achievement is we get to *stop*," ZeroDarkness said, dropping his daggers as he flopped on the ground in exhaustion.

The rest of the raiders followed suit, falling to the ground or leaning on their weapons. The casters didn't even eat. They were simply too tired, flopping on their backs on the bloody stone. Tina wanted desperately to follow suit. Her whole body felt as heavy as stone, and not in the usual good way. But she didn't dare let her guard down yet. They'd killed off the bosses, but the actual point of all this fighting wasn't finished yet.

"Mana up," she ordered her raid. "And move out of the way. We've got people coming through."

The raid grumbled, but they did as she said, moving out of the way of the main gates Gregory was already yelling at his men on the walls to open. A minute later, the colossal doors to the royal castle opened with a groan, and the mass of refugees they'd been protecting all this time surged inside.

Tina slumped against her shield as the torrent of dirty, frightened people flooded past. She hadn't realized how much the responsibility of protecting them had weighed on her until it was suddenly gone. Now that they were inside the castle, they were under the king's protection, and while that didn't let her off the hook, she was no longer the one in charge of all the lives in Camp Comeback.

The relief of that was like a dam breaking inside her. Tina had to fight to stay upright, clinging to her shield as all the refugees and lowbies scurried into the protective shell of the castle, where they joined an already enormous crowd. As she stared at the wall of people packed into the castle's giant paved courtyard, it took Tina's poor, exhausted brain several moments to realize these must be the NPC refugees from the Diplomatic Quarter--the actual citizens of Bastion.

She stared at them in wonder. This was the first time since getting trapped that she'd seen regular people--not players, not soldiers, not knights or monsters or corpses or kings but average everyday people.

Other than being terrified, they looked surprisingly ordinary. Some were fat, some thin, some young, some old. Some had possessions in their arms. Others had nothing. There were parents carrying their children, an older woman protecting a very pregnant younger one with a kitchen knife. There was a girl with her puppy and a balding man clutching his terrified obese cat. They all just looked like people you'd see anywhere, but there were so many of them, and they were so scared.

For the first time since she'd arrived at the Order's Fortress, a stab of pity punctured Tina's anger. Of course these people were afraid. Their world was ending before their damn eyes. Even if they hadn't been trapped in the Nightmare, they'd come back to find their homes on fire and the dead marching on their city, and they couldn't do anything to save themselves. Tina couldn't imagine what it would be like to be low level and gearless, forced to hide inside walls from monsters who could swat you like a fly. How terrified they would feel and how helpless. No wonder they hated the players, Tina realized with a jolt. If she'd been stuck inside those walls, she'd hate the people who'd done this to her world too.

She was still reeling from that unexpected moment of empathy when a ghostly horn sounded in the air. The noise sent a wave of fear down Tina's spine, making her shoot bolt upright. All the other veteran Roughnecks jumped as well. Even SilentBlayde came out of the shadows, appearing right beside her as a deep voice shouted though the now-still city.

"*You will all feed the great pyre!*"

"Crap!" Tina swore, yanking her shield off the ground. "That's Sanguilar!"

"Sangu-who?" Frank asked numbly, sitting up from where he'd been lying on the ground.

"The Once King's Blood General!" Tina yelled back, reaching down to yank the other tank back to his feet. "He's the next-to-last boss in the Dead Mountain Fortress, the one directly before the Once King himself!"

"And that's bad?" Frank asked.

511

"Hella bad," Tina confirmed, holding up her red-runed sword. "He's the guy who dropped this. Sanguilar was the Roughnecks' world-first kill. We were one of the only guilds in the world who could take him, but that was with the *original* Roughneck Raiders guild back in the game."

"You think we can't take him?" Killbox said, insulted.

"No," Tina said curtly, looking the Berserker dead in the eyes. "Don't get me wrong. We've come a hell of a long way since the Deadlands, but this fight is stupid hard even for veteran raiders, and we don't get to try again if we wipe. We'll just be *dead*. Even if I had the best raiders in the world, though, I don't think it's possible to beat Sanguilar in these conditions."

"Why not?" Killbox asked.

It took everything Tina had not to roll her eyes. "Dude, did you do *any* research on the DMF fights before you got into my raid?"

"Nope," Killbox said proudly. "Now why can't we kill this fool? We killed Grel!"

Tina reached up to rub her suddenly throbbing temples. "Because Grel was relatively simple. Tough and hit like a truck, but he wasn't actually that complicated to fight. Sanguilar is *completely* different. One of his abilities is that he heals whenever anything dies within a hundred feet of him. Back in the game, we got around that by just not dying and by off-tanking all of his stupid endless skeletal soldiers way off to the side, where their deaths wouldn't pump him back up. On a battlefield like this, we don't have that kind of control."

She pointed back at Cinco and Assets's lines, which had already been pushed back almost to the gates by the ever-increasing army of undead, which was now picking up new recruits as the ghostfire from the zombies spread to the dead soldiers and knights at their feet, raising new undead to serve the Once King's will.

"If we don't kill the lesser undead, we'll get swarmed under," Tina said. "And if we *do* kill them, Sanguilar will out-heal any damage we can do to him. He'll be completely unkillable! Which is a problem since he's a five-skull motherfucker who hits even harder than Grel. *Worse,* unlike these stupid zombies, the Blood General's intelligent, which means I won't be able to tank him any better than I could tank Malakai. If he just decides to go and slaughter the healers, there ain't shit I can do about it."

"But--"

"But nothing," she snapped. "It doesn't matter how good or how geared we are. If we fight Sanguilar under these conditions, we are going to *lose,* then we're going to *die.* Our only hope is to not fight him at all." She turned around. "ZeroDarkness! Go find the king and tell him time's up. We're pulling everyone in *now,* and he needs to be ready with the Bastion."

The Assassin, who was still lying on the ground where he'd fallen earlier, lifted his arm weakly and vanished into the growing afternoon shadows.

"How the hell are we going to do that?" Frank asked as ZeroDarkness disappeared. "You can tell people to get inside all you want, but we've still got a lot of refugees to move through. They're already running for their lives, so it ain't as if they aren't hustlin'. It just takes time to move that many people."

Tina looked nervously at the crowd. There were still a lot of people outside the gates, not to mention all the players holding the line to protect them. She'd been hoping they could move in the defenders as the area they had to protect shrank, but a few Dead Mountain patrols had started appearing, mixed in with the normal low-level zombies. A pair of level eighty-two two-skull skeletons had already clawed their way through the Trade Company shield line before Cinco's people had hacked them down, and Tina could hear more screaming in the crowd. If they didn't want to lose all the people they'd just busted their asses protecting, they needed more defenders, not fewer.

"Roughnecks, move up to reinforce the shield line!" she ordered, her voice heavy. "We can't let them break."

513

Her raiders grumbled, hauling themselves off the ground to obey. Tina felt the same way. They'd finally made it to the castle. They were supposed to be *done*. But they couldn't rest yet. It would only be a bit longer, just until the last of the refugees made it through the gates. After that, they could all fall back and let the Sun or whatever take care of the rest. Until then, there was nothing for it but to suck it up, so Tina pushed her aching body into motion and jogged out to join Cinco on the front line.

It was terrifying work. Fighting the zombie horde wasn't as hard or as tricky as the bosses had been, but the pressure never let up. The Once King's army was endless and relentless, and now that they'd been in one place for a while, Tina was starting to see familiar faces in the crowd. Men in the armor of the knights and players she'd seen at Camp Comeback were appearing among the dead, their eyes glowing with the blue-white ghostfire. She knew cutting them down was a mercy, but that didn't make it any easier to run her sword through people she'd known--people she'd failed. She was focusing on just holding on when someone shrieked behind her.

A second later, she saw why. A red mist was rising in the hazy late-afternoon sunshine. It was subtle, but it was growing fast, the red mist condensing on the cool bodies of the zombies like bloody dew.

"Shit," Tina snarled then chopped down the undead knight in front of her before turning to bellow at the top of her lungs. "Time's up! Everyone inside!"

The whole square broke into a panic as the defensive lines began to collapse. Fighters and refugees rushed the castle doors together as the undead surged in. Still hacking at zombies, Tina shouted for her people to hold position until everyone else was in. She was still fighting when she felt someone step through her shadow, then ZeroDarkness was right beside her, his face pale.

"Please tell me the Bastion's about to go up," she begged.

The jubatus Assassin shook his head. "The king's in position, but the shield was lower than he thought. He's recharging it right now with the Dawnblade and a bunch of Clerics, but he said he doesn't know how long it'll be until..."

He trailed off, voice going quiet. When Tina looked up from her latest kill, she saw why. Ahead of them, across the now-packed square, the zombie army was parting, making way for an undead elf nearly as tall as she was. He was dressed in gleaming black armor almost as thick as hers, and his skin was as pale as a corpse's. His hair was a red so deep it looked almost black, and his eyes were an even less comforting shade. They were the same vivid crimson as arterial blood, the bright shade made even brighter by the light of the ghostfire flickering out from his pupils.

"He's here!" Tina called to her raiders, readying her shield.

The undead elf lifted a sleek, wet-looking eyebrow. "As grand entrances go, I was hoping for better than 'He's here,'" Sanguilar sneered. "But it is gratifying to be recognized after so long. I certainly recognize *you.*" His thin lips pulled back in a bloodthirsty smile as he kicked the remaining zombies shambling between them out of the way. "You were the first to kill me in the Nightmare. The only one left in this world who wields my blade." He lifted his sword, which was indeed a perfect copy of her red-glowing sword, right down to the unnecessary serrations that ran down the back. "You are the leader of the army that defeated my poor beast, Grel'Darm. Roxxy, I believe."

"It's *not* a pleasure," Tina snarled over the top of her shield. Then-- because every second he spent talking was a second he wasn't killing them--she went on. "But I'm happy you remember who killed you. That way, you can't say you're surprised when it happens again."

The general chuckled. "I think this time will be a little different from our previous encounters in the Nightmare," he taunted. "But if you want a rematch, I'm more than happy to oblige. Loser serves for eternity."

Before Tina could tell him to shove off, the elf lunged forward, charging her shield with lightning speed. Setting her teeth, Tina braced for

515

impact, crossing her sword behind her shield to give it extra support. But the general's blow didn't force her back as she expected. It took her clean off her feet, launching her into the air.

She landed three feet back with a crunch that cracked the paving stones, but at least she landed on her feet. Even so, she barely got her shield up before he struck again. She couldn't hold this time, either, but at least she had the presence of mind to tilt her shield down, letting the force of the blow bang her bulwark against the ground rather than launching her again.

When he realized the same trick wouldn't work twice, Sanguilar went for her shield. But Tina had seen Malakai pull that stunt too many times to fall for it now, and she whipped it out of the way. Crimson eyes flashing even redder with delight at a good challenge, the towering elf stabbed at Tina through the gap she'd created in her defense. But she was ready there, too, blocking his strike with the sword she'd had waiting there ever since she'd first braced her shield.

Identical crimson blades locked together as she caught his point with her cross-guard in the best parry of her life. Then she turned her wrist, twisting the strike away with every bit of leverage and strength she could muster. The general's blade flew off to the left, and Tina seized the opportunity to snatch her shield back into position. She barely made it in time before the black-armored elf slashed at her again, using a rising strike this time with both of his hands on the sword hilt.

The added force of both arms sent her tower shield flying upward. Unable to stop it, Tina let the momentum carry her instead, leaping upward to follow her shield with all her strength. The blood general's sword passed through the air under her feet as Tina came back down, crushing her boot into his face as she went.

The satisfying crunch of his nose breaking under her metal heel was short-lived. She was still digging her heel into his face when the Blood General took one hand off his sword to grab her leg instead. Tina felt as though her whole limb was going to pop out of joint as he snatched her

516

out of the air and slammed her into the ground. He was raising his boot to stomp her in return when Tina pincered his standing leg with both her feet and rolled sideways.

Caught off guard, the Blood General lost his balance and crashed to the ground, scattering zombies. Scrambling back to her feet, Tina was almost glad she'd had to go two rounds with Malakai now. Any less practice against such a Superman-level opponent, and she was pretty sure she'd be dead already. It still pissed her off how, with all of Roxxy's weight and strength, the four- and five-skull bosses could practically juggle her. She was only staying one step ahead of execution like this.

When the general pushed to his feet, she saw her opening. His eyes were still on the ground as he rose, undoubtedly expecting another trip, so Tina attacked his upper body instead, stabbing her runed blade straight through his sword arm. She swung her shield up to slam the edge into his throat at the same time, driving it down so hard, the wet crunch of his breaking windpipe could be heard even over the din of battle.

When she stepped back again, his whole neck was caved in, and his arm was pouring blood, which was enough to make her grin. Without hit points, there was no way to know how much damage she'd actually done, but it looked like a lot. Then again, for all his crazy-overpowered abilities, Tina recalled that the Blood General actually had a relatively small health pool for a raid boss. Maybe if she could just keep tearing him down, they wouldn't be doomed after all.

But her wild hope was short-lived. She'd barely finished admiring her damage when Sanguilar flashed her a bloody smile, almost as if he was showing it off. It turned out that that was *exactly* what he was doing, because the blood began to roll back into him before Tina's eyes. As if there were a whole raid of healers throwing spells at him, the Blood General's body put itself back together. The hole in his arm vanished, and his neck popped back into place. Even the bloodstains and the holes in his armor disappeared, leaving him looking exactly as he had before their fight started.

"You see?" he said, his voice mocking. "Your allies give me strength." He glanced at the battle, which was still raging around them. "It's not as if they can *stop* dying, and I won't let you isolate me in the corner of my room like you could back in the Nightmare. Like I said, *very* different, but you seem to be behind the times. I'm trying to have a real fight, and you're still playing nothing but defense. Do you even know how to do anything other than tank-and-spank?"

To drive his point home, the huge elf whipped his leg up with impossible speed to kick her in the shield. To her horror, Tina let him, leaning back frantically to keep her shield from smacking her in the face. She thought she'd saved it until she realized the kick had knocked her several feet into the air. She was fighting the urge to windmill her arms-- which would help her balance but leave her totally unguarded for the attack that was absolutely going to come next--when her fall suddenly stopped. Firm, armored hands grabbed her shoulders, and she looked back frantically to see she'd been caught by the combined effort of Killbox and Frank.

Seeing them behind her gave Tina a marvelous idea, and a grin burst across her face. "We've picked up a few new tricks of our own, asshole," Tina said as they set her back down on her feet. "Killbox, Frank, we're gonna Grel'Darm this guy."

The Blood General looked insulted. "If you think *I* will fall for any of the same tricks as that empty-skulled construct, you have not been paying attention."

Tina just flashed him another smile. "Get Team Hulk moving over there," she told Killbox, nodding at the tall buildings near the edge of the square where they were fighting, which were already on the verge of collapse. When he nodded, she lifted her voice. "Neko! Can you do that thing James did with the mud?"

"Yeah!" Neko called back. "I saw him do it! It's just water and earth. Easy peasy, Blood General squeezy!"

"Great," Tina said. "Wait for my signal."

518

"Oooh," the Blood General said, faking a shiver. "Water and earth, so mysterious! What's the little healer going to do? Make me a mud pie?"

Tina slashed at the jerk to shut him up, but the arrogant elf didn't even bother to parry. He just let her cut him then held out his arms so she could watch the wound heal.

"Come now," he taunted. "I know you can hit harder than that. What about your damage-dealing players? Surely they want to take a shot."

"No one else wants to waste their time," Tina informed him, slicing open another wound on his arm. "I'm the only one in a bad enough mood to play with you."

Sanguilar looked unimpressed. "You know I'm not bound by the game anymore. The only reason I'm bothering to fight a tank is out of recognition for your prowess during the Nightmare. But now I'm starting to find you boring." His smile grew cruel. "I think I might go kill someone else. Just to see you panic."

"Try it and see," Tina snarled, stabbing him straight in the stomach. It was just going to heal, but getting stabbed in the guts still had to hurt. Especially when she twisted her sword, widening the wound as much as she could. He wasn't mad enough yet. She needed him furious, angry enough to do something dumb. "You're not as hot-shit as you think, elf boy."

With a sneer, the Blood General reached out to grab her shield again. Tina whipped it out of the way, flicking her sword up to slice off his ear. It grew back instantly but not before he hissed in annoyance.

"Foul wench!" he said, lashing out at her.

Tina danced away. "*Wench?*" she repeated, laughing at him. "Dude, just because you're an ancient elf doesn't mean you have to talk like one. Get with the times!"

"I will do no such thing!" he snarled. "*We* are the originals, the celestials! We remember the days before the Sun's betrayal. You are all just twisted shadows of us! You know *nothing*!"

"You're a has-been," Tina said. "Just another farm-status raid boss. The only thing you've ever been good for was giving us a world-first kill and being a loot sack."

Sanguilar bared his bloody teeth at her, and Frank gulped.

"Are you sure it's smart to piss this guy off?" he whispered from Tina's side. "I know taunting is our tank thing, but he seems a bit unstable."

"He's mega-unstable," Tina replied in a loud voice, keeping her eyes on the Blood General. "The dude's older than dirt. He's gotta be senile by now, especially since he's undead. You know zombies all have worms for brains. I bet the Once King's even more degraded, not that he was very impressive to begin wi--"

"*Enough!*" Sanguilar roared, pointing his sword at her. "You shall not defile my king with your ignorant opinions! I'd hoped you'd be a worthy challenge outside the Nightmare's bounds, but now I see that the heroes of this banal age are beneath even my lowest expectations. Killing you so that you may know the glory of service to the Once King's ghostfire is a privilege you do not deserve!"

"So you're not going to try, then?" Tina shrugged. "That's cool, man. I don't mind if you give up and let us hack you to--"

The Blood General charged her with a roar, his red-runed sword swinging for her head. Even knowing it was coming, Tina still only dodged it by inches, jumping back out of range to force the enraged Blood General to follow her. When her back hit the crumbling front of the old guild registration building, she knew she was in the right spot.

"*Now, Neko!*"

Magic surged behind her and landed just as Sanguilar lunged forward to continue his attack. As his boot came down on the ground in front of Tina, though, a slick of soupy, wet mud bubbled up through the cracked paving stones to meet it. With no traction in the slick mud, the towering elf's foot went out from under him, sending him to the ground.

He was struggling to get back up when Tina and Frank both turned and started sprinting all out toward the castle gate.

"Killbox!" she yelled as she ran. "*Drop it!*"

At her order, Killbox and all her other Berserkers stepped away from the crumbling building she'd pointed at earlier, the one whose foundations they'd been hacking at with their axes the whole time she'd been taunting the Blood General. At this point, the whole edifice was held up only by the Berserkers' monstrous strength. The moment they stepped away, it started to fall. Killbox gave it a kick for good measure, collapsing three stories of limestone and heavy timber construction directly on top of the still-scrambling Sanguilar.

"Great job, guys!" Tina said.

"You know it!" Killbox called back, flexing as the rest of his Berserkers cheered and gave each other a round of high fives. "One problem, though. This guy's not a giant like Grel was. I can't even see him buried under there. How the hell are we going to hit him through all that rock?"

"We're not," Tina said, her grin growing wider. "The dude's unkillable, remember? Fuck him. He can rot under that building for all I care. We're going inside."

"Hell yeah!" NekoBaby cheered, making an obscene gesture at the rubble pile the Blood General was buried under. "See ya, sucka!"

"Roughnecks, retreat!" Tina called, pointing her sword at the castle gates. "Everyone inside!"

Bashing the remaining zombies and skeletons out of their way, the whole raid turned and charged the castle gates. The guards inside had already closed the heavy doors nearly all the way, but a squad of heavily armored former knights had stayed out to guard the Roughnecks' retreat. They were nearly bowled over for their trouble as all the players rushed inside at full speed. Tina was the last one through. She walked in backward, fending off zombies with her shield and sword the whole way until, at last, she crossed the threshold. She planted her feet there, blocking the last gap in the door with her shield as teams of men pushed on the gates to close them. They were almost done when Tina spotted something moving through the sea of zombies throwing themselves frantically at the gates.

It *looked* like an armored hill--a big, arched brown shape with scuffed metal plates nailed to its surface. Squinting at it through the narrowing gates, Tina realized that was wrong. It wasn't a hill. It was Butamon, the giant undead boar boss from the Dead Mountain Fortress courtyard. The monster pig looked even bigger across the field of zombies, its empty eyes flaring with ghostfire as it squealed and started to charge, plowing through the zombies like a freight train headed straight for the castle gate.

"*Frank!*" Tina screamed frantically, bracing her shield against the gap in the slowly closing doors. "Help me!"

Her fellow tank ran up behind her, locking his shield with hers.

"Ground on three," Tina ordered, staring down the boar that was plowing toward them. "One, two, *three*! Steady Ground!"

"Steady Ground!" Frank yelled a heartbeat later.

The two of them became one with the ground below the paving stones just in time. The giant boar crashed into the gates like a runaway school bus. Even with Steady Ground, the impact was still enough to slam Tina's shield back into her, cracking her in the jaw so hard she blacked out for a second. It was only her Steady Ground ability that kept her from failing in her job as the world's most epic doorstop. Outside, the giant boar screamed and rammed its metal-capped tusks into the doors, raining splinters and chunks of zombie down on top of her as the closing gates stopped then started moving back inward.

"Everyone push!" Tina yelled, bracing against the doors, which the boar's attacks were pounding back open. "Don't let them in!"

Bodies slammed into her back as the crowd behind her--her Roughnecks, Cinco's Red Sands, random members of the king's guard, everyone--crammed in behind the gates and pushed with all their strength.

Outside, arrows--normal ones from the castle guards and glowing ones from the player Rangers--rained down from the battlements onto the giant boar's back.

The raid boss squealed and snorted as the damage poured down, but it didn't let up. It was still going strong when Tina and Frank's Steady Ground faded, and they began to slide back.

"Push harder!" Tina yelled, shoving her shield into the monster boar's rotting snout. "Don't let up!"

By this point, the whole courtyard was pushing together. Thousands of people--players and non-players--were all shoving together, but the boar had help as well. Mountains of zombies were piling up on either side of the boar, crawling on top of each other to press their combined weight against the gates. As more and more piled on, the gates began to buckle inward. Staring up at the giant boar and the wall of zombies around it, Tina began to worry that this was the end. She was putting all her strength into her shield for a final shield slam before she was crushed when a burst of golden light flashed in the sky.

Tina felt the magic before she saw it. The Bastion's golden light spread out from the castle in a wave of power, covering the castle and pushing back the undead. All at once, the pressure on Tina's shield vanished. The doors they'd been so desperately fighting to hold slammed shut a second later, then Tina was crushed against the wood by the combined force of everyone behind her. She was still getting up when two twelve-man teams of castle guards rushed forward, carrying giant wooden crossbeams, which they wedged against the doors.

More beams followed. By the time the castle guard was done, every piece of wood in the castle seemed to be braced against the front gates. Smiling at the ridiculous woodpile, Tina looked up to see the golden shield of the Bastion covering the castle like a bell jar. It didn't go much past the castle walls--a far cry from the city-covering shield that had gone up two days ago--but it didn't need to. Everyone left alive in the city was here, safe inside the barrier. And from the furious screams of the damned, the undead knew it.

"Huh." Killbox snorted, looking up the wall at the deafening wailing going on outside. "What a bunch of sore losers."

Tina looked around at the crowded courtyard, which wasn't nearly as packed as it should have been. Bastion was supposed to be a city of hundreds of thousands, but there couldn't have been a tenth that many in here, including the players.

"More like sore winners," she said quietly, nodding at the Bastion's golden shield. "We stopped them for now, but this thing's already on its last legs. When the shield goes down, where are we going to go?"

The Berserker had no answer for that. He just stood next to her, both of them propping up Frank, whose legs had given out now that the battle was finally over, and stared at the reinforced gate, which was never going to hold once the Bastion's golden protection vanished.

Chapter 23

James

The ride up the Royal Mile was one of the most terrifying experiences of James's life.

After helping move everyone out of Tina's island, referred to by everyone who lived there as Camp Comeback, he, Ar'Bati, and Flameboyant had loaded up one of Malakai's siege wagons with everyone too injured to walk--plus a few other items--and started toward the castle. Since they were bringing up the rear, James missed the majority of the fighting for the Mile, but the aftermath told him it had been brutal. Their rolling infirmary picked up several more injured players as they creaked their way north through the corridor lined with players using stolen knight shields to fend off the hordes of mindless undead.

When they reached the palace, they passed Tina's raid, which was busy massacring what appeared to be every single dungeon boss in the game. From the mess on the ground, he knew they'd been at it for a while, but while there were still a lot more to kill, they'd already cleared the way enough for the king's forces to secure the castle gate, which was what mattered.

"Where is King Gregory?" James asked when they reached the heavily guarded doors.

"Activating the Bastion," the guards told him as they started helping wounded players off his wagon. "It's not up yet because everyone's not inside, but it will be, Sun save us all."

"Sun save us all," Ar'Bati echoed as he handed down the injured. "Has the Diplomatic Quarter been evacuated already?"

"Almost," the guard said. "They were still moving the infirmary patients, last I heard, but Captain Hightower just went by to check on the progress himself--and to make sure all the players were let out of their cages--so it should be nearly done."

That was a great relief to hear. "Our cart should be the last from the south," James told him. "Once we get the fighters inside, we can close the gates."

"Thank the Sun for that," the guard said as they pulled the last of the injured down and passed them to the Clerics--player and NPC--who were managing the massive infirmary that had popped up in the center of the castle courtyard. "The undead are getting thicker by the minute. If we don't close up soon, I'm worried even the Bastion won't be..." He stopped, thick eyebrows furrowing under the brim of his leather helmet. "Oy, what's this?"

The guard yanked the tarp off the cart bed the injured had been riding in to reveal twelve barrels marked with stark black-and-white striping. "This is wind-fire powder!"

"It's for use against the undead," James explained quickly. "We found it at the player camp, and--"

"You can't bring that in here!" the guard cried, making a ward against evil as he stepped back. "It's bloody dangerous! You've got enough there to blow the whole castle sky high three times over. And that barrel's *cracked*!"

"It's got a ward on it," Flameboyant explained, pointing at the magical markings.

"Don't matter," the guard snapped, grabbing their horses by the reins. "Even if we weren't under siege, I can't be letting such a dangerous thing into the castle. Now get off, and I'll wheel this thing right back out--"

"You can't put it out there with the undead!" Ar'Bati snarled.

"Well, it can't be in here!" the guard snarled back.

James winced and held up his hands. Before he could think of something to say to de-escalate the situation, though, a large voice boomed behind them.

"It's fine, Sergeant. Let them in."

526

The guard stopped yelling and whirled around, then his eyes widened. "Captain Hightower, sir!" he said, slapping his hand to his forehead in salute as the captain of the city guard marched over.

"Begging your pardon, sir," the guard said nervously. "I don't mean no disobedience, but this player has wind-fire powder. Regulations strictly forbid--"

"I'm giving special permission," the captain said, nodding at James. "This player has the king's trust. Whatever he's got, I trust him to handle it with care. Let them in, and get this cart out of the gate. We've got soldiers coming in!"

"Yes, sir," the guard said, giving James a final dirty look before letting go of the reins.

After nodding respectfully to the guard, James flicked the reins and drove them in. When they were safely out of the way, he hopped down and bowed to Captain Hightower. "Thank you so much for your assistance back there."

"They're just trying to do their jobs," the captain said dismissively, then his dark eyebrows drew into a scowl. "But what are you about, bringing wind-fire powder in here?"

"I know it's dangerous," James said. "But our backs are to the wall here. I couldn't leave such a powerful weapon behind."

The captain snorted. "Desperate times, desperate measures, I suppose. Just make sure you keep a lid on it. It'd be just our luck if we escaped the undead only to blow ourselves up."

James was about to assure the captain he would never allow such a thing when a huge cry went up outside. A few seconds later, players started flooding in through the door. The Roughnecks came in last, with Tina herself bringing up the rear, using her shield to block the door against something horrible. He couldn't see what from this angle, but it bashed against the gate. Tina was screaming for people to help her shut the door as everyone piled on. James helped, too, as did Ar'Bati. Since he was a

527

ranged damage-dealer, Flameboyant ran up on the walls with the other Sorcerers to help attack.

From way in the back, James couldn't see what was going on, but they seemed to have fought whatever was outside to a standstill when a flash of gold went off in the sky, then the Bastion exploded overhead, covering the castle in a golden shield that drove back the undead.

"Thanks be to the Holy King," Ar'Bati said, panting as he craned his neck back to look up at the golden light shining from the highest tower. "He did it!"

"He did it," James agreed though far less enthusiastically. Everyone in the courtyard was cheering and celebrating, but James couldn't miss how much smaller the Bastion was this time. The golden dome that had once covered the entire city now barely reached past the castle wall. He hoped the smaller radius was a power-saving strategy that would allow the shield to stand indefinitely, but he feared what they were seeing was all the power the Bastion had left. He didn't want to voice his fears out loud, though, so he looked around for the king instead.

Fortunately, the eight-foot-tall Gregory was easy to find. With just a little looking, James spotted him up on the battlements. After making Ar'Bati swear to guard the wind-fire powder with his life, James scrambled up the stairs to the king and quickly discovered he wasn't the only one.

"Hey, T," he said, grinning up at the stonekin standing in front of him. "Glad you made it."

"You too, James," Tina said, though she didn't return his smile.

James could see why. His sister looked like she'd been through hell. Her towering body and armor were covered in blood of every sort, including a worrisome amount of her stonekin's silver. She also looked exhausted, making him wonder when was the last time she'd slept.

The king wasn't much better. Gregory looked like he'd aged a decade since he'd come to get James this morning. He stood at the edge of the covered battlement above the castle's front gates, staring out at the sea of undead that now filled the Royal Mile. And it was a *sea*. There were so many zombies and skeletons and undead gnolls and reanimated animals out there, James couldn't even see the pavement. Up in the sky, the undead Birds were still fighting Xthr, and though the oldest living Bird seemed to be gaining the upper claw, the southern half of the city was on fire yet again beneath them. From up here, Bastion didn't even look like a city anymore. It looked like a wasteland, and no one seemed to feel it more than Gregory himself.

"We are finished," he whispered.

"We're not finished," Tina said irritably.

"We are cornered in a castle with no way out," the king said bitterly, glaring at her. "Even in this diminished capacity, the Bastion won't last much longer. When it goes down, the undead will storm the gates again. And the walls. And the sewers and the waterways and the old mines. I chose the castle to make our stand because it was the only safe place, but I didn't know how great the enemy's force would be. Didn't think." He dragged his giant hands through his wild red hair. "I fear I've ordered my people to their grave."

"It's only a grave if we let it be," Tina said, crossing her arms over her chest. "This castle was built to take a siege. There are only a few real doors in. With a bit of rest, my Roughnecks can hold those no problem. I don't know what your food and water supply is here, but if your men and the other players can take care of the walls, we should be able to hold out long enough to come up with another plan."

"What other plan?" Gregory demanded. "There's no rescue coming! This is the Last Bastion! If we fall, no one is coming to help us." He put his head in his hands. "I have failed."

"It's not failure to lose a fight you never could have won in the first place," James said firmly, reaching up to place his hand on the king's giant shoulder. "That doesn't mean we're dead, though. We just have to come up with a new plan, and I think I've got one."

The king and Tina both turned to look at him. Neither of them looked surprised, but James was shocked when no one tried to cut him off.

They just motioned for him to continue, so with a deep breath, James went all in. "We can use wind-fire powder."

"Oh my *god,*" Tina groaned.

"Just hear me out," James pleaded. "I know it sounds crazy, but--"

"I don't think it's crazy at all," his sister said quickly, looking like she didn't know whether to laugh or to cry. "I'm just dying from the irony because wind-fire powder was *my* plan."

"I know," James said, giving her a smile. "I saw the fire ward you put on Trainers' Hall. I want to know who came up with that, and can they do it again?"

"It's Richard's work, so you'd have to ask him," Tina said. "But I don't see why not."

"My Sorcerers can ward against fire as well," Gregory offered. "But why? What do you mean to do?"

James took a deep breath. "I mean to burn it all." He pointed down at the courtyard, where Ar'Bati was keeping everyone away from the wagon with bared fangs and claws. "We have twelve barrels of wind-fire powder down there. That's enough to scorch this whole city if the wind is blowing in the right direction. If we put a fire ward on the castle walls, we can burn the undead to ash without burning ourselves. Wind-fire will burn anything, even raid bosses. If we can get a big-enough inferno going, we can destroy the Once King's entire army without even having to open the doors."

The king stepped back, eyes wide with horror. "Are you seriously suggesting we *burn* all of Bastion?"

"No," James said. "Because all of Bastion is here." He waved his hand at the people huddling in the courtyard. "The citizens, the soldiers, the players, you and me--*we* are Bastion. All that stuff out there is just empty, ruined houses that are now crawling with undead. Cities can be rebuilt, but your people can't." He looked at Tina. "Even if the Roughnecks could hold the doors when the Bastion goes down, it would take you weeks to kill that many zombies, and that's assuming the Once King doesn't just bring in more. Even if you pulled it off perfectly, there's not enough food and water in here to keep us alive that long. We cannot withstand this siege! Our only hope is to kill the enemy before they kill us, and wind-fire powder is the surest way."

"You won't get an argument from me," Tina said bitterly. "I've been ready to burn this place since I got here."

James winced at the truth of those words, but he kept his eyes on the king. As happy as he was to have his sister's backing, Gregory was the one he needed to convince. He was the only one who could give the word, and from the look on his face, he'd rather eat his sword.

"My legacy is already bad enough," he said desperately, putting his head in his hands. "I can't go down in history as the king who burned his own capital."

"What history will there be if we die here?" James pointed out. "If Bastion falls, that's it. The Once King's army will sweep over this continent. The Savanna can't stand against an army like this! It's Bastion's duty to protect all the other lands that have sworn fealty to you. If Bastion won't fight to the last breath to save those who depend on it, what good is it?"

That at last seemed to get through. "What good, indeed," Gregory said wearily, dropping his hands to look out again over the undead swarming across what had once been his beautiful capital city. "Are you sure they'll all burn?"

"No, but I've yet to find the thing wind-fire powder won't burn," James said. "It's worth a try, at least. What have we got to lose?"

"Nothing," the king admitted with a sad sigh. "I'll get my sorcerers on it."

"And I'll get mine," Tina said, then her face broke into a wicked grin. "Oh man, I'm so gonna love watching this. Dibs on getting to throw one of those barrels!"

James was glad someone was happy about this. Even though it was his idea, he still felt sick to his stomach as he went to tell Ar'Bati the plan was on. While they carefully moved the barrels up to the battlements, Tina and the king gathered all their Sorcerers and other knowledgeable magical types in front of the castle's main tower. James would have given his tail to hear what the Arch-Sorcerer, High Priest Raffestain, and Richard--*the* Richard--were talking about, but he didn't dare leave the wind-fire powder to anyone else. In the end, the group split, and all the Sorcerers went up on the walls to start grabbing magic out of the air.

When all the deadly barrels were in position, James went down to round up people strong enough to throw them far enough to actually do some good. That meant raid-geared strength players, so his first stop was the Roughneck camp. When he got down to the front gate, he found his sister's guild sitting on the ground in a circle, stuffing their faces with rations like they would never eat again. The only one who wasn't eating was SilentBlayde. He was sitting apart from the others, hugging his knees on top of a crate and staring off into space with a blank, shell-shocked expression. Every now and then, NekoBaby or the other tank--Frank, James thought his name was--would come over and try to get him to eat, but he just shook his head and turned away.

It was painful to watch. James knew his sister and Haruto had fought because he'd voted against her for the Forlorn Hope, but he would have thought they'd have made up by now. Tina was quick to get mad, but she didn't normally stay that way for long, especially not at SB. Of the few falling-outs they'd had over their years of being inseparable, James could only remember one that had lasted more than an hour. He was about to go over and ask SB what the problem was a giant hand grabbed his shoulder.

He jumped a foot in the air, hissing under his breath before whirling around to find his sister staring at him.

"Dude," she said, "you startle like cat."

"I do a lot of things like a cat these days," James said huffily. "What's up?"

Tina jerked her thumb over her shoulder at the wall. "Richard and the others are done with the ward."

James blinked. "Really? That was fast."

"Apparently, it's a lot easier to do something if you've already done it once," Tina said with a shrug. "At least that's what Richard said. I'm just happy it's up, 'cause the Bastion is looking sad."

The golden dome was indeed starting to flicker, its golden glow going in and out like a bulb about to burn out. "Then we'd better get moving."

His sister nodded and turned to her raid. "Killbox!" she yelled. "Frank! Get your Knights and Berserkers and follow me up to the walls. We've got some barrels to throw!"

Several huge armored figures heaved to their feet and started jogging up the steps to the battlements. Tina followed, barking orders for everyone to stand in front of one of the barrels James and Ar'Bati had carefully arranged at strategic points around the castle. Not wanting to miss this, James ran after her and stuck to his sister's side as she picked up her barrel--the cracked one set on the battlement above the front gate-- and hefted it onto her shoulder.

"Richard!" she yelled to the tall, thin human Sorcerer who was still poking at fire magic just down the wall. "We clear?"

The Sorcerer lifted his hands over his head with a thumbs-up. A second later, the whole castle was bathed in warm magic as the fire ward activated.

"On my mark!" Tina yelled, her stonekin's giant voice booming across the battlements. All around the castle, eleven other Berserkers and Knights picked up their barrels. Killbox lifted his one-handed, hefting the thing like a baseball as he took aim at one of the particularly huge raid bosses moving in the distance.

"Aim!" Tina ordered, hauling her barrel back over her shoulder. "And *throw*!"

On her command, twelve barrels launched off the battlements. Even knowing how much strength the raiders were packing, it was still astonishing to see it in action. The barrels rocketed off the castle like missiles before falling in an arc onto the undead army below, and wherever they landed, hell followed.

The first blast almost blew James off the battlements. The fire ward protected them from the heat, but nothing could stop the shockwave caused by the vacuum of so much oxygen being consumed at once. All over the city, the barrels went off like nuclear weapons, sparking raging fires that grew into all-consuming storms of flame before his eyes, burning everything they touched.

"*Wooo!*" Tina screamed as the zombies were consumed. "Burn, fuckers, burn!"

The undead obeyed. Their shambling bodies burned like kindling, creating spinning updrafts of flame that rose into the sky to form tornadoes. Even Xthr took notice. With a scream of victory, the giant Bird kicked his last remaining opponent into the flames, casting the undead Bird into the fires that burned everything else, before diving into the safety of the Lightless Realm.

And just in time--now that the initial blasts were over, the fires were starting to feed on themselves. The entire Royal Mile was a river of fire. The flames rose to the sky, so high they blocked the sun. Whirlpools of smoke formed as the fires sucked down fresh oxygen with infinite hunger, but what surprised James the most was that it was beautiful.

Being a Naturalist, he couldn't use or see the tendrils of fire magic. He could see all the others, though, and that was more than enough. The power of the fire pulled all the other magic with it, spinning the tendrils of power into huge threads bigger than anything he'd ever seen before. It was incredible to behold and *enormous*. Within moments, the spiraling magic-- and the tornado of flames that fed it--had grown to encompass the entire city, turning the world red-orange with its light as sky and ground vanished into flame.

Everywhere he looked, he saw nothing but flame, yet James felt no uncomfortable heat. In the sea of flame, the castle was a protected island, whole and unscarred thanks to the fire ward shimmering along its walls.

But then, just as James started to let himself believe that they'd actually pulled it off--that there was no *way* the Once King's army could survive the sea of flame--he felt the stomach-twisting lurch of a portal opening.

He whirled around in the direction of the Room of Arrivals only to realize he couldn't see the blasted building through the wall of flame. A heartbeat later, though, that ceased to matter as the wall of red-orange flame was pierced by a new pillar of fire, a ghostly blue-white one.

James stumbled backward as the ghostfire flared, cutting through the glare of the firestorm and creating a column of cold safety for the figure that rose inside it. Even from this distance, James could see it was a man--an elf, to be precise, rising through the ghostfire on ash-gray wings. He was still staring at it when someone behind him asked, "Who's that?"

James dragged his eyes away from the winged figure to see King Gregory on the stairs behind him. The giant king was frozen, his eyes locked on the figure flying up through the ghostfire.

"What is that?" he demanded, voice shaking. "I've never seen a winged elf except in books and paintings."

James had. He knew who that was, but he couldn't speak. Fear had stolen his voice. Fortunately, his sister had no such problem.

"It's him," she said, awed. "It's the Once King!"

"It can't be the Once King," Richard said frantically. "He never leaves his mountain!"

"You know any other giant winged elves?" Tina demanded, throwing out her arm. "Dude, your guild fought him just like mine did! That's the Once King in the flesh!"

Richard's reply to that was to go even paler than usual.

"What do we do?" squeaked Gregory.

James had no idea. Tina was oddly silent as well. Then before anyone could answer, a voice filled the air--a very *familiar* voice.

"Foolish, ignorant children," the Once King said, hovering on his wings as he pointed through the fire at the figures on the battlements. "You think you can stop death with mere *fire*?"

Every word he spoke rang through the city like a bell, resonating with some ancient part of James's jubatus body, the deep buried corner that still remembered Creation's first true King. But while there was definitely something metaphysical about the Once King's voice, what really made James shake was the fact that he knew it already. It was the same voice he'd heard through his Eclipsed Steel Staff, the one that was always telling him to kill himself.

James cursed himself for a fool. This whole time, he'd thought his weapon had some sort of vague malign intelligence. But the staff had come from the Dead Mountain, and it was made of Eclipsed Steel, a corrupted form of sun metal that only the Once King himself could create. When he thought back on their conversations, the idea that he'd been actually talking to the Once King this whole time was the only thing that made sense. No wonder it claimed to be so old. The Once King was the first born of creation, created by the Sun itself. It also explained why the staff had felt oddly empty when he'd used it to fight Tina. The Once King hadn't had time to taunt him like usual because he'd been preparing his invasion. Preparing to come *here*.

Feeling like an absolute idiot, James reached up to rip the cursed weapon off his back. He was about to hurl the hateful thing off the wall into the flames when the Once King clutched a hand to his chest. James forgot all about the staff after that. He was too shocked to even feel afraid as he watched the winged elf pull a mass of sky blue from inside his body. *Pure* mana--not the tendrils James worked with, but actual magic from inside his own life. James had never even heard of someone working with pure mana other than to spend it on other things, but the Once King wielded the power like an old, old hand, working the spire of magic that came from his body until it was as tall as a Dubai skyscraper.

When the power pierced the sky itself, the Once King flicked his fingers, and the lovely blue mana coalesced into a blade. The elf king grabbed it with both hands and swung the mountain of mana like an executioner's blade. Down, down, down it fell through the burning city, cutting through stone and rock, through every strand of magic, through the fire itself. In one clean slice, the river of flame covering the city was ripped in half, and as it split, the fire died.

Richard gasped beside them. James felt it too. All those giant cords of magic the fire had swirled together had just been severed. As they frayed and vanished, the flames--the magical combustion sparked by the wind-fire powder--died as quickly as it had risen. The wind went flat, the river stilled, and even the smoke scattered, leaving James staring in awe at the clear city, the clean air, and the elf who was flying above it all.

For a silent moment, the Once King smiled at them. Then as if he hadn't just cleaved all the magic from heaven to earth, he furled his wings and dove through the broken dome of the Room of Arrivals, swooping back through the portal from whence he'd come.

"Holy shit," was all James could say.

"What the hell was that?" Tina shouted at the same time. "If he can just come out and do that shit, why does he need all this crap?" She waved a middle finger at the sea of undead they'd just burned, an alarming number of which were starting to get back up.

"I think it's because of 'all this crap' that he had to come out," James said, looking down at the Eclipsed Steel staff he was still clutching in his hands. "The wiki... that is, legend says the Once King hasn't left the Dead Mountain Fortress since it was made. That would make this his first appearance in centuries. There's probably a good reason for that, because if he's powerful enough to do shit like this, he certainly wouldn't bother with an army, but I don't know why." He scowled, scratching his whiskers thoughtfully. "I need to talk to SB. He's the one who knows all the elven histories inside and out. I'm sure he'll have a theory."

He was turning to go find the Assassin when Tina grabbed him by the shoulder. "Lore shit can wait," she growled. "We've got bigger problems. Look."

She pointed at the sky above them--the lovely, clear, empty sky the Once King's attack had revealed. A *blue* sky without a hint of gold.

"Holy Sun," Gregory whispered, shaking in his giant boots.

"The Bastion's down," Tina confirmed. "It happened during the firestorm. I didn't say shit at the time 'cause hey, everything was burning. But now we've got no fire *and* no shield, which means we're fucked."

"Can you get it back up?" James asked the king.

Gregory shook his head. "I barely managed to raise it last time! But we've used it too much. There's simply nothing left."

Down in the scorched streets, the undead were picking themselves back up. Many were little more than burned husks, but the ones who'd been buried underneath the top layers were still terrifyingly unscathed. Some were already starting to claw at the front door again, dragging their broken fingers across the deep gouges the undead boar boss had left in the wood.

"I gotta get back to those gates," Tina said then lifted her voice. "Roughnecks! On the gates!"

All along the walls, players stopped staring in horror at their failure and hopped down to obey. When she'd made sure everyone was moving, Tina turned to Gregory and James. "We'll hold things here as long as we can," she said. "You two put your heads together and figure out another way to survive this. Throw mana potions at the Bastion. I don't care. Just figure out something brilliant, because you're the last hope we've got."

With that, Tina saluted and ran down the stairs, nearly knocking Richard over as she raced to take her position at the front gates, which were already rocking despite the enormous pile of wooden braces the guards had wedged behind them. The rest of her raid fell in behind her with practiced swiftness, their faces calm and determined despite the doom they'd just witnessed.

"How does she do it?" King Gregory whispered, his face stricken as he watched Tina adjust Frank's position beside her. "She has only to speak, and people forget their fear as they rush to follow her lead. Even I felt we could do it, if only so I wouldn't disappoint her faith in me." His shoulders slumped. "She'd be a better king than I am."

"Roxxy's more experienced than you are," James said gently. "Never forget, she's been leading armies for seven years. Her guild was world ranked before this happened. Those skills don't just go away. If anyone can hold that door, she can. Our job is to use the time she's going to buy us to figure a way out of this."

"But we don't have one," Gregory said, sounding desperate. "The once-great army of Bastion is broken, and my strongest captain is raving mad and locked in a dungeon. The Bastion's drained dry, and the Dawnblade is just one sword. The wind-fire powder was supposed to be a last resort, and now it's failed too. What is left to try?"

"There has to be something," James said stubbornly.

"What?"

James's ears went flat. He was still working on an answer when Ar'Bati bounded up the stairs.

"All is not lost, your majesty!" the cat warrior said, grabbing the king so fiercely that both Gregory and James startled. "Windy Lake still stands! The savanna to the south still has its armies, *and* we've already defeated the undead menace at Red Canyon. The four clans are still Bastion's allies! If we can find a way to break through this siege and escape, I know they will help you."

The king gave James's brother a weak smile. "Thank you," he said. "But your people are days away by mount. Even if we could break through, the undead would swarm us over before we reached safety. I can't say how much it means to hear we have strong allies still, but they do us no good if we cannot reach them."

"Actually, I think Fangs is on to something," James said excitedly. "The castle might be lost, but it's not the only safe place left in the world. The savanna is still ours. We just have to get to it."

"Could we portal there?" Ar'Bati asked. "We portaled here."

539

"That is impossible, I'm afraid," the king said, shaking his head. "I already asked my Portal Keepers about this days ago when we feared the players' ability to open portals. They assured me that without the Room of Arrivals to act as an anchor, creating a portal into or out of Bastion is impossible without a prohibitive amount of mana. Sadly, this is still the case. Even if we only went a short distance, opening a gateway for so many people would take more mana than all my Sorcerers put together possess. I don't know how the addition of players would change that, but I can't imagine it would be enough to open a doorway all the way to the Windy Lake."

"Just because we don't have a portal doesn't mean running still isn't a good plan," James said. "We just need to break out of this siege."

"But we're surrounded on all sides," Ar'Bati reminded him. "I just went to the back of the palace to check, and the undead are there as well. There's no escape."

"Ah," James said. "But there *is* one force left in this city that hasn't yet joined the fight. Maybe they can get us unstuck."

"Who?" Gregory asked.

James turned and pointed down the Royal Mile at the stone pillar that was barely visible above the buildings. "The bank."

***

Twenty minutes later, the king's Arch-Sorcerer blinked James into the middle of the Bank of Bastion. The old ichthyian caster sagged with fatigue the moment they arrived, almost falling to the floor before James caught him.

"You are fortunate that I know more about teleportation than players do," he wheezed as James helped him up. "I hope whatever you're after here is worth sacrificing half my mana for. I'll be empty when I get back and useless for the battle."

"I promise not to waste your efforts," James said.

The old fish-man straightened with a harrumph. "See that you don't," he said, then the Arch-Sorcerer vanished in a pop of purple magic exactly like the one Flameboyant left behind when he teleported. James was wondering what other variations on the standard spells the old NPCs knew when he suddenly became aware of his surroundings.

As promised when the Arch-Sorcerer reluctantly agreed to teleport him in a line across the city, he was standing in the gold-and-crystal lobby of the bank. Like everything else in FFO, the Schtumple Bank of Bastion had gotten much bigger when the game became real. The already-cavernous main teller area was now the size of an amphitheater. The glowing crystals that shed light from the curved roof were now as numerous as stars, while the elaborately carved gold support columns that held the whole thing up were the size of old-growth oak trees. The walls were still covered in golden murals of schtumple history, but the gilded images were now *much* more ornate, depicting the ancient schtumples fighting alongside the Birds against hordes of winged elves so vividly, James could almost hear their battle cries.

But though much was different, some things hadn't changed at all. Ahead of him, the polished stone floor was still divided into lanes for each teller window by red velvet ropes, not that any player had ever waited in line to actually speak to a teller. They'd just piled on top of each other to get close enough to click on the NPC and opened the bank interface. There were no tellers in the boxes now, though. James was wondering where everyone was when a voice behind him shrieked.

"*A player!*"

James whirled around to see a short, round schtumple in very impressive-looking black-and-gold armor shouting the alarm. He was raising his hands to explain himself when a giant metal hand grabbed him from behind. James yowled in surprise as what he'd assumed was a *carving* of a ten-foot-tall golem stepped out of its nook in the intricately carved golden support column to yank him off his feet. When he tried to wiggle his way free, the magical automaton simply grabbed him with its other

541

hand, pinning him in place against its body as a line of armored schtumples poured through a door at the back of the lobby to surround him with a ring of short--but *very* sharp--yellow-glowing pikes.

"How did it get in?" cried one of the schtumple guards, poking James in the leg with his weapon.

"All the doors should be blocked," agreed another, prodding James as well. "Someone check the wards!"

"Peace, peace!" James cried, fending off the sharp points with his feet. "I was sent here by the king!"

The schtumple in front of him--a salty-looking little creature with a long scar over one of its sideways-tilted pug eyes--lifted his visor to give James a skeptical once-over. As the schtumple studied him, James realized that *all* the schtumples surrounding him were wearing identical sets of glossy black plate armor embossed with veins of gold so bright, it almost seemed to glow.

Shit. These weren't just any guards. These were the Black Golds, the level-eighty-one crack troops of the Grand Schtump's army. They were only one-skull rated, but they were famous for having nasty abilities specifically designed to swiftly murder any player stupid enough to open fire in a bank.

A drop of sweat slid down James's whiskers. He smiled nervously, wiggling his right hand at the wrist to draw attention to the folded paper tucked into his belt since the golem was still pinning his arms. "That's a letter from King Gregory," he said quickly. "Please read it. It should explain everything."

Scowling, the schtumple who'd been studying him reached out to snatch the letter with stubby armored fingers. He read it quickly, nose wrinkling, then he handed it to the schtumple on his right. One by one, all the Black Golds read the letter Gregory had written, then the group stepped away from James to huddle in a little circle and discuss what should be done.

542

Most of their conversation was too quiet for even James's cat ears. In the end, though, they seemed to reach a consensus.

"We can't kill it without approval," said the one-eyed warrior who seemed to be their leader. "You there, go and fetch the Grand One."

"Yes, sir!" said the soldier to his left, who ran off and vanished down the ornate hallway at the back of the lobby.

When he was gone, the officer returned his steady gaze to James. The rest of the Black Golds held just as still. If they hadn't been breathing and blinking, James would have thought they'd turned to statues like the golem. He was fighting not to fidget when he heard shuffling from the rear hallway, then a booming voice echoed through the lobby.

"You'd best hope this player didn't get in through a fault in your ward," it warned. "If so, I might have to *fire* you."

The word *fire* was said with such dreadful gravity that James was unsure if it involved literal fire or not.

"I say, Grand One, that there is no fault!" replied a shrill, defiant voice.

The booming voice harrumphed, then the largest schtumple James had ever seen stepped into the lobby. He wasn't as tall as King Gregory, but he still dwarfed James at seven feet. He was almost as wide, too, huge and round and sporting the first and only V-necked breast plate James had ever seen, which revealed a tuft of bronze chest hair. Beneath the armor, the rest of his bulk was draped in a golden tunic that was cut to show off his arms, which were surprisingly muscular. His legs must have been just as strong, because he practically bounded across the polished stone floor, bouncing with lightness that belied his size as he walked over to get a better look at James.

James did his best to smile back. This, he realized belatedly, must be the Grand Schtump, the schtumples' racial leader. Other than his size, the Grand One looked like every other schtumple. He had a round, bald head and pug-like eyes set too far apart on the sides of his face. Beside him, a much shorter--which was to say perfectly normal-sized--schtumple

543

wearing a purple wizard robe and carrying an abacus was quivering frantically, turning his round head to glare at James with each of his eyes in turn.

"I know not how he got in, your Grandness," he said angrily. "On my title as Head Financial Wizard, there are no flaws in my wards! The player must have used a hax. It is a skill of theirs!"

"Not anymore," the Grand Schtump said, shoving the wizard away. "There are no more hacks now. Go check your books!"

The robed wizard bowed and shuffled away, shooting murderous glances at James over his shoulder as he went. With another harrumph, the Grand Schtump pushed past the ring of Black Golds to stand in front of James himself.

"How'd you get in here?" he demanded in a rumbling, dangerous voice.

"The Arch-Sorcerer teleported me," James replied immediately. "I've come on behalf of the king. I wouldn't have burst in uninvited, but we desperately needed to speak with you, and your doors are locked."

"He had this letter, Grand One," said the Black Golds' officer.

The giant schtumple grabbed the folded paper and held it up in front of his wide face, scratching his tuft of chest hair idly as he read. "Hmm," he said when he'd finished, tossing the letter on the floor, where one of the Black Golds retrieved it. "You must be very savvy to get the king on your side." He glanced at the golem. "Put the player down."

The golden automaton obeyed, dropping James on the floor. As always, his jubatus instincts landed him neatly on his feet, and he used that accidental grace to sweep into a low bow. "Grand Schtump," he said. "It is an honor to meet such a wealthy one as yourself."

The Grand Schtump arched a wispy eyebrow. "Very savvy," he muttered, tilting his perfectly round head sideways. "Gregory's letter asks only that I listen to you. This is a cheap way to get a favor, so I will listen. Speak, player."

There was no more compelling argument he could think of than the truth, so that was what James went with. "Bastion is overrun by the Once King's armies. Other than your forces here, all the other living in the city have forted up in the castle, but it will fall within the hour if nothing is done. Therefore, the Holy King humbly requests your aid to save his people from undeath."

The schtumples must have been much more isolated here in the bank than James had realized, because his words went off like a bomb. One of the younger Black Golds actually fainted dead away when he heard, and even the Grand Schtump looked horrified, his small, floppy ears pulling back in distress.

"How can the castle fall?" he demanded. "What about the Bastion?"

"The Bastion has been exhausted," James reported grimly. "We have nothing left."

"We are doomed!" cried one of the Black Golds.

"They'll come for us next!" cried another, his ball-like eyes going even rounder. "What can we do?"

"Work with us," James said desperately. "You're the only fighting force left who hasn't entered the battle. If you help us, we might yet push the Once King back!"

The guards' pikes began to wave through the air as the schtumples all pulled in to whisper to each other. In the middle of the circle, the Grand Schtump crossed his arms tight across his chest.

"Hrmmm, hrrmm!" he said as his Black Golds whispered to him. "*Hrrrmmm!*"

James had no idea if that was a good "hrmmm" or a bad one. It must not have been a no, though, because the enormous schtumple pushed his way back out of the circle. "If we helped you, what sort of help would you want?"

"You have masses of two- and three-skull level-eighty-one golems in this bank," James said, rushing the words in his eagerness. "You also have the famous Black Golds, led by your illustrious self. If you rallied your full force and attacked the enemy from behind, it might be enough to break the siege on the castle and get us a chance to escape."

James finished with a big, hopeful smile, but the Grand Schtump was already shaking his rounded head.

"We cannot do this," he said. "We would help if we could, but are duty bound to protect the bank and honor our clients' deposits. Even to help the king, we cannot leave this building unguarded. To do so would violate our contracts and endanger the power of gold."

"I don't think your clients will care about their deposits if they're *dead*," James said hotly. "What about just letting us into our vaults? Several of us have flying mounts stockpiled here, and Xthr's already killed the Once King's undead Birds. If we could get even a few flying mounts together, we could load people up and escape by air!"

The Grand Schtump's wide face squished in a massive frown. "No withdrawals," he said tersely.

The "*What?*" shot out of him before James could stop it. "You're denying us access to our vaults?" he cried. "Isn't that breaking your oaths?"

"Yes and no," replied the giant schtumple. "They are your vaults, but you entrusted them to us when you opened an account, and it is our opinion that players have gone crazy. Therefore, as the trustees of your possessions, it the decision of the bank that your wealth must be protected from you until you are proved to be whole of mind again."

"Oh," James said, digging into his backpack for his copy of the Forlorn Hope agreement. "Well, problem solved, then. The players are cool now. We even partnered up with the king, see?"

He handed the scroll to the Grand Schtump, who read it so thoroughly, James could have sworn he was finding extra meaning in the ink blotches.

"It is a clever agreement," he admitted at last, handing the scroll back. "But the answer is still no. Signing up for a suicide squad is not proof of sanity."

"Oh, come on!" James cried. "It's *our* stuff! You have no right to keep it from us!"

The Grand Schtump hrrrmed and harrumphed, his round eyes looking at everything but James, and the longer he stalled, the more suspicious James became.

"That's not the real reason, is it?" he said, crossing his arms over his chest. "You're not just keeping us from our vaults because you think we're crazy. There's something else."

The giant schtumple shuffled his feet. "There are many factors to any--"

"My sister could be dying as we speak!" James cried. "If you can't help us and you can't give me the stuff *I* deposited, the least you can do is tell me why!"

The Grand Schtump's round face fell. "It is owed, yes," he muttered under his breath. "And what is owed must be paid." That seemed to decide him, and the Grand Schtump straightened up. "You *are* crazy," he said apologetically. "But that's not the only reason we can't let you in. Players cannot be allowed to make withdrawals because players have too much gold."

"Wait," James said, rubbing his ears, because there was no way he'd heard that right. "Too much gold? You won't help us because we have too *much* gold?"

"It is a critical problem," the Grand Schtump said nervously. "The Nightmare showered wealth upon your kind like it was nothing. There is one player who has one billion gold in his accounts. One *billion*! Such numbers were unimaginable before the Nightmare. Players have more money than this world can support. If we let you take it out of the bank all at once, gold would become worthless, and we schtumples would be ruined!"

James bared his fangs. And to think, he'd defended schtumples to Ar'Bati when the warrior had called them greedy. "We're all about to die, and you're worried about *inflation*?" he yelled. "The Once King is about to conquer Bastion! This whole continent will be a giant grave crawling with undead! Who cares about *gold*?"

"*We* care about gold!" the Grand Schtump bellowed, his huge voice echoing through the cavernous lobby. "Gold is our magic, our purpose! We are not like you, cat-elf. You and all those descended from the first elves were born with the blue mana of the Boundless Sky within you. You are beloved by the Sun, beloved by the Wind and the Water, but we are different! We schtumples were born from the Moon as the Birds were, but the Moon has long been silent. There is no god looking out for schtumples now, only gold."

He slammed his fist against his inch-thick golden breastplate as his guards nodded in reverent awe. "Gold is ours!" the Grand Schtump cried, throwing his brawny arm up at the mural on the wall of the winged elves descending on the ancient schtumples like vultures. "We remember the day the elves came from the sky. Greedy, arrogant creatures! They had the whole Boundless Sky, and they *still* wanted what was ours. So they took it. They took our land, took our *gold*, the only source of magic that belonged to us alone!"

The Grand Schtump turned back to James with a defiant look. "My great ancestors sacrificed everything to make this vault. We made this place specifically so that we could preserve and protect the value of gold. This is not just a safe house for valuables. You stand in the heart of the schtumple people! The only fortress that preserves our place in this world! And now you--you twisted little elf-cat-player-*thing*--have the gall to ask me to save the elves by letting them steal our power again? To ruin gold?" He scoffed. "I would rather die."

James bit his lip. "But the Once King--"

"The elf called King is the first and last of the celestial elves," the Grand Schtump said bitterly. "They're the ones who broke this world. Let them finish the job. He cares only for the descendants of celestials, anyway, the humans and jubatus and fish-men and such. Not schtumples." The enormous schtumple shrugged. "Let him come. Whatever he does, it can't be worse than losing gold."

James's mouth opened and closed several times, but no words came. There was so much to sort out that he'd never heard or read about before, like mana being the essence of the Boundless Sky or the Schtumples not being descended from elves. He was desperate to know more, like how the elves had come here and why they'd stayed. All the celestial elven stuff he'd read in the game had depicted the Boundless Sky as a lost paradise, a home they could never return to. But if they'd landed of their own accord, why couldn't they just go back? The Once King still had his wings, even. If he was so miserable, why couldn't he just fly home instead of trying to kill everyone?

He was itching to ask the Grand Schtump for more details. He also wanted to interrogate his eclipsed steel staff since it was apparently a telephone to the Once King. There was clearly *way* more going on with the history of this world than the game lore had explained. He was sure the answer to why all of this had happened in the first place--and more importantly, how it might be *stopped*--was in there somewhere, just beyond his reach. Just a little more knowledge, and it might all fall together, but they had no time. Tina and the others might already be dead--or worse, undead. He'd come to the schtumples in a last-ditch Hail Mary for help. He still wasn't entirely sure what gold meant to them, but if he couldn't find a way to make this work, everything was lost.

"Thank you for telling me all of this," James said when he could speak again. "I was ignorant of how important gold was to the schtumples, and I didn't know what I was asking. I'd never demand that you sacrifice your people for ours, but we need your help. Please."

The Grand Schtump sighed. "It isn't that we don't wish to help," he said. "We have lived here in peace for many generations now. Despite our history, the humans and elves of Bastion have been good customers to us for a long time. We do not wish to see you die, but the costs of saving you are just too great. I'm sure you understand."

James did understand, but he couldn't accept it. He'd known this was a long shot, but if the bank couldn't help, then he was utterly out of ideas. It didn't help that he'd started everything off on the wrong foot. He'd barged in and made assumptions despite knowing nothing of the schtumples' actual history. He wasn't even that familiar with their in-game lore since he'd always dismissed them as a joke race.

If he'd been less arrogant, he might know something he could use, some trick or loophole that would convince the schtumples to overcome their reservations and help. There had to be *something*. The bank was in Bastion, after all, and doing business with the outside world seemed to be core to their racial identity. They might not be willing to die for Bastion, but surely there was something they could do. Something he could get.

"'Put your money where your mouth is' is a schtumple saying, right?" he asked, looking hopefully at the Grand Schtump. "I understand that opening the bank to all players would destroy the value of gold, but what about just *one*? I'm already in here. Could you let me access just *my* vault?"

The Grand Schtump blinked at him, then he began to laugh. "You speak like a schtumple, indeed," he said, flashing James a gold-toothed smile. "I think we could weather one account. What is the name?"

"James Anderson," James replied, then he grew worried. "At least, that's what it was on the TrueID system, if that's still even a thing."

The Grand Schtump clapped his gold-ringed fingers, and several normal-sized schtumples suddenly appeared in the teller windows, their round eyes wobbling as they peeked at James through the golden bars.

"Bring me the account ledger for James Anderson!" the Grand Schtump ordered, then he glanced down. "You want account-level access, yes?"

"Yes," James said firmly. If he was going to do this, he was getting the vaults for *all* of his characters, even the low-level ones.

"Bring it all," the big schtumple bellowed.

550

The teller schtumples nodded and scrambled into action, wheeling out ladders and climbing up to access the glittering walls of filing cabinets behind the teller windows. A few moments later, an older schtumple wearing an elegant burgundy velvet coat and a gold nameplate that read Bank Front Manager shuffled out to bow before the Grand Schtump before reverently handing him a golden clipboard.

"Very good," the Grand Schtump said, turning to walk toward the enormous vault door that took up the entire wall to the left of the tellers. "You come with me, Mr. Anderson. I will give you the personal treatment today!"

Feeing quite honored, James followed the trundling ball of schtumple out of the lobby. He was surprised at the complete turnaround in the Grand Schtumple's attitude, but he supposed it made sense. The Grand Schtump had said he'd wanted to help but just didn't know how. Now James had given him a potential way out of becoming the First Bank of the Undead that didn't require crushing his own people. No wonder the big schtumple was whistling as he unlocked the huge vault door with a complicated code sequence.

Even with the Grand Schtump's impressive strength, it still took the assistance of all the Black Golds to actually open the three-foot-thick door. Inside was a long stone hallway lined with what appeared to be mirrors. Since he'd only ever accessed his vault through the teller interface, James had never seen the bank's inner workings before, and he watched in awe as the Grand Schtump followed the clipboard he'd been given to one of the largest mirrors in the middle. After checking his reflection in the eight-foot-wide span of glass, the Grand Schtump pulled a gold coin out of his pocket. Flipping it in his stubby fingers, he cleared his throat and spoke in a ringing voice.

"James Anderson."

He flipped the coin at the glass as he spoke. As it hit, the surface of the silver mirror rippled like water, then the distortions cleared to reveal a single stone room the size of a Wal-Mart. Acres of wooden racks filled the smooth-sanded, dark-stone floor, their tops rising all the way to the vaulted ceiling overhead, and on their shelves was James's stuff--*all* of it.

The room grew hazy as tears filled James's eyes. His gear, his pets, his mounts and weapons, toys and collectibles--they were all here! One long wall was lined with huge bins full of his ores, minerals, crystals, herbs, and other crafting supplies all organized by profession, just as he'd left them. On the other side, huge chests held his entire account's worth of gold. He'd only ever seen it as a number on an interface before. Seeing it now in person--the weight of it all, the size, the stacks of glittering coins-- was overwhelming. He'd never seen so much wealth in his life, and it was all *his.*

"After you," the Grand Schtump said, holding out his hand.

James didn't wait to be asked twice. He vaulted through the door where the mirror had been and ran straight to the armor stands, which were here as tasteful glass display cases with recessed lighting. The very first one held his Vitas Gloria Raiment set. Staring at the silk robe, belt, bracers, boots, and pants through the glass, James could have sworn he could see the green stitched leaves waving in time with the life magic that floated through the cavern. Beside them, the Vitas Gloria Staff glowed like summer sunlight shining through a leafy canopy light from its weapon rack, shedding an endless stream of feather-shaped green leaves that sparkled and vanished before they hit the ground.

James really did cry then. The Vitas Gloria Raiment wasn't as highly stat-ed as the Dead Mountain raid-healing set he'd lost when the Nightmare had eaten his backpack, but it was infinitely more precious. The six-piece set and matching weapon had taken him a year of grinding elite quests in the Verdancy to obtain. He was one of only a handful of players in the world who'd managed to collect the whole thing so far. He was about to rip the glass door open and put it on right there when he realized that, while the set would make him infinitely more powerful--and much better dressed--it wouldn't actually do anything to fix their situation.

Removing his hands from the armor case reluctantly, James forced himself to turn around and look at his wealth--*really* look. In addition to the sets inside the glass cases, there was a ton of gear on the shelves, but he couldn't actually let anyone else use it since all the pieces were bound to him, either on this character or one of his alts. The three giant shelves full of potions would have been useful, but he'd need a dump truck to transport them back to the castle. His rack of mount items looked more promising, but when he picked up his Reins of the Sand Serpent, they felt like normal leather, not magical at all.

He gave the reins a shake, just to be sure, but no giant snake made of sand appeared. Apparently, whatever magic made summoned mounts work had been an in-game-only power just like their bottomless backpacks and the ability to instantly message across dimensions.

James hung the useless reins back on their hook with a sigh of bitter disappointment. So much for his aerial evacuation plan. But as he scrambled to think of a way he could actually use all of this amazing stuff to save the people in the castle, a new plan entered his mind, one he didn't like at all.

"In the game," he said slowly, turning to look at the Grand Schtump, who was still standing outside the vault, staring at James's gold with open hunger, "schtumple players were always depicted as mercenaries. Is that true?"

The Grand Schtump nodded. "All schtumple soldiers are mercenaries, even the Black Golds. If it's not for gold, why fight?"

"Great," James said, pointing at his chests of gold. "How much would it cost me to buy your help against the Once King?"

"More than you can afford," the big schtumple said sternly. "Helping you would leave the bank unprotected, which would endanger our entire race. There is no price I can put on that."

"What about some other kind of help?" James pressed, refusing to give up. "If you won't fight the undead with us, then is there something you can do to help us escape? We've got tens of thousands of people

trapped in the castle, but if we can just get them somewhere else--
somewhere safe, like Windy Lake--that would be almost as good. Is there
anything you can sell me that can make that happen?"

The Grand Schtump's round, jowly face screwed up as he thought
that through. "Hrmmm," he said, stomping his feet. "*Hrmmm!*" The hrmms
got louder and louder until, at last, the big schtumple snapped his fingers.
"I have a maybe," he informed James excitedly, then he lifted his booming
voice. "Fetch me the Senior Financial Wizard!"

The teller schtumples, who'd been hovering at the threshold of the
giant vault door, scrambled to obey. A minute later, the purple-robed
schtumple with the abacus who'd been with the Grand Schtump when
James arrived hopped through the door and scuttled down the hall.

"You called for your employee, Grand One?"

"Indeed," the Grand Schtump said, flipping through the papers of
James's account ledger with greedy fingers. "Can we still do the Anywhere
Portal?"

James's eyebrows shot up. Anywhere Portal scrolls were
convenience items that bypassed the normal Bastion portal network
restrictions. Using one would open a portal from wherever you were to
any of a long list of pre-allowed locations in the game, including leveling
hubs like Windy Lake. The only catch was that Anywhere Scrolls couldn't
be made or bought using gold. To get one, you had to spend real-world
money in the FFO web store, which, now that James thought about it, had
been run by schtumples. He'd thought that was just because the game devs
used schtumple avatars for everything involving money, including telling
you when your monthly subscription was about to expire. If their joke
money grubbing had real parallels in this world, though, then they might
be saved!

"*Please* tell me you can do it," he begged. "I still have an account set
up with the store! I'll gladly buy a portal!"

"There is no more store," the Financial Wizard informed him
crisply. "It vanished along with the Nightmare, thank the Moon. But many

of the items offered are still in their display cases, including the Anywhere Portal scrolls."

James's hopes shot up so high and fast he actually became physically dizzy. "How much do they cost?"

"Five platinum," the Financial Wizard said without missing a beat. "Each."

James's soaring hopes crashed. Platinum was the secondary currency FFO used as a stand-in for real cash in the game to avoid all the various local tax laws. It was also way outside of James's budget as a lowly assistant martial arts instructor with a six-figure debt. "But I don't have any platinum."

"That's fine," the Grand Schtump said. "First law of schtumple magic: all things have a gold value. Even platinum. We just have to figure out the proper exchange rate. If the Nightmare were still going, we could use trade chat to estimate fair market value. Now, though, we'll just have to guess."

"Okay," James said, keeping a good hold on his hopes this time. "How much do you think it'll be?"

The Grand Schtump looked at his Financial Wizard, who frowned. "Let's see," he said, flicking the stone beads back and forth. "The current supply of platinum is zero, but demand is greater than zero, so the gold value of platinum is..." He clicked his beads a few more times. "Priceless."

James's ears flattened against his scalp. "*Priceless?* You mean I can't buy it?"

"No, no, Mr. James Anderson," the Grand Schtump said quickly. "Second law of schtumple magic: Everything has a price. It may be more than you can afford, but there's nothing that can't be bought."

James thought about that for a minute, then he looked over his shoulder at his vault, the great room filled with all the treasures he'd hoarded over his time playing FFO. "What about eight years of my life? Is that priceless enough?"

The Grand Schtump and his Financial Wizard put their heads together. After several moments of whispering and checking the abacus, the Grand Schtump straightened back up. "Probably."

James slumped. "Probably?"

The Grand One shrugged. "Priceless is a hard price to pin down. We won't know for sure until we try." He waved his gold-ringed hand, and a scroll of fine parchment appeared in front of James's face. A golden fountain pen followed, floating in the air above his fingers, ready to be used.

"If you're serious about this, sign your vault back over to us," the Grand Schtump said. "We'll conduct the purchasing ritual using the objects in this room. If it's enough, the Anywhere Portal scrolls will appear. If it's not..." He shrugged. "No refunds."

James looked back at his glittering collection. He looked at the racks of legendary weapons and the wreath of golden laurels that had only been given out to winners of the FFO Olympians event four years ago. He looked at the sun-metal music box that played the entire ichthyian ballad "The Song of the Sea." He looked at the oil lamp containing his Fire Rabbit, the rarest pet in the game. He looked at all of it, the priceless hoard of treasures he'd won with blood and sweat and endless patience. In eight long, horrible years of failure, this was the only thing he'd succeeded at, the only evidence that his time in FFO hadn't been a waste--that *he* hadn't been a waste.

Even now, after everything had changed, seeing it filled him with pride. In the end, though, the glittering vault was still just a room full of stuff. It wasn't worth a sister or a friend or a kingdom. James knew that, but it didn't stop his hand from shaking as he turned and grabbed the golden pen and signed his name in a messy rush on the golden line.

The moment the contract was signed, the Grand Schtump whisked it away. "Prepare the ritual!" he bellowed.

Schtumples began rushing madly in all directions. James was forced to step back into the hall as a team of tellers unhooked the mirror that connected to his vault to the outside world and carried it into the lobby. When they'd propped it up in the center of the cavernous room, the Senior Financial Wizard brought a pair of platinum-embossed scrolls as long as James's arms out from a heavily secured room in the back.

"Two?" James asked nervously.

"It has to be two," the wizard explained as he set the Anywhere Portal scrolls down on either side of James's vault mirror. "All your people are stuck in the castle, so it does you no good to open a portal to Windy Lake from here. Unless you want to walk back to the palace through the city, you'll have to make two portals: one connecting the castle to the bank, and one connecting the bank to Windy Lake."

That was information James would have loved to know *before* he'd signed the contract, but done was done. Either his vault would be enough, or it wouldn't, so he stood back and let the schtumples work. When everything was in position, the Senior Financial Wizard positioned himself in front of the mirror to James's vault and began to read the contract James had just signed, speaking the words with great emotion as if the legalese were a magic spell.

James's fur began to prickle as the power in the room built. When it was almost too much for him to take, the Financial Wizard threw the contract at the vault mirror with a flourish, and golden magic exploded outward, engulfing James in a wave of metallic-smelling power. He was still waving his hands in surprise when the Grand Schtump bellowed, "The price is paid! *Use the scrolls!*"

The Financial Wizard thrust the two platinum scrolls--which were now glowing like rolls of Christmas lights with sparkling rainbow magic-- into James's hands. Fighting to keep his head in the vortex of swirling alien magic, James unrolled the first one and spoke his destination.

"Windy Lake!"

The scroll vanished from his fingers. The next moment, a doorway opened to his left, letting in a shaft of blazing sunlight followed by the hot, familiar wind of the Savanna. Satisfied that the portal had worked, James grabbed the next scroll and squeezed it in his fist as he yelled, "The royal castle of Bastion!"

The second scroll vanished just like the first, and a new doorway appeared on his right. It looked exactly like the opening to Windy Lake, only instead of warm sunlight and pleasant grassland breezes, this portal opened into the roar of battle. Through it, James could see the palace courtyard and the hordes of undead that were pouring through the shattered remains of the front gates. A ring of players and knights had formed to fill the gaps between the outer keep buildings while terrified people stared out from inside, watching through the windows as death crept closer.

Off to one side, James spotted Tina and King Gregory fighting side by side, trading blows with the massive form of the Blood General. The High Priest and the Arch-Sorcerer had taken the field as well, fighting with the rest of the Roughnecks against the giant undead boar boss Frank was barely holding back. Only a few Sorcerers were still throwing spells, and healing seemed to be nonexistent.

He tried to get their attention, but no one could hear him over the din. Frustrated, James looked for his brother and spotted Ar'Bati fighting shoulder to shoulder with the three-skulled Knight trainer, Fiona Steelwall, against one of the Dead Mountain's skeleton patrols. With the help of a few player Rangers, they got the skeletons down and were moving on to the next threat when James screamed his brother's name.

"*Fangs!*"

Ar'Bati's cat ears twitched, and he looked up at last to see James waving frantically at him through the portal.

"I got us a way out!" he screamed. "Tell everyone to run straight through both portals, no stopping! Go!"

Ar'Bati raised his sword in acknowledgment and started bellowing at the people behind him to move. They didn't need much encouragement. The moment the refugees saw their way out, they charged the portal, almost bowling James over in their rush to escape.

Scrambling out of the way, James jumped back to stand with the schtumples who'd formed a corridor with their bodies between the two portals, undoubtedly to keep the frantic, bloody people from accidentally fleeing into their bank. Not that James minded. The rows of armored guards were a perfect funnel to keep people moving between the two doors he'd just paid everything for, and the faster they moved, the better.

"Go straight through!" he yelled as the refugees flooded past. "There are two portals. Don't stop between them. Just keep running! You're going to make it!"

He repeated the instructions over and over as thousands of men, women, and children of every race stampeded past. Whenever someone tripped or otherwise failed to go at maximum speed between the portals, the schtumple Black Golds grabbed them and tossed them through the Windy Lake side to keep the path clear.

James was grateful for their haste. With each second that ticked by, the vault on the other side of the mirror grew emptier. Shelf by shelf, James's treasured collection was disappearing as the metals and gold and irreplaceable magical items were consumed by the schtumple magic powering the portals. By the time the courtyard was half empty, his vault was more than two thirds gone, and James was starting to panic.

"We're running out of time!" he shouted, looking back through the portal at all the players still fighting the undead. "*Tina!*"

She didn't even seem to hear him. Cursing, James left the evacuation to the schtumples and the former knights and jumped through the portal himself, racing across the bloody paving stones toward the front lines.

"*Tina!*" he screamed at the top of his lungs.

Again, she didn't seem to notice. James wasn't sure if that was because he still wasn't loud enough or if the fight was so intense she couldn't spare attention for anything else. The Blood General, however, *did* turn around. James flinched as the horrible red eyes bright with ghostfire locked on him, but at least his sister finally seemed to see him, turning her bloody, punch-drunk face in his direction.

"*Portal!*" James screamed, pointing backward at the giant magical doorway the whole courtyard was scrambling to run through.

His sister's eyes widened with recognition, then the Blood General booted her shield into her face. Terrified, James sucked in a breath as her guard was thrown open, leaving her front unprotected as the raid boss swung his sword toward her exposed throat.

He would have cut clean through it, but Gregory got there first, blocking the Blood General's red sword with the golden Dawnblade as he cried out, "Retreat! Everyone fall back to the portal!"

The king's command caught the attention of all the fighters who hadn't yet noticed the castle emptying out behind them. With a last volley of attacks, the players and soldiers fighting the undead turned and bolted for the portal. All the refugees were through at this point and someone had even seen fit to drag Malakai along. It was just the fighters now, but they couldn't all retreat at once, or the undead would follow. Instead, they collapsed on the portals, the front lines holding back the horde while the rear guard dove for safety. Even the king retreated, sweeping his Dawnblade in front of him in massive arcs to hold back the undead so the last of the players and former knights could jump through the portal.

The only one who didn't move was Tina. She was still exactly where she'd started, going toe to toe with the Blood General. She seemed to be holding her own, more or less, but without the others to hold them back, the lesser undead were slowly starting to surround her. If she didn't move fast, she'd be cut off.

"Tina!" James screamed at her. "There's no time! You have to fall back!"

She nodded and started to move, but the Blood General cut her off, using his sword to push her toward the far wall instead. Grabbing his staff, James was about to run out and help her when an iron arm wrapped around his middle as Ar'Bati yanked him back.

"Don't be stupid!" the warrior yelled. "The portals are about to close! You have to get through *now*!"

"*No!*" James screamed, fighting his brother's hold. "We can't leave her!" He couldn't lose Tina again. Not like this.

Something flickered in the shadows behind Tina, then the Blood General's throat exploded in a shower of crimson as shadow-wreathed SilentBlayde sprang from the Lightless Realm. Silver swords flashing in the smoky sunlight, he moved faster than James's eyes could follow, driving the Blood General away from Tina with a relentless attack. Now that the courtyard was nearly empty of players, the general's wounds were much slower to close, and when the pain made him stagger, Tina took the opportunity to break free, sprinting across the bloody courtyard toward the portal.

When she'd made it thirty feet, SilentBlayde vanished off the Blood General and re-emerged in James's shadow--and just stood there.

"What are you doing?" James yelled at him. "Get through the portal!"

"Not without her!" SB yelled back, his blue eyes going frantically to Tina, who was still sprinting across the courtyard with the Blood General hot on her heels. The huge elf was reaching out to grab her when King Gregory suddenly reemerged from the portal.

"*Get down!*"

James and SB both dropped as the king swept his Dawnblade in an arc over their heads, sending out a wave of golden light that knocked the undead over like bowling pins. Even the Blood General stumbled, his fingers missing Tina's copper hair by inches as she charged ahead.

"Mr. James Anderson!" the Grand Schtump yelled.

James looked back to see the giant schtumple gesturing at his vault, which was now almost completely empty. The only thing left was the Vitas Gloria Raiment, and it was disappearing before his eyes, the vivid green silk unraveling at a terrifying rate as the portal magic devoured it.

"Go, your highness!" James yelled at the king. "The portal's about to close!"

King Gregory nodded and jumped back through, clearing the distance between the two portals in one giant step.

"We need to get out of the way too!" he yelled at SB, stepping through the portal himself.

The elf didn't look happy about that, but SilentBlayde wasn't stupid enough to lie there on the ground while Tina was charging at them. He dove through the portal after James, rolling neatly across the bank's smooth floor to pop up on the Windy Lake side. James, however, stayed in the bank, thrusting his hand through the portal to grab his sister. She was almost to him, almost in reach, when she suddenly went down with a crash that shook James's teeth. For a horrible second, James had no idea why, then he saw the Blood General's sword sticking out of her back.

"Not that easily!" the bloody elf roared, yanking his weapon free to stab her again. "You'll never escape death that--"

He cut off with a choking sound as Tina flipped herself over and planted her boot right in the middle of his chest. The blow sent the general crashing into the wall of zombies behind him. Before he could recover, Tina scrambled onto her hands and knees and tossed herself at the portal, but she only made it halfway. With no one to keep them back, zombies had flooded into every inch of the castle courtyard. They grabbed her kicking legs, biting and clawing at her sun-metal armor as she struggled to get free. She was still kicking at them when the last green thread of James's Vitas Gloria Raiment vanished, and the portals began to collapse.

"*No!*" James screamed, lurching forward only to be caught by Ar'Bati, who was still standing behind him. He watched in petrified horror as the shimmering portals collapsed toward his struggling sister, the gleaming edge falling like a guillotine to cut her in half. James's heart stopped as a horrible wet noise filled the air, but it wasn't Tina.

It was a tooth. A large, bloody, golden tooth had hit the mirror of James's vault. It vanished the moment it landed, filling the bank with golden light and stopping the portal's collapse just long enough for the team of Black Golds to grab Tina and drag her through. She was still kicking off zombies when she landed on the floor. They would have surged in after her, but the schtumple Black Golds blocked the hole with their spears, shoving back the undead with astonishing strength. Staring at them in wonder, James turned to look at the Grand Schtump, who flashed him a wide smile that was now short one golden tooth.

"The proper form of the saying is 'My money, my mouth,'" the giant schtumple informed him, pointing at the Windy Lake portal, where the king and SilentBlayde were watching them desperately. "I've bought you a few more seconds. Use them to finish the job. We'll hold back the undead."

"Thank you," James choked out, reaching down to grab Tina, but she was too heavy.

He was still struggling when the Grand Schtump reached down and picked up Roxxy one-handed, then he tossed her through the portal onto the grass at the king's feet.

"Go," the schtumple ordered. "And thank you for doing business with the Bank of Bastion."

James could only nod in reply as Ar'Bati dragged him through the portal. King Gregory was already helping a dazed Tina back to her feet when the silvery portal fizzled out of existence for good, cutting off the din of battle and leaving everyone panting in the hot, dusty silence. It was only then that James saw they were standing in a field surrounded by thousands of armed cat-people, crushed yurts, and a furious-looking Gray Fang, whose green eyes lit up the moment she spotted James.

"*You!*" she yelled, hobbling forward. "What in the name of the Winds is going on here?"

Chapter 24

Tina and James

The last few hours of Tina's life had been an angry blur. She knew they'd made an epic last stand, but she couldn't actually remember anything clearly. It was all just slashing swords and flying blood and godlike monsters trying to kill her. The last five minutes had been even worse. All she could recall was the Blood General, trying not to die, and everyone screaming at her. She was pretty sure she'd nearly been cut in half by a portal, but she'd been hit in the head so many times, it was hard to be certain of anything, especially now.

Standing on her feet in the hot, dusty road with a vast blue sky overhead, Tina had to wonder if she'd actually died. Maybe they all had, because the other players and the king's soldiers were there as well. If this was the afterlife, though, it was a weird one. Thanks to Roxxy's height, she was tall enough to look over the crowd of players and knights to see the thousands of furious puffy-tailed cat-warriors that surrounded them. She was starting to worry she'd have to fight in death too when an old gray-furred cheetah-lady stepped forward, using her walking stick like a club to shove her way through the crowd straight toward them.

"You!" she yelled, pointing her stick at James. "What in the name of the Winds is going on here?"

Tina opened her mouth to state the obvious, but the king beat her to it.

"Please forgive our sudden imposition, Elder..."

"Gray Fang," James whispered.

"Elder Gray Fang," the king finished, giving her a stately bow. "I am King Gregory Heraldsford of Bastion."

Elder Gray Fang gave him a skeptical look, but behind her, the jubatus warriors were freaking their fur.

"It's the Holy King!" someone cried.

"I *told* you those were Royal Knights!" hissed another.

"Why's the king here?" a third asked. "Who's in Bastion?"

Gray Fang made a warning sound deep in her throat, and the peanut gallery fell silent. When it was clear there would be no more interruptions, the old cat bowed as far as her stooped back would allow.

"Your Majesty," she said reverently. "We are always honored by your presence, however sudden. But you have clearly come to us in much haste and need."

"Indeed," the king said, looking around at the refugees, who now looked even more pathetic than they had back at the castle. "My people are in dire need of assistance."

"Then we shall help them," Gray Fang promised, waving to the warriors behind her. "The four clans will see to it that their immediate needs are met. Meanwhile, if you'd please follow me to the Lodge, there is much to discuss."

"We are most grateful for the hospitality of Windy Lake," Gregory said earnestly, reducing his giant strides to teeny steps as he matched the elder's pace. Tina was still watching the two racial leaders walk awkwardly away when a new cat-person--a scarred warrior with graying fur and keen eyes--elbowed his way into the crowd.

"My boys!" he cried, running straight past her to grab James and Ar'Bati in a crushing hug.

"I'm so proud!" the old cat yelled, lifting them both off the ground in his excitement. "You came back, and you brought the king! You've brought our family so much honor this day!"

"Thank you, Father," said Ar'Bati, his stiff jaw trembling with something that looked suspiciously close to tears.

"We saw the smoke the day after you left for Bastion," the old jubatus went on, setting them down at last. "It was a week old, but we knew you'd gone into trouble." He hugged them both again. "I'm so glad you're both home safe!"

"Us too, Father," James said, causing Tina to arch an eyebrow. She was about to demand to know what the hell this was all about when the jubatus everyone was calling Dad turned to glare at her. "Who is this?" he demanded. "The king and his men are without question, of course, but what are you doing with all these *players?*"

As usual, he said that word like a curse, and Tina sighed. Great, a new place, a new batch of NPCs who hated their guts. She was about to tell Angry Cat Senior to piss off when James pushed his way between them.

"These players are good, Dad," James assured him, putting a hand on Tina's arm. "This is my sister, Christina Anderson, leader of the Roughnecks, who fought the undead and saved the people of Bastion. Tina, this is my adopted father, Rends Iron Hides."

Rends Iron Hides's expression changed completely as her brother spoke. "Defender of the kingdom, you say? Well, well, *well.*" The old cat flashed Tina a giant fanged smile and held out his hand. "Sorry to have doubted you. Age is clearly getting the better of me. I should have guessed you were no ordinary player the moment you showed up with the king. I'm delighted to meet you, Christina, sister of James."

"Just Tina is fine," Tina said awkwardly.

She was reaching out to take the jubatus's rough-padded hand when she realized that her glove was drenched in sticky red blood. Grimacing, she pulled her hand back to wipe it off on her armor, but that just added *her* blood to the mix. She was staring at the mess in exhausted defeat, trying to figure out what to do, when Rend reached out and grabbed her hand anyway.

"Any sister of James's is family to me," he said proudly, squeezing her filthy glove without so much as a flinch. "Would you like to be Claw Born too? Stonekin's not a problem these days. Speaking of, are you single? 'Cause I could pay the Water Born to adopt you instead, then you can marry my boy Fangs here--"

"*Dad!*" Ar'Bati growled.

"Too soon?" Rend asked.

566

Everyone glared at him, even James, and the old jubatus sighed.

"All right, all right," he said, then he gave Tina a wink. "Just think about it. In the meanwhile, let's get you taken care of."

He gave a whistle, and more old jubatus came forward, including several who seemed to be important. Tina tried to listen to what they said, leaning heavily on her shield for support, but she was so tired she couldn't follow the words. Something good must have come of it, though, because a few minutes later, James was leading her and all the other players to the outskirts of the yurt-city that was Windy Lake.

As they walked through town, a pack of jubatus stuck their heads out of their white tents to glare at her suspiciously. But while she and the other players got the hairy eyeball, James and Ar'Bati were being treated like celebrities. At one point, a lithe young lady in leather armor ran over, gave both Ar'Bati and James a hug, then ran off. Ar'Bati smiled. James blushed. And Tina rolled her eyes.

"What the heck is going on?" she mumbled, looking around for SB before she remembered he wasn't there.

She was still recovering from that when NekoBaby said, "I dunno, but it looks like James is wildly popular around here."

Tina glanced over her shoulder, blinking in surprise when she realized the Naturalist wasn't just walking behind her. Neko was practically plastered to her back, keeping so close, Tina was amazed she hadn't stepped on the cat girl's paws yet.

"What's up with you?"

The healer clutched her magical staff to her tightly bound chest and moved even closer. "It's this place! People keep staring at me."

"Of course they're staring at us," Tina said. "We're an invading army."

"I didn't say *us*," Neko hissed. "I said *me*. Every dude in this damn village is looking at me like I'm a piece of meat! There's a whole pack of them over behind that yurt that keep moving to new gawking positions as we go."

Tina almost burst out laughing at that. Almost. That would have been cruel to Neko, though, so she kept it to a mere snort. "They've probably never seen a girl like you before," she said, looking pointedly down at Neko's ridiculous body. "You're curves-by-Photoshop, remember? That's high ordinance."

"It's creepy is what it is!" Neko hissed, giving up all pretext as she climbed up onto Tina's shield to ride on the safety of the stonekin's back. "Normally, I'd just Taser them, but I'm OOM, and it's freaking me out. I'm getting a majorly rapey vibe here. These are medieval guys, after all. I bet one tries to knock me out and drag me off to be his cat-wife!"

"Relax, Neko," Tina said. "This a newb zone. Those guys are all level twenty at best. But if it bothers you that much, just make sure you stay by a friend at all times. Also, don't forget to cast Cure Poison on anything anyone gives you to eat or drink. The same goes for anytime you walk away and come back to your cup or plate. We probably won't be here for long, so just stay vigilant, and you'll be okay."

"Fuck that!" Neko cried. "They're the assholes, not me! Why should I have to do all that crap?"

"You know girls have to do that stuff back home all the time, right?" Tina snapped. "Only we don't have lightning magic or Cure Poison. I never left my cup alone at parties or bars, and I never got on an elevator that was only guys, either."

"Well, it fucking sucks," Neko said angrily.

"Tell me about it," Tina agreed.

The cat-girl shot another murderous look at the group of young jubatus males, who did indeed seem to be following them. "The moment I get my mana back, I'm electrocuting all of them."

Tina sighed. "You can't attack them just for looking. They probably don't know any better. Like you said, this isn't an enlightened time."

"Then I'll have to en*light*en them myself," Neko said darkly, curling her fingers menacingly at the jubatus guys, who waved back eagerly.

"You're making it worse," Tina warned. "Just stay away from--" She stopped mid-step, blinking at the sight that had just come into view. "Wait, are those *gnolls?*"

Her balance wobbled as Neko lurched over to her other shoulder, jubatus admirers forgotten.

"Holy crap, they *are*," Neko said, astonished.

Sure enough, the field just beyond Windy Lake had been taken over by an entire encampment of hyena people. Their surprisingly orderly camp was the picture of military discipline, complete with guard patrols and orderly paths between the tent blocks. James exchanged friendly waves with the gnoll soldiers on duty. The soldiers waved back then flipped over to battle mode as they pointed their short spears at Tina and the others. She blinked back, surprisingly intimidated. They might only come up to her knee, but the gnolls' beady black eyes did the squinty, mean-look thing *really* well.

"Is Thunder Paw still here?" James asked the gnoll guarding the entrance to the camp. The gnoll replied in a series of barks and yips, and James nodded. "Great. Can you please ask him to halt the anti-bandit expedition? We'll explain more later."

The guard gnoll looked at James sideways, so James barked and yipped. This made the guards howl with laughter, and they ran off, running into the orderly camp on all fours.

"When did you learn gnoll?" Ar'Bati asked as the group moved on.

James tapped his black staff against his head. "Vocabulary is all memorization, which Intelligence gear amps up. I learned a lot of words from Thunder Paw on our trip back from Red Canyon, but I don't understand the grammar yet." He smiled. "I bet I said something pretty weird just now, but it worked, so I can't complain."

Ar'Bati looked insulted. "That is..." He faded off with a scowl. "What's the player term for egregious cheating?"

"Hax," Tina supplied.

"That is *hax*," Ar'Bati finished.

James shrugged. "Play the hand you're dealt."

He came to a stop after that in the middle of a large, empty field.

"What's this?" Tina asked, looking around in confusion.

James gave her a sheepish look. "Where you're staying, I'm afraid. These are the festival grounds. It looks like an empty field, I know, but it has outhouses for a crowd, and it's inside the magical influence of the Naturalist Lodge. Fangs and I are going back to see about finding you some spare tents, but we're a very large group, so I doubt Windy Lake has enough for everyone. Still, it's not like it rains much here. My main concern is sun stroke, but there's some trees beside the lake." He pointed at a line of scrubby trees beside the water. "If we put the wounded in the shade, they should be okay until we get something better set up."

"Thanks, J," Tina said. "We'll manage. I'm just happy nothing's trying to kill us. But where are you going to be?" She'd already gotten the hint that James had no plans of hanging out with her and the other players, not that she could blame him now that he was a cat-village rock star.

"The main lodge," he replied. "Gotta see what the situation is before I crash."

"We'll be here, then," Tina said, waving goodbye. James waved back and turned toward the village again, falling into step behind Ar'Bati, who'd already gotten a head start.

The moment her brother--or maybe brothers, who the fuck knew--were gone, Tina collapsed on the ground, causing Neko to jump away with a yowl. The army of players around her immediately followed suit. Sighs of relief filled the air as people sat down, fell down, or splayed out on the ground. Some dug immediately into their packs for food and water. Others ran to the outhouses, which quickly acquired massive lines.

Happy she didn't have to worry about such fleshy concerns, Tina just lay on her back, staring up at the painfully bright deep-blue sky. She'd had no healing since the undead had broken through the gates, and her whole body hurt from head to toe. Her shield arm was numb from all the hits, and the muscles in her sword hand burned and twitched even when resting. The only parts of her that weren't throbbing with pain were the parts touching the ground.

Being flat on the dusty earth felt *lovely*. This was the first really clean, wild ground she'd encountered since the transition. The dirt particles clung to her comfortingly, as if the ground itself were hugging her. She was fighting the urge to bury herself like a hibernating toad when she felt someone with very quiet feet coming over.

Tina froze, not even daring to open her eyes as whoever it was sat down in the grass beside her. Then they sighed, and her suspicions were confirmed. Over a mic or live in this world, it didn't matter. Even with her eyes closed, she'd know SB's sigh anywhere.

"Tina..." he said quietly when it became obvious she wasn't going to look at him. "I--"

She rolled over, putting the wall of her stonekin's back between them. It wasn't the best reaction, but she was too spent to deal with him right now. Just knowing he was close brought a hot, angry wetness to her eyes, so Tina kept them closed, lying in silence until his presence vanished silently from behind her--and was immediately replaced by NekoBaby's loud huff.

"*Damn*, girl," the jubatus healer said. "That was the most ultimate cold shoulder I've ever seen."

"Don't 'damn, girl' me, cat-boy," Tina said bitterly, curling her body into a ball. "Just go away."

That earned her a hiss as Neko's puffy tail lashed out to whap Tina in the face. "What the hell are you doing?" the Naturalist demanded. "I voted against you, too, you know. So did Killbox, Frank, Zen, Anders, and Richard, but I don't see you giving any of us the silent treatment. I know you and SB have history or whatever, but for the record, I think this whole blow-up of yours is bullshit. Everyone has secrets. You need to get over it."

Tina squeezed her eyes tighter. "You don't know what you're talking about, Neko, so please, shut up. I've nearly died like fifty times today, and I can't handle this."

A weight landed on her shoulder as Neko jumped on top of her. "Look at me, Roxxy," she said, leaning down to shove her face right in front of Tina's. "I might be really bad at romance and women and shit, but I'd have to be stupid to miss this. *Anyone* can tell you and SB want to doink each other so bad it hurts. Hurts him, hurts you, hurts to fucking watch, oh my *god*."

"Don't want to hear it, Neko," Tina said through clenched teeth.

"No," Neko said angrily, grabbing Tina's face in her hands. "I'm gonna say this, 'cause I owe you both big time, and someone has to take the hit to tell you."

"Tell me what?" Tina said in a dangerous voice.

"That you're being an *idiot*," the cat-girl hissed at her. "I subscribe to your video channel, so I've seen you IRL. You're damn cute, so maybe you've got that hot college-girl thing where you think you can get away with shit like this, but trust me. It's gonna be *your* fault when he walks away."

Tina started to shake.

"Us guys will go through hell and high water to get laid," NekoBaby went on. "SB's more determined than most. He's had it super bad for you for, like, six years straight. But if you keep demanding shit he can't give and pushing him away, he's gonna give up and go chase some other tail. Don't try to pretend it's not gonna hurt like all fuck when you see him with another girl one day. You have to give to get, you know, so cut him some slack."

Neko finished with a huff, but Tina couldn't even lift her arms to push the jubatus away. She was just so tired, and it hurt so much. She knew Neko was only trying to help, but the jubatus didn't know how brutally unfair those words were. How utterly *wrong*.

"That's not it," she whispered at last. "I gave him everything I had, but it still wasn't good enough. *I* wasn't good enough."

"Huh? What was that?" Neko leaned closer, cupping her huge fluffy ears. "My hearing's good but not *that* good. Say it again."

572

Tina couldn't. Speaking the truth out loud once had already torn back open the wound she'd tried her best to beat closed during the defense of Bastion. If she said it again, she would tear herself to pieces. From the way her body was shaking, Tina wasn't sure she hadn't already.

"Oh shit," Neko said. "Are you *crying?*"

Tina pressed her face into the ground, and the Naturalist began to panic. "Craaap," she moaned. "This is why I suck at relationships! Anyway, that's all I had to say, so I'm gonna go hang with Killbox for a bit. He hits on me like a teen boy who's too into rap, but... yeah. Sorry, Roxxy!"

Neko patted her awkwardly on the shoulder one last time and bolted. When she was gone, Tina slumped into the welcoming dirt.

She lay there and shook for a long time. How long, she had no idea, but the ground was much quieter when she felt another pair of boots coming toward her across the barren field.

"Roxxy?" Zen asked softly. "You still awake?"

Tina considered not answering, but the Ranger only came to her when it was important. The flaming wreckage of her personal life had already dinged her performance as a raid leader enough for one day, so she forced herself to stop shaking and sit up, wiping the dust off her face so she could look at Zen properly.

It must not have been enough, because the Ranger jerked back. "Whoa," she said softly, then her leaf-green eyes softened. "You want to talk about it?"

"No," Tina said flatly. "What do you need? Is there trouble?"

Zen shook her head, her curly green hair bobbing. "Everyone's too tired for trouble. We've been fighting for twelve hours straight. But since we never seem to be able to get rest for long, I wanted to take this chance to talk."

Tina winced inwardly. "About what?"

"I just wanted to tell you that, despite the drama, I really respected how you accepted the vote and led everyone out of Camp Comeback," the Ranger said. "I've seen how hard you've been trying to lead the

573

Roughnecks without relying on threats, and I wanted you to know how much that's meant to all of us. Especially me. I know you and I butt heads a lot, but you've never taken our disagreements out on me personally. I know how hard that is to do. I've certainly had some very unkind things to say about you, but I want you to know that after today, I'm glad you're the leader of the Roughnecks. You proved you're still the best for the job, and even if we don't always agree, there's no one else I'd rather follow."

Tina squirmed uncomfortably at the praise. Then, because she felt she needed to say something nice back, she added, "Hearing that from you means a lot. You're the only officer other than..." She stopped, unable to even get SB's name out of her mouth. "You're the only one I trust to do things without constant supervision," she finished at last.

"Um, thanks?"

Tina winced as she realized how backhanded that compliment sounded. "What I mean is I trust you not to do anything stupid or crazy," she amended then winced again. That *still* sounded awful, as if she was praising Zen for not being an idiot when Tina really just wanted to convey how much she had come to trust and respect the former nurse. "What I'm trying to say is--"

Zen laughed and leaned over to pat Tina's knee. "I think you're too tired for this conversation," she said gently.

"It's all coming out wrong," Tina said, covering her face with a sigh. "Can you just spot me this one?"

"Sure," Zen said, settling down in the dirt beside her with her bow across her knees. "Tell you what--why don't you get some sleep, and I'll sit here and keep anyone from bothering you. Okay?"

"Sounds great," Tina said, flopping back into the blessed dirt. "Thank you, Zen."

The Ranger nodded, but Tina was already out, her stone body sinking to the earth as she fell asleep for the first time in three days.

***

"You know," James said, using his Eclipsed Steel Staff as a walking stick as he and Ar'Bati hobbled slowly toward the Naturalist Lodge. "Someday, I'd love to arrive in Windy Lake *not* on the heels of crisis or the edge of death."

"Pah," Fangs said dismissively. "What kind of lazy life is that?"

"A lovely one?" James said, looking wistfully up at the sunny sky. "I've been a cat-person for a week straight, and I haven't had one nap in a sunbeam yet. Not one! Or warm laundry. If it does end up that I actually am stuck here forever, I'm inventing the electric dryer just so I can try sleeping on warm laundry."

"I don't know what an 'electric dryer' is," Ar'Bati replied huffily. "But sunbeams are quite nice in winter. Not that I've ever lazed in one, of course, but I've heard about them. You know, from friends."

"Suuure," James said, chuckling. He was about to ask if any of Ar'Bati's "friends" had ever tried sitting in a box when he spotted a strange shape on the horizon. His head snapped up so fast his neck popped.

Fangs was even quicker, baring his teeth in a hiss as his arm shot out to point at the huge shadow flying down from the north. "What is that?"

James put his hands over his eyes to block the sun. "I think it's *Xthr*."

"The Bird?" Fangs cried, panicked. "What's he doing here? I thought his favor was spent."

So had James. "We'd better warn the king."

Ar'Bati nodded, and the two of them bolted toward the lodge. They'd just finished climbing the wooden steps when Gregory himself came out through the curtain door.

"Your Majesty!" James cried, pointing at the shadow in the sky, which the rest of the town was now starting to notice.

"I know," the king said, giving James a tired smile. "Don't worry. He's here at my behest. He's not free of his ancient debt until he saves

575

Bastion, and while we are all here, there's still one very important aspect my kingdom cannot be said to be whole without."

Before James could ask him what that was, the king strode away down the dirt street toward the front of town. Scowling, James and Ar'Bati jogged after him, sticking close to the king as he walked out of the yurt city and into the grasslands that swept around the lake itself.

They made it just in time to see Xthr land. The giant Bird swept in like an aircraft carrier, his beating wings whipping the blue waters of the Windy Lake into foot-tall waves, and in his claws, clutched as delicately as an egg, was a glowing golden crystal as tall as Gregory.

James's eyes widened. "Is that...?"

"Yes," Gregory said, his face showing his relief in the crystal's shimmering light. "Removing the Bastion from Bastion is a sacrilege that will stain my name for all of history, I'm sure, but I couldn't leave it to the Once King. At least here, I can use its power to defend Windy Lake. After it's recovered, of course."

That struck James as a very practical way to go about things. He just hoped Xthr didn't crush the Bastion before he set it down. From the look on his monstrous face, the Bird was definitely considering it. In the end, though, all he actually managed was a disgusted sigh as he dropped the Bastion in the grass beside the king.

"*I truly regret granting your ancestor that favor now,*" the old Bird rumbled. "*All these years, I've dreamed of crushing that hateful bit of sunshine, and now I find myself its savior.*" He huffed a blast of purple fire high into the air. "*I told you fate had a sense of irony.*"

"I am glad of it," Gregory said, bowing low. "Thank you, Great Bird. In our darkest hour, you honored your vow. All that truly matters in Bastion has now been saved. Your debt is now paid in full."

"*Such careless words,*" Xthr boomed, lowering his huge head to glare at the king with his purple-faceted eyes. "*You're lucky that I am a creature of the Moon. If my magic weren't so rooted in cycles, I would have betrayed you.*"

The king grinned back. "That is why my forefathers trusted you," he said. "And why they taught me to call on you in our time of need. But our alliance doesn't have to end at one favor. You and the Once King have been enemies since the dawn of time. If you wished to continue--"

The ground shook as the giant Bird laughed.

"*Never!*" Xthr cried. "*I've already made myself a laughingstock, helping your doomed kingdom as much as I have. But I didn't get this old by throwing myself in with lost causes. Bastion may have escaped, but the Once King still has the upper hand. His lichs are already reanimating Bastion's dead, using your own troops to replace what you have killed. Once they have sufficient reinforcements, the Blood General will march down here in pursuit of you. Vanguard units were already departing when I left.*"

The Bird reached out to tap a giant claw against the Bastion. "*You saved what matters most, Buffoon King. I'll give you that. But it will not save you. I shall be sorry to see your end, but in the scope of my long, long life, it makes no difference at all. The Quiet Moon will protect me if the Once King seeks more than just your annihilation, which is all that matters to me.*" He lifted his head back up with sad smile. "*Farewell, Bastion's Last King. May you have a painless death.*"

The king's shoulders slumped as the giant Bird spread his wings, but it did not return to the sky. Instead, Xthr's enormous body slid into the Lightless Realm, leaving them standing alone in the grass beside the ruffled lake.

"Well," Gregory said, shoulders slumping, "that didn't go entirely as I'd hoped."

"At least we have the Bastion," James said optimistically. "That's not nothing. But can I ask you a question about what Xthr said? It was very close to something the Grand Schtump said as well, but I don't know enough about this world to understand it."

"I will try to answer as best I can," the king promised. "What troubles you?"

James looked up at the clear blue sky. "Xthr spoke of being born of the Moon, but FFO has no moon. So far as I know from the wiki, it's *never* had a moon, so what are they talking about?"

Gregory sighed and ran a hand through his tousled red hair. "I know and I don't know, I'm afraid. I wish I had some secret to tell you, but the only gods I know of are the Sun, the Wind, the Water, and the Moon, the same as everyone else. I've read that we are all descended of the celestial elves, children of the Sun, but other than as pertains to the Birds, specifically Xthr, I've never heard of the Moon as anything other than a myth or legend. Frankly, I presumed it was a long-dead god of the Lightless Realm, but I have no evidence of that." He looked hopefully at James. "Are you familiar with the word?"

"It's a pretty big thing in our world," James said, scrubbing his hands through his fur. "But I'm not sure that means anything here, and we've got too many problems on our hands to go adding new mysteries. I was just hoping you had an easy answer."

"Sorry to disappoint," the king replied. Then he looked at the Bastion. "I seem to be doing that a lot, but we must make use of today's sacrifices to ensure our future. If the Once King is coming here, then we must be prepared."

"Prepared for what?" an old voice asked. "To run or to fight?"

James and the king both turned around to see Grey Fang watching them. More specifically, she was staring at the Bastion, her eyes filled with wonder.

"I heard what the Bird said, but I put no truck in the cowardice of Lightless creatures. The Once King used betrayal to destroy Bastion the city, but now that we have the Bastion itself--and its king and its armies and the players--he will not find us such easy prey."

That struck James as an extraordinarily optimistic way to view their situation, but at least it perked Gregory up.

"Then shall we plan our strategy?" the king asked.

"In the morning," the old cat assured him, shooting a pointed look at the king's bloody armor and tired face. "With respect, Your Majesty, Bastion is five hundred miles away. If the enemy is coming, it will not arrive tonight, and you and your armies need rest. Tomorrow, at dawn, we can discuss how to turn back this invasion, but for now at least, you should rest."

Gregory didn't look as though he wanted to rest, but Gray Fang's grandma voice seemed to be universal. When she said, "Go to bed," even kings listened.

"If that is what you feel is wise, then we shall adjourn for the evening."

"An excellent choice," the elder said, nodding back at the Lodge. "You shall have our best room."

Gregory nodded, then to everyone's shock, he turned and picked up the Bastion, carrying the giant crystal with him like a lover all the way back to the Naturalist Lodge.

"That is a sight I never thought to see," Ar'Bati whispered.

"Me, neither," James said, eyes wide. "It's the heart of his kingdom, though, and he *is* super strong. Makes sense."

Ar'Bati could only blow out a breath at that. James was about to suggest they follow when Lilac ran up to tell them they'd found tents for the players.

***

The rest of the evening was spent distributing supplies. Eager to show off their hospitality to the king, Windy Lake had turned itself upside down, finding food, blankets, fresh clothes, and medical supplies for the remaining population of Bastion. As the only one who was both a player and a member of the tribes, James was often called upon to act as an intermediary. He was delivering tents on behalf of the Water Born clan to the masses of low-level players when Flameboyant found him.

"There you are, James!" the Sorcerer said, running up to him.

"Flame!" James said, grinning. "I was worried you hadn't made it through the portal. I'm sorry I wasn't able to find you."

"It's all good," Flameboyant assured him. "I'm not here to scold or anything. I just wanted to say thank you for everything."

"Everything?" James raised an eyebrow. "You sound like you're leaving."

The elf nodded, his face sheepish. "If you don't mind, I'd like to join the other low-levels. I'm just too under-powered for all the fighting that's going on, and I think my chances of survival are higher if I stick closer to my own level."

"Of course," James said. "You don't need my approval. It's not like you're my retainer or something. I'm just happy to know you'll be safe."

Flameboyant looked at the ground. "I knew you'd say that," he muttered. "But I still feel like I'm bailing. I still haven't paid you back for saving my life."

"Dude," James said. "You jumped through a window with me to crash the king's war meeting and shoved a bag over Malakai's head. That *has* to make us even. I might even owe *you* now."

"Well, when you put it that way..."

James stepped forward and hugged Flameboyant, making the red-haired elf jump.

"Stay safe," James said. "When this is all over, let's go drinking or something."

Flameboyant hugged him tight. "You too, James," he whispered. "Don't die, okay?"

James promised he would not, and the elf walked away, his arms piled high with blankets for the lowbie camp.

It was several more hours before James managed to return to the Naturalist Lodge to crash for the night. He managed to sleep until dawn, but the king was up bright and early the next morning, as were all the clan heads, Gray Fang, the captains of the garrison and the City Guard, the high

580

priest Raffestain, and the Arch-Sorcerer. By the time James had emptied his bladder, the lodge was overflowing with concerned-looking old people. He was wondering what good he'd be to all of this when Gray Fang grabbed him by a sleeve.

"James," she said sharply. "The meeting is about to begin. Since this will decide everyone's fate, we'll need the players' leaders to attend as well. Go and fetch them here, and be polite."

"Yes, ma'am," James said and ran off, leaving the room full of old cats shaking hands with Bastion bigwigs.

Running through town in the warm morning, he saw a new collection of tents set up down by the lakeshore that was packed to bursting with knights and soldiers. The Bastion civilian refugees were there as well, camped out as far from the players as possible. The positioning bothered him, but that kind of hate didn't just go away. It would take time to mend the wounds Malakai had made, but the fact that the heads of Bastion wanted the players at their meeting was a good start, so James picked up the pace, dropping to all fours as he raced to the edge of town, where Tina and the others were encamped.

When he got to the tent city filled with his fellow players, though, James realized he had no idea which one belonged to Tina. He tried poking his head into a few, but this turned out to be a terrible idea when he stumbled on two people sleeping naked on their spread-out blankets, arms and legs tangled together.

Blushing so hard he was amazed his fur didn't start smoking, James jumped back and started scanning the camp for someone else who could just *tell* him where Tina was and save him the embarrassment of walking in on any more naked shenanigans. Unfortunately, no one was up this early. James was beginning to despair when he spotted Tina's off-tank, Frank, heading for the outhouses.

"Frank!" he cried, running over. "Man, am I glad to see you."

"Good morning to you, too, James," Frank said with a grin. "You a fellow early riser?"

"No, but the king is," James said, lowering his voice. "We have a situation. Do you know which tent is Tina's?"

Frank's expression turned grim. "Son, it's best if you just stop right there. Not that I'd ever speak ill of your sister, but it's a stupid man who steps into that wolverine's den."

"She'll be more pissed if I leave her out," James said. "But I guess I don't technically have to have her. I just need someone who can speak on behalf of the players."

"Then why don't ya take SilentBlayde?" Frank suggested, his eyes suspiciously sly. "He's the Roughnecks' second-in-command, and frankly, you'd be doing the poor boy a favor."

James winced at the mention of SB's name. He still had no idea what had happened between him and Tina, but he didn't think he'd make it better by bringing the Assassin with him to the meeting. Also, their last encounter hadn't exactly been friendly. But he still didn't know where Tina was, and Frank was already shoving him toward a lone acacia tree at the edge of camp with a dark shape hunched in its branches.

"Thanks for taking care of him," Frank said, slapping James on the back. "I gotta wizz something fierce. Go talk SB down and give him a task to take his mind off things. You'll be doing us all a solid."

Before James could object, the knight vanished into the outhouse and began to noisily relieve himself. Left with no other options, James sighed and walked over to the base of the sandy-barked tree.

"Harut--" He stopped. SB didn't like to be called by his real name anymore. "Blayde?" he tried instead. "You up there?"

No answer.

Shaking his head, James flexed his claws and started climbing. He found the elf sitting on the topmost branch, staring out at the endless waving grass.

"SB?" James said, waving his hand in front of his friend's face. "You awake?"

His blue eyes were open, but that didn't necessarily mean anyone was home inside. He certainly looked shell-shocked. Even though his face was half-hidden by his mask, he looked utterly exhausted, and he was still dressed in his dirty, bloody armor. The Haruto James knew was a neat freak of the first order, but SB didn't even look like he'd been down to the lake to sluice off.

"Hey," James said, clinging to the tree trunk since he didn't trust that branch with the weight of both of them. "I need your help. Can you come down?"

"What's the point?" SilentBlayde replied quietly. "I've ruined everything."

James sighed. "I'm sure it's not--"

"It is," SB said sharply, then he put his head in his hands. "You were right," he whispered. "I am a horrible person. I had everything. I had a *miracle*, and I destroyed it all." His voice began to tremble. "There's nothing left for me in this world anymore."

James went still. He'd heard words like those before, in a different place from a different person. This time, though, he knew to take them seriously.

"I don't think you're horrible," he said gently, easing himself onto the branch despite the way it creaked. "I'm not even mad at you anymore, so why don't you tell me what happened."

SB dropped his hands with a bleak sigh. "She was wrong," he whispered. "And I voted against her because of it."

"Are you talking about the Forlorn Hope?"

SilentBlayde nodded. "She thought we were stupid to work with the king, that it would be easier to just burn them all and save ourselves. But she hadn't seen what I'd seen. She didn't know what that fire would really do, who it would hurt. I did." He clenched his bloody gloves tight. "I did it for her."

James was sure Tina hadn't seen it that way, but something about this still rang false. "Is that why she blew up at you?" he asked skeptically. "I

583

mean, I'm sure she was angry, but Tina's not the sort to stop talking to someone just because they disagree with her. All the other officers voted against her as well, and she's still talking to them. Did something else happen?"

SB hunched his shoulders and slid a little farther down the branch, which was answer enough.

"You know," James said, pinching the bridge of his nose, "this feels a lot like the last time she stopped talking to you."

SilentBlayde curled up even tighter at the mention of the old incident, and James winced. *Bingo.*

"You want to tell me what's going on?"

"No," whispered the sad ball SB had rolled himself into.

"I think it would help," James said encouragingly. "I know you hate it when people pry into your private life, but you broke my sister's heart one day and never told anyone why. Now it looks like you've done it again, but you seem to be the one suffering, so maybe this is a good time to just let it out."

SilentBlayde shook his head frantically. "I can't."

"Why not?" James asked. "We're trapped in an alternate universe in our alternate egos. We don't know why we're here or if we'll ever be able to get back home. Whatever secret you're carrying, there's no way it can reach you here. What if, instead of letting your past ruin your future, you just told Tina the truth?"

SB peeked over his folded arms to give James the bitterest look he'd ever seen. "Can you tell Tina the real reason you failed out of college?"

James looked down at the ground, instantly defeated. "Of course not," he muttered. "I wish I'd never told *you*."

"There you go," SB said, staring back out at the grass. "Some things stick with us no matter where we go. Even in another world, even with another name, there's no running from what's inside." He dropped his head back to his arms with a shudder. "Just leave me alone."

He sounded so hopeless, James's heart broke for him, but he didn't know how to fix things. He didn't know if this *could* be fixed, but there was absolutely no way he was leaving SB alone right now.

"You're coming with me," James said firmly, grabbing his arm. "I need you to represent the Roughnecks at a war meeting."

"I don't care."

"You should," James said sharply. "I know things look bad right now, but Tina's not going to be mad at you forever. I cooked her with lightning yesterday, and she's already forgiven me. She'll forgive you too if you give her a chance, but if we don't get our game together, there won't be time for that, 'cause we're all going to be *dead*. So if you want a second chance, come down and help me make one."

He finished with an encouraging smile, but SilentBlayde just scooted farther down the branch, which was starting to dip dangerously.

"That's it," James said, moving back to the main trunk. "You're coming with me. No more brooding in trees."

"Are you deaf?" the elf growled. "I said leave me a--"

James kicked the tree branch. With SilentBlayde sitting so far out on the edge already, one good whack was all it took. The moment his foot touched it, the branch snapped in half, and SB went toppling backward to the ground, where he crashed gracelessly into a bush, confirming James's suspicions.

"Well, well," James said, hopping down to grab SilentBlayde by his collar. "Looks like someone spent all night sulking instead of sleeping and is now too tired to stop me."

"Let me go!" SB yelled, struggling feebly.

"No," James said, dragging the elf behind him as he turned back toward the lodge. "I have work to do. Maybe you'll help me with it, maybe you won't, but like hell am I leaving you here alone."

SilentBlayde fought for a few more seconds, then he just seemed to give up, going limp in defeat as James dragged him across the dusty field. "Why do you care?" he muttered. "I thought we weren't friends anymore."

"You're the only one who said that," James replied. "But if it makes you feel better, knowing you voted against Tina for the Forlorn Hope is better than any apology you could have offered. I couldn't ask for better proof that you've stopped being her yes-man. Now if you'll just say you're sorry for trying to kill me, we'll be square."

"I *am* sorry, James," SilentBlayde said in a small voice. "More than you'll ever know. I was desperate and stupid, and I am ashamed of my actions. I hope you can forgive me."

"Apology accepted," James said, lifting the Assassin out of the dirt. "Can you walk now, or do I have to keep dragging you?"

"I can walk," SB said tiredly.

James set the elf back on his feet, though he didn't let go. SB didn't comment on the hand James kept on his wrist. He just quietly brushed the dirt and dust off his armor, wincing when this only served to reveal more blood.

"I'm what the cat's dragged in today, I'm afraid," he muttered, reaching up to straighten his mask.

"Meow," James said.

The joking sound came out painfully close to an *actual* meow, and James slapped his hands over his mouth in horror. SB stared at him for a moment, then he burst out laughing, falling back into the dirt as he pointed at James and cackled. A few seconds later, James joined in, doubling over as they both laughed and laughed, drawing curses and thrown rocks from the still-sleeping players around them.

"Oh man," James said when he finally got ahold of himself. "I think we've been through too much. We're starting to lose our marbles here."

"What do you mean, 'starting?'" SB said, getting back to his feet. "We've been like this for a while now."

James couldn't argue with that.

"So," the Assassin said, brushing his hands over his filthy clothes one more time before giving up. "What's this about a war meeting?"

586

"Oh crap!" James glanced at the sky, which was much lighter than it should have been. Getting SB had taken way longer than he'd anticipated, which meant the king and all the clan heads might be waiting for them right now. That was not a comfortable thought, so James grabbed SB and booked it, dragging the elf all the way back through Windy Lake and up the steps to the Naturalist Lodge.

When he burst through the curtained door, an entire room full of the most important people on the continent stopped talking to look at him. He was trying to think of what to say when someone barked, "Where's Roxxy?"

"She's still sleeping," James said, yanking SB up beside him. "This is SilentBlayde, FFO's top Assassin and second-in-command of the Roughnecks. He'll be handling things until Roxxy's back on her feet."

This announcement was followed by a long, tense silence. As it stretched, James realized just how nuts he sounded. The exhausted elf at his side was caked in dirt and dried blood. His eyes were ringed with deep dark circles, and he smelled of ash and death. He looked more like a bandit than a respected second-in-command. James was frantically searching for something to say when SB cleared his throat.

"I apologize for my appearance," he said, his silvery voice as smooth as ever as he bowed from the waist. "I've had a lot to take care of since we fled Bastion."

That was a bald-faced lie, but it seemed to work.

"Not all of us are so lucky as to be pampered kings," King Gregory said sympathetically, waving at the open space beside him in the circle around the fire. "Thank you for making time for us. Please sit."

SB walked over and sat beside the king, though it turned into more of a plop as his exhausted legs gave out and dropped him on the pillow. James sat down next to him, squeezing himself into the space between Gregory and his friend. When they were both seated, the old jubatus who'd been talking when they entered stood back up and resumed.

It wasn't the meeting James had hoped for. He'd been eager for an actual plan, but since no one here actually knew each other beyond basic reputation, the "war meeting" ended up being mostly introductions, stating of positions, and mutual bemoaning about how little information everyone had. There was also a great deal of time spent talking about how to feed everyone.

This turned out to be quite the problem. Unlike the well-prepared players of Camp Comeback, who still had their prepackaged rations, the armies and citizens of Bastion had come through the portal with nothing but what was in their pockets. Supplying so many on such short notice was no easy task, and all the clan heads had different ideas as to how it could be accomplished. They were still bickering about it when Gregory leaned over.

"James," he whispered, glancing pointedly at Thunder Paw, who'd spent most of the meeting listening politely and being glared at by the jubatus. "What can you tell me of the gnolls? I'm only familiar with them as a threat to the kingdom. I know very little concerning them as potential allies, and the jubatus aren't a good source of information for obvious reasons."

James smiled. He'd wanted to bring this up with the king anyway. "They're good people," he said earnestly. "The gnolls care immensely for family and pack. They're also very clever and as tough as nails in a fight. You couldn't ask for more tenacious allies."

Gregory nodded. "Excellent. What are their needs? Specifically, what of Bastion's now extremely limited resources could I offer that would tempt them into an alliance?"

"You're in luck on that score," James said. "They want legitimacy. Their ancestors came to the savanna as refugees and were immediately branded as bandits. We've cleared that up somewhat, but after so many years of bad blood, peace is still very fragile in the savanna." He glanced at the circle of angry old cat-people, who were now growling at each other like lions. "Frankly, I'm amazed the alliance hasn't blown up already."

"I can work with that," the king said, then he stood up, an action James got the impression Gregory had been avoiding the whole meeting.

The room went quiet as the Holy King rose to his full height. James tried to catch Thunder Paw's eye to give the old Naturalist a hint that something was coming his way, but it was a no-go. All the eyes in the room, including Thunder Paw's lone remaining good one, were locked on the king.

"Chieftain Thunder Paw," Gregory said, his voice deep and respectful. "Your people still have outlaw status in Bastion, and I know there is much to be sorted out here between Windy Lake and the Grand Pack. That said, since our arrival, I've seen you acting steadfastly as our ally, despite our history. I am most humbled and impressed by your wisdom and generosity, and I would like to make you an offer."

Thunder Paw bowed as much as an old, hunched hyena-man could, but this seemed mostly a cover to let him flick his one good eye at James, who gave him a thumbs-up.

"We would gladly hear your offer, great king," said Thunder Paw.

"Excellent," Gregory replied, pulling a battered scroll from the satchel at his belt. "It's called the Forlorn Hope..."

***

The meeting broke up shortly after that. Thunder Paw wanted to discuss the Forlorn Hope with his pack, and everyone else was frantic to put the logistics they'd nearly come to blows over into practice. James was about to slip away as well when the king touched his shoulder.

"James, SilentBlayde, if you could stay a moment."

When the lodge had emptied of even Gray Fang, the towering king turned and offered them the scroll he'd just showed Thunder Paw to SilentBlayde. "It's already signed," he said at SilentBlayde's confused look. "Please tell Roxxy and all the other players that your Forlorn Hope contract has been met in full. As promised, I hereby pardon all players of past crimes and formally recognize them as citizens of Bastion."

By the time he finished, SB's eyes were huge above his mask. "Thank you, Your Highness," he said, bowing with what appeared to be true sincerity. "This means a great deal to all of us. To me, especially."

"I'm glad to hear it," Gregory said, smiling. "Bastion needs heroes now more than ever." With that, the king's smile fell. "It pains me to ask, but can I count on the Roughnecks for the coming battles? I have heard that you are mercenaries. Now that our previous arrangement is concluded, I was hoping I might hire you to continue to defend us against the Once King."

James's head whipped around to watch SB. He'd never even considered that the Roughnecks wouldn't fight until the king had mentioned it. Now that the idea was in his head, though, he realized he wasn't sure. Tina was always so goal-focused, and her goal right now was to get home. Fighting a losing battle when they were no longer trapped wasn't part of that, but surely she wouldn't leave them here to die.

SilentBlayde fiddled nervously with his face wrap. "*I* would fight," he said at last. "As would others who have a stake in this world's future, but I can't speak for Roxxy. We didn't get what we came to Bastion to find, so I'm not sure where she plans to lead us next. There hasn't been time to talk about it."

"James said that you were looking for way home," Gregory said, nodding. "I don't know if they can help, but I brought all of my subjects from the castle with us, including the remaining Portal Keepers. I was thinking of selling access to them in exchange for further Roughneck employment, but I already promised Roxxy a meeting in exchange for Malakai's life." He scowled, thinking the problem through. "Do you think she'd take an arranged marriage as payment if I made it good enough? For a boon as great as the Roughnecks' help, lands and titles are not out of the question."

James bit his lip and glanced at SB, who was clutching his fists so tight, his leather gloves creaked.

"That would be a disastrous plan," the Assassin said in a flat, deadly voice.

"Really?" Gregory replied, completely failing to pick up on--or else politely ignoring--the elf's obviously personal motives. "A pity. Making her a duchess would solve many problems."

"Can we see the Portal Keepers?" James asked excitedly. "Tina... I mean Roxxy's still sleeping, but she's never been much for lore. I don't think she'd mind if SB and I spoke to the Portal Keepers on her behalf. Also, if we're able to get answers and have them ready for her by the time she wakes up, that will probably put her in a *much* better mood when she comes to speak to you."

The king brightened noticeably at that prospect. "An excellent idea," he said, rubbing his hands together. "If you don't think she'd mind, I'd be happy to let you speak with the keepers. There's one in particular I think you'll be very interested to meet. Just be sure to inform Roxxy that I honored my debt."

"We will," James promised, eager to finally speak with someone who might actually be able to tell him what was going on. "Where are the Portal Keepers now?"

"In the army camp with the rest of my subjects," the king said, walking them out of the lodge. "The guard will show you the way. You there!" He pointed at one of the disgraced former knights standing at attention in the square in front of the Naturalist Lodge. "Escort these men to the Portal Keepers' tent."

The soldier--a young, earnest-looking man with sandy-brown hair and a painfully honest smile--hurried forward to obey his king. With a final nod at both of them, Gregory stepped back into the lodge. Eager to get to the Portal Keepers--and hopefully some answers--James grabbed SB's arm and started down the stairs, but the elf didn't move. He just stood there staring at the young ex-knight who'd come forward like he'd seen a ghost. James was opening his mouth to ask his friend what was wrong when SB suddenly whirled around.

"One more thing, Your Majesty!"

"Yes?" the king said, poking his head back out.

James looked at SilentBlayde in confusion. He had no idea what was going on, but the elf was vibrating like a high-tension wire.

"I know you've stripped most of your knights of their titles," SB said, his voice strained with what was clearly a desperate attempt not to get emotional. "But I must speak on behalf of one whom I know does not deserve such punishment."

Gregory raised a bushy red eyebrow and stepped out onto the lodge's porch. "He must be some knight indeed for you to say so. What is this exemplary person's name?"

SilentBlayde pulled himself very straight. "Sir Jamie Tillerson."

The young former knight SB had just been staring at jumped with a high-pitched gasp. "Oh no, my lord!" he said desperately, almost falling on his face in his rush to kneel before the king. "I was at the battle against the players the same as my fellows. I am not deserving of any special favor!"

The king frowned, puzzled. "Are you Jamie Tillerson?"

"I am, my king," the young man said, head still down. "But I know not why this player should single me out so. I have never even met this SilentBlayde! It is not possible that he can give such account of me."

At this, SilentBlayde whirled around and yanked his mask off his face. Now it was James's turn to gasp. He'd *never* seen SB take off his face mask. Ever.

"I know you, Sir Jamie," SilentBlayde said, his voice cracking as the emotion he'd been so desperately trying to keep down finally broke through. "You saved me in Bastion when your fellow knights would have murdered me for no reason other than that they didn't like my face."

He reached up to pull back his filthy hair, and the young man gasped. "Master Sky!" he cried, shocked. "Is it really you?"

"It's really me," SB said sadly. "But I'm not Sky of Highcloud. I lied to keep you from guessing that I was a player. But while Sir Dan and the others would have killed me anyway, you didn't let them. You didn't know that I deserved their vengeance. The reason I was wounded wasn't because I'd been beaten by players. It was because I'd just killed eight of your fellow knights in an alley. I *was* the monster Sir Dan accused me of being, but you didn't see that. All you saw was a hurt man who needed your help, so you risked your life for me. I bet you looked for the Highcloud family as you promised, didn't you?"

"I did look," Jamie said, still confused. "But I never did find them."

"Because they don't exist," SB said desperately. "Only me. Your compassion and dedication to your knightly duty saved my life that night. It's because of *you* that I survived to help the Roughnecks destroy the Once King's raid bosses and defend Bastion." He turned back to Gregory, his bare face stark. "Please, Your Majesty, I beg you to return this man's knighthood. There's no one who deserves his title more or does it more honor than Sir Jamie."

The king sighed, then the morning was filled with the pure ring of the Dawnblade as he drew his sword. "I cannot ignore such a heartfelt defense," Gregory said, reaching out to tap the still-kneeling Jamie Tillerson on the shoulders with his golden sword. "On the word of this player, I, Gregory Heraldsford, hereby restore the title of Knight of the Crown to Jamie Tillerson in recognition of his ceaseless devotion to the oaths of knighthood. May you continue to serve as a good example to your fellows in these dark times."

Tears were running down Sir Jamie's face by the time the king finished. James was feeling dangerously close to breaking down himself. But though the king had clearly been moved by SB's story, his face was furious when he sheathed his blade.

"You're very lucky that your past crimes have already been forgiven, Assassin," Gregory said quietly. "You just confessed to murdering eight of my knights in front of me. Fortunately for you, I am not my father. He would have had you beheaded for waiting until after your absolution to pull this ploy."

"I'm sorry. That was not my intention," SilentBlayde said, bowing deeply from his waist. "Please believe that I truly regret what I've done in Bastion."

He looked pointedly at James as he finished. Smiling, James nodded back. He knew SB was sorry. He was *always* sorry, but James was hopeful he'd actually learned something from it this time.

"Yes, well, it has already been forgiven," the king said angrily. "I can't punish you without violating my oaths. But I would still like to know whom you killed, seeing how they died in my name."

"It was a patrol led by Sir Roals near the Diplomatic Quarter," SilentBlayde answered without hesitation. "I understand you can't give me the punishment I deserve, but when this is over, I'd like to make reparations to their families if I may."

"It will be costly," Gregory warned. "The lives of knights are not cheaply bought."

SB shook his head. "I don't care about cost. It's the very least I can do to atone for my crimes."

"Very well, then," the king said with a sigh. "I'll hold you to it once this war is concluded."

"Thank you, Your Majesty," SB said, bowing low again as the king turned and walked back into the lodge. When he straightened up, James had to fight the urge to slap his friend on the back in congratulations. He was so proud of Blayde he could burst, but this wasn't the time or place for his emotions. Now that the king was gone, the knight SB had saved had fallen into the dirt, his whole body shaking as the sobs he'd been so desperately trying to hide from the king finally broke free.

"Sir Jamie?" Blayde said nervously, crouching down to put a hand on the young man's shoulder. "Are you all right?"

"Oh yes," Sir Jamie said, hiccupping. "I'm sorry, Master Sky-- Master Blayde!" He stopped to scrub his face, but the tears kept coming.

"This is a terrible way to repay your kindness. I'm just... My mum and dad worked so hard to get me my chance at knighthood. I didn't know how I was going to tell them that I'd lost my title and disgraced our family. I didn't know if I *could* go home again after this, but you saved me." He looked at SB with heartfelt gratitude. "Thank you."

James watched in quiet amusement as SilentBlayde awkwardly patted the crying knight on the shoulder. Neither of them seemed to know what to say after that, though, so James stepped in to fill the gap before the silence got awkward.

"Well, sounds to me like you two are even," he suggested, reaching down to help the newly re-knighted Sir Jamie back to his feet. "You should shake on it to make it official."

He elbowed SB in the ribs until SilentBlayde offered the knight his hand. Sir Jamie took it, and they shook. When it was over, Sir Jamie pulled out a dirty handkerchief to wipe his nose, looking very much like the kid he was only a few years away from being.

"So, sirs," he said, his voice still wavering. "What now?"

"Portal Keepers?" James suggested.

"Right," Sir Jamie said, wiping his nose one last time before he pulled himself straight again, as befitted a knight. "Please follow me."

James happily fell into step behind Sir Jamie as they walked through the village. On the way, the young knight asked about Forever Fantasy Online the game. Happy to have a safe topic, James eagerly launched into his now very well-polished rundown of FFO's main concepts, slang, and terms, covering SB's uncharacteristic silence all the way to the knights' area by the lake.

"You're so good at this, you should write a book," SB said when James finished his rundown. "'Forever Fantasy Online for NPCs.'" He frowned. "Wait, no, NPC is racist now. Or would that be playerist? Non-playerist?" He shook his head. "We need a new term."

"We need a lot of stuff," James said, suddenly serious. "So many of our problems are just misunderstandings caused by ignorance. We're not

595

the only ones who got shoved into a new world. The people who lived here have also suffered catastrophic changes, and it's not over yet." He looked around at the tents where Bastion's soldiers and former knights were glaring at them with open hate. "Even if we defeat the Once King, it'll be a long time before this world heals."

"We can make it," Sir Jamie said confidently, smiling over his shoulder. "If I can be forgiven, anyone can."

"You did nothing that needed forgiving," SB said firmly, but he looked much more hopeful than he had this morning, and that made James hopeful too. He was patting his friend on the shoulder when Sir Jamie stopped them in front of a tent that was very different from the others.

Like the players, most of the soldiers were living in the small, white portable tents the jubatus used for hunting. This one was much bigger, a richly decorated yurt that had clearly been donated by one of the richer families of the four clans. When Sir Jamie opened the flap, three people--two men and a woman--put down the books they'd been reading and stood up. James recognized them at once. Not by face--he wasn't *that* attentive--but they were all wearing the exact same purple silk robes decorated with constellations every Portal Keeper had sported back in the game.

"These players have won the trust of the king," Sir Jamie announced formally. "His Majesty requests that you answer any questions they may have."

The two male portal keepers looked at James--and the still dreadfully bloody and dirty SilentBlayde--with open terror, but the woman grinned.

"Ooh, players!" she said with a distinctly New York accent. "You're going to want to talk to me."

"Very much so," James said, incredibly intrigued, because while the slender, brown-haired, middle-aged woman in front of him was clearly a Portal Keeper, which meant an NPC, she *talked* like a player. "Who are you?"

The woman grinned as she stuck out her hand. "I'm Leylia."

The End

Book 2 of 3

Thank you for reading **Last Bastion**! If you enjoyed the story, or even if you didn't, we hope you'll consider leaving a review. Reviews, good and bad, are vital to any author's career, and Travis and I would be extremely grateful if you'd consider writing one for us.

Not ready for the ride to end? The final book in the FFO trilogy, **The Once King**, is out now!

If you want to be the first to know when new books are available, sign up for our New Release Mailing List over at rachelaaron.net. List members are the first to hear about any new projects, and you get bonus content, including the list-exclusive Heartstrikers short story, *Mother of the Year*! The list is free, and we promise never to spam you or give your info to anyone else, so sign up and join the fun! You can also follow us on Twitter @Rachel_Aaron and @TravBach.

Liked FFO and want something new to read right now? Check out one of Rachel's other completed series! Just visit www.rachelaaron.net for the full list of Rachel's novels complete with their beautiful covers, links to reviews, and free sample chapters!

Thank you again for reading, and we hope you'll be back soon!

Yours sincerely,
Rachel Aaron and Travis Bach

Glossary of Terms

Forever Fantasy Online is a full-immersion Virtual Reality game. It uses the proprietary Sensorium Engine to hijack players' senses and convey a fake world to them. For safety and health reasons, players can still feel about 10% of their normal senses (sans sight) while in VR.

FFO is a massively multi-player game set in a high-fantasy world involving millions of players across the globe. Though once the unrivaled juggernaut of VR gaming, eight years after its launch populations have declined in favor of newer full sensory VR games. The active player-base of FFO is now estimated to be around 5 million with about 200,000+ players online at any one time.

Unlike some MMOs, FFO doesn't have its player community divided up across multiple servers. Instead, it favors a dynamic zone-based system. Whenever there are too many people in a zone (like the Deadlands), the game will load another zone-server and start assigning newcomers to that version of the zone instead. So a million players could all be in the Deadlands at the same time, but the game would split them across 10,000 different servers to keep the load down.

Game Terms

HP & MP - Health Pool and Mana Pool, aka Hit Points and Mana Points. Damaging attacks reduce the health pool. If HP hits 0, the character is killed and must either be raised by an allied healer's spell or they must relinquish their current location in favor of respawning at a safe graveyard or shrine. No matter where they pop up, dead players always respawn with all of their gear and inventory.

Mana points are used to fuel magical abilities and are only possessed by the spell-casting classes *(Sorcerers, Naturalists, and Clerics. See below.)* Casting spells uses up mana. When a character is out-of-mana (aka OOM), they must wait to recover before casting any more.

Character Class - All players in Forever Fantasy Online must choose from one of seven classes: Knight, Berserker, Assassin, Ranger, Sorcerer, Cleric, and Naturalist.

Each class has a fixed set of abilities and equipment they have access to. For example, all Berserkers have the same stun abilities and use two-handed weapons, while spell-caster classes such as Sorcerers must wear cloth armor and use caster weapons such as staffs or wands.

While abilities and equipment vary, character classes all fit into the three general roles of FFO combat.

Tank (Role) - Heavily armored characters whose job it is to keep enemies from attacking less durable players. Tanks are not good at dealing damage, but they take it very well, making them hard to kill and easy to heal. To keep enemies on them, and not attacking the more vulnerable players, Tanks have abilities called "taunts"--such as Roxxy's *Ground Stomp*--which force monsters to attack them.

Healer (Role) - A magical character who specializes in healing spells. They can also remove status effects such as poisons, curses, diseases, bindings, and even bring players back from the dead. Healers do have some damage-dealing abilities so that they can quest and level on their own, but while they aren't completely helpless, they will never do as much damage as the specialized damage-dealing classes.

Damage / DPS (Role) - Damage dealers are the most numerous classes of character in FFO. Berserkers, Sorcerers, Assassins, and Rangers are all high-damage classes. Tanks can keep monsters at bay while healers heal them, but it is the damage dealer's job to actually kill the attacking enemy.

Group / Party - a small team of two to five players. Used by friends to play together or strangers to tackle challenges too great for a solo player to handle. There are many dungeons and quests in Forever Fantasy Online which require five players to beat. (Ex: The Red Canyon's Lich Lab dungeon.)

Raid – a group of up to fifty players. Typically subdivided into ten parties of five, raids are basically player "armies" created to fight massively epic battles against foes no small party could hope to handle.

Raiding is a big part of the FFO endgame since the coordination required to get fifty players together and to fight well together is very hard. Because of all that work, the rewards for killing raid bosses are among the best in the game.

NPC - non-player character. Any computer-controlled character in the game. NPCs can be friendly or hostile and are generally humanoid and/or intelligent. Note that this term is not usually applied to monsters.

PVE - Players vs. Environment. PVE content is any gameplay that involves the players fighting computer-generated enemies. Completing quests, fighting through a dungeon, and participating in a raid are all examples of PVE content.

PVP - Player vs Player. Some players consider fighting computer opponents too easy. They prefer to fight other real human players in specialized combat called "PVP." FFO has a couple of options for those who wish to only fight human-controlled opponents, including dueling, and participating in ranked gladiatorial combat leagues for special PVP equipment. (There's also an opt-in system for conducting PVP in quest zones.)

Dungeon / Instance - Dedicated group content is often arranged in self-contained areas called dungeons or instances. When a party or raid enters such an area, usually marked by a portal, the game will create a unique instance of that dungeon just for them. So 1000 groups can all be in the Red Canyon dungeon, but it will be a fresh storyline and battle for each and no group can see another in there. The same goes for the Dead Mountain Fortress and other raids.

Aggro - A term used to mean "a monster's attention." When a monster is attacking a player, that player is said to have aggro. Tanks have special abilities to draw monsters' aggro, or attention, to themselves to prevent the monsters from attacking more vulnerable classes.

Levels - Every monster and character in FFO has a power level. Player characters can range from level 1 to level 80 depending on how much they've played the game. Some monsters can be above level 80, such as the skeleton knights of the Dead Mountain Fortress and other monsters in the Deadlands. This is to provide a stiff challenge for powerful veteran players.

Skull Ratings – In addition to levels, all monsters and NPCs in FFO have a skull rating. The number of skulls a monster has beside their level shows how many players the developers think it will take to kill that monster. All beings in FFO are one-skull by default, meaning they can be killed with moderate ease by one same-level player, but there are many harder enemies that require coordinated player effort to take down. For example:

- Two-skull monsters are designed to be a challenge for two players.
- Three-skull monsters are designed to be a challenge for five players.
- Four-skull monsters are designed to be a challenge for ten-player raids.
- Five-skull monsters are for fifty-player raids only.

Two-skull monsters are often called bosses or sub-bosses. Four and five skull monsters are called raid bosses since any group larger than five players is considered a raid.

Gear / Loot – To help them master the world of FFO, player characters have magical equipment, which gives them about 90% of their power. Gear can be looted off the corpses of defeated enemy monsters, earned through completing quests, or won from defeating dungeons or raids. Magical equipment comes in the form of rings, amulets, weapons, and armor. Armor is broken down into nine different "slots" - head, shoulders, chest, belt, legs, feet, bracers, hands, and cloak. Player characters can equip one of each type of gear, but they can't wear more than one piece in the same slot at a time.

Enjoyed *Last Bastion?*
Need a new book *right now*?!

Try one of Rachel's other completed series! Go to
www.rachelaaron.net
for full sample chapters, links to reviews, and lovely covers in
high resolution!

Keep reading to see the covers and blurbs to my first-in-the-
series.

Minimum Wage Magic

The DFZ, the metropolis formerly known as Detroit, is the world's most magical city with a population of nine million and zero public safety laws. That's a lot of mages, cybernetically enhanced chrome heads, and mythical beasties who die, get into debt, and otherwise fail to pay their rent. When they can't pay their bills, their stuff gets sold to the highest bidder to cover the tab.

That's when they call me. My name is Opal Yong-ae, and I'm a Cleaner: a freelance mage with an art history degree who's employed by the DFZ to sort through the mountains of magical junk people leave behind. It's not a pretty job, or a safe one-- there's a reason I wear bite-proof gloves-- but when you're deep in debt in a lawless city where gods are real, dragons are traffic hazards, and buildings move around on their own, you don't get to be picky about where your money comes from. You just have to make it work, even when the only thing of value in your latest repossessed apartment is the dead body of the mage who used to live there.

"A catchy title, a plucky protagonist and a maximum effort by the author, honestly readers can't ask for more in the urban fantasy genre."- **Fantasy Book Critic**

"I love what Rachel Aaron has done with this novel to expand her stories within this unique world of her creation. I have developed a trust in her ability to write engaging stories of great characters which I feel most comfortable and eager to spend time with, and this book is no exception." - **TS Chan**

The Heartstrikers Series

As the smallest dragon in the Heartstriker clan, Julius survives by a simple code: stay quiet, don't cause trouble, and keep out of the way of bigger dragons. But this meek behavior doesn't cut it in a family of ambitious predators, and his mother, Bethesda the Heartstriker, has finally reached the end of her patience.

Now, sealed in human form and banished to the DFZ--a vertical metropolis built on the ruins of Old Detroit--Julius has one month to prove to his mother that he can be a ruthless dragon or lose his true shape forever. But in a city of modern mages and vengeful spirits where dragons are seen as monsters to be exterminated, he's going to need some serious help to survive this test.

He just hopes humans are more trustworthy than dragons.

"*Super fun, fast paced, urban fantasy full of heart, and plenty of magic, charm and humor to spare, this self published gem was one of my favorite discoveries this year!*" - **The Midnight Garden**

"*A deliriously smart and funny beginning to a new urban fantasy series about dragons in the ruins of Detroit...inventive, uproariously clever, and completely un-put-down-able!*" - **SF Signal**

The Legend of Eli Monpress

Eli Monpress is talented. He's charming. And he's the greatest thief in the world.

He's also a wizard, and with the help of his partners in crime--a swordsman with the world's most powerful magic sword (but no magical ability of his own) and a demonseed who can step through shadows and punch through walls--he's getting ready to pull off the heist of his career. To start, though, he'll just steal something small. Something no one will miss.

Something like... a king.

"I cannot be less than 110% in love with this book. I loved it. I love it still. Already I sort of want to read it again. Considering my fairly epic Godzilla-sized To Read list, that's just about the highest compliment I can give a book" - **CSI: Librarian**

"Fast and fun, The Spirit Thief introduces a fascinating new world and a complex magical system based on cooperation with the spirits who reside in all living objects. Aaron's characters are fully fleshed and possess complex personalities, motivations, and backstories that are only gradually revealed. Fans of Scott Lynch's Lies of Locke Lamora (2006) will be thrilled with Eli Monpress. Highly recommended for all fantasy readers." - **Booklist, Starred Review**

The Paradox Trilogy

(written as Rachel Bach)

Devi Morris isn't your average mercenary. She has plans. Big ones. And a ton of ambition. It's a combination that's going to get her killed one day - but not just yet.

That is, until she just gets a job on a tiny trade ship with a nasty reputation for surprises. The Glorious Fool isn't misnamed: it likes to get into trouble, so much so that one year of security work under its captain is equal to five years everywhere else. With odds like that, Devi knows she's found the perfect way to get the jump on the next part of her Plan. But the Fool doesn't give up its secrets without a fight, and one year on this ship might be more than even Devi can handle.

"*Firefly-esque in its concept of a rogue-ish spaceship family... The narrative never quite goes where you expect it to, in a good way... Devi is a badass with a heart.*" - **Locus Magazine**

"*If you liked* Star Wars, *if you like our books, and if you are waiting for* Guardians of the Galaxy *to hit the theaters, this is your book.*" - **Ilona Andrews**

"*I JUST LOVED IT! Perfect light sci-fi. If you like space stuff that isn't that complicated but highly entertaining, I give two thumbs up!*" - **Felicia Day**

About the Authors

Rachel Aaron and **Travis Bach**
are two giant nerds who love gaming,
reading, writing, and hiking through the
great outdoors while talking about gaming,
reading, and writing! When they're not
terrifying the wildlife, Rachel and Travis
enjoy anime, manga, MMOs, table top
gaming, cooking, pampering their old lady
dog, and helping their son build secret
bases in Minecraft.

Rachel and Travis live in Athens, GA, but dream of moving out
west where the humidity isn't 90% all year long. If you love gaming and
manga as much as we do, hit us up on twitter at

@Rachel_Aaron
@TravBach

Or send us a note at www.rachelaaron.net!

Cover Illustration by Daniel Schmelling
Cover Design by Rachel Aaron
Editing provided by Red Adept Editing

As always, this book would not have been nearly as good without my amazing beta readers! Thank you so, so much to Michele Fry, Laligin, and Kevin Swearingen.
Y'all are the BEST!